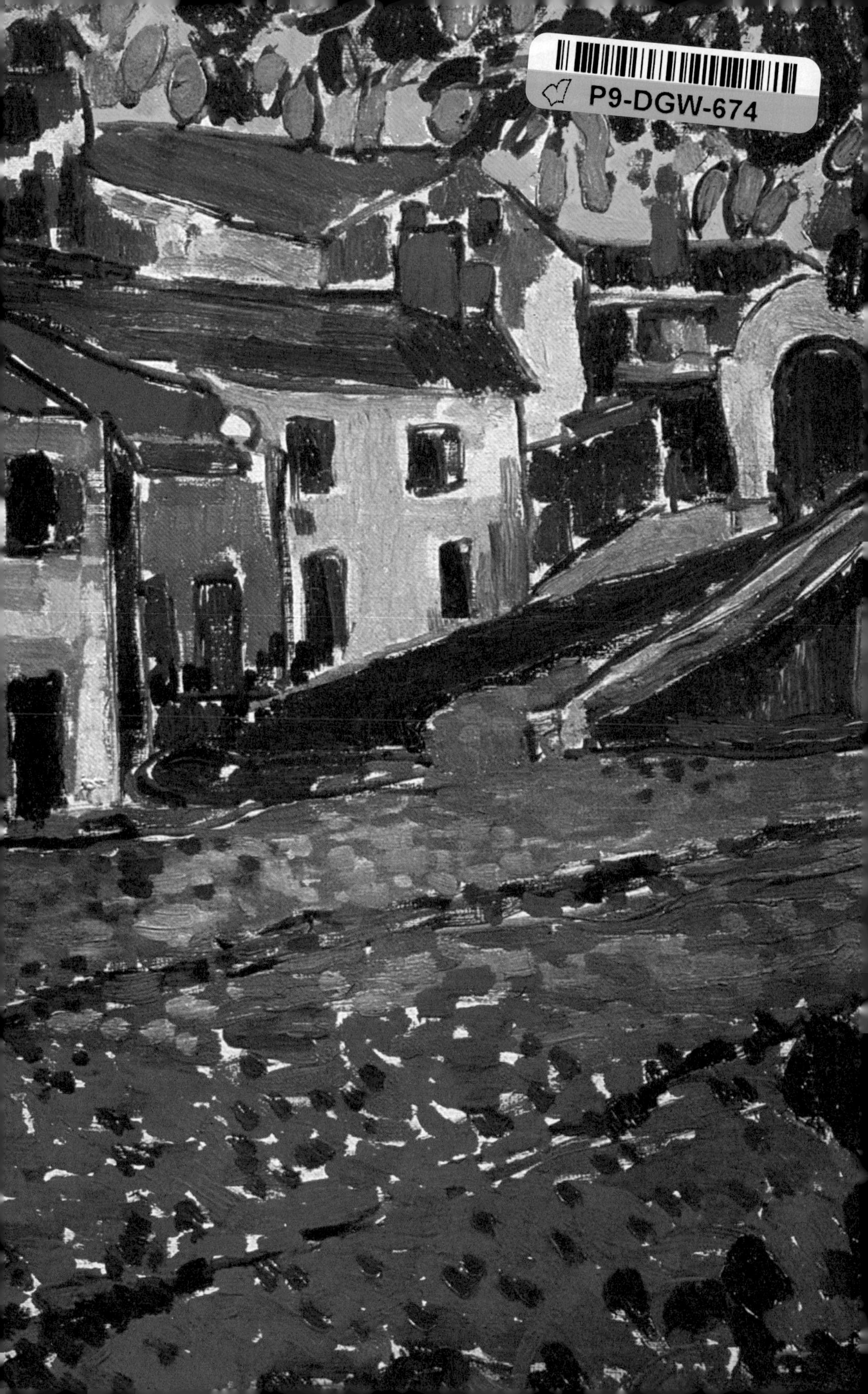

TARA ROAD

By the same author

THE RETURN JOURNEY
EVENING CLASS
THIS YEAR IT WILL BE DIFFERENT
THE GLASS LAKE
THE COPPER BEECH
THE LILAC BUS
CIRCLE OF FRIENDS
SILVER WEDDING
FIREFLY SUMMER
ECHOES
LIGHT A PENNY CANDLE
LONDON TRANSPORTS

TARA ROAD

Maeve Binchy

Delacorte Press

Published by
Delacorte Press
Random House, Inc.
1540 Broadway
New York, New York 10036

This book was first published in Great Britain by Orion Books, Ltd.

Library of Congress Cataloging in Publication Data
Binchy, Maeve.
    Tara Road / by Maeve Binchy.
      p.   cm.
    ISBN 0-385-33395-1
    I. Title.
    PR6052.I7728T37   1999   98-33768
    823'.914—dc21   CIP

Designed by Virginia Norey

Manufactured in the United States of America
March 1999

10 9 8 7 6 5 4 3 2 1

BVG

To dearest Gordon with all my love

TARA ROAD

CHAPTER

O N E

RIA'S MOTHER HAD ALWAYS BEEN very fond of film stars. It was a matter of sadness to her that Clark Gable had died on the day Ria was born. Tyrone Power had died on the day Hilary had been born just two years earlier. But somehow that wasn't as bad. Hilary hadn't seen off the great king of cinema as Ria had. Ria could never see *Gone With the Wind* without feeling somehow guilty.

She told this to Ken Murray, the first boy who kissed her. She told him in the cinema. Just as he was kissing her, in fact.

"You're very boring," he said, trying to open her blouse.

"I'm not boring," Ria cried with some spirit. "Clark Gable is there on the screen and I've told you something interesting. A coincidence. It's not boring."

Ken Murray was embarrassed, as so much attention had been called to them. People were shushing them and others were laughing. Ken moved away and huddled down in his seat as if he didn't want to be seen with her.

Ria could have kicked herself. She was almost sixteen. Everyone at school liked kissing, or said they did. Now she was starting to do it and she had made such a mess of it. She reached out her hand for him.

"I thought you wanted to look at the film," he muttered.

"I thought *you* wanted to put your arm around me," Ria said hopefully.

He took out a bag of toffees and ate one. Without even passing her the bag. The romantic bit was over.

Sometimes you could talk to Hilary, Ria had noticed. This wasn't one of those nights.

"Should you not talk when people kiss you?" she asked her sister.

"Jesus, Mary, and Holy St. Joseph," said Hilary, who was getting dressed to go out.

"I just asked," Ria said. "You'd know, with all your experience with fellows."

Hilary looked around nervously in case anyone had heard. "Will you *shut up* about my experience with fellows," she hissed. "Mam will hear you and that will be the end of either of us going anywhere ever again."

Their mother had warned them many times that she was not going to stand for any cheap behavior in the family. A widow woman left with two daughters had enough to worry her without thinking that her girls were tramps and would never get a husband. She would die happy if Hilary and Ria had nice respectable men and homes of their own. Nice homes, in a classier part of Dublin, places with a garden even. Nora Johnson had great hopes that they would all be able to move a little upward. Somewhere nicer than the big, sprawling housing estate where they lived now. And the way to find a good man was not by flaunting yourself at every man that came along.

"Sorry, Hilary." Ria looked contrite. "But anyway she didn't hear, she's watching TV."

Their mother did little else during an evening. She was tired, she said, when she got back from the dry cleaners where she worked at the counter. All day on your feet, it was nice to sit down and get transported to another world. Mam wouldn't have heard anything untoward from upstairs about experience with fellows.

Hilary forgave her—after all she needed Ria to help her tonight. Mam had a system that as soon as Hilary got in she was to leave her handbag on the landing floor. That way when Mam got up to go to the bathroom in the night she'd know Hilary was home and would go to sleep happily. Sometimes it was Ria's job to leave the handbag out there at midnight, allowing Hilary to creep in at any hour, having taken only her keys and lipstick in her pocket.

"Who'll do it for me when the time comes?" Ria wondered.

"You won't need it if you're going to be blabbing and yattering on to fellows when they try to kiss you," Hilary said. "You'll not want to stay out late because you'll have nowhere to go."

"I bet I will," Ria said, but she didn't feel as confident as she sounded. There was a stinging behind her eyes.

She was sure she didn't look *too* bad. Her friends at school said she was very lucky to have all that dark curly hair and blue eyes. She wasn't fat or anything and her spots weren't out of control. But people didn't pick her out; she didn't have any kind of sparkle like other girls in the class did.

Hilary saw her despondent face. "Listen, you're fine, you've got naturally curly hair, that's a plus for a start. And you're small, fellows like that. It will get better. Sixteen is the worst age, no matter what they tell you." Sometimes Hilary could be very nice indeed. Usually on the nights she wanted her handbag left on the landing.

And of course Hilary was right. It *did* get better. Ria left school and like her elder sister took a secretarial course. There were plenty of fellows, it turned out. Nobody particularly special, but she wasn't in any rush. She would possibly travel the world before she settled down to marry.

"Not too much traveling," her mother warned.

Nora Johnson thought that men might regard travel as fast. Men preferred to marry safer, calmer women. Women who didn't go gallivanting too much. It was only sensible to have advance information about men, Nora Johnson told her daughters. This way you could go armed into the struggle. There was a hint that she may not have been adequately informed herself. The late Mr. Johnson, though he had a bright smile and wore his hat at a rakish angle, was not a good provider. He had not been a believer in life insurance policies. Nora Johnson worked in a dry cleaners and lived in a shabby, run-down housing estate. She did not want the same thing for her daughters when the time came.

"When do you think the time will come?" Ria asked Hilary.

"For what?" Hilary was frowning a lot at her reflection in the mirror. The thing about applying blusher was that you had to get it just right. Too much and you looked consumptive, too little and you looked dirty and as if you hadn't washed your face.

"I mean, when do you think either of us will get married? You know the way Mam's always talking about when the time comes."

"Well I hope it comes to me first, I'm the elder. You're not even to consider doing it ahead of me."

"No, I have nobody in mind. It's just I'd love to be able to look into the future and see where we'll be in two years' time. Wouldn't it be great if we could have a peep."

"Well, go to a fortune-teller then, if you're that anxious."

"They don't know anything." Ria was scornful.

"It depends. If you get the right one they do. A lot of the girls at work found this great one. It would make you shiver the way she knows things."

"You've never been to her?" Ria was astounded.

"Yes, I have actually, just for fun. The others were all going, I didn't want to be the only one disapproving."

"And?"

"And what?"

"What did she tell you? Don't be mean, go on." Ria's eyes were dancing.

"She said I would marry within two years. . . ."

"Great, can I be the bridesmaid?"

"And that I'd live in a place surrounded by trees and that his name began with an *M,* and that we'd both have good health all our lives."

"Michael, Matthew, Maurice, Marcello?" Ria rolled them all around to try them out. "How many children?"

"She said no children," Hilary said.

"You don't believe her, do you?"

"Of course I do, what's the point giving up a week's wages if I don't believe her."

"You *never* paid that!"

"She's good. You know, she has the gift."

"Come *on.*"

"No, she does have a gift. All kinds of high-up people consult her. They wouldn't if she didn't have the power."

"And where did she see all this good health and the fellow called M and no children? In tea leaves?"

"No, on my hand. Look at the little lines under your little finger around the side of your hand. You've got two, I've got none."

"Hilary, don't be ridiculous. Mam has three lines. . . ."

"And remember there was another baby who died, so that makes three, right."

"You are serious! You do believe it."

"You asked so I'm telling you."

"And everyone who is going to have children has those little lines and those who aren't haven't?"

"You have to know how to look." Hilary was defensive.

"You have to know how to charge, it seems." Ria was distressed to see the normally levelheaded Hilary so easily taken in.

"It's not that dear when you consider—" Hilary began.

"Ah, Hilary, please. A week's wages to hear that kind of rubbish! Where does she live, in a penthouse?"

"No, a caravan as it happens, on a caravan halting site."

"You're joking me."

"True, she doesn't care about money. It's not a racket or a job, it's a gift."

"Yeah."

"So it looks like I can do what I like without getting pregnant." Hilary sounded very confident.

"It might be dangerous to throw out the Pill," said Ria. "I wouldn't rely totally on Madam Fifi or whatever she's called."

"Mrs. Connor."

"Mrs. Connor," Ria repeated. "Isn't that amazing? Mam used to consult St. Anne or someone when she was young. We thought that was mad enough, now it's Mrs. Connor in the halting site."

"Wait until you need to know something, you'll be along to her like a flash."

It was very hard to know what a job was going to be like until you were in it and then it was too late.

Hilary had office jobs in a bakery, a laundry, and then settled in a school. There wasn't much chance of meeting a husband there, she said, but the pay was a bit better and she got her lunch free, which meant she could save a bit more. She was determined to have something to put toward a house when the time came.

Ria was saving too, but to travel the world. She worked first in the office of a hardware shop, then in a company that made hairdressing supplies. And then settled in a big, busy real estate agency. Ria was on the reception desk and answered the phone. It was a world she knew nothing of when she went in, but it was obviously a business with a huge buzz. Prosperity had come to Ireland in the early eighties and the property market was the first to reflect this. There was huge competition between the various real estate agents and Ria found they worked closely as a team.

On the first day she met Rosemary. Slim, blond, and gorgeous, but as friendly as any of the girls she had ever met at school or secretarial college. Rosemary also lived at home with her mother and sister, so there was an immediate bond. Rosemary was so confident and well up in everything that was happening, Ria assumed that she must be a graduate or someone with huge knowledge of the whole property market. But no, Rosemary had only worked there for six months; it was her second job.

"There's no point in working anywhere unless we know what it's all about," Rosemary said. "It makes it twice as interesting if you know all that's going on."

It also made Rosemary twice as interesting to all the fellows who worked there. They found it very difficult to get to first base with her. In fact, Ria had heard that there was a sweepstake being run secretly on who would be the first to score. Rosemary had heard this too. She and Ria laughed over it.

"It's only a game," Rosemary said. "They don't really want me at all." Ria was not sure that she was right; almost any man in the office would have been proud to escort Rosemary Ryan. But she was adamant: a career first, fellows later. Ria listened with interest. It was such a different message than the one she got at home, where her mother and Hilary seemed to put a much greater emphasis on the marriage side of things.

Ria's mother said that 1982 was a terrible year for film stars dying. Ingrid Bergman died, and Romy Schneider and Henry Fonda, then there was the terrible accident when Princess Grace was killed. All the people you really wanted to see, they were dying off like flies.

It was also the year that Hilary Johnson got engaged to Martin Moran, a teacher at the school where she worked in the office.

Martin was pale and anxious and originally from the West of Ireland. He always said his father was a small farmer, not just a farmer but a *small* one. Since Martin was six feet one it was hard to imagine this. He was courteous and obviously very fond of Hilary, yet there was something about him that lacked enthusiasm and fire. He looked slightly worried about things and spoke pessimistically when he came to the house for Sunday lunch.

There was a problem connected with everything. The Pope would get assassinated when he visited England, Martin was sure of it. And when he didn't, it was just lucky and his visit hadn't done all the good that people had hoped it would. The war in the Falklands would have repercussions for Ireland, mark his word. And the trouble in the Middle East was going to get worse, and the IRA bombs in London were only the tip of the iceberg. Teachers' salaries were too low; house prices were too high.

Ria looked with wonder at the man her sister was going to marry.

Hilary, who had once been able to throw away a week's salary on a fortune-teller, was now talking about the cost of having shoes repaired and the folly of making a telephone call outside the cheap times.

Eventually a selection was made and a deposit was paid. It was a very small house. It was impossible to imagine what the area might look like in the future. At present it was full of mud, cement mixers, diggers, unfinished roads, and unmade footpaths. And yet it seemed exactly what her elder sister wanted out of life. Never had she seen her so happy.

Hilary was always smiling and holding Martin's hand as they talked, even on very worrying subjects like stamp duty and the real estate agent's fees. She kept turning and examining the very small diamond that had been very carefully chosen and bought from a jeweler where Martin's cousin worked so that a good price had been arranged.

Hilary was excited about the wedding day, which would be on the day before her twenty-fourth birthday. For Hilary the time had come. She celebrated it with manic frugality. She and Martin vied with each other to save money on the whole project.

An autumn wedding was much more sensible. Hilary could wear a cream-colored suit and hat, something that could be worn again and again, and eventually dyed a dark color and worn still further. As a wedding feast they would have a small lunch in a Dublin hotel, just family. Martin's father and brothers, being small farmers, could not afford to be away from the land for any longer than a day. It would be impossible to be anything but pleased for her. It was so obviously what Hilary wanted. But Ria knew that it was nothing at all like what she wanted herself.

Ria wore a bright scarlet-colored coat to the wedding, and a red velvet hair band and bow in her black curly hair. She must have been one of the most colorful bridesmaids at the drabbest wedding in Europe, she thought.

Next day she decided to wear her scarlet bridesmaid's coat to the office. Rosemary was amazed. "Hey, you look *terrific*. I've never seen you dressed up before, Ria. Seriously, you should get interested in clothes, you know. What a pity we have nowhere to go to lunch and show you off, we mustn't waste this."

"Come on, Rosemary, it's only clothes." Ria was embarrassed. She felt now that she must have been dressed like a tramp before.

"No, I'm not joking. You must always wear those knock-them-dead colors. I bet you were the hit of the wedding!"

"I'd like to think so, but maybe I was a bit too loud, made them color-blind. You've no idea what Martin's people were like."

"Like Martin?" Rosemary guessed.

"Compared to them Martin's a ball of fire," Ria said.

"Look, I can't believe you're the same person as yesterday." Rosemary stood in her immaculate lilac-colored knitted suit, her makeup perfect and amazed admiration written all over her.

"Well, you've really put it up to me. Now I'll have to get a whole new wardrobe." Ria twirled around once more before taking off her new scarlet coat, and caught the eye of the new man in the office.

She had heard there was a Mr. Lynch coming from the Cork branch. He had obviously arrived. He wasn't tall, about her own height. He was handsome, and he had blue eyes and straight fair hair that fell into them. He had a smile that lit up the room. "Hallo, I'm Danny Lynch," he said. Ria looked at him, embarrassed to have been caught pirouetting around in her new coat. "Aren't you just *gorgeous*?" he said. She felt a very odd sensation in her throat, as if she had been running up a hill and couldn't catch her breath.

Rosemary spoke, which was just as well because Ria would not have been able to answer at all.

"Well *hallo* there, Danny Lynch," she said with a bit of a smile. "And you are very welcome to our office. You know, we *were* told that there was a Mr. Lynch arriving, but why did we think it was going to be some old guy?"

Ria felt a pang of jealousy as she had never before felt about her friend. Why did Rosemary always know exactly what to say, how to be funny and flattering and warm at the same time?

"I'm Rosemary, this is Ria, and we are the workforce that keeps this place going, so you have to be very nice to us."

"Oh, I will," Danny promised.

And Ria knew he would probably join the sweepstake as to who would score first with Rosemary. Probably would win, as well. Oddly he seemed to be talking to Ria when he spoke, but maybe she was just imagining it. Rosemary went on. "We were just looking for somewhere to go out and celebrate Ria's new coat."

"Great! Well, we have the excuse, all we need is the place and to know how long a lunch break so that I don't make a bad impression on my first day." His extraordinary smile went from one to the other; they were the only three people in the world.

Ria couldn't say anything; her mouth was totally dry.

"If we're out and back in under an hour then I think we'll do well," said Rosemary.

"So now it's only where?" Danny Lynch said, looking straight at Ria. This time there were only two of them in the world. She still couldn't speak.

"There's an Italian place across the road," Rosemary said. "It would cut down on time getting there and back."

"Let's go there," said Danny Lynch, without taking his eyes away from Ria Johnson.

Afterward Ria could remember nothing of the lunch. Rosemary told her they talked about work, the houses on their books.

Danny was twenty-three. His uncle had been a real estate agent. Well, he had been a bit of everything in a small town, a publican, an undertaker, but he also had an agent's license and that's where Danny had gone to work when he left school. They had sold grain and fertilizer and hay as well as cattle and small farms, but as Ireland changed, property became important. And then he had gone to Cork City and he loved it all, and now he had just gotten this job in Dublin.

He was as excited as a child on Christmas Day, and Rosemary and Ria were carried along with him all the way. He said he hated being in the office and loved being out with clients, but then didn't everyone? He knew it would take time before he'd get that kind of freedom in Dublin. He had been to Dublin often but never lived there.

And where was he staying? Rosemary had never seemed so interested in anyone before. Ria watched glumly. Every man in the office would have killed to see the light in the eyes, the interest in every word. She never inquired where any of her other colleagues lived, she didn't seem to know if they had any accommodation at all. But with Danny it was different. "Tell us now that you don't live miles and miles away, do you?" Rosemary had her head on one side. No man on earth could resist giving Rosemary his address and finding out where *she* lived too. But Danny didn't seem to regard it as a personal exchange; it was part of the general conversation. He spoke looking from one to the other as he told them how he had fallen on his feet. He really had the most amazing bit of luck. There was this man he had met, a sort of madman really called Sean O'Brien, old and confused. A real recluse. And he had inherited a great big house on Tara Road, and he wasn't capable of doing it up, and he didn't want all the bother and the discussing of it and all so what he really wanted was a few fellows to go in and live there. Fellows were easier than girls, they didn't want things neat and clean and organized. He smiled apologetically at them as if to say he knew that fellows were hopeless.

So that's where he and two other lads lived. They had a room each, and kept an eye on the place until poor old Sean decided what he was going to do. Suited everybody.

What kind of a house was it, the girls wanted to know?

Tara Road was very higgledy-piggledy. Big houses with gardens full of trees, small houses facing right on the street. No. 16 was a great old house, Danny said. Falling down, damp, shabby now. Poor Sean O'Brien's old uncle must have been a bit of a no-hoper like Sean himself, it must have been a great house once. You got a feel for houses, didn't you? Otherwise, why be in this business at all.

Ria sat with her chin in her hands listening to Danny and looking at him and looking at him. He was so enthusiastic. The place had a big overrun garden, and an orchard even at the back. It was one of those houses that just put out its arms and hugged you.

Rosemary must have kept the conversation going and called for the check. They walked across the road back to work and Ria sat down at her desk. Things don't happen like this in real life. It's only a crush or an infatuation. He's a perfectly ordinary small guy with a line of chatter. He is exactly like this to everyone else. So why on earth did she feel that he was totally special, and that if he got to share all his plans and dreams with anyone else she would kill the other person. This wasn't the kind of way people went on. Then she remembered her sister's wedding the day before. *That* wasn't the way people went on either.

Before the office closed Ria went over to Danny Lynch's desk. "I'm going to be twenty-two tomorrow," she said. "I wondered . . ." Then she got stuck.

He helped her out. "Are you having a party?"

"Not really, no."

"Then can we celebrate it together. Today the coat, tomorrow being twenty-two. Who knows what we'll have to celebrate by Wednesday?"

And then Ria knew that it wasn't a crush or an infatuation, it was love. The kind of thing she had only read about, heard about, sung about, or seen at the cinema. And it had come to find her in her own office.

At first she tried to keep him to herself, not tell anyone about him, not share him with other people. She clung to him in the car as if she never wanted him to leave her arms.

"You're sending me very funny signals, my Maria," he said to her. "You want to be with me and yet you don't. Or am I just a thick man who can't understand?" His head was on one side, looking at her quizzically.

"That's exactly the way I feel," she said simply. "Very confused."

"Well, we can simplify it all, can't we?"

"Not really. You see for me it would be a very big step. I don't want to make a production out of it all, but you see I *haven't* with anyone else. Yet, I mean . . ." She bit her lip. She didn't dare tell him that she wouldn't sleep with him until she knew that he loved her. It would be putting words in his mouth.

Danny Lynch held her face in his hands. "I love you, Ria, you are utterly adorable."

"*Do* you love me?"

"You know I do."

The next time he asked her to go back to the big rambling house she would go. And oddly he didn't ask her at all in the days and nights that followed. He told her about himself, his time at school where he was picked on because he was small, and how his elder brothers taught him to fight. His brothers were in London, both of them. One married, one living with a girl. They didn't come home much. Usually went to Spain or Greece on their holidays now.

His parents lived in the same house as they always had. They were very self-contained, went for long walks with their red setter. She felt that he didn't get on well with his father, but even though she ached to ask she didn't probe. Men hated that kind of intimate chat. She and Rosemary knew this from reading magazine articles and even from their own experience. Fellows didn't like being questioned about feelings. So she did not ask him about his childhood and why he spoke so little of his parents and rarely went to see them.

Danny didn't ask questions about her family, so she forced herself not to prattle about how her father had died when she was eight, how her mother was still bitter and disappointed by the memory of him. And how dull Hilary and Martin's wedding had been.

There was no shortage of things to talk about in those heady days. Danny did ask about what music she liked, and what she read and where she had been on holidays, and what films she went to see, and what kind of houses she liked. He showed her books about houses, and pointed out things that she would never have noticed. He would love to own the old house, No. 16 Tara Road, he told her. He would do it up and take such care of it. He would put so much love into the house that the house would return his love.

It was wonderful having Rosemary to talk to. At first Ria held back.

She was so afraid that if Rosemary smiled just once more, that Danny would leave Ria's side and join her but as the days went by she began to have a little more confidence. And then she told Rosemary everything, where they went, what he was interested in, about his strange lonely family in the country.

Rosemary listened with interest. "You've got it very bad," she said eventually.

"Do you think it's foolish, just a crush or something? You know a lot about these things." Ria wished so much for an oval face and high cheekbones so desperately it almost hurt.

"He seems to have it just as bad," Rosemary pronounced.

"He *says* he loves me, certainly," Ria said. She was answering Rosemary's question but she didn't want to sound too confident.

"Of course he loves you, that was obvious the very first day," Rosemary said, twirling her long blond hair around her finger. "It's the most romantic thing I've ever seen. I can't tell you how envious we all are. Total love at first sight and the whole office knows. What nobody knows is are you sleeping with him?"

"No," said Ria firmly. And then in a much smaller voice, "Not yet."

Ria's mother wondered was she ever going to meet him.

"Soon, Mam. Don't rush things, please."

"I'm not rushing anything, Ria. I'm just pointing out that you have been going out with this fellow every single night week after week and common courtesy would suggest that you might invite him home with you once in a while."

"I will, Mam. Honestly."

"I mean, Hilary brought Martin back to meet us, didn't she?"

"Oh, she did, Mam."

"So?"

"So, I will."

"Are you going home for Christmas?" Ria asked Danny.

"Here is home." He embraced all of Dublin in a gesture.

"Yes, I know. I meant to your parents' home."

"I don't know yet."

"Won't they expect you to go back?"

"They'll leave it to me."

She wanted to ask about his brothers over in England and what kind of a family *was* it if they didn't all gather around a table for a turkey on Christmas Day. But she knew she must not probe and sound too inquisitive. "Sure," she said unconvincingly.

Danny took both her hands in his. "Listen to me, Ria. It will be different when you and I have a home. It will be a real home, one that people will want to come running back to. That's what I see ahead for us. Don't you?"

"Oh, yes, Danny," she said with her face glowing. She did understand. The real Danny was a loving person like herself. She was the luckiest woman in the world.

"Ask him for Christmas Day so that we can get a look at him," her mother begged.

"No, Mam. Thank you, but no."

"Is he going back down the country to his own people?"

"I'm not sure, he's not sure."

"He sounds a real fly-by-night to me," her mother sniffed.

"No, Mam, he's not that."

"Well, a mystery man . . . that he won't even put in an appearance to give the time of day to his girlfriend's family."

"He will, Mam, when the time comes," Ria said.

Someone always behaved badly at the office party.

This year it was Orla King, a girl who had drunk half a bottle of vodka before the festivities had even started. She tried to sing, "In the jungle the mighty jungle the lion sleeps tonight."

"Get her out before the top guys see her," Danny hissed.

It was easier said than done. Ria tried to urge Orla to come with her to the ladies' room.

"Piss off!" was the response.

Danny was there. "Hey, sweetheart, you and I have never danced," he said.

Orla looked at him with interest. "That's true," she agreed.

"Why don't we go out and dance a bit where there's more room?"

"Yesh," said the girl, surprised and pleased.

In seconds Danny had her out on the street. Ria brought her coat. The cold fresh air made her feel sick. They directed her to a quiet corner.

"I want to go home," she cried afterward.

"Come on, we'll walk you," Danny said.

Between them they supported her. From time to time Orla tried a chorus of "The lion sleeps tonight" without much success.

When they let her in the door of her flat she looked at them in surprise. "How did I get home?" she asked with interest.

"You're fine, sweetheart," Danny said soothingly.

"Will you come in with me?" Orla ignored Ria entirely.

"No, honey, see you tomorrow," he said, and they were gone.

"You saved her job, getting her out of there," Ria said as they walked back to the office party. "She's such a clown . . . I hope she knows how much she owes you."

"She's not a clown, she's just young and lonely," he said.

Ria got a stab of jealousy as sharp as a real pain. Orla was eighteen and pretty, even drunk with a tearstained face she looked well. Suppose Danny was attracted to her? No, don't suppose that.

Back at the party they hadn't been missed. "That was very smart of you, Danny," Rosemary said with approval. "And even smarter, you avoided the speeches."

"Anything we should know?"

"Oh, that we had a profitable year and there would be a bonus. Onward and upward sort of thing."

Rosemary looked magnificent, with her blond hair swept up in a jeweled comb, a white satin blouse, tight black skirt, and those long slim legs. For the second time Ria felt a pang of envy. She was dumpy and fuzzy-looking. How could she keep a man as gorgeous as Danny Lynch? She was foolish even to try.

He whispered in her ear. "Let's circulate, talk to the suits for a bit and then get away."

She watched him joke easily with the senior figures in the agency, nod respectfully to the managing director, listen courteously to their wives. Danny had only been there a matter of weeks. Already they liked him and thought he would do well.

"I'm getting the Christmas Eve bus tomorrow."

"I'm sure it'll be nice, lots of returned emigrants and everything," she said.

"I'll miss you," he said.

"Me too."

"I'll hitchhike back the day after Christmas . . . there's no buses."

"That's great."

"I wonder, could I come and see you at home, and you know, meet your mother maybe?"

He was asking, she hadn't dragged him or forced him.

"That would be great. Come and have lunch with us on Tuesday." All she had to do now was force herself not to be ashamed of her mother and her sister and her dreary brother-in-law.

It wasn't a military inspection on Tuesday. It was only lunch. They were going to have soup and sandwiches.

Ria tried to see the house through Danny's eyes. It was not the kind of place that he would have liked to live, a corner house on a long, sprawling road of a big estate. He's coming to see me, not the house, she told herself. Her mother said she hoped he wouldn't stay after three because there was a great movie starting on the television then. Ria gritted her teeth and said no indeed she was sure that he wouldn't.

Hilary said that she was sure he was used to fancier meals but he'd have to put up with this like anyone else. With a huge effort Ria said that he would be delighted to put up with it. Martin read the paper and didn't look up at all.

She wondered if Danny would bring a bottle of wine or a box of chocolates or a plant. Or maybe bring nothing at all. Three times she changed her dress. That was too smart, this was too dowdy. She was struggling into the third outfit when she heard the doorbell ring.

He had arrived.

"Hallo, Nora, I'm Danny," she heard him say. Oh, God, he was calling her mother by her first name. Martin always called her Mrs. J. Mam would just hate this.

But she heard in her mother's voice the kind of pleased response that Danny always got. "You're very, very welcome," she said, in a tone that hadn't been used in that house for as long as Ria could remember.

And the magic worked with Hilary and Martin too. Eager to hear about their wedding, interested in the school where they worked, relaxed and easygoing. Ria watched the whole thing with amazement.

And he had brought no wine, chocolates, or flowers. Instead he gave them a game of Trivial Pursuit. Ria's heart sank when she saw it. This was not a family where games were played. But she had reckoned without Danny. Their heads were bent over the questions. Nora knew all the ones about film stars and Martin shone in general knowledge.

"What hope have I against a teacher?" Danny said in despair.

He said he was leaving long before they wanted him to go. "Ria promised to come and see the place I live," he said apologetically. "I want us to go while there's still light."

"He's gorgeous," Hilary whispered.

"Very nice manners," her mother hissed.

And then they were free.

"That was a lovely lunch," Danny said as they waited for the bus to Tara Road. And that was all he would say. There would be no analysis, no defining. Men like Danny were straightforward and not complicated.

And then they were there. And they stood together in the overgrown front garden and looked up at the house on Tara Road. "Look at the shape of the house," Danny begged her. "See how perfect the proportions are. It was built in 1870, a gentleman's residence." The steps up to the hall door were huge blocks of granite. "Look how even they were, they were perfectly matched." The bow windows had all the original woodwork. "Those shutters are over a hundred years old. The leaded glass over the door has no cracks in it. This house was a jewel," Danny Lynch said.

There he was, living in it, well, more or less camping in a room in it.

"Let's remember today, the first day that we walked together into this house," he said. His eyes were bright. He was just as sentimental and romantic as she was in so many ways. He was about to open the peeling front door with his key and paused to kiss her. "This will be our home, Ria, won't it? Tell me you love it too." He meant it. He wanted to marry her. Danny Lynch, a man who could have any woman. And he meant he was going to own a huge house like this. A boy of twenty-three with no assets. Only rich people could buy houses like this, even one in such poor repair.

Ria didn't want to pour cold water on his dreams, and particularly she didn't want to sound too like her sister, Hilary, and this new obsession with the cost of everything. But this was fantasy. "It's not possible to own a place like this, surely?" she said.

"When you come in and see it you'll know this is where we are going to live. And we'll find a way to buy it." He talked her through the hallway with its high ceiling. He pointed out the original moldings on the ceiling to take her eyes off the bicycles clogging the hallway. He showed her the gentle curve of the stairs, and made no mention of the rotting floorboards. They passed the big room with its folding doors. They couldn't go into it. Sean O'Brien, the eccentric landlord, was using it as some kind of storeroom for giant-size containers.

They went down the steps to the huge kitchen with its old black range. There was a side door here out to the garden, and numerous storage rooms, pantries, and sculleries. The magnitude of it all was too great for Ria to take in. This boy with the laughing eyes really thought that he and she could find the money and skills to do up a house of this size.

If it were on their books back at the office it would have the customary warnings printed all over it. In need of extensive renovation, suitable for structural remodeling, ready for inventive redesign. Only a builder or developer or someone with real money would buy a property like this.

The kitchen had an uneven tiled floor. A small, cheap tabletop range had been laid on the old black one.

"I'll make us some coffee," Danny said. "And in years to come we'll remember the first time we had coffee here together on Tara Road . . ." At that moment, as if on some kind of cue, the kitchen was suddenly lit up with one of those rays of watery winter sunshine. It came slanting in the window through all the briars and brambles. It was like a sign.

"Yes, yes I will remember my first coffee with you on Tara Road," Ria said.

"We'll be able to tell people it was a lovely sunny day, December twenty-eighth, 1982," said Danny.

As it happened, it also turned out to be the date of the first time Ria Johnson ever made love to anybody. And as she lay beside Danny in the small narrow bed she wished she could see into the future. Just for a moment. A quick look to see would they live here together for years and have children and make it the home of their dreams.

She wondered if Hilary's friend Mrs. Connor, the fortune-teller on the halting site, would know. She smiled at the thought of going to consult her. Danny stirred from his sleep on her shoulder, and saw her smiling.

"Are you happy?" he asked.

"Never more so."

"I love you, Ria. I'll never let you down," he promised.

She was the luckiest woman in the country. No, she told herself, think generously, who was luckier anywhere? Make that the world.

The next weeks went by in a blur.

They knew that Sean O'Brien would be glad to get rid of the place.

They knew that he would prefer to deal with them, young people who wouldn't make a fuss about the damp and the roof, and would not tut-tut over the decay. But they still had to give him what the house was worth. So how could they get it together?

There were sheets of paper building up into piles as they did their sums. Four rented rooms upstairs would bring in enough to pay the mortgage. It would have to be done very quietly of course. No need to burden the planning authorities with any details, or indeed the tax people either. Then they would approach the bank with their proposition. Ria had a thousand pounds saved; Danny had two and a half thousand. They had both seen couples with less than they had get their hands on property. It all depended on timing and presentation. They would do it.

They invested the price of a bottle of whiskey when inviting the landlord to discuss the future. Sean O'Brien proved to be no trouble. He told them again and again the story they knew already. He had inherited the house when his uncle died some years back. He didn't want to live in it, he had a small cottage by a lake in Wicklow where he fished and drank with congenial people. That's where he wanted to be. He'd only held on to Tara Road in case there was going to be a property boom. And indeed there had been. It was worth much more now than it had been ten years ago, so he had been clever, hadn't he? A lot of people said he was an eejit but that wasn't so. Danny and Ria nodded and praised him and filled his glass.

Sean O'Brien said he had never been able to keep the house up to any standard. It was too much effort and he didn't have the skills to restore it and let it properly to people who would look after it. That was why he had been happy to hand it to young fellows like Danny and his pals. But he took their point that it wasn't going to be such a great investment if it kept falling down and deteriorating the way it was.

He thought that the going rate would be in the neighborhood of seventy thousand pounds. He had asked around and this is what he had heard. However, he would take sixty thousand for quick sale, and he'd get rid of all the old furniture and containers and boxes that he was storing for friends. Danny could have it when he produced sixty thousand.

It would have been a bargain for anyone with the money to restore it. For Danny and Ria it was impossible. For a start they would need fifteen percent of the price as a deposit. And nine thousand pounds was like nine million to them.

Ria was prepared to change the dream, not Danny. He didn't fret or complain. He just wouldn't let go of the idea. It was too good a house, too beautiful a place to let slip from their hands into the possession of some builder. Now that Sean O'Brien had faced the notion of selling, he would want to sell.

It was hard to keep their minds on the sales they had to handle in the office. Doubly hard because every day they were dealing with people who could buy the house on Tara Road without any trouble at all.

People like Barney McCarthy, for example. The big, bluff business-man who had made his money in England as a builder and who bought and sold houses almost on whim. He was in the process of selling a large mansion that had been a mistake. One of his rare mistakes.

He was so unexpectedly honest that he knew why it was a mistake. He saw himself momentarily a country squire, living in a huge Georgian house with a tree-lined avenue. The house was indeed elegant but it turned out to be too remote, too far from Dublin. It had been an ill-considered decision and he was prepared to lose a little on the whole deal, but not a lot. He needed to sell this white elephant.

He had already bought the comfortable big square family residence that he should have bought in the first place. His wife was settled there. He was involved in buying pubs and investing in golf courses but the main issue was to sell the mansion, which now seemed just like a monument to his folly. He was a man who cared about the public image of himself.

He also loved to drop the names of famous people he had met, and in the real estate agency they were greatly in awe of him. But they had a huge problem in selling this property at anything like the price he expected. Quite simply, Barney had spent too much on it and there simply were not the buyers. He was not going to see a profit, and he was a man who hated to take a humiliating loss on this deal. Senior partners in the agency, smooth-talking men, pointed out to Barney that the upkeep of such a house was enormous and that they could count on the fingers of one hand the likely buyers in Ireland. They had indeed looked outside the country too, but with no success.

There was a conference in the agency about it. Danny and Ria sat with the others listening to the worrying news that Barney might be taking his business elsewhere. Ria's mind was far from Barney's problems and more on their own. But Danny was thinking. He opened his mouth to say something and then changed his mind.

"What is it, Danny?" He was popular and successful. They wanted to hear what he would say.

"No, it's nothing. You've thought of all the angles," Danny said.

And the conversation went around aimlessly in the same circle for another half an hour.

Ria knew that Danny had thought of something. She knew the way his eyes danced. After the meeting he whispered that he had to get out of the office. She was to cover for him.

"If you pray to anyone, pray now," he said.

"Tell me, Danny. Tell me."

"I can't, there isn't time. Say I got a phone call . . . from the nuns down the road. Anything."

"I can't sit here and not know."

"I've got an idea how Barney can sell his house."

"Why didn't you tell them?"

"I'm telling *him*. That's how we'll get our money. If I tell them we'll only get a pat on the back."

"Oh God, Danny. Be careful, they could sack you."

"If I'm right it won't matter," he said. And he was gone.

———

Rosemary called Ria. "Come into the ladies' room. I want to tell you something."

"I can't. I'm waiting for a call." Ria couldn't leave her post in case he rang, or needed her cooperation.

"Orla can cover for you, come on, it's important," Rosemary said.

"No, tell me here, there's no one around."

"Well, it's very hush-hush."

"Speak in a whisper, then."

"I'm leaving, I've got a new job." Rosemary pulled back, waiting to see the amazement and shock on Ria's face. She saw very little reaction at all. Perhaps she hadn't explained it properly.

She explained it all again. It had just been agreed. It was very exciting. She would tell them here in the agency this evening. She had been offered a better job in a printing company. It wasn't far away; they could still have lunch. Ria barely listened she was so sick with worry. Rosemary was not unnaturally offended. "Well, if you can't be bothered to listen," she said.

"I'm sorry, Rosemary, really I am. It's just that I have something on my mind."

"God, you're so bloody dull, Ria. You've nothing on your mind but Danny this, Danny that. It's like as if you were his mother. Do you know that you haven't the remotest interest in anyone else these days!"

Ria was stricken. "Look, I can't tell you how sorry I am. Please forgive me. Tell me again."

"No, I won't tell you again. You don't care if I go or stay. You're *still* not listening to me. You've your eyes on the door in case he's coming back in. Where is he, by the way?"

"With the nuns, they rang."

"No, they didn't. I was talking to them an hour ago. There's no movement there, they have to wait for some Mother General to say yes from Rome."

"I'll tell you all about it later. Please tell me about your new job, please."

"Ria, will you *shut up?*" Rosemary hissed. "I haven't told them yet and there you go bleating about my new job. I think you're unhinged."

She saw him come in the door, walking quickly, lightly as he always did. She knew by his face that it was all right. He slid into his desk and gave her a thumbs-up sign. Immediately she dialed his phone extension.

"Don't say you were with the nuns. Apparently there's nothing happening on that sale," she whispered.

"Thanks, you're brilliant."

"What happens now, Danny?"

"We sit tight for a week. Then all systems go."

Ria hung up. She thought the day would never end, the hands of the clock were crawling past. Rosemary went in and came out having given her notice. Everything seemed to be in slow motion. Across the room Danny seemed to be perfectly normal in his conversations, chatting to people, laughing, working on the phone. Only Ria, who knew his every heartbeat, could see the suppressed excitement.

They went to the pub across the road and without asking her what she wanted, he bought them both large brandies.

"I told Barney McCarthy he should put in a soundproofed recording studio, with all that stuff on the walls. Cost him another twenty thousand."

"Why on earth . . . ?"

"He could sell it to pop stars. It's the kind of a place they'd want, carve out a helicopter pad as well."

"And he thought it was a good idea?" Ria was weak.

"He asked why did those swanky agents I worked for not come up with this idea."

"What did you say?"

"I said they would probably think it was a bit of a young man's idea, that they were more conservative. And Ria, wait for this, I looked him in the eye and I said, 'And another thing, Mr. McCarthy, I thought if I came to you directly with this idea that maybe I could sell it for you myself.'" Danny sipped his brandy. "He asked me was I trying to take his business away from my employers. I said yes, I was, and he said he'd give me a week."

"Oh, God, Danny."

"I know. Isn't it wonderful? Well, we can't do it from their place so I'll develop flu tomorrow, after I've taken all the addresses and contacts I need home. I've begun to make a list already and then I'll get on the phone. I may need you to send some faxes from the office for me."

"We'll be killed."

"Don't be ridiculous, of course we won't. This is what business is about."

"How much will . . . ?"

"If I sell Barney's bloody house by next week we'll have the deposit on Tara Road and more. *Then* we can go to the bank, honeybun. *Then* we can go to the bank."

"But they'll sack you, you won't have a job."

"If I have Barney McCarthy's business, any agency in Ireland will take me. Just a week of iron-hard nerve, Ria, and we're there."

"Iron nerve," she agreed.

"And remember this day, sweetheart. March twenty-fifth, 1983, the day our luck changed."

"Will Danny be back for my going-away drinks?" Rosemary asked Ria.

"Yes, I think his flu will be better by then," Ria said loudly.

"Sorry, it slipped out. How is he, by the way?"

"Fine, he rings at night." Ria didn't say how often he telephoned during the day too, asking for information.

"And did he find what he's looking for?" Rosemary asked.

Ria thought for a moment. "He sounds cheerful enough. I think he is just in the process of finding it," she said.

An hour previously Danny had rung to say that Barney's forces had soundproofed a wine cellar already and the equipment was being installed today. Tomorrow the manager of a legendary pop group was flying over to inspect it; Danny would be traveling with him. It was looking very good.

And it was very good. Barney McCarthy got his price. And Danny Lynch got his commission. And Sean O'Brien got his sixty thousand pounds. And Danny told his employers what he had done, and that he would leave as soon as they wanted him to. They invited him to stay and keep Barney's business with them, but Danny said it would be awkward. They would always be watching him, he would feel uneasy.

They parted on good terms, as Danny Lynch did with everyone and everything in life.

———

They were like excited children as they wandered about the house planning this and that.

"This front room could be something *really* special," Danny said. Now that the boxes and containers that held the secrets of poor old Sean O'Brien and his friends had been moved out, anyone could see what perfect proportions it had: the high ceiling, the tall windows, the big fireplace.

It didn't matter at all that a naked bulb hung on an old, knotted electric cord from the middle of the ceiling, or that some windowpanes had been broken in the past and replaced with cheap and irregular bits of glass.

The stained and chipped mantelpiece could be renewed and made to look as it must once have when it was a gentleman's residence.

"We'll get a gorgeous soft wool Indian carpet," Danny said. "And look here beside the fireplace, do you know what we'll have—one of those big Japanese Imari vases. Perfect for a room like this."

Ria looked at him with stunned admiration.

"How on earth do you know all this, Danny? You sound as if you'd done a course in fine arts or something."

"I look at places, sweetheart, I'm in and out of houses like this all day. I see what people with taste and style have done, I just look, that's all."

"A lot of people look but they don't see properly."

"We'll have such a good time doing it up." His eyes were shining.

Ria nodded, not trusting herself to speak.

The excitement of it all was nearly too much for her. Sometimes she felt dizzy, physically dizzy with the magnitude of what they were taking on.

The pregnancy test was positive. The timing could not be worse. As she lay awake at night, either in her mother's home or in the shambles that was now Tara Road, she rehearsed how she would tell him that she was pregnant.

The fear that he might not want the child was so great it stopped her opening her mouth. The days went by and Ria felt she was acting everywhere and to everyone, and that she had long ceased to be a real person with normal responses.

When she did tell him it was completely by accident. Danny said that the hall was much bigger than they had thought now that they had got the bicycles out of it and into the shed. Maybe they should have a painting party at the weekend, get everyone to do a bit of wall each. It wouldn't be permanent or anything but it might give them a bit of pride in the place.

"What do you think, sweetheart? I know the smell of paint will make us all sick for a day or two but it will be worth it."

"I'm going to have a baby," she said suddenly.

"What?"

"Yes, I mean it. Oh Jesus, Danny, I'm so sorry. I'm so sorry now in the middle of all this." And she burst into tears.

He laid down his coffee cup and came over to hold her tight. "Ria, Ria. Stop, stop. Don't cry."

But she went on sobbing and shaking in his arms. He stroked her hair and soothed her as you would a child. "Shush, shush, Ria. I'm here, it's all right."

"No, it's not all right, it couldn't be worse. What a time for this to happen. I don't know how it happened."

"I do, and it was all lovely," he said.

"Oh, Danny, please don't make a joke about it, it's a nightmare. I've never been so upset. I couldn't tell you, not with all this going on."

"Why is it a nightmare?" he asked.

Oh, please, please may he not say that an abortion was no trouble. That he had the money now. They could go to London at the weekend. Please may he not say that. Because Ria knew that she didn't trust herself. She might do it just to keep him. Then she would hate him as well as love him, which would be absurd but she could see it happening.

He was smiling his big wide smile. "Where's the nightmare, Ria, my sweet sweetheart? We wanted children. We were going to get married. So it happened sooner rather than later. That's all."

She looked at him in wonder. In as much as she could understand anything, he really did seem overjoyed.

"Danny . . ."

"What were all the tears about?"

"I thought, I thought . . ."

"Shush."

"Rosemary? Can we have lunch? I've some marvelous news."

"What makes me think it has to do with lover boy?" Rosemary laughed.

"Lunch or not?"

"Of course."

They went to the Italian restaurant where they had gone that day with Danny, only a few months ago last November, and imagine all that had happened since.

Rosemary looked better than ever. How it was that no drop of oil or spill of sauce would ever land on her light gray cashmere sweater Ria would never know.

"Well, tell me," Rosemary said. "Stop pretending to look at the menu."

"Danny and I are getting married, and we want you to be the bridesmaid." Rosemary was speechless. "Yes, isn't it wonderful? We own the house and we thought it silly to wait any longer."

"Married?" Rosemary said. "Well, aren't you the dark horse. All I can say is well done, Ria. Well done!"

Ria felt slightly that she would have preferred Rosemary to say that this was great; *well done* sort of implied that she had won by trickery. "Yes. Aren't you happy for us?"

"Of course I am." Rosemary hugged her. "Stunned but very happy for you. You got the man of your dreams *and* a beautiful house as well."

Ria decided to play it down a little. "There's years of work to get it right. No one else but us would be as mad as to take it on."

"Nonsense, it's worth a fortune; you and Danny know that. You certainly moved fast on that one, you got the bargain of the century." She spoke with true praise.

Ria felt a stab of guilt as if they had somehow conned poor Sean O'Brien and given him less than he deserved.

"Nobody's seen the house yet but you. I'm almost afraid of what the families will say when they do." Ria could see the jealousy in Hilary's face already.

"Nonsense, they'll be dead impressed. What are they like, Danny's parents?"

"I haven't met them yet, but I gather not at all like Danny," Ria said.

Rosemary made a face, "Still, maybe the brothers are okay. Are they coming home from England? I might make off with one of them. Bridesmaid's privilege, you know!"

"No mention of their coming back."

"Never mind. I'll find something to entertain me. Now, down to serious things. What will we wear?"

"Rosemary?"

"What?"

"You know I'm pregnant?"

"I thought you might be. But that's good, isn't it? It's what you want?"

"Yes, it is."

"So?"

"So, we shouldn't really be thinking of big white weddings and veils and all that stuff. And anyway, his family is very quiet, low-key. It wouldn't work."

"What would Danny like? Isn't that all that matters? Would he like the whole works or a few sandwiches in the pub?"

Ria didn't even pause to think. "He'd like the full works," she said.

"Then that is exactly what we'll have," said Rosemary, getting out pen and paper and starting to make a list.

She met Barney McCarthy before she met Danny's parents. She was invited to lunch. In fact it was a little like a royal command.

Danny was excited. "You'll like him, Ria, he's marvelous. And he'll love you, I know he will."

"I'm nervous of going to that restaurant, it will all be in French and we won't know what all the things are."

"Nonsense, just be yourself. And never apologize or put yourself down. We are as good as anyone else. Barney knows that, that's how he got on, by knowing it about himself." She noticed with a little stab of worry that Danny seemed more anxious about her meeting Barney than his parents. "Oh, we'll go down to them anytime," he said.

Nora Johnson was amazed at the news. "You do surprise me," she said twice.

Ria felt very irritated by this response. "Why do I surprise you, Mam? You know I love him, you know he loves me. What else would we do but get married?"

"Oh, certainly, certainly."

"What have you against him, Mam? You said you liked him, you admired the fact that he bought a big house and is planning to do it up. He's got good prospects, we won't be penniless. What objection do you have to him?"

"He's too good-looking," her mother said.

Hilary was no more enthusiastic. "You'd want to be careful of him, Ria," she said.

"Thank you very much, Hilary. When you were marrying Martin I didn't say that to you. I said I was delighted for you and I was sure you were going to be very happy."

"But that was true." Hilary was smug in her excellent choice of a mate.

"It's true for me too," Ria cried.

"Yes, Ria. But you'd have to watch him; he's a high flier. He's not going to be content with earning a living like normal people do; he'll want the moon. It's written all over him."

Danny, who never fussed about anything, went to great trouble discussing what Ria should wear when meeting Barney McCarthy.

Eventually it made her impatient. "Listen, you were the one who said I should be myself. I'll wear something nice and smart and I'll be myself. It's not a fashion parade or a beauty contest, it's a lunch." Her eyes flashed with the kind of spirit she hadn't shown for a while.

He looked at her admiringly. "That's my girl, that's the way to go," he said. She wore the scarlet coat she had bought for Hilary's wedding, and a new silk scarf that Rosemary had helped her to choose.

Barney McCarthy was a large square man of about forty-five in a very well-cut suit. He wore an expensive watch and he carried himself well and confidently. Slightly balding, he had the face of a working man, someone who had been out in all weathers. He had an easy manner; he was neither impressed by the restaurant nor trying to put it down. They talked effortlessly, all three of them.

Still, despite the pleasant, inconsequential conversation, Ria couldn't avoid the feeling that she was being given an interview. And with a sense of satisfaction after the coffee she realized that she had done very well.

Orla King was the one who told her that people in the office didn't really like Ria's working there anymore. Not now that she was engaged to marry Danny Lynch. People said that she would be telling him everything, giving him leads.

"I had no idea." Ria was shocked.

"Well, I'm only telling you because you two were very nice to me when I was being an eejit last Christmas." Orla was very nice. She couldn't help looking so good.

Ria wondered why she had felt so stupidly jealous of her.

Danny told Barney McCarthy that Ria had decided to leave the company, to go before they asked her to.

Barney was unexpectedly sympathetic. "That's very hard on her. She was in that firm long before you went in and rocked the boat."

"That's true," Danny said, surprised. He hadn't thought of it that way.

"So is she upset?"

"A little, but you know Ria, she's out looking for another job already." He was proud of her.

"Maybe I'd have a job for her," said Barney McCarthy.

One of his business interests was a new dress rental firm. A very classy outfit called Polly's. They took Ria immediately.

"Should I not have a week's trial or something?" Ria asked Gertie, the tall, pale manager with long dark hair tied in a simple ribbon behind her neck.

"No need," said Gertie with a grin. "Instructions from Mr. McCarthy to hire you, so you're hired."

"I'm sorry. That's an awful way to come in anywhere," Ria apologized.

"Listen, it's fine, and you're fine and we'll get along great," said Gertie. "I'm only telling it to you the way it is."

———

They went to see Danny's parents. It was a three-hour journey by bus. Ria felt very sick but forced herself to be in good spirits. Danny's father waited in the square where the bus came in. He drove an old shabby van with a trailer attached to it.

"This is my Ria, Dad." Danny was proud and pleased to show her off.

"You're very welcome." The man looked old, stooped, and shabby. He had worked all his life for his older and brighter brother, the man who had given Danny a start in the business. Danny's father was involved in delivering canisters of bottled gas around the countryside. He could be younger than Barney McCarthy but he looked a different generation.

They drove the two miles through narrow roads with high hedges to where Danny had been born. Ria looked around her, pleased to know his past and the place that had made him. But Danny hardly looked out at all.

"Did you have friends living in these places we pass by?"

"I knew them, yes," Danny said. "I went to school with them."

"And will we meet them?" she wanted to know.

"They've all gone away, nearly everyone emigrated," he said.

His mother seemed old too, much older than Ria had expected. They had ham and tomatoes, shop bread, and a packet of chocolate biscuits. They were not really sure if they could come to Dublin for the wedding, it was a long way and there might be work here that would be hard to get away from.

It was obvious that this was not so. Ria protested, "It would be wonderful to have you there for such a big day. We're going to have the reception on Tara Road and you'll see the new house."

"We're not great people for parties," Danny's mother said.

"But this is family," Ria begged.

"You know, it's a bit rattley in the bus and my back isn't what it was."

Ria looked at Danny. To her surprise he wasn't pushing and coaxing as much as she was. Surely he wanted them there. Didn't he? She waited for him to speak.

"Ah, go on. Come on, can't you? It's only once in a lifetime." They looked at each other doubtfully. "Now, I know you didn't go to Rich's wedding because that was in London," Danny began.

"But London's much farther away than here, and that would have meant planes and boats," Ria cried.

But the Lynches had been thrown the life belt they needed, the excuse not to go to the wedding.

"You see, child . . ." Danny's mother said, clutching Ria's arm. "You see, if we didn't go to the one wedding it would look like favoring Danny more if we went to the other."

"And we'll come up and see the house another time," Danny's father said.

They looked at her hopefully and there was no more to be said.

"Of course you will," she said soothingly. And they all smiled, Danny as much as anyone.

"Did you not want them to come?" she asked on the long bus journey home.

"Sweetheart, you could see yourself they didn't want to come," he said.

She felt disappointed in him. He should have persuaded them. But then men were different, everyone knew this.

After only a week in Polly's, Gertie told her something most unexpected. She told her that as one of the perks of the job Ria could rent a wedding dress for herself, free.

"Are you serious?" Ria's face lit up with joy. She would never have been able to afford anything like this.

"I tell you it straight up . . . Mr. McCarthy's instructions," said Gertie. "The whole wedding party is to be kitted out, so choose what you like. Go on, Ria, it's what he wants. Take it."

Danny took a morning suit for himself and his best man. Rosemary chose a slinky silver dress with little pearl buttons. Ria had a few problems convincing her mother and sister that they should pick something for the day.

"Come on, Mam, Hilary. It's free, for heaven's sake. We'll never get an opportunity like this again," she pleaded. She was nearly there. "And why doesn't Martin wear a morning suit?" Ria suggested. "He'd look terrific in it. Go on, Hilary, you know he would."

That's what did it. Her mother wore a smart gray coat and jacket, with a black feathered hat, Hilary a wine-colored suit with pale pink lapels, and a huge pink hat.

Since there was no outlay on wedding clothes, they paid for a tenor to sing "Panis Angelicus" *and* a soprano to sing "Ave Maria."

It was a very mixed gathering. They invited Orla from the old office and Gertie from Polly's. One of Danny's brothers, Larry, came over from London and was best man. He looked like Danny, same fair hair and lopsided smile, only taller, and spoke now with a London accent.

"Will you be going home to see your parents?" Ria asked.

"Not this time," Larry said. He hadn't been back to the place where he grew up to see his father and mother for four years.

Ria knew this, but she knew not to comment even by a glance. "There'll be plenty of other times," she said.

Larry looked at her with approval. "That's it, Ria," he said.

To Ria's huge relief she heard her sister and brother-in-law make no mention at all of anything being a waste of money. The smell of paint had well left Tara Road and the big trestle tables covered with long white tablecloths held chicken salads and ice cream as well as the big wedding cake.

Barney McCarthy was there. He apologized that his wife, Mona, had not been able to come. She had gone to Lourdes with three friends, it had been long arranged. Gertie had giggled a bit at this information, but Ria had hushed her quickly. Barney had sent two cases of champagne in advance and he stood chatting easily among the forty people who toasted the bride and groom, handsome Danny Lynch and his beautiful bride.

Ria had never thought she could look as well as this with her dark curls swept up into a headdress and a long veil trailing behind her. The dress had never been worn before, thick embroidery and lace from head to toe, the richest fabric she had ever seen.

Rosemary had been there to advise and suggest throughout. "Stand very straight, Ria. Hold your shoulders right back. Don't scuttle up the church; when you get in there walk much more slowly."

"Look, it's not Westminster Abbey," Ria protested.

"It's your day, every eye in the place is on you, walk like you want to give them something to look at."

"That's easy if you look like *you*. With me it's different. They'd die if they thought I was taking myself seriously." Ria felt nervous, as if she was going to look affected, as if she were playing a part. She was so afraid of having them all laugh at her.

"Why shouldn't you take yourself seriously? You look gorgeous. You've got proper makeup on for once. You're a dream, go for it, Ria." The bridesmaid's enthusiasm was very infectious. Ria walked almost regally into the church on the arm of her brother-in-law, who was giving her away.

Danny had actually gasped when she came up the aisle.

"I love you so much," he said as they posed by the wedding cake for pictures. And Ria suddenly felt sorry for whoever else was going to wear this dress when it was cleaned and back out in the shop.

No other bride could ever look as well or be so happy.

They had no honeymoon. Danny went back to looking for work and Ria went back to her job in Polly's. She enjoyed the work and the extraordinarily varied streams of customers they met. There were many more rich people in Dublin than she had known about, and also people who were not rich but who were prepared to spend huge amounts on a wedding day.

Gertie was kind to the brides and didn't fuss them. She helped them choose but didn't steer them toward the most expensive. She encouraged them to be more daring. A wedding was for dressing up, she said, like a rainbow or fireworks.

"Why is it called Polly's? It's a silly name," a bride asked Ria one day.

"I think it's to do with Pretty Polly . . . something like that," Ria explained.

"That was very diplomatic," Gertie said admiringly afterward.

"What do you mean? I hadn't a clue why he called it Polly's. Do you know?"

"After his fancy woman. It's hers; he bought it for her. You know that."

"I didn't, actually. I hardly know him at all. I thought he was pillar of the church and all that."

"Oh, yes, he is when he's with the wife. But with Polly Callaghan . . . that's something else."

"Oh, that's why the checks are all to P. Callaghan. I see."

"What did you think it was?"

"I thought it might be a tax thing."

"But wasn't he at your wedding and all? I thought you were great pals with him."

"No, Danny sold his house for him, that's all."

"Well, he told me to give you the job and to organize all the gear for your wedding, so he must think very highly of your Danny."

"He's not the only one. Danny's out at lunch today with two fellows who are thinking of setting up their own firm. They want him to join them."

"And will he?"

"I hope not, Gertie, it would be too risky. He has no capital; he'd have to put the house up with a second mortgage as a security or something. It would be very dangerous. I'd love him to go somewhere where he'd be paid."

"Do you tell him this?" Gertie asked.

"Not really. He's such a dreamer, and he thinks big, and he's been right so often. I stay out of it a lot of the time. I don't want to be the one who is holding him back."

"You have it all worked out," Gertie said with admiration. Gertie had a boyfriend, Jack, who drank too much. She had tried to finish with him many times, but she always went back.

"No, I don't really have it worked out," Ria said. "I *look* placid, you see, that's why people think I'm fine. Inside I worry a lot."

"Did you say yes to them?" Ria hoped that Danny couldn't hear the anxiety in her voice.

"No, I didn't. Actually, I didn't say anything. I listened to them instead."

Danny was good at that. It looked as if he was talking but in fact he was nodding his head and listening.

"And what did you hear?"

"How much they wanted Barney's business and how seriously they thought I could deliver it. They know all about him, like what he eats for breakfast sort of thing. They told me about companies and businesses he has that I never knew about."

"And what are you going to do?"

"I've done it," Danny said.

"What on earth did you do?"

"I went to Barney. I told him that anything I had was due to him and that I had this offer from fellows who knew a bit too much about him for his comfort."

"And what did he say?"

"He thanked me and said he'd come back to me."

"Danny, aren't you amazing! And when will he come back to you?"

"I don't know. I had to pretend not to mind. Maybe next week, maybe tomorrow. You see, he might advise me to take it or not to. I'll listen to him. He could ring tomorrow. I might be wrong but I feel he'll ring tomorrow."

Danny was wrong. Barney McCarthy called that night. He had been thinking of setting up a small real estate agency himself. All he really needed was to be prompted to do it. Now he had. Would Danny Lynch manage it for him? On a salary of course, but part of the profits as well.

Not long after this they were invited to a party at the McCarthys' home. Ria recognized a lot of faces there. Politicians, a man who read the news on television, a well-known golfer.

Barney's wife was a large, comfortable-looking woman. Mona moved with ease and confidence among the guests. She wore a navy wool dress and had what must have been real pearls around her plump neck. She was probably in her mid-forties, like her husband. Could Barney *really* have a fancy woman called Polly Callaghan, Ria wondered. A settled, married man with this comfortable home and grown-up children? It seemed unlikely. Yet Gertie had been very definite about it. Ria tried to imagine what Polly Callaghan looked like, what age she was.

Just at that moment Mona McCarthy came up to her. "I understand you work at Polly's," she said pleasantly.

Ria suddenly felt an insane urge to deny it and say she had never heard of Polly. She told Barney McCarthy's wife that it was a most interesting job and that she and Gertie loved getting involved in all the dramas of the people who came in and out.

"Will you continue working after you've had the baby?" Mona asked.

"Oh, yes, we need the money and we thought we'd give a foreign student one of the single rooms and she could look after the baby."

Mona frowned. "You don't need the money, surely?"

"Well, Mrs. McCarthy, your husband has been most generous to Danny but we have a huge house to keep up."

"When Barney was starting out I went to work. It was to make money to keep Barney's builder's van on the road. I always regret it. The children grew up without me. You can't have that time back again."

"I'm sure you're right, we'll certainly talk about it. Maybe the moment I see the baby I won't want to go out to work ever again."

"I didn't certainly, but I went out after six weeks."

"Was he very grateful, Mr. McCarthy? Did he know how hard it was for you?"

"Grateful? No, I don't think so. Things were different then. We were so anxious to make a go of it, you know, we just did what had to be done."

She was nice, this woman. No airs and graces, and they must have been a little like herself and Danny years ago. How sad that now when they were old he fancied someone else.

She looked across the room. Danny was at the center of a little circle telling some funny story.

Danny's parents could never have been guests in a house like this. Barney McCarthy, when he was growing up, would not have been in a place of this grandeur. Perhaps he saw in Danny some of the same push and drive that he had in his youth, and that was why he was encouraging him. In years to come they might be entertaining at Tara Road and everyone would know that Danny had another lady somewhere.

She gave a little shiver. Nobody knew what the future had in store.

"What does she look like, this Polly?" Ria asked Gertie.

"About thirty, I imagine. Red hair, very smart, keeps herself well. She comes in about once a month. You'll like her, she's really nice."

"I don't think I will like her. I liked the wife."

"But she's old, the wife, isn't she, I mean really old?"

"I suppose she's about the same age as her husband. She went out to work, you know, so that he could afford a van."

Gertie shrugged. "That's life," she said. "It's hard on old Polly too. At Christmastime and Sunday lunches, he doing the family man bit. I suppose I should be congratulating myself that at least my Jack is single. He may not be much else but single he is."

Gertie was back with Jack again. He was meant to be seriously off the drink this time but nobody was holding her breath.

———

Barney McCarthy was looking at some land in Galway and he needed Danny to go with him. Barney drove fast and they crossed the country quickly.

A table had been booked in advance and waiting for them was an attractive woman in a cream-colored suit.

"This is Polly Callaghan." Barney gave her a kiss on the cheek and introduced her to Danny.

Danny swallowed. He had heard about her from Ria. He hadn't expected her to be so glamorous.

"How do you do?" he said.

"The boy wonder, I'm told." She smiled at him.

"No, just born lucky."

"Was it Napoleon who said he wanted generals that were lucky?" she asked.

"He was bloody right if that's what he said," Barney offered. "Now, what drinks?"

"Diet Coke, please," Danny said.

"No vices at all?" she asked.

"I want to keep a clear head if I'm to work out how much apartments would go for in the area."

"You weren't born lucky," Polly Callaghan said. "You were born sharp, that's much better."

"And did they have the same room?" Ria asked.

"I don't know, I didn't check."

"But, you know, were they lovey-dovey?" She was eager to know.

"Not so you'd notice. They were more like a married couple really. They acted as if they knew each other very well."

"Poor Mona, I wonder does she know," Ria said.

"Poor Mona, as you call her, probably doesn't give a damn. Hasn't she a palace of a house and everything she wants?"

"She may want not to share him with a mistress."

"I liked Polly Callaghan, actually. She was nice."

"I'm sure," said Ria, a little sourly.

———

Polly came into the shop the next day. "I met your husband in Galway, did he tell you?"

"No, Mrs. Callaghan, he didn't." For some reason Ria lied.

Polly seemed pleased, she nodded approvingly. "Discreet as well as everything else, or maybe you are. Anyway he's a bright lad."

"He is indeed." Ria smiled proudly.

Polly looked at Gertie carefully. "What happened to your face, Gertie? That's a terrible bruise."

"I know, Mrs. Callaghan. Didn't I have a fall off my bicycle. I hoped it wasn't too noticeable."

"Did you have to have a stitch?"

"Two, but it's nothing. Will I get you a cup of coffee?"

"Please." Polly looked after Gertie as she went upstairs for the coffee tray. "Are you two friends, Ria?"

"Yes, yes indeed."

"Then talk her out of that lout she's involved with. He did that to her, you know."

"Oh, he couldn't have . . ." Ria was shocked.

"Well, he did it before, that's why she wears her hair long, to hide it. He'll kill her in the end. But she won't be told, not by me anyway. She thinks I'm an interfering old bat. She might listen to you."

"Where's *Mister* Callaghan?" Ria asked Gertie when Polly had left the shop.

"There never was one, it's only a courtesy title. Did she tell you that Jack did this to me?"

"Yes. How do you know?"

"Because I see it in your face. And she's always on me to get rid of him."

"But you can't go back to him if he hit you."

"He doesn't mean it. He's so sorry, you have no idea."

"Did he just come in and punch you in the face?"

"No, it wasn't like that. It was an argument, he lost his temper. He didn't mean it."

"You can't take him back."

"Look, everyone in the world's given up on Jack, I'm not going to."

"But you can see why everyone in the world's given up."

"I tell you, he cried like a baby he was so ashamed. He said he didn't remember picking up the chair."

"He hit you with a chair? Jesus, Mary, and Joseph."

"Don't start, Ria. Please don't start. I've had my mother and my friends and Polly Callaghan. Not you as well."

Just then Rosemary came in to look at wedding hats and the matter had to be dropped. Rosemary had been invited to a society wedding, she said. It was now seriously time to get a man. She wanted a hat that would take every eye in the place away from the bride.

"Poor bride," said Ria.

"It's a jungle out there," said Rosemary.

The baby was due in the first week of October.

"That will be Libra, that's a good star sign. It's got to do with being balanced," Gertie said.

"You don't believe all of that, do you?"

"Of course I do."

Ria laughed. "You're as bad as my sister, Hilary. She and her friends spent a fortune on some woman in a caravan, they believed every word out of her."

"Oh, where is she? Let's go to her."

"Wild horses couldn't get me there."

"She might tell you if it's going to be a girl or a boy."

"Stop it. I don't want to know that badly."

"Ah, come on. And we'll get Rosemary to come too. What'll she say?"

"She'll tell me that I'm pregnant, she'll see that from my stomach. That you're involved with a fellow who can't keep his fists to himself; she'll see that from your face. And that Rosemary's going to marry a rich man, it's written all over her. And we'll have given her good money for that."

"*Please,*" Gertie said. "It'll be a laugh."

Mrs. Connor had a thin, haunted face. She did not look like someone who was being handed fistfuls of fivers and tenners by foolish women for a bit of news about the future. She looked like someone who had seen too much. Maybe that was all part of the mystique, Ria thought, as she sat down and stretched out her hand.

The baby would be a girl, a healthy girl, followed some years later by a boy.

"Aren't there going to be three? I have three little lines here," Ria asked.

"No, one of them isn't a real child line. It could be a miscarriage, I don't know."

"And my husband's business, is it going to do well?"

"I'd have to see his hand for that. Your own business will do well, I can see there's a lot of travel, across the sea. Yes, a lot of travel."

Ria giggled to herself. It was twenty pounds wasted, and the baby would probably be a boy. She wondered how the others got on.

"Well, Gertie, what did she tell you?"

"Not much, you were right. She was no good, really."

Rosemary and Ria looked at each other. Rosemary was aware of Jack and his lifestyle by now.

"I expect she told you to walk on out on your current dark stranger," Rosemary said.

"Don't be so cruel, Rosemary, she did *not* say that." Gertie's voice sounded shaky.

"Listen, I didn't mean it," Rosemary said.

There was a silence.

"And what about you, Rosemary?" Ria wanted to break the tension.

"A load of old nonsense, nothing I wanted to know at all."

"No husband?"

"No, but a whole rake of other problems. You don't want to be bothered with it." She fell silent again and concentrated on driving the car. As an outing it had not been a success.

"I told you we were mad to go," Ria said.

The others said nothing at all.

Barney McCarthy was a frequent visitor to Tara Road. Ria learned that he had two married daughters who lived in big modern houses out near the sea. Barney said that neither house had a tenth of the character that this one had. But the girls had insisted. They wanted places that had never heard of damp. They got no pleasure from going to auctions and sales and finding treasures. They just liked to accept delivery of brand-new suites of furniture, fitted kitchens, built-in bedroom cupboards. He spoke with an air of resignation, it was simply the way people were.

"It sounds as if he pays for it all," Ria suggested.

"You can be sure he does, those two guys aren't lighting any fires anywhere—getting married to rich women, that's the only energy they used up."

"Are they nice?"

"Not really, anyway not to me. And why should they be? They're not in business with him like I am. They resent me like hell."

"Don't you mind?"

Danny shrugged.

"Why should I mind? Listen, Barney's got us a perfect Victorian brass fender from an old house his people are demolishing, and proper fire irons. He says they're just right, the genuine article; the fender would cost two hundred pounds at a sale."

"And why do we get them for nothing?" Ria asked.

"Because to everyone else they're just junk from a house. They'd go on a scrap pile. We really are getting that front room into shape."

Danny was right. It was unrecognizable now. Ria often wondered what would happen if old Sean came back and saw what they had done to his shabby storeroom. They hadn't gotten the carpet of Danny's dreams yet, though they kept looking, and they *had* found what they thought was the perfect table. It was called a "mahogany tripodular breakfast table" in the catalog. That meant it had three feet, they realized; it was exactly right for this room. They discussed it for ages. Was it too small, should they go for a real, *proper* dining table? But four could sit around it easily and even six at a pinch. They would be entertaining more as time went on.

Ria said that she had lost all contact with what was real and what was fantasy.

"I never saw ourselves as owning anything like this, Danny."

Her arms swept in the whole house. "I never thought we'd have a front room like this in a million years. How do I know whether we might end up with a dining table for twelve and a butler?"

They laughed and hugged each other.

Danny Lynch from the broken-down cottage in the back of beyond, and Ria Johnson from the corner house in the big, shabby estate were not only living like gentry in a big Tara Road mansion, they were actually debating what style of dining table to buy.

The day the round table was delivered they brought up two kitchen chairs and a bowl of flowers and sat across from each other holding hands. It was a warm evening, their hall door was open, and when Barney McCarthy called he stood for a few moments looking in at them, happy and excited.

"You do my heart good, the pair of you," he said.

And Ria realized how his two sons-in-law must indeed hate Danny, the favored one, in many ways the heir apparent.

Barney said that Danny and Ria needed a car. They began to look at the ads for secondhand motors. "I meant a company car," he said. And they got a new one.

"I'm really afraid to let Hilary see this," Ria said, patting the new upholstery.

"Let me think . . . she'll say that the depreciation starts the moment you put it on the road," Danny guessed.

"And my mother would say there was a car like this in *Coronation Street* or something." Ria laughed. "I wonder what *your* parents would say if they saw it."

Danny thought for moment. "It would worry them. It would be too much. They'd have to put coats on and take the dog for a walk." He sounded sad but accepting that this is the way things would always be.

"They'll become more joyful in time. We won't give up on them," Ria said. She thought she sounded a bit like Gertie, who despite everything was not going to give up on Jack. She was actually wearing his ring now and they would marry soon. That would give him confidence, she said.

They were invited to Sunday lunch at the McCarthys. Not a big party this time, just the four of them. Barney and Danny talked buildings and property all the time. Mona and Ria talked about the baby.

"I thought about your advice, and I think I am going to stay at home and look after the baby," Ria said.

"Will you be able to rely on grandmothers for a bit of help?"

"Not really. My mother goes out to work and Danny's parents are miles down the country."

"But they'll come up to see the child?"

"I hope so. They're very quiet you know, not like Danny."

Mona nodded as if she understood very well. "They'll mellow when the baby arrives."

"Did that happen with you too?" You could ask Mona McCarthy anything, and she never minded talking about their humble origins.

"Yes, you see Barney was very different from the rest of his family. I think his parents didn't understand why he pushed himself so hard. They didn't do much; his father just made tea in the builder's yard all his life. But they loved it when we brought the children round at a weekend. I used to be tired and could have done without it. They never knew why Barney worked so hard and they couldn't understand his head for business. But it's different when it comes to grandchildren. Maybe it will be the same in their case."

Ria wished this kind woman didn't have the smart, groomed Polly Callaghan as a rival. For the hundredth time she wondered whether Mona McCarthy knew about the situation. Almost everyone else in Dublin did.

Danny had to go to London with Barney. Ria drove him to the airport. Just as she kissed him good-bye she saw the smart figure of Polly Callaghan get out of a taxi. Ria deliberately looked the other way.

But Polly had no such niceties; she came straight over. "So this is the new car. Very nice too."

"Oh hallo, Mrs. Callaghan. Danny, I'm not meant to park here, I should move off. Anyway, I should be at work."

"I'll keep an eye on him for you in London. I won't let him get distracted by any little glamour-puss over there."

"Thanks," Ria gulped.

"Come on, Danny. The great man has the tickets, he'll start to fuss in a moment." They were gone.

Ria thought of Mona McCarthy and how she had taken Barney's children every weekend to see their grandparents even though she was tired from working all week.

Life was hard on people.

Ria gave up work a week before the baby was due. They were all very supportive, these people she had not even known a year ago. Barney McCarthy said that Danny must be around Dublin, not touring the country so that he would be nearby for the birth. Mona said that they shouldn't waste money buying cots and prams. She had kept plenty for grandchildren; it was just that her own daughters hadn't provided her with any yet.

Polly Callaghan said that Ria must know there would always be a part-time job for her when and if she wanted to come back, and gave her an outlandish pink and black bed jacket to wear in the hospital.

Rosemary, who had been promoted to run a bigger branch of the printing company, came to see her from time to time.

"I'm just no good at all this deep breathing and waters breaking and everything," Rosemary apologized. "I've no experience of it."

"Nor I," Ria said ruefully. "I've never had anything to do with it either, and I'm the one who's going to have to go through with it."

"Ah, well." Rosemary wagged her finger as if to say that we all knew why. "Does Danny go to these prenatal classes with you? I can't imagine him . . ."

"Yes, he's as good as gold, it's idiotic really, but very exciting all the same; he loves it in a way."

"Of course he does, and he'll love you too again when you get your figure back." Rosemary was wearing her very slim-fitting trouser suit and looked like a long, elegant reed. She meant it to be reassuring, Ria thought, but because she felt like a tank herself it was unsettling.

As were the visits from pretty little Orla from the big real estate agency that would have been greatly frowned on had her bosses known of them. And Ria's mother came too, full of advice and warnings.

The only one who didn't come was Hilary. She was so envious of Tara Road that it pained her to come inside the door and see the renovations. Ria had tried to involve her in the whole business of looking for bargains at auctions, but that didn't work either. Hilary became so discontented at the size and scope of her own house compared to Ria's that the outings would end in disaster. The wonderful day when they saw the huge sideboard was almost ruined because of Hilary's tantrum.

"It's so unfair," she said. "Just because you have a great big empty room, you can buy great furniture dirt cheap. It's only because nobody else has these mansions that nobody wants them."

"Well, isn't that our good luck?" Ria was stung.

"No, it's the system—you're going to get that sideboard for nothing. . . ."

"Shush, Hilary, it's coming up in a minute. I have to concentrate. Danny says we can go to three hundred pounds—it's worth eight hundred, he thinks."

"You're going to pay three *hundred* pounds for one piece of furniture for a parlor you don't even use? You're completely mad."

"Hilary, *please,* people are looking at us."

"And so well they might be looking at us, that thing could be crawling with woodworm."

"It's not, I checked."

"It's daft, this, believe me."

The bidding had started. Nobody was interested. One dealer who Ria knew by sight was raising it slowly against a man who ran a secondhand furniture shop. But they would both have the same problem unloading it. Whose house would have room for it?

"A hundred and fifty." Ria's voice was clear and strong.

The others stayed in for a minute or two and then dropped out. She had the Victorian serving table, as it was described, for one hundred and eighty pounds.

"Now! Wasn't that marvelous?" Ria said, but the dead, disappointed face of her sister gave no answering flicker.

"Look, Hilary, I just saved a hundred and twenty pounds, why don't we celebrate? Isn't there something you'd like—you and Martin. Go on, we'll bid for that if there is."

"No, thank you." The voice was stiff.

Ria thought of the huge celebration there would be at Tara Road when she told Danny the good news about the sideboard. She couldn't bear to think of her only sister going back to that strange, pokey little house, to that sad, joyless Martin. But she knew there was nothing she could do. She would have liked to stay, and with the money she had saved maybe spend fifty pounds on some nice glass. There were a couple of decanters there that might go cheaply. But the mockery would be too great. Hilary would remind her that they were people who had had tomato ketchup and a bottle of Chef mayonnaise on their sideboard when they were young. Not a ship's decanter. It would take the joy out of it.

"Let's go then, Hilary," she said.

And since then, Hilary had not been around to the house at all. It was childish and hurtful, but Ria felt that she had been given so much she could afford to be forgiving and tolerant. She wanted to see her sister and talk to her the way they used to before all this money and style got in the way.

Danny was working late in the office, there were still five days to go before the baby. Ria decided she would drive to see Hilary. She didn't care what snide remarks would be made by her sister about the smart car. She wanted to talk to her.

Martin was out; he was at a residents' meeting where they were organizing a protest. Hilary looked tired and discontented.

"Oh, it's you," she said when she saw Ria. Her eye was drawn to the car at the gate. "Hope that will still have tires on it when you leave," she added.

"Hilary, can I come in?"

"Sure."

"You and I didn't have a fight about anything, did we?"

"What are you going on about?"

"Well, it's just that you never come and see me. I ask you so often it's embarrassing. You're not there when I go to Mam. Not one word of good wishes over all this. We used to be pals. What happened?"

Hilary's face was mutinous like a child. "You don't need pals anymore."

Ria was not going to let this go. "Like hell I don't need a pal. I'm scared stiff of having the baby in the first place. People say it's terrifying and that no one admits it. I'm worried that I mightn't be able to look after it properly and I'm afraid that Danny's taken on too much and that we'll lose everything. At times I'm afraid he'll stop loving me if I start whining about things, and you *dare* to tell me I don't need a pal."

Things changed then. Hilary's frown had gone. "I'll put on the kettle," she said.

Orla called round to Tara Road. One of the tenants explained that both the Lynches were out. Danny was probably at his office. Ria had taken the car somewhere. Orla thought she would call on Danny at his office. She had been drinking since she left work; she didn't feel like going home yet. And Danny might like to go for a pint. And he was extraordinarily attractive.

Nora Johnson read the letter for the third time. They were selling the shop where she worked. There were some expressions of regret. And explanations of the changing needs of consumers. But the bottom line was that come the beginning of November, Nora Johnson was going to have no job.

Rosemary smiled at the man across the table. He was a big customer at the print shop. He had asked her out many times. Tonight was the first time she had said yes and they were having dinner in a very expensive restaurant. They were doing a color brochure for him. It was for a charity heavily supported by businessmen. It would be a good point of contact. Others might see and admire their work. Rosemary had spent a lot of time and trouble making sure that the finished product would be right.

"And do you have the full list of your sponsors so that we can set them out for you with some suitable artwork?"

"I have them back at my hotel," he said.

"But you don't have a hotel room," Rosemary said. "You *live* in Dublin."

"That's right." He had an easy confident smile. "But tonight I have a hotel room." He raised his glass at her.

Rosemary raised her glass back. "What an extravagant gesture," she said.

"You're worth only the very best," he said.

"I meant extravagant not to have checked first whether the room would be called on."

He laughed at what he thought was her grudging admiration. "You know, I had this premonition that you would come to dinner with me and end the evening with a drink back at the hotel."

"And your premonition was exactly half right. Thank you for a delightful dinner." She stood up, ready to leave.

He was genuinely amazed. "What makes you come on like this, all promises and teasing and then a bucket of cold water?"

Rosemary spoke clearly. She could be heard at the nearby tables. "There were no promises and no teasings. There was an invitation to dinner to discuss business, which was accepted. There was no question of going to your hotel room. We don't need business that badly."

She walked head high from the restaurant, with all the confidence that being twenty-three, blond, and beautiful brings with it.

"I didn't mean to be standoffish," Hilary was saying. "It's just that you have everything, Ria, really everything . . . a fellow like a film star . . . Mam says he's too good-looking. . . ."

"What does Mam know about men?"

"*And* you've got that house and the flashy car outside the door here and you go to places and meet celebrities. How was I to know that you might want someone like me around?"

As she was about to answer Ria got the dart of pain that she knew was waiting for her sometime next week. The baby was on the way.

Gertie had been out to get fish and chips. She laid the package on the kitchen table while she went to get the plates that were warming in the bottom of the oven. She had a tray with tomato ketchup, knives, forks, and napkins ready.

She had not understood Jack's humor. With his arm he swept the paper-wrapped parcel off the table. "You're only a slut," he shouted at her. "You're not fit for any decent man's house. A woman who can't put dinner on the table but has to go out to the chipper to buy it."

"Oh, no. Jack, please, *please,*" Gertie cried.

He had picked up what was nearest at hand. As ill luck would have it, it was a heavy, long-handled scrubbing brush.

When Martin came back from the residents' association a young boy from next door was waiting with the news. "There's a baby being born," he said excitedly. "Your missus didn't know how to drive the car so my da drove them to the hospital. You missed all the fun."

They couldn't find Danny. He wasn't at Tara Road. He wasn't at the office. Ria gave Hilary Barney McCarthy's telephone number in case he might be there, but Mona said that he wasn't at home, and she hadn't seen Danny at all. He had wanted to be at the hospital. They had been through it all so often.

Ria wanted him beside her now. *"Danny!"* she screamed with her eyes closed. He had said so often that this was *their* baby, he would be there for the birth. Where in God's name was he?

Danny had been about to leave his office when Orla King arrived. Pretty as a picture but definitely slurring her words. He didn't need a conversation with her just now. But Danny Lynch was never rude.

"Would you like to go to the pub for one?" Orla asked.

"No, sweetheart. I'm bushed," he said.

"A pub livens you up. Come on, please."

"You'll have to forgive me tonight, Orla."

"What night then?" she asked. She ran her tongue over her lips as she smiled at him.

He could either go at once, risking a scene and possibly leaving unfinished business, or he could offer her a drink from the bottle of brandy he kept for Barney. "A small brandy then, Orla. But just three minutes to drink it then we both have to go."

She had won, she thought. She sat on his desk with her legs crossed as Danny went to the cupboard and found the bottle. Just then the phone rang.

"Oh, leave it, Danny. It's only work," Orla pleaded.

"Not this time at night," he said, picking it up.

"Danny, are you alone? This is Polly Callaghan. It's urgent."

"Not really, no."

"Can you be alone?"

"It will take a few minutes."

"I haven't time. . . . Can you just listen?"

"Of course."

"Have you your car?"

"No."

"Right, Barney's here. He has chest pains. I can't call the cardiac ambulance to come here, I want to call it to your house."

"Yes, of course."

"But it's a question of my getting him there."

"I'll get a taxi to you. I'll make the other call first."

At this stage the petulant voice of Orla could be heard. "*Dan-ny,* come off the phone, come over here."

"And you'll get rid of whatever companion you have with you?"

"Yes." He was clipped.

And even more clipped dealing with Orla. "I'm sorry, Orla, sweetheart. Brandy's over . . . I have an emergency."

"You don't call me sweetheart and then ask me to leave," she began.

She found herself propelled toward the door, while Danny grabbed his jacket and phoned an ambulance all at the same time.

She heard him give the Tara Road address. "Who's sick? Is it the baby arriving?" she asked, frightened by his intensity.

"Good-bye, Orla," he said, and she saw him running down the street to hail a taxi.

Barney was a very gray shade of white. He sat in a chair beside the bed. Polly had made unsuccessful attempts to dress him.

"Don't worry about the tie," Danny barked. "Go down and tell the taxi man to come up . . . to help me get him down the stairs."

Polly hesitated for a second. "You know the way Barney hates anyone knowing his business."

"This is a taxi man, for Christ's sake, Polly. Not MI5. Barney'd want to get there quicker."

Barney spoke with his hand firmly holding his chest. "Don't talk about me as if I'm not here, for Christ's sake. Yes, get the taxi man, Polly, quick as you can." To Danny he spoke gently. "Thank you for getting here, thank you for sorting it out."

"You're going to be fine." Danny supported the older man easily and warmly in a way he would never have been able to hold his own father.

"You'll look after everything for me, the way it should be?"

"You'll be doing it yourself in forty-eight hours," Danny said.

"But just in case . . ."

"Just in case, then. Yes, I will." Danny spoke briskly, knowing that was what was wanted.

At that moment the taxi man arrived. If he recognized the face of

Barney McCarthy he gave no sign. Instead he got down to the job of easing a heavy man with heart pains down the narrow stairs of an expensive apartment block to take him to another address from which the ambulance would collect him. If he had worked out the situation he had seen too much and been too long in the taxi game to let on anything at all.

Hilary waited in the big shabby room outside the Labor Ward. From time to time she made further unsuccessful stabs at finding Danny. There was no reply from her mother's house when Hilary rang. She didn't know her mother was sitting there with the letter telling her that her working life was over.

Nora Johnson was too despondent to answer the telephone until she had pulled herself together and decided what she would do next.

"Danny!" That was the scream before the baby's head appeared. The nurse was speaking and she could hardly hear. "All right, Ria. It's over, you have a beautiful little baby girl. She's perfect."

Ria felt more tired than she had ever been. Danny had not been here to see his daughter born. The fortune-teller had been right, it *was* a little girl.

Orla King felt that she was now losing her mind because of drink. Not only did the guilt of trying to seduce a man on the night that his wife was having their first baby hang heavily on her, but the subsequent confusion in her brain worried her. She knew that Ria must have been at home because she heard Danny call the ambulance to Tara Road. But then she heard from everyone else that Ria was at her sister's house and they had to get a neighbor to drive Ria's car to the hospital as Hilary couldn't drive. Orla knew now that she was hallucinating and having memory failure. She went to her first Alcoholics Anonymous meeting.

And on the first night she met a man called Colm Barry. He was single, handsome, and worked at a bank. Colm had dark curly hair, which he wore a little long on his collar. He had dark sad eyes.

"You don't look like a banker," Orla said to him.

"I don't feel like a bank clerk. I'd rather be a chef."

"I don't feel like being a typist in a real estate agency. I'd like to be a model or a singer," Orla said.

"There's no reason why we shouldn't be these things, is there?" Colm asked with a smile.

Orla didn't know whether he was making fun of her or being nice, but she didn't mind. He was going to make these meetings bearable.

On that night when Gertie saw Jack raising the great scrubbing brush that might have split her head, she picked up a knife and stuck it straight into his arm. They both watched helplessly and amazed as the blood poured onto the packet of fish and chips he had flung to the floor. Then she took off her engagement ring, laid it on the table, got her coat, and walked out of the house. From a phone booth at the corner of the road, she rang the police and told them what she had done. In the Emergency Ward, Jack assured everyone that it had been purely domestic and that nobody was making any accusation against anyone whatsoever.

For a very long time, Gertie refused to see Jack, and then to everyone's disappointment she agreed to meet him just once. She found a chastened and sober man. They talked and she remembered why she loved him. They asked two strangers to be their witnesses and they were married in a cold church at eight o'clock one morning. Jack was put off the road for drunken driving and consequently sacked from his job.

Gertie left Polly's just before Polly Callaghan sacked her. She was absent too often; it was no longer reasonable to expect them to keep her on the payroll. Jack had bouts of sobriety, never lasting very long. Gertie grew white-faced and anxious. She got a job in a launderette where there was a flat upstairs. It was a living but only a bare living.

Gertie's own mother washed her hands of the whole situation. She said that she just hoped Gertie had good friends that would tide her over when times got really bad. Gertie had one friend who tided her over a great deal: Ria Lynch.

Hilary Moran never fully forgave Danny Lynch for not being with his wife that night. Oh, she had heard that there were explanations and confidences that had to be kept, and Ria certainly bore no grudge. But nobody else had heard the great wailing as Ria had waited for him to come to her during the long hours of labor. It made her feel even more strongly that she had gotten a good man in Martin. He might never reach the dizzying heights of Danny Lynch; he was certainly not as easy on the eye. But you could rely on him. He would always be there. And when Hilary had a child Martin would not be missing. She hoped that they would have children. The fortune-teller had been wrong about living amid trees. She might be wrong about them having no children as well.

Barney McCarthy recovered from his heart attack. Everyone said that it had been so fortunate to have come upon him when he was with quick-witted, resourceful Danny Lynch who wasted no time in getting him to the hospital. He had to take things a little more easily these days.

He had wanted to involve Danny more in his business, but met with an unexpected resistance from his family. Perfectly natural resentment, Barney thought to himself. They obviously feared that Danny was getting too close to him. He would have to be more diplomatic. Show them that he was not going outside the family.

Sometimes he felt that his daughters seemed sharper with him, less loving. Less uncritically supportive. But Barney did not allow himself the luxury of brooding about people's moods. These girls owed him everything. He had slaved long hours and years to get them their superior educations and degrees. Even if they had heard something about Polly Callaghan they were unlikely to rock the boat. They knew that he would not leave Mona, that the household would continue undisturbed. He enjoyed his dealings with Danny Lynch, but for everyone's sake he just had to make sure they were less public as time went on.

For Nora Johnson, the day that her granddaughter was born was also the date that she had been told her job was over. She made a decision not to tell any of the family about it, not until she had tried to find another position at any rate. But it wasn't easy, and in the first weeks of Annie Lynch's life her grandmother was facing rejection after rejection. There were few openings for a woman of fifty-one with no qualifications.

Wearily and without much hope she went for an interview as a carer companion to an elderly lady who lived in a little granny cottage in the grounds of a big house around the corner from Tara Road. It turned out extremely well. They took to each other on sight. When it became known that Nora had a daughter living on Tara Road the old lady's family suggested that maybe the post should be a residential one. Nora could sell her own house, have a nest egg and live around the corner from her daughter Ria.

Ah, but what about her security and her future, Nora had wondered. Where would she live when in the fullness of time the old lady she was looking after had left this earth? It was arranged that she should have first refusal on buying the house when that day came.

Polly Callaghan remembered the night that child was born because it was the night she thought she was going to lose Barney forever. She had loved him without pausing to count the cost for twelve years, since she was twenty-five years old. Not once did she stop and say that it was folly to love a man who would never be free.

She did not weigh up the very likely possibility of finding herself a single man who would be delighted to provide her with a home and family. Polly Callaghan, glamorous, articulate, and successful, would have been the object of interest to many a man.

But the thought had not crossed her mind. She knew she had a lucky escape that night. Barney had only just gotten to Intensive Care in time, but he had agreed to change his lifestyle, give up the cigarettes and brandy. Walk more, behave like he might actually be mortal instead of invincible. Polly had been urging this for years, while his wife had provided comfort food and no such structure.

Now at last he had gotten the warning that he needed to jolt him into action. Barney McCarthy was only in his forties; he had years of living ahead of him.

Polly had been grateful to Danny Lynch for his speedy response. Grateful yet disappointed in him. He obviously had a girl with him in his office when she had called that night. Polly had heard her giggling. Polly was not one to sit in judgment on a man having an affair outside marriage. But she thought that Danny was fairly young to have started. *And* it was, after all, a night when you might have expected him to be with his young wife, who was having their first baby. Still, Polly was philosophical. That's men.

Rosemary remembered very well the time that Annie Lynch was born. It had been something of a turning point in her life. First there was that loutish man who had booked a hotel bedroom and had assumed that she was going to share it. And this was the time she felt unexpectedly attracted to a man called Colm Barry who worked in the bank near where she worked. He had always been helpful and encouraging about how she should handle her business. Unlike some people in that branch, he had never encouraged caution and restraint, which was the immediate response of others in the bank. He seemed even a little disenchanted with the whole idea of the bank. He was just genuinely helpful, and seemed admiring of Rosemary's skills in expanding the business. He must be about thirty, a tall man with dark curly hair which he wore longish. The bank didn't approve, he said with some satisfaction.

"Does it bother you what the bank thinks?" Rosemary asked.

"Not a bit. Does it bother *you* what other people think?" he asked in return.

"It has to a bit at work because if they see a youngish woman they're inclined to ask to speak to a man. Still! In this day and age I have to try and give off some kind of vibes of confidence I suppose. So in *that* way it bothers me. Not about other things though."

He was easy to talk to. Some men had that way of listening to you and looking at you, men who really liked women. Men like Danny Lynch. Colm had sad eyes, Rosemary thought. But she really liked him. Why should women always wait to be asked out? She invited Colm Barry to have dinner with her.

"I'd love to," he said. "But sadly I'm going to a meeting tonight."

"Come on, Colm. The bank will survive without your being at one meeting," she said.

"No, it's AA," he said.

"Really, what kind of car do you have?" she asked.

"No, the other lot, Alcoholics," he said simply.

"Oops."

"No, don't worry. Think me lucky that I do go, that I get the support that's there. That's why I'm able to refuse a beautiful blonde like you."

"For tonight," she said with a big smile. "There'll be another night, won't there?"

"Yes, of course there could be another night. But now that you know the score you might be just a little less interested in having dinner with me." He was wry but not apologetic, just preparing himself for a change in attitude. Rosemary paused. Just long enough for Colm to feel he could speak again and end things before they had begun. "We both know that you must find someone who is . . . let's say, substantial. Don't waste time on a loser like a drinky bank clerk."

"You're very cynical," Rosemary said.

"And very realistic. I'll watch you with interest."

"I'll watch you with interest too," she said.

Mona McCarthy always remembered where she was when she heard that Barney had been taken into intensive care. She was in the attic rooting out a children's cot for young Ria Lynch. She had just got an anxious phone call from Ria's sister saying that the girl had gone into labor and they were looking for Danny. Then half an hour later Danny had rung to say that Barney was absolutely fine but they had thought it wise to err on the side of caution and have an EKG. And she could come to the hospital whenever she liked; he was sending a car for her straightaway.

"Where did it happen? Is it bad?" Mona asked.

Danny was calm and soothing. "He was at home with me, at Tara Road, we were working all evening. It's fine, Mona. Believe me, he's in great shape, telling you not to worry. You'll see for yourself when you come in."

She felt better already. He was an amazing boy, Danny, so well able to calm her down while he should be in high panic himself over his wife's labor.

"And, Danny, I'm delighted to hear the baby's on the way, how is she?"

"What?"

"Ria's sister brought her in, she . . ."

"Oh shit, I don't believe it." He had hung up.

"Danny?" Mona McCarthy was confused. Hilary had said she couldn't find Danny at Tara Road. Now Danny had said he had been there all evening. It was a mystery.

Whenever Mona McCarthy had been faced with a mystery she reminded herself that she was not a detective and there was probably some explanation. And then she put it out of her mind. She had found this to be a satisfactory way of coping with a few mysteries over the years. And after Barney recovered, she never asked him any details about the night.

Any more than she ever asked him to tell her about where he had dinner when he came home late or how he spent his time in hotels when he traveled. On several occasions she had to sidestep conversations with her husband, conversations that looked as if they were heading toward a definition of mysteries and even confrontations. Mona McCarthy was much less simpleminded than most people believed.

Danny Lynch never forgot the frantic rush from one hospital to the other. And the look of reproach in his sister-in-law's face and the sight of his little daughter in the arms of an exhausted and tearful Ria.

He cried into Ria's dark hair and took the baby gingerly into his arms. "I'll never be able to make it up to you but there *is* a reason." And of course she understood. He had to do what he did, he hadn't known her time had come.

He had not known it was possible to love a little human being as he loved Annie. He was going to make his little princess a home that was like a palace. Princesses deserve palaces, he said.

"You'd never think we lived in a republic with all this chat about princesses," Ria would tease him.

"You know what I mean, it's all like a fairy tale," Danny would say. And in so many ways it was.

There was enough business coming in. It meant plenty of hard work but Danny was able for that. Barney was being a little more discreet about his involvement with him.

Ria was wonderful with little Annie. She even put her into the car regularly and drove her down to see her grandparents in the country. Danny's parents seemed very touched by that. His mother knitted the baby silly hats and his father carved her little toys. There had been no knitted hats and carved toys when Danny and his brothers were growing up.

He had a truly beautiful daughter, a house that someone of his education and chances could only have dreamed about. He had a wife who was loving and good to him.

Life had been very good to Danny Lynch.

Ria had never forgotten that Danny was not at her side when the baby was born, but she had heard the story of how Barney McCarthy's life and reputation had been saved. There was no way Danny could have known that the baby would come so early. Ria had very mixed feelings about the way Barney was being protected in his double life. She hated being a party to deceiving the kindly Mona McCarthy.

But all this took very much the backseat compared to her love for the new baby. Ann Hilary Lynch weighed seven pounds one ounce at birth and was adorable. She looked up trustingly at Ria with her huge eyes. She smiled at everyone and they passed her around from one to another, a sea of delighted faces, all of them thinking that they were special to the baby.

And all Ria's fears and worries that she had blurted out to her sister, Hilary, seemed to have been groundless. She was able to manage her baby, and Danny loved her more and more as time went on. He was a doting father and her heart was full as she saw him take his little daughter by the hand through the big wild garden that they had never tamed. There were too many other things to do and so little time.

She grew up a sunny child in a happy home, her blond straight hair like her father's, falling into her eyes.

There had never been proper pictures of Ria as she grew up. Often she had wished she had snapshots of herself as a toddler, as a ten-year-old, as a teenager. But apart from the occasional picture of a first communion, confirmation, and a visit to the zoo, her mother had not kept any real record. It would be different for Annie. Everything would be there, from the hospital to her triumphant arrival at Tara Road, her first Christmas at home . . . all the way along the line.

And she took pictures of the house too. So that they would all remember the changes, so that Annie would not grow up thinking things had always been luxurious. Ria wanted her to see how she and the house had in a way grown together.

The day before the carpet arrived and then the day it was in place; the day they finally got the Japanese vase Danny had always known would be right; the huge velvet curtains that Danny had spotted on the windows of a house that was being sold at an executor's sale. They measured them and found they fitted exactly. Danny knew they'd go for nothing, it was always the same when distant relatives were selling up. They just wanted the place cleared quickly; there were massive bargains to be found.

Ria sometimes felt a little guilty about it, but Danny said that was nonsense. Things were only valuable to those who wanted them.

Most of their life was lived in the big warm kitchen downstairs, but Danny and Ria spent time every day in the drawing room, the room they had created from their dreams. They delighted in finding further little treasures for it. When Danny got a raise in salary they went out and bought something else. The old candlesticks that were transformed into lamps, more glass, a French clock.

There was no sense that this room was kept to impress people. It was not a parlor, as Hilary had so scornfully dismissed it. The heavy, framed portraits that they bought for the walls were other people's ancestors, not their own. But there was no pretense, they were just big pictures of people who had been forgotten by their own. Now they came to rest on Danny and Ria's walls.

Ria did not go back to work. There were so many reasons why it made more sense to be at home. There was always a need to drive someone somewhere, or pick them up. She spent one day a week in a charity shop and another morning in the hospital helping to entertain the children who had come there with their mothers who had nobody else to mind them.

Danny's office wasn't far away. Sometimes he liked to come home to lunch, or even to have a cup of coffee and relax. Barney McCarthy came to see him there too. For some reason the two of them didn't meet in hotels as much as they used to. She knew the kind of food he liked to eat nowadays and always gave him a healthy salad and some poached chicken breast.

Ria would leave the men to talk.

Barney McCarthy often said admiringly in her presence, "You were very lucky in the wife you got, Danny. I hope you appreciate her."

Danny always said he did, and as the years went by Ria Lynch knew this was true.

CHAPTER

TWO

ROSEMARY'S MOTHER SAID that Ria Lynch was as sharp a little madam as you'd meet in a day's walk.

"I don't know why you say that," Rosemary said. But she knew very well what caused her mother's irritation. Ria was married, well married too. This is what Mrs. Ryan wanted for her daughter and transferred her disappointment to attacking Ria Lynch.

"Well, she came from nothing, from nowhere, a corporation estate. And look at her now, mixing with Barney McCarthy and the wife and living in a big house on Tara Road." Mrs. Ryan sniffed with disapproval.

"Honestly you'd find fault with anyone, Mother." Since she was a toddler Rosemary had been told to say "Mother," not "Mam" like other girls did. They were people with class, she had been led to believe.

But as she grew up, Rosemary realized that there really wasn't much sign of classiness in their lives. It was much more in her mother's mind and dreams, memories of a grander lifestyle when she was young and resentment that her husband had never lived up to her hopes.

Rosemary's father was a salesman who spent more and more time away from a home where he never felt welcome. His two daughters grew up hardly knowing him except through the severe, thin-lipped disappointment of their mother, who managed to make sure they realized that he had let them all down.

Mrs. Ryan had great hopes for her two elegant daughters, and believed that they would marry well and restore her to some kind of position in Dublin society.

She was bitterly let down when Rosemary's sister, Eileen, announced that she was going to live with a woman from work called Stephanie, and that they were lovers. They were lesbians and there would be no secrecy or glossing anything over. This was the 1980s and not the Dark Ages. Mrs. Ryan cried for weeks over it and agonized as to where she had gone wrong. Her elder daughter was having unnatural sex with a woman. And Rosemary was showing no sign at all of landing the kind of husband who might change everyone's fortunes.

No wonder she resented the good luck of Ria; a successful husband, a house in a part of Dublin that was becoming increasingly elegant, and an entry to the best homes in the city because of the patronage of the McCarthys.

Rosemary had moved into a small flat as soon as she could afford to. Life at home was no fun at all, but Rosemary visited her mother every week for a lecture and a harangue about her failure to deliver the goods.

"I'm sure you're sleeping with men," Mrs. Ryan would say. "A mother knows these things. It's such a foolish way to go on, letting yourself be cheap and easily available. Why should anyone want to marry you if they can get it for free?"

"Mother, don't be ridiculous," Rosemary said, neither confirming nor denying anything that had been said. There was not a great deal to confirm or deny. Rosemary had slept with very few men, only three in fact. This was more because of her own personality, which was aloof and distant, than from any sense of virtue or innate cunning.

She had enjoyed sex with a young French student and had not enjoyed it with an office colleague. She had been drunk on the two occasions when she had made love with a well-known journalist after Christmas parties, but then he had been drunk too, so she didn't imagine it had been very successful.

But she didn't burden her mother with any of these details.

"I saw that Ria coming out of the Shelbourne Hotel as if she owned it the other day," Mrs. Ryan said.

"Why don't you like her, Mother?"

"I didn't say I didn't like her, I just said she played her cards right. That's all."

"I think she played them accidentally," Rosemary said thoughtfully. "Ria had no idea it was all going to turn out for her as well as it did."

"That kind always know they don't take a step without seeing where it leads. I suppose she was pregnant when she married him."

"I don't really know, Mother," Rosemary said wearily.

"Of course you know. Still, she was lucky, he could easily have left her there."

"They're very happy, Mother."

"So you say."

"Would you like to come out and have lunch in Quentin's one day next week, Mother?"

"What for?"

"To cheer you up. We could get dressed up, look at all the famous people there."

"There's no point, Rosemary. You mean well but who would know us? Who would know what we came from or anything about us? We'd just be two women sitting there. It's all jumped-up people these days, we'd only be on the outside looking in."

"I have lunch there about once a week. I like it. It's expensive, of course, but then I don't eat lunch any other day so it works out fine."

"You have lunch there every week and you haven't found a husband yet?"

Rosemary laughed. "I'm not going there looking for a husband, it's not that kind of a place. But you do see a different world there. Come on. Say yes, you'd enjoy it."

Her mother agreed. They would go on Wednesday. It would be something to look forward to in a world that held few other pleasures.

In Quentin's, Rosemary pointed out to her mother the tucked-away booth where people went when they were being discreet. A government minister and his lady friend often dined there. It was a place that businessmen took someone from a rival organization if they were going to offer him a job.

"I wonder who's in there today," her mother said, drawn in to the excitement of it all.

"I'll have a peep when I go to the loo," Rosemary promised.

At a window table she saw Barney McCarthy and Polly Callaghan. They never bothered with a private booth. Their relationship was known to everyone in the business world. She saw the journalist whom she had met so spectacularly at two Christmas parties; he was interviewing an author and taking some scrawled notes that he would probably never decipher later. She saw a television personality and pointed him out to her mother who was pleased to note that he was much smaller and more insignificant than he looked on the box.

Eventually she went to the ladies' room, deliberately taking the wrong route so that she could pass the secluded table. You would have to look in carefully to see who was there. With a shock that was like a physical blow Rosemary saw Danny Lynch and Orla King from the office.

"Who was there?" her mother asked when Rosemary returned to the table.

"Nobody at all, two old bankers or something."

"Jumped-up people," her mother said.

"Exactly," said Rosemary.

Ria was anxious to show off the new cappuccino machine to Rosemary. "It's magic, but I'll still have mine black," Rosemary said, patting her slim hips.

"You have a will of iron," Ria said, looking at her friend with admiration. Rosemary, so tall and blond and groomed, even at the end of a day when everyone else would be flaking. "Barney McCarthy brought it round, he's so generous you wouldn't believe it."

"He must think very highly of you." Rosemary managed to lay a tea towel across her lap just in time to avoid Annie's little sticky fingers getting on her pale skirt.

"Well, of course Danny nearly kills himself working all the hours God sends."

"Of course." Rosemary was grim.

"He's so tired when he gets home he often falls asleep in the chair before I can put his supper on the table for him."

"Imagine," Rosemary said.

"Still, it's well worth it, and he loves the work, and you're just the same; you don't mind how many hours you put in to be successful in the end."

"Ah, yes, but I take time off too. I reward myself, go out to smart places as a treat."

Ria smiled fondly at the armchair where Danny often slept after all the tiring things he had been doing. "I think after the busy day, Danny regards getting back to Number Sixteen Tara Road as a treat. He has everything he wants here."

"Yes, of course he has," said Rosemary Ryan.

Hilary told Ria that one of the girls in fourth year was pregnant. A bold strap of fourteen, and she was the heroine of the hour. All the children envied her, and the staff said wasn't it great that she didn't go to England and have an abortion. The girl's mother would bring up the baby as her own so that the fourteen-year-old could return to her studies. Wasn't it very unfair, Hilary said, that some people could have a child quick as a wink while others in stable marriages who could give a child everything didn't seem to be so lucky?

"I'm not complaining," Hilary said, even though she rarely did anything but complain. "But it does seem an odd way for God to have sorted out the whole business of continuing the human race. Wouldn't you think He would have arranged something much more sensible like people going to an agency and giving proof that they could bring up a child properly, instead of teenagers getting pregnant from gropings in the bicycle sheds."

"Yes, in a way," Ria said.

"I don't expect *you* to agree with me. Look at what getting pregnant did for you, a marriage to a fellow like a film star, a house like something out of *Homes and Gardens* . . ."

"Now hardly that, Hilary," Ria laughed.

Nora Johnson pushed her granddaughter up and down Tara Road in a pram, getting to know the neighbors and everyone's business. She had settled very well into the compact mews at No. 48 Tara Road. Small, dark, energetic, birdlike, she was an authority on almost everything. Ria was amazed at how much her mother discovered about people.

"You just need to be interested, that's all," Nora said.

In fact, as Ria knew very well, you just needed to be outrageously inquisitive and direct in your approach. Her mother told her about the Sullivan family in No. 26; he was a dentist, she ran a thrift shop. They had a daughter called Kitty, just a year older than Annie, who might be a nice playmate in time. She told about the old people's home, St. Rita's, where she called from time to time. It did old people a lot of good to see a baby; it made them think there was some continuity in life. Too many of them saw little of their own grandchildren and great-grandchildren.

She brought her clothes to Gertie's launderette for the sociability of it, she said. She knew she could use Ria's washing machine but there was a great buzz in a place like that. She said that Jack Brennan should be strung up from a lamppost and Gertie was that extraordinary mixture of half-eejit half-saint for putting up with him. Gertie's little boy, John, spent most of his time with his grandmother.

She reported that the big house, No. 1 on the corner, was for sale, and people said it might be a restaurant. Imagine having their own restaurant on Tara Road! Nora hoped it would be one they could all afford, not something fancy, but she doubted it. The place was becoming trendy, she said darkly.

Nora Johnson was soon much in demand as a baby-sitter, a dog walker, and an ironer. She had always loved the smell of clean shirts, she said, and why not turn an interest into a little pocket money?

She seemed to know well in advance who was going to sell, who was going to build. Danny said she was invaluable. His eyes and ears on the road. He had managed to get two sales through his mother-in-law. He called her his secret weapon.

He also pretended a far greater interest in film stars than he really felt. Ria loved to watch him struggling for a name or to remember who played opposite Grace Kelly in this film or who Lana Turner's leading man was in that one.

"You remind me very much of Audrey Hepburn, Mother-in-law," he said once to her.

"Nonsense, Danny." She was brisk.

"No, I mean it. You have the same-shaped face, honestly, and long neck, doesn't she, Ria?"

"Well, Mam has a grand swan's neck all right. Hilary and I were always jealous of that," Ria said.

"That's what I mean, like Audrey Hepburn in *Breakfast at Tiffany's*." Nora was pleased but she wouldn't show it. Danny Lynch was a professional charmer; he wouldn't get round her. No way would she fall for his patter. But he insisted. He showed her a picture of Audrey Hepburn with her hand under her chin. "Go on, pose like that and I'll take a snap of you and then you'll see what I mean . . . put your hand under your chin, come on, Holly. . . ."

"What are you calling me?"

"Holly Golightly, the part Audrey plays in the film, you look just like her." He called her Holly from that day on.

Nora Johnson who wouldn't fall for that kind of patter was totally under his spell.

Rosemary went to the bank on Friday mornings. The girls there admired her a lot. Always dressed immaculately, and it seemed as if she were wearing a different outfit each time until you looked carefully. She had three very well-cut jackets and a lot of different-colored blouses and scarves. That's why it looked different. And she was so much on top of her business. The man who ran the print shop left everything to her. It was Rosemary Ryan who arranged the rates for deposit and the loans for new machinery. It was Rosemary who got the statement for the tax returns, and who tendered successfully for the bank calendar.

Young bank officials looked at her enviously. She was only the same age as they were and look at all the power and responsibility she had managed to get for herself. They thought she sort of mildly fancied Colm Barry, but then that couldn't be possible. Colm was the last man someone like Rosemary Ryan would go for. He had no ambition or sense of survival, even in the bank. He never kept from his boss the fact that he didn't really admire the ethics of the bank and that he went to Alcoholics Anonymous meetings. And these kinds of revelations were not the road to promotion. Rosemary would want a much higher achiever than Colm Barry even if she did always wait until his window was empty and asked for him if he wasn't there.

Rosemary had all her documentation done before she came to the bank each weekend. As she stood in line she saw to her amazement Orla King in animated conversation with Colm Barry over the desk. Orla had what Rosemary considered cheap and obvious good looks. Too tight a top, too short a skirt, the heels on her shoes too high. Still, men didn't see anything too flashy in it; they appeared to like it. As Orla was leaving she saw Rosemary and her face lit up. "Well now, it's a small world. I was only talking about you last night," she said.

Rosemary's face was cold and disapproving, but she forced her public smile. Orla must know she had been spotted in the private booth of Quentin's. "All full of praise I hope?" she said lightly.

"Well yes, praise and puzzlement. Why such a beautiful woman like you isn't married. That was one of the strands."

"What an extraordinary thing to talk about." Rosemary was very cold.

Orla didn't seem to notice the tone. "No, you're quite well known now, even people who don't know you know of you. They were all interested."

"What very empty lives they must all live," Rosemary said.

"You know the way people go on, they didn't mean any harm."

"Oh, I'm certain that's true, why should they?" Her voice was so disdainful anyone but Orla would have been put off.

"Well, why is it, Rosemary?"

"Probably, like you, I haven't found the right person yet." Rosemary hoped her voice wasn't as glacial as it felt from inside.

"Ah yeah, but I'm just a fun girl, you're a serious woman."

"We're both in our twenties, Orla. Hardly over-the-hill yet."

"No, but this man said, and honestly he was out for your good, he wasn't putting you down or anything, he said that you'd want to be looking round soon, the millionaires will be looking for younger models, next year's models, if you don't get in there quick." Orla laughed happily. She meant no insult. In fact talking to someone as beautiful as Rosemary you could only assume that saying such a thing was a joke and not to be taken seriously.

But Rosemary's face was cold. That was exactly what Danny Lynch had said to her jokingly only a few days ago at Sunday lunch at Tara Road. Rosemary hadn't minded then, but she minded now. She minded very much that he was saying such things about her to Orla King last night, especially when he had told Ria that he would be working with Barney.

Orla was heading off for work without a care in the world. "Cheers, Colm, see you Tuesday night," she called.

"I gather that you and the lovely Ms. King are going out socially," Rosemary said to Colm.

"Yes, well that's right, sort of . . ." He was vague.

Rosemary realized that it must be at an AA meeting. People would tell you of their own involvement but they never told you who else went to the meetings. She was glad in a way that he had not fallen immediately for the tight sweaters and the skirt stretched across the small round bottom. "Anyway, it's a very small forest, Dublin, isn't it? We all find out about everyone else sooner or later." She was only making conversation but she saw a wary look come across his face.

"What do you mean?" he asked.

"I only meant if we were in London or New York we'd never know half the queue in the bank, that's all."

"Sure. By the way, I'm leaving here at the end of the month."

"Are you, Colm? Where are they sending you?"

"I'm brave as a lion. I'm leaving the bank altogether," he said.

"Now that *is* brave. Are there farewell drinks or anything?" She could have bitten off her tongue.

"No, but I'll tell you what there will be. I'm going to open a restaurant on Tara Road. And as soon as I get started I'll send you an invitation to the launch."

"I'll tell you what I'll do, I'll print the invites for you as a present," she said.

"It's a done deal," he said, and they shook hands warmly. He had a lovely smile. What a pity he was such a loser, Rosemary thought. He would have been a very restful man to have teamed up with. But a restaurant on Tara Road? He must be out of his mind. There would be no local demand and no passing trade either. As an enterprise it was doomed before it began.

Danny and Barney McCarthy were going to look at property very near Danny's old home.

"Will we all go together and take Annie to see her grandparents?" Ria suggested.

"No, love. It's not a good idea this time. I'm going to be flat out looking at places, and making notes, meeting local fellows who are all mad to make a quick killing. There's going to be nothing but meetings and more meetings in the hotel."

"Well, you will go and see them?"

"I might, I might not. You know the way it's more hurtful to go in somewhere for five minutes than not to go at all."

Ria didn't know. "You could drive down a couple of hours earlier."

"I have to go when Barney goes, sweetheart."

Ria knew not to push it. "Fine, when the weather gets better I'll drive her down to see them, we might both go."

"What? Yes, great." She knew he wouldn't. He had separated himself from them a long time ago, they were no longer part of his life. Sometimes Danny and his singlemindedness were a mystery and a slight worry to Ria.

"Would you like to drive down to the country with me to see Danny's parents?" Ria asked her mother.

"Well, maybe. Would Annie be carsick?"

"Not at all, doesn't she love going in the car? Will you make them an apple tart?"

"Why?"

"Oh, Mam, out of niceness, that's why. They'll be apologizing about everything. You know the way they go on. And if I bring too much they get sort of overwhelmed. You bringing an apple tart is different somehow."

"You're very complicated, Ria. You always were," said Nora, but she was pleased to make one, and did a lot of fancy lattice work with the pastry.

Ria had written well in advance and the Lynches were expecting them. They were pleased to see little Annie, and Ria took a picture of them to add to the ones she had already framed and given to them. They *would* be part of Annie's life and future in spite of their distance and reserve. She had resolved this. They never saw their other grandchild in England. Rich didn't come back. It was hard, they said. Ria wondered why it was hard for a man who was meant to be doing well in London to come home just even once and show his son to his own parents.

Rosemary had said she should leave them to it and be glad that she didn't have nagging in-laws. But Ria was determined that they stay involved.

They had cold ham, tomatoes, and shop bread, which was all they ever served. "Will I warm up the apple tart, do you think?" Mrs. Lynch asked fearfully, as if faced with an insuperable problem.

How had these timid people begotten Danny Lynch, who traveled the country with Barney McCarthy, confident and authoritative, talking to businessmen and county families that would have his parents doffing their caps and bending their knee?

"And you were down here a few weeks ago and never told us?" Danny's father said.

"No, indeed I was not. I think Danny may have been nearby, but of course he would have to stay with Barney McCarthy all the time." Ria was annoyed. She had known that somehow it would get back to them. He had only been a few short miles away, why couldn't he have come over for an hour?

"Well, now, when I was in the creamery there, Marty was saying that his daughter works in the hotel and that the pair of you were there."

"No, it was Barney who was with him," Ria said patiently. "She got it wrong."

"Oh well, fair enough," said Danny's father. The incident had lost any interest for him.

Ria knew what had confused the girl; Barney McCarthy had brought Polly with him on the trip. So that's where the mistake lay.

In September 1987, shortly before Annie's fourth birthday party, they were planning a party for the grown-ups at Tara Road.

Danny and Ria were making the list, and Rosemary was there as she so often was.

"Remember a few millionaires for me, I'm getting to my sell-by date," Rosemary said.

"Oh that will be the day," Ria laughed.

"Seriously though, has Barney any friends?"

"No, they're all sharks. You'd hate them, Rosemary," Danny laughed.

"Okay, who else is on the list?"

"Gertie," said Ria.

"No," said Danny.

"Of course, Gertie," said Ria.

"You can't have a party and not have Gertie." Rosemary supported her.

"But that mad eejit Jack Brennan will turn up looking for a fight or a bottle of brandy or both," Danny protested.

"Let him, we've coped before," Ria said. There were the tenants, they'd be in the house anyway, and they were nice lads. They would ask Martin and Hilary, who would not come but would need the invitation. Ria's mother would come just for half an hour and stay all night. "Barney and Mona, obviously," Ria said.

"Barney and Polly, actually," Danny said.

There was a two-second pause and then Ria wrote down Barney and Polly.

"Jimmy Sullivan, the dentist, and his wife," Ria suggested. "And let's ask Orla King."

Both Danny and Rosemary frowned. "Too drinky," Rosemary said. "Unreliable."

"No, she's in AA now. But still too unpredictable," Danny agreed.

"No, I like her. She's fun." Ria wrote her down.

"We could ask Colm Barry, the fellow who's going to open a restaurant in the house on the corner."

"In his dreams he is," Danny said.

"He *is*, you know, I'm doing the invitations to the first night."

"Which may easily be his last night," Danny said.

Rosemary was annoyed at the way he dismissed Colm, even if it was exactly her own feeling about it all. She decided to say something to irritate Danny. "Let's ask him anyway, Ria. He has the hots for Orla King, like all those fellows who see no further than the sticky-out bosom and bum."

Ria giggled. "We're all turning into matchmakers, aren't we?" she said happily.

Rosemary felt a great wish to smack Ria. Very hard. There she stood, cozy and smug in her married state. She was totally confident and sure of her husband and it never occurred to her that a man like Danny would have many people attracted to him. Orla King might not be the only player on the stage. But did Ria do anything about it? Make any attempt at all to keep his interest and attention?

Of course not. She filled this big kitchen with people and casseroles and trays of fattening cakes. She polished the furniture they bought at auctions for their front room upstairs, but the beautiful round table was covered with catalogues and papers. Ria wouldn't think in a million years of lighting two candles and putting on a good dress to cook dinner for Danny and serve it there.

No, it was this big noisy kitchen with half the road passing through and Danny's armchair for him to fall asleep in when he came home from whatever the day had brought. She looked at Danny and admired his handsome, smiling face. He stood there in the kitchen of his big house holding his beautiful daughter in his arms while his wife planned a party for him. A man so confident that he could take a girlfriend to within a few short miles of where his own mother and father lived. And in front of Barney McCarthy too. Rosemary had heard the laughing tale of how Ria's father-in-law had got the wrong end of the stick as usual. Why was it that some men led such lucky lives that nobody would blow a whistle on them? Things were very, very unfair.

Ria baked night and day to have a great spread for the party. Twice she had to refuse invitations from Mona McCarthy and remember not to tell her why she was so busy. She hated doing this to the kind woman who had shown her such generosity. But Danny had been adamant. This was a do that Polly would enjoy. The party would not be mentioned to Mona.

Ria's mother knew the score and would not say anything untoward. Living now so close to Ria meant that she was a constant visitor and aware of everything that went on in the household. Nora Johnson never came to No. 16 Tara Road for an actual meal, she was not a lunch guest or a dinner guest. That way you made yourself unpopular, she always said. Instead she was a presence just before or after every meal, hovering, rattling her keys, planning her departure and next visit. It would have been vastly easier had she come in properly and sat down with everyone else. Ria sighed over it but she put up with her mother. It was comforting too to have someone around who knew the whole background to things. Like the Barney McCarthy saga.

"Close your eyes to it, Ria," she advised on several occasions. "Men like that have their needs, you know." It seemed unusually tolerant and forgiving on her mother's part. Usually people's needs were dismissed with a sniff. But Nora Johnson was a very practical person. She said once to Ria and Hilary that she would have forgiven her late husband much more if he had his needs and dealt with them rather than doing what he did, which was failing to provide her with an adequate life insurance or pension.

"We must have plenty of soft drinks," Ria said on the morning of the party.

"Sure, with people like Orla and Colm off the sauce," he agreed.

"How did you know she was in AA?" Ria asked.

"I don't know, didn't you or Rosemary say? Someone did."

"I didn't know; I won't say anything," Ria said.

"Neither will I," Danny promised her.

As it happened it was a night when Orla lapsed from her rule. She had arrived early, the first guest in fact, to find Danny Lynch and the wife who he had said meant nothing to him in a deep embrace in their kitchen. The home where Danny Lynch claimed he felt stifled was decorated, warm and welcoming and about to fill up with their friends. The little girl in a new dress toddled around. She would be four shortly, she told everyone, and she thought that this was her party. She was constantly trying to hold her daddy's hand. This was not the scene that Orla had expected. She thought she might have one whiskey.

When Colm arrived she was already very drunk. "Let me take you home," he begged.

"No, I don't want anyone to preach at me," Orla said, tears running down her face.

"I won't preach, I'll just stay with you. You'd do that for me," he said.

"No, I wouldn't, I'd support you if your fellow was behaving like a shit. If your fellow was here and behaving like a hypocritical rat I'd have a whiskey with you, that's what I'd do, not a rake of sanctimonious claptrap about Higher Powers."

"I don't have a fellow." He made a weak joke.

"You don't have anything, Colm, that's your problem."

"Could be," he said.

"Where's your sister?"

"Why do you ask?"

"Because she's the only one you give a tuppenny damn about. I expect you're sleeping with her."

"Orla, this isn't helping you and it isn't hurting me."

"You've never loved anybody."

"Yes, I have." Colm was aware that Rosemary was beside them. He looked at her for help. "Should we try to find whoever this fellow is that she thinks she loves?"

"No, that would be singularly inappropriate," Rosemary said.

"Why?"

"It's the host," she said succinctly.

"I see." He gave a grin. "What do you suggest?"

Rosemary wasted no time. "A further couple of drinks until she passes out," she suggested.

"I couldn't go along with that, I really couldn't."

"Okay, look the other way. I'll do it."

"No."

"Go, Colm. You're not helping."

"You think I'm very weak," he said.

"No, I don't for Christ's sake. If you're in AA you're not meant to get a fellow member to pass out, I'll do it." He stood aside and watched. Rosemary poured a large whiskey. "Go on, drink it, it's only tonight, Orla. One day at a time, isn't that what they say? Tomorrow you need have none. But tonight you need one."

"I love him," wept Orla.

"I know you do, but he's a liar, Orla. He takes you to Quentin's; he takes you down the country to hotels with Barney McCarthy and then he plays housey-housey with his wife in front of you. It's not fair."

"How do you know all this?" Orla was round-mouthed.

"You *told* me, remember?"

"I never told you. You're Ria's friend."

"Of course you told me, Orla. How else would I know?"

"When did I tell . . . ?"

"A while back. Listen, come up here and sit in this alcove, it's very quiet and you and I'll have a drink."

"I hate talking to women at parties."

"I know, Orla, so do I. But not for long. I'll send one of those nice boys who lives in this house up to talk to you. They were all asking who you were."

"Were they?"

"Yes, everyone is. You don't want to waste your time on Danny Lynch, professional liar."

"You're right, Rosemary."

"I am, believe me."

"I always thought you were stuck-up, I'm sorry."

"No, you didn't. You always liked me deep down." Rosemary went to find the boys who rented the rooms in Danny and Ria's house. "There's a real goer-up in the alcove on the stairs, she keeps asking where are the good-looking men she met when she came in."

Colm moved out of the background. "You should be in the United Nations," he said to Rosemary.

"But you don't fancy me?" she said archly.

"I admire you too much, I'd be afraid of you."

"Then you'd be no use to me." She laughed, and kissed him gently on the cheek.

"I don't sleep with my sister, you know," he said.

"I didn't think you did for a minute. Don't I know you're having a thing with that publican's wife?"

"How do you know that?" he was amazed.

"I told you it's a small forest and I know everything," she said with a laugh.

Nora Johnson said afterward it was amazing how much drink they put away, young, fresh-faced people. And wasn't it extraordinary that young, very drunk girl shouting at everyone. And she had gone into one of the tenants' rooms. And what a funny chance that someone had opened the door and they had been seen in bed. Danny had said he hadn't thought that any of it was funny. Orla was obviously unused to drink and had reacted badly. She hadn't meant to go to bed with one of those kids. It was out of character for her.

"Oh, come on, Danny. She's anybody's, we all knew that when we worked back in the agency," Rosemary said in her cool voice.

"I didn't know." He was clipped.

"Oh, she was." Rosemary listed half a dozen names.

"I thought you said that nice man Colm Barry fancied her," Ria said.

"Oh, I think he did a bit back awhile, but not after last night's performance." Rosemary seemed to know everything.

Danny glowered about it all.

"Didn't you enjoy last night?" Ria looked anxiously at him.

"Yes, yes of course I did." But he was absent, distracted. He had been startled, frightened even, by Orla's behavior. Barney had been unexpectedly cold and asked him to get her out as quickly and quietly as possible. Polly had looked at him as if he had somehow broken the rules.

That weak Colm Barry had been no help at all. The kids who rented the rooms had been useful at the time but why, oh why, had someone left the door of a bedroom open? Only Rosemary Ryan had been of any practical use at all, shepherding people on- and offstage as if she knew everything that was going on. Which of course she couldn't have.

Hilary wasn't able to come to the party for Annie's fourth birthday, but she came with a present a couple of weeks later. The first thing she wanted to know was if Barney McCarthy had been wiped out in the stock market crash.

"I don't think so; Danny never said a word." Ria was surprised at such a thought.

"Martin said that fellows like Barney who make all their money in England always keep it there, that he'd have lost his shirt," Hilary said grimly.

"Well, it can't have been because we'd have known," Ria said. "He seems to be doing just as much if not more."

"Oh, well, that's all right then," said Hilary.

Sometimes Ria felt that Hilary would have been pleased if there was bad news—she and Martin, who had no money at all, watched the ebb and flow of a stock market with so much interest.

Gertie had been quiet and watchful during the party on Tara Road. Jack was with her, dressed in his one good suit. They had a baby-sitter and they couldn't stay late. Jack drank orange juice. Gertie's sister, Sheila, was going to come home from the United States this Christmas. It had never been made clear to Sheila and her American husband, Max, the extent of the problems with Jack Brennan.

Sheila was inclined to be boastful of her life in New England. Their wealth and status was always treated to an impressive show by her family when she came back. The fact that Gertie had married such an unstable man had never been mentioned in letters or phone calls. Gertie was hoping that the three-week visit could hold without one of Jack's moods.

It depressed her to see that pretty girl Orla behaving so badly. If someone like that could lose control, what hope was there for her Jack? But against all the odds he remained sober. Restless and anxious, but sober. There was a God after all, Gertie confided to Ria as she helped her serve the hot spicy soup and pita bread.

"I know, Gertie, I know. Every time I look at Danny and little Annie I know this."

Gertie had winced slightly because she heard one of the girls who worked for her at the launderette say that the good-looking Danny Lynch who lived in the posh end of Tara Road had a fancy woman just like his boss Barney McCarthy did. Gertie had so much wanted it not to be true, she had refused to listen or inquire anything at all about it.

Barney McCarthy never again mentioned the behavior of Orla King at the party on Tara Road. He had assumed that the relationship would now be at an end. And he had assumed correctly. Danny called to Orla's flat to tell her so. He spoke very directly and left no area for doubt.

"You don't think you're going to get rid of me like that," she had cried. She had indeed managed to stay sober after the upsetting events of the night in Tara Road, but this news was not helping her resolution.

"I don't know what you mean," Danny said. "We both went into this knowing the limitations, I was never going to leave Ria for you, we agreed that it would be fun and would hurt nobody."

"I never agreed to that," Orla wept.

"Yes, you did, Orla."

"Well, I don't feel that way now," she said. "I love you. You're treating me like shit."

"No, that's not true, and if anyone is treating anyone like shit, it's you.

You come to my house, you get as pissed as a fart, you insult my boss, you go to bed with at least one and possibly two of my tenants in full view of everyone. Who's treating whom badly, may I ask?"

"You've not done with me, Danny Lynch. I can still make trouble for you," Orla said.

"Who'd believe you, Orla? After your behavior in our house, who'd believe I touched you? Even with a forty-foot pole?"

"Hallo, Rosemary? Orla King here."

"Hi, Orla. Feeling okay again?"

"Yes, I didn't go back on the drink."

"There. I knew you wouldn't. I told you, didn't I?"

"Yes, you did. I'm not a good judge of people as it turns out. I didn't know you were so nice."

"Come on, of course you did."

"No, I didn't. Danny Lynch is a cheat and a liar and I'm going round to his house to tell his wife what he's been up to."

"Don't do that, Orla."

"Why not, he *is* a liar. She should know."

"Listen. You've just agreed I'm your friend, so listen to the advice of a friend."

"Okay. What is it?"

"Danny's very dangerous. Suppose you did that, he'd hit back. He'd get you sacked."

"He couldn't do that."

"He could, Orla, he really could. He could tell your bosses that you photocopied stuff for him, gave them details of deals that were coming up."

"He wouldn't."

"What has he to lose? He's secure with Barney. Barney doesn't owe you any favors for what you said to him about that trip to the country."

"Oh God, did I?"

"Yes, I'm afraid you did."

"I don't remember."

"That's the problem, isn't it? Listen, believe me, I haven't steered you wrong. You're going to give yourself nothing but grief if you go round to Tara Road with the story. Danny will go for you bald-headed. You know how determined he is. You know how ambitious, how much he wants to get ahead, he won't let you stand in his way."

"So what do you think . . . ?"

"I think you should let him know you'd like to cool it a bit, men love that sort of thing. Agree to keep it on the back burner, some phrase like that, and once he knows you won't be any problem he'll start coming round to see you again and it will all restore itself to where it was."

Rosemary could hear the tears of gratitude in Orla's voice. "You're really so helpful, Rosemary. I don't know why I thought you were stuck-up and difficult. That's exactly what I'll do. And of course he'll come round when he knows there's going to be no drama."

"That's it, it may take a bit of time, of course," Rosemary warned.

"How much time do you think?"

"Who knows with men? Maybe a few weeks."

"*Weeks?*" Orla sounded horrified.

"I know, but it's for the best in the end, isn't it?"

"You're right." Orla hung up.

Nora Johnson had been to bridge lessons. She was greatly taken by the game and somewhat inclined to tell lengthy tales about some hand that was dealt, called, and played. She seemed to have the same kind of recall for the game as she had about every film star she had ever seen on the screen.

Ria had refused absolutely to learn. "I've seen too many people get obsessed by it, Mam. I'm bad enough already, I don't want myself spending five hours every afternoon wondering are all the diamonds out or who has the seven of spades."

"It's not like that at all," Nora scoffed. "But it's your loss. I'm going to suggest that I get some games going for them up in St. Rita's."

And it was a huge success. There were demon bridge sessions in one of the resident's lounges, often with as many as three tables playing. Nora Johnson played there almost every afternoon wherever they needed to make up a four. There were not enough hours in the day for her.

And as well as organizing their games, she organized the lives of the residents, advising them, cajoling and contradicting them. She was never happier than laying down rules and making decisions for other people. Including her daughter Ria.

"I wish you'd pray to St. Anne," Nora Johnson told her daughter.

"Oh Mam, there's no St. Anne," Ria said, exasperated.

"Of course there's a St. Anne," said her mother scornfully. "Who else do you think was the mother of Our Lady. And her husband was St. Joachim. St. Anne's feast is the end of July and I always pray to her for you then, and say that basically you're a good girl and you'll remember your name day."

"But it's *not* my name day. We're not in Russia or Greece, Mam, we're in Ireland and my name is Ria, anyway, or Maria. Not Ann."

"You were baptized Ann Maria, your own daughter is called Ann after the mother of Our Lady."

"No, it's because we like the name."

"There!" Her mother was triumphant.

"But what should I be praying for, even supposing she was there listening? Haven't we got everything?"

"You need another child." Her mother spoke with pursed lips. "St. Anne could do it. You may think it's superstitious but believe me it's true."

Ria knew that if she stopped taking the Pill that would do it too. Something she had been thinking about a lot, and must discuss with Danny. He had seemed preoccupied about business recently, but maybe this was the time to bring the subject up.

"I might pray to St. Anne," she said gently to her mother.

"That's the girl," said Nora Johnson.

Gertie's sister, Sheila, came home for Christmas.

"I must have her to a lunch here," said Ria.

"Oh God, no," Danny said. "Not over Christmas. Not that fellow with his fists here over Christmas, please."

"Don't give a dog a bad name, Danny. Wasn't he great at the party?"

"Well, if standing like a block of wood was great, then he was."

"Don't be an old grouch, it's not like you."

Danny sighed. "Sweetheart, you're always filling the house with people. We get no peace."

"I am not." She was hurt.

"But you are, this is one of the few times there's just us and Annie here. There are people coming and going all the time."

"That's the meanest thing I ever heard. Who's here more often than Barney? He's here about four times a week, and with Polly one day or Mona another. Now, I don't ask them, do I?"

"No."

"So?"

"So it's not very restful, that's all."

"Forget Gertie's sister then," Ria said. "It was just an idea."

"Look . . . I don't mean . . ."

"No, I said forget it, we'll be restful."

"Ria, come here . . ." He dragged her toward him. "You are the world's worst sulker," he said and kissed her on the nose. "All right, what day will we have them?"

"I knew you'd be reasonable. What about the Sunday after Christmas Day?"

"No, that's the McCarthys. We can't miss that."

"Right, the Monday then, no one will have gone back to work. It will be stay at home Ireland. Will we ask your mother and father?"

"What for?" Danny asked.

"They can see Annie, see all that we've done to the place, meet these Americans, you know."

"They'd be no good, and honestly I don't think they'd enjoy it," Danny said.

Ria paused. "Sure," she said. And after all she had won over Gertie's sister.

Sheila Maine and her husband, Max, had not been in Ireland for six years. Not since their wedding day. They now had a son, Sean, the same age as Annie. Sheila seemed astounded at how well Ireland was doing, how prosperous the people were, and how successful were the small businesses she saw everywhere. When she had left to go to America to seek her fortune at the age of eighteen, Ireland had been a much poorer country. "Look what has happened in less than ten years!"

Ria felt that not unlike her own sister, Hilary, who seemed to rejoice in bad news rather than good, Sheila Maine was not entirely pleased to see the upturn in the economy. What Sheila really seemed to resent was the great social life that people had in Dublin. "It's not at all like this in the States," she confided on the evening before Christmas Eve, when there was a girls' dinner out in Colm's new restaurant. "I can't imagine all these people laughing and talking to each other at different tables. It's all changed a great deal from my time."

Colm had been having a series of rehearsals, inexpensive meals where friends would try out the recipes and the ambience at a very reduced cost. This way they could iron out some of the wrinkles before the restaurant opened officially in March. Only those who were within his group were allowed in. Colm's beautiful and silent sister, Caroline, worked with him, serving and acting as hostess. "Smile a little more, Caroline," they heard him urging her from time to time. She was a nervous girl, she might never see to fronting a successful restaurant for her brother.

Sheila was thrilled with it all. And on Christmas Eve they were going in to Grafton Street where a live radio broadcast was done on *The Gay Byrne Show*. Perhaps she might even be called upon to speak as a returned emigrant. Anything was possible in the Ireland of today. Look at all of Gertie's smart friends, with their good jobs or their beautiful houses. Gertie herself was not particularly well-off; her launderette was at the less smart end of Tara Road. And her husband, Jack, though charming and handsome, seemed vague about his prospects. But they had a business, and a two-year-old baby boy. And everyone was so confident. Sheila Maine's sigh was so like Hilary Moran's sigh that Ria could hardly wait for the two women to meet at lunch in her house.

And indeed they did get on very well. Gertie and Ria stood back and watched them bonding together. The quiet husband, Max Maine, who came from a Ukrainian background and knew little or nothing about Ireland, seemed ill at ease. Only Danny, of course, was able to draw him out with his warm smile and his huge interest in everything new. "Tell me about the kind of houses you have out there in New England, Max. Connecticut, isn't it? Are they all that white board we see pictures of?"

Max was frank and explained that the house he and Sheila lived in did not fit the dreamy ideal of a house in its own grounds. Danny was equally frank and expanded on how they had managed to get a big house like this one on Tara Road by being in the right place at the right time, and by having three of their rooms occupied by youngsters who helped to pay the rent. Visibly Max relaxed with half a bottle of Russian vodka, which they sipped from small glasses. Ria watched as Danny captivated her friend's brother-in-law. He hadn't wanted them to come and yet he was now giving his all. Jack, having been frightened into some kind of truce, sat drinkless and wordless in a corner.

Afterward as they washed up, Ria gave Danny a hug. "You are marvelous, and weren't you rewarded in the end? He is a nice man, Max, isn't he?"

"Sweetheart, he hasn't a word to throw to a dog. But you're so good to people when they come here for me, I thought I'd be nice to him for you, and for poor Gertie, who isn't a bad old stick. That's all."

Somehow Ria felt cheated. She had really believed that Danny was enjoying his conversation with Max Maine. It was upsetting to realize that it had all been an act.

Sheila wanted to know was there a good fortune-teller around before she went back home. A lot of her neighbors in America went to psychics, some of them very powerful, but they wouldn't know you like an Irish woman would. "I'll take all you three girls . . . my treat," she said. You had to like Sheila. Bigger and much more untidy than Gertie, she had the same anxious eyes and the edges of her mouth turned down in sadness to leave this place where everyone was having such a good time.

Ria longed to tell her that they were all putting on a show for her, but that would have let Gertie down.

"Come on, let's all go to Mrs. Connor," Gertie suggested.

"She didn't get things right for me years back, but I hear she's red-hot at the moment. Why not, it's an adventure isn't it?" Rosemary agreed. The last time they had been there, Rosemary had said nothing about what had been predicted, just that it was not relevant to her life plans. Maybe it would be different now.

"Well, she did tell me my baby would be a girl. I know it was a fifty-fifty chance, but she was right. Let's go to her," Ria said. She had stopped taking the Pill back in September. But as yet the time had not been ripe to tell Danny. She was waiting for the proper moment.

Mrs. Connor must have had five or ten people a night coming to her since they were there last. Hundreds of eager faces watching her, thousands of hopeful hands held out and many more thousands of paper banknotes crossing the table. There was no evidence whatsoever of any increased affluence in her caravan. Her face showed no sign of any contentment in having seen the futures of so many people.

She told Sheila, having heard her accent, that she lived across the sea, possibly in the United States, that she was married reasonably happily, but that she would like to live back in Ireland.

"And will I live back in Ireland?" Sheila asked beseechingly.

"Your future is in your own hands," Mrs. Connor said gravely, and somehow this cheered Sheila a lot. She considered the money well spent.

To Gertie with her anxious eyes, Mrs. Connor said that there was an element of sadness and danger in her life and she should be watchful of those she loved. Since Gertie was never anything but watchful of Jack, this seemed a good summing-up of affairs.

Rosemary sat and held out her hand, marveling as she looked around her at the squalor of the surroundings. This woman must take in tax-free something like a hundred thousand pounds a year. How could she bear to live like this? "You were here before," the woman said to her.

"That's right, some years back."

"And did what I saw happen for you?"

"No, you saw me in deep trouble, with no friends, no success. It couldn't have been more wrong. I'm in no trouble, I have lots of friends and my business is thriving. But you can't win them all, and you got the others right." Rosemary smiled at her, one professional woman to another.

Mrs. Connor raised her eyes from the palm. "I didn't see that, I saw you had no real friends, and that there was something you wanted that you couldn't get. That's what I still see." Her voice was certain and sad.

Rosemary was a little shaken. "Well, do you see me getting married?" she asked, forcing a lightness into her voice.

"No," Mrs. Connor said.

Ria was the last to go in. She looked at the fortune-teller with sympathy. "Aren't you very damp here, that old heater isn't great for you?"

"I'm fine," Mrs. Connor said.

"Couldn't you live somewhere better, Mrs. Connor? Can't you see that in your hand?" Ria was concerned.

"We don't read our own hands. It's a tradition."

"Well, somebody else might. . . ."

"Can you show me your palm, please, lady. We're here for you to know are you pregnant again."

Ria's jaw fell open in amazement. "And am I?" she said in a whisper.

"Yes, you are, lady. A little boy this time." Ria felt a stinging behind her eyes. No more than her mother's famous St. Anne, dead and gone for two thousand years, Mrs. Connor barely alive in her caravan couldn't know the future, but she was mightily convincing. She had been right about Annie, remember, and right about Hilary having no children at all. Possibly there were ways outside the normal channels of knowing these things. She stood up as if to go. "Don't you want to hear about your business and the travel overseas?"

"No, that's not on. That's somebody else's life creeping in on my palm," Ria said kindly.

Mrs. Connor shrugged. "I see it, you know. A successful business, where you are very good at it and happy too."

Ria laughed. "Well, my husband will be pleased, I'll tell him. He's working very hard these days, he'll be glad I'm going to be a tycoon."

"And tell him about the baby that's coming, lady. He doesn't know that yet," said Mrs. Connor, coughing, and drawing her cardigan around her for warmth.

Danny was not really pleased when he heard the news. "This was something we said we would discuss together, sweetheart."

"I know, but there never is time to discuss anything, Danny, you work so hard."

"Well, isn't that all the more reason we *should* discuss things? Barney's so stretched these days, money is tight, and some of the projects have huge risk attached to them. We might not be able to *afford* another baby."

"Be reasonable. How much is a baby going to cost? We have all the baby things for him. We don't have to get a crib, a pram, or any of the things that cost money." She was stung with disappointment.

"Ria, it's not that I don't want another child—you know that—but it's just that we did agree to discuss it, and this isn't the best time. In three or four years we could afford it better."

"We won't have to pay anything for him, I tell you, until he is three or four."

"Stop calling it him, Ria. We can't know at this stage."

"I know already."

"Because of some fortune-teller! Sweetheart, will you give me a break?"

"She was right about my being pregnant. I went to the doctor next day."

"So much for joint decisions."

"Danny, that's not fair. That's the most unfair thing I ever heard. Do I ask to be part of all the decisions you make for this house? I do bloody not. I don't know when you're going to be in or out, when Barney McCarthy will come and closet himself with you for hours. I don't know if we are to see his wife or his mistress with him each time he turns up. I don't ask to discuss if I can go out to work again, and let Mam look after Annie for us, because you like the house comfortable for you whatever time you come home. I'd like a cat but you're not crazy about them, so that's that. I'd like us to have more time on our own, the two of us, but you need to have Barney around, so that's *that*. And I forgot to take the Pill for a bit and suddenly it's a matter of joint decisions. Where are the other joint decisions, I ask you? Where are they?" The tears were running down her face. The delight in the new life that was starting inside her seemed almost wiped out.

Danny looked at her in amazement. His own face crumpled as he realized the extent of her loneliness and how much she had felt excluded. "I can't tell you how sorry I am. I truly can't tell you how cheap and selfish I feel listening to you. Everything you say is true. I have been ludicrous about work. I worry so much in case we'll lose what we've got. I'm so sorry, Ria." He buried his face in her and she stroked his head with sounds of reassurance. "And I'm delighted we're having a little boy. And suppose the little boy's a little girl like Annie I'll be delighted with that too."

Ria thought about telling him what the fortune-teller had said about her having a business of her own one day, and overseas travel. But she decided it would break the mood. And it was nonsense anyway.

"I know you're pregnant again, Ria. Mam told me," Hilary said when she came to call.

"I was about to tell you. I forgot what a Bush Telegraph Mam is. It's probably being broadcast on the midday news by now," Ria said apologetically.

"Are you pleased?" Hilary asked.

"Very. And it will be good for Annie to have someone to play with, though she'll probably hate him at first."

"Him?"

"Yes, I'm pretty sure. Listen, Hilary it's hard for me to talk about this with you. You never want to talk about, well, about your own situation, and there was a time when we could talk about anything, you and I."

"I don't mind talking about it." Hilary was offhand.

"Well, have you thought of adopting a baby?"

"I have," Hilary said. "But Martin hasn't."

"Why ever not?"

"It might be too expensive. He thinks that the cost of educating and clothing a child is prohibitive these days. And suppose it went to third level education, well, you're talking thousands and thousands over a lifetime."

"But if you'd had your own you'd have paid that."

"With difficulty, you know, and the other way there'd be the feeling we're doing it for someone else's child."

"Oh, there wouldn't. Of course there wouldn't. Once you get the baby it's yours."

"So they say, but I don't know." Hilary nodded doubtfully over her mug of tea.

"And is it easy to adopt?" Ria persisted.

"Not nowadays, they're all keeping their kids you see, and getting an allowance from the state. I'd put an end to that, I tell you."

"And have them terrified out of their lives, like when we were young."

"It didn't terrify *you*," Hilary said as she so often did.

"Well, I mean the generation before us then. Remember all the stories, girls committing suicide or running off to England and everything, never knowing what happened. Surely it's much better the way it is?"

"Easy for you to say, Ria. If you saw that little hussy up at the school, with her stomach stuck out in front of her, and now it appears that her mother doesn't want to bring it up, so there's more drama."

"Maybe you and Martin . . ."

"Live in the real world, Ria. Could you imagine us working in that school, bringing up that little tinker's baby, paying through the nose for everything for it? Right pair of laughingstocks we'd be."

Ria thought that Hilary found the world too harsh and unloving a place, but then she was in a poor position to try and console her sister. Ria had so much and in many ways Hilary really did have so little.

Orla King was back at her AA meetings again. Colm was as friendly to her as ever. But she felt awkward, particularly with imperfect recollection of the party at Tara Road. Finally she brought the subject up. "I meant to thank you for trying to help me that night, Colm." It wasn't easy to find the words.

"It's okay, Orla. We all go through it, that's why we're here. That was then, this is now."

"Now is a bit bleak, though."

"Only if you allow it to be. Try something different. I've felt so tired since I left the bank, trying to set up this restaurant business, that I haven't had time to miss the drink and feel sorry for myself."

"What can I do except type?"

"You said once you'd like to be a model."

"I'm too old and too fat, you have to be sixteen and look half-starved."

"You don't sing badly. Can you play the piano?"

"Yes, but I only sing when I'm drunk."

"Have you tried it sober? It might be more tuneful and you'd remember the words."

"Sorry to be so helpless, Colm. I'm like a tiresome child, I know. But suppose I *could* get a few songs together, then where would I try for a job?"

"I could give you the odd spot when my place opens . . . not real money, but you might get discovered. And of course Rosemary knows half of Dublin. She might know people in restaurants, hotels, clubs."

"I don't think Rosemary's too keen on me these days. I did fool around with her best friend's husband."

Colm grinned. "Well, at least that's all you're describing it as now, fooling around, not the great love affair of the century."

"He's a shit," Orla said.

"He's all right, really, he just couldn't resist you. Very few of us could." He grinned at her and she thought again what an attractive man he was. Since he had left the bank he wore much more casual clothes, open-necked shirts in bright colors, his black curly hair and big dark eyes make him look slightly foreign, Spanish or Italian. And he was a rock of sense too. Handsome, single, sensible.

Orla sighed. "You make me feel much better, Colm. Why couldn't I fall in love with someone normal like you."

"Oh, I'm not normal at all, we all know that," Colm joked.

A look of unease crossed Orla's pretty, round face. She hoped that when she had been drunk she had said nothing about the overprotectiveness Colm always had about his silent, beautiful sister. No, surely bad and all as she had been that night she'd never have hinted at anything as dark as that.

Brian was born on June 15th and this time Danny was beside Ria and holding her hand.

Annie said to everyone that she was quite pleased with her new brother, but not *very* pleased. This made people laugh so she said it over and over. Brian was all right, she said, but he wasn't able to go to the bathroom on his own, and he couldn't talk and he took up a lot of Mum and Dad's time. Still, Dad had assured her over and over that she was his little princess, the only princess he would ever have or want. And Mum had said that Annie was the very best girl not only in Ireland, or Europe, but on Earth and quite possibly the planets as well. So Annie Lynch didn't have anything to worry about. And Brian was going to take ages before he could do anything like catch up on her. So she was very relaxed about the whole thing.

Gertie's baby, Katy, was born just after Brian, and Sheila Maine's daughter, Kelly, around the same time.

"Maybe they'll all be friends when they grow older." The future was always happy and filled with people for Ria.

"They might all hate each other, you can just see Brian saying 'She wants me to be friends with these awful people. . . .' They'll make their own friends no matter what you say."

"I know, it's just that it would be nice."

Rosemary showed her irritation. "Ria, you're amazing, you're so into never changing things, never moving on. It's ridiculous. You're not friendly with the children of your mother's friends, are you?"

"Mam didn't have any friends," Ria said.

"Nonsense, I never met anyone with more friends, she knows the whole neighborhood."

"They're only acquaintances," Ria said. "Anyway, there's nothing wrong with my hoping that friendships will continue into the next generation."

"No, but not very adventurous."

"When *you* have children, won't you want them to be friends with Annie and Brian?"

"They'll be far too young if they ever materialize, which is unlikely," Rosemary said.

Annie had been listening carefully; these days she understood a lot of what was going on. "Why don't you have children?" she asked.

"Because I'm too busy," Rosemary said truthfully. "I work very hard and it takes up a lot of time. You see all the time your mummy spends on you and Brian? I don't think I could be unselfish enough to do that."

"I bet you'd love it if you tried it," Ria said.

"Stop it, Ria. You sound like my mother."

"I mean it."

"So does she. So does Gertie, for God's sake, she was trying to get me broody the other day. Imagine the Brennan family being held up to anyone as an example of domestic bliss!"

Gertie didn't bring her own children to Tara Road. They lived over the launderette not far away, but she always felt that they would be discontented if they saw how others lived. Also, the atmosphere in Ria's house was so peaceful. A big kitchen where everyone gathered, something always cooking in the big stove, the smell of newly baked cinnamon cakes or fresh herb bread.

Not like Gertie's house, where nothing was ever left out on a gas cooker. Just in case, just in case it might coincide with one of the times that Jack was upset. Because if Jack was upset it could be thrown at anyone. But Gertie came on her own to Tara Road from time to time and did a little housework for Ria. Anything that would give her the few pounds that Jack didn't know about. Just something that might tide them over when there was trouble.

Rosemary's business was now very high-profile. She was often photographed at the races, gallery openings, or at theater first nights. She dressed very well and she kept her clothes immaculate. Ria had even taken to offering her a nylon housecoat to wear in case the children smeared her with whatever they had their hands in.

"Come on, that's going a bit far," Rosemary laughed the first time.

"No, it isn't. I'm the one who'd have to spend six years apologizing if they got ice cream or pureed carrots all over that gorgeous cream wool. Put it on, Rosemary, and give me some peace."

Rosemary thought they could have more peace if they went upstairs to that magnificent front room and drank their wine there rather than being in what was like a giant playpen with children's toys and things all over the floor and Ria leaping up to stir things and lift more and more trays of baking out of the oven. But it was useless to try and change her ways. Ria Lynch believed that the world revolved around her family and her kitchen.

Danny saw her in the pink nylon coat and was annoyed. "Rosemary, you don't need to dress up to play with the children."

"Your wife's idea," Rosemary shrugged.

"I didn't want them messing up her lovely clothes."

"Wait till she has kids of her own," Danny said darkly. "Then we'll see some messed-up clothes."

"I wouldn't bet on it, Danny," Rosemary said. Her smile was bright, but she felt that she was being put under a lot of pressure from all sides. It wasn't enough apparently to look well, dress well, and run a successful business. No, not nearly enough. Apparently there was no such thing as a private life in this city. Rosemary resented the excessive interest people had in marrying others off. Why was she not allowed to have a lover that no one knew of, or indeed, a series of them? She was successful and glamorous but so what? You had to find a mate and breed children as well, otherwise it counted for nothing in people's eyes. She was getting it everywhere, but particularly on her weekly visits to her mother's house.

Mrs. Ryan was becoming intolerable. Rosemary was now in her late twenties and no marriage prospects. Her sister, Eileen, was no consolation to her. Just be yourself, be free. Don't listen to the old voices, Eileen would say if ever Rosemary grumbled about their mother. Which was fine for Eileen, living as she did with the powerful Stephanie, a lawyer, and working for her as her clerk. They had an apartment where they had a regular Sunday afternoon drinks party. It was almost like a salon where everyone was welcome, men and women, but Rosemary felt they despised her for dressing so well. The term "frocky" was used a lot as a derogatory description for women that Eileen and Stephanie thought were dressing just to please male egos.

Yet in ways Rosemary envied them. They were sure and happy in their lives and they wished her well. "I'm demented with Eileen and Stephanie producing soulful ladies for me, my mother despairing that I'm a lost cause, and every customer that I'm nice to thinking I'm about to perform every known kind of sexual favor to keep his business."

"Why don't you sign up with a marriage agency?" Ria said unexpectedly.

"You have to be joking me! Now you've joined them all."

"No, I mean it. At least you'd meet the right kind of person, someone who wants to settle down."

"You're daft as a brush, Ria," Rosemary said.

"I know, but you did ask me what I thought." Ria shrugged. It seemed perfectly sensible to her.

Rosemary met Polly Callaghan at several gatherings. Their paths would cross at press receptions and the openings of art galleries, or even theater first nights. "Did you ever think of a marriage agency? No, I'm not joking, someone suggested it to me as a reasonable option and I wonder, is it barking mad?"

"Depends on what you want, I suppose." Polly took the suggestion seriously. "You don't look like the kind of woman who wants to be dependent on a man."

"No, I don't think I am," Rosemary said thoughtfully.

But it *would* be nice to have someone to come home to in the evening. Someone who was interested and in your corner, someone who would fight your battles. Somehow Rosemary had always thought he would turn up. But this was ridiculous, why should he? Business opportunities didn't fall into your lap, you had to make them.

Good dress sense wasn't just guesswork, you had to consult experts. Rosemary was on first-name terms with all the buyers in the smart Dublin shops. She told them exactly how much she could spend and discussed what she needed. They enjoyed doing the research for her, an elegant woman like that who paid them the courtesy of recognizing that they were indeed experts in their field.

So why shouldn't she go to a marriage agency?

She approached it in her usual businesslike way and went to meet her first introduction. He was handsome in a slightly disheveled way, came from a wealthy family, but it took her forty minutes to realize that he was a compulsive gambler. With her practiced charm she managed to maneuver the conversation far away from the actual reason why they were meeting—possible marriage. Instead she discussed stock markets, horse racing, the greyhound track. Then at the coffee stage she looked at her watch and said she had to have an early night; it had been delightful and she hoped they would meet again. She left without having given him her address or phone number but also without his having asked for it. She was pleased that she had handled it so well, but annoyed that she had wasted a night.

Her second introduction was to Richard Roche, the head of an advertising agency. She met him in Quentin's and they talked easily about a wide range of subjects. He was a pleasant, easy dinner companion; she felt that he found her attractive. Nothing prepared her for the way it ended.

"I can't tell you when I've enjoyed a meal as much," he began.

"I feel the same." She smiled warmly.

"So I do hope we remain friends."

"Well, yes."

"You're not at all interested in getting married, Rosemary, but we can regard this dinner as a happy accident. All friends have to meet somewhere." His smile was very warm and sincere.

"What do you mean I'm not interested in getting married?"

"Of course you're not, you don't want children, a home, anything like that."

"Is that what you think?"

"It's what I can see. But as I say, it was my good fortune to meet you and as I continue my search I'm sure I'll be unlikely to have such an elegant and charming dinner companion again."

He was saying he didn't want her. Men didn't do that to Rosemary Ryan. "You're playing hard to get, Richard," she said, looking at him from under her eyelashes.

"No, you're the mystery woman. You must have a thousand friends and yet you chose to have dinner with a stranger. I'm what I say I am, a man who wants a wife and children, you are the puzzle."

He was serious. He didn't want to continue. Well, she would get out with dignity if it killed her. "It makes life a little adventurous, don't you think, to dine with a stranger?" She would *not* let him see how humiliated she felt, she would end the evening with style.

She nodded at Brenda Brennan to get her a taxi, and somehow got herself home.

She sat shaking in her small apartment. How dare he treat her like that! Damn him to hell. She had been prepared to go a bit of the distance with this Richard Roche. What made him think he could tell her she didn't want marriage and children?

She resolved to watch the paper for news of his eventual wedding plans and she would manage to circulate the news that he had found his bride through an introduction agency; she would let his colleagues know. She would wipe this night of embarrassment and failure from her mind. She would get a new apartment, somewhere elegant where she could relax. Nobody was going to treat Rosemary Ryan like this.

A year later she did see a gossip column item about him. He was going to marry a glamorous widow with two small children. They had met in Galway, apparently, with mutual friends. Rosemary didn't write to his colleagues or the wedding guests. The rage and hurt had long died down. She had taken up no further introductions after that night, but instead concentrated on looking for somewhere new to live.

Colm's restaurant started very slowly. He devised the menus and did most of the cooking himself; and he had a sous chef, a waiter, a washer-up, and his sister, Caroline, to help him. But it didn't take off as he had hoped it would. This was 1989, a lot of new restaurants were opening in Dublin. Rosemary invited as many influential people as she could rustle up to come to the opening.

Ria was disappointed that Danny would not try to do the same. "You know an awful lot of people through Barney," she said pleadingly.

"Sweetheart, let's wait until it's a success, then we'll invite lots of people there."

"But it's now he needs them, otherwise how else will it *be* a success?"

"I don't suppose for a moment that Colm is expecting the charity of his friends. In fact he'd probably find that just a little patronizing."

Ria didn't agree, she thought it was small-minded and overcautious of him. Don't risk getting your name associated with something that might fail. It was a shabby attitude, out of character with Danny's cheerful optimistic approach to life, and she said as much to Rosemary.

"Now don't be so quick to attack him. He may be right in a way. Much more useful to take businesspeople there for meals when it's up and running." Rosemary spoke soothingly, but in reality she knew very well why Danny Lynch didn't want to go to the opening and why he forced Ria to go to a business dinner that night.

Danny knew that Orla King was going to sit at the piano in the background and sing well-established favorites. She would not have a spotlight, but if the place was successful she would have a platform.

Orla had worn a demure black dress and sipped a Diet Coke through the many rehearsals. But she had proved herself once to be a very loose cannon, and unpredictability was the last thing Danny Lynch wanted around him. Especially since Barney McCarthy's finances had taken such a battering and there were heavy rumors of much speculative building to try and recoup the losses.

Rosemary went to Colm's opening night and reported that it had been very successful. A lot of the customers had been neighbors; it boded well for the future.

"This really is a great area, you two were very lucky to come in here when you did," Rosemary said approvingly.

Ria wished that she didn't sound so surprised, as if she hadn't expected it of them.

"Not lucky, just far-seeing," said Danny, who must have felt the same.

"Not a bit of it. The secret of the universe is timing, you know that," Rosemary laughed. She wasn't letting them away with anything except random good fortune. "Isn't it a pity that there aren't any proper apartments or little mews flats around here? I could become your neighbor!"

"You could afford a whole house on the road the way you're going," Danny said.

"I don't *need* a whole house. I don't want to be worrying about tenants. What I need is a house just like the one your mother has, Ria, a little mews like that."

"Oh that's a one-off," Danny explained. "Holly was certainly in the right place at the right time. You see, she looked after the old trout who lived in the big house and then when she went to her reward the family were grateful and sold Holly the little mews. It's so valuable now you wouldn't believe it."

"Would she like to sell and move in with you?" Rosemary wondered.

"No way," Ria said. "She loves her independence."

"And we want ours too," Danny added. "Much as I love Holly, and I do love her, I wouldn't want her here all the time."

"Well, if there are no more of those around perhaps something like a penthouse, for want of a better word, something with a nice view."

"Not too many of those on a Victorian road."

"But there are a lot of conversions happening." Rosemary knew the property scene as well as anyone.

"Indeed there are, expensive but you'd always see your money back. Two-bedroom?" Danny was into sales mode now.

"Yes, and a big room for entertaining, I could have a lot of functions there. A roof garden I'd like if possible."

"There's nothing like that around here at the moment, but a lot of the upcoming sales are going to want to do huge renovations," Danny said.

"Keep an eye out for me, Danny; it doesn't have to be Tara Road, somewhere nearby."

"I'll get it for you," Danny promised.

In three weeks Danny came back with news of two properties. Neither owner was willing to build. It would be a question of Barney McCarthy buying the building, his men doing the renovation, and subject to planning, permission to get a penthouse-style apartment custom-built for Rosemary. They could start drawing up plans as soon as she liked.

Danny expected Rosemary to be very pleased but she was cool. "We are talking about an outright buy, not just renting? And I could see the titles for all the other flats in the house?"

"Well, yes," Danny said.

"And my architect and surveyor could look at the plans?"

"Yes, of course."

"And inspect the building specifications and work throughout?"

"I don't see why not."

"What's the word on a roof garden?"

"If there's not too much heavy earth brought up there the structural engineers say that both houses could take the load."

Rosemary smiled one of her all-embracing smiles that lit up the whole room. "Well, Danny, that's great, lead me to the properties," she said.

Ria was shocked that Rosemary had been so ungracious about it all. "Imagine her interrogating you like that!" she said, outraged, to Danny.

"I didn't mind," he said.

"But you're a friend, you went out on a limb for her, persuaded Barney to buy a place." Ria was still stunned by the ingratitude.

"Nonsense, Ria, Barney doesn't do things just for friendship; it's a business thing for him too, you know."

"But the way she said it, saying she'd have to inspect Barney's building method and everything . . . I didn't know where to look when she said it."

Danny laughed. "Sweetheart, Barney has been known to cut corners with the best of them. Rosemary would know that. She's just thorough, covering everything. That's what has her where she is."

Hilary sniffed when she heard that Rosemary was coming to live on Tara Road. "That's the final seal of approval, if *she's* coming to live in the area," she said.

"Why don't you like her? She never says a word against you," Ria complained.

"Did I say a word against her?" Hilary asked innocently.

"No, but it's the tone of voice. I think Rosemary is quite lonely, you know. It's all very well for you, you have Martin, and I have the children . . . and Danny too when I see him, but she doesn't have anybody."

"Well, I'm sure she's had offers," Hilary said.

"Yes, I'm sure she has, and so had you and I in a way when we were young, but they were no use if they were from an eejit like Ken Murray."

"Rosemary could get better than Ken Murray interested in her."

"Yes, but she hasn't found the right one, so isn't it grand that she's coming to live here halfway between Mam and ourselves? All we need is for you to come and live here too then we'd have taken over."

"Where would Martin and I get the repayment for a house on Tara Road?" Hilary began.

Ria moved off the subject. "Gertie's mother's being difficult."

"All mothers are difficult," Hilary said.

"Ours isn't too bad."

"That's because she baby-sits for you all the time," Hilary said.

"No, very rarely, she's got far too busy a life. But Gertie's mother won't take the children anymore, she says if she'd wanted a late family she'd have had one."

"What will Gertie do?"

"Struggle like she always has. I told her they could come here for a while but . . ." Ria paused and bit her lip.

"But Danny wouldn't like it."

"He's afraid Jack Brennan will come round looking for them and for a fight and that it would frighten Annie and Brian."

"So what happens now?"

"I go up and take them out for the day for her, but you see it's the nights are the really bad times. That's the time she wants them out of the house."

"What a desperate mess," Hilary said, her face soft in sympathy and quite unlike the envious Hilary, who normally talked about how much everybody earned.

"You'd never take them for this weekend, you and Martin, just till their grandmother comes round, or that lunatic breaks his skull with drink and has to go to the hospital again? I know Gertie would die with gratitude."

"All right," said Hilary surprisingly. "What kind of things do they eat?"

"Beans and fish fingers, chips and ice cream," Ria said.

"We can manage that."

"I'd love to have them myself," Ria apologized. She did in fact sound wistful.

Hilary forgave her. "I know you would, but it just happens that I'm married to a much more generous man than you are, that's the way things turn out."

Ria paused to think of the spontaneous, loving Danny Lynch being considered less generous than the amazingly mean, penny-pinching Martin Moran. Wasn't it wonderful the way people saw their own situations?

"So Lady Ryan is going to grace us with her presence on the Road," Nora Johnson said. She had come to introduce the new element in her life, a puppy of indeterminate breed. Even the children, who loved animals, were puzzled by it. It seemed to have too many legs, yet there were only four; its head looked as if it were bigger than its body but that could not possibly be so. It flopped unsteadily around the kitchen and then ran upstairs to relieve itself against the legs of the chairs in the front room. Annie reported this gleefully and Brian thought it was the funniest thing he had ever known.

Ria hid her irritation. "Does it have a name, Mam?" she asked.

"Oh it's just thirty-two, no fancy name."

"You're going to call the dog Thirty-two?" Ria was astounded.

"No, I mean where Lady Ryan's penthouse is being built. The dog is called Pliers, I told you that." She hadn't but it didn't matter. "They all know she's coming to Tara Road, everyone's heard of her."

"That's good, anyway they'd know her from visiting."

"No, they read about her in the papers. There's as much about her as there is about your friend Barney McCarthy." Nora didn't approve of him either so there was another sniff.

"It's extraordinary, Rosemary being so famous," Ria said. "You know her mother thinks of her still as a thirteen-year-old and says she should be more like me. Rosemary of all people."

Rosemary Ryan was featured now in the financial pages as well as the women's pages. The company was going from strength to strength, and had taken on several foreign contracts as well. They printed picture postcards for some of the major tourist resorts in the Mediterranean, they had successfully tendered for sporting events as far afield as the West Coast of America. She had bought shares in it and it was a matter of time before she would take it over entirely. The man who had employed her as a young girl to help in a very small print shop looked in amazement at the confident, poised woman who had transformed his business. He was more interested in lowering his golf handicap nowadays than taking the early morning train to Belfast, having two meetings a lunch and coming back on the afternoon train with a signed contract for work worth more than he ever dreamed possible.

Rosemary saw no reason at all why people in Northern Ireland should not have their printing done in the South, if the service was professional, the price was right, and the quality high. She had long ago persuaded the company to change its name from Shamrock Printing to the more generally acceptable if equally meaningless Partners Printing.

And still no man. Well, there were plenty of men but no one man. Or at least no one available man. She puzzled people, so attractive, flirtatious even. It was not that she was frigid, she quite enjoyed dalliances and encounters on the few occasions that she allowed them to develop. People thought she had a much more adventurous and colorful sex life than she had. And Rosemary allowed this view to be widely held.

For one thing, it discouraged people from thinking that she was a lesbian like her sister. "Would that be so terrible if they thought you were?" Eileen had asked.

"No. And don't get all sensitive and prickly on me, of course it wouldn't. It's just that if I'm not then there's no point in having to carry all the defensive stuff that goes with it. You and Stephanie can do that because it's part of your life, it's not my cause."

"Fair enough," Eileen said. "But I don't see what you're so hot under the collar about. It's not the 1950s for heaven's sake, you're free to do your own thing."

"Sure. It's people's expectations that annoy me."

"Maybe you've met him already and didn't know."

"What do you mean?"

"Maybe Mr. Perfect is out there under your nose, and you just didn't recognize him. One night you'll fall into each other's arms."

Rosemary considered it. "It's possible," she said.

"So who do you think it might be? It can't be anyone who rejected you because nobody could, Ro. Maybe someone you never started with . . . can you think of anyone?"

Rosemary had told nobody about Richard, her date from the introductions agency that she had met briefly at various gatherings. It had been so hurtful when he claimed to read in her face that she had no interest in finding a life mate. "I did fancy that Colm Barry a bit, you know, the one who has the restaurant. But I don't think he's the marrying kind."

"Gay?" Eileen said.

"No, just messy, complicated."

"I'd leave it, Ro, honestly. Stick to doing up this palace and building the business."

"I think I will," Rosemary agreed.

When Gertie had another "accident" her mother gave in and took the children back to live with her. "You think I'm doing this for you, but I'm not, I'm doing it for those two defenseless children that you and that drunken sot managed to produce."

"You're not helping me, Mam."

"I am helping. I'm taking two children out of a possible death house. If you were a normal woman instead of half-crazed yourself, you'd be able to realize that what I'm doing is helping you."

"I have other friends, Mam, who would take them when Jack's upset."

"Jack is upset every day and every night of the week these days. And decent though that Moran pair are, the odd weekend is all they'll manage."

"You're very good, Mam, it's just that you don't understand."

"You can say that again! Indeed I don't understand, two terrified little children who jump at the slightest sound, and you won't get a barring order and throw that lout out of their lives."

"You're the religious one, you believe in a vow, for better for worse. We'd all stay when it's for better, it's when it's for worse it's harder, you see."

"It's harder on a lot of people, all right." Her mother's mouth was a thin hard line as she packed John and Katy's things for yet another trip to their granny's in their disturbed young lives.

Rosemary came round to Danny and Ria's several evenings a week. There were always plans to be discussed, reports to be given. She never stayed long, only long enough for everyone to know she was on the case and that no shoddy workmanship would escape her sharp eye. Ria tried to give her supper but she always said she had eaten a gigantic lunch and couldn't possibly swallow another thing. Ria knew this was not true. Once a week Rosemary went to Quentin's, the rest of the time she had low-fat yoghurt and an apple at her desk. Business meetings that had a social side to them would involve a wine and soda spritzer at the Shelbourne Hotel. Rosemary Ryan didn't remain greyhound slim without an effort of will. Sometimes Ria wondered why on earth she did it, why she pushed herself so hard. The gym and a swim before work, the jogging on the weekends, the permanent diet, the early nights, the regular hair appointments. What was it all *for*?

Rosemary would say it was for personal satisfaction, if she asked her. But it seemed such an odd and even a lonely answer that Ria didn't ask anymore. It was like the way they didn't talk about sex these days. Once they talked of nothing else. That was way back, before Ria had slept with Danny, but now they never mentioned the subject at all. Ria never said how Danny still had the power to thrill her just like the early days. And Rosemary didn't tell of her numerous conquests. Ria knew that she was on the Pill and she had a lot of lovers. She had seen the plans for the large bedroom in Rosemary's apartment with its luxurious bathroom, Jacuzzi, and twin handbasins. This wasn't the bathroom of a woman who went to bed too often on her own. Ria longed to ask but didn't. If Rosemary wanted to tell her she would.

"It's all taking longer than we thought," Rosemary said.

"Look at the contract, you'll see there are contingency clauses," Danny laughed.

"*You* covered your back, didn't you?" She was admiring.

"No more than you did."

"I just insured against shoddy workmanship."

"And I just insured against wet weather, which indeed we had," he said.

Ria was cutting out pastry shapes at the kitchen table with the children. Brian just wanted them round, Annie liked to shape hers.

"What are they talking about?" Brian asked.

"Business," Annie explained. "Daddy and Rosemary are talking business."

"Why are they talking it in the kitchen? The kitchen's for playing in," Brian said loudly.

"He's right," said Rosemary. "Let's take all these papers up to the beautiful room upstairs. If I had a room like that I wouldn't let it grow cold and musty like an old-fashioned parlor, I tell you that for nothing."

Good-naturedly, Danny carried the papers upstairs.

Ria stood with her hands floury and her eyes stinging. How *dare* Rosemary make her feel like that? In front of everybody! A woman who had let an upstairs parlor get musty. Tomorrow she would make sure that that room was never again allowed to lie idle. Possibly Rosemary had done her a favor.

"Are you okay, Mam?" Annie asked.

"Sure I am, of course."

"Would you like to be in business too?"

For no reason Ria remembered the fortune-teller, Mrs. Connor, prophesying that she would run a successful company or something. "Not really, darling," Ria said. "But thanks all the same for asking."

The next day Gertie came. She looked very tired and had huge black circles under her eyes.

"Don't start on me. *Please,* Ria."

"I hadn't a notion of it, we all lead our own lives."

"Well, that's a change in the way the wind blows, I'm very glad to say."

"Gertie, I want us both to tidy the front room, air it, and polish it up properly."

"Is anyone coming?" Gertie asked innocently.

"No," said Ria crisply. Gertie paused and looked at her. "Sorry," said Ria.

"Okay, you're kind enough not to ask me my business, I won't ask you yours."

They worked in silence, Gertie doing the brass on the fender, Ria rubbing beeswax into the chairs. Ria put down her cloth. "It's just I feel so useless, so wet and stupid."

"*You* do?" Gertie was amazed.

"I do. We have this gorgeous room and we never sit in it." Gertie looked at her thoughtfully. Someone had upset Ria. It wasn't her mother; Nora Johnson's stream of consciousness just washed over her all the time. It was hardly Frances Sullivan, Kitty's mother; she wouldn't upset anyone. Hilary talked about nothing except the cost of this and the price of that; Ria wasn't going to get put down by her own sister. It had to be Rosemary. Gertie opened her mouth and closed it again. Ria never heard a word against her friend; there was nothing Gertie would say that would be helpful.

"Well, don't you agree it's idiotic?" Ria asked.

Gertie spoke slowly. "You know, compared to what I have, this whole house is a palace, and everyone respects it. That would be enough for me. But on top of all that you and Danny went out and found all this beautiful furniture. And maybe you're right . . . you *should* use this room more. Why not start tonight?"

"I'd be afraid the children would pull it to bits."

"No, they won't. Make it into a sort of a treat for them to come up here. Like a halfway house to bed or something. If they're beautifully behaved here they can stay up a bit longer. Do you think that might work?" Gertie's eyes were enormous in her dark, haunted face.

Ria wanted to cry. "That's a great idea," she said briskly. "Right, let's finish this lot in twenty minutes then we'll go downstairs and have hot currant bread."

"Barney's coming round for a drink before dinner this evening, we'll go to my study," Danny said.

"Why don't you go to the front room instead, I'll leave coffee for you there. Gertie and I cleaned it up today and it looks terrific. I tidied away a lot of the rubbish. The table's free for you to put your papers."

Together they went up to examine the room. The six o'clock sunshine was slanting in the window. There were flowers on the mantelpiece.

"It's almost as if you were psychic. This isn't an easy discussion so it's good to have it in a nice place."

"Nothing wrong?" She was anxious.

"Not really, just the perpetual Barney McCarthy cash flow problem. Never lasts long but it would give you ulcers while it's there."

"Is it best if I just keep the kids downstairs out of the way?"

"That would be terrific, sweetheart." He looked tired and strained.

Barney came at seven and left at eight.

Ria had the children tidy and ready for bed. When they heard the hall door close they came up the stairs together, all three of them, the children slightly tentative. This room wasn't part of their territory. They sat and played a game of snakes and ladders. And possibly because they were overawed by the room, Annie and Brian didn't shout at each other. They played carefully, as if it were a very important game. When the children were going to bed, for once without protest, Danny hugged them both very tight.

"You make everything worthwhile, all of you," he said in a slightly choked voice.

Ria said she would be up to see that they had brushed teeth. "Was it bad?"

"No, not bad at all. Typical Barney, must have it now. Must have everything this minute. Overextended himself yet again. He's desperate to make Number Thirty-two a real show house, you know. It's going to be his flagship, people will take him seriously with this one. It's just that it's costing a packet."

"So?"

"So he needed a personal guarantee, you know, putting this house up as collateral."

"*This* house?"

"Yes, his own are all in the frame already."

"And what did you say?" Ria was frightened. Barney was a gambler; they could lose everything if he went down.

"I told him we owned it jointly, that I'd ask you."

"Well you'd better ring him straightaway and say that I said it's fine," she said.

"Do you mean that?"

"Listen, we wouldn't have ever had this place without him; we wouldn't have had anything without him. You should have told me earlier. Ring him on his mobile. So that he'll know we're not debating it."

That night after they had made love Ria couldn't sleep. Suppose the cash flow problem was serious this time. Suppose they lost their beautiful home. Danny lay beside her in an untroubled sleep. Several times she looked at his face and by the time dawn came she knew that even if they did lose the house it wouldn't matter just as long as she didn't lose Danny.

"Come on, Mam, we'll have our tea in the front room," Ria said to her mother.

"It's far from a place like this you were reared." Nora Johnson looked around the room that Ria had now resolved to use properly. She still smarted slightly from Rosemary's remark, yet in a way her friend had done her a favor. Danny didn't fall asleep when he sat here, he looked around him with pleasure at the treasures they had managed to gather. The children were quieter and kept their games neatly in one of the sideboard drawers rather than leaving them strewn around the place. Gertie enjoyed cleaning the room, she said it was like stepping into the cover of a magazine. Hilary went through the cost of every item of furniture and pronounced that they had made a killing.

Even Ria's mother seemed happy to sit there, although she would never admit it. She compared it to rooms in other houses where she ironed and said it was much more elegant. She wouldn't allow the dog to come into this territory, and so Pliers slept glumly in a basket in the kitchen. When Rosemary called she always admired the room. She had probably forgotten her cruel words. Instead she saw virtue in its high ceilings, its two tall windows, its lovely warm colors. It was a real gem, she said several times over.

Ria realized that there was great satisfaction in having lovely possessions. If you couldn't have a streamlined figure, flawless makeup, and exquisite clothes, then having a perfect room was a substitute. For the first time she knew why people bought books on style and decoration and period furniture.

It was interesting, however, to see that Rosemary's own design plans were as different from the room she admired so much in No. 16 Tara Road as could possibly be. No. 32 had gutted entirely and the long, top-floor apartment had a wraparound roof garden with a view stretching out toward the Dublin mountains. At night it would look magnificent with all the city lights in between. The interiors were cool and spare, a lot of empty wall space, pale wooden floors, kitchen fittings that were uncluttered and minimalist.

It was about as unlike Ria's house as anyone could imagine. Ria fought to like the clean lines seen in the artist's impressions, and as the project proceeded she visited the site often and forced out words of praise for a place that seemed to her like a modern art gallery.

———

Danny spent a lot of time in No. 32. Sometimes, Ria felt, too much time. There were other properties out there, this was only one of them.

"I told you if we get the right kind of tenants in here, Barney's home and dry. He's into the prestige end of things, not the Mickey Mouse conversion. We need a good write-up in the property pages, and Rosemary can organize that. We need a politician, a showbiz person, a sports star or something to buy up the other flats."

"Can you pick and choose?"

"Not really, but we want the word to get about. I asked Colm to tell the nobs who come into his restaurant."

"And has he?"

"Yes, but sadly his ignoramus brother-in-law, Monto Mackey, is the only one who came inquiring."

"Monto and Caroline want to live in a flat on Tara Road?"

"I know. I didn't think he'd have the cash but he does. And cash is what he offered, you know, suitcases of it."

"No!" Ria was astounded. Colm's beautiful but withdrawn sister was married to an unattractive car dealer, a large, florid man interested more in going to race meetings than in his wife or his business. He seemed the last kind of person to buy a property like this.

"Barney was delighted of course, always a man for the suitcase of money, but I convinced him to watch it, that it was quality we wanted here, not dross like Monto Mackey."

"And did he listen? Are things all right with him these days?" Ria never actually said aloud that she was anxious about the guarantee they had given to Barney, but it was always there.

"Don't worry, sweetheart, the bailiffs aren't at the door. Barney's fine, just has to be steered away from quick money without the small annoyance of tax." Danny seemed amused and quite unimpressed by his boss. They had a very relaxed relationship.

When Rosemary spoke in front of Barney about getting some garden furniture he offered an introduction to a friend. "No need to trouble the tax man at all, pay cash and everyone's happy," Barney had said.

"Not everyone." Rosemary had been cool. "Not the government, not the people who have to pay tax, not my accountant."

"Oh, pardon *me*," Barney had said. But nobody had been embarrassed. You met all sorts in this world. That's what business was about.

"Is Lady Ryan having a housewarming party? She might like me to take the coats for her." Nora wanted to know every last detail of it all.

"Don't stir up trouble, Holly." Danny was affectionate to his mother-in-law. "You only call her Lady Ryan to get a rise out of Ria. No, I didn't hear of any party. She didn't say anything to you, did she, sweetheart?"

"She's going to wait until she has a proper roof garden, apparently," Ria explained. "She says the place will look nothing until she has lighting and tubs of this and trellises of that. She's such a perfectionist."

"How long will that take her? It took me three years to get anything to grow in my place," Nora Johnson said.

"Oh, Holly, we're just not in Rosemary Ryan's world. The garden will be ready in three weeks, that's part of the schedule."

"It can't be," Nora gasped.

"Yes it can, if you hire good nurseries and have everything in containers."

"I wonder, could I clean for Rosemary, do you think?" Gertie asked Ria.

"Gertie, you run a business, you haven't time to. You don't *have* to either."

"I do." Gertie was short.

"But who's looking after the launderette?"

"I told you, it looks after itself; your mother's dog Pliers could run it. I have kids in there doing it for me, I make much more per hour cleaning than I pay them."

"That's ludicrous."

"Has she got anyone already to clean?"

"Ask her, Gertie."

"No, Ria, you ask her for me, will you? As a friend?" said Gertie.

"Of course I won't have Gertie cleaning for me. She should be managing that run-down washeteria of hers for a start, and minding her own children for another thing."

"She'd like the hours."

"You give her the hours then."

"I can't. Danny wonders what on earth I do all day that I then have to go and pay Gertie."

"Yes. Quite."

"Rosemary, go on, you need someone you can trust."

"I'll have a firm, contract cleaners twice a week."

"But they're total strangers, they might steal everything, root around among your things."

"Oh, Ria, please. How do you think these places survive? They have to employ honest people, you're absolutely guaranteed that. Otherwise they go out of business."

And that was it as far as Rosemary was concerned. She was now much more interested in creating her garden. The trellis arrived and was erected instantly. Days later the instant climbers in containers were carried upstairs.

"Lots of roses, of course," Rosemary explained to Ria. "Bush Rambler, that's a nice pink here on this side and Muscosa and Madame Pierre Oger, all on this side. What else do you think?" She consulted Ria as if she wanted her view.

"Well, I see you have Golden Showers, that's nice." Ria picked the only name she recognized.

"Yes, but that's yellow. I thought I'd go for blocks of color, more dramatic to look out at."

Rosemary never once said that it would look well or tasteful or dramatic for other people, it was always for herself. But surely she'd want other people to admire it too, Ria thought. She wasn't sure. She wasn't sure of anything about Rosemary sometimes. Ria knew for a fact that Rosemary hadn't known one flower from another three months ago and here she was helping the men from the nurseries to trail the honeysuckle, the jasmine, the wisteria as if she had been doing nothing else all her life. It was amazing the grasp she had of anything she touched.

She did indeed have a housewarming. Ria knew hardly anybody there; Danny and Barney knew a few. Polly was in attendance that night, so Ria had to be sure not to mention the party to Mona. Colm had hoped that he might tender to do the catering but Rosemary had chosen some other firm. "Clients, you know," she said lightly, as if that covered everything.

Gertie asked her directly did she want any help at all during the function and Rosemary had answered equally directly that she didn't. "I can't risk having Jack turn up looking for his conjugal rights or his dinner or both," she said.

Rosemary's mother and Eileen and Stephanie were there. "Do you know any of this crowd?" Mrs. Ryan asked her daughter querulously.

"No, Mother. I only know lawyers these days and protesters, and Rosemary *is* in business."

"I don't think they come from anything, you know." Eileen sighed. Rosemary was passing behind her mother. She mouthed the phrase at her sister that she knew was hovering on her mother's lips. "Jumped-up people, you know." Eileen and Stephanie burst out laughing. Mrs. Ryan was startled. "Look, you two are eccentric enough already, don't be drawing attention to yourselves."

"At least we didn't wear our boiler suits, Mrs. R.," said Stephanie who was willowy with long chestnut hair and quite gorgeous.

"Or our bowler hats," giggled Eileen.

Mrs. Ryan sighed. Nobody had her problems, nobody at all. For all this wealth and style there wasn't a whisper of a husband for Rosemary anywhere in sight. There were, however, photographers there, and Rosemary was photographed with a politician. Barney and Danny were taken with an actress, out on the roof garden with a bank of flowers and a panoramic view in the background. Rosemary was on the financial pages, the others on the property pages. Inquiries about No. 32 Tara Road came flooding in. Everyone was happy.

Because she was now such a near neighbor, Danny and Ria saw a lot more of Rosemary. She often called in around seven in the evening for an hour or so and they would all have a glass of wine mixed with soda in the front room. Ria made hot cheese savories, or bacon slices wrapped around almonds and prunes. It didn't matter that Rosemary waved them away; Danny would have a few, she and the children would eat the rest, and anyway it gave her a chance to bring out the Victorian china that she had bought at auctions.

The children stayed down in the kitchen, with strict warnings not to fight and not to touch anything on the stove. Ria found herself fixing her hair regularly and putting on some makeup. She really couldn't face the elegant Rosemary night after night without making some effort.

"Dressing up for Lady Ryan!" her mother scoffed.

"You always dress nicely, Mother, I note," Ria said.

Her mother had taken to wearing little pillbox hats like Audrey Hepburn's headgear. She bought these in thrift shops. Danny had commented on them with huge admiration. "Now you dare tell me, Holly, that you don't look like Audrey Hepburn. You could be her younger sister."

Gertie was also disapproving of Rosemary's visits. "You wait on her as if you were her maid, Ria," she said.

"I do nothing of the sort, I don't go out to work and they do, that's all. Anyway, it's nice for me to have a room to show off and everything."

"Sure." Gertie had gone off Rosemary. It would have been a handy few quid just down the road, and she would like to have seen the inside of a place that had featured in the papers. Even as a cleaner. "Is it lovely above there in Number Thirty-two?" Gertie asked Ria. It would be nice to tell the customers in the launderette about it, even secondhand.

Ria didn't often take Brian up to Rosemary's apartment. He was three now; he upset the calm of this place. She felt she was apologizing for his endless noise and perpetual toddling and constant sticky hugs and demands for attention. Annie wouldn't have wanted to come. There was nothing to entertain her at Rosemary's and too many areas that seemed off-limits.

"You *must* bring the children with you," Rosemary would insist. But Ria knew that it was easier not to. She loved them so much that it would kill her to apologize for what she considered their totally natural behavior. So instead she left the children with her mother on one of the many Saturday afternoons that Danny was working, and walked up to see Rosemary on her own. It was so peaceful and elegant, as if she hadn't unmade a bed, cooked a meal, or done any washing since the day it had been shown off at the housewarming. Even the roof garden looked as if every flower had been painted into place.

Despite the smart surroundings, Rosemary was in so many ways exactly the same as she had been years ago when they had started work in the real estate agency. She could still laugh in the same infectious way about the things that had made them laugh back then: Hilary's obsession with money, Mrs. Ryan's fear of jumped-up people, Nora Johnson's living her life through the world of movies.

Rosemary had told Ria about some of the problems at work, the girl who was excellent at everything and would have been a superb personal assistant but had such bad body odor she had to let her go, the man who had changed his mind at the last moment and canceled a huge print job and Rosemary had to take him to court, charity leaflets she had printed for nothing for a function that turned out to be a rave where everyone was on Ecstasy and the police were called.

They would sit on the terrace with their feet up, and the heavy scent of the flowers all around them.

"What's that lovely green one with the gorgeous smell?" Ria asked.

"Tobacco plant," Rosemary said.

"And the big purple one a bit like lilac?"

"Solanum crispum."

"How on earth do you know them all, and remember them, Rosemary? You have so many other things in your mind as well."

"It's all in a book, Ria. There's no point in having these things if you don't know what they are." Rosemary's voice was slightly impatient.

Ria knew how to head impatience off at the pass. "You're absolutely right. I've got plenty of books, next time I'll talk just as authoritatively as you do."

"That's my girl." Rosemary was approving. The moment of irritation was over.

Maybe if their place was less untamed and wild, she and Danny could sit like this on a Saturday afternoon and watch the children play. Maybe they could just talk to each other, read the papers together sometimes. It had been so long since they sat in their garden.

"Is there a lot of work keeping all this the way it is?"

"No, I have a man once a week for four hours, that's all."

"And how do you know what to tell him to do?"

"I don't. I hired him from a garden center, *he* knows what to do. But you see, the whole trick was in making it labor-saving. It was the builders who did it all. Once you don't have sprawling herbaceous borders to break your back weeding, you're fine. Just nice easy-care bushes and shrubs that sort of bring themselves up." It always seemed so effortless when Rosemary described things.

As she walked down Tara Road, Ria thought about it. Brian was old enough now, she could get a job, but Danny didn't seem to want her to. "Sweetheart, isn't it wonderful for me to know you are here and in charge of everything," he would say if she brought up the subject. Or else he would frown with worry and concern. "Aren't you happy, love? That's terrible. I suppose I'm very selfish, I thought your life seemed very full, lots of friends and everything . . . but of course we'll talk about it."

That wasn't what she wanted either.

It was a particularly lovely road just as the summer was starting. The cherry trees were in bloom everywhere, their petals starting to make a pink carpet. She never stopped marveling at the variety of life you could find on Tara Road—houses where students lived in great numbers in small flats, and tenants, their bicycles up against the railings just as it had been in their own house with their tenants until this year when Danny and Ria had been able to reclaim all the rented rooms for themselves. Then on past the small lock-up workshop and the road changed again into big houses on their own grounds until it came to the corner with a busy street. And around the corner to where Gertie lived and worked, where the handy launderette had plenty of clientele among the tenants. And where Gertie and Jack lived their mysterious life where you were considered a much better friend if you asked no questions.

If she turned right outside Rosemary's house the road would go past equally mixed housing, high houses like their own, lower ones half hidden by trees, then a terrace of six houses where the Sullivans lived, where Jimmy had his dental surgery. And on to the corner where Colm's restaurant was struggling along.

Her mind full of gardens, Ria noticed that almost every house had made more effort than they had. But it was so hard to know where to start. Some of that undergrowth really needed someone with a saw to cut it down, and then what? She didn't want to be one of those women who, leaving a friend's house, immediately wanted new kitchen work surfaces or a change of curtains, but it seemed ludicrous that she and Danny had managed to close their eyes somehow to a huge aspect of the life they could have together.

Ria didn't want to admit it to herself, but she knew that she had gotten out of the habit of initiating things. When they were first married she would go down to the main road, buy two pots of polish and the scullery would be immaculate when Danny got back from work. Now perhaps he had higher standards. He bought and sold and therefore got to know the houses of the rich and those with taste and style. She would never go ahead on her own with any plan. Yet if Danny didn't see that their garden was dragging the place down, perhaps it was up to her to make the move.

Barney McCarthy was just parking his car in their cluttered driveway. It wasn't an easy maneuver, he had to negotiate it in beside their car, Annie's bicycle, Brian's tricycle, a wheelbarrow that had been there for weeks, and several crates that had been ignored by the dustmen but had never been taken to the dump.

"You look lovely, Ria," he said as he got out. He was a man who admired women but he never paid an idle compliment. If he said you looked well he meant it.

Ria patted her hair, pleased. "Thank you, Barney. I don't feel lovely, actually I feel a bit annoyed with myself. I think I'm getting rather slovenly."

"You?" He was amazed.

"When you think that we have lived here for nearly nine years and it's still a bit like a building site."

"Oh no, no," Barney murmured soothingly.

"But it *is*, Barney. And I'm the one who's around here all the time. I should be doing something about it, and I'm going to, I've decided that. Poor Danny shouldn't have to take that on as well as everything else. Already he works all the hours God sends . . ." She thought Barney looked at her sympathetically.

"Ria, you can't go talking like that, there's years of undergrowth there."

"Don't I know it? No, I meant maybe you could tell me how much it would cost to get your men to come in and clear the place out, then we could arrange what to plant . . . just tell me what it will be, don't bother Danny at all, and I'll build it into the household expenses. At least that's something I'd be able to do."

"I think we should bring Danny in on this, ask him what he wants."

"But he'll say, 'In time, in time,' and we'll never get it done. Let's just clear it, Barney, and then we can decide what we should plant and how to decorate it."

Barney stood stroking his chin. "I don't know, Ria, there's a lot to be thought of before you bring in the diggers. Suppose you wanted to build here, for example. It would be silly to have put in a lot of fancy flower beds and such, which would only have to be taken out again."

"Build?" Ria was astonished. "But what would we want to build? Haven't we a huge three and a half story house already! We haven't any furniture in some of the tenants' rooms yet. We're going to make a bigger study for Danny and maybe a playroom for the children, but we don't need any more space."

"You never know how people's plans change as the years go on," Barney said.

She felt a chill. She didn't want things to change, only get better. She made a sudden decision. She was not going to discuss it anymore with this man. Much as he liked and admired her, he thought of her only as Danny's little wife. Pretty, possibly a good mother and homemaker, tactful and always ready with the right kind of food when they needed it, equally pleasant to his wife and his mistress. He did not consider her a person who would be able to make a decision about the home she lived in.

"You're absolutely right, Barney, I don't know what got into me," she said. "Will I make a little snack for you and Danny? Iced tea, maybe, and a tomato sandwich on whole meal bread?"

"You're a genius," he said.

Ria's mother was in the kitchen with the children. "Oh, there you are, back from Lady Ryan's place."

Ria had now forgotten where her mother's resentment began and why. She had long ceased to try to convince her of Rosemary's worth. "Yes indeed, and she was asking for you too, Mam."

"Huh," snorted Nora Johnson. "Was that Barney I heard you talking to?"

Ria was bending over to see the picture that Annie had been painting; there was water all over the kitchen. "I painted a picture of you, Mam," she said proudly. A creature like a golliwog stood surrounded by saucepans and frying pans.

"Lovely," said Ria. "That's really beautiful, Annie, you're so clever."

"I'm a clever boy," Brian insisted.

"No, you're a very stupid boy," Annie said.

"Annie, really! Brian's very clever indeed."

"I don't think he has a brain in his head," Annie said seriously. "If you don't give him any paints he screams and if you do he just makes big splashes."

"Rubbish, Annie. He's just not as old as you are, that's all. Wait until he's your age, he'll be able to do all the same things."

"When you get older will you be as clever as Gran?" Annie asked.

"I hope so." Ria smiled.

"Never in a million years," her mother said. "I expect you'll be whipping up some little delicacy for that adulterer upstairs with Danny."

"It's a word I don't use really in general conversation myself," Ria said, flashing her a look.

Annie was learning new phrases all the time. "What a dutterer?" she asked.

"Oh, a dutterer is like a sort of drain, you know another word for a gutter," Ria said quickly.

Annie accepted this and went back to her painting.

"Sorry," her mother said a little later.

Ria patted her on the arm. "It doesn't matter, I agree with you as it happens. Then I would, wouldn't I? Wives always do. Can you get me those big iced tea glasses please, Mam?"

"Mad idea, this, you should either have a nice cold gin and tonic or a nice hot cup of tea, I say, not mixing the two up. It's not natural."

Later that evening, Ria said to Danny that they should really try to do something with the wilderness of the garden.

"Not now, sweetheart," Danny said, as she knew he was going to.

"I'm not going to nag, let *me* do it. I'll ask Barney for a price."

"You already did," Danny said.

"That's because I was trying to take things off your shoulders."

"Sweetheart, don't do that, please. He'd only do it for nothing, and it's not necessary."

"But, Danny, you're the one who says we must keep up the value of the property."

"We don't know what were going to *do* with it yet, Ria."

"Do with it? We want a place for people to park their cars when they come to see us, for us to park our car without it being like an obstacle course . . . we want it to look like a home where people are settling down for their life. Not some kind of a transit camp."

"But we haven't thought it through . . . what the future may bring."

"Now don't start talking like Barney about building here." Ria was very cross.

"Barney said that?"

"Yes, and I don't know what the hell he was talking about."

Danny saw her red angry face and her confusion. "Listen, if there is any building to be done, it's way, way down the road yet. You're right. We must do something . . . a sort of patch-up job on it."

"But what do we need to build?"

"Nothing yet, you're quite right."

"Yet? Haven't we got a huge house?"

"Who knows what the future will bring?"

"That's not fair, Danny. I must know what you think the future will bring."

"Okay then, I'll tell you what I mean. Suppose, just suppose we fell on hard times, we wouldn't want to lose this house. If we had a chance to build in the garden, maybe a small unit, two self-contained flats, little maisonettes they used to be called, or town houses, there would be room. . . ."

"Two flats in our garden? Outside our front door?" Ria looked at him as if he were mad.

"If we left the possibility of doing so then it would be like an insurance policy."

"But it would be terrible."

"Better than losing the house if that were the choice. It's not, but suppose it were."

"Why should I suppose any such thing? You're always looking on the bright side, why are we looking at doom and gloom and building horrible flats in our garden in case we're poor? If there's something you're not telling me, then you'd better tell me now. It's not fair to leave me not bothering my pretty little head. It's not fair and I won't stand for it."

Danny took her in his arms. "I swear I'm not hiding things from you. It's just in this business you see so many people who believed that the future was going to be fine and that everything would go on slightly upwards each year . . . and then something happens, some swing in the market, and they lose everything."

"But we don't have any stocks and shares, Danny."

"I know sweetheart, *we* don't."

"What does that mean?"

"Barney does, did, and our fortunes are very tied in with his."

"But you said that the whole business of the guarantee was over, that once he made his money on Number Thirty-two that he'd got out of that worry."

"And he has." Danny was soothing. "So he's more cautious now."

"Barney was never cautious in his life. He had a heart attack and he still smokes and drinks brandy, and anyway why does it mean that *we* should be cautious and edgy?"

"Because our fortunes are very much tied up with his. He knows that and he wants the best for us, so *that's* why he likes to think there's a chance of our building . . . suppose things go badly for him . . . of us getting more bricks and mortar, the only thing that's definitely going to keep its value. Do you see?"

"Not really, to be honest," Ria said. "If Barney's business collapsed, couldn't you work in any agency in town?"

"Yes, I suppose I could," Danny said with that quick bright smile that Ria had learned to dread. It was the kind of smile he had when he was showing somebody a doubtful property. When he was anxious to close on something, when he had a completion date but not an exchange date, when he was afraid that the chain wouldn't hold and somebody some-where along the line wouldn't get their loan and so it would all collapse like a house of cards.

But there was no more to be discovered or discussed or gained. A patch-up job and a legacy of worry for the future. That was what had come out of the conversation.

Sheila Maine wrote from America to say that the papers were full of the great opportunities in Ireland, and the numbers of people who were relocating there. She wondered if any of the girls she knew in Dublin would advise her. She had so much enjoyed meeting them all when she had been there. And hadn't that been a fun day when they had gone to the psychic in her caravan? Mrs. Connor had told Sheila that her future was in her own hands and really and truly this was very sound. Everywhere she looked now she read the same advice, the same counsel. Why hadn't they known it years ago when they were just swept along with what everyone else thought, and did what other people did?

Sheila wrote that her son, Sean, who was now eight was learning Irish dancing at a nearby class, and her daughter, Kelly, who was a very demanding three-year-old, would join the babies class in it next year. She was determined that the children would not grow up ignorant of their Irish heritage. She copied the letter to her sister, Gertie, to Rosemary, to Ria, and to Hilary. Sheila had particularly liked Hilary during her visit to Ireland and she urged her to come out to visit her in the school holidays.

Hilary showed the invitation. "How could I do that? She must be mad, they've no idea of money over there."

"I don't know, Hilary." Ria sometimes felt that she spent her life assuring her sister that some things actually *were* within her reach. "Suppose you were to book three months in advance, you'd get a great reduction and Sheila says it would cost you nothing out there."

"But what about Martin?" Hilary always had an argument against everything that was suggested.

"Well, he could go with you if he'd like two weeks out in New England, which he very well might, or else go home to see his parents in the country. You know he says he wants to go back there more than you do."

Hilary frowned. It made sense only if you were as rich as Ria and Danny, with no financial worries at all. Life was very strange the way the cards were dealt, she said again.

Ria's patience was limited that day. Mona McCarthy had been around wondering would Ria help at a coffee morning, which was fine except that it meant she would have to ask someone to look after Brian for her. She couldn't ask her mother. Nora Johnson had such a network of social and professional activities that you had to book her days in advance. Today she would be ironing in one place, delivering leaflets about the Bring and Buy sale in aid of the animal refuge, visiting some of the old ladies in St. Rita's. She couldn't break into all that.

Gertie said it wasn't a good morning to leave Brian at the launderette for a couple of hours, because . . . well, let's say . . . it wasn't a good morning. Gertie's own children were with her mother. That said it all. And never in a million years would Ria ask a neighbor like Frances Sullivan to look after him. It would be admitting that even as a nonworking wife she couldn't organize her life. If only that pale, wan Caroline, the strange sister of Colm in the restaurant, was more together then she could be drafted in for a couple of hours, but it always took her about three seconds too long to understand what you were saying, and Ria hadn't the time for it today.

Hilary sat there turning the letter this way and that. Ria decided to take the chance. "I'm going to ask you a favor, say no if you want to. I am very eager to go up to Mona McCarthy's house for a variety of reasons."

"I'm sure you are," Hilary sniffed.

"None of them like you think, but it would suit me greatly if you minded Brian for me for three hours, then I'll come back and make you a huge, gorgeous lunch. Yes or no?"

"Why do you want to go there?"

"That's a 'no,' I suppose," Ria said.

"Not necessarily. If you tell me why you want to go, then I'll stay."

"All right I will. I'm worried that the McCarthys might be in some kind of financial trouble. I want to see what I can find out, because if they are then it will affect Danny. Now that's the truth—take it or leave it. Yes or no?"

"Yes," said Hilary with a smile.

Ria phoned a taxi, put on her good suit and her best silk scarf, took a freshly baked walnut cake from the wire tray where it was cooling, and headed off to the McCarthys' large house six miles from Dublin. The drive was filled with smart cars, and the sound of women's chatter was loud as she approached the door. It was touching to see Mona's face light up when she came in. Ria slipped out of her jacket and began to help with the practiced smile of one who had been to many coffee mornings. It was all about making sure these comfortably off and often lonely women had a good time and were warmly welcomed into a group. Their ten-pound entrance fee was not in itself so important as making them feel they belonged. This way they could later be persuaded to part with much larger sums of money at fashion shows, at glittering dinner dances, at film premieres.

An elegant woman was introduced to Ria as Margaret Murray, 'You may know my husband, Ken. He's in the property business," she said.

Ria longed to tell her that Ken Murray was the first boy she had ever kissed many years ago, when she was fifteen and a half. That it had been horrible and he had told her she was boring. But she thought that Margaret Murray might not find this as funny in retrospect as she did, so she said nothing but had a little giggle to herself.

"You're in good form," Mona McCarthy said approvingly.

"Remind me to tell you why later. This is all going very well, isn't it?"

"Yes, I think they like coming here as a curiosity," Mona said.

"Why so?"

"Well they speculate a lot, you know, about whether we are still solvent or not. Rumors around the place have us in the poorhouse." Mona looked remarkably calm as she refilled the coffeepot from the two percolators.

"And aren't you worried about this?" Ria asked.

"No, Ria, if I worried every time that I hear something about Barney I'd be a very worried woman indeed. We've been poor before, and if it happens I imagine we could cope with it again. But I don't think it will happen. Barney is always a contingency plan person, I feel sure there are a lot of safety nets along the way." She was serene, almost like a ship as she sailed back into the room full of women who she knew to be rather overinterested in what kept this extravagant lifestyle afloat.

Colm Barry called when Ria and Hilary were having the promised enormous lunch. "Well, you two don't stint yourselves, I'm glad to see." He sat down and accepted their offer.

"Oh, Ria can afford to buy the best cuts of meat," Hilary said, reverting to type.

"It's what she does with them that's so delicious." Colm appreciated the cooking. "And the way they're served."

"It's hard to get good fresh vegetables round here," Ria said. "They're very tired up at the corner and nowhere else is in a pram's walk, really."

"Why don't you grow your own?" Colm suggested.

"Oh Lord, no. It would be such work digging it all out back there.

Even to get the front tidied up was a major undertaking. Neither Danny nor I have the souls of gardeners, I'm afraid."

"I'd do it for you at the back if you like," Colm offered.

"Oh, you can't do that," Ria protested.

"I have an ulterior motive. Suppose I was to make a proper kitchen garden out there and grow all the things I want for the restaurant in it, then you could have some too."

"Would it work?"

"Yes, of course it would, that is if you don't have plans to have velvet lawns, water features, fountains, or pergolas out there."

"No. I think we can safely say those aren't on the agenda," Ria laughed easily.

"Great, then we'll do it."

Ria noted with pleasure that Colm hadn't said they should wait to consult Danny. Unlike Barney McCarthy, he seemed to regard her as a responsible adult capable of making a decision on her own. "Will it be much heavy work, preparing the soil?"

"I don't know yet."

"It's such a wilderness out there, we have no real idea how much awful stuff there might be buried with old roots and rubble."

"But I need the exercise anyway, so it's going to be something that benefits everyone. We all win, no one loses."

"Very few of those deals about, let me tell you," Hilary said.

And from that time on Colm became part of the background in their house on Tara Road. He let himself in silently through the wooden door that went onto the back lane; he kept his gardening tools in a small makeshift hut at the back. He dug an area half the width of the house and the whole length of the garden. This left plenty of space for the children to play in. And as the months went on, he erected a fence and covered it with a plant he called Mile-a-minute, or Russian vine.

"It really looks rather nice, you know," Danny said thoughtfully one day. "And the whole notion of 'Mature Kitchen Garden at rear' is a good selling point."

"If we were to sell, which we're not going to do. I wish you wouldn't frighten me saying things like that, Danny," Ria complained.

"Listen, sweetheart, if you worked all day and all night as I do in a world where hardly anything else is discussed then you'd talk in real estate–speak too." He was right, and what's more he was good-tempered and happy. He was very loving to Ria sometimes, dashing home from work saying he thought of her so much and deeply that he couldn't concentrate on anything else. They would go upstairs and draw the curtains. Once or twice Ria wondered what Colm working in the garden might think.

They didn't talk much about it but she knew that in Gertie's case it was a nightmare, usually only attempted by Jack when drunk. For Hilary it had almost ceased to exist. Martin had once said the only real reason for a man and woman to mate was the hope of producing a child, and that the urge and impetus just weren't there otherwise. He had only said it once, and afterward confessed that he had been a bit depressed at the time and didn't really mean it, Hilary confided. But somehow it was there always in the air.

Ria didn't know any details of Rosemary's sex life. But she was sure it must be very active in those perfect surroundings that she had created for herself. Everywhere they went men were attracted to her. Ria had sometimes seen Rosemary leave parties with men. Did she take them home, upstairs to that apartment that had been featured in so many magazines? Probably. Rosemary wouldn't live like a nun. Still, it must be very unsettling to have to get to know different people in that way. To learn the intricacies and familiarities of another body instead of knowing exactly what worked for you. And for Danny. Ria knew that she was very, very lucky.

The anxiety over the McCarthy finances seemed to have subsided. Danny didn't work so late at night. He took his little princess, Annie, out on walks and visits to the sea. He held the hand of his chubby son, Brian, as the child changed from stumbling to waddling and eventually to running away ahead of them.

The back garden changed slowly and laboriously. Ria knew that it was much easier to learn the names of twenty plants for containers on a roof terrace than to understand Colm's discussion about double-cropping and pest-proof barriers. She tried to sympathize when his sprouts all failed, when his great bamboo bean supports blew down in the wind, and when the peas that he had tried to grow in hanging baskets produced hardly anything at all.

"Why didn't you grow them in the ground?" Ria had asked innocently.

"I was trying to make it nice for you to look out on. You know, a lot of hanging baskets on the back wall. They looked good, I thought." He was very disappointed.

She wished she could share his enthusiasm but to her it was back-breaking and unyielding and there were mountains of healthy sprouts and peas in the shop. Still, he battled on and he even gave the children little tubs where they could grow tomatoes and peppers. He was good with Annie and Brian, and seemed to understand the age difference between them well. Brian got a simple tomato plant that just had to be watered; Annie was encouraged to grow lettuce and basil. But mainly he didn't take part in their lives, he kept to himself on his side of the huge Russian vine fence.

On the other side there was a swing, a garden seat, and even a home-made barbecue pit. At the front of the house the area had been macad-amized by Barney's men, and what had been described as a patch-up job had blossomed well. People admired the colored heathers that grew in the makeshift flower bed.

"I don't know where the heathers came from, honestly," Ria said once.

"You *must* have planted them, sweetheart. As little as I know about gardening, I know that flowers don't appear by magic! And anyway, don't you have to have special soil for heathers?"

Colm was there as they spoke. "That's me, I'm afraid. I bought a bag of the wrong kind of soil, you know, ericaceous, lime-hating." They didn't know but they nodded sagely. "So I had to put it somewhere and I dumped it there. Hope it's all right."

"It's great." Danny approved. "And did you plant the heathers too?"

"Someone gave me a present of them. You see, because I put on the menu that all vegetables are homegrown, the customers think I have a great deal of land behind my place. They often give me plants instead of a tip."

"But we should pay you for those. . . ." Ria began.

"Nonsense, Ria, Danny, as I told you I have a very good deal being able to use your garden and honestly the vegetables are a huge success. I have rows of zucchini planted this week, the trick is to come up with some clever recipes for them now."

"You're doing better these days?" Danny was interested.

"Much better, and we got a great review. That helped a lot." Colm never complained, even when times were slack. "I was even wondering if you'd consider a small greenhouse an eyesore. I'd disguise it well you know, build it up against the back wall. . . ."

"Go ahead, Colm. Do you want a contribution?"

"Only the right to use a bit of electricity for it, it won't take much."

"Oh, would that all business deals could be like this!" Danny said, shaking Colm's hand.

Brian was seven in the summer of 1995. Danny and Ria had a barbecue for his friends. They only wanted sausages, Brian said. People didn't eat other things.

"Not lovely lamb chops?" Danny said. He liked the idea of standing with an apron and chef's hat turning something a little more ambitious than sausages.

"Ugh," Brian said.

"Or those lovely green peppers Colm grew, we could thread them all on a skewer and make kebabs."

"My friends don't like kebabs," Brian said.

"Your friends have never had kebabs," Annie said. She was close to being twelve, only just over three months away from it. It was very hard having to deal with someone as infantile as Brian, really. Very strangely it seemed that her mother and father appeared equally delighted with his babyish ramblings as they were with anything she said.

The arrangements for his party were very tedious. Annie had suggested giving Brian two pounds of cooked sausages and letting all his friends heat them up. They'd never know the difference and all they cared about was lots of tomato ketchup.

"No, it must be right. We had a great party for your seventh birthday, don't you remember?" her mother said.

Annie didn't remember, all the birthdays had merged into one. But she knew that they must have made a fuss over it like over all celebrations. "That's right, it was terrific," she said grudgingly.

"You are beautiful, Annie Lynch, you're an adorable girl." Her mother hugged her until it hurt.

"I'm awful, look at my desperate straight hair."

"And I spend my life saying look at my frizzy hair," Ria said. "It's a very annoying part of being a woman, we're never really satisfied with the way we look."

"Some people are."

"Oh, all the film stars your gran goes on about, all these beauties, I expect they're happy with themselves, but nobody *we* know."

"I'd say that Rosemary is okay with the way she looks."

Rosemary Ryan had refused to be called "Auntie" by her friends' children. She said she was quite old enough already without any of that sort of thing, thank you. "She's super-looking, I know, but she's always on this diet or that diet so maybe in her heart she isn't totally satisfied either."

"No she's very pleased with her appearance, you can see it the way she looks at herself in mirrors."

"What?"

"She sort of smiles at herself, Mam. You must see it, not only in mirrors, but in pictures, anywhere there's glass."

Ria laughed. "Aren't you a funny little article, Annie, the things you see."

Annie didn't like being patted on the head. "It's true, isn't it, Dad?"

"Totally true, Princess," said Danny.

"You didn't hear what was said," they both accused him.

"Yes I did. Annie said Rosemary smiles at her reflection in mirrors and indeed she does, always has. Years ago in the old agency she was at it."

Annie looked pleased, Ria felt put out. It was such a criticism of her friend and she had never been aware of it. "Well, she's so good-looking she's entitled to admire herself," she said eventually.

"Good-looking? I think she's like a bird of prey," Annie said.

"A handsome bird of prey, though," Danny corrected her.

"Mam looks much better," Annie said.

"That goes without saying," Danny said, kissing each of them on the tops of their heads.

It was a very sunny day on Brian's birthday. The preparations went on all morning. Nora Johnson was there fussing, Gertie had come to ask could she help. She looked as if she hadn't slept for a month.

"Only if you stay for the party properly, if you go home and get the children," Ria said.

"No, not today." She was so strained it almost hurt to look at her.

"What's wrong, Gertie?"

"Nothing." The word was like a scream.

"Where are the children?"

"With my mother."

"Who's running the launderette?"

"A sixteen-year-old schoolgirl who wants a holiday job. Have you finished the interrogation, Ria? Can I get on with helping you?"

"Hey, that's not fair, it's not an interrogation." Ria looked upset.

"No, sorry."

"It's just you don't look too well. Why do you want to help here?"

"Why do you think?"

"Gertie, I don't know. Truly I don't."

"Then you're as thick as two short planks, Ria. I need the money."

Ria's face paled. "You're my friend, for God's sake. If you want some money, ask me, don't come round expecting me to be inspired. How much do you want?" She reached for her handbag.

"I won't take money from you, Ria."

"Am I going mad, didn't you just ask for it?"

"Yes, but I won't take it as charity."

"Well, all right. Pay it back to me sometime."

"I won't be able to do that."

"So, it doesn't matter then."

"It does. I want to earn it, I want to scrub and clean. I'll start with the oven, then I'll do all the kitchen surfaces and the bathrooms. I need the tenner."

Ria sat down with the shock of it all. "You must have ten pounds. You *must* have that much, Gertie. You run a business, for God's sake."

"I have to keep the float in the shop, he knows that. I told him I'd be back with ten pounds before lunch, he won't go near the shop."

"Jesus Christ, Gertie, take the ten pounds. Do you think I'm going to watch you for two hours earning this?"

"I won't take it."

"Well, get out then."

"What?"

"You heard me. You're my friend, I'm not going to pay you five pounds an hour for sloshing about in my kitchen, and putting a brush down my lavatories today. I'm sorry but that's it." Ria's eyes were blazing.

Gertie had tears in her eyes. "Oh, Ria, don't be full of principle, have a little understanding instead."

"I have plenty of understanding . . . why don't you have a little dignity?"

"I'm trying to, you're taking it away from me." Gertie looked as if a puff of wind would blow her over. "You're very upset."

"Of course I am upset. Now will you please take the ten-pound note and if you try to give it back to me or lift one hand toward any cleaning whatsoever I'll ram the bloody money down your throat."

"You have no reason to be upset with me or with anyone, Ria. You have a charmed life. I don't envy it to you, you deserve it and you work hard for it, and you're nice to everybody, but everything's going right for you. You might just *think* about how hard it might be when everything's going wrong."

Ria swallowed. "It's my son's seventh birthday, the sun is shining, of course I'm happy. I'm not happy every day, nobody is. Listen, you are my friend. You and I know everything about each other."

"We don't know everything about each other," Gertie said quietly. "We're not schoolgirls anymore, we are women in our mid-thirties, grown-ups. I thought that if I did the work somehow we'd be quits. I'm sorry. And I'm also sorry for upsetting you on Brian's birthday." She turned to leave.

"If you don't take the ten pounds you'll have really upset me."

"Sure. Thank you, Ria."

"No, not coldly. With a bit of a hug anyway." There was a stiff little hug. Gertie's thin body was like a board. "You know what would be the best? If you were to come back later with the kids. Would you do that?"

"No, thank you. But not because of sulking or anything. Just no."

"Sure. Right."

"Thanks again, Ria."

"You're full of dignity, you always have been."

"You deserve all you have, and even more. Enjoy the day." She was gone.

Nora Johnson came into the kitchen from the garden. "I've been tying the balloons to the front gate so that they'll know where the party is and I see Lady Ryan coming down the road wearing a designer outfit. Coming to help, no doubt. Where's Gertie got to? She said she was going to clean some of those old baking tins for the sausages."

"She had to go home, Mam."

"Well, honestly, talk about helpful friends when you need them! If you hadn't Hilary and myself you'd be lost."

"Haven't I always said it, Mam?"

"And will Annie help to entertain them when they get here?"

"No, I don't think a dozen seven-year-old boys is Annie's idea of a good summer afternoon. She'll keep her distance. Danny has a whole lot of games planned for them."

"He's not off about His Master's Business then, is he?" Nora sniffed.

"No, Mam, he's not."

"You look a bit pale, are you all right?"

"Never better."

Ria escaped in relief to greet Rosemary, who had come to count heads. She had bought a great number of individually wrapped chocolate ice creams, they were at home in her freezer. "I'll come back in an hour so you don't have to bother putting them into the freezer. Was there a problem with Gertie?"

"Why do you ask?" Ria wanted to know.

"She ran past me on the road crying and she didn't see me, she genuinely didn't."

"Oh, nothing more than the usual." Ria looked grim.

"Roll on the Divorce Referendum," Rosemary said.

"You don't think that's going to make the slightest difference in Gertie's way of thinking, do you?" Ria asked. "I mean, if there was divorce introduced into this country tomorrow morning, you don't think she'd leave Jack? Abandon him? Give up on him, like everyone else has? Of course she wouldn't."

"Well, what's the point of having it on the statute books at all if people are going to react like that?" Rosemary wondered.

"Search me." Ria was at a loss. "The two families we know who should avail of it won't go near it. You don't think Barney McCarthy is going to disturb his nice comfortable little situation if divorce is introduced, do you?"

"No, I don't indeed, but I didn't know that *you* would see things so clearly." Rosemary laughed almost admiringly. Sometimes Ria could be very surprising. Rosemary went back to No. 32 to change into something more suitable for a children's party.

The party guests had begun to arrive. Very soon they were punching each other good-naturedly. All of them. There didn't seem to be any reason for this, no real aggression or gangs or hostility, that was the way boys behaved. Annie's friends were much gentler, Ria said to her mother as they separated one pair of warring boys before they crashed into Colm's vegetable garden locked into their fight.

"Where *is* Annie, by the way?"

"In her room, I think. There's no point in dragging her down to join them. She's too old for them and not old enough to find them funny. She'll come when she hears there's birthday cake."

"Or sausages. Two to one she gets the smell of sausages and she's down like a greyhound out of a trap," said Nora sagely.

Annie was not in her room, as it happened; she had gone out the back gate and was walking up the lane that ran parallel to Tara Road. She had seen a small, thin orange kitten there the other day. It might not belong to anyone. It had looked frightened, not as if it were used to being petted. Perhaps it was abandoned and she might keep it. They would say no, of course, as people said no to everything. If she could get it into her room for a few days without anyone noticing, give it a litter tray and some food, then they wouldn't have the heart to turn it out. Today would be a good day to smuggle it in, nobody would notice. There was so much fuss about Brian and all his brain-dead friends, shouting and pushing and shoving around the garden. You could bring a giraffe upstairs today and no one would notice. Annie tried to remember which was the back gate where she had seen the little kitten. It wasn't as far up the road as Rosemary's. It was hard to identify them from the back.

Annie Lynch stood in the lane in her blue checked summer dress squinting into the afternoon sun, pushing her straight blond hair out of her eyes. Perhaps she could peep through the keyholes of these wooden doors. Some of them were quite rickety and it was easy to see through the cracks anyway. One of the back gates was new, it was a smart painted wooden door you couldn't see through at all. Annie stood back a little. This must be No. 32 where Rosemary Ryan lived.

She had a very posh garden upstairs on the roof but there was a garden with an ornamental pool and a summer house at the back. This might well be where the poor kitten had wandered in to have a look at the fish in the pond.

Annie knelt down and looked in the keyhole. No sign of a cat. But there were people there in the summer house. They seemed to be fighting over something. She looked more carefully. It was Rosemary Ryan struggling with a man. Annie's heart leaped in her throat. Was she being attacked? Should Annie rattle at the gate and shout, or would the attacker come out and hurt her as well? Rosemary Ryan had her skirt right up around her waist, and the man was pushing at her. With an even greater shock than the first one Annie realized what they were doing. But this wasn't the way it was done. Not what she and Kitty Sullivan had giggled about in school. Not what people almost did at the cinema and on television. It was different. They kissed each other and lay down, it was all gentle. It wasn't like this all this shoving and grunting. Rosemary Ryan couldn't be making love with someone. This isn't the way it was meant to be. The whole thing wasn't possible!

Annie pulled back from the keyhole, her heart racing. She tried to make sense of the situation. To be honest nobody *could* see them unless they were actually looking through the keyhole of the back gate. The summerhouse faced away from the main house and toward the back wall.

Annie couldn't see who the man was; he had his back to her. All she had seen was Rosemary's face. All screwed up and angry, upset. Not dreamy like it was in the movies. Maybe she had got it totally wrong, this mightn't be what they were doing at all. Annie looked once more.

Rosemary's arms were around the man's neck, her eyes were closed, she wasn't pushing him away she was pulling him toward her. "That's it, yes, yes, that's it," she was crying out.

Annie straightened up in horror. She couldn't believe what she had seen. She started to run down the lane. When passing No. 16 she heard the sounds of shouting and screaming from Brian's party. But she didn't stop. She didn't want to go in knowing what she knew now. She couldn't bear them all expecting her to be normal. Things would never be the same again and she could never tell anybody. On she ran, tears blinding her eyes until just as she was getting to the main road and back to normality she fell, one of those unexpected falls where the earth just jumped up to meet you with a thud.

It winded her totally and she had trouble getting her breath. When she struggled to stand she saw she had grazed both knees, which were bleeding, and her arm. She leaned against the wall and sobbed as if her heart would break.

Colm heard the noise and came out. "Annie, what happened?" No reply, just heaving shoulders. "Annie, I'll run and get your mother."

"*No.* Please don't. *Please,* Colm."

Colm wasn't like other grown-ups, he didn't always automatically know what was best for you. "Okay, but look at you . . . you've had a horrible fall, let me see." He held her arm gently. "No, it's only the skin, what about your knees? Don't you look at them, I'll examine them without touching, and I'll report to you."

Annie stood there while he knelt down and studied them. Eventually he said, "Lots of blood but I don't think you need a stitch. Let me walk you home, Annie."

She shook her head. "No. Brian's having a party, I don't want to go home."

Colm took this onboard. "If you like you could come into my house, into the bathroom and wash your poor knees. I'll be in the restaurant out of your way but there if you need me, and you could come in and out and I'll give you a nice lemonade or whatever you like." He smiled at her.

It worked. "Yes, I'd like that, Colm."

Together they went in, and he showed her the bathroom. "There's a whole lot of face cloths there, and if you put a little disinfectant in the water . . ." She seemed helpless, unsure of how to start. "If you like I could dab them for you, take any grit out?"

"I don't know. . . ."

"Yes, sometimes it's easier if you do it yourself. Would I stay here on this chair while you do it, and tell you if I see more bits that need to be done?"

He got the first smile. "That would be great." He watched while the child touched her knee tentatively with the diluted disinfectant, and wiped away all the grit and earth. It was only a surface scratch, the bleeding was slight. "I can't reach my elbow, will you do that, Colm?"

Gently he cleaned her arm and handed her a big fluffy towel. "Now, pat it dry."

"There might be spots of blood on the towel?" She looked anxious.

"All the more work for Gertie's launderette then," he smiled.

They went into the cool dark bar of his restaurant. At the bar there were four high stools. He gestured her to one of them. "Now, Miss Lynch, what's your pleasure?" he said to her.

"What do you think is nice, Colm?"

"Well, they say that in times of shock something with a lot of sugar is good. In fact they always recommend hot, sweet tea."

"Ugh," said Annie.

"I know, that's my view too. I'll tell you . . . what I always have is a St. Clements. It's a mixture of orange and lemon. How does that sound?"

"Great. I'd like that," said Annie. "Do you not drink real drinks, then?"

"No, you see they don't agree with me. Something to do with my personality or metabolism or whatever . . . it's not clear exactly what causes it but they don't suit me."

"How did you find out they didn't suit you?"

"I got a few little hints, like once I started I couldn't stop." He smiled wryly.

"Like drugs?" Annie asked, interested.

"Just like drugs. So I had to stop altogether."

"Do you miss not being able to drink real drinks, at parties and things?" Annie was interested.

"Do I miss it? No. I don't miss the way I was, which was out of control, I'm very glad not to be like that. But I suppose I wish I was the way other people are, you know, having a nice glass of wine or two of an evening, a couple of beers on a summer day. But I'm not able to stop after that so I can't start." Annie looked sympathetic. "However, there are lots of things I can do that others can't," Colm said cheerfully. "I can make wonderful sauces and great desserts that would take the sight out of your eyes."

"Brian's awful friends want ice creams in silver paper wrappers! Imagine!" Annie said disparagingly.

"I know. Isn't it disgusting!" Colm said, and they both began to laugh. Annie's laugh had a slightly hysterical tinge in it.

"Nothing happened out in the lane to make you fall, did it?" Colm asked.

The child's eyes looked wary. "No. Why?"

"No reason. Listen, will I walk home with you now?"

"I'm all right really, Colm."

"Of course you are, don't we know that? But I have to go for a walk every day, all chefs must, it's a kind of rule, stops them getting big stomachs that keep falling into their saucepans."

Annie laughed. It wasn't possible to think of Colm Barry having a tummy like that. He was nearly as slim as Dad. They set off together. Just as they came to the gate they saw Rosemary Ryan unloading the ice creams in a cool bag from the back of her car. Annie stiffened. Colm noticed but said nothing.

"Heavens, Annie, what a terrible cut! Did you fall?"

"Yes."

"She's okay now," Colm said.

"It looks dreadful, where did it happen?"

"On the road in front of Colm's restaurant," Annie said quickly.

Colm was surprised.

"And Colm came to your rescue." Rosemary always smiled at Colm flirtatiously, though it never did her any good.

"Exactly, I can't have people falling down in front of my premises. Bad for business," he joked.

"You were lucky you didn't fall in front of the traffic." Rosemary had lost interest in it, now she was hauling the boxes of ice creams out. They could hear the shouting and screaming of Brian's friends from the back garden. "My public is waiting for me and the ice cream," Rosemary laughed. "I think we know which they are waiting for more." She moved ahead of them through the basement and out to the back.

"Thanks, Colm," Annie said.

"Don't mention it."

"It's just that it's . . . well, it's nobody's business really where I fell, is it?"

"Absolutely not."

She felt he was owed some kind of explanation. "I was looking for a cat, you see. I thought if I got a kitten and sort of kept it secretly for a bit . . . you know?"

"I know." Colm was grave.

"So thanks for all the St. Clements and everything."

"I'll see you round, Annie."

Gran was terrific, she had kept sausages for Annie. "I didn't see you around so I put them in the oven to keep warm."

"You're great, where are they all?"

"They're about to have the cake. Lady Ryan arranged sparklers."

"Mam hates it when you call her that." Annie giggled and then she winced at the pain in her elbow.

Her grandmother was full of concern. "Let me wash that for you."

"It's okay, Gran, it's done. Look at Auntie Hilary with all those awful boys."

"She loves them, she's brought a big dartboard where you throw rings on. There's fierce competition."

"What's the prize?"

"Oh, some game. Hilary knows what electronic games children of that age want from being up at the school, you know."

"Why didn't Auntie Hilary have any children, Gran?"

"The Lord didn't send her any, that's all."

"The Lord doesn't send children, Gran, you know that."

"No, not directly, but indirectly He does, and in your Auntie Hilary's case He just didn't."

"Maybe she didn't like mating," Annie said thoughtfully.

"What?" Nora Johnson was at a loss for a word, which was very unlike her.

"Maybe she decided not to go through the whole business of getting them, like cats and rabbits, you know. There must be some people who just don't like the thought of it."

"Not many," her grandmother said dryly.

"I bet that's it, you could ask her."

"It's not the thing you ask people, Annie, believe me."

"I do, Gran, I know you couldn't ask her. There are some things you don't talk about at all, you just put away at the back of your mind. Isn't that right?"

"Absolutely right," her grandmother said with enormous relief.

Later on the parents of Brian's friends came to collect their sons, and they stood in the warm summer evening in the back garden of Tara Road while the boys played and pummeled on, tiring themselves and each other out for bedtime. Annie watched her mother and father stand there in the center of the group, passing around a tray of wine and little smoked salmon sandwiches. Dad's arm was around Mam's shoulder a lot of the time. Ria knew from the girls at school that parents still want to be with each other and make love and all that, even when they didn't want children. It seemed such an unlikely thing to want to do. Horrible even.

There was much sympathy about the grazed knee, and when she went to bed, Mam came into her room. She sat in Annie's big armchair, moving the furry toy animals out of the way.

"You've been very quiet all afternoon and evening, Annie. Are those knees all right?"

"Fine, Mam, don't fuss."

"I'm not fussing, I'm just sorry for your poor old knees and your elbow too. Like you would be if I fell."

"I know, Mam. Sorry. You weren't fussing, but I'm fine."

"And how did it happen?"

"I was running, I told you."

"It's not like you to fall, you're such a graceful girl. When Hilary and I were your age we were falling all the time, but you never do. I think it's because your dad calls you a princess you decided to behave like one."

Her mother's look was so fond and warm that Annie reached out for her hand. "Thanks, Mam," she said, eyes full.

"I was so exhausted out there today, Annie, with those boys. Honestly they're like young bullocks head-butting each other, not like children at all. When I think what an ease it's always been to have your friends, but that's the difference between the sexes for you. Would you like a hot drink? You've had a bad shock today."

"What do you mean?" Annie's eyes were wary.

"The fall, it jars the system even at your age."

"Oh, that. No, no, I'm fine."

Ria kissed her daughter's flushed face and closed the door.

She had spoken only the truth, it *had* been a killing day. But then wasn't she so well off compared to everyone else? Her mother going home alone with that absurd little dog. Hilary crossing the city with her dartboard in a big carrier bag to a man who wouldn't hold her in his arms anymore because they couldn't make children. Gertie facing who-knew-what horrors in the flat above the launderette. Rosemary alone in that marble palace of a penthouse.

While she, Ria, had everything she could ever have wanted.

CHAPTER

THREE

SOMETIMES THEY SAW MOTHERS and daughters together in the shops. Talking normally, holding up a skirt or a dress. Nodding or frowning but concerned. Like friends. One going into a cubicle to try something on, the other holding four more outfits outside. Perhaps they weren't real people, Ria told herself. Maybe they were actresses or from advertising. Judging from the eleven confrontations she had with her own daughter in an hour and a half it was very hard to believe that any fourteen-year-old girl and her mother would go shopping together from choice. These other people were only playing at being Happy Families. Surely?

Annie had this gift token from her grandmother. It was for more money than she had ever spent before on clothes. Up to now Annie had only bought shoes, jeans, and T-shirts on her own. But this was different, it was for something to wear for all the parties this summer. It had seemed normal for Ria to go with her and help her choose. It had even seemed like fun. That was some hours ago. Now it seemed like the most foolish thing either of them had ever done in their lives.

When Annie had looked at something with leather and chains, Ria had gasped aloud. "I knew you were going to be like that, I knew it in my bones," Annie cried.

"No, I mean, it's just . . . I thought . . ." Ria was wordless.

"*What* did you think. Go on, Mam, say what you thought, don't just stand there gulping." Annie's face was red and angry.

Ria was not going to say the outfit looked like an illustration from a magazine article called "Sadomasochistic Wardrobe Unearthed."

"Why don't you try it on?" she said weakly.

"If you think I'm going to put it on now that I've seen your face, and let you make fun of me . . ."

"Annie, I'm *not* making fun of you. We don't know what it looks like until you put it on, maybe it's . . ."

"Oh, Mam, for God's sake."

"But I mean it, and it's your token."

"I know it is. Gran gave it to me to buy something I liked, not some awful, revolting thing with a butch tartan waistcoat like you want me to wear."

"No, no. Be reasonable, Annie, I haven't steered you toward anything at all, have I?"

"Well, what are you here for then, Mam? Answer me that. If you have nothing to suggest, what are you doing? What are *we* doing here?"

"Well, I thought we were looking . . ."

"But you never look. You never look at anything or anyone, otherwise you wouldn't wear the kind of clothes you do."

"Look, I know you don't want the same clothes as I do."

"*Nobody* wants the same clothes as you do, Mam, honestly. I mean, have you thought about it for one minute?"

Ria looked at one of the many mirrors around. She saw reflected a flushed angry teenager, slim with straight blond hair, holding what appeared to be a bondage garment. Beside her was a tired-looking woman with a great head of frizzy hair tumbling onto her shoulders, and a black velvet V-neck sweater worn over a flowing black and white skirt. She had put on comfortable flat shoes for shopping. This was not a day when Ria had rushed thoughtlessly out of the house; she had remembered the mirrors that came on you suddenly in dress shops. She had combed her hair, put on makeup, and even rubbed shoe cream into her shoes and handbag. It had all looked fine in the hall mirror before they had left Tara Road. It didn't look great here.

"I mean, it's not even as if you were really old," Annie said. "Lots of people your age haven't given up."

With great difficulty Ria forced herself not to take her daughter by the hair and drag her from the shop. Instead she looked thoughtfully back into the mirror. She was thirty-seven. How old did she look? Thirty-five? That's all. Her curly hair made her young, she didn't look forty or anything. But then what did she know?

"Oh, Mam, stop sucking in your cheeks and making silly faces, you look ridiculous." When had it happened, whatever it was that made Annie hate her, scorn her? They used to get on so well.

Ria made one more superhuman effort. "Listen, we mustn't talk about me, it's *your* treat, your gran wants you to get something nice and suitable."

"No, she doesn't, Mam. Do you never listen? She said I was to get whatever I wanted, she never said one word about it being suitable."

"I meant . . ."

"You mean anything that would look well on a poodle at a dog show." Annie turned away with tears in her eyes.

Nearby a woman and her daughter were looking through a rail of shirts. "They must have a yellow one," the girl was saying excitedly. "Come on, we'll ask the assistant. You look terrific in yellow. Then we'll go and have a coffee."

They seemed an ordinary mother and daughter, not just a couple sent over by central casting to depress real people. Ria turned away so that nobody could see the tears of envy in her eyes.

Danny had organized the people to deliver the sander at eleven o'clock. Ria wanted to be home to greet them. It was such a peculiar idea, to take up their carpets and bring out the beauty of the wooden floors. They didn't look a bit beautiful to her, full of nails and discoloration. But Danny knew about these things, she accepted this. His work and his skill was selling houses to people who knew everything, and these people knew that exposed wooden floors and carefully chosen rugs were good, while wall-to-wall carpeting was bad, and obviously concealed unmerciful horrors beneath. You could rent a sander for a weekend and walk around behind it while it juddered and peeled off the worst bit of your floor. That was what lay ahead today and tomorrow.

Would Annie think she was sulking if she left her now? Would she be relieved? "Annie, you know your father arranged that this sanding machine to come today?" she began tentatively.

"Mam, I'm *not* spending the weekend doing that, it's not fair."

"No, no, of course not, I wasn't going to suggest it. I was going to say I should go home and be there when they arrive, but I don't want to abandon you." Annie stared at her wordlessly. "Not that I'm much help, really I'm inclined to get confused when I see a lot of clothes together," Ria said.

Annie's face changed. Suddenly she reached out and gave her mother an unexpected hug. "You're not the worst, Mam," she said grudgingly. From Annie this was high, high praise these days.

Ria went home with a lighter heart.

Ria had just got in the door of her house on Tara Road when she heard the gate rattle and the familiar cry: "Ree-ya, Ree-ya." A call known all over the area, as regular as the Angelus or the sound of the ice cream van. It was her mother and the dog, the misshapen and unsettled animal Pliers, a dog never at ease in Ria and Danny's home on Tara Road, but because of circumstances forced to spend a lot of his disturbed life there. Ria's mother was always going somewhere where dogs weren't allowed, and Pliers pined if left at home alone. Pliers yowled in Ria's house, but for some reason this was not regarded as pining and was considered preferable.

Ria's mother never came in unannounced or uninvited. She made a great production out of this from the time she had moved to the little house near them. Never assume that you are automatically welcome in your children's homes. That was her motto, she always said. It seemed a loveless kind of motto and also totally inappropriate since she called unannounced and uninvited almost every single day. She thought that this shout at the gate was somehow enough warning and preparation. Today reminded Ria of being back at school when her mother would come to the playground or to the park where her pals had gathered, always calling "Ree-ya." Her school friends used to take up the cry. And now here she was, a middle-aged woman and nothing had changed, her mother still calling her name as if it were some kind of a war cry.

"Come in, Mam." She tried to put a welcome in her voice. The dog would worry at the sanding machine when it arrived and bark at it, then he would set up one of his yowls so plaintively that they would assume his paw had been trapped in it. Of all days to have to baby-sit Pliers, this must be one of the worst.

Nora Johnson bustled in, sure as always of her welcome. Hadn't she called out from the gate to say she was on her way? "There was a young pup on the bus, asked me for my bus pass. I said to him to keep a civil tongue in his head." Ria wondered why her mother, such a known dog lover, always used the word pup as a term of abuse. There were pups everywhere these days, in shops, driving vans, hanging about.

"What was so bad about him asking you that?"

"How dare he assume that I am at the age to have a bus pass? There's no way that he should think with only half a look out of his slits of eyes that I am a pensioner." Of course, Ria's mother, despite her lemon-colored linen suit and black polka dot scarf, looked exactly the age she was, the young pup on the bus had just been thoughtless. At his age he assumed everyone over forty was geriatric. But there was no point in trying to explain any of this to her mother. Ria busied herself getting out the tray of shortbread she had made the night before. The coffee mugs were ready. Soon the kitchen would be full of people, the men with the sanding machine, Danny wanting to learn how it worked, Brian and some of his school friends, there was always something on offer to eat in the Lynches' kitchen, unlike their own. Annie might be back with some amazing outfit and Kitty Sullivan, whom she had met in the shopping mall.

Rosemary always came in on a Saturday, and sometimes Gertie escaped from the flat over the launderette. Gertie came twice a week to do the cleaning, it was a professional arrangement. But she could drop in socially on a Saturday. There would always be an excuse, she had left something behind or she wanted to check the time of next week.

Colm Barry might come in with vegetables. Every Saturday he brought them by the armful. Sometimes he even scrubbed big, earth-covered parsnips and carrots, or trimmed spinach for them. Ria made soups and casseroles with the freshest produce possible, all grown with no effort a few feet away from her own kitchen.

Other people came and went. Ria Lynch's kitchen was a place with a welcome. So unlike the way things had been when Ria was young herself and nobody was allowed out to their kitchen, a dark murky place with its torn linoleum on the floor. Visitors weren't really encouraged to come to her mother's house at all. Her mother, and from what she could remember, her father also, were restless people, unable to relax themselves and incapable of seeing that others might want to.

Even when her mother visited her here on Tara Road she hardly ever settled, she was constantly rattling keys or struggling out of or into coats, just arriving or about to leave, unable to give in to the magic of this warm, welcoming place.

It had been the same in Danny's family. His mother and father had sat in their very functional farmhouse kitchen drinking mug after mug of tea and inviting in no company and welcoming no disturbance. Their sons grew up out of doors or in their own rooms, and lived their own lives. To this day Danny's parents lived that kind of life; though they were over seventy, they didn't mix with neighbors or friends, they held no family gatherings. Ria looked around with pride at her big, cheerful kitchen, where there was always life and company, and where she presided over everything at its heart.

Danny never noticed Nora Johnson's key rattling, nor was he irritated by the way she called from the gate. He seemed delighted to see his mother-in-law when he came into the kitchen and gave her a big hug. He wore a scarlet sports shirt that he had bought for himself when he was in London. It was the kind of thing that Ria would never have chosen for him in a million years, yet she had to admit it made him look impossibly young, like a handsome schoolboy. Perhaps she *was* the worst in the world at choosing clothes. She tugged uneasily at the floppy velvet top that Annie had mocked.

"Holly, I know why you're here, you came to help with the sanding," Danny said. "Not only do you give our daughter a small fortune for clothes but now you're coming to help us do the floors."

"I did not, Daniel. I came to leave poor Pliers with you for an hour. They're so intolerant down at St. Rita's, they won't allow a dog inside the door, and isn't it just what those old people there need, four-legged company! But those young pups of doctors say it's unhygienic, or that they'd fall over animals. Typical."

"But it's our gain to have Pliers here. Hallo, fellow." Could Danny really like the terrible hound about to open his mouth and drown everything with his wail? Pliers's teeth were stained and yellow, there were flecks of foam around his mouth. Danny looked at him with what definitely seemed like affection. But then so much of Danny's life depended on being polite to those who wanted to buy or sell property, it was hard to know when he was being genuinely enthusiastic or faking it. His was not a world where you said what you thought too positively.

Ria's mother had downed her coffee and was on her way. She had become very involved in the whole life of St. Rita's, the nearby retirement home. Hilary was convinced that their mother was actually ready to book herself in as a resident. Nora had taught Annie to play bridge and sometimes took her granddaughter along to St. Rita's to join in the game. Annie said it was marvelous fun, the old people were as noisy as anyone at school and had just the same kind of feuds and squabbles. Annie reported that everyone in the home held Grannie in high regard. Of course, compared to them, Grannie was very young.

Nora said it was only sensible to examine the options about aging. She dropped many hints that Ria should do the same; one day she too would be old and on her own, she would be sorry then that she hadn't given more time to the elderly. It wasn't as if she had any real work to go out to like other people; she had plenty of time on her hands.

"You must drive the old fellows mad down in St. Rita's, a young spring chicken like yourself in polka dots coming in to dazzle them," Danny said.

"Go on with your flattery, Danny." But Nora Johnson loved it.

"I mean it, Holly, you'd take the sight out of their eyes," Danny teased her. Pleased, his mother-in-law patted her hair and bustled out again, smart and trim in her lemon suit. "Your mother's wearing well," Danny said. "We'd be lucky to look as spry at her age."

"I'm sure we will. And aren't you like a boy rather than a man freewheeling down to forty," Ria laughed. But Danny didn't laugh back. That had been the wrong thing to say. He was thirty-seven going on thirty-eight. Foolish Ria, to have made a joke that annoyed him. She pretended not to have noticed her mistake. "And look at me, you said that when you met me first you took a good look at my mother before you let yourself fancy me—women always turn into their mothers, you said." Ria was babbling a lot but she wanted to take that strained look off his face.

"Did I say that?" He sounded surprised.

"Yes, you did. You must remember?"

"No."

Ria wished she hadn't begun this, he seemed confused and not at all flattered by her total recall. "I must ring Rosemary," she said suddenly.

"Why?"

The real reason was so that she didn't stand alone with him in the kitchen with a feeling of dread that she was boring him, irritating him. "To see is she coming round," Ria said brightly.

"She's always coming round," said Danny. "Like half the world." He seemed to say that in mock impatience but Ria knew he loved it all, the busy, warm laughing life of their kitchen on Tara Road, so different from the loveless house where he had grown up in the country, with the crows cawing to each other in the trees outside.

Danny was as happy here as she was: it was the life of their dreams. It was a pity they were so tired and rushed that they had not been making love as often as they used to, but this was just because there was so much happening at the moment. Things would be back to normal soon enough.

Rosemary wanted to know all about the shopping expedition when she arrived. "It's wonderful seeing them coming into their own," she said. "Knowing what they want, and defining their style." She didn't sit down, she prowled around the kitchen picking up bits of pottery and looking at the name underneath, fingering the strings of onions on the wall, reading the recipe taped to the fridge, examining everything and vaguely admiring it all.

She clutched her mug of black coffee with such gratitude you would think that nobody had ever handed her one before in her life. Naturally she waved away the shortbread, she had just stood up from a disgustingly huge breakfast she said, even though her slim hips and girlish figure showed anyone that this was unlikely to have been the truth. Rosemary wore smart, well-cut jeans and a white silk shirt, what she called weekend clothes. Her hair was freshly done, the salon's first client every Saturday morning, week in week out. Rosemary always sighed enviously over those people who could go any day of the week, lucky people like Ria who didn't go out to work.

Rosemary now owned the printing company. She had won a small-business award. If she were not her longest-standing best friend, Ria could have choked her. She seemed to be the actual proof that a woman could do everything and look terrific as well. But then, she and Rosemary went back a long way. She had been there the very day Ria had met Danny, for heaven's sake. She had listened to all the dramas over the years, as Ria had listened to hers. They had very few secrets.

In fact, Gertie was the only subject where they really differed.

"You're only encouraging her to think her lifestyle is normal by giving her tenners for that drunk."

"She's not going to leave him. You could put all kinds of work her way, I wish you would," Ria pleaded.

"No, Ria, can't you see you're making the situation worse. If Gertie thinks you go along with this business of her head being like a punching bag and her terrified children living up in her mother's house, then you're just making sure the whole scene goes on and on. Suppose you said one day, 'Enough is enough,' it would bring her to her senses, give her courage."

"No, it wouldn't, it would only make her feel she hadn't one friend left on earth."

Rosemary would sigh. They agreed on so much, the sheer impossibility of mothers, the problems with sisters, the wisdom of living on the lovely, tree-lined Tara Road. And Rosemary had always been incredibly supportive of Ria, about everything. Too many other women told Ria straight out that they would go mad if they didn't have a job to go to and money that they earned themselves. Rosemary never did that, any more than she would ask Ria like other working wives often did, "What do you *do* all day?" especially in front of Danny.

For the last five years, of course, Annie and Brian didn't need as much minding, but somehow the thought of a job outside the home had not really been a serious one. And anyway, realistically, what job could Ria have done? There was no real training or qualification to fall back on. Better by far to keep the show on the road here. Ria rarely felt defensive about being a stay-at-home wife, and she genuinely felt that it must be a good life if Rosemary, who had everything that it was possible to have in life, said she envied her.

"Well go on, Ria, tell me, what did she buy?" Rosemary really thought it had been fun and that Annie and she had agreed and bought something.

"I'm no good at knowing what to look for, where to point her," Ria said, biting her lip.

She thought she saw a small flash of impatience in Rosemary's face. "Of course you are. Haven't you all the time in the world to look around shops?"

Then the van containing the sander arrived and the men who delivered it were offered coffee, and nine-year-old Brian, looking as if he had been sent out as child labor digging in a builder's site instead of having just got out of bed, came in with his two even scruffier friends, scooping up cans of Coke and shortbread to take upstairs. And Gertie, with her big, anxious eyes and some rambling explanation about how she hadn't cleaned the copper saucepan yesterday, began to scrub at its base, which meant that she needed a loan of at least five pounds.

Pliers whined and there on cue was Ria's mother, back unexpectedly from St. Rita's. They hadn't told her that there was a funeral there that morning so she wasn't needed after all. And Colm Barry knocked on the window to show her that he was leaving her a large basket of vegetables. She waved him in to join the group and felt the customary surge of pride at being the center of such a happy home. She saw Danny standing at the kitchen door watching everything. He was so boyish and handsome, why had she made that silly remark about him approaching forty?

Still, he had gotten over it, it had passed. His face didn't look troubled now, he just stood there watching, almost as if he were an objective observer, as if he were an outsider, someone viewing it all for the first time. They all took turns at doing the floors, and it wasn't as easy as it looked. Not just a matter of standing behind a machine that knew its own mind, you had to steer it and point it and negotiate corners and heavy objects. Danny supervised it, full of enthusiasm. This was going to change the house, he said. Ria felt an unexpected shiver in her back. The house was wonderful, why did he want to change it?

Ria's mother wouldn't stay for lunch. "I don't care how many tons of vegetables you say that Colm left out for you, I know what troubles result from people moving in on top of other people. Sit down with your own family, Ria, and look after that husband of yours. It's a miracle that you've held on to him so long. I've always said that you were born lucky, to catch a man like Danny Lynch when all was said and done."

"Now, Holly, stop giving me a swollen head, I'm a very mixed blessing, let me tell you. Here, if you really won't stay, let me get you some of Colm's tomatoes to take with you. I can just see you serving delicate, thin tomato sandwiches and vodka martinis to gentlemen callers all afternoon."

Nora Johnson pealed with laughter. "Oh, chance would be a fine thing, but I will take some of those tomatoes to get them out of your way." Ria's mother could never take anything that was offered to her graciously, she would only accept something if there was an air of doing you a favor about it.

Rosemary was disappointed that there were no clothes to examine. She wondered had they caught sight of the gorgeous outfit in the corner window just where the two streets joined. No? Absolutely heavenly, no good for people of our age, Rosemary said, patting her own flat stomach, but great for someone like Annie who had a figure like an angel and wasn't getting droppy and droopy like the rest of us. Rosemary must have known that she wasn't getting droppy and droopy. She must have.

Brian and his friends Dekko and Myles had a problem. They had been going to watch a match on cable television up in Dekko's house but there was a new baby and so the television couldn't be put on.

"Can't you watch it here?" Ria had asked.

Brian looked at her, embarrassed. "No. Do you not understand anything? We can't watch it here."

"But of course you can. It's your home as much as Dad's and mine, you can take a tray into the sitting room."

Brian's face was purple trying to explain. "*We don't have it here, Ma,* we don't have cable like Dekko's family."

Ria remembered. There had been a long argument some months ago, she and Danny had said the children already watched too much television.

"Not that it's any good having it now," Dekko said glumly. "Not if we can't turn it on because of the awful baby."

"Come on, Dekko, a little brother can't be awful," Ria said.

"It is, Mrs. Lynch, it's disgusting and embarrassing. What on earth did they have to have one for after all these years? I'm ten, for heaven's sake." The boys shook their heads and began to debate the possibilities of getting an extension cord to add to the electric cord. If they moved it twelve feet outside the house and kept the sound down lowish, would that do? Dekko was doubtful. His mother had gone ballistic about this desperate baby.

This was not good news for Ria. She had been thinking long and hard about their having another child. The agency was now going from strength to strength. Danny had been made Agent of the Year. They were still so young, they had a big house, another baby was just what she had been hoping they might consider.

The copper saucepan was gleaming. Gertie showed it proudly to Ria. "You could look at your face in it, Ria, and it would be better than a mirror."

Ria wondered why anyone would want to lift a huge saucepan to look at a reflection but didn't say so. Neither did she say anything about the bruise down the side of Gertie's face, a dark mark that she was trying to hide with her hair. "My goodness, it's shining like gold. You are so good to come in on a Saturday, Gertie." The routine was that Ria would now offer the money and Gertie would refuse, but then take it. It was a matter of dignity, and that was the way they played it now.

But not today. "You know why I did."

"Well, I mean it's still very good of you." Ria reached for her handbag, surprised by the directness.

"Ria, we both know I'm desperate. Can I have ten pounds, please? I'll work it all off next week."

"Don't give it to him, Gertie."

Gertie held back her hair until Ria could see the long red scab of a cut. "Please, Ria."

"He'll only do it again. Leave him, it's the only thing."

"And go where, tell me that? Where could I go with two kids?"

"Change the locks, get a barring order."

"Ria, I'm on my knees to you, he's waiting on the road."

Ria gave her the ten pounds.

From the hall Ria could hear Annie speaking to her friend Kitty. "No, of course we didn't get anything, what do you think? Just standing there gasping, eyes rolling up to heaven, you're *not* going to wear this, you're *not* going to wear that . . . no, not actually saying it but written all over her face . . . It was gross I tell you. No I'm not going to get anything at all. I swear it's the easiest. It's not worth the hassle. I don't know what I'll tell Gran, though, she's so generous and *she* doesn't mind what I wear."

Ria looked for Danny. Just to be with him for a moment would make her feel better, it might mean a return to some of the strength and confidence that seemed to be seeping out of her. He was bent slightly over the sanding machine, his body juddering with it as it ground through to the good wood he wanted to expose. He was totally involved in it and yet there was something about him that seemed as if he were doing it for somebody else, as if he had been asked by one of his clients to improve a property.

Ria found her hand going to her throat and wondered was she getting flu. This was a marvelous Saturday morning on Tara Road. Why was everything upsetting her? Ria wondered what would happen if she were to write to a problem page? Or talk to a counselor? Would the advice be that she should go out and get a job? Yes, that would on the face of it be a very reasonable response. Outside people would think that a job took your mind off things, less time to brood, might make you feel a bit more independent, important. It would seem like nitpicking to explain that it wasn't the answer. Ria *had* a job. There was no sense in going out somewhere every morning just for the sake of it, to make some point. And Danny had often said that a working wife would play hell with his tax situation. And there were ways that the children needed a home presence even more than ever at this stage.

And her mother needed her to be there when she came in every day. And Gertie did, not just for the few pounds she earned from cleaning but for the solidarity. And who would do the charity work if Ria were to have a full-time job? It had nothing to do with smart fund-raising lunches like how some middle-class women spent their time. It was real work, serving in a shop, selling things, making money, turning up in a hospital minding the toddlers whose mothers were being told they had breast cancer. It was collecting old clothes, storing them in the garage, then getting them dry-cleaned at a cheap bulk rate, it was finding containers and making chutneys and sauces, it was standing outside the supermarket for four hours with a charity tin.

And the house itself needed her. Danny had said so often that she was a one-person line of defense, rooting out woodworm, fighting damp, dry rot. And suppose, just suppose that getting a job *was* the answer, what job would she do? The very mention of the Internet sent a chill through Ria. She would have to learn the basic keyboard and how to use office machines before she could even ask for a job as some kind of a receptionist.

Perhaps the empty, anxious feeling would go. Maybe the solution had nothing to do with looking for a job. The answer could be as old as time. In fact, Ria was sure that it was. She wanted another baby, a little head cradled at her breast, two trusting eyes looking up at her, Danny at her side. It wasn't a ridiculous notion, it was exactly what they needed. Despite the scorn and ridicule that would come from Brian and his friends, it was time to have another baby.

They were having dinner with Rosemary. Tonight it was not a party, there were just the three of them. Ria knew what would be served: a chilled soup, grilled fish, and salad. Fruit and cheese afterward, served by the big picture window that looked out onto the large, well-lit roof garden.

Rosemary's immaculate apartment, No. 32 Tara Road, was worth a small fortune now, Danny always said. With the success of Rosemary's company there was no shortage of money and even though she was not a serious cook like Ria, Rosemary could always put an elegant meal on the table without any apparent effort.

Ria would know, of course, how much had come directly from the delicacies shop, but nobody else would. When people praised the delicious brown bread, Rosemary would just smile. And it was always arranged so well. Grapes and figs tumbling around on some cool, modernistic tray, a huge, tall blue glass jug of ice water, white tulips in a black vase. Stylish beyond anyone's dreams. Modern jazz at a low volume and Rosemary dressed as if she were going out to a premiere.

Ria was constantly amazed at her energy and her high standards. She walked with Danny along Tara Road. Sometimes she wished he didn't speculate so much about what the retail value of each house was. But then that was his business. It was only natural. As they had said to each other so often, this road stood out alone in Dublin. Any other street was either up-market or down-market, this was the exception. There were houses on Tara Road that changed hands for fortunes. There were still dilapidated terraces, each house having seven tenants, where the dustbins and the bicycles spelled out shabby rented property. There were redbrick middle-class houses where civil servants and bank officials had lived for generations, there were more and more houses like their own, places that had been splendid once and were gradually coming back to the elegance they had previously known.

There was a row of shops down by the launderette on the corner where Gertie lived, the shops getting gradually smarter as the years went by. There was Colm Barry's chic restaurant on its own grounds. There were little places like her mother's, which defied description and definition.

Every time Ria came in the gate of No. 32, she marveled at how elegant the whole front looked. Her thought processes went in exactly the same well-traveled channels. She would love their house to have a big, expansive welcoming area like this, a place where more than one car could park, where everything seemed to sweep up toward the door, flowers getting taller and turning into bushes as they approached the granite steps. As if the house were some kind of temple. In their own house there was no air of permanency. It was as if the whole place could be dismantled in minutes. True, a few years back Danny had agreed to some small rockeries and a basic tarmacadam on the surface. But compared to No. 32, theirs was absolutely nothing.

Then Ria would ask herself again why she cared. She wasn't competitive, she reminded herself that she never envied other people with their kitchen appliances, their sofas, their curtains. Possibly because it signified some kind of permanency. Nobody would imagine that anyone in No. 32 would ever build flats or anything in their drive, but anything could happen in the Lynch establishment, the way it looked now. Danny had said several times that this just added to the charm, mystery, and value of their property. Ria had said the money value of your property was only important when you came to sell it, otherwise the value was surely only what made you feel good while you were there. They talked about this from time to time but it was one of the rare subjects where Ria had never been able to communicate how strongly she felt about it all. Wanting to make a more defined, permanent entrance to the house always seemed superficial, like nagging or envying what someone else had.

Ria liked to think that she was able to know what was really important and what wasn't. She would use all her powers of persuasion to suggest that he should be a father again. A garden was much lower on the list of priorities and she didn't want to hassle him about everything. He had been looking tired and pale lately. He worked too hard.

Ria looked around her as Rosemary went out to get them their drinks. This was a truly perfect setting for her friend. No sign whatsoever that the owner was a shrewd businesswoman. Rosemary kept all her files and work at the office. Tara Road was for relaxing. And it looked as pristine as the day she had moved in. The paintwork was not scuffed, the furniture had not known the wear and tear of the young. Ria noticed that there were art books and magazines arranged on a low table. They wouldn't remain there long in her house, they would be covered with someone's homework or jacket or tennis shoes or the evening newspaper. Always Ria felt that Rosemary's house didn't really feel like a home. More like something you would photograph for a magazine.

She was about to say that to Danny as they walked home along Tara Road, peering in at the other houses as they passed by and as always complimenting themselves at having been so clever as to buy in this area when they were young and desperate. But Danny spoke first. "I love going to that house," he said unexpectedly. "It's so calm and peaceful, there are no demands on you."

Ria looked at him walking with his jacket half over his shoulder in the warm spring evening, his hair falling into his eyes as always, no barber had ever been able to deal with it. Why did he like the feel of Rosemary's apartment? It wasn't Danny's taste at all. Much too spare. It was probably just because it was valuable. You couldn't spend all your working day dealing with property prices and not be affected by it. But deep down Danny wanted a house with warm colors, and full of people.

If they had been having Rosemary to dinner tonight it would have been seven or eight people all around the kitchen table. The children would have come in and out with their friends. Gertie might have come to help serve and eventually join them at the table. There would be music in the background, the telephone ringing, possibly Clement, Annie's inquisitive cat, would come in and examine the guest list, people would shout and interrupt each other. There would be large bottles of wine already open on each end of the table, a big fish chowder filled with mussels to start, large prawns, and thick, chunky bread. A roast as a main course and at least two desserts. Ria always made a wonderful treacle tart that no one could resist. That was the kind of evening they all enjoyed. Not something that could have been part of a tasteful French movie.

But it was a silly thing to argue about and it might seem as if she were trying to praise herself, so Ria, as she did so often, took the point of view she thought would please him. She tucked her arm into Danny's and said he was right. It had been nice to be able to sit and talk in such a relaxed way. Nothing about thinking that Rosemary was dressed and made-up as if she were going to a television interview rather than to welcome Danny and Ria, the people probably closest to her.

"We're lucky we have such good friends and neighbors," she said with a sigh of pleasure. That much she meant. As they turned into their own garden, they saw that the light was on in the sitting room.

"They're still up." Danny sounded pleased.

"I hope they are nothing of the sort, it's nearly one o'clock."

"Well, if it's not the children then we have burglars." Danny sounded not at all worried. Burglars would hardly be watching television and waiting for the occupants to return.

Ria was annoyed. She had hoped that tonight she and Danny could have a drink together in the kitchen and they might talk about another baby. She had her arguments ready in case there was resistance. They had been close tonight, physically anyway, even if she would never understand his pleasure in that cool, remote home of Rosemary's. Why did the children have to be up tonight of all nights?

It was Annie, of course, and her friend Kitty. There had been no mention of Kitty's coming around, no request that they could take Ria's bottles of nail polish to paint each other's toenails or borrow her fitness video, which was blaring from the machine. They looked up as if mildly annoyed to see the adults returning to their own home.

"Hi, Mr. Lynch," said Kitty, who rarely acknowledged other women but smiled broadly at any man she saw. Kitty looked like something in a documentary television program about the dangers of life in a big city.

She was waif-thin and had dark circles under her eyes. These were a result of late nights at the disco. Ria knew just how many because Annie had railed at the unfairness of not being able to get similar freedom.

Danny thought she was a funny little thing, a real character. "Hi, Kitty, hi, Annie, why look, you've painted each toenail a different color. How marvelous!"

The girls smiled at him, pleased. "Of course, there isn't a great range," Annie said apologetically. "No blues and black or anything. Just pink and reds." Kitty's frown of disapproval was terrible to see.

"Oh, I *am* sorry," Ria said sarcastically, but somehow it came out all sharp and bitter. She had meant it to be exasperated, funny, but it sounded wrong. The unfairness of this annoyed her. It was *her* makeup drawer they had ransacked without permission, and she was meant to be flattered but also inadequate at not having a Technicolor choice for them. The girls shrugged and looked at Danny for some kind of backup. "Brian in bed?" she asked crisply before Danny said anything that would make it all worse.

"No, he's taken the car, and he and Myles and Dekko have gone out to a few clubs," Annie said.

"Annie, really."

"Oh, Mam, what do you expect? You don't think Kitty or I know where Brian is, or care, do you?"

Kitty decided to rescue it. "Now, please don't worry about a thing, Mrs. Lynch, he went to bed at nine o'clock. He's all tucked up and asleep. Really he is." She managed to cast Ria in the role of a fussing geriatric mother who wasn't all there in the head.

"Of course that's where he is, Ria." Danny had joined in patting her down.

"Was it a nice night?" Annie asked her father. Not because she wanted to know but because she wanted to punish her mother.

"Lovely. No fussing, no rushing around."

"Um." Even in her present mood of doing anything to annoy her mother, Annie couldn't appear to see much to enthuse about there.

Ria decided not to notice the angry resentment that Annie felt about everything these days. Like so many things she let it pass. "Well, I suppose you'll both want to go to bed now. Is Kitty staying the night?"

"It's Saturday, Mam. You *do* realize there's no school tomorrow."

"We still have some sit-ups to do." Kitty's voice was whining, whee-dling, as if she feared that Mrs. Lynch might strike her a blow.

"You girls don't need sit-ups." Danny's smile was flattering but yet couldn't be accepted. He was after all a doting and elderly father.

"Oh, Dad, but we do."

"Come here, let's see what she tells us to do."

Ria stood with a small hard smile and watched her husband doing a ridiculous exercise to flatten his already flat stomach with two teenage girls. They all laughed at each other's attempts as they fell over. She would not join them, nor would she leave them. It was probably only ten minutes yet it felt like two hours. And then there was no warm chat in the kitchen, and no chance of loving when they went upstairs. Danny said he needed a shower. He was so unfit, so out of training these days, a few minutes of mild exercise nearly knocked him out. "I'm turning into a real middle-aged tub of lard," he said.

"No, you're not, you're beautiful," she said to him truthfully, as he took off his clothes and she yearned for him to come straight to bed. But instead he went to shower and came back in pajamas; there would be no loving tonight. Just before she went to sleep Ria remembered how long it had been since there had been any loving. But she wasn't going to start worrying about that now on top of everything else. It's just that they were busy. Everyone said that's what happened to people for a while, and then it sorted itself out.

On Sunday, Danny was gone all day. There were clients looking at the new apartments. They were aiming for a young professional kind of market, Danny had said. The developers had asked why bother having a health club and coffee bar attached unless the young singles could meet similarly minded people there. He had to go and supervise the whole sales approach. No, he wouldn't be back for lunch.

Brian was going to Dekko's house; there was a christening. Dekko wasn't going to go at all but there would be his grandmother and people from his mum and dad's work there, and apparently it was essential that he be there. For some reason. Anyway it had been agreed that if Myles and Brian and he wore clean shirts and passed round the sandwiches, they would get five pounds each.

"It's a lot of money," Dekko said solemnly. "They must be mad investing fifteen pounds in us all being there."

"I would have thought normal people would have paid us fifteen pounds for us all *not* to be there," Brian said.

"Nobody's normal in a house where there's a baby," Dekko had said sagely, and they all sighed.

Annie said that she and Kitty were going to the career forum at school and that of course they had told everyone this ages ago, over and over. It was just that nobody ever listened.

"You didn't go to any of the other career forums," her mother protested.

"But those were only about the bank, and insurance and law and awful things." Annie was amazed that it wasn't clear.

"And what is it this week that you have to go?"

"Well it's real careers, like the music industry and modeling and things."

"What about your lunch, Annie? I defrosted a whole leg of lamb and now it seems there'll be no one here."

"Only you, Mam, would think that an old leg of lamb was important compared to someone's whole future." She banged out of the room in a temper.

Ria rang her mother.

"No, don't be ridiculous, Ria, why would I drop everything and come to eat huge quantities of red meat with you? Why did you defrost it anyway until you knew whether your family was going to be there to eat it? That's you all over, you never think about anything."

Ria rang Gertie. Jack answered. "What?"

"Oh . . . um . . . Jack, it's Ria Lynch."

"What do you want? As if I didn't know."

"Well, I wanted to talk to Gertie."

"Yeah, with a load of feminist advice, I suppose."

"No, I was going to invite her to lunch, as it happens."

"Well, we can't go."

"*She* might be able to go."

"She's not able to go, Mrs. Burn-your-bra."

"Perhaps she and I could talk about that, Jack."

"Perhaps you'd like to go and take a—" There was the sound of a scuffle.

"Ria, it's Gertie . . . sorry, I can't go."

"You can't go to what?"

"To whatever it is you're asking me to . . . thanks but I can't."

"It was only lunch, Gertie, just a bloody leg of lamb."

There was a sob at the other end. Then, "If that's all it bloody was, Ria, why on earth did you ring me and cause all this trouble?"

"This is Martin and Hilary's answering machine, please leave a message after the beep."

"It's nothing, Hilary, it's only Ria. If you're not there on a Sunday at ten o'clock in the morning then it's not likely you'll be there at lunchtime . . . heigh-ho, no message."

Ria rang Colm Barry at the restaurant. He was always there on a Sunday, he had told her that he took advantage of the peace and quiet to do his accounts and paperwork.

"Hallo." Colm's sister, Caroline, always spoke so softly you had to strain to hear what she said. She said that Colm wasn't there, he had gone out to do something, well, he wasn't there. Caroline sounded so unsure Ria began to wonder whether Colm was actually standing beside her mouthing that he wouldn't take the call.

"It doesn't matter, I was just going to ask him if he'd like to come to lunch, that's all."

"Lunch? Today?" Caroline managed to make both words contain an amazing amount of incredulity.

"Well, yes."

"With your family?"

"Here, yes."

"And had you asked him? Did he forget?"

"No, it was a spur of the moment thing, you too, of course, if you were free."

Caroline seemed totally incapable of taking in such a concept. "Lunch? Today?"

She said the words again and Ria wanted to smack her very hard. "Forget it, Caroline, it was just a passing idea."

"I'm sure Colm will be very sorry to have missed the invitation. He loves going to your house, it's just that he's . . . well, he is . . . well, he's out."

"Yes I know, doing something, you said." Ria felt her voice had sounded unduly impatient. "And you're not free, Caroline, yourself? You and Monto?" She hoped fervently that they were not free. And she was in luck.

"No, I'm very sorry, truly I am, Ria, I can't tell you how sorry I am but it's just not possible today. Any other day would have been."

"That's fine, Caroline. It was short notice, as I said." Ria hung up.

The phone rang and Ria answered it hopefully.

"Ria? Barney McCarthy."

"Oh, he's already gone to meet you there, Barney."

"He has?"

"Yes, up at the new development, the posh flats."

"Oh, of course, yes."

"Are you not there?"

"No, I was delayed. If he calls back tell him that. I'll catch him up along the way."

"Sure."

"And you're fine, Ria?"

"Fine," she lied.

Would she cook the lamb anyway, and have it cold with salad when they all came home? Gertie said you could refreeze things if they hadn't thawed completely. But what did Gertie know? Colm would know but he was out somewhere doing something according to that dithering sister of his. Rosemary would know but Ria hated having to ask her. Was she in fact becoming very boring, as Annie had said? Was she as thoughtless as her mother had suggested? Ria knew now why people who lived on their own found Sunday a long, lonely day. It would be different when they had a new baby . . . there wouldn't be enough hours in the day.

Brian had been sick at the christening. He said it was bad enough to let him off school. He was pretty sure that Myles and Dekko would have kinder, more understanding families who wouldn't force invalids to go out when they were feeling rotten. Annie said that it was just a punishment since they had all been drinking champagne and obviously they were sick. Brian, red-faced with annoyance, said that she had no proof of this at all. That she was only trying to make trouble to take attention away from the fact that she and Kitty had been out so late and caused such alarm.

"I was talking about my career, about the future, jobs and things, something a drunk like you will never have," Annie said coldly to Brian.

Ria tried to keep the peace, looking in vain for any support from Danny, who had his head stuck in brochures and press releases about the new apartment blocks. He had been tired when he came back last night. Too tired to respond when she reached out for him. It had been a long day, he said. For Ria too it had been a long day, a long, lonely day pushing a heavy sanding machine around the floor, but she hadn't complained. Now they were back in familiar territory, a big noisy breakfast, a real family starting the week together in the big, bright kitchen.

And everything had simmered down by the time they were ready to leave. Brian said he thought he *could* face school, possibly the fresh air would do him good and there was no proof that any court of law would accept that any alcohol had been taken. Annie said that possibly yes she *should* have telephoned to say that it was all going on longer, but she hadn't thought that anyone would be waiting. Honestly.

Danny dragged himself out of the world of executive apartments. "You couldn't *give* away anything with carpet wall-to-wall nowadays," he said. "Everything has to have sprung oak floors or they won't consider it. Where did all the money come from in this society? Tell me that and I'll die happy."

"Not for decades yet, I have great plans for you first," Ria laughed.

"Yes, well none for tonight, I hope," he said. "There's a dinner, investors, I have to be there."

"Oh, not again!"

"Oh, yes again. And many times again before we're through with this. If the real estate agents don't go to the promotions then what confidence will they think we have in it all."

She made a face. "I know, I know. And after all it won't be for long."

"What do you mean?"

"Well, eventually they'll all be sold, won't they? Isn't that what it's about?"

"This phase . . . but this is only phase one, remember we were talking about it on Saturday with Barney?"

"Did Barney get you yesterday?"

"No, why?"

"He got delayed, I told him he'd find you at the development."

"I was with people all day. I expect someone took a message. I'll get it when I get into the office and ring him then."

"You work too hard, Danny."

"So do you." His smile was sympathetic. "Look, I brought home that sander and you had to do most of it as it turned out."

"Still, if you think it looks nice?" Ria was doubtful.

"Sweetheart, no question. It adds thousands to the resale value already and that's only in one weekend. Wait till we get those children of ours working properly, nice bit of slave labor, and do the upstairs as well. This place will be worth a fortune."

"But we don't want to sell it," Ria said, alarmed.

"I know, I know. But one day when we're old and gray and we want a nice apartment by the sea or on the planet Mars, or something . . ." He ruffled her hair and left.

Ria smiled to herself. Things were normal again.

"Ree-ya?"

"Hallo, Mam. Where's Pliers?"

"I see. You have no interest in seeing your own mother anymore, only the dog."

"No, I just thought he'd be with you, that's all."

"Well, he's not. Your friend Gertie's taken him for a walk, that's where he is. Gone for a nice morning run down by the canal."

"Gertie?"

"Yes, she said that she heard dogs like Pliers needed a run now and then to shake them up. And, of course, though I have been able to keep myself reasonably trim, I'm not really able to do anything like that for Pliers anymore, so Gertie offered." Ria was astounded. Gertie didn't run, she barely walked these days living in such dread of her drunken husband. Ria's mother had lost interest in the conversation. "Anyway, I only came in because I was passing to tell Annie that it's seven o'clock tonight."

"What is?"

"They're coming down to St. Rita's with me this evening, Annie and her friend Kitty. We're teaching bridge."

Ria's mind was churning. Annie going to the old people's home. Bridge? "But that will be during supper."

"I suppose they manage to think that some things are more important because they're nice and normal and they actually like people," said Ria's mother. She sat at her daughter's table waiting for coffee to be served to her, her face thunderous with the heavy implication that Ria was neither nice nor normal and positively hated meeting people.

The washing machine had just begun to swirl and hum when Rosemary rang. "Oh Lord, Ria, how I envy you, relaxed in your own home while I'm stuck at work."

"That's the way things are." Ria knew there was an edge to her voice. She was becoming sharp with people for no reason. She rushed on to take the harm out of her words. "We all think the grass is greener in the other place. Often when I'm picking up things from the floor here I envy you being at work and out of the house all day."

"No, of course you don't."

"Why do you say that?"

"Because, as I keep telling you, if you *did* feel like that, cabin fever and everything, then you'd *get* a job. Listen, what I rang to say is that I saw Jack being taken off in a police car this morning, some disturbance outside a pub. I thought you'd want to know. If you have nothing to do you might check whether Gertie's in bits or anything."

"Gertie's not in bits, she's out walking my mother's dog."

"You're not serious. Aren't people amazing?" Rosemary sounded pleased at this surprise news. "She didn't ask for a dog-walking fee, did she?"

"No, I don't think so, my mother would have said."

"Oh, well, that's all right then. It's not as if she's doing it to get a couple of quid to buy him more drink when the fuzz lets him go."

"Mrs. Lynch?"

"Yes, that's right." All day odd things had been happening.

"Mrs. Danny Lynch?"

"Yes?"

"Oh, oh, I'm sorry. No, I think I may have the wrong number."

"No, that's who I am, Ria Lynch." The phone went dead.

Hilary rang just then. "You sounded like the Mother of Sorrows on the answering machine," she said.

"No, I didn't. I just spoke and said it didn't matter. We both say that people who don't leave messages should be hanged."

"I keep saying that the answering machine was a sheer waste of money. Who ever calls? What messages are there that you'd want to hear?"

"Thanks, Hilary."

Hilary was unaware of any sarcasm. "What was it you wanted to talk about anyway? Mam, I suppose?"

"No, not at all."

"She's really going loopy you know, Ria. You don't see that because you don't want to. You always want to believe that everything's fine in the world, there's no famine, no war, politicians are all honest and mean well, and the climate's great."

"Hilary, did you ring up just to attack me in general or is there anything specific?"

"Very funny. But going back to Mam, I worry about her."

"But why? We've been over this a dozen times, she's fit and healthy, she's busy and happy."

"Well, she should feel needed by her own family."

"Hilary, she is needed by her family. Isn't she in here every single day of her life, sometimes twice a day? I ask her to stay to meals, I ask her to stay the night. She is out with Annie and Brian more than I am. . . ."

"I suppose you're saying now that I don't do enough."

"I'm not saying anything of the sort, and she's never done talking about you and Martin and how good you are to her."

"Well, that's as may be."

"So what is it really that's worrying you?"

"She's trying to sell her house."

There was a silence. "Of course she's not, Hilary, she'd have talked to Danny about it."

"Only if she were selling it through him."

"Well, who else would she go to? No, Hilary, you've got this all wrong."

"We'll see," said Hilary, and hung up.

———

"Sweetheart?"

"Yes, Danny?"

"Was anyone looking for me at home, any peculiar sort of person?"

"No. Nobody at all, why?"

"Oh there's some crazy woman ringing up about the apartments, she says she's being refused as a client . . . total paranoia. She's ringing everyone at home as well."

"A woman did ring, but she didn't leave any message. That might have been her. . . ."

"What did she say?"

"Nothing, just kept checking who I was."

"And who did you say you were?"

Suddenly Ria snapped. It had been a stressful weekend, filled with silly unrelated things that just didn't make sense. "I told her that I was an ax murderer passing through. God, Danny, who do you think I told her I was? She asked was I Mrs. Lynch and I said I was. Then she said she had the wrong number and hung up."

"I'm telling the police about it, it's nuisance calls."

"And did you say that in the office . . . you know who she is?"

"Listen, honey, I'll be late tonight, you know I told you."

"A dinner, yes I know."

"I have to run, sweetheart."

He called everyone sweetheart. There was nothing particularly special about it. It was ludicrous but she would have to make an appointment with her husband to discuss having a baby, and a further appointment to do something about it if he agreed that it *was* a good idea.

Ria had a mug of soup and a slice of toast for her supper at seven o'clock. She sat alone in her enormous kitchen. The blustery April wind blew the washing on the line, but she left it there. Brian had gone to Dekko's house to do his homework. Annie was going to have a pizza with her gran after bridge at St. Rita's, hugely preferable to spending any time at all with her mother, obviously. Even sharing space with an unwelcome baby seemed like a better bet for Brian than his own house. Colm Barry had waved to her from the vegetable garden before he left for his restaurant. Her friend Rosemary was at home cooking something minimalist. Her other friend Gertie had been avoiding a drunken husband by walking that ridiculous dog all day, or so Ria's mother said. How had it happened . . . the empty nest? Why was there nobody at home anymore?

They all came back together when she least expected it. Annie and her grandmother, laughing as if they were the same age. There was over half a century between them and yet they were relaxed and easy together. The ladies had been great fun, Annie said. They were going to lend her some genuine fifties clothes, even one of those fun fake furs. Some of them had come with them to the pizza house.

"They're allowed out?" Ria said in surprise.

"It's not a prison, Ria, it's a retirement home. And people are very lucky who can get in there."

"But you're too young to go to a place like that, much too young," Ria said.

"I was speaking generally." Her mother looked lofty.

"So you're not planning to go in there yourself?"

Her mother looked astounded. "Are you interrogating me?" she asked.

"Oh, Mam, for heaven's sake, don't always cause a row about everything," Annie groaned.

Brian came in. He seemed pleased but not surprised to see his grandmother. "I saw Pliers tied to the gate, I knew you were here."

"Pliers? Tied to the gate?" Ria's mother was out of the house like a shot. "Poor dog, darling Pliers. Did she abandon you?"

They heard the sound of a car. Danny was home. Early, unexpected.

"Dad, Dad, do you know where we'd find the colors of the flags of Italy and Hungary and India? Dekko's father doesn't know. It would be great if you knew, Dad."

"That friend of yours is even more scattered than you are, Ria." Nora Johnson was still smarting over the dog. "Imagine Gertie left poor Pliers tied to the gate. He could have been there for hours."

"He wasn't there when we came in a few minutes ago, Gran," Annie reassured her.

"No, I saw Gertie running up Tara Road. It could only be a couple of minutes at the most." Danny was reassuring too. "Hey, where's supper anyway?"

"No one came home." Ria's voice sounded small and tired. "You said you had a business dinner."

"I canceled it." He was eager, like a child.

Ria had an idea. "Why don't we go to Colm's restaurant, the two of us?"

"Oh, well I don't know, anything will do. . . ."

"No, I'd love to, I'd simply love to. It would be a treat for me."

"It would be a treat for *anyone* to go to Colm's," Annie sniffed. "Better than a pizza."

"Better than sausages in Dekko's," Brian grumbled.

"Wish I'd been able to go out to four-star restaurants when I didn't feel like cooking," said her mother.

"I'll phone him and book a table." Ria was on her feet.

"Honestly, sweetheart, anything . . . a steak, an omelette . . ."

"It wouldn't do you at all. No, *you* deserve a treat too."

"I eat out too much, being at home's a treat for me," he begged.

But she had the phone to her ear and made the booking. Then she ran lightly upstairs and changed into her black dress and put on her gold chain. Ria would have loved the time to have a bath and dress properly but she knew she must seize the moment. This was the very best chance she would have to talk to her husband about future plans. Ria moved very swiftly before she could be sabotaged by either her mother or daughter putting sausages and tinned beans in front of Danny.

They walked companionably down Tara Road to the corner. The lights of Colm's restaurant were welcoming. Ria admired the way that it was done. You couldn't really see who was inside but you got the impression of people sitting down together. She was glad that Colm seemed to have tables full on a Monday night. It would be so dispiriting to cook for people and have shining glassware and silver out there and then for nobody to turn up. That was one of the reasons she would never like to run a restaurant, you would feel so hurt if people didn't come to it.

"Very few cars outside," said Danny, cutting across her thoughts. "I wonder how he makes any kind of living."

"He loves cooking," Ria said.

"Well, just as well that he does because there can't be much profit in tonight's takings from the look of the place." She hated when Danny reduced everything to money. It seemed to be his only way of measuring things nowadays.

Caroline took their coats. She was dressed in a smart black dress with long sleeves and she wore a black turban covering her hair. Only someone with beautiful bone structure could get away with something as severe, Ria thought to herself. "You look so elegant tonight, the turban's a new touch." Was she imagining it or did Caroline's hand fly to her face defensively?

"Yes, well, I thought that perhaps . . ." She didn't finish her sentence.

She had been so odd on the telephone yesterday, Ria had wondered if there was anything seriously wrong. And even tonight, despite the serene way she smiled and seemed to glide across the floor to show them to their table, there was something tense and pent-up there. They were a strange pair, the brother and sister, Caroline with her handsome husband, Monto Mackey, always in a smart suit and an even smarter car, Colm with his discreet relationship. He was nowadays involved with the wife of a well-known businessman, but it was something that was never spoken of. Colm and Caroline seemed to look out for each other, as if the world was somehow preparing to do one of them down.

Ria would have liked that kind of loyalty. Hilary was a complicated sister; she blew hot and cold, sometimes envious and carping, sometimes surprisingly understanding. But there was never this united front that Colm and Caroline wore.

"You're miles away," Danny said to her.

She glanced over at him, handsome, tired-looking, boyish still, puzzling over the menu. Wondering if he would go for the crispy duck or be sensible about his health and have the grilled sole. She could read the decisions all over his face. "I was just thinking about my sister, Hilary," she said.

"What has she done now?"

"Nothing, except get the wrong end of the stick about everything as usual. Burbling on about you and about Mam wanting to sell the house."

"She told you that?"

"You know Hilary, she never listens to anyone."

"She said I wanted to sell the house?"

"She said Mam wasn't even asking you, that she wanted to sell it herself."

"I don't understand."

"Would anyone? The whole thing is nonsense."

"Your *mother's* house! I see."

"Well, you see more than I do, it's totally cracked."

Colm came to the table to greet them. He made a point of spending only forty seconds and putting a huge amount of warmth and information into that time. "There's some very nice Wicklow lamb, and I got fish straight off the boat down at the harbor this morning. The vegetables as you know come from the finest garden in the land, and if you're not sick of eating them yourselves, I suggest zucchini. Can I give you a glass of champagne to welcome you? And then I'll get out of your way and let you enjoy your evening."

Colm had once told Ria that too many restaurant owners made the great mistake of believing that the guests enjoyed the Mine Host figure spending a lot of time at the table. He always felt that if people had come out to dine then that's what they should be allowed to do. Tonight she valued it especially.

She chose the lamb and Danny said that because he really was as fat as a fool these days he must have plain grilled fish with lemon juice and no creamy sauce. "You're not fat, Danny, you're beautiful. You know you are, I told you the other night."

He looked embarrassed. "A man can't be beautiful, sweetheart," he said awkwardly.

"Yes, indeed he can, and you are." She reached out and touched his hand. Danny looked around. "It's all right, we're allowed to hold hands, we're married. Now that couple over there, they're the ones who shouldn't be caught." She laughed over at a couple where the older man was being very playful with his much younger companion.

"Ria?" Danny said.

"Listen let me speak first. I'm delighted your dinner was canceled tonight, delighted. I wanted you on your own without half the country being in our kitchen and all joining in."

"But that's what you like," he said.

"Yes, it's what I like a lot of the time but not tonight. I wanted to talk to you. We don't have time to talk these days, no time to do anything, not even make love."

"Ria!"

"I know. I'm not blaming either of us, it just happens, but what I wanted to tell you was this . . . and I needed time and space to tell you . . . what I wanted to say was . . ." She stopped suddenly, unsure how to go on. Danny was looking at her, confused. "You know how I said you look young? I mean it. You *are* young, you *are* like a boy, you could pass for someone in his twenties. You're just like you looked when Annie was a baby, with your hair falling into your eyes, unable to believe that you could be a father. You have that look in your eyes."

"What are you saying? What in God's name are you saying?"

"I'm saying that honestly, Danny, I can see these things. It's time for another baby. Another start of a life. You're more sure and comfortable now, you want to see another son or daughter grow up." A waiter approached them with plates of fig and parma ham, but something about the way they sat facing each other made him veer away. These were cold starters, they could wait a little. "It's *time* for you to have another child, to be a father again. I'm not thinking of myself only but of you, that's all I'm saying," Ria said, smiling at the strange shocked look on Danny's face.

"Why are you saying it like this?" His voice was barely above a whisper. His face was snow-white. Surely he couldn't find it such a staggering idea. On and off she had been saying this over the years. Only this time she had phrased it in terms of fatherhood rather than her own need or joint life with a new baby.

"Danny, let me explain. . . ."

"I don't believe you're saying this. Why? Why this way?"

"But I'm just saying that it's the right time. That's all. I'm thinking of you and your future, your life."

"But you're so calm . . . this isn't happening." He shook his head as if to clear it.

"Well, of course, I want it too, you know that, but I swear I'm thinking of you. A baby is what you need just now. It will put things into perspective, you won't be rushing and fussing about developments and market share and everything, not with a new baby."

"How long have you known?" he asked.

It was an odd question. "Well, I suppose I've always known that with the other two grown-up almost, the day would come."

"They'll always be special, nothing would change that." His voice was choked.

"Well don't I *know* that, for heaven's sake, this would be different, not better." Ria sat back from her position hunched up and leaning over the table. The waiter seized the opportunity and slid in their plates without any comment. Ria picked up her fork but Danny didn't move.

"I can't understand why you're so calm, so bloody calm," he said. His voice trembled, he could hardly speak.

Ria looked at her husband in astonishment. "I'm not very calm, Danny, my darling, I'm telling you I think it's time we had another baby and you seem to agree . . . so I'm very excited."

"You're telling me *what*?"

"Danny, keep your voice down. We don't want the whole restaurant to know." She was a little alarmed by his face.

"Oh, my God," he said. "Oh God, I don't believe it."

"What is it?" Now her alarm was very real. He had his head in his hands. "Danny what is it? Please? Stop making that sound, please."

"You said you understood. You said you'd been thinking about my future and my life. And now you say that *you* want another baby! That *you* do, that's what you were talking about." He looked anguished.

Ria was going to say that the way it normally happened was that the woman had the baby but something stopped her. In a voice that came from very far away she heard herself ask the question that she knew was going to change her life. "What exactly were *you* talking about, Danny?"

"I thought you had found out and for a mad moment I thought you were going along with it."

"What?" Her voice was impossibly steady.

"You know, Ria, you must know that I'm seeing someone, and well, we've just discovered she's pregnant. I am going to be a father again. She's going to have a baby and we are very happy about it. I was going to tell you next weekend. I thought suddenly that you must have known."

The noise in the restaurant changed. People's cutlery started to clatter more and bang loudly off people's plates. Glasses tinkled and seemed about to smash. Voices came and went in a roar. The sound of laughter from the tables was very raucous. She could hear his voice from far away. "Ria. Listen to me, Ree-ah." She couldn't have said anything. "I wouldn't have had this happen for the world, it wasn't part of any plan. I wanted us to be . . . I didn't go looking for something like this. . . ."

He looked boyish all right, helplessly boyish. This was too much to cope with. It wasn't fair that she should have to cope with something like this. "Tell me it's not true," she said.

"You know it's true, Ria, sweetheart. You know we haven't been getting on, you know there's nothing there anymore."

"I don't believe it. I *won't* believe it."

"I didn't think it would happen either, I thought we'd grow old together, like people did."

"And indeed like people do," she said.

"Yes, some do. But we're different people, we're not the same people who married all those years ago. We have different needs."

"How old is she?"

"Ria, this has nothing to do with . . ."

"How old?"

"Twenty-two, not that it matters . . . or has anything to do with anything."

"Of course not," she said dully.

"I was going to tell you, maybe it's better that it's out now." There was a silence. "We have to talk about it, Ria." Still she said nothing. "Aren't you going to say anything, anything at all?" he begged.

"Eight years older than your daughter."

"Sweetheart, can I tell you, this has nothing to do with age."

"No?"

"I don't want to hurt you." Silence. "Any more than I already have hurt you and honestly I was wondering, could we be the only two people in the whole world who'd do it right? Could we manage to be the couple who actually *don't* tear each other to pieces . . . ?"

"What?"

"We love Annie and we love Brian. This is going to be hell for them. We won't make it a worse hell, tell me we won't."

"Pardon?"

"What?"

"I said, I beg your pardon. What am I to tell you? I didn't understand."

"Sweetheart."

Ria stood up. She was trembling and had to hold the table to keep upright. She spoke in a very low, carrying voice. "If you ever . . . if *ever* in your life you call me sweetheart again I will take a fork in my hand, just like this one, and I will stick it into your eye." She walked unsteadily toward the door of the restaurant while Danny stood helplessly at the table watching her go. But her legs felt weak, and she began to sway. She wasn't going to make the door after all. Colm Barry put down two plates hastily and moved toward her. He caught her just as she fell, and moving swiftly he pulled her into the kitchen.

Danny had followed them in and watched, standing uncertainly as Ria's face and wrists were sponged with cold water by Caroline.

"Are you part of the problem, Danny? Is this about you?" Colm asked.

"Yes, in a way."

"Then perhaps you should leave." Colm was perfectly courteous but firm.

"What do you mean . . . ?"

"I'll take her home. When she's ready and if she wants to go, that is."

"Where else would she go?"

"Please, Danny." Colm's voice was firm. This was his kitchen, his territory.

Danny left. He let himself into the house with his front door key. In the kitchen Danny's mother-in-law, her dog, and the two children were watching television. He paused in the hall for a minute, considering what explanation to make. But this was Ria's choice, not his, how to tell and what to tell. Quietly he moved up the stairs. He stood in the bedroom, uncertain again. After all, she might not want him here when she returned. But suppose he went elsewhere? Might not this be another blow? He wrote a letter and left it on her pillow.

Ria, I am ready to talk whenever you are. I didn't think you'd want me here so I've taken a duvet to the study. Wake me anytime. Believe me I'm more sorry about all this than you'll ever know. You will always be very, very dear to me and I want the best for you.

Danny

He reached for the phone and made the first of two calls.

"Hallo, Caroline, it's Danny Lynch. Can I speak to Colm?"

"I'll see."

"Well, can you ask him to tell her that I've said nothing to the children and I'm in the study at home. Not the bedroom, the study, if she wants to talk to me. Thank you, Caroline."

Then he dialed another number. "Hallo, sweetheart, it's me . . . Yes, I told her . . . Not great . . . Yes, of course about the baby . . . I don't know . . . No, she's not here . . . No, I can't come over, I have to wait for her to get back . . . Sweetheart, if you think I'm going to change my mind now . . . I love you too, honey."

In the kitchen of Colm's restaurant the business of preparing and serving food went on around them. Colm gave Ria a small brandy. She sipped it slowly, her face blank. He asked her nothing about what happened.

"I should go," she said from time to time.

"No hurry," Colm said.

Eventually she said it with more determination. "The children will worry," she said.

"I'll get your coat."

They walked from the restaurant in silence. At the gate of the house she stopped and looked at him. "It's as if it's happening to other people," Ria said. "Not to me at all."

"I know."

"Do you, Colm?"

"Yes, it's to cushion the shock or something. We think first that it's all happening to someone else."

"And then?"

"I suppose then we realize it's not," he said.

"That's what I thought," Ria said.

They could have been talking about the vegetables or when to spray the fruit trees. There was no hug of solidarity or even a word of goodbye. Colm went back to his restaurant, and Ria went into her home.

She sat down in her kitchen. The table had crumbs and some apple cores in a dish. A carton of milk had been left out of the fridge. There were newspapers and magazines on the chairs. Ria saw everything very clearly, but not from where she was sitting. It was if she were way up in the sky and looking down. She saw herself, a tiny figure sitting down there in this untidy kitchen in the dark house where everyone else slept. She watched as the old clock chimed hour after hour. She didn't think about what to do now. It was as if it hadn't sunk in that it was happening to her.

"Mam, it's the drill display today," Annie said.

"Is it?"

"Where's breakfast, Mam?"

"I don't know."

"Oh, Mam, not today. I need a white shirt, there isn't one ironed."

"No?"

"Where were you, were you at the shops?"

"Why?"

"You're in your coat. I could iron it myself, I suppose."

"Yes."

"Has Dad gone yet?"

"I don't know, is his car there?"

"Hey, Mam, why isn't there any breakfast?" Brian wanted to know.

Annie turned on him. "Don't be such a pig, Brian. Are you too drunk to get your own breakfast for once?"

"I'm not drunk."

"You were yesterday, you stank of drink." They looked at Ria, waiting for her to stop the fight. She said nothing. "Put on the kettle, Brian, you big useless lump," Annie said.

"You're just sucking up to Mam because you want her to do something, make you sandwiches, drive you somewhere, iron something. You're never nice to Mam."

"I am nice to her. Aren't I nice to you, Mam?"

"What?" Ria asked.

"Aw here, where's the iron?" Annie said in desperation.

"Why have you got your coat on, Mam?" Brian asked.

"Get the corn flakes and shut up, Brian," Annie said. Ria didn't have any tea or coffee. "She had some before she went out," Annie explained.

"Where did she go?" Brian, struggling with cutting the bread, seemed puzzled.

"She doesn't have to account to you for her movements," Annie said. Her voice sounded very far away.

"Bye, Mam."

"What?"

"I said, good-bye, Mam." Brian looked at Annie for reassurance.

"Oh, good-bye, love, bye, Annie."

They went round to get their bicycles. Usually they did everything to avoid leaving the house together but today was different.

"What is it do you think?" Brian asked.

Annie was nonchalant. "They could be drunk, they went out to Colm's restaurant, maybe the pair of them got pissed. Dad's not up yet, you'll note."

"That's probably it, all right," said Brian sagely.

Danny came in to the kitchen. "I waited until the children left," he said.

"What?"

"I didn't know what you'd want to say to them. You know? I thought it was better to talk to you first." He looked anxious and uneasy. Danny's hair was tousled and his face pale and unshaven. He had slept in his clothes. She still felt the strange sense of not being here, of watching it all happen. That feeling hadn't gone during the long, wakeful hours of night. She said nothing but looked at him expectantly.

"Ria, are you all right? Why have you your coat on?"

"I don't think I took it off," she said, rising from her chair.

"What? Not even to go to bed?"

"I didn't go to bed. Did you?"

"Sit down, sweetheart. . . ."

"What?"

"I know, I'm sorry, it doesn't mean anything. It's just something I call you. I meant sit down, Ria."

Suddenly her head began to clear. They were no longer little matchstick figures way down below, people she was watching from far away. She was here in this messy kitchen wearing her coat over her good black party dress. Danny, her husband, the only man she had ever loved, had gotten some twenty-two-year-old pregnant and was going to leave home and set up a new family. He was actually trying to tell her to sit down in her own house. A very great coldness came over her. "Go now, Danny, please. Leave the house and go to work."

"You can't order me out, Ria, and take this attitude . . . we have to talk. We have to plan what to do, what to say."

"I will take whatever attitude I like to take, and I would like you not to be here anymore until I am ready to talk to you." Her voice sounded very normal from inside. Possibly to him too.

He nodded, relieved. "When will that be? When will you be . . . ready to talk?"

"I don't know, I'll let you know."

"Do you mean today? Tonight, or . . . um . . . later?"

"I'm not sure yet."

"But Ria, listen sweet . . . listen, Ria, there are things you have to know. I have to tell you what happened."

"I think you did."

"No, no. No, I have to tell you what it was about and discuss what we do."

"I imagine I know what happened."

"I want to explain. . . ."

"Go now." He was undecided. "Now," she said again.

He went upstairs and she stood listening to the sound of a quick splash wash, and his opening drawers to get clean clothes. He didn't shave, he looked hangdog and at a loss. "Will you be all right?" he asked. She looked at him witheringly. "No, I know it sounds a stupid thing . . . but I do care and you won't let me talk. You don't want to know what happened, or anything."

She spoke slowly. "Just her name."

"Bernadette," he said.

"Bernadette," she repeated slowly. There was a long silence, then Ria looked at the door and Danny walked out, got into his car, and drove away.

When he had gone, Ria realized that she was very hungry. She'd had eaten nothing since lunchtime yesterday. The figs and parma ham had not been touched last night. She cleared the table swiftly and got a tray ready. She would need all her strength for what lay ahead, this was no time to think about diets and calories. She cut two slices of a wholemeal bread and a banana. She made some strong coffee. Whatever happened now she would need some fuel to give her energy.

She had just begun to eat when she heard a tap at the back door. Rosemary came in carrying a yellow dress. It was something they had discussed the other night. Was that only Saturday night? Less than three days ago? Rosemary always dressed for work as if she were going to be on prime-time television, groomed and made-up. Her short straight hair with its immaculate cut looked as if she had come from a salon. The dress that she had brought to lend to Ria was one she had bought but hardly ever worn. She didn't have the right coloring she had said, it needed someone dark.

Rosemary held the dress out as if she were in a dress shop convincing a doubtful buyer. "It looks nothing in the hand but try it on, it's absolutely right for the opening of the flats." Ria looked at her wordlessly. "No, don't give me that look, you think it's too wishy-washy but honestly with your dark hair and, say, a black scarf . . ." Rosemary stopped suddenly and looked at Ria properly. She was sitting white-faced wearing a black velvet dress and gold chain, and eating a huge banana sandwich at eight-thirty in the morning. "What is it?" Rosemary's voice was a whisper.

"Nothing, why?"

"Ria, what's happened. What are you doing?"

"I'm having my breakfast, what do you think I'm doing?"

"What is it? Your dress . . . ?"

"You're not the only one who can get dressed in the mornings," Ria said, her lip trembling. Her voice sounded to her a bit like a mutinous five-year-old. She saw Rosemary look at her face, aghast. Then it was all too much. "Oh God, Rosemary, he has a girlfriend, a girlfriend who's pregnant. She's twenty-two, she's going to have his baby."

"No!" Rosemary had dropped the dress on the floor and come over to embrace her.

"*Yes.* It's true. She's called Bernadette." Ria's voice was high now and hysterical. "Bernadette! Can you imagine it! I didn't know they still called people of twenty-two that. He's left me, he's going to live with her. It's all over. Danny's gone. Oh, Jesus, Rosemary, what am I going to do? I love him so much, Rosemary. What am I going to do?"

Rosemary held her friend in her arms and muttered into the dark curly hair. "Shush, shush, it can't be over, it's all right, it's all right."

Ria pulled away. "It's not going to be all right. He's leaving me. For her. For Bernadette."

"And would you have him back?" Rosemary was always very practical.

"Of course I would. You know that." Ria wept.

"Then we must *get* him back," said Rosemary, picking up a table napkin and wiping Ria's tearstained face just as you would a baby's.

"Gertie, can I come in?"

"Oh, Rosemary, it's not such a good time. I wonder if I could leave it to another time . . . it's just . . ." Rosemary walked past her. Gertie's home was a mess. That was nothing new but this time there actually seemed to be broken furniture. A lamp was at a rakish angle and a small table now in three pieces stood in the corner. Broken china and glass seemed to have been swept to one side. There was a stain of spilled coffee or something on the carpet.

"I'm sorry, you see—" Gertie began.

"Gertie I haven't come here at nine o'clock in the morning to give your home marks. I've come for your help."

"What is it?" Gertie was justifiably alarmed. What kind of help could she possibly give to Rosemary Ryan, who ran her life like clockwork, who looked like a fashion model, had a home like something from a magazine and a successful job?

"You're needed up in Ria's house now. You have to come, I'll drive you. Come on, get your coat."

"I can't, I can't today."

"You have to, Gertie. It's as simple as this, Ria needs you. Look at all she does for you when you need her."

"No, not now. You see, there was a bit of trouble here last night."

"You do surprise me." Rosemary looked around the room scornfully.

"And we made it all up and I said to Jack I wouldn't go running to the two of you anymore." Gertie lowered her voice. "He said that it was the women friends I had who were coming between us . . . making the problems."

"Bullshit," Rosemary said.

"Shush, he's asleep. Don't wake him."

"I don't care if he wakes or not, your friend who has never once asked you a favor in her whole life wants you to come round to her house and you're bloody coming."

"Not today, tell her I'm sorry. She'll understand. Ria knows what the problems are in this house, she'll forgive me for not coming this once."

"She might, I won't. Ever."

"But friends forgive and understand. Ria's my friend, you're my friend."

"And that big ignorant bruiser in a drunken sleep is not a friend, we have to assume? Is that what you're telling me? Get sense, Gertie, what's the worst he can do to you? Another couple of teeth? Maybe you should have them *all* out next time you go to Jimmy Sullivan. Make it easier. Just whip out your dentures as soon as lover boy starts looking crooked."

"You're a very hard, cruel woman, Rosemary," Gertie said.

"Am I? A moment ago I was a sympathetic, understanding friend. Well, I'll tell you what you are, Gertie. You are a weak, selfish, whinging victim and you deserve to get beaten up as much as you do, and possibly more because you haven't a shred of kindness or decency in you. If someone told anyone else on God's earth that Ria Lynch needed them they'd be there like a shot. But not you of course, not Gertie."

Rosemary had never been so angry. She walked to the door without even looking behind to see how Gertie was taking it. Before she got to her car she heard steps behind her. Out in the daylight she saw the marks on Gertie's face, bruises that had not been visible indoors because of the dim light in the house. The women looked at each other for a moment.

"He's left her. The bastard."

"Danny? Never! He wouldn't."

"He has," said Rosemary, starting up the car.

Ria was still sitting in her party dress. That more than anything underlined the seriousness of it all. "I haven't told Gertie anything except that Danny *says* he's moving out. I don't know any more, anyway, and we don't want to, or have to. All we want is to help you get through today." Rosemary was completely in charge.

"You're very good to come, Gertie." Ria's voice was small.

"Why wouldn't I? Look at all you do for me." Gertie looked at the floor as she spoke, hating to catch Rosemary's eye. "So where do we start?"

"I don't know." The normally confident Ria was at a loss. "It's just that I couldn't bear to talk to anyone else except you two."

"Well, who might come in on top of you? Colm?"

"No, he stays in the garden. He knows anyway. I fainted in the restaurant last night."

Rosemary and Gertie exchanged quick glances. "So who else is likely to come?" Rosemary asked and then with one voice she and Gertie said, "Your mother!"

"Oh, sweet Jesus, I couldn't face my mother today," Ria said.

"Right," Gertie said. "Do we head her off at the pass? I could do that. I could go and thank her for lending me the dog, tell her I'm sorry I tied him up at the gate."

"Why did you want him?" Ria asked.

It was no time for disguises. "For protection. Jack's a bit afraid of dogs. He was very upset yesterday what with being taken in by the police."

"But not *kept* in, unfortunately," said Rosemary.

"Yes, but what kind of jails would they need if you took in every drunk?" Gertie was philosophical. "I could tell your mother you had flu or something."

Rosemary shook her head. "No, that would be worse than ever. She'd come over like Florence Nightingale with potions and try to book you into that geriatric home of hers. We could say you'd gone out shopping, that there'd be no one at home. Or would that be an odd sort of thing to say?"

Ria didn't seem to know. "She might come round to see what I bought," she said.

"Could you say you have to go out and meet someone?"

"Who?" Ria asked. There was a silence.

Rosemary spoke. "We'll say that there's a free voucher in Quentin's, that you and I were meant to be going there today but now we can't. And since it's only valid today your mother and Hilary are to go instead. How about that?" She was crisp and decisive, as she must be at work, looking around to see how the suggestion was received.

"You don't know how slow they are," Ria said. "They'd never do anything unexpected like that."

"Hilary would hate to miss the bargain, she'd go just to get value. Your mother would love to see the styles. They'll go. I'll book it."

Gertie was reassuring. "Anyone would get dressed up and go to Quentin's. I'd even stir myself for that, and that's saying something." She managed a watery smile from her poor bruised face.

Ria felt a lump in her throat. "Sure, sure they'll go," she said.

"I'll pick up Annie and Brian from school and take them back to my place, to have supper and watch a video." Rosemary saw the look of doubt on Ria's face about this and said quickly, "I'll make it such a good video that they won't be able to refuse, oh, and I'll invite the awful Kitty as well." Ria grinned. That would do it. "And lastly, Ria, I'll also book you a hair appointment in my place, they really are very good."

"It's too late for hairdos and makeovers, Rosemary. We're way beyond all that. I couldn't do it, it would be meaningless to me."

"How else are you going to fill in the hours until he comes home?" she asked. There was no answer. Rosemary made two brisk phone calls to busy professionals like herself. No time was wasted in long, detailed explanations. To Brenda in Quentin's who heard that a Mrs. Johnson and Mrs. Moran would be going as her guests, and were to be treated royally as winners of a voucher, given everything they asked for. Then to the hairdressing salon, where she booked Mrs. Lynch for a style cut and shampoo and also a manicure.

"I'm not usually so feeble, but I don't think I have the energy to explain all this about Quentin's to my mother and Hilary," Ria began.

"You don't have to, I will," Rosemary said.

"The house is a mess."

"It won't be when you get back," promised Gertie.

"I don't believe any of this is happening," Ria said slowly.

"That's what happens, it's nature's way of coping. It's so you can get on with other things," said Gertie, who knew what she was talking about.

"It's like an anesthetic, you have to go on autopilot for a while," said Rosemary, who had an explanation for everything but would have had no idea what it felt like to see a huge pit of despair open in front of you.

Ria didn't really remember the visit to the hairdressing salon. She told them she was very tired and hadn't slept all night, they would have to excuse her if she was a little distracted. She tried to show an interest in the hot oil treatment for her thick curly hair, and tried to make a decision about the shape and color of her nails. But mainly she let them get on with it, and when it came to pay they said that it was on Rosemary Ryan's account.

Ria looked at her watch. It was lunchtime. If everything had gone according to plan her mother and sister would be sitting in one of Dublin's grandest restaurants having a meal they believed to be free. It was yet one more extraordinary aspect to this totally unreal day.

In Quentin's, Hilary and her mother were offered an Irish coffee after their lunch. "Do you think it's included on the voucher?" Mrs. Johnson hissed. Emboldened by the excellent Italian wine Hilary decided to be assertive. "I very much think it is. A place like this wouldn't stint on little extras." It turned out to be very much included, the elegant lady who ran the place told them, and a second was brought to the table without their having to decide.

While they waited for the taxi, they were asked as a favor to taste a new liqueur that the restaurant was thinking of putting on the menu; they needed some valued customers' views before they made a final decision. The taxi journey back to Nora Johnson's house was something of a blur. She was relieved to have been told by that bossy Rosemary that Ria wouldn't be at home. Otherwise she might have felt she should call around and give a report on how the lunch had gone. She would telephone instead, when she had a little rest.

There were two more hours before Danny came home. Ria had never known time to pass so slowly. She walked aimlessly around the house touching things, the table in the hall where Danny left his keys, the back of the chair where he sat at night and often fell asleep with papers from work on his lap. She picked up the glass jug he had given her for her birthday. It had the word *Ria* engraved on it. He had loved her enough in January to have her name put on a jug and yet in April another woman was pregnant with his child. It was too much to take in.

Ria looked at the cushion she had embroidered for him. The two words, *Danny Boy*. It had taken her weeks of redoing the stitches to finish it. She could remember his face when she gave it to him. "You must love me nearly as much as I love you to do something like that for me," he had said. Nearly as much!

She looked at their new music center. Only last Christmas, less than five months ago, he had spent hour after hour testing where the speakers would be best. He had bought her so many compact discs, all the Ella Fitzgeralds she had loved, and she had got him the big band sound he liked, the Dorsey Brothers, Glenn Miller. The children had groaned at their taste. Perhaps the youthful Bernadette played the strange music that Annie and Kitty liked. Perhaps Danny Lynch pretended he liked it too. Soon he would be home to tell her things like this.

Ria saw Colm Barry in the garden. He was turning the soil but in a desultory way, as if he weren't really there to dig vegetables but to look after her in case she needed it.

Gertie phoned Rosemary at seven o'clock. "I just rang to say . . . well, I don't know why I rang," she said.

"You know why you rang, you rang because it's seven o'clock and we're both mad with worry."

"Are the children there?"

"Yes, that bit worked anyway. I nearly had to give my body to get that video but I got it."

"That'll keep them entertained. Do you think they'll patch it up?"

"They'll have to," said Rosemary. "They've too much to lose, both of them."

"But what about the baby? The girl who's pregnant?"

"That's probably what they're talking about this minute."

"Do you say prayers at all, Rosemary?"

"No, not these days. Do you?"

"No, I do deals, I suppose. I promise God to do things if Jack stops, whatever."

Rosemary bit her lip. It must have cost Gertie a lot to admit this. "Do they work, these deals?"

"What do *you* think?"

"No, I suppose not all the time." Rosemary was being diplomatic.

"I've done a deal today. I've told God that if he gets Danny back for Ria, I'll, well . . . I'll do something I've been promising to do for a long time."

"I hope it's not to turn the other cheek again or anything," Rosemary said before she could stop herself.

"No, quite the contrary as it happens," Gertie said and hung up.

At seven o'clock Ria turned down the volume control on the answering machine. She didn't want to be disturbed by any more drunken messages from her mother and sister, who appeared to have become legless at the restaurant where they had lunch. There were also messages from other people. A query from her brother-in-law, Martin, to know where Hilary was. Dekko's mother to say that there would be a babysitting opportunity for Brian at the weekend. The hire shop confirming the rental of the sanding machine for next weekend. A woman organizing a class reunion lunch who wanted addresses of others who had been at school with them.

Ria would not have been able to talk to any one of them today. What *did* people do without answering machines? She remembered the day they had installed it and how they had laughed at Danny's attempts to record a convincing message. "We have to face it, I'm just not an actor," he had said. But he had been an actor, a very successful one for months. Years maybe.

She sat down and waited for Danny Lynch to come back to Tara Road.

He didn't call out as he usually did. There was no, "Yoo-hoo, sweetheart, I'm back." He didn't leave his keys on the hall table. He looked pale and anxious. If things were normal she would have worried, wondered if he was getting the flu, begged him to take more time off from the office, to relax more. But things were not normal so she just looked at him and waited for him to speak.

"It's very quiet here," he said eventually.

"Yes, isn't it?"

They could have been strangers who had just met. He sat down and put his head in his hands. Ria said nothing. "How do you want to do this?" he said.

"You said we must talk, Danny, so talk."

"You're making it very hard for me."

"I'm sorry, did you say that *I* am making it hard? Is that what you said?"

"Please, I'm going to try to be as honest as I can, there will be no more lies or hiding things. I'm not proud of any of this but don't try and trip me up with words and phrases. It's only going to make it worse." She looked at him and said nothing. "Ria, I beg you. We know each other too well, we know what every word means, every silence even."

She spoke slowly and carefully. "No, I don't know you at all. You say there'll be no more lies, no more hiding things. You see, I didn't know there had been any lies or any hiding things, I thought we were fine."

"No, you didn't. You can't have. Be honest."

"I am, Danny. I'm being as honest as I ever have been. If you know me as you claim you do, then you must see that."

"You thought that this was all there was."

"Yes."

"And you didn't think it had all changed. You thought we were just the same as when we got married?" He seemed astounded.

"Yes, the same. Older, busier. More tired, but mainly the same."

"But . . ." He couldn't go on.

"But what?"

"But we have nothing to say to each other anymore, Ria. We make household arrangements, we rent a sander, we get things out of the freezer, we make lists. That's not living. That's not a real life."

"You rented the sander," she said. "I never wanted it."

"That's about the level of our conversation nowadays, sweetheart. You know this, you're just not admitting it."

"You're going to leave, leave this house and me and Annie and Brian . . . is that what's happening?"

"You know it's not the same anymore, like it was."

"I don't, I don't know that."

"You can't tell me that for you everything's perfect?"

"It's not totally perfect, you work too hard. Well, you're out too much, maybe it's not work after all. I thought it was."

"A lot of it is," he said ruefully.

"But apart from that I thought everything was fine, and I had no idea that you weren't happy here with us all."

"It's not that."

She leaned over and looked him right in the eyes. "But *what* is it, Danny? Please? Look, you wanted to talk, we're talking. You wanted me to be calm, I'm being calm. I'm being as honest as you are. What is it? If you say you weren't unhappy then why are you going? Tell me so that I'll understand. Tell me."

"There's nothing left, Ria. It's nobody's fault, it happens all the time to people."

"It hasn't happened to me," she said simply.

"Yes, it has, but you won't face it. You just want to go on acting."

"I was never acting, not for one minute."

"I don't mean in a bad sense, I mean playing Happy Family."

"But we *are* a happy family, Danny."

"No, sweetheart, there's more, for both of us. We're not old people, we don't have to rein ourselves in and put up with the way it all turned out."

"It turned out fine. Don't we have the most marvelous children and a lovely home? Tell me, what more do you want?"

"Oh, Ria, Ria. I want to be somebody, to have a future and a dream and to start over and get things right."

"And a new baby?"

"That's part of it, yes, a new beginning."

"Will you tell me about her, about Bernadette? About what you and she have that we don't have? I don't mean glorious sex, of course. Calm I may be, but not quite calm enough to hear about that."

"I beg you, don't bring bitter accusing words into it."

"I beg *you* to think about what you say. Is there anything bitter and accusing about asking you in a totally nonhysterical way why you are suddenly ending a life that I thought was perfectly satisfactory? I just asked you to tell me what you are going to that's so much better. I'm sorry I mentioned sex but you did tell me that you and Bernadette are going to have a child and so forgive me but there must have been some sex involved."

"I hate you to be sarcastic like this. I know you so well and you know me, we shouldn't be talking like this. We shouldn't, truly."

"Danny, is this just something that's happened to us, something that we might sort of get through like people do? I know it's serious and there's a child involved, but people have survived such things."

"No, it's not like that."

"You can't feel that it's all over. You got involved with somebody much younger, you were flattered. Of course I'm furious and upset but I can get over it, we all get over things. It doesn't have to be the end."

"All day I said to myself . . . please may Ria be calm. I don't expect her to forgive me but may she be calm enough for us to discuss this and see what's best for the children. You are calm, I don't deserve this but it's the wrong kind of calm. You think it's just a fling."

"A fling?" she said.

"Yes, remember we used to go through all the degrees of relationships, a whirl, a fling, a romance, a relationship, and then the real thing." He smiled as he said this. He was looking at his wife very affectionately.

Ria was bewildered. "So?"

"So this is not a fling, it's the real thing. I love Bernadette, I want to spend the rest of my life with her, and she with me."

Ria nodded as if this was a reasonable thing for the man she loved to be saying about somebody else. She spoke carefully. "During the day when you were thinking please let her be calm, what else did you think? What did you think would be the best end to this discussion?"

"Oh, Ria, please. Don't play games."

"I have never felt less like playing games in my life. I mean this utterly seriously, how do you want it to end?"

"With dignity I suppose. With respect for each other."

"What?"

"No, you asked me, you asked what did I hope for. I suppose I hoped you'd agree that what we had was very good at the time but it was over and that . . . we could talk about what to do that would hurt Annie and Brian least."

"I've done nothing at all to hurt them."

"I know."

"And you didn't think there was anything that you and I could talk about that would get us back together the way it used to be, well, used to be for you."

"No, love, that's over, that's gone."

"So when you said talk, it wasn't talk about us, it was talk about what I am to do when you go, is that it?"

"About what we both do. It's not their fault, Annie and Brian don't deserve any hardship."

"No, they don't. Do I, though?"

"That's different, Ria. You and I fell out of love."

"I didn't."

"You did, you just won't admit it."

"That's not true. And I won't say I did to make you feel better."

"Please."

"No, I love you. I love the way you look and the way you smile, I love your face and I want to have your arms around me and hear you telling me that this is all a nightmare."

"This isn't the way it is, Ria, it's the way it was."

"You don't love me anymore?"

"I'll always admire you."

"I don't want your admiration, I want you to love me."

"You only think you do . . . deep down you don't."

"Don't give me this, Danny, trying to make me say that I'm tired of it all too."

"We can't have everything we want," he began.

"You're having a pretty good stab at it though."

"I want us to be civilized, decide what we'll do about where we all live. . . ."

"What do you mean?"

"Before we tell the children, we should be able to give them an idea what the future is going to be like."

"I'm not telling the children anything, I have nothing to tell them. You tell them what you want to."

"But the whole point is not to upset them. . . ."

"Then stay at home and live with them and give up this other thing . . . that's the way not to upset them."

"I can't do that, Ria," Danny said. "My mind's made up."

That was the moment she believed that all this was actually happening. Up to then it had all been words, and nightmares. Now she knew and she felt very, very weary. "Right," she said. "Your mind's made up."

He seemed relieved at the change in her. He was right, they did know each other very well, he could see that somehow she had accepted it was going to happen. Their conversation would now be on a different level, the level he had wanted, discussion of details, who would live where.

"There wouldn't be any hurry to move and change everything immediately, disrupting their school term, but maybe by the end of the summer?"

"Maybe what by the end of the summer?" Ria asked.

"We should have thought of what will happen, where we'll all live."

"I'll be living here, won't I?" Ria said, surprised.

"Well, sweetheart, we'll have to sell the place. I mean it would be much too big for . . ."

"Sell Tara Road?" She was astounded.

"Eventually of course, because . . ."

"But, Danny, this is our home. This is where we live, we can't sell it."

"We're going to have to. How else can, well . . . everybody be provided for?"

"I'm not moving from here so that you can provide for a twenty-two-year-old."

"Please Ria, we must think what we tell Annie and Brian."

"No, *you* must think. I've told you I'm telling them nothing, and I am not moving out of my home."

There was a silence.

"Is this how you're going to play it?" he said eventually. "Daddy, wicked monster Daddy, is going away and abandoning you, and good saintly poor Mummy is staying. . . ."

"Well that's more or less the way it *is,* Danny."

He was angry now. "No, it's not. We're meant to be trying to be constructive and make things more bearable for them."

"Okay, let's wait here until they come home and let's watch you making it bearable for them."

"Where are they?"

"At Rosemary's, watching a video."

"Does Rosemary know?"

"Yes."

"And what time will they be back?"

Ria shrugged. "Nine or ten, I imagine."

"Can you ring and get them back sooner?"

"You mean you can't even wait a couple of hours in your own home for them."

"I don't mean that, it's just if you're going to be so hostile . . . I suppose I'm afraid it will make things worse."

"I won't be hostile. I'll sit and read or something."

He looked around wonderingly. "You know I've never known this house so peaceful, I've never known you to sit and read. The place is always like a shopping center in the city with doors opening and closing, people coming in and out and food and cups of coffee. It's always like a beer garden here, with your mother and the dog and Gertie and Rosemary and all the children's friends. This of all times must be the very first time in this house that you can hear yourself think."

"I thought you liked the place being full of people."

"There was never any calm here, Ria, too much rushing round playing house."

"I don't believe this, you're just rewriting history." She got up from the table and went over to the big armchair. She still felt this huge tiredness. She closed her eyes and knew that she could sleep, there and then, in the middle of this conversation that was about to end her marriage and the life she had lived up to now. Her eyelids were very heavy.

"I'm so sorry, Ria," he said. She said nothing. "Will I go and pack some things, do you think?"

"I don't know, Danny. Do whatever you think."

"I'm happy to sit and talk to you."

Her eyes were still closed. "Well, do then."

"But there's nothing more to say," he said sadly. "I can't keep on saying that I'm sorry things turned out like this, I can't keep saying that over and over."

"No, no you can't," she agreed.

"So maybe it *would* be better if I were to go up and pack a few things."

"Maybe it would."

"Ria?"

"Yes?"

"Nothing."

For a while she could hear him upstairs moving from his study to the bedroom. And then she fell asleep in the chair.

———

She woke to the sound of voices in the kitchen.

"Usually it's Dad fast asleep," said Brian.

"Did you have a nice time?" Ria asked.

"It's not even in the cinemas for another three weeks." Brian's eyes were shining.

"And you, Annie?"

"It was okay. Can Kitty stay the night?" Annie asked.

"No, not tonight."

"But Mam, *why*? Why do you always make life hell for everyone? We told Kitty's mother that she'd be staying."

"Not tonight. Your father and I want to talk to you and Brian about something."

"Kitty can talk too."

"You heard me, Annie." There was something about her voice. Something different. Grudgingly, Annie escorted her friend to the door. Ria could hear muttered remarks about people who spoiled everything.

Danny had come downstairs. He looked pale and anxious. "We want to talk to you, your mother and I," he began. "But I'll do most of the talking because this is about . . . well, it's up to me to explain it all, really." He looked from one to the other as they stood alarmed by the table. Ria still sat in her armchair. "It's very hard to know where to start, so if you don't think it's very sentimental and slushy I'll start saying that we love you very, very much, you're a smashing daughter and son. . . ."

"You're not sick or anything, Daddy?" Annie interrupted.

"No, no, nothing like that."

"Or going to jail? You have that kind of voice."

"No, sweetheart. But there are going to be some changes, and I wanted to tell—"

"I *know* what it is." Brian's face was contorted with horror. "I know. It was just the same in Dekko's house when they told him, they told *him* they loved him. Are we going to have a baby? Is that it?"

Annie looked revolted. "Don't be disgusting, Brian."

But they both looked at Ria for confirmation that this wasn't the problem. She gave a funny little laugh. "*We're* not, but Daddy is," she said.

"Ria!" He looked as if she had hit him. His face was ashen. "Ria, how could you?"

"I answered a question. You said we should answer their questions."

"What is it, Daddy? What are you saying?" Annie looked from one to the other.

"I'm saying that for some of the time I won't be living here anymore, well for most of the time really. And that in the future, well, we'll all probably have to move, but you will have a place with me and also with Mummy for as long as you like, always, forever and ever. So nothing about us will change as far as you're concerned."

"Are you getting divorced?" Brian asked.

"Eventually, yes. But that's a long way down the line. The main thing to establish is that everyone knows everything and there are no secrets, nobody getting hurt."

"That's what your father wants to establish," Ria said.

"Ria, please . . ." He looked hurt and annoyed.

"And is Mam making it up about you having a baby? That's not true, is it, Dad?"

Danny looked at Ria in exasperation. "That's not the point at the moment. The point is that you are my children and nothing can change that, nothing at all. You are my daughter and my son."

"So it *is* true!" Annie said in horror.

"Not a baby!" Brian said.

"Shut up, Brian, the baby's not coming here. Dad's going away to it. Isn't that what's happening?" Danny said nothing just looked miserably at the two stricken young faces. "Well, is it, Dad? Are you going to leave us for someone else?"

"I can never leave you, Annie. You're my daughter, we never leave each other."

"But you're leaving home and going to live with someone who's pregnant?"

"Your mother and I have agreed that we are not the same people we once were . . . we have different needs. . . ."

Ria gave a little strangled laugh from the armchair.

"Who is she, Daddy? Do we know her?"

"No, Annie, not yet."

"Don't you care, Mam? Won't you stop him? Won't you tell him you don't want him to go?" Annie was blazing with rage.

Ria wanted to leap up and hold her hurt, angry daughter to her and tell her just how bad it all was, how unreal. "No, Annie. Your father knows that already, but he has made up his mind."

"Ah, Ria, we agreed, you promised that this shouldn't be a slanging match between us."

"We agreed nothing, I promised nothing. I am not telling my children that I have 'different needs.' It's just not true. I need you and want you at home."

"Oh, Mam, everything's ending, Mam." Brian's face was white. He had never heard his capable mother admitting that she was adrift.

"Brian, it's all right, that's what I'm trying to say to you. Nothing's changing. I'm still Dad, still the same Dad I was all the time."

"You can't leave Mam, Dad. You can't go off with some other one, and leave Mam and us here." Brian was very near tears.

Annie spoke. "She doesn't care, Mam doesn't give a damn. She's just letting him go, she's letting him walk out. She's not even trying to stop him."

"Thank you very much, Ria, that was terrific." Danny was near to tears.

She found her voice. "I will not tell the children that I don't mind and that it's all fine. It is *not* all fine, Danny."

"You promised . . ." he began.

"I promised nothing."

"We said we didn't want to hurt the children."

"I'm not walking out on them, I'm not talking about selling this house over their heads. Where am I hurting them? I only heard about your plans last night and suddenly I'm meant to be all sweetness and light. Saying this is all for the best; we're different people with different needs. I'm the *same* person, I have the same needs. I need you to stay here with us."

"Ria, have some dignity, *please*," he shouted at her.

They seemed to realize that the children hadn't spoken. They looked at the faces of their son and daughter, white and disbelieving and both of them with tears falling unchecked. They were beginning to realize that their life on Tara Road was over. Nothing would ever be the same. An eerie stillness settled on the kitchen. They watched each other fearfully. It was always Ria who broke a silence, who made the first move, who jollied people along. But not tonight. It was as if she were more shocked than any of them.

Danny spoke eventually. "I don't know what to do for the best," he said helplessly. "I wanted it told differently but maybe there's no good way of telling it." They said nothing. "What would you like me to do? Will I stay here in the study tonight so things will be sort of normal, or will I leave and come back tomorrow? You tell me and I'll do what you say."

It was obvious that Ria was going to say nothing.

He looked at the children. "Go," said Brian. "Stay," said Annie. "Not if you're going to leave anyway, go now," Brian said. They all looked at Annie. She shrugged. "Why not?" she said in a small, hurt voice. "If you're going to leave tomorrow, what's the point of hanging about?"

"It's not good-bye, sweetheart. . . ." Danny began. "Can you understand that?"

"No, I can't, Daddy, to be honest," she said. She picked up her schoolbag and without a backward glance went out the kitchen door and up the stairs.

Brian watched her go. "What's going to happen to us all?" he asked.

"We'll all survive," Danny said. "People do."

"Mam?" Her son looked at her.

"As your dad says . . . people do, we will too." The look that Danny gave her was grateful. She didn't want his gratitude. "The children have said they'd like you to go, Danny. Will you, please?"

He went quietly and the three of them heard him starting his car and driving down Tara Road.

Ria had a little speech ready for them at breakfast.

"I wasn't much help last night," she said.

"Is it all really going to happen, Mam? Isn't there anything we can do to stop it?" Brian's face was hopeful.

"Apparently it *is* going to happen, but I wanted to tell you it's not quite as sad and awful as it seemed last night."

"What *do* you mean?" Annie was scornful.

"I mean that what your father said was quite true. We both do love you very much and we'll be here, or around if not here, whenever you need us until you get bored with us and want lives of your own. But until then I'm not going to shout at your father like I did and he's not going to sneer at me. And if you want to be with him, at a weekend say, then that's where you'll be and if you want to be with me, then I'll be here or wherever and delighted for you to be with me. That's a promise." They didn't rate it much. "And what I suggest is that you ring your dad at the office today and ask him where he'd like to meet you and talk to you and tell you about everything."

"Can't you tell us, Mam?" Brian begged.

"I can't really, Brian. I don't know it all and I'd tell it wrong. Let him tell you, then you won't feel worried and there won't be any gray areas."

"But if he tells us one thing and you tell us another?" Annie wanted to know.

"We'll try not to do that anymore."

"And does everyone know about it?"

"No, I don't think many people do."

"Well, do they or don't they?" Annie was abrupt and rude. "I mean does Gran know, Aunt Hilary, Mr. McCarthy, people like that?"

"Gran and Hilary don't know, but I expect Mr. McCarthy does. I didn't think of it before, but I imagine he knows all about it." Her face was like stone.

"And are we to tell anyone? Do I tell Kitty what's happened or is it all a terrible secret?"

"Kitty's your friend. You must tell her whatever you want to, Annie."

"I don't want to tell Dekko and Myles, they'd tell the whole class," Brian said.

"Well, don't tell them then, for goodness' sake." Annie was impatient.

"Do you get custody of us, Mam, or does Dad?"

"I've told you we won't fight over you, you'll be welcome with both of us always. But I would think you would probably live with me during the week, through the school year."

"Because she wouldn't want us, is that it?" Annie was instantly suspicious.

"No, no. She knows your father has two children, she must want to welcome them."

"But she's having her own," Brian grumbled.

"What's her name?" Annie wanted to know.

"I don't know." Ria lied.

"You *must* know, of course you know," Annie persisted.

"I don't. Ask your father."

"Why won't you tell us?" Annie wouldn't let go.

"Leave Mam alone. Why do you think she knows?"

"Because it's the first thing I'd have asked, that anyone would ask," said Annie.

Danny used to laugh at the way Ria made lists of things to do. She always headed it "List". Old habits die hard. She headed it "List" and sat at the table when the children had gone. Their hugs had been awkward but some pretense at normality had been restored. The tears and silences of last night were over. The list covered many phone calls.

She must ring her mother first and prevent her coming anywhere near the house, then ring Hilary, then at ten o'clock when the charity shop where she was meant to be working opened she would ring and cancel her shift. She would ring Rosemary at the printing company and Gertie at the launderette, and Colm to thank him for looking after her.

And lastly she would ring Danny. Beside Danny's name she wrote firmly: Do not apologize.

Nora Johnson started to explain about the lunch. "There may be a question on the bill at the restaurant. They *said* we could have three Irish coffees. In fact, Ria, they more or less insisted. But if there's any dispute . . ."

"Mam, could you stop talking, *please?*"

"That's an extraordinary tone to take with your own mother."

"Listen to me please, Mam. This is not a good day for me. Danny and I are going to have a trial separation. We told the children last night. It didn't go well."

"And has he moved out?" Her mother sounded very calm.

"Yes. We haven't decided what to do about the house yet but he has moved out for the moment."

"Keep the house," her mother said in a voice like a trap closing.

"Well, all that has to be discussed. If you don't mind, I don't feel much like talking about it now."

"No, but talk to a lawyer and keep that property."

"Ah, Mam, that's not the point. The point is that Danny's leaving. Aren't you sorry? Aren't you upset for me?"

"I suppose I saw it coming."

"No, you couldn't have seen it coming."

"He had very small eyes," said Ria's mother.

"Can I speak to Mrs. Hilary Moran?"

"Jesus, Ria, think yourself lucky you didn't use that voucher. I have such a hangover."

"Listen, can you talk?"

"Of course I can't talk. I can't think and I certainly can't be in a school with all these screeching voices but this is where I am, and where I have to stay until four-thirty. God, you don't know how lucky you are having nothing to do at all day but sit in a big house—"

"Hilary, shut up and listen to me."

"What?"

"Danny has another woman, a girl he got pregnant."

"I don't believe it."

"It's true. I wanted to tell you before Mam did, she's possibly trying to ring you at this minute." Ria felt her voice tremble a little.

"I'm very sorry, Ria, more sorry than I can say."

"I know you are."

"And what happens now?"

"We sell the house, I suppose. He goes his way, I go mine. I don't *know* what happens now."

"And the children?"

"Angry, of course. In total shock, as am I."

"You didn't know or suspect anything?"

"No, and if you tell me he has small eyes like Mam did I'll go round and kill you."

They giggled. In the middle of it all they were able to laugh at their mother.

"I could tell them I'm sick and come round to you." Hilary was doubtful.

"No, honestly, I have a million things to do."

"I hope one of them's getting your hands on the deeds of that house," Hilary said before they hung up.

Frances Sullivan ran the charity shop. "Ria . . . of course . . . we'll find someone else for this morning, don't give it a thought. Going anywhere nice?"

"No, bit of a family crisis, something I want to work out."

"You do that. Is it Annie and my Kitty?"

"No, why do you say that?" Alarm bells sounded in Ria's head.

"Nothing." Frances was backing off.

"Go on, Frances. I'd tell you if *I* knew."

"It's probably nothing, it's just that Kitty let out that she and Annie were going off on a motorbike rally next Saturday. I wondered had you'd found out."

"Not next Saturday, surely? They have another careers forum."

"I think not," said Frances Sullivan. "But you didn't hear it from me."

Rosemary's secretary put her through at once. "Is it a good time, Rosemary?"

"Is he giving her up?" Rosemary said.

"No, not a chance."

"And the children?"

"Took it very badly, of course. Danny and I made a real mess of it."

"Are you all right, Ria?"

"I am at the moment. I'm on autopilot. And thank you so much for all the things, I forgot to thank you for anything."

"Like what?"

"The hairdo, the lunch for Mam and Hilary—they got pissed there by the way, the bill might be a bit more than we thought."

"Oh, for heaven's sake, Ria."

"And for coming around, and all the encouragement. That's the best bit, I'm sorry for not making a better go of it."

"You and he'll be back together."

"No, it's not likely."

"You're still in Tara Road, aren't you?"

"Yes, for the moment."

"Stay there, Ria. He's not going to leave that house."

"Gertie, I truly appreciated your coming round, I knew it wasn't such a good day for you."

"And you sorted it all out, didn't you?"

"No, I'm afraid not."

"Listen there's nothing I don't know about family rows, he'll be as sorry as anything, he'll put it right. He'll let whoever she is have her baby or an abortion or whatever. You and he are . . . well, I know you don't like the example but, you're like Jack and myself. Some people are meant for each other."

"I know you think this is helping, Gertie, but—"

"Listen, can you ever imagine either of you living anywhere on earth but Tara Road? You're made for that house, that's a sure guarantee it will work out all right."

"Colm? It's Ria Lynch."

"Ah yes, Ria."

"You were very kind to me. I realized I never thanked you."

"There's no need for thanks between friends, it's assumed."

"Yes, but we don't want to take friends for granted either."

"You wouldn't do that."

"I don't know. I seem to have been a bit spaced out."

"There's days we're all like that," he said.

"Thank you for not inquiring if it sorted itself out."

"These things take time." He was so soothing, making no demands that she tell him. After all the others that she had talked to, this was very restful.

"Danny?"

"It was awful," he said. "I'm so sorry."

Ria looked at her little piece of paper. Do not apologize, it ordered her. She had wanted to cry and say she was sorry, that they were not the kind of people who snarled at each other like that. She wanted him to come home and wrap her in his arms. Do not apologize, she read, and she knew she had been right to write it down. Danny was not coming home to her. Ever.

"There was hardly any way it couldn't have been awful," she said in a matter-of-fact tone. "Now, let's see what we can salvage. I've told the children to call you today and that maybe you could meet them one evening on some neutral ground. Tell them about things, tell them what it's going to be like. The summer and everything."

"But it's all still so up in the air, you and I have to—"

"No, you must tell them what they can expect. Whether you'll be able to cook dinner for them, have them to stay for weekends. You see, they know they'll be welcome here, they don't know what you can offer them."

"But you won't want to let them . . . ?"

"Danny, they're nine and fourteen. Do you think I'm going to try to tell people of that age where they can go to see their father and where they can't? Nor would I want to. They must hear as much good news from you as possible."

"You sound very calm." He was impressed.

"Of course I'm not calm. But you will let them know they're welcome with you wherever you go, not just phrases, actual plans?"

"Plans?"

"Well, you do have a place to live, I imagine?"

"Yes, yes."

"And would it have enough room for them to stay?"

"Stay?"

"When they go to see you."

"It's just a small flat at the moment."

"And is it nearby?" She kept her voice interested and without any emotion.

"It's in Bantry Court, you know the block . . . that we . . . that Barney developed a few years back?"

"I do," Ria said. "That was handy, your being able to get a flat in Bantry Court." She hoped the bitterness wasn't too obvious in her voice.

"No, it's not mine, it's Bernadette's. She got it from her father when she was eighteen. You see, it was an investment."

"It certainly was," Ria said grimly.

"He's dead now," Danny said.

"Oh, I see."

"And her mother's sort of worried about the whole situation."

"I imagine so."

"She rang you that time, you know the woman that didn't give her name? She was sort of checking up on me, I suppose."

"But she knew you were married, I presume?"

"Yes." He sounded wretched.

Ria continued to speak brightly. "And you're getting a house soon, is that right?"

"Yes, you know, a house. For everybody."

"For everybody. Quite."

There was a silence. He spoke again. "You know it will take time to get everything sorted out."

"I think they'd love to know some immediate sort of plans so that they'll know they haven't lost you."

"But won't you . . . ?"

"I'll have them lots. And the same about summer. Tell them the weeks you can take them away. Remember you once talked of renting a boat on the Shannon?"

"Do you think they'd like that? I mean, you know, without you?"

"Without me? But they're going to have to learn that it will be without me from now on when it's with you. We *all* have to learn that. Let them learn it soon before they panic and think that you have gone away."

At no stage did Ria mention Bernadette's name nor the child that was expected. It was clear that she expected Annie and Brian would be part of the new household. She wanted only that he would close no doors on his daughter and son.

"Another thing. Do your parents know about . . . about all this?"

"Lord no," he said, startled at the very idea.

"Don't worry. I'll tell them in time," she said.

"I don't know what to say. . . ." he began.

"Oh, and Barney and Mona and Polly and people . . . do they know?"

"Not Mona," Danny Lynch said quickly.

"But Barney is up-to-date?"

"Yes, well, he helped us to get a house, you see."

"Like he helped to get us this one," Ria said. A wave of irritation about Barney McCarthy swept over her. She realized she had never liked him. She had liked both of his women but not him. How odd that she hadn't known this before. She decided to change the subject. "Children are easily distracted, be sure to emphasize holidays to them."

"But what would you do? If we all went away?"

"I'd go on a holiday myself maybe."

"But, sweetheart . . . where would you—?"

"Danny, can I ask you not to call me that?"

"I'm so sorry. Yes, you did ask me, but you know it means nothing."

"I know *now* it means nothing. I didn't always."

"Please, Ria."

"Okay, Danny. We'll say good-bye now."

"Where will I take them, McDonald's, Planet Hollywood?"

"I don't know. It might be a bit difficult to talk in those places, but decide, all of you."

They hung up.

It had been less upsetting than she had thought. Funny how annoyed she was about Barney's complicity. It wasn't unreasonable to be annoyed. After all, she and Danny had kept Barney's secret for years. They had never told Mona McCarthy where her husband really was on the night that little Annie Lynch was born.

CHAPTER

FOUR

Ria lost all sense of time. Sometimes when she went to bed she awoke thinking it was morning and realizing that she had only been asleep for half an hour. The empty side of the bed seemed an enormous, vast space. Ria would get up and walk to the window, hugging herself as if to try to ease the pain. Just after midnight and he was asleep in some apartment block wrapped around this child. It was too much to bear. Perhaps her mind would give up under the strain. That's what happened to people. As she sat long hours staring out the window while stars disappeared and dawn came, Ria thought that perhaps her mind had actually broken down already without her noticing it. Yet she appeared to function during daylight hours. The house was cleaned, the meals were cooked, people came and went. She spoke normally, she believed, to those who spoke to her.

But it was all totally unreal. And she couldn't remember anything at all from a day just over. Was it today that Myles and Dekko had brought three frogs to play in the bath—or was that yesterday or last week? Which was the day that she had the huge row with Annie about Kitty? And how had it started? Had Hilary come with six parsnips and a request that Ria make a parsnip soup to take home with her, or had Ria just imagined this?

He was going to come back of course, that was obvious. But when?

How long did this humiliating, hurtful waiting period have to go on before he threw his keys onto the hall table and said, Sweetheart, I'm home. Everyone has a silly fling and mine is over, now will you forgive me or will I have to walk on my knees?

And she would forgive him immediately. A great hug, a holiday maybe. The name of Bernadette would not be mentioned for a while and then it would come into the conversation as a kind of risqué joke.

But when was all this healing process going to start? Sometimes during the day Ria would stop whatever she was doing with a physical sense of shock as she remembered something else that had been a lie. That colored shirt that he had bought in London. The girl had chosen it for him, hadn't she? Bernadette had been in London with him. Ria had to sit down when she realized that. Then the bill for the mobile phone. Almost every call was to her number, the number that was his now in case of emergencies. The duty-free perfume, a guilt present from a trip with Bernadette. The day when they were all at the zoo, just going into the lion house and he got a call to go back to the office. That wasn't the office, that had been Bernadette. There were so many times and Ria had never suspected. What a fool, what a simple, trusting fool she had been. Then she would argue that view. Who wanted to be a jailer, watching every move? If you loved someone you trusted him. Surely it was as simple as that.

And everyone knew, of course they did. When she telephoned him at work they must have raised their eyes to heaven, in sympathy as well as irritation. The staid, stay-at-home wife who didn't know her husband had another woman. Even Trudy, the girl who answered the phone, must have put Bernadette through as often as Ria. Possibly Bernadette knew her name too, and asked about her diet, which was a way of getting into her good graces.

And then of course there was Barney McCarthy coming to this house praising Ria's delicious food. He had been out many, many times with Danny and Bernadette. In Quentin's where Ria went once a year on their wedding anniversary, that nice Brenda Brennan who ran the place would have known too. She must really have pitied Ria, the once-a-year mousy wife who suspected nothing.

And Polly knew, and of course she must have scorned, not pitied Ria, because she was in exactly the same position as Mona. Mona? Did she know? Ria had spent so long deceiving Mona and hiding Polly's existence and all the time Mona might have been doing just the same about Bernadette.

It would be funny if it were not so terrible. And when you thought about it, if all these people knew, didn't Rosemary know? She knew everything that happened in Dublin. But no, Ria had to believe that her performance could not have been an act. And a true friend would have told her. If Rosemary and Gertie had known, they would have had to give Ria some warning and not allow her world to be blown apart. From time to time Ria wondered if Rosemary *had* been giving her warnings. Was all this advice about clothes and getting a job some kind of hint that all was not well?

The Sullivans obviously knew. Frances had been brisk and supportive. "It's probably a passing thing, Ria. Men approaching forty behave very oddly. If you can sit it out then I'm sure it will all be for the best."

"Did you know?" Ria had asked her directly.

The answer had not been equally straightforward. "This is a city full of rumors and stories. You would be addled in the head if you listened to them all. I have enough problems of my own trying to keep Kitty on the rails."

Colm Barry probably hadn't known. Danny wouldn't have been so foolish as to take that child to a restaurant a few doors from his own house. But so many others did know. It was humiliating to think just how many. Taxi drivers would have known, the man in the petrol station, Larry the bank manager, he probably knew. Maybe Bernadette had moved her account to Larry's branch for togetherness.

The window cleaner asked about Danny. "Where's himself?" he inquired. It was a day when she felt in a mood to talk.

"He's gone, he left me for a young one as it happens."

"He always had a bit of a roving eye, your man had, you're well rid of him," the window cleaner had said. Now why had he said that? *Why?*

Why did people in the thrift shop press her hand and say that she was a great woman. Who had told them? Had they always known? Oh, how she wished she could get away from all these people who knew. People who pitied her, patted her on the head and talked about her. She *knew* it would end when he gave up Bernadette and came home, but how long would she have to wait while all these people smiled indulgently as if Danny had a dose of the flu?

And of course she had to cope with the children. Annie's mood swings went the whole way from blaming her mother to blaming herself. "If you'd only been a bit more normal, Mam, you know, if you'd stopped yacking and cooking he wouldn't have gone away." The next day it might be, "It's all my fault . . . he called me his princess but I didn't spend any time with him, I was always at Kitty's house. He knew I didn't love him enough, that's why he went and found someone else not much older than me."

Once or twice she asked Ria if they might write a letter to Dad saying how lonely they were without him. "I don't think he knows," Annie wept.

"He knows." Ria was stony.

"If he knows, why doesn't he come back?" Annie asked.

"He will, but only when he's ready. Honestly, Annie, I don't think we can hurry him up." And for once she noticed Annie nodding as if on this rare occasion she agreed with her mother.

Brian had his views as well. "It was probably all my fault, Mam. I didn't really wash enough, I know."

"I don't think that was it, Brian."

"No, it could have been, you know the way Dad was always washing himself and wearing a clean shirt every day and everything?"

"People do that, you know."

"Well, could we tell him that I wash more now? And I will, I promise."

"If Dad left just because you were filthy he'd have left ages ago, you've been filthy for years," Annie said gloomily.

Then Brian decided that his father had left on account of sex. "That's what Myles and Dekko say. They say that he went off to her because she's interested in having sex night and day."

"I don't think that's right," Ria said.

"No, but it might be part of it. Could you telephone him and say you'd be interested in having it night and day too?" He looked a bit embarrassed and awkward to be talking to his mother about such things, but he obviously felt that they had to be said.

"Not really, Brian." Ria was glad that Annie wasn't in the room.

Annie was in the room, however, when Brian came up with his trump card. "Mam, *I* know how to get Dad back," he said.

"This should be interesting," Annie said.

"You and he should have a baby." The silence was deafening. "You could," Brian went on. "And I wouldn't mind, I've talked about it with Myles and Dekko, it's not as bad as you'd think. And we could baby-sit, Myles, Dekko, and myself. It would be a great way of getting pocket money." He looked at his mother's stricken face. "Or listen, Mam, if Dad came back, I'd do it for nothing. No charge at all," he said.

Wouldn't it be wonderful, Ria thought, if she could be miles away from here, not to have to reassure people that she was fine, and that everything was fine, when in fact the whole world was as far from fine as it would ever be? She put off going out because of the people she would meet, yet she knew it was dangerous to hole up on Tara Road and be the reclusive, betrayed wife.

She heard a sound at the hall door and her heart lifted for a moment. Sometimes Danny used to run back during the day. "Missed you, sweetheart, have you a cuddle for a working man?" And she always had. When had it stopped? Why had she not noticed? How could the sound of a leaflet being pushed through a hall door still make her think that he had come back? She must make a big effort today to live in the real world. Like knowing what she was doing and what time it was. She looked at the clock automatically when she heard the Angelus bell ringing. Everyone did that, it was almost as if you were checking whether the church had got it right. At the same time the telephone rang.

It was a woman with an American accent. "I hope you'll forgive me calling a private home, but this was the only listing I could get for a Mr. Danny Lynch, Realtor and Estate Agent. Information didn't have a business listing."

"Yes?" Ria was lackluster.

"Briefly, my name is Marilyn Vine and we were in Ireland fifteen years ago. We met Mr. Danny Lynch and he tried to interest us in some property. . . ."

"Yes, well, do you mind if I give you his office number, he's not here at the moment. . . ."

"Of course, but if I could take one more minute of your time to ask you if this is something he might do. There isn't really any money in it."

"Oh, then I doubt it very much," Ria said.

"I'm sorry?"

"I mean he only cares about the value of this and the price of that nowadays—but then I'm just a little jaundiced today."

"I beg your pardon, did I get you at a bad time?"

"There aren't going to be any good times from now on, but that's neither here nor there. What exactly was it that you wanted Danny to do for charity?"

"It wasn't that, precisely. He was such a pleasant, personable young man that I wondered if he knew anyone who might like to do a house exchange this summer. I can offer a comfortable and I think pleasant home with a swimming pool in Stoneyfield, Connecticut; it's a quiet New England college town. And I was looking for somewhere within walking distance of the city, but with a garden . . ."

"This summer?" Ria asked.

"Yes. July and August. I know it's not much notice . . . but I really felt that I wanted to be there last night. I couldn't sleep and I thought I'd make this call, just in case."

"And why did you think of Danny?" Ria asked in a slow, measured voice.

"He was so knowledgeable and he was my only contact. I felt sure he might put me in touch with someone else if it wasn't his particular scene."

"And would it be a big house or a small house you'd want?" Ria asked.

"I don't really mind. I wouldn't be lonely in a large place and anyone coming here to Stoneyfield would have a house with plenty of room for four or five people. They could have the car too, of course, and there are very attractive places to go."

"And aren't there agencies and things?"

"Yes, of course, and I can go through the Internet . . . it's just that when you actually meet a person all those years ago, and remember a friendly face, it seems a little easier. He wouldn't remember me, us, at all. But it's just at the moment I don't feel like talking to strangers much, negotiating with them. I guess it does sound a little odd."

"No, oddly enough I know exactly how you feel."

"Am I talking to Mrs. Lynch?"

"I don't know."

"I beg your pardon?"

"We are going to get separated, divorced. There's divorce now in Ireland, did you know that?"

"This really was not a good time to ring. I can't tell you how sorry I am."

"No, it was a great time. We'll do it."

"Do what?"

"I'll go to your house, you come to mine, July and August. It's a deal."

"Well, I suppose we should—"

"Of course we should, I'll send you a photo of it and all the details. It's lovely; you'll love it. It's on Tara Road, it's got all kinds of trees in the garden and lovely, polished wooden floors and it's got some old stained-glass windows, and . . . and . . . and . . . the original moldings on the ceilings and . . . and . . ." She was crying now. There was a silence at the other end of the line. Ria pulled herself together. "Please forgive me. Marion, is it?"

"Marilyn. Marilyn Vine."

"I'm Ria Lynch and I can't think of anything I'd like to do more than get away from here and go to a quiet place with a swimming pool and nice drives. I could take my children for one month and the other month I could spend on my own, thinking out my future. That's why I got a bit carried away."

"Your house sounds like just what I want, Ria. Let's do it."

You might not have known from her voice three thousand miles away that she was standing in her kitchen looking out of her white wooden house and tears were running down her face also. When Marilyn Vine at last put down the telephone on her kitchen counter, she went out into her garden with her cup of coffee. She sat by the pool where she had swum earlier. Fifteen laps morning and afternoon; it was as routine now as brushing her teeth. It was ten minutes past seven in the morning. She had just agreed to exchange houses with an extremely agitated woman going through some kind of life crisis. A woman whom she had never met who lived three thousand miles away. A woman who might well not have the right to exchange houses, whose property could be under some kind of legal review pending divorce.

All Marilyn knew was that it was very foolish to make early-morning, spontaneous, spur-of-the-moment decisions. It was so unlike her to make a telephone call like that at this hour of the morning. And even less like her to go along with the plans of the hysterical woman at the other end of the line. She would never do anything remotely like this again. The only question now was whether she should call back and undo it before it was too late. Or should she just write a letter?

She could call immediately, it might be a cleaner break, and say the home exchange was no longer possible from her end, that she had family duties that she could not ignore. Marilyn smiled wryly at the thought of her being someone with family responsibilities. But Ria in Ireland wouldn't know this. It would be easier to write or send an E-mail— anything not to have to hear the disappointment in that voice. But there was no technology on Tara Road and Ria Lynch would not have had access to her husband's office, where presumably such things existed.

She had sounded gutsy and lively as well as slightly unhinged. Marilyn tried to work out how old she was. That good-looking young real estate agent must be about forty now, this woman was probably the same age. She mentioned having a daughter of fourteen and a son who was almost ten. Marilyn's face hardened. So her marriage was ending, but she hated her husband: that much was obvious—she spoke about him so disparagingly to a total stranger. She was going to be much better off without him.

Marilyn would not allow herself to brood. Very soon now she would need to go to work. She would drive up to the college campus and take her place in the parking lot. Then, greeting this person and that, she would walk to her job at the alumni office, cool and self-sufficient in her crisp linen suit.

They would look at her with interest. How strange she hadn't gone to Hawaii with her husband. Greg Vine's visiting lectureship had seemed exactly what the couple needed. But Marilyn had been adamant she would not go, and had been equally resolute in giving no explanation to her colleagues and friends. By now they had stopped inquiring and trying to persuade her. She knew she was an object of interest and speculation. Their interest was genuine but so was their mystification that she would not go to a sunny island with the urging of a loving husband and the support of a caring department at the university that would hold the job open for her until her return.

What would they say if they knew what an extraordinary alternative she had been contemplating? To exchange homes for two months with a woman who owned, or claimed she owned, a four-story Victorian house in Dublin. They would say it was a foolish decision, and she must under no circumstances be allowed to go ahead.

Marilyn finished her coffee, straightened her shoulders, and squared up to what she had done. She was an adult woman, very adult indeed.

She would have her fortieth birthday on August first this summer. She would make whatever decisions she felt like making. Who else was going to tell her what was best for her?

She nodded toward the telephone as if affirming the conversation she had made on it earlier. She looked at her reflection in the hall mirror. Short auburn hair, cut so that she could swim and leave it to dry naturally, anxious green eyes, tense shoulders, but otherwise perfectly normal. Not at all the kind of person who would have decided something totally unbalanced.

Marilyn picked up her keys and drove to work.

Ria sat down and held on to the table very tightly. Not since she was a teenager had she been abroad alone. And with Danny very few times. Well, at least she had a passport and a few weeks to get everything organized at this end.

Marilyn had said she was perfectly happy to feed Annie's cat. The children would love a trip to America, a house with a swimming pool. Marilyn said it was easy to learn to drive on the wrong side of the road because the place was so quiet. Ria had warned Marilyn against any such foolhardy courage in Dublin, which was filled with traffic hazards and mad drivers.

Marilyn had said she would prefer to walk anyway.

From force of habit, Ria got a piece of paper, wrote the word *List,* and underlined it. As she began to write down what she had to do, her chest tightened. Was she totally mad? She knew nothing about this woman. Nothing at all except they had both cried on the telephone. When you paused to think about it, wasn't it very odd that she should approach the business of exchanging her house this way? There were agencies, firms specializing in such things. There was the whole Internet waiting for the opportunity to match people together, find them the ideal house swap.

What kind of a person would remember Danny's handsome face from years ago and try to track him down? Perhaps she had fancied him all that time ago; he was a striking-looking man after all. Maybe she had in fact been closer to him than she was saying; it might have been a fling, a whirl or whatever. This whole idea of taking his house could be a ploy, a ruse to get involved in his life.

Ria had seen so many movies where mad people sounded totally plausible, where innocent, trusting folk admitted them willingly into their lives. These could be the first hours of a nightmare that could wreck them. She must try and be rational about all this and work out what she wanted. Why did it seem such a good idea? Was it only so that she wouldn't have to look at Hilary, her mother, Rosemary, Frances, and Gertie and see the sympathy in their eyes? Was there any other reason that was taking her across the Atlantic Ocean?

I might half-forget him out there, Ria told herself. I might actually not see his face everywhere I look. Suppose she was sleeping in a strange bed in America, she might not wake up at four o'clock frightened, thinking he was very late, could he have been in a car crash, and then the even more sickening realization that he was not coming back at all. America might cure that.

And the awful belief that there may have been other Bernadettes. People always said that the man doesn't leave on the first affair. There could have been other people entertained in this house who had even slept with her husband. How great to go to a place where nobody had met Danny nor heard of him, and certainly not slept with him.

But still it was a very sudden decision to have made. Promising a total stranger that she could live here on Tara Road. In normal times she would not have done anything so wildly lacking in caution. But these were not normal times, they were times when two months in America might actually be what she needed. And it was idiotic really to think that this woman Marilyn might be a serial killer.

Ria remembered that Marilyn had not wanted this house, she had wanted a lot of other houses, and it was Ria who had pushed Tara Road. Marilyn had sounded apologetic and had tried several times to end the conversation, it was Ria who had made all the running. Marilyn had said she would send photographs and banker references, and Ria would do the same. Of course she was above board and normal. She wanted to escape and have time to get her head together; that was American-speak for exactly what Ria wanted to do. It wasn't *so* outrageous a coincidence that two people with identical needs should meet accidentally at the right time.

Why do I want it so much? Ria asked herself. When I got up this morning I hadn't a notion of going to a house in New England for the summer. Is it for the children, so that I'll be able to offer them something the equivalent of their father's trip on the Shannon? Is it that I want to be somewhere where Danny Lynch isn't the center of the world and we are all waiting for what he will do next so that we can react?

She felt the answer was a mixture of all these things, but she still wasn't sure that she had the strength to go ahead with it. Should she talk to Rosemary about it? Rosemary was so clearheaded, she cut straight to the chase on everything.

But Ria firmed up her shoulders. She *was* a strong person, despite a lot of evidence to the contrary. She would not allow circumstances to turn her into one of those dithering women she despised so much when she served them at the charity shop. The ones who couldn't make up their minds between a blue tablecloth and a yellow one; they'd have to talk to a husband, a daughter, a neighbor about it all before they came back and paid three whole pounds.

She liked the sound of Marilyn; this woman was not a psychotic, deranged killer coming over to waste the neighborhood of Tara Road. She was someone who had appeared just when she was needed. With bleak determination Ria applied herself to the list.

The meal with Annie and Brian was not going well.

Danny had taken them to Quentin's, which he thought would be a treat for them, but was turning out to be a great mistake. For one thing they weren't dressed properly. Any other young people having an early dinner there with parents and grandparents were elegantly turned out. Brian wore scruffy jeans and a very grubby T-shirt. His zipped jacket had a lot of writing on it, the names of footballers and dead pop stars; he looked very like a young runaway who might have been harassing tourists on Grafton Street. Annie was also in jeans, far too tight in Danny's opinion. Her blond hair was not washed and shiny, it was greasy and pushed behind her ears. She wore an old, sequined jacket to which she was inordinately attached. It belonged to some old lady in St. Rita's and was described as a genuine fifties garment if you commented on it at all.

"Would you look at the prices!" Brian said, astounded. "*Look* what they charge for steak and kidney pie. Mam makes that for free at home."

"Not for free, you eejit," Annie said. "She has to buy the steak and the kidney and the flour and the butter for the pastry."

"But that's all there already," Brian protested.

"No, it's not. It doesn't grow in the kitchen, you fool. That's so typical of a man. She has to go out and pay for it in the shops and then there's the cost of her labor; that *has* to be taken into consideration."

Danny saw that in a way Annie was trying to justify the cost of the expensive meal that he was treating them to, but as a conversation it was going nowhere. "Right, now do we see anything we like?" He looked from one of them to the other hopefully.

"What are porcini, is it roast pork?" Brian asked.

"No, it's mushrooms," his father explained.

"Eejit," Annie said again, even though she hadn't known either.

"I might have a hamburger but I don't see it on the menu," Brian said.

Danny hid his annoyance. "Look here, they say ground beef served with a tomato and basil salsa, that's more or less it," he pointed it out.

"Why don't they *call* it a burger, like normal places?" Brian grumbled.

"They expect people to be able to read and understand things," Annie said dismissively. "Do they have vegetarian things, Dad?"

Eventually they made their choices and Brenda Brennan, the suave manager, came and took their order personally.

"Pleasure to see you with your family, Mr. Lynch," she said, showing not an iota of displeasure at the fact that the children were dressed like tramps.

Danny smiled his gratitude.

"Is that her?" Brian whispered when Brenda Brennan had gone.

"Who?" Danny was genuinely bewildered.

"The one, the one who's going to have the baby, the one that you're going to live with?"

"Don't be *ridiculous,* Brian." Annie's patience was now exhausted. "She's as old as Mam, for God's sake. Of course she's not the one."

Danny felt the time had come to reclaim the purpose of the evening. "Your mother and I have had a very good conversation today, very good. We had none of those silly fights that have been so upsetting for us and indeed especially for you."

"Well, that makes a change," Annie grumbled.

"Yes, it *does* make a change, these have been a bad couple of days for us all, but now we're all able to talk again."

"Are you coming back?" Brian asked hopefully.

"Brian, this is what your mother and I were talking about. It's a question of what words we use. I've not gone away, I haven't left you two, of course I haven't. I'm going to be living in a different place, that's all."

"What kind of place?" Annie asked.

"Well it's only a flat at the moment, but it will be a house very soon and you'll come to stay there as often as you like. It's got a lovely garden, and it will be your home too."

"We've got a lovely garden on Tara Road," Annie said.

"Yes, well now you'll have two." He beamed with pleasure at the thought of it.

They looked at him doubtfully.

"Will we each have our own room?" Annie asked.

"Yes, of course. Not quite immediately, not the day we move in, but there'll be alterations done. Mr. McCarthy's people will divide a room for you. In the meantime when you come to stay one of you can sleep on the sofa in the sitting room."

"Doesn't sound much like a second home to me, sleeping on the sofa," Annie said.

"No, well, it's only temporary and then it will be sorted out." He kept his smile bright.

"And how many days will we stay there, in the house with the divided room?" Brian asked.

"As many as you like. Your mother and I talked about that very thing today. You'll be delighted when you go home and discuss it with her, we both agree that you are the important people in all this. . . ."

Annie cut across his speech. "And could one of us stay in one place, and one in the other? I mean I don't have to be joined at the hip to Brian or anything?"

"No, of course not."

Annie looked pleased by this.

"And when the baby comes if it's crying and annoying us, can we go back to Tara Road?" Brian asked.

"Yes of course."

"Well, that's all right then." Brian seemed satisfied.

"And will she be like Mam and saying keep your room tidy and you can't come in at this hour."

"Bernadette will make you very welcome. She's so looking forward to meeting you. When will we arrange that, do you think?"

"You didn't say if she'd be making rules and regulations," Annie persisted.

"You'll be as courteous and helpful in this new house as you are on Tara Road. That's all that's expected of you."

"But we're *not* helpful on Tara Road," Brian said, as if this was something his father had misunderstood.

Danny sighed. "Suppose we decide a time and place to meet Bernadette?"

"Does she have a big bump? Does she look very pregnant?" Annie wanted to know.

"Not particularly. Why do you ask?"

Annie shrugged. "Does it make any difference where we meet?" Danny felt a tic of impatience; this was much harder than he had expected it would be. "Do we have to meet her?" Annie asked. "Wouldn't it be better to wait until the baby's born and everything, get all that out of the way?"

"Of course you'll meet her," Danny cried. "We're all going away on a boat on the Shannon for a holiday, all of us. We want to meet together long before that."

They looked at him, dumbfounded.

"The Shannon?" Annie said.

"All of us?" Brian asked.

"Can Kitty come too?" Annie put in quickly. "And don't even think of asking about Myles and Dekko, Brian, don't think of it."

"I don't honestly think Mam would like a holiday with . . . you know, *her* coming too," Brian said slowly.

Annie and her father exchanged glances. It was the one moment of solidarity in a nightmare meal. At least his daughter understood some of the problems ahead. Annie said nothing about Brian being brain-dead. Instead they both began to explain to the boy who was, after all only nine years of age, that his mother would not be coming with them on this long planned, much-discussed holiday.

In Marilyn's office there was much talk of the annual alumni picnic in August. They had to get a list of accommodation addresses ready. Hotels, guest houses, dormitories, private homes where the past students could stay. Many of them looked forward to this weekend as the high spot of the year. It was a highly successful fund-raiser for the college and maintained close contacts between present and past.

It had always been a tradition that those who worked in the alumni office would offer hospitality in their own homes. Marilyn and Greg had hosted many a family at 1024 Tudor Drive. Pleasant people all of them. They had always been delighted with the pool in the hot August weather and many had kept in touch over the years. The Vines had invitations in return to stay in Boston, New York City, and Washington, D.C., any time they liked.

The plans for the picnic were under way, the wording of the appeal in the first notifications, the details of tax deductions in any gift made to an alumni library and arts center. They would have to debate the nature of the entertainment, the number of people allowed to address the gathering, the need to keep the speeches short. Soon work would be apportioned. Marilyn knew she must speak before then. She would not accept any tasks and projects that she would be unable to carry through.

She cleared her throat and addressed the professor of education, who was running the meeting. "I must explain that I will not be here during the months of July and August. I have accepted the leave of absence the college so kindly offered to me. I leave at the end of June and will be back after Labor Day, so may I ask you to give me a full load of work now, since I won't be here for the event itself?"

A group of faces looked up smiling. This was good news. The taut, tense Marilyn Vine was finally giving in. At last she was going to join Greg her bewildered husband in Hawaii.

Almost two months before she left. That would give Ria plenty of time. And she wouldn't tell anybody anything until she was ready. The list had been invaluable. She couldn't understand why Danny had laughed at her, ruffled her hair, and said she was a funny little thing. It was what people *did,* for heaven's sake. All right, if they were at work or in an office they used computers, personal organizers, Filofaxes. But basically the process was the same. You wrote down what had to be done, and you clutched it to you. That way you didn't forget anything.

It would take a week at least before she got the documents from Marilyn. She didn't want to spring this on everyone without evidence that this was a good idea. She had prepared a little dossier of her own, which she would send off today or tomorrow. She had photographs of the house both inside and out and cuttings from the *Irish Times* newspaper's property section showing the kind of place that Tara Road was. She put in a map of Dublin, an up-to-date tourist guide to the city, a restaurant guide, a list of books Marilyn might like to read before she came. She gave the address of her bank, the name, telephone number, and fax of their bank manager. Also a terse and unemotional note to say that the house was owned jointly by her and Danny; its ownership was not in dispute. He would look after the children for the month of July and later she would send a list of friends and contacts who would be of help to Marilyn when she arrived.

Perhaps a week was too optimistic; she might have to keep her secret for a little longer than she had hoped. She imagined that the whole business could even take as long as ten days. But Ria had reckoned without knowing how fast things moved along in the United States. A FedEx van turned up the very next day at her house with all of Marilyn's details. Hardly daring to breathe she looked at the pictures of the swimming pool, the low white house with the flowers on the porch, the map of the area, the local newspaper, and the details of the car, shopping facilities, and membership in a recreation center and club that could be transferred to Ria while she was in residence. There were golf, tennis, and bowling nearby, and Marilyn also said she would give her a list of telephone numbers for any emergency that might occur.

In a note as terse and unemotional as Ria's own letter, Marilyn explained that she needed some space to think out her future. She had not joined her husband on a short sabbatical in Hawaii because there were still matters she had to think through. With her bank details she also added that she had not yet told her husband about the exchange but that there would be no problem and she would confirm this within twenty-four hours. She didn't want to call him and tell him it had been organized just like that. Some things need a little diplomacy, as she was sure Ria would understand.

Ria understood. She still had to tell Danny. Did they all know in his office, she wondered, as she rang and asked to be put through to him? It was very, very hard to dial the office now. As Danny's wife she had had some kind of automatic status in their eyes; now what had she? It was easy to read sympathy, scorn, or embarrassment into the voice of the receptionist. Perhaps it was none of these things.

"Can you come around and collect your things soon, Danny? I want to try to organize the place a bit."

"There's no huge hurry, is there?"

"No, not from my point of view, but for the children . . . they really should get used to knowing that your things are where you stay."

"Well, as I said, the flat's a bit small at the moment."

"But didn't you say Barney was organizing you a new house?"

"Finding us one I said, not buying one, Ria."

"Sure I know that, but doesn't it exist?"

"It's not in great shape yet."

"But it's probably in good enough shape to hold your golf clubs, your books, the rest of your clothes . . . you know, the music center, that's yours."

"No, sweet . . . no it's not *mine,* it's ours. We're not down to dividing things up item by item."

"We have to sometime."

"But not . . . no, not this minute."

"Come today if you can, with the car. And there are a few other things

I want to talk to you about anyway. Come before the children get back, won't you?"

"But I'd like to see them."

"Sure, and you can anytime, but it's not a good idea to see them here."

"Ria, don't start laying down rules."

"But we agreed not to confuse them; they're to be equally welcome in each home. I'm not going to be over in your place when they visit you, and it makes sense for you not to be in my place."

There was a silence.

"It's a bit different."

"No, it's not, there'll be no sign of me or all my makeup and clothes and sewing machine dotted around in Bernadette's house, so why should all your things be here?"

"I'll come over," Danny said.

Heidi Franks could hardly wait for the alumni picnic meeting to be over so that she could talk to Marilyn. She was overjoyed to know that the woman had finally seen sense. She would offer to go and keep an eye on her garden for her. She knew it was Marilyn's pride and joy and that the neighbors didn't have green thumbs. But this decision had been long in the making. Heidi would not rush in with cries of delight; she would take it as casually as Marilyn herself. That announcement at the meeting had been very deliberately cool and unfussy, even in an environment where she knew they were all very interested and concerned about her plans.

"I'll be happy to drop in and adjust the sprinklers for you," she said as soon as they had a moment to talk.

"You're too good, Heidi, but truly they are totally automatic; they work themselves."

"Well, just to make sure that there are no little bugs or aphids attacking all your lovely beds."

"No, actually there'll be someone there, that's why I couldn't offer any accommodation for the picnic."

"Really, someone to house-sit? That's a good idea. Who's going to do it?"

"Oh, you wouldn't know her, she's from Ireland—Ria Lynch."

"Ireland?" Heidi said.

"I know. I think she'll find it very different here. I must rush, Heidi, I have to hand this stuff in. I'll talk to you later and tell you all about it." She had left the office.

Heidi smiled fondly after her. Greg would be so pleased. He had been distraught when Marilyn wouldn't accompany him. He had moved heaven and earth to get the position and the professorial exchange; once it had been achieved he couldn't go back on it. Now Marilyn was going to join him at last.

Ria had never used a courier service before. It was surprisingly easy; they just came around and took the package. How foolish she had been, thinking that people used ordinary mail anymore when things were important. She had a lot to learn. But maybe this summer would teach her quite a few of them.

She saw Colm in the garden being watched through sleepy eyes by Clement, the cat that he had given to Annie when it was a little kitten. He worked so hard and was always so even-tempered and pleasant. She yearned to invite him in for coffee and tell him her plans.

But she couldn't, not until she had spoken to Danny. Danny, who was going to go through the roof when he heard how she intended to spend the summer. Danny, who had obviously had a disastrous evening with the children at Quentin's . . . what a stupid place to have taken them in the first place. They hadn't told her it was bad but they didn't have to, it was written all over their faces.

Heidi picked up the telephone on Marilyn's desk.

"Good afternoon, Marilyn Vine's phone, Heidi Franks speaking . . . Oh, Greg, nice to talk with you, no, you've just missed her. She'll be back in ten minutes. Can I take a message? Sure, sure. I'll tell her. Oh, and Greg we're all thrilled she's going out to you. It's a great decision. Today. At the meeting. Yes, for July and August. No? You don't? Could it be a surprise or anything? Oh, I'm really so sorry I spoke. No, I don't *think* I got it wrong, Greg. She says there's an Irish woman coming to house-sit up on Tudor Drive while she's out with you. Listen, better let her talk to you about it. I know, Greg. Things *do* get confused." Heidi replaced the receiver slowly and turned around.

At the door stood Marilyn listening with a white face. *Why* had she told the faculty before she had told Greg? She was such a fool. It was partly because of the time difference between here and Hawaii, partly because she had been considering what to say. Now things would be worse than ever.

Danny didn't even lift the envelope of pictures, brochure, and maps. He just looked at Ria astounded.

"This is *not* going to happen. Believe me, this is so mad that I can't even take it in."

Ria was calm. On her list she had written: Don't plead, don't beg. It was working, she was doing neither.

"It's only going to cost our fares, and I've been to the travel agency. They're not crippling."

"And what exactly would you call crippling, might I ask?" he said with a sneer in his voice.

"The price of a meal at Quentin's for two children who only wanted a burger and a pizza," she said.

"Aha, I *knew* something like this would come up, I *knew* it," he said triumphantly.

"Good, it's nice to be proved right," Ria said.

"I beg of you, don't get all silly and smug on me. We're trying, God damn it, we're trying for the kids' sake not to make them into footballs. You sounded fine on the phone. Why have you changed?"

"I'm still fine. I haven't changed. I *am* thinking of the children. You're going to be able to hire a lovely cruiser on the Shannon for them; I don't have the money for that. In fact I don't know *what* money I'll have so I've arranged a grand holiday for them in a place with a lovely pool. *Look* at it, Danny, at no cost except the fare. We'll just go out to the grocery and I'll cook there instead of here. I thought you'd be pleased."

"*Pleased?* You thought I'd be pleased to let a madwoman that none of us knows into my house. . . ."

"Our house . . ."

"It's not on, Ria, believe me."

"We've arranged it."

"Then unarrange it."

"Will you explain to the children that there'll be no holiday for them with me, no chance to see the United States? Will you look after them for two months instead of one? Well, *will* you, Danny? That's what this is about."

"No, it's not about this, it's about you putting a gun to my head, that what it's about."

"I am *not* doing that, I am trying my very best to pick up all the pieces that *you* broke. I was perfectly happy to go on here forever and ever. You weren't. *That's* what it's all about." She was as flushed as he was.

His voice was calmer now, and she noticed that he wasn't calling her "sweetheart" anymore. That much had sunk in anyway. "We don't know anything about this person, Ria, even suppose for a moment that I thought it was a good idea. Running away is never a good idea." She looked at him quizzically, her head on one side. "I didn't run away, I made a decision about life and I told you openly and honestly," he blustered slightly.

"Yes, I forgot. Of course you did." She was totally calm now.

"So now will you agree that maybe *some* year we could talk about your doing this, you know, organizing a house exchange to the States? It's a big market actually, and safer than time share. Barney was only talking—"

"I'm going on July first, she's coming that day. The children can come out to me on August first. I've checked the flights, there are seats available, but we need to book soon." Her voice was very steady and she seemed very sure of what she saying.

Danny reached out and unwillingly dragged Marilyn Vine's envelope to him to look at the contents. That was the moment when Ria knew she had won and that the trip was on.

Marilyn sent a very short E-mail to Greg at the university in Hawaii.

> *Very much regret not getting in touch about my summer plans.*
> *Please call me at home tonight at any time that suits you and*
> *I will explain everything.*
>
> > *Again many regrets,*
> > *Marilyn.*

He called at eight p.m. She was waiting and answered immediately.

"It must be about two o'clock in the afternoon there," Marilyn said.

"Marilyn, I didn't call to discuss the different time zones. What's happening?"

"I'm truly very sorry and Heidi is distraught over it all as you can imagine. Another hour and I would have E-mailed you asking you to call."

"Well, I'm calling now."

"I want to get away from here. I find it very stifling."

"I know, so did I. That's why I arranged for us to come here." His voice was uncomprehending. He had been so sure she would go to Hawaii with him, so devastated when she had said she wasn't able to face it.

"We've been through all that before, Greg."

"We have most certainly *not* been through it, as you say. I am sitting out here five thousand miles away without any understanding of why you are not here with me."

"Please, Greg?"

"No, you can't just say 'Please, Greg' and expect me to understand, to be somehow inspired. And what *are* your summer plans as you call them? Am I going to be told about them or must I wait for more conflicting messages from half the faculty to tell me that you're joining me here or not?"

"I can't apologize enough for that."

"Where are you going, Marilyn?" His voice was cold now.

"I'm going to Ireland on July first."

"*Ireland?*" he said.

She could see his face, lined and suntanned, and his glasses pushed up on his forehead, his hair beginning to thin a little in the front. He would be wearing a pair of faded chinos and maybe one of those very bright primary color shirts that looked just fine in the glare and heat of the islands but looked overdone and touristy anywhere else.

"We were there years ago together. Do you remember?"

"Of course I remember, we were on a conference for three days and then three days touring the west, where it rained all the time."

"I'm not going for the weather, I'm going for some peace."

"Marilyn, it's very dangerous in your state of mind to go and bury yourself in some cabin on the side of a mountain there."

"No I'm not doing that. It's a big suburban house actually, in a classy part of Dublin, an old Victorian building. It looks lovely, four stories altogether and there's a big garden. I'll be very happy there."

"You can't be serious."

"But I am. I've arranged an exchange with the woman who owns it, she's coming here to Tudor Drive."

"You're giving our house to a total stranger?"

"I've told her that you may possibly come back, that it's not likely but that work may bring you back, she realizes that."

"Oh, very generous of her, and will her husband be coming back from time to time to visit you, possibly?"

"No, they're separated."

"Like us, I suppose," he said. "For all the phrases we wrap it up in, we are separated, aren't we, Marilyn?" He sounded very bleak.

"Not in my mind, we're not. We are just spending some time apart this year; we've been through that a hundred times. Do you want to hear about Ria?"

"Who?"

"Ria Lynch, the woman who's coming."

"No, I don't." Greg hung up.

Heidi Franks was so upset at having opened her mouth to Greg Vine in Hawaii that she had to go to the rest room and weep at her own stupidity. She had obviously created a very awkward situation. And yet how was she meant to have been inspired that the husband knew nothing of the wife's plans?

They were an immensely compatible couple, and nobody thought for a moment that this temporary separation while Greg was in Hawaii meant any rift in the marriage. For one thing, he called and sent E-mails regularly, and also sent postcards to various faculty members, always reporting some little bit of news he had learned from Marilyn. So how could *anyone* be blamed for assuming that Greg knew his wife's plans?

Still, it was very upsetting, and that gray drained look on Marilyn's face as she realized that Heidi had been blabbing away on the telephone would be hard to forget. Heidi dabbed her eyes; her face looked blotchy and dry. Her hair was a mess. Oh, how she wished that Marilyn were the kind of person that she could apologize to properly. And maybe they might even both be a bit tearful together. Then Marilyn would tell her what it was all about, swear her to secrecy over whatever it was that was happening, and Heidi would be totally diplomatic. Because the maddening thing was that normally she actually *was* discreet. But this would not happen. Marilyn was stoic and unbending. Nonsense, she had said. Please don't mention it, it was a matter of timing. Then the subject had been closed.

Heidi felt wretched. Tonight there was a cocktail party to say farewell to a lecturer in the math department. Henry had said he would like her to go. These were occasions when the older wives always dressed up to kill. Heidi looked once more with displeasure at her flaking skin and bird's-nest hair. It would take more than cold eye pads to restore those sad red eyes to anything approaching elegance. She made a sudden and rare decision to take the afternoon off and go to Carlotta's Beauty Salon. Carlotta, who specialized in "Treatments for the Maturer Skin," would look after her.

It was wonderful to lie back and let Carlotta get on with the repair job. Heidi felt herself relaxing and feeling better by the moment. Carlotta, with her big dark eyes, was both attractive and motherly-looking at the same time. She was immaculately groomed, a perfect advertisement for her own salon. She had come to live in Stoneyfield from California over ten years ago and opened a very smart and successful salon, employing six local women.

She had been married, it was rumored, at least three times in her youth. No children spoken of. There was no husband around at the present time. But everyone knew that if Carlotta wanted one, one would appear. One might even detach himself from where he was already meant to be secured. She was a very exotic, charming, not to mention financially secure woman. Whichever side of forty she was, and this was often debated in Stoneyfield, Carlotta would have few problems in finding husband number four when she set out to look for him.

She suggested an herbal facial for Heidi, and a scalp massage. Nothing too rushed, nothing too expensive. Heidi vowed that she would come to this restful place regularly. She owed it to herself. Henry had his golf; it was only fair that she should have something relaxing also. As the firm, capable hands massaged her throat and neck, Heidi began to forget the sad, strained face of Marilyn Vine, who had planned to take two months off traveling somewhere without informing her husband.

"How is Marilyn getting along these days?" Carlotta asked unexpectedly.

Carlotta lived next door to the Vines. Heidi had totally forgotten. But she was not going to be caught twice in one day. This time she would say absolutely nothing about Marilyn's plan and intentions. "I do see her from time to time in the office, but I don't really know how she's getting along. She keeps very much to herself. You know her much better than I do, Carlotta, living so near and everything. Do you see much of her?"

Carlotta spoke easily about everyone but she never actually gave out any detailed information. She spoke in warm generalities. They were wonderful neighbors, she said. You couldn't live beside better people than the Vines. And they kept their property so well. Everyone else on Tudor Drive had begun to smarten themselves up since Marilyn got going. She just loved those trees and flowers.

"Does she come to the salon?" Heidi asked.

"No, she's not really into skin care."

"Still, this would be such a treat for her," Heidi said.

"I'm glad you feel it relaxing." Carlotta was pleased. "But anyway, even if I were thinking about it, this isn't the time with her trip and everything."

"Her trip?"

"Didn't she tell you? She's going to Ireland for two months, exchanging homes with a friend of hers there or something."

"*When* did she tell you this?"

"This morning, when we were putting out the trash. She had just fixed it up, she seemed very pleased. Longest conversation I've had with her for a long time."

"Ireland . . ." Heidi said thoughtfully. "What on earth is taking her all the way to Ireland?"

"America!" said Rosemary. "I don't believe it."

"I hardly believe it myself," Ria admitted.

"And what does everyone say?" Rosemary wanted to know.

"You mean what does Danny say?"

"Yes, I suppose I do, to be honest."

"Well, he's horrified, of course. But mainly I think because of having the children for a month, that doesn't suit the little love nest at all."

"So what's he going to do?"

"Well, *he* is going to have to work that out. I'll be at Kennedy Airport to meet them on August first. July is *his* business." She sounded much stronger, more resourceful somehow.

Rosemary looked at her with admiration. "You really have thought this through, haven't you? You'll have the whole place sussed out by the time the children get there, you'll know where to take them, how to entertain them and everything. You'll really *need* a month to get it together."

"I need the month to get myself together. This month is for me, they'll find plenty to do when they get there. Here, let me show you pictures of the house."

Rosemary was as fascinated with the change in her friend as she was with pictures of a beautiful garden and a swimming pool in a small college town in Connecticut. It might be just false energy but Ria certainly looked as if she had some life in her. Up to now she had been like somebody sleepwalking.

"I'm not going," Annie said.

"Fine," her mother replied.

This startled Annie. She had expected that she would be persuaded and coaxed. Things were certainly changing round here.

Brian was looking at the photographs. "Look, they have a basket beside their garage, I wonder, do they have a ball or should we bring one?"

"Of course they have a ball," Annie said loftily.

"Look at the pool, it's like something in a hotel."

Annie reached for the picture again. But her face was still mutinous. "It's ridiculous, us going out there," she said.

Ria said nothing in reply, she just continued to set the table for breakfast. She had moved the big chair with the carved arms where Danny used to sit. Not a big public statement, she had just put it in a corner with a pile of magazines and newspapers on it. She always sat at different parts of the table herself trying to vary things, trying not to leave the yawning gap where the children's father used to sit.

It was surprising how she still expected him to come in the door saying: "Sweetheart, did I have one awful day, it's good to be home." Had he said that on the days when he had been making love to Bernadette? The thought made her shiver sometimes. How little she had known him and what he wanted in life. Ria found it almost impossible to concentrate on the trip to America at times, there was so much buzzing around in her head. Those times he had been working late, she had been so understanding and planned food that wouldn't be dried up when he came back. All those nights when he fell asleep exhausted in the big chair, perhaps it was exhaustion from making love to a young girl. Weeks of waking with a shock at four a.m. in her empty bed and trying to remember the last time they had made love there, and what he thought as he was planning to leave her and live in another home.

If she lived on her own, Ria knew that she would almost certainly be quite mad by now. It was having to put on a face for the children that kept some hold of her sanity. She looked at them as they sat at the table, Brian looking at the pictures of a big basketball net fixed to a wall and the swimming pool with its tiled surrounds, Annie pushing the cuttings and pictures around sulkily. A wave of pity for them came over her. These were children who were having to face an entirely different summer than the one they had a right to expect. Ria would be very gentle with them.

She answered Annie thoughtfully. "Yes, I know it sounds ridiculous to go there, but it has a lot going for it as well. It would be a new experience for us all to see America and with no hotel bills to pay. And then, of course, there would be someone who would come here and mind this house for us all, that's important."

"But who is she?" Annie groused.

"It's all there in the letter, love. I left it for you to read."

"It doesn't *tell* us anything," Annie said.

And in a way she was right. It didn't tell all that much. It didn't say why Marilyn wanted to leave this paradise and come to Dublin, and whether her husband would come too. It didn't speak of any friends or relations in Stoneyfield, nothing about a circle of people she knew, just an emergency list of locksmiths, plumbers, electricians, and gardeners.

Ria's list had been much more people-oriented. But nothing would please Annie anyway so this wasn't relevant. She was shuffling the papers around on the kitchen table, her face discontented.

"Has Dad fixed up the date of the Shannon trip?" Ria asked them.

They looked at each other guiltily as if there was something to hide.

"He says the boats are all booked," Brian said.

"Ah, surely not?"

"That's what he *says,*" Annie said.

"Well, there must have been great demand for them then," Ria said, pretending not to notice the disbelief.

"But he may be making it up," Brian said.

"No, Brian, of course he wouldn't make it up, he's dying for a trip on the Shannon."

"Yeah, but *she* wasn't," Annie said.

"We don't know that now." Ria struggled to be fair.

"We do actually, Mam."

"Did she tell you to your faces?"

"No, we haven't met her yet," Brian said.

"Well, then . . ."

"We're meeting her today," Annie said. "After school."

"That's good," Ria said emptily.

"Why is it good?" Annie would fight with her shadow today.

"It's good because if you're going to be spending July with her, then the sooner you meet Bernadette the better. So that you'll get to know her."

"I don't want to know her," Annie said.

"Neither do I." Brian was in a rare agreement with his sister.

"Where are you all meeting?"

"Her flat, well, their flat," Annie said. "For tea, apparently." She made it sound like the most unusual and bizarre thing to offer in the afternoon.

Part of Ria was pleased to see the resentment against the woman who had taken their father away. Yet another part of her knew that the only hope of peace ahead was if the children were cooperative. "You know it would be nice if . . ." she began. She had been about to say that they should take a little potted plant or a small gift. It would break the ice and please Danny as well. But then she stopped herself. This was ridiculous. She would *not* make smooth the path of the meeting between her children and their father's pregnant mistress. Let Danny do it whatever way he wanted to.

"What would be nice?" Annie sensed a change of heart.

"If all this hadn't happened I suppose, but it has so we have to cope as best we can." She was brisk.

She scooped up all the contents of Marilyn's envelope.

"Are you putting those away?" Annie asked.

"Yes, Brian's seen them, you're not coming with us so I'll just keep them with my things. Okay?"

"What will I do while you're there?"

"I don't know, Annie. Stay with Dad and Bernadette, I suppose. You'll work it out." She knew it was unfair, but she just wasn't going to go down the road of pleading and begging.

Annie would go to Stoneyfield when the time came, they all knew that.

Bernadette lived in Bantry Court, the apartment block that Barney had developed about five years back. Danny had sold many of them. Perhaps this was how he had met Bernadette. Ria had never asked. There were so many questions she had not asked. Such as what she looked like. What they talked about. What she cooked for him. If she held him and stroked his forehead when he woke with a nightmare and his heart racing.

She had coped by pushing these things out of her mind. But today her daughter and son were going to this woman's apartment for tea. Somehow it was important that she had to see Bernadette first. Before Annie and Brian did.

As soon as they left for school Ria got into her car and drove there. She noticed that it took fifteen minutes. On the many nights when he came home so late, Danny must have driven this route. Had he hated coming back to Tara Road all that time or was he happy to keep both lives going? If this girl had not become pregnant would it have just gone along like that forever? Bantry Court, Tara Road, two different compartments of his life?

She parked in the forecourt and looked up at the windows. Behind one of those sat Bernadette, who was going to entertain Danny's children to tea this afternoon and get to know them, tell them about the new half sister or brother who would be born. Would she call Danny darling or even sweetheart? Would she upset them by putting her hand on his arm?

They weren't going to like her no matter what she did. There was no way she could get it right. Annie and Brian wanted what they could never have because Bernadette existed. They wanted things to be the way they were.

Her name was Bernadette Dunne. That much Ria did know. The children had told her. The name was stuck there at the back of her mind. Like a weight, a very heavy object.

Ria went to the list of bells. There it was. Dunne, No. 12, top floor. Would she press it? What would she say? Suppose Bernadette let her in, which she very probably would not, what on earth would Ria say? She realized that she hadn't thought it out at all, she had come here purely on instinct.

So she paused and moved back a little and while she did a woman came along and went up to the row of bells. She pressed No. 12.

A voice answered. "Halloo!" A thin young voice.

"Ber, it's Mummy," the woman said.

"Oh, good." She must have pressed a buzzer because the door snapped open.

Ria shrank back.

"Are you coming in?" The woman was pleasant and a little puzzled at Ria dithering and hovering there.

"What? Oh, no, no. I've changed my mind. Thank you." Ria turned to go back to her car but first she looked hard at Danny's new mother-in-law. Small and quite smart, wearing a beige suit and a white blouse, and carrying a large brown leather handbag. She had short, well-cut brown hair, and copper-colored high-heeled shoes. She looked somewhere between forty and forty-five. Not much older than Ria and Danny. And she was Bernadette's mother.

Ria sat in the car. It had been very foolish to come here and upset herself. Now she was too shaky to drive. She would have to sit in this parking lot until she felt calm enough to move. What had possessed her to come and realize that Mrs. Dunne visiting her pregnant daughter was of their generation, not an older woman like her own mother or Danny's mother?

How did Danny rationalize this to himself? Or was he so besotted that he didn't even notice? She had not got very far along this road of thought when she saw the woman coming out the big glass doors of Bantry Court. This time she was with her daughter. Ria strained forward to see. The girl had long straight hair, shiny and soft like an advertisement for shampoo. Ria felt her own hand go automatically to her frizzy curls.

She had a pale, heart-shaped face, and dark eyes. It was the kind of face you might see on the front of a CD of some folk singer. It was a soulful face. She wore a long black velvet sweater, a short pink skirt, and childish black shoes with pink laces in them. Ria knew that Bernadette Dunne was twenty-two going on twenty-three and that she was a music teacher. She looked about seventeen and being marched to school by her mother who found her playing truant. They got into the smart new Toyota Starlet and Bernadette's mother backed expertly out.

Ria found her strength and her car key, and followed them as they drove out of Bantry Court. She simply had to know where they were going, nothing else mattered. The two cars went slowly in the morning traffic through the crowded street, and then the one in front gave a signal and stopped. Bernadette leaped out and waved as her mother went to find a parking place. She didn't look remotely pregnant yet, but possibly the big floppy sweater hid that. Ria noticed where she was going. A big, well-known delicacies shop. She was buying the supper for her stepchildren. She was going to make a spread for Annie and Brian Lynch tonight.

Ria ached to park her car on the footpath, leaving its hazard lights on, and run into the shop. Then she would point out the vegetarian pâté that Annie would like, the little chorizo sausage that was Brian's current favorite, and nice, runny Brie with bran biscuits for Danny. Or else she could just stand there and get drawn into conversation with this girl, as people do in shops.

But it was dangerous. Possibly Bernadette had seen a picture of Ria and knew what she looked like. And anyway her mother would be back shortly to help and advise about the purchases. She would recognize Ria as the dithering woman outside Bantry Court. What kind of a mother was she anyway, encouraging her daughter in breaking up another man's family, having the baby of a married man? Some help and example she must have been to Bernadette if this is the way things turned out.

But then Ria realized that it could not have been what that woman wanted for her daughter either. Possibly she had been horrified by it all as Ria would be horrified if her own Annie were to get involved with a middle-aged married man. Possibly the mother hadn't been told that Danny was married at the start. And had then become suspicious.

Suddenly Ria remembered the woman who had telephoned her, the voice demanding to know if she was Mrs. Danny Lynch. This was the woman. Danny had concocted some cock-and-bull story at the time, but had later admitted it. Ria would have done the same if Annie were to be involved with a married man. She would have called the house to check if his wife really existed. To speak to the enemy. This woman probably loved her daughter too. She would have wished for a boyfriend who was young and single. But who could know what a daughter was going to do?

Was seeing Bernadette better than not seeing her? She sat in the car biting her lip and wondering. Possibly better. It meant that now there was no more imagining. It had cleared that area of speculation from her mind. It didn't make it any more bearable that she was so young. Or forgivable.

There was a knock on the car window and Ria jumped. For a mad moment she thought Bernadette and her mother were about to confront her. But it was the anxious face of a traffic warden. "You were not even thinking about parking here, were you?" she asked.

"No, I was thinking about men and women and how they want different things."

"Well, you chose an extraordinary place to sit and think about that." The warden looked as if she were itching to take out her notebook and issue a ticket.

"You're right," Ria agreed. "But these thoughts come on you suddenly. However, I'm out of here now."

"Very wise." The traffic warden put her notebook away regretfully.

At noon Ria telephoned Marilyn.

"Nothing wrong, is there?" Marilyn's voice sounded anxious.

"No, I just wanted to check that it's all still on track at your end, that's all. I'm sorry, is it too early? I thought you might be up."

"No, no. That's fine, I've just had a swim, this is a good time for me. So you're making all your plans?"

"Yes, yes I am indeed." Ria's voice sounded very down.

"Nothing's changed, has it?"

"No, it's just something not connected. I saw the woman my husband is leaving me for today; she's just a child. It was a bit of a shock you see."

"I'm so sorry."

"Thank you. I wanted to tell someone."

"I can understand that."

Ria's eyes filled with tears: it was as if this woman genuinely understood. She must reassure her that she wasn't going to be an emotional drain on her. "I'm not cracking up or anything," Ria began. "I don't want you to get that impression, I just wanted to reassure myself that it's all going to happen, this business of going to the United States. You know, I wanted something to hang on to."

"Sure it's going to happen," Marilyn said. "Because if it doesn't then I'm going to crack up also. I've had the worst telephone conversation with my husband, such coldness, and bitter things we said . . . and I don't want to tell anyone about it here because they'd try to calm me down and say it didn't matter. But it did."

"Of course it did. How did it end?"

"He hung up."

"And you couldn't call him back because it would only be more of the same."

"Precisely," Marilyn said.

There was a silence between them. Neither of them offered a consolation.

"What kind of a day are you going to have?" Ria asked.

"A busy one, I'm filling up every moment of time. It may not be healthy but it's all I can do. And you?"

"Almost exactly the same, no point in sitting down to have a rest, taking it easy as they all say. The pictures keep coming back to your mind if you start taking things easy, I find."

"Yes, I find that's exactly what they do," Marilyn agreed.

There was no more to say. They said good-bye easily, like old friends who have shorthand between them.

Ria made good her promise to have a busy day. She would clean out cupboards first; it was an ideal opportunity for some hard physical work. Now that a stranger was coming to live in her house, all those long-promised clearances would be made. Most of Danny's things were gone already, but she would get the last lot out now. There would be no sentimental pausing to remember when times were better. It would be as if she were part of a removals business.

She began with the big airing cupboard in the bathroom. There were still some of his pajamas, socks, and old T-shirts. *She* was not going to look after them, let Bernadette find the space for them now. All were neatly folded and placed in one of the specially bought carrier bags with handles. Danny could not say that she had flung them into a garbage bag, they were as carefully arranged as if he were taking them on a vacation. She included old sports towels of his, a winter dressing gown, a shabby tracksuit and some very out-of-date swimming trunks. He would not thank her for these things but still he could not fault her.

Then she telephoned her mother and asked her to come for lunch.

"Have you got over this nonsensical idea of emigrating to the USA?" Nora Johnson asked.

"Two months holidays, Mam, a rest, a change, it's exactly what I need. Do me all the good in the world."

"Well, it's certainly cheered you up a bit," her mother admitted unwillingly.

"Come up to me, Mam, I need your help. I'm sorting out the kitchen cupboards, it needs two."

"You're mad, Ria, you know that, clinically mad. Imagine tidying the kitchen cupboards at a time like this."

"What would you prefer, that I get Danny arrested for not loving me anymore? That I lie on a long sofa and weep?"

"No."

"All right, I'll make us a great energy-giving soup and we'll have it as a reward after an hour and a half's work." Ria was killing two birds with one stone. Her mother would need time and explanations and reassurance that this was not a mad endeavor. What better time to do it than while they were sorting out her kitchen?

She was utterly exhausted when it was over. But at least her mother was placated, reassured of the sanity of the enterprise, cordially invited to come out and visit Stoneyfield, and also had helped in the clearing out of kitchen cupboards.

But still Ria would not stop, she wanted to wear herself out. She didn't want to lie wakeful in that big lonely bed tonight and think of Danny and that child asleep in Bantry Court. She wanted to fall straight into a weary sleep the moment she got there. So after her mother had left Ria called Gertie. She was another who needed a one-to-one explanation of what Ria was doing. Better by far to do it while they were working. "Gertie, I know I sound like the Diary of a Mad Housewife, but I don't suppose that if you could get away you could give me two hours this afternoon? It would be such a help. I need to polish all the silver, wrap it up, and put it into the safe deposit vault. Marilyn doesn't want the responsibility of having it around when she comes. And anyway, I suppose I'll have to divide it with Danny later so it's no harm that it's all put away."

"I'd love to, because I want to talk to you about something else, and it's fairly quiet here just now. I could come up now, straightaway?"

"Great, and listen Gertie, I can give you twenty quid. It's worth that to me, honestly."

"You don't have to. . . ."

"No, this is a professional agreement; you're doing me a service."

Gertie came, pale as ever, eyes darting anxiously round her. "There's nobody here, is there?"

"No one but me."

"You know what I wanted to tell you. This place you're going to, I looked it up on the map. It's only about thirty miles away from where Sheila lives."

"Sheila? Your sister? Isn't that marvelous." Ria was delighted. "I'll be able to see her."

Gertie wasn't so pleased. "You'd never tell her would you, Ria? You'd never let anything slip?"

"About what?"

"About me and Jack. You know, about the situation?" Gertie's eyes were haunted-looking.

Ria felt such a wave of pity for her friend that she could hardly speak. "Of course I wouldn't, Gertie, you know that."

"It's just that you being out on your own there and a bit low and everything after all you've been through, you know the way people confide . . . ?"

"No, Gertie, I *wouldn't* confide, believe me."

"It's hard to say this, Ria, but you see it sort of keeps me going that Sheila envies me; nobody else does. It's nice to hold on to the fact that my smart sister who went out to the United States thinks that I have a great life back here, handsome husband, terrific family, great friends, and all."

"But in many ways you *do* have all that, Gertie," Ria said. And was rewarded by the old smile, the smile Gertie used to have when she worked at Polly's.

"I do," she said. "You're quite right. I do have all that, depending on how you look at it."

Together they polished the silver, and kept off topics that would hurt either of them. When it was done Ria handed over an envelope.

"I hate taking this because I've enjoyed it so much. This is a lovely happy house, that man is so stupid. What can he get from her that he can't have here?"

"Another crack at being young, I think," Ria said. "That's all I can make of it."

"You're tired, Ria. Aren't you going to take a rest before the children come home?"

"No, I'm not tired, and anyway they're with their father this evening."

"Is he taking them to Quentin's again, I wonder?"

"No. He's taking them to meet their stepmother, as it happens," Ria said in a dangerously calm voice.

"She'll *never* be that, mark my words. That will all be blown over long before there's any question of marriage, divorce referendum or no divorce referendum."

"That doesn't help any, Gertie. Really, it doesn't," Ria pleaded.

"It wasn't meant to help, it's just a fact, it's what's going to happen. Polly met her apparently, she says she gives it three months."

Ria hated the thought of Polly talking about her, but not nearly as much as she hated the thought of Barney and Polly having met Bernadette socially. Probably many times, as a foursome. It made Ria want to do some very hard work indeed, until her brain stopped functioning. She wondered would she scrub the kitchen floor when Gertie went, or was that going over the top entirely?

As a compromise, she went into the front room and sat at the circular table looking around. What would the American woman make of this old-fashioned room? Her place seemed to be so modern and open. She would possibly consider this a fussy, silly room with its heavy framed pictures and the overformal sideboard. But these pieces had been bought with love and care over the years. She remembered the day that each of them had been eased through the doors. They were polished regularly by Gertie, when she came to earn Jack's extra drinking money. Surely Marilyn would like them. And feel happy in this room.

Ria opened the drawers of the sideboard. It would be interesting to know what they *should* contain. Possibly this was the place for table napkins, corkscrews, salad servers. But then since they had their meals in the kitchen, what was the point of stacking things you needed where you didn't eat? Ria wondered what the drawers actually did contain.

The answer was, in fact, everything that had no place there. There were children's drawings, a broken watch, pencils, an old calendar, a knitted beret that her mother had made, sticky tape, a torch without a battery, a restaurant guide, a tape of Bob Marley songs, some cheap plastic toys from Christmas crackers, an old diary of Annie's, a couple of receipts, and a picture of Ria and Hilary when they were in their teens. Ria put everything on a tray and cleaned out the drawer with a damp cloth. She would put nothing back in again; none of these things belonged there.

Idly she picked up Annie's diary; the funny, slanted writing was small and crowded so that she could fit more in. Ria smiled over the lists of hit singles, the Top Ten, the names and birthdays of various singers. Then there were bits about school and the fact that Annie wasn't allowed to sit beside Kitty because they all talked too much. Some of the teachers were hateful, some weren't too bad but a bit pathetic. It was exactly the kind of thing that Ria used to write herself. She wondered where her old diaries were and whether her mother had ever read them.

Then she came to Brian's barbecue birthday party. The writing was very small and crabbed here, as if every word was important and it must all be included. It was very hard to understand as well as to read.

Ria felt no compunction at all about reading the private diary. She had to know what had occurred that day. Annie wrote about it in veiled terms. Whatever it was it had happened in the lane and nobody knew and it was truly the most horrifying thing in the world. She wrote that it most definitely was not her fault. All she had been doing was looking for a kitten. There was no crime in that.

> *I don't care how marvelous Kitty says it is, I don't care what these feelings are. I don't believe them. Her face was all screwed up as if she was cross about something. I wouldn't tell Kitty because she'd laugh, and of course I couldn't tell Mam because she wouldn't believe me or she'd make some awful remark. I nearly told Colm. He's so nice, he knew something was wrong. But I couldn't tell him. He has too many things to worry about anyway and it's not a thing you could* tell *anybody. There aren't words to tell it. It was something I wish I'd never seen. But I did and I can't unsee it now. I didn't know that's the way it was done, I thought you did it lying down. And* her *of all people. I never liked her, and I like her less now. In fact I think she's disgusting. There's ways I'd like her to know I saw, have some power over her, but that's not right either. She'd just laugh and be superior about it as she is about everything.*

Ria caught her breath. What could Annie have seen? Who was it? And where? It couldn't have been Kitty since she was mentioned in other contexts. The memory of the day of Brian's birthday came back to Ria. Annie had come home after a fall outside Colm's restaurant. Could she have seen Colm Barry and that businessman's wife? No, she mentioned Colm as a nice person, and it was the woman she resented, someone superior, someone scornful. Possibly it was Caroline. Could she have stumbled across that strange, withdrawn sister of Colm and her big, ignorant husband? Or even Caroline and someone else? Would there be any clue?

Ria read on.

> *I don't care how marvelous they say love is, I'm not going to have any part of it. I wish Daddy would stop saying that one day some man will come and carry away his little princess. It's not going to happen. Sometimes I wish I had never been born.*

Ria sat down suddenly at the table that was strewn with all the clutter from the sideboard. She would have to return it all to where it came from. Annie must have stuffed the diary away hastily one time and meant to collect it later. Annie must never know that her mother had seen this diary.

Marilyn looked around her house with an objective eye. How would it appear to someone who lived in a house that was over a hundred years old? The items of furniture pictured in Ria's home looked as if they were all antiques. That Danny Lynch must have done very well at his business.

This house had been built in the early 1970s. Tudor Drive was part of an area developed for the increasing number of academics and business-people. The homes all stood on their own grounds; the lawns and front-age were communally looked after. It was an affluent neighborhood. Here and there small white wooden churches dotted around made it look like a picture postcard saying "Welcome to New England." But it would all look very new and recent to someone who came from a civilization as old as the one that Ria was leaving.

In one of the books about Dublin that she was reading, Marilyn saw that they recommended an outing to see where St. Kevin lived the life of a hermit on a beautiful lake south of Dublin. That was in the year six something, not sixteen something but the actual seventh century, and it was on their doorstep. Marilyn hoped that Ria and their children wouldn't think that they had seen everything that Stoneyfield could offer in the first half hour and would then wonder how to spend the rest of the time.

Marilyn was tired from her constant clearing out of closets and leaving things ready for the new family. There would be plenty of room for them all. Ria would sleep in the main bedroom, and there were three other bedrooms. The people who designed this house must have had a more sociable and hospitable family than the Vines in mind.

The guest rooms had hardly ever been used. They had been so content on their own that they rarely invited visitors. Family came at Thanksgiving, and they put up people for the alumni picnic, but that was all. Now two Irish children would sleep in these rooms and play in the garden. The boy was ten. Marilyn hoped he wouldn't kick a soccer ball or any-thing through her flower beds, but it wasn't something you could actually make rules about. It would be suggesting to Ria that she thought the boy would be out of control. Better to assume perfect behavior rather than try and legislate for it.

Marilyn paused with her hand on the door of one room. Should she lock it? Yes, of course she should. She didn't want strangers in here among these things. They wouldn't want to see it either. They would respect her for keeping her private memories behind a locked door. They would not feel excluded. But then wasn't it *odd* somehow to lock a room in the house that was meant to be these people's home?

Marilyn wished there were someone she could ask, someone whose advice she would seek out and take. But who would she ask? Not Greg, he was still very cold and hurt. Mystified by her decision to go to Ireland, irritated by Ria's coming to Tudor Drive, and unable to talk about any of it.

Not Carlotta next door, who had been forever eager to come in and be part of their lives. Marilyn had spent a long time carefully and courteously building up a relationship based on distance and respect rather than neighborly visits. She could not ruin it now by asking advice on a matter so intimate and personal that it would change everything between them.

Not Heidi at the office. Whatever she did she must not encourage Heidi, who was always asking Marilyn to join this or that, beginners bridge, fen shui groups, embroidery circles. Heidi and Henry were so kind they would have come around to Tudor Drive every single evening to pick her up to take her somewhere if she had allowed them to. But they had never really known what it was like to feel so restless. They had both been married before and now found contentment in a mature second marriage. They were always entertaining in their home and attending the college functions. They couldn't understand someone who wanted to be alone. Marilyn thought she might lock the room but leave the key somewhere for Ria so that it didn't look so like an action of exclusion. She wouldn't decide now, she'd see how she felt the morning she left.

And the time raced by. Summer came to Tara Road and Tudor Drive. Ria marshaled her troops well in advance and encouraged them to welcome Marilyn and invite her into their homes. That's what Americans liked, visiting someone's home.

"Even mine?" Hilary was unsure.

"Particularly yours. I want her to meet my sister and get to know her."

"Isn't she getting enough? Do you know what someone would pay for the use of that fine house for two months? Martin and I were saying that if you rent it in Horse Show week alone you'd get a small fortune."

"Sure, Hilary. I wish you'd come out to see me there, we could meet Sheila Maine and have great times."

"Millionaires can have great times, certainly," Hilary said.

Ria ignored her. "You will keep an eye out for Marilyn, won't you?"

"Ah, don't you know I will."

And all the others had promised too. Her mother was going to take Marilyn to visit St. Rita's; she might enjoy meeting elderly Irish people with lots of memories. Frances Sullivan would ask her to tea and possibly to come to the theater one night. Rosemary was having a summer party, she would include Marilyn.

Polly Callaghan came by unexpectedly. "I hear there's an American woman coming to stay here; if she wants any chauffeuring around at weekends tell her to get in touch."

"How did you know she was coming?" Ria asked.

"Danny told me."

"Danny doesn't approve."

Polly shrugged. "He can't have it every way."

"He mainly has, I think."

"Bernadette's not going to stay the distance, Ria," Polly said.

Ria's heart leaped up. This was what she so desperately wanted to hear. Someone who knew them all and could make a judgment on who would win in the end. Someone like Polly who would be in her corner and tell her what was going on in the enemy camp. Ria was about to ask her what they were like together. Was it true that Bernadette didn't talk at all but sat with her hair falling over her face? She yearned to know that Danny looked sad and lost and like a man who had made a wrong turning.

But she pulled herself together sharply. Polly was Barney McCarthy's woman, she was in their camp when all was said and done. Ria must not give in to the need she felt to confide. "Who knows whether it will last or not? Anyway, it's not important. He wants her, we're not enough for him, so be it."

"All men want more than they can have. Who knows that better than I do?"

"Well, you went the distance, Polly. You and Barney lasted, didn't you?" It was the first time Ria had ever mentioned the relationship and she felt a little nervous at having done so.

"Yes, true, but only unofficially. I mean, I'm still the woman in the background; that's all I'll ever be. Mona is the wife, the person of status."

"I don't think so actually, I think Mona is a fool," Ria said. "If he loved you then she should have let him go to you."

Polly pealed with laughter. "Come on, you know better than that, he didn't *want* to leave her, he wanted us both. Just like Danny possibly wants you both, you and the girl as well."

Ria played that conversation over in her mind many times. She didn't think that Polly was correct. Danny had been anxious to leave, to start again. And of course times were so different now from what they were when Barney McCarthy and Polly Callaghan had fallen in love.

She was surprised to get a telephone call from Mona wishing her luck in the States and offering her a loan of suitcases. "You have great courage, Ria. I admire you more than I can say."

"No, you don't, Mona, you think I'm running away, making a feeble gesture—that's what most of Danny's friends think."

"I hope I'm your friend too. I didn't know one thing about this other woman, you know, I wasn't part of any cover-up."

"No, I'm sure that's true, Mona." Ria felt guilty then. For years she herself had been part of a cover-up.

"And, Ria, I think you are quite right to take a strong stand, I wish I had done that years ago, I really do."

Ria could hardly believe this conversation was taking place. All the taboos with Polly and Mona suddenly broken after all the years. "You did what was right then," she said.

"I only did what made fewer waves, it wasn't necessarily what was right," Mona said. "But great good luck to you out there, and if I can take your American friend anywhere just ask her to call me."

Yes, they were all going to rally round when Marilyn arrived. Gertie was going to come and clean for her. Colm had said he would invite her to the restaurant, introduce her to a few people.

"Colm, can I ask you a strange question?"

"Anything."

"It's ages ago now, but Annie had a fall outside your restaurant; it was on the day of Brian's birthday and you cleaned up her knee for her."

"Yes, I remember."

"And you made her a nice drink called a St. Clements, and that's why she called the cat Clement."

"Yes?" He looked wary.

"It's just that . . . well, do you think Annie was upset by anything else that day? Not just the fall. Like some incident or something?"

"Why do you ask all this, Ria?"

"It's hard to say. Something came to my notice, as they say, and I was just wondering if you could throw any light on it."

"Well, couldn't you ask her yourself?"

"No." There was a silence. "It came to my notice reading her diary," Ria admitted.

"Ah."

"You're shocked," she said.

"Not really, a little maybe."

"Every mother does, believe me."

"I'm sure you're right. But what did you learn?"

"That she saw something that upset her, that's all."

"She didn't tell me. And I hope you don't think that I upset her?" He looked stern now.

"God, no. I've made a desperate mess of this. No, no, of course I don't think that. She said in her diary that you were so kind and helpful and she was going to tell you about it but couldn't. I just wondered did she see anything here?"

"Here?"

"She fell outside your restaurant, didn't she?"

Colm remembered that Annie had fallen in the back lane. But that was her secret, which he had kept. One she obviously had not shared with anyone except what she thought was her private diary.

"No," Colm said thoughtfully. "There was nothing upsetting she could have seen here. Nothing at all."

Ria pulled herself together. "I feel very cheap admitting all this but you'll have to forgive me. I'm saying good-bye to the children for a month tonight. It's a bit emotional."

"They seem to be coping very well, you are too." He admired her.

"Oh, who knows how people cope?" Ria said. "When my father died years and years ago I used to keep searching the house in case he had left us some treasure and then my mother would stop going on about him and how badly he had provided for us. But to the outside world people thought I had gotten over it fine."

"I know." Colm was sympathetic. "Caroline and I had a very drunken father, and I used to wish that there was some kind of magic potion that we could give him and that he would stop drinking and be a real dad. But there wasn't." His face was empty as he spoke.

Ria had never known this about his background. "We *do* let our children down, we read their diaries, we lose their fathers . . . we're hopeless! I think I'll be able to make their world all right just by having a barbecue in the garden for them tonight." She gave a little laugh.

"No, it will be fine. I'll bring over some vegetables for Annie, she's still into that, isn't she?"

"She is, Colm. Thank you, you've been a great friend through all this."

"I'll miss you."

"Maybe Marilyn will be a dish and you and she will be a number when I get back."

"I'll let you know," he promised.

And Ria went home to face the evening where she would say good-bye to her children.

They had told her little or nothing about their meeting with Berna-dette. Ria had been longing to know every detail but wouldn't ask. She must not make them feel that they had to report back from one camp to another. She learned only practical things, like that the holiday on the Shannon cruiser was back on course, that the new house had been hur-ried on—Barney McCarthy's men were there night and day finishing the renovations and it was now finally ready. Smelling of paint but ready; they would sleep there tomorrow night.

Ria learned that there would be two beds in Annie's room and there was a bunk bed being installed for Brian in a sort of outhouse that was once going to have appliances, whatever they were. Washing machines, dryers, Ria had explained. Brian was disappointed; he thought they might be scientific things.

And they had met Bernadette's mother, who was all right really and would drive them to a swimming pool for a course of six lessons. It was so that they could get themselves ready for the one in America. Ria felt she knew everything and yet nothing about the life that her children would live without her. It was an uncanny feeling, as if she had died and was hovering overhead like a ghost, anxious to intervene but unable to speak because she didn't have a body.

They had supper in the garden, kebabs, with sausages for Brian and lots of little vegetables that Colm had left in a basket for Annie. Clement seemed to know they were going; he came and looked at them all reproachfully.

"I hope she'll play with him, you know, entertain him a bit," Annie said. "Clement is not a cat who should be left to brood too much; it doesn't suit him."

"Well, you can come and visit Marilyn and tell her about his personality, can't you?" Ria suggested.

"This isn't our house anymore, not after tomorrow morning when you go," Annie said.

"No, that's true, but on the other hand it will be lived in by someone whose own house *you* are going to visit and it would be nice to introduce yourselves to her."

"Do we have to?" Brian saw tedious conversations with adults ahead.

"No, of course not, it might be nice, that's all."

"Anyway, Colm will keep an eye on Clement. Colm loves him as much as I do," Annie said, cheering up.

There was no point whatsoever in hoping for any confidences from Annie. And she must never in a million years confide what she had read. Any possible trust that might ever grow between them would have been destroyed if that were ever known.

They talked on easily in the warm night about plans.

Most of the children's things were already in Danny's new house. Rosemary had offered to drive them there tomorrow morning early so that Ria would have time to leave the house unfussed. When they left for America it would not be from Tara Road but from this new house. Ria had left them lists of clothes that they were to pack taped to the inside of their suitcases. They were to check that carefully before they left.

"She said you were very organized," Brian said.

"Bernadette said that?" Ria tried not to sound too interested.

"When she saw the suitcases, and Dad said you were the Queen of the Lists." Brian looked at her eagerly hoping she would be pleased. But Annie who was sharper knew that her mother would not like to hear of this discussion.

"And so I am, your dad's right," Ria said with a brightness she certainly didn't feel. She hated the thought of Danny mocking her list-making activities with this child Bernadette.

"Dad's coming round here later to say good-bye, isn't he?" Brian was still hoping for some reassurance that things were normal.

"That's right, when you've gone to bed, there are a few last-minute things we have to discuss."

"You won't have awful fights or anything?" Annie checked.

"No, we don't do that anymore, you know that."

"Not in front of us you don't, but you obviously drive each other crazy," Annie pronounced.

"I don't think that's so at all, but then we all look at people's lives differently. I often think that your gran is crazy to spend so much time with those old people in St. Rita's instead of with people of her own age but she's as happy as a songbird there."

"Well that's because they depend on her there, they need her. And she's only a young thing up in St. Rita's, not an old bag as she is with other people," said Annie as if it were dead simple to understand.

Ria told them she would telephone every Saturday and they could ring anytime because there was an answering machine. But not to waste Dad and Bernadette's money on long calls.

"I don't think she has much money," Brian said. "I think it's mainly Dad's."

"Brian, you have the brain of a flea," Annie said.

Danny arrived at ten o'clock. With a shock Ria realized how physically attractive he was to her and would always be. Nothing had changed very much since those first days when she had met him at the real estate agency and the heady discovery that he had eyes for her rather than for Rosemary. The line of his face had something about it that made you want to stroke him. She had to control herself before she stretched out a hand to touch him. She must behave calmly, he must not know how much power he had to move her.

"We'll go out to the garden in a minute, it's so peaceful. But first what would you like? Tea? A drink?"

"Any lager?"

"Sorry, no. Is that a new taste?"

"I'll have tea," he said.

"Do we drive each other mad?" Ria asked companionably as she put on the kettle.

"No, I don't think so. Why do you ask?"

"The kids think we do."

"What do they know?" He grinned.

"They say the new house is very nice," she said.

"Good, good."

"Can I ask you to keep a sharp eye on that Kitty? All right, so we know I never liked her, but she is a little madam and she really could lead Annie astray."

"Sure, anything else?"

"Brian is by nature filthy, I mean truly filthy. You wouldn't believe it, it could be very unpleasant in close quarters like a boat. You might just *insist* on clean clothes every day, otherwise he'll wear the same things for a month."

Danny smiled. "I'll note that."

"And is there anything for me to look out for when they come to Stoneyfield? Is there anything you don't want them to do?"

He looked surprised to be asked. And pleased. "I don't know. The traffic, I imagine, to warn them that it will be coming from a different side when they cross the road."

"That's very sensible, I will warn them all the time."

"And maybe they could do some educational things there, you know, museums or art galleries. Things that would help them at school."

"Sure, Danny."

They brought their mugs of tea out to the garden and sat on the stone bench. There was a silence.

"About money," he said.

"Well, *I* bought *my* air ticket, you've bought theirs. The rest is just as if we were here, isn't it? I mean the same household expenses except I'll be paying them there."

"Yes." His voice seemed a bit flat.

"That's all right, isn't it?"

"Yes, of course."

"And the electricity, gas, and phone are all paid by banker's order here . . ."

"Yes," he said again.

"So that's money sorted out, is it?" Ria asked.

"I suppose so."

"And I hope you all have a lovely time on the Shannon. Are you going south or north when you get on the boat?"

"South to Lough Derg. Lots of lovely little places to moor, it would be fabulous if we got good weather."

They were talking like two strangers.

"I'm sure you will, the long range forecast is good," Ria said cheerfully.

Another silence.

"And I hope this place works out very well for you too," he said.

"I'm sure it will Danny, thank you for accepting it all. I appreciate that."

"No, no, it's only fair," he said.

"I've left your telephone number for Marilyn."

"Good, good."

"And perhaps you might bring the children round here to meet her one day?"

"What? Oh, yes, certainly."

"Probably best to ring in advance."

"Indeed."

There was nothing left to say. They walked up the stairs and stood awkwardly in the hall that had been full of crates and boxes and bicycles on the day they had vowed to make it a great home forever and ever.

Now the polished floor with its two good rugs glowed warmly in the evening light. The door to the front room was open. There on their table was a bowl of roses that Colm had picked to welcome the American guest. They reflected in the wood, the clock on the mantelpiece chimed and the wind moved the heavy velvet curtains.

Danny went in and looked round him. Surely he was full of regret, not just for these pieces but for the time and energy and love that had gone into gathering them. He seemed to be swallowing as he looked around. He was very still. None of his usual quick movement and almost quivering approach to the world. He was like a photograph of himself.

Ria knew she would never forget him standing here like this, his hand on the back of one of the chairs. He looked as if he had just thought of the one final thing that this room needed. Maybe a grandfather clock? Possibly another mirror to reflect the window. His face had that kind of look. He did *not* look like a man about to go away from all that he had built up here to stay with a pregnant girl called Bernadette. He looked like someone about to put down his car keys and say he was home and that it had all been a ridiculous mistake. It would be too late now, of course, to stop Marilyn, but they would find her another place to stay and everything would be as it was. And they wouldn't wake the children now to tell them, let them find out tomorrow. That was the kind of look he had and the aura that surrounded him.

Ria said nothing; she stood holding her breath as if waiting for him to begin to rebuild the dream. It was very important not to say the wrong thing now. She had been brilliant so far this evening, calm and undramatic. She knew he had valued it. His smile was warm, not strained. He had laughed aloud when she told him how smelly and dirty his son was, his arm had brushed against hers on the stairs and he had not flinched away as he had done during all their prickly conversations.

He stood almost transfixed in this room, Ria didn't know for how long; it felt like a long time. The room was working a magic of its own. He would speak, he would say it was madness, all of this total madness, he was so sorry that he had hurt so many people. And she would forgive him, gently and soothingly, but he would know that he had come back home where he belonged.

Why was he taking so long to find the words? Should she help him, give him a pointer in the right direction? And then he looked at her directly and she saw he was biting his lip, he really was struggling to say what was almost too huge to be said. How could she let him know how great would be her forgiveness and understanding, how much she would do to have him home with her again?

Words had been her undoing in the past apparently; he had thought she was babbling and prattling. Horrible, horrible phrases when she thought she had been talking, confiding. She knew that whatever the temptation she must say nothing. Their whole future depended on this.

She moved very slightly toward him, just one step, and it seemed to have been enough. He came and put his arms around her, his head on her shoulder. He wasn't actually crying but he was trembling and shaking so heavily that she could feel it all through his body.

"Ria, Ria what a mess, what a waste and a mess," he said.

"It doesn't have to be," she said gently.

"Oh God, I wish it had all been different. I wish that so much." He wasn't looking at her, still talking to her hair.

"It can be. It can all be what we make it," she said.

Slowly Ria, slowly, she warned herself. Don't gabble; don't come out with a long list of promises and resolutions and entreaties. Let him do the asking and say yes. Stroke his forehead and say that it will be all right in the end; that's what he wants to hear. He moved his face from her neck and he was about to kiss her.

She must respond as the old passionate Ria would have. She raised her arms from his shaking shoulders and almost clenched him around the neck. Her lips sought his, searching and demanding. It was so good to hold him again. She felt herself carried away in what could only be called a flood of passion, and didn't realize for an instant that he was tugging at her hands behind his neck.

"Ria, what are you doing? Ria, stop!" He seemed shocked and appalled.

She pulled away mystified. He had reached for her; he had lain on her shoulder and said it was a waste, a mess. He had said he wanted to undo it, hadn't he? Why was he looking at her like this?

"It will be all right," she said, flustered now but sure that her role must still be one of making smooth his homecoming. "I promise you Danny it will be all right, it will all sort itself out. This is where you belong."

"*Ria!*" He was horrified now.

"This is your room, you created this. It's yours, like we are your family, you know that."

"I beg you, Ria . . ."

"And I beg *you* . . . come back. We won't talk about it now, just stay, it will all be as it was. I'll understand you have responsibilities to Bernadette and even affection. . . ."

"Stop this . . ."

"She'll get over it, Danny. She's a child, she has her whole life ahead of her, with someone of her own age. She'll look back on it as something foolish, wonderful but foolish . . . and we'll just accept it into our lives the way people do."

"This is not possible . . . that you should . . . I don't know, suddenly change like this." He did look bewildered.

But this was madness. *He* was the one who had reached out for her. "You held me. You told me it was all a mess and a mistake and a waste and you were sorry you did it."

"I didn't, Ria. I said I was sorry that so many people got hurt, I didn't say the other things."

"You said you wished it hadn't turned out like this, I'm saying come back. I won't ask you where you are if you stay out late, I swear I won't. Please, Danny. Please." The tears were pouring down her face now and he was standing there horrified. "Danny, I love you so much I'd forgive anything you did, you *know* that. I'd do anything on earth that it takes to have you back." She was gulping now and she stretched her arms out to him.

He took her hand in both of his. "Look, love, I'm going now. This minute. You don't mean any of this, not a word of it. You meant all the things we talked about for half an hour in the garden. You meant about wishing us all a good holiday on the Shannon and I meant about hoping it goes well for you in America." He looked at her hopefully as if praying that his nice, practical, soothing words would stop her tears and prevent the danger of her clutching him again.

"I'll always be here waiting for you to come back, just remember that."

"No, you won't, you'll be in America having a great time." He tried to jolly her along. "A strange woman will be here trying to make head or tail of our funny ways."

"I'll be here, this room will always be here for you."

"No, Ria, that's not the way things are, and I'm going now but I want you to know how . . ."

"How what?" she asked.

"How generous it would have been of you to make that offer, if there had been any question of it. It would have been a very unselfish thing to do."

She looked at him in amazement. He didn't see that there was no unselfishness or generosity involved. It was what she ached for. He would never realize that, and now she had made a total fool of herself on top of everything else.

The weeks of planning and driving herself and discipline had been thrown away. Why had they come into this room anyway? If she had not seen that look on his face she might not have seen a possible lifeline. But she had seen it; she had not imagined it. That's what she would hug to herself always.

"Yes it's late, of course you must go," she said. The tears had stopped. She was not the calm Ria who had walked up the stairs from the kitchen with him, her face was too tearstained for that. But she was in control again, and she could sense his relief.

"Safe journey," he said to her on the steps.

"Oh yes, thank you, I'm sure it will be fine."

"And we did make a lovely house, Ria, we really did." He looked past her back into the hall.

"Yes, yes indeed, and two marvelous children," she said.

On the steps of the house they had spent so long creating, Danny and Ria kissed each other cautiously on the cheek. Then Danny got into his car and drove away and Ria went into her home on Tara Road and sat for a long time at her round table, staring sightless in front of her.

CHAPTER

FIVE

"THEY DIDN'T FIGHT," Annie said to Brian as she helped him close his suitcase.

"How do you know?"

"I listened for a bit at the bathroom window, they talked about holidays."

"Oh, good," Brian said.

"She said to Dad that you were filthy, though."

Brian looked surprised but unconvinced. "No, she didn't, she wouldn't say that about me. What would make her say that?" His face looked round with worry.

Annie took pity on him. "No, I made it up," she lied.

"I knew." Brian's faith in his mother was restored.

"I wish she weren't going," Annie said.

"So do I."

It was such a rare thing for the brother and sister to be joined in any emotion that it startled them. They looked at each other uncertainly. These were very troubled times.

Rosemary arrived earlier than expected. Ria handed her a cup of coffee.

"You look fine," Rosemary said approvingly.

"Sure."

"I came early to leave you less time for tearful farewells. Where are they anyway?"

"Finishing their packing." Ria sounded very muted.

"They'll be okay."

"I know."

Rosemary looked at her friend sharply. "Was it all right last night with Danny and everything?"

"What? Oh yes, very civilized." Never in a million years would anyone know how it had been last night with Danny. Ria would not allow it to be spoken of even in her own heart.

"Well, then that's good." There was a silence. "Ria?"

"Yes?"

"You know they'll never see Bernadette as anything . . . as anything except what she is."

"I know, of course."

"They won't bond with her or anything like that. Can you *imagine* what she feels like having to replace you for a month? What a task that would be for anyone, let alone a dumb kid like that." There was no reply so Rosemary just carried on. "You know, I did think this whole jaunt to America was mad, but now I think it's the cleverest thing you could have done. You're really much sharper than anyone gives you credit for. Hey, here come the kids. What do you want, lingering or brisk?"

"Brisk, and you're wonderful," Ria said gratefully.

In minutes Ria was waving good-bye as Rosemary drove the children to stay in a strange house for the month of July. Who would ever have believed that any of this could happen? And what was even more incredible was that Rosemary actually thought that Ria had been somehow clever to engineer this situation.

Bernadette's mother was sitting at the kitchen table in the new house. "Well, she's a fine hard-hearted-Hannah, isn't she, sweeping off to the United States and leaving you to look after her children."

"I know, Mum, but in a way it's for the best."

"How is it for the best?" Finola Dunne couldn't see any silver lining.

"Well, I suppose she won't be there on Tara Road anymore as a kind of center for him, you know."

"She wasn't much of a center for him when she was there, judging from the amount of time he spent with you." Bernadette's mother always managed to sound both disapproving of her daughter's affair with a married man while equally proud that the matter had been so satisfactorily sorted out.

"It was his home for sixteen years, it still has a great draw for him, the place."

"This place will too in time, child. Wait till it gets a bit more settled." Finola Dunne looked around the luxury-fitted kitchen that Barney McCarthy's men had installed at double speed. This was an expensive house in one of the more fashionable southern suburbs of Dublin. It must have cost a packet. It was a sheltered avenue, a good place to bring up a new baby, and there were a lot of other young couples around.

Finola Dunne knew that Danny Lynch was a hotshot real estate agent. But she felt the sooner he sold this Tara Road house, realized his money, and got some small, more suitable place for his first wife, the better. The boy worked hard, she gave him that, and he obviously adored Bernadette, but he would wear himself out unless he sorted out his finances. He had left this morning for a meeting at six a.m. to avoid the traffic.

"Any mention of his selling Tara Road?" she asked.

"No, and it's not something I ask about. I think he was more attached to that house than to any woman. It gives me the shivers," Bernadette said.

"No time for that, they'll be here any minute and a long summer of entertaining them begins."

"Only thirty days, and they're not too bad," said Bernadette with a grin.

Ria's children were very quiet in Rosemary's car.

"What kind of things will you do all day, do you imagine?" Rosemary asked brightly.

"No idea," Annie shrugged.

"They don't have cable television," Brian said.

"Maybe they'll take you out to places?" Rosemary was optimistic.

"She's very quiet, she doesn't go to places," Brian said.

"Is she nice, I mean interesting to talk to?"

"Not very," Brian said.

"She's okay, just, you know, nothing much to say," Annie said.

"I prefer her mother actually," Brian said. "You'd like her, Rosemary, she's full of chat and more your age."

"I'm sure I would," said Rosemary Ryan, who could cope with any boardroom committee meeting or television discussion, but was finding this conversation very hard going indeed.

At Dublin Airport, Ria looked around. So many people heading off in so many directions. She wondered whether any of them could be traveling in such a confused state of mind as she was. In the line next to her she saw a good-looking man with the collar of his raincoat turned up. He had fair hair that fell into his eyes. She looked at him wildly. For an instant she thought it was Danny, racing out to stop her leaving, a last-minute plea that she change her mind. She remembered with the feeling of a cold shower of water that this was the last thing on earth he would do. She could still feel him tugging at her hands, which she had clasped around his neck. Her face burned at the shame of it.

She walked through the duty-free shop wondering what she should buy. It seemed such a pity to waste the value on all those shelves. But she didn't smoke, she drank little, she didn't need anything electronic. Marilyn's house would be full of more equipment than she would ever learn to use. She stopped by the perfumes.

"I want something very new, something I've never smelled before, which will have no memories," she said.

The assistant seemed used to such requests. Together they examined the new scents, and settled on one that was light and flowery. It cost forty pounds.

"It seems rather a lot," Ria said doubtfully.

"Well it is, but then it depends. Do you *have* that kind of money to spend on a good perfume?" The girl clearly wanted to move on.

"I don't know whether I do or not," Ria spoke with wonder. "Isn't that odd? I actually don't know what my financial situation will be. I never thought about it until this minute. I might be the kind of person who could afford this and more, or I might never be able to buy anything remotely like it in my whole life."

"You should take it then," said the sales assistant, quickly trying to head off too much philosophy.

"You're right, I will," said Ria.

She fell asleep on the plane and dreamed that Marilyn had not left Tudor Drive after all but was sitting waiting for her in the garden. Marilyn had brown hair and copper shoes and was wearing a beige suit just like Bernadette's mother had worn. She spoke with a cackle when Ria arrived. "I'm not Marilyn, you stupid woman, I'm Danny's new mother-in-law. I've got you out here so that they can all move into Tara Road. It was all a trick, a trick, a trick." Ria woke sweating. Her heart was racing. It was an extraordinary sensation to be on a plane thousands of feet up in the air, people around her eating lunch.

The air hostess was concerned. "Are you all right? You're as white as anything."

"Yes . . . I had a bad dream, that's all." Ria smiled her gratitude for the concern.

"Have you anyone meeting you at Kennedy?"

"No, but I know what to do—take the Stoneyfield limo. I'll be fine."

"A holiday, is it?"

"Yes, I think it is, I'm sure that's what you'd call it, what I call it. It will be certainly a holiday." Ria saw the nervous smile of the courteous girl in her stewardess uniform. Really, she must stop this habit of analyzing what she was doing. It was just that simple questions caught her unawares.

She lay back and closed her eyes. How ridiculous to have made Marilyn look like Bernadette's mother when of course she looked totally different. Ria opened her eyes suddenly in shock. She had no idea whatsoever what Marilyn looked like. She knew the measurements of her swimming pool, the voltage of her electricity, the weight of laundry that the dryer could handle, the times of church services in Stoneyfield, and the days of the week the garbage was collected. She had the names and phone numbers of two women called Carlotta and Heidi. She had photographs of the rock garden, the main bedroom, the swimming pool, and carport.

She knew that Marilyn would have her fortieth birthday while she was in Ireland but she did not know whether she was fair or dark, tall or small, thin or fat. Extraordinary to think that an entirely unknown woman had set out for Tara Road last night and nobody knew what she looked like.

The flights to Dublin were at night and there was a coach service to Kennedy from a nearby town. Marilyn accepted Heidi's offer to drive her there. She closed the door and left the keys and an envelope of instructions with Carlotta. Ria would call to collect them when she arrived in the early evening. She had left her house in perfect order. Clean, freshly laundered linen and towels everywhere, food in the fridge, flowers on the table and the breakfast bar.

She decided about locking the room only when she heard Heidi's car pull up outside the house. She left the door closed but not locked. Ria would understand; she would treat it appropriately. She would probably dust it and open the windows during the two months. There were some things you didn't need to say or to write down.

Heidi chattered and asked questions all the way to the Stoneyfield limo. Did Ria play bridge by any chance? Would Marilyn take any courses in Trinity College while she was in Dublin? What was the weather going to be like? And casually, very casually, would Greg be joining her there at all? Or would he be coming back to Stoneyfield during the vacation? To none of these questions did Marilyn give any satisfactory reply. But she did hug her friend Heidi just before she got in the van.

"You're very generous, and I do hope to be generous myself one day, when I come out of this forest, this awful forest."

Heidi looked after the van as it pulled out of the station. Marilyn sat there, bolt upright and reading a letter. Her eyes were very bright. It was the nearest that Marilyn had come to being human for a long time.

Marilyn read the letter to Greg again and again.

She had put as much of her soul into it as she could and she realized that she was still holding back a lot. It was as if there was some kind of brake refusing her permission to explain too much. Or maybe there was no more to explain. It was quite possible that she had lost the capacity to love and care anymore and that this is how she was going to be for the rest of her life.

She took out the little wallet of pictures that Ria had sent. Every one of them had people in them. And little notes on the back. Annie doing her homework in our front room. Brian serving a pizza in the kitchen.

My mother and sister, Hilary. Me with my friend Gertie who also helps with the cleaning, hanging out the washing. Our friend Rosemary who lives up the road. Colm Barry who runs a kitchen garden at the back of our house and a restaurant at the corner of Tara Road. The best picture of the house itself also showed a family of four squinting into the sun. On the back Ria had written "In Happier Times."

Marilyn studied Danny Lynch carefully. He was handsome, certainly. And very unchanged from the boyish, enthusiastic salesman she had met all those years ago. Then she looked at Ria, small, dark, and always smiling. Her whole face was lit up with goodwill in every single snapshot. Very different in a lot of ways to the voice she talked to on the phone. There Ria sounded tense and anxious. Anxious to please, that her house should be good enough, anxious to reassure that her children were going to be no trouble when they came to Stoneyfield.

And most of all anxious that Marilyn would be swept immediately into this huge group of family friends and acquaintances. Never had anything been a more unlikely starter. Marilyn Vine, who kept herself so withdrawn from colleagues, family, friends, and neighbors that they all called her a recluse. Marilyn Vine, unable to talk to her own husband and tell him why she was making this strange journey. She would be polite to these people, of course, but she didn't want anything at all to do with their lives.

"Can I ask Kitty to supper please, Bernadette?" Annie asked.

Bernadette raised her eyes from the book she was reading. "No, sorry, your father said no."

"She always comes at home. When Dad was at home he liked her."

"Well, he must have gone off her." Bernadette was not very concerned.

"Will Mam be in America yet?" asked Brian.

"Don't go on about Mam," Annie corrected him.

"It's okay." Bernadette shrugged. She was back in her book. She really didn't seem to mind.

"Well, will she?" Brian wanted his question answered.

Bernadette looked up again perfectly pleasantly but they felt she would have preferred there to be silence in the house. "Let me see, it takes about five or six hours. Yes, I'd say she'd be there now, on a bus to wherever the place is she's going."

"Stoneyfield," Annie said.

"Yes, that's right." Bernadette was reading again.

There didn't seem to be any more to say. Dad wouldn't be home until eight o'clock. It was a long sort of an evening. Out of sheer desperation Annie took out *Animal Farm*, one of the books that her mother had given her to pack. I don't think I'd like it, Annie had said at the time, but surprisingly she did, very much. And Brian read his book of soccer heroes.

So when Danny came home tired and apprehensive he found them all sitting in armchairs reading peacefully. Annie looked up and saw the pleasure in her father's face. This was so different from Tara Road. But he must miss it all there, surely he did, even if he didn't love Mam anymore, and preferred Bernadette and all that. There was no bustle of dinner being prepared here, Bernadette would take out two frozen dishes shortly and put them in the microwave. There was no endless stream of people passing through. No Gertie coming and going. No Rosemary popping in and out, no Kitty, no awful Myles and Dekko, no Gran with Pliers or Colm with his basket of vegetables. Surely Dad must miss all that very much.

But as Annie looked at her father she knew with a great certainty that he preferred things like this. He laid his keys in a long oval dish. "I'm home," he said and everyone sprang into action to welcome him. When he said he was home on Tara Road there was so much going on that nobody seemed to notice.

All the instructions had worked like a dream. The Stoneyfield Airport Limo was where Marilyn had said it would be, the fare was exactly as she had described. The weather was warm and sunny, much hotter than back in Dublin. The noise and the variety of people everywhere were extraordinary. Yet despite it all Ria felt well able to cope, she had expert guidelines and the whole system seemed to be working perfectly.

The driver announced that they were approaching Stoneyfield and Ria took a deep breath. This was going to be her home now. She almost wanted to look at it unobserved for a while, so when she got off she took her two suitcases into an ice cream parlor and sat down to get her bearings. The menu was so exotic—Marilyn would find the range of ice cream sodas, floats, and specials so much less extensive in Dublin. Still, she wasn't going there for ice cream. Ria watched the people come and go. A lot of them knew each other. The woman behind the counter seemed a real personality, wisecracking with the customers just like they did in the television comedies.

She was in America now, she would not start comparing and contrasting everything with the way it was at home. She would even try to think in dollars rather than converting it back to pounds all the time. From her window seat in the Happy Soda House, Ria could see Carlotta's Beauty Salon. It looked elegant, a discreet sort of place where a woman might go in, and behind those heavy, cream-colored curtains and all that gold lettering get good advice about keeping old age at bay and keeping your man at home. She wondered what Carlotta herself looked like; there had been no pictures, no pictures of any person at all.

Steeling herself, Ria crossed the road, her dark green traveling outfit of jumper and skirt and her two suitcases looking out of place here. Everyone else seemed to wear Bermuda shorts or crisp cotton dresses. They all looked as if they had been to beauty salons already. Ria felt travel-stained and tired. She pushed the door to Carlotta's and went in. Carlotta was the tall, full-bosomed, exotic-looking woman at the desk. She excused herself from the client she was talking to and came over at once.

"Ria, welcome to the United States, I hope you're going to love Stoneyfield. We are just delighted that you're here." It was so warm, so genuine, and so utterly unexpected that Ria felt a prickle of tears in her eyes. Carlotta was looking at her with an expert eye. "I was keeping an eye out for the limo, they come every forty-five minutes or so but I guess it must have come now without my noticing it."

"I went into the Happy Soda House," Ria confessed. She realized it was a dull and indeed ungracious thing to say in response to all this welcome and kindness. And Ria did want to respond. This woman was so outgoing compared to Marilyn, who had sometimes been a little terse on the telephone. Carlotta was making such overtures of friendship that Ria was appalled at her own inability to find the proper words. "You'll have to forgive me, I seem to be sort of shell-shocked. I'm not used to long flights and things. . . ." Her voice trailed away.

"Do you know what I was going to suggest to you, Ria? Suppose you relax here, have a nice shower, a relaxing aromatherapy massage—Katie doesn't have a client at the moment—then you go and take a rest in a dark room and I come and wake you up in a couple of hours and we go back home? Or would you prefer if I drove you straight out to Marilyn's home? Either is fine with me."

Ria thought that she would love to stay in the salon.

Katie was one of those women who made no small talk and asked no questions. Ria felt no need to apologize for her tired, neglected skin, for the lines appearing around her eyes, for the chin that was definitely more slack than it used to be. The healing, soothing oils were gently and insistently massaged into the various pressure points, temples, shoulders, scalp. It felt wonderful. Once before Ria had gone for aromatherapy with Rosemary as a treat, and Ria had promised it to herself every month. Twelve times a year. But she never had. It was too expensive and there were always things she wanted to buy for the children or the house. Her mind started to go down that channel again about what she could afford from now on but she forced it back. Anyway, here in this cool dark place with that wonderful rhythmic massage of her shoulders and back, with that intense satisfying smell of the oils, it was easy to banish worries and to fall into a deep sleep.

"I hated to wake you up." Carlotta was handing her a glass of fruit juice. "But otherwise your sleeping pattern will be off."

Ria was now her old self again. She got up from her relaxation bed in the pink cotton robe Katie had given her and came out to shake Carlotta's hand. "I can't thank you enough for this terrific welcome. It was exactly what I needed and I didn't know. You couldn't have arranged anything that I would have liked more."

Carlotta knew genuine appreciation when she saw it. "Get your clothes on, Ria, and I'll take you home. You're going to have a great summer here, believe me."

Ria was about to leave when Katie handed her a piece of paper. She wondered if it was some advice about future skin care that she would study later, but she looked at it anyway. It was a bill for an amount of money that Ria would never in her whole life have spent in a beauty salon. She had thought it was a complimentary treatment. How humiliating. She must show no hint that she was surprised.

"Of course," she said.

"Carlotta wanted you to have a fifteen percent discount so that's all built into the check and service is included," Katie said.

Ria handed over the money with a sickening feeling that she was a great fool. Why should she have thought that this woman was giving her a free treatment? She was living among people who took beauty salons as a matter of course. Possibly if she had done so years ago she might not be in the position she was in now.

Gertie had arranged to be in Tara Road when Marilyn arrived. Ria had said that there just had to be someone here to open the door. It was a high priority.

"Suppose, just suppose, Gertie, that there's any crisis or anything, you will make sure that my mother's installed here instead of you, won't you?"

"Crisis?" Gertie had asked as if such a thing had never occurred in her life.

"Well you know, anything could happen."

"Listen, there's going to be someone to meet her." Gertie spoke very definitely. And just as Gertie was leaving her house to head to Ria's she got the message that Jack was in the hospital. There had been a fight somewhere last night and Jack had only recovered consciousness now. Gertie ran down the road to the little house where Nora Johnson lived but she wasn't at home. Possibly gone to St. Rita's, her neighbor didn't know. Gertie damned Danny Lynch to the pit of hell. All her anger was directed at him. If he hadn't abandoned his wife for some pale-faced child none of this would be happening. Gertie would not be running from house to house looking for someone to open Ria's door and greet some American woman. Jimmy Sullivan said that Frances was at the thrift shop and wouldn't be able to get away.

Gertie ran to the restaurant. Please, please let Colm not have gone to a market or anything. Please, God, if you are there, and really I know you are there, let Colm Barry be at home. He's fond of the Lynches, he'd do it. And he'd be nice to the woman. Please.

Gertie never prayed to God to ask him to make Jack behave like a normal man. Some things were too big, even for the Almighty to undertake. But something like Colm being in could happen. And did happen. "Let me drive you somewhere first, Gertie. She won't be in for another half hour."

"No, no, I couldn't let Ria down."

"We know she's going to come in to the city, look around for a few hours, and then come here at twelve, that's the arrangement."

"She might come early. Anyway I can go on the bus."

"I'll drive you. Which hospital?"

As they sat in the car Gertie twisted a handkerchief in her hands, but there was no conversation. "You're very restful, Colm, really you are. Anyone else would be asking questions."

"What's there to ask?"

"Like why does he do it?"

"Why ask that question? I did it for so long myself, people were possibly asking that question fairly uselessly about me all over the shop." He was very reassuring, just what she needed. She stopped tearing at the piece of cotton in her hands.

"Maybe people would ask why I stay with him."

"Oh well, that's easy. He's very lucky, that's all."

"How do you mean?"

"I had nobody to stay with me, no one to cushion things, so eventually I had to face it, what a lousy life I had."

"Well, doesn't that mean being on your own might have made you strong?" Gertie's face was anguished. "That's what my mother's always telling me. She says give him up and he'll come to his senses."

Colm shrugged. "It could work, who knows. But I'll tell you one thing, coming to *my* senses was no bloody fun at all because all I came to was a hollow, empty life." He left her at the gate of the hospital and drove back to welcome Ria's American.

Marilyn told herself that Ria's instructions about what to do on arriving in Dublin had been excellent. They had agreed not to meet, since it would be a rushed, hopeless meeting, with one arriving and the other leaving. Marilyn's overnight plane would be in by seven o'clock, Ria advised that she should get a bus to the city, leave her bags at the bus station, and walk up to have breakfast in a Grafton Street coffee shop.

This way she would pass O'Connell Bridge on the River Liffey, the entrance to Trinity College, and she would see the various bookshops and gift stores which she might like to explore later. After breakfast she should go up and walk around St. Stephen's Green. A few statues and points of interest were listed and a gentle itinerary, ending up at a taxi stand where she should take a cab, pick up her luggage, and head for Tara Road. One of the people already mentioned would be there to welcome her in and show her around.

It had all gone extremely well. The city began to fall back into place for Marilyn; she had not properly remembered the whole layout from the brief visit before. It had certainly changed and become much more prosperous in the intervening years. The traffic was much denser, the cars bigger, the people better dressed. Around her were foreign accents, different languages. It was not only the American tourists who came to the craft shops nowadays, the places seemed full of other Europeans.

Around eleven-thirty her feet were beginning to feel tired. Ria would be boarding her plane just about now. It was time to find her new home. The taxi driver told her a long complicated tale of woe about there being too many taxis allowed on the streets of the city and not enough work for them. He said that most people were on the take all the world over, that he was sorry that he hadn't emigrated to America like his brother who now had a toupee and a German wife. He said that Tara Road was the fastest-moving bit of property in Dublin. A regular gold mine.

"If your friends own that house, ma'am, they're sitting on half a million," he said confidently as he drove in the gateway and drew up at the foot of the steps.

The door was opened by a dark, good-looking man in his early forties. He came down the steps, hand stretched out. "On Ria's behalf you're very welcome to Tara Road," he said, while Marilyn frantically searched for his name from the cast of thousands she had been presented with. Somehow she had thought it would be the sister, Hilary, or one of the two women friends. "I'm Colm Barry, neighbor and friend. I also dig the back garden but I use a back gate so I'll be no intrusion in your time here."

Marilyn looked at him gratefully. He seemed to tell her what she needed to know and not too much. He was courteous but also cool in a way that she very much liked. "Indeed, the man who runs the restaurant," she said, placing him at last.

"The very one," he agreed. He carried her suitcases up the granite steps.

Ria's photographs had not lied. The hall was glorious with its deep glowing wooden floor, and elegant hall table. The door to a front room was open, Colm pushed it slightly. "If it were my house I would never leave this room," he said simply. "It runs the whole depth of the house, windows at each end. It's just lovely." On the table was a huge bowl of roses. "Ria asked me to leave those for you."

Marilyn felt a gulp in her voice as she thanked him. The place was so beautiful and these rich pink and red roses on such a beautiful table were the final touch.

He carried her bag upstairs and showed her the main bedroom. "I expect this is where you'll be, I'm sure all the details were written out for you. Ria's been getting ready for weeks. I know she's gone to huge trouble."

Marilyn knew it too. Her eyes took in the immaculate white bedspread, brand new, must have been put on this morning, the folded towels, the shiny paintwork and the empty closet. This woman had worked at getting her house ready. Marilyn hoped guiltily that hers would match up. They went down to the kitchen and at that moment the cat door opened and a large orange cat came in.

"This is Clement." Colm introduced the cat formally. "An excellent cat, he has a little weakness sometimes of killing a perfectly innocent bird and then he'll bring it back to you as a trophy."

"I know, I have to say well done, Clement, how nice," Marilyn said with a smile.

"Good, just so long as you know the drill. Anyway, Clement isn't very competitive, usually he just opens one eye and looks at the birds, then goes back to sleep." Colm continued his tour of the kitchen, opening the fridge. "Ah, she's left you some basics I see, including a soup made from vegetables grown in that very garden. Shall I take some out for you to heat up? You've had a long journey, you'll want to settle in." And he was gone.

What a calm, pleasant neighbor, Marilyn thought, exactly the person she would like to live near. There would be no problem in keeping someone like Colm Barry out of your life. He would never be like Carlotta, aching to come over the fence and get involved. And he was right, she did want to settle in. She was pleased that it had been this man rather than one of the women she had expected. He was a fellow spirit, a soul mate. He somehow understood that she wanted to be alone. She was glad he had been there to welcome her.

She wandered slowly around the house that would be hers until September. The children's rooms had been tidied, pictures of soccer players on Brian's wall, pop stars on Annie's. Plastic models of wrestlers on Brian's windowsills, soft furry toys on Annie's. Two well-kept bathrooms, one with what looked like genuine Victorian bathroom fixtures. And one empty, lifeless room, a lot of shelving on the wall but nothing on display. This must have been a study or office that belonged to Danny in what Ria would have called happier times.

A warm, almost crowded kitchen, shelves of cookbooks, cupboards full of pans and baking dishes, a kitchen where people baked, ate, and lived. A house full of beautiful objects but first and foremost a home. There was very little wall space that did not have pictures of the family, mainly of the children but some that included the handsome Danny Lynch as well. He had not been cut out of their lives because he had gone away. Marilyn looked at his face for some clues about this man. One thing she knew from being in his home: he must love this new woman very much or have been very unhappy in his marriage to Ria to enable him to leave this beautiful home without a backward glance.

"I wonder, should I go and call on her?" Nora Johnson said to Hilary.

"Ah, isn't she perfectly all right where she is? Hasn't she a valuable house worth a fortune to sit in all summer for nothing?" Hilary sniffed.

"Yes, well, she still might be a bit lonely, and Ria said—"

"Oh Ria said, Ria said . . . there's many people she could have given that house to, to mind, if she had wanted to."

Nora looked at her elder daughter with a flash of impatience. "Listen to me, Hilary, if you're suggesting that you could have looked after the house and fed that very dim cat for Ria . . ."

"Yes, or you could have, Mam. She didn't have to go and get a perfectly strange American."

"But Hilary, you great silly girl, the whole point of it was that Ria wanted to go to America. She didn't want to exchange houses with me down the road, and you across the city."

Hilary listened, feeling very foolish. Somehow in her flurry of resentment she had forgotten this fact. "We should give her tonight and tomorrow to rest anyway and maybe we might get in touch then," she said.

"I'd hate her to think she wasn't welcome," Ria's mother said. While Ria's sister hid the sniff she had been about to indulge in.

Carlotta pointed out all the amenities as she drove Ria to Tudor Drive.

Ria marveled as they passed all the houses with their communal lawns in front. "No fences," she noticed.

"Well, it's neighborly, I guess," Carlotta said.

"Is it like that on Tudor Drive?"

"Not our part, no, it's more closed in."

Carlotta told her the names of streets and drives that would become familiar in the next days and weeks. She pointed out the two hotels, the club and the library, the good gas station, the one where the guy was a pain in the butt, the two antique shops, the florist, the okay deli, the truly great gourmet shop. And of course the Garden Center, Carlotta gestured triumphantly.

"Oh well, that's not going to be of much interest to me, I barely know flower from weed."

Carlotta was puzzled. "But I thought you were crazy about gardening, that that's how you got to know each other."

"Not at all, the reverse in fact."

"Well, well, well. Just goes to show how you can get things wrong. It's just that Marilyn doesn't have any other interests, so I just assumed . . ."

They were nearly there.

"Look, I'd love you to come in and have something to eat and drink with me in my place, but you're here for the summer, you'll want to get into your own place, and see what it's like." Carlotta took out the envelope with the keys in it and prepared to hand them over.

"But aren't you going to come in with me?" Ria was surprised.

"Well, no, honey, not really. I mean this is your house, Marilyn and Greg's house."

"No, come in please, I'd love you to come in and show me around, won't you?"

Carlotta bit her lip in indecision. "I don't really know where their things are. . . ." she began.

"Oh please do, Carlotta. I'd feel much more at home if you showed me everything. And Marilyn said she was going to leave me a bottle of wine in her fridge. I left her one in mine. So it would be a lovely start for me."

"I wouldn't want her to think . . ."

But further protest was useless. Ria was already out of the car and looking up at her new home. "Do we go in this little gate or round by the carport do you think?"

"I'm not sure." The previously suave and confident Carlotta looked flustered.

"But which way is the front door?"

"Ria, I've never been in this house in my life," said Carlotta.

The pause was minimal. Then Ria spoke. "So, it will be a new experience for both of us," she said.

And taking a suitcase each they went in to explore Number 1024 Tudor Drive, home of the Vines.

"Heidi? It's Greg Vine."

"Oh, hello, Greg. How are you?" Heidi was so relieved that he was still speaking to her after her indiscretion to him on the telephone some weeks back she didn't even pause to wonder why he had called.

"Well, I'm basically okay, Heidi, but a little confused. You did see Marilyn off to the airport, didn't you? I mean, she *did* go?"

"Yes, yes of course. And you do have her number there? She said you did." Heidi's voice was rising a little anxiously.

"Yes, I have it all. I was just wondering if this person . . . has arrived in Stoneyfield. You know, the one who'll be living in our home."

"I'm not sure of all the details, but I think she should have arrived there an hour or two ago, Greg." Heidi wasn't saying it but it had been like pulling teeth getting any information out of Marilyn whatsoever about the arrival of Ria.

"I see."

"Was there anything?"

"No, not really." He sounded very bleak. Despairing almost.

Heidi's heart went out to him. She tried hard to guess what he might want to know. "You'd like to know if she arrived safely and got in, is that it?"

"In a way, I suppose," he said.

"So would you like *me* to call to see if she is there?"

"I believe the answering machine will be on for the first week with our message on it, and then if this person wants to change it she may." He sounded very bitter and hurt.

"You want to know if she has arrived and what she's like, what kind of a person she is, Greg? Is *that* it?"

"Well, I think it's more it than anything I've come up with so far," he said. And there was a wry near-laugh in his voice.

"I'm not sure if I should drive by, she may be asleep. But if I call and then it's only the machine . . . ?"

"Look, whenever you can, Heidi, that's all. I feel so helpless out here, it's so strange, things sort of multiply in your mind."

"I know." She was sympathetic.

"I don't think you do. You and Henry can talk about anything and I think we used to once also. But now we can talk about nothing without upsetting each other . . ." he broke off.

"It'll get better, Greg."

"I'm sorry, I sound like someone on *Oprah.*"

"Is that so bad?"

"No, it's just not the way I am. Listen, I don't want to upset any kind of confidence between you and Marilyn, believe me I don't."

"There is nothing to upset, just give me the numbers to call and I'll get in touch as soon as I have something to report."

"Call collect, Heidi."

"No, I won't do that, but you buy me a nice bright-colored muumuu to wear at the alumni picnic."

"Oh God, I'd forgotten that."

"You'll be back for it, Greg. You've never missed one yet. We rely on the history department."

"But where would I live if I did come back for it?" He sounded totally bewildered.

"Listen, Greg, that's not for weeks yet. Let me report on the situation on Tudor Drive before you make any decisions."

"You're a real friend, Heidi."

"We all were and all will be, the four of us, mark my words," she said, with no conviction whatsoever.

Carlotta and Ria toured the house.

"Everything is so beautiful and she had no help coming in, she must have had contract cleaners," Carlotta said admiringly.

They moved from the big open living room with its colored rugs on the floor and three white leather sofas encircling an open fireplace into the huge kitchen with its breakfast bar and dining table into Greg's study room lined with books from ceiling to floor on three walls and with a red leather desk and big black swivel chair under one window. There was no room for pictures on the walls but three tables stood around, all of them with little sculptures, ornaments, treasures of some sort.

"What a beautiful room," Ria said. "If you could see *my* husband's study now . . . it's like, well, it's like a shell."

"Why is that?" Carlotta asked reasonably.

Ria paused and looked at her. "Sorry, he's my ex-husband, and he's just moved out so his study's empty. But it was never like this, not even in our heyday. Should we tour the garden, do you think?"

"The garden will be there tomorrow," Carlotta said.

"Then let's hit Marilyn's bottle of Chardonnay," Ria suggested.

"If aromatherapy can cope with jet lag like the way it's working with you, we're only in the foothills of discovery," Carlotta said and they went into the kitchen.

Just at that moment there was a knock on the door. Carlotta and Ria looked at each other, and went together to answer it. A woman in her forties stood there carrying a gift-wrapped bottle.

"I'm Heidi Franks, I work with Marilyn and I wanted to welcome you . . . well, hello, Carlotta, I didn't know you'd be here. . . ."

"Ria insisted that I come by." Carlotta seemed to be apologizing, as if she had been discovered intruding.

"Come on in, Heidi," Ria said. "You arrived at a great time, we were just about to have a drink."

"Well, I don't really like to . . ."

Ria wondered what made them both apologize for coming into this home. Americans were legendary for their friendliness and their ease yet both Carlotta and Heidi seemed to be looking over their shoulders in case the shadow of Marilyn Vine might fall on the place and they would have to run away.

She put away the fanciful thoughts and ushered them into the kitchen.

Marilyn unpacked everything and had her soup. And a glass of the expensive French wine that Ria had left her. Then she lay for a long time upstairs in the claw-foot bath and soaked away the hours of travel followed by hours of walking around Dublin.

She thought she might sleep, but no, all during the long afternoon her eyes were open and her mind was racing. Why had she come to this house, full of the past and the future? This was a Victorian house, for heaven's sake. Marilyn didn't know exactly what date it was, but people could well have lived here when the Civil War was taking place, when Gettysburg was being fought!

There was hope in this house that there was never going to be in 1024 Tudor Drive. Two sunny children smiled out of photographs in every room. A boy with a grin as wide as a watermelon, and a girl who would be almost the same age as Dale. Marilyn lay under the white bedspread in the master bedroom of this house, which had everything, and thought of her life, which had nothing.

There was a small sound and the anxious face of the great marmalade cat came around the door. With a leap he landed and laid himself on the bed beside her. He had a purr like the engine of a small boat on the lakes in upper New York State. Marilyn neither loved nor hated cats, she approved of all animals in a vague way. But Clement was a knowing sort of cat. He seemed to understand that she was not happy. He nestled in beside her, purring louder and louder. Like some kind of lullaby or a mantra it sent Marilyn Vine to sleep and when she woke it was midnight.

In Stoneyfield it must be seven o'clock in the evening. She would call Ria and thank her for this restful home. The arrangement was that Ria would pick up if she wanted to answer the call. Marilyn dialed the number. After three rings she heard her own voice respond. "It's Marilyn," she said. "It's midnight here and everything's wonderful. I just wanted to thank you."

Then Ria's voice came on the line. "It's only twilight here, but it's even more wonderful. Thank you very, very much."

"You found the Chardonnay?" Marilyn asked.

"Yes, indeed I finished it, and you found the Chablis?"

"Sure I did. I haven't finished it yet but I will."

"And Gertie let you in?"

"I got in fine and I love the place. You have one beautiful home. And Carlotta gave you the keys and everything?"

"She did, it's a dream house, you undersold it."

There was a little pause. Then they both said good night. Marilyn did not know why she had pretended Gertie was there. Ria had no idea why she did not say to Marilyn that her friends Carlotta and Heidi were about to open the third bottle of wine. If anyone had asked them they would have been hard put to explain.

"I'm going to see my grannie today, Bernadette."

"Oh, good."

"So I don't know *exactly* what time I'll be back."

"Sure."

Annie gathered up her tote bag of things which included a very short lycra skirt and a halter top.

"Before you go, call your dad in the office, will you?"

"Why should I do that?"

"Because you forgot to tell him at breakfast that you were going to your grandmother's."

"Oh, he doesn't want to be bothered with every detail."

"He does, actually."

"I'll tell him tonight."

"Would you prefer *me* to tell him for you?" Bernadette's voice was without any threat. It sounded like a simple question, which it most definitely was not.

"There's no need to behave like a jailer, Bernadette."

"And there's no need to lie to me either, Annie. You're not going to your grandmother's with all that gear. You and Kitty are off somewhere entirely different."

"What's it to you if we are?"

"It's nothing to me, I couldn't care less where you go or what you do, but your father's going to be upset and *that* I don't want."

It was the longest sentence that Annie had ever heard from Bernadette. She considered it for a while then she said inquiringly, "He won't be upset if he doesn't know."

"Nice try. No way," Bernadette said.

"I have to ring Kitty," Annie said, defeated.

Bernadette nodded to the phone. "Go ahead," she said and went back to her book.

Annie looked around once or twice during the conversation but there was no evidence that Bernadette was listening. "No, I can't explain," Annie said mutinously. "Of course I tried. Don't you think I did? Who do you think? Yeah. Yeah. Even worse than Mam if you ask me."

She hung up disconsolately and looked over at Bernadette curled up in her armchair. She thought she had seen a flicker of a smile but she might have only imagined it.

"What's she like?" Myles and Dekko wanted to know.

"She's all right, I suppose," Brian said grudgingly.

"Do they have lots of sex all the time?"

"Oh no, of course they don't."

"Well, why else did he go and live with her and get her pregnant?" Dekko asked.

"That was all in the past. I don't think they do that sort of thing now." Brian was puzzled at the notion.

"They never stop doing it." Myles was still gloomy about the new baby that had blighted his own life. "They go on and on until they drop dead from it."

"Do they?" Dekko was interested.

"I know they do." Myles was an authority on this. "But in your house, Brian, they must be at it all the time. What with the situation and everything."

"Yeah, I see what you mean." Brian considered it carefully.

"Don't you hear them gasping and being out of breath from it?"

"No," he shook his head. "Not in front of us anyway."

"Of course it's not in front of you, you eejit. It's when they go to bed
. . . that's when you'd hear it."

"No, they just talk in low voices about money."

"How do you know?"

"Annie and I listened. We wanted to know if they were talking about
Mam, but they never mentioned her, not once."

"What kind of talk about money?"

"Oh, desperate boring things about second mortgages. For hours and
hours," said Brian.

"Are they total monsters?" Finola Dunne asked her daughter on the
phone.

Bernadette laughed. "They're not too bad, very loud of course, and
restless."

"That's all ahead of you," her mother said sagely.

"I know."

"Anyway, it's swimming today. I'll be able to report myself. I like the
boy, he's got a sense of humor."

"It's much harder on Annie." Bernadette sounded sympathetic.

"Yes, she needs watching."

"That's always been your motto, Mum."

"Fine lot of good it did me with you!" Bernadette's mother rang off.

At the swimming pool Annie was astounded to see her friend Kitty.

"What a coincidence!" she said four times.

Kitty was equally amazed. "Who would have thought it?" she asked
the air around her.

"This is my friend Mary, Mrs. Dunne." Annie introduced her. "She's
been feeding my cat, Clement. Can I go around to Tara Road with her to
see Clement after the swimming lesson?"

"I don't see why not," Finola Dunne said. There was an easy bus
service back to Danny and Ria's house. Mary seemed a nice little thing,
kind of the child to feed the cat.

"Why are you calling her Mary?" Brian asked.

"Because it's her name, you fool," Annie hissed.

"It never was before," Brian protested.

"It is now, so will you shut up?"

The swimming coach was blowing a whistle to get their attention.

"See you later, Kitty," Annie called.

"I'm sorry, I got her name wrong, I called her Mary," Finola Dunne said.

"Oh um she's both . . . really." Annie's face was red.

Brian grinned in triumph.

While the swimming lesson was in progress Finola Dunne made a phone call. Her eyes were steely when it was time to go. "Tell Mary that the American lady is feeding the cat on Tara Road and that you won't need to go and visit it at all."

Annie hung her head. "Did you ring Bernadette?" she said eventually.

"Yes, and she had a message for you."

"What did she say?" Annie was apprehensive.

"She said I was to say to you nice second try, third try your dad deals with it."

Heidi and Carlotta told Ria that they had never in their whole lives drunk a bottle of wine each. They were astounded with themselves and each other. They blamed it entirely, they said, on the bad influence of their new Irish friend. Ria assured them that she had never done anything so outrageous herself and that at home she was very much a one drink a night person.

"But this is the United States," wailed Carlotta. "We count units, we count calories, we all know people, like about half my clients in the salon at a rough guess, who are in recovery and detox and now we're heading that way ourselves."

"And I'm a middle-aged faculty wife. We all hear tales of how *they* go on the bottle at exactly this time of life. And rot away. Our husbands don't have the salary to get us into the Betty Ford Clinic."

"Ah, but I'm a sadder case than either of you," Ria laughed. "I'm a deserted wife from Ireland over here to sort out my head and on my first day in America I fall in with two lushes and get pissed out of my brains."

They had learned a great deal about each other—about Carlotta's alimony from her three husbands, all paid at the time in large, agreed-to lump sums and even of the details of how well it had been invested. Heidi's first marriage had been to a man so totally unsatisfactory in every way that he was only equaled in horror by Henry's first wife. It would have been a wonderful poetic justice if they had met and married each other but they had gone on to marry and upset other people. And of course Danny Lynch was introduced to Stoneyfield—how Ria met him the day before her twenty-second birthday, of the afternoon she first slept with him on Tara Road and of the night he told her that he was indeed planning to be a father but not of her baby.

"Let's see what Marilyn left in the fridge," Heidi said.

They could have talked forever. But when they had eaten a spinach quiche they found in the freezer, and had two sobering cups of coffee, Ria felt Carlotta and Heidi were slightly guilty and even embarrassed at the confidences shared. It was not that they regretted having talked so openly, more that this was an inappropriate place to have done so. She was disappointed to see the warmth of the evening beginning to trickle away. She thought that she had found two wonderful new friends the moment she arrived. Perhaps it wasn't going to be like that. She must learn to move more slowly, not to assume huge warmth where it might not exist. She let the evening wind down without begging to meet them again. This seemed to suit them. And Ria also felt they were very pleased she had not mentioned to Marilyn that they were all sitting together having a little party at 1024 Tudor Drive. In all their revelations and discussions and debates, they had mentioned not once the woman who lived in this house.

When they left at about ten o'clock, which was three o'clock in the morning at home, Ria walked slowly around Marilyn's house. In Ireland her husband, Danny, was in bed with a child who was expecting his child. Her son, Brian, was lying on his back with the bedclothes in a twist at the end of the bed, and the light on. Her daughter, Annie, would have filled her diary with impossible plans of how to escape to somewhere dangerous with Kitty. Her mother would sleep surrounded by pictures of the saints and vague unformed plans to sell her little house and move herself into St. Rita's.

Hilary and Martin would be asleep in their strange, poky little house in the bed they bought at a fire sale, the bed where they no longer made love because Martin said that unless you thought you were conceiving a child there was no point in it. Their big round red alarm clock would be set for six-thirty. During the school vacation Hilary still had to go up to the school to do secretarial work and Martin had a job marking exam papers to make ends meet. Rosemary would be asleep now for four hours and as Gertie's life had obviously been tranquil enough to allow her to be at Tara Road to welcome Marilyn, so perhaps she too was asleep beside the big drunken boor that she thought of as some kind of precious and fragile treasure, which it was her mission to protect.

Clement would be asleep somewhere in the kitchen on a chair. He chose a different one every night with great care, and a sense of hurt. He was never allowed upstairs to the bedrooms no matter how much he had tried or no matter how often Annie had pleaded.

Was Marilyn asleep? Maybe she was awake thinking about her. Ria went into the room that she had just glimpsed before she had somehow instinctively shut the door against Carlotta. She turned on the light. The walls were covered with pictures of motorbikes, Electra Glides, Hondas.

A bed had boy's clothes strewn on it, jackets, jeans, big shoes . . . as if a fifteen-year-old had come in, rummaged for something to wear, and then gone out. The closet had clothes hanging neatly on a rail and on the shelves were piles of shirts and shorts and socks. The desk at the window had school papers on it, magazines, books. There were photographs too, of a boy, a good-looking teenage boy with hair that stuck up in spikes and a smile not at all impaired by the braces on his teeth, always with a group of friends. They were playing basketball in one, they were swimming in another, they were out in the snow, they were in costume for a school play. The pictures were laid out casually.

She looked at the photographs. It must have been intentional. She longed to know more about the woman who was asleep in her bed back on Tara Road. There must be something in this house that would give her an image of what Marilyn Vine looked like. And then she found it. It was attached with sticky tape to the inside of his sports bag. A summer picture of a threesome; the boy in tennis clothes, all smiles with his arms around the shoulders of a man with thinning hair and an open-necked checked shirt. The woman was tall and thin and she wore a yellow running suit. She had high cheekbones, short, darkish hair and she wore her sunglasses on her head. They were like an advertisement for healthy living, all three of them.

Rosemary left a note in the letterbox.

> *Dear Marilyn,*
> *Welcome to Dublin. When you wake up I'm sure you may want to go straight back to sleep and not to get involved with nosy neighbors, but this is just a word to say that whenever you would like to come round for a drink or even to have a lunch with me in Quentin's, which you might enjoy, all you have to do is telephone.*
> *I don't want to overpower you with invitations and demands but I do want you to know that as Ria's oldest and I hope dearest friend I wanted to welcome you and hope you have a good time here. I know she is very excited about going to your home.*
> *Most sincerely,*
> *Rosemary Ryan.*

Marilyn had the note in her hand before Rosemary had run back to her car, which was parked outside the gate. She had felt wide awake after her conversation with Ria in the night, and knew that sleep would not come again, despite the hugely affectionate purring of Clement, who had reluctantly come downstairs again to be with her and sat on one of the chairs in this beautiful old room. Through the window Marilyn saw the tall blond elegant woman in a very well cut suit that was most definitely power dressing. With a flash of very elegant smoky tights and high heels she was getting into a black BMW and driving away. This was the woman whom Ria had described in her letters as her great friend, a business tycoon and Ms. Perfect but absolutely delightful at the same time.

Marilyn read the letter with approval. No pressure but generous. This was a woman who went to work at six-thirty in the morning, owned her own business, and looked like a film star. Rosemary Ryan drove the streets in her BMW. Marilyn read the note again. She didn't want to meet this woman, make conversation with her. It didn't matter how important these people were in Ria's life, they weren't part of hers. She would leave the letter unanswered and eventually if Rosemary called again they would have a brief meeting.

Marilyn hadn't come to Ireland to make a whole set of superficial acquaintances.

"I dreamed about you, Colm," Orla King said as he came into the restaurant.

"No, you didn't. You decided you wanted to ask me could you sing here on Saturday and you needed an excuse to come and see me." He smiled at her to take the harm out of his words.

Orla laughed good-naturedly. "Of course I want to sing here on Saturday, and also every night in August during Horse Show week when you'll be full. But I actually did dream about you."

"Was I a successful restaurant owner, tell me that?"

"No, you were in jail for life for murdering your brother-in-law, Monto," Orla said.

"Always very melodramatic, Orla," Colm said, but his smile didn't quite go to his eyes.

"Yeah, but we don't choose what we dream, it just happens," Orla said with a shrug. "It must mean something."

"I don't *think* I murdered my brother-in-law," Colm said as if trying to remember. "No, I'm sure I didn't. He was here last night with a big crowd from the races."

"He's a real shit, isn't he?" Orla said.

"I'm not crazy about him certainly, but I definitely didn't murder him." Colm seemed to find it hard to hold on to the light banter of this conversation.

"No, I know you didn't, he was on the phone to me today trying to get me to go to a stag night. Singing, he said. We all know what he means by singing at a stag night."

"What *does* he mean, Orla?"

"It means show us your tits, Orla."

"How unpleasant," Colm said.

"Not everyone thinks so, Colm."

"No, I mean how deeply unpleasant of the man who is married to my sister asking a professional singer to do anything like that at a stag night. You misunderstood me totally. I'm obviously sure that the sight of your breasts would be a great delight to anyone but not under such circumstances."

"You speak like a barrister sometimes."

"Well, I might need one if your dream comes true." Colm spoke in a slightly tinny voice.

"Monto told me that . . . well he sort of said that . . ." Orla stopped.

"Yes?"

"He sort of hinted that he had a few problems with your sister, Caroline."

"Yes, I think he has a problem remembering he is married to her."

"He says more than that. He sort of says there's a dark secret."

"There is, you know, it's called Bad Judgment. She married a man whom you so rightly describe as a shit. Not much of a dark secret, but there you go. Anyway Orla, you'd like to sing on Saturday? A couple of pointers. You sing as background, not as foreground. They want to talk to each other as well as listen to you. Is that understood?"

"Right, boss."

"You'll sing much more Ella and lots less Lloyd Webber. Okay?"

"You're wrong, but yes, boss."

"You keep your hands and eyes off Danny Lynch. He'll be here with his new wife and his two kids and his mother-in-law."

"It's not a new wife, it's his pregnant girlfriend so don't be pompous, Colm."

"Hands and eyes. A promise or no slot and you never work again here or anywhere else."

"A promise, boss."

Colm wondered why he had warned Orla off, after all it might be some small pleasure for Ria out in America to hear that the love nest was less secure than everyone imagined. But business was business and who wanted a scene in a restaurant on a Saturday night.

"We're going to take Mrs. Dunne out to dinner on Saturday night," Danny told his children.

"Mam's going to ring on Saturday night," Brian objected.

"She told us to call her Finola, not Mrs. Dunne," Annie objected.

"She told *me* to call her Finola, she didn't tell you."

"Yes, she did."

"No, Annie, she didn't. She's a different generation."

"We call Rosemary Rosemary, don't we?"

"Yes, but that's because she's a feminist."

"But Finola's a feminist too, she said she was," Annie insisted.

"Okay, so she's Finola. Fine, fine. Now I thought we might go to Quentin's, but it turns out that she . . . Finola . . . wants to go to Colm's so that's where we're going."

"Dead right too," Annie said. "Colm has proper vegetarian food, not some awful, poncy thing that costs what would keep a poor family for a month like the token vegetarian dish in Quentin's costs."

"But what if Mam rings?" Brian asked.

"There's an answering machine and if we miss her we'll call her back." Danny was bright about it all.

"She might have been looking forward to talking to us though," Brian said.

"We could change the message and say we were all at Colm's maybe?" Annie suggested.

"No, I think we'll leave the message as it is." Danny was firm.

"But it's so easy, Dad."

"People ring Bernadette too, and they wouldn't want to hear all about our fumblings and fusterings."

"It's not fumbling just to let Mam know that we hadn't forgotten she was going to call," Annie said.

"Well, call her! Say we're going out."

"We can't afford to phone her," Brian said.

"I just told you you can. A quick call, okay?"

"But what about the second mortgage and all the debts and everything?" Brian asked.

"What do you mean?" His father was anxious.

Annie spoke quickly. "You know you often said that everything costs so much we might have to get a second mortgage, but Brian doesn't realize how cheap it is to call for thirty seconds."

"I didn't say anything about—"

"Dad, we're just going to love a night out in Colm's, and Finola will love it and so will you. Stop worrying about Brian, who as I have so often told you, is totally brain-dead. And let's get on with it."

"You're a great girl, Princess," he said. "I look around Dublin and I see all the bright young men who are going to take you away from me one day."

"Come on, Dad, who are you fooling? You don't meet kids of my age anywhere."

"No, but you're not going to run off with a kid, are you, Princess?" her father asked.

"You did, Dad."

There was a silence.

"Who will I marry?" Brian asked.

"A person who has been deprived of all her senses, but very particularly the sense of smell," Annie said.

"That's not right, is it, Dad?"

"Of course not, Brian. Your sister is only making a joke. You'll marry a great person when the time comes."

"A lady wrestler, maybe," Annie suggested.

Brian ignored her again. "Is there any way of knowing it's the right person, Dad?"

"You'll know." His father was soothing.

"You didn't, Dad. You thought Mam was the right person and she turned out not to be."

"She was the right person at the time, Brian."

"And how long's the right time, Dad?" Brian asked.

"About sixteen years, apparently," Annie said.

"Supper everyone, I have bought lovely fish and chips," Bernadette called from the kitchen.

Marilyn had taken a chair and a cup of coffee out to the front steps; she sat in the sun examining the garden.

There was so much that could be done with it. Such a pity they hadn't given it any real love and care, unlike the house itself. She saw there *had* been interesting trees planted. Somebody at some stage had known what would flourish and had wanted to make an impression, but the Arbutus had not been pruned or shaped, it had been allowed to become rough and woody, it was almost beyond saving. The palm tree was scraggy and untidy and almost unseen because other bushes had grown up around it and almost taken it over.

Outside the gate she noticed a woman in her sixties with a very mis-shapen and unattractive dog. The woman was staring in with interest.

"Good morning," Marilyn said politely.

"And good morning to you too, I expect you're the American visitor."

"Yes, I'm Marilyn Vine. Are you a neighbor?"

"I'm Ria's mother, Nora, and this is Pliers."

"How do you do?" Marilyn said.

"Ria said most definitely that we should not call in on top of you unannounced." Nora had come up the step to continue the conversation but she looked doubtful. Pliers gave a wide and very unpleasant yawn as if he could sense a tedious exchange of courtesies ahead. Marilyn remem-bered her from the photograph, she knew the woman lived nearby. "I can tell you one thing for a start, Ria didn't grow up in a home like this with all those antiques around her."

Marilyn could hear the resentment in the woman's voice. "Really, Mrs. Johnson?"

Nora looked at her watch with a scream and said she'd be late for St. Rita's. "You must come with me one day . . . it's an old people's home, a visit would be a great thing," she said.

"It's very kind of you but *why* exactly?" Marilyn was bewildered.

"Well, they like unusual things to happen in their day. I take my grandchildren there sometimes, and I once brought a juggler I met on Grafton Street. They like Pliers as a new face, I'm sure they'd enjoy meeting an American, it would be different anyway."

"Well, thank you. Sometime, perhaps."

"Has Lady Ryan been around yet?"

"I beg your pardon?"

"Ria's friend, Rosemary?"

"No, she left a note though. People have been so kind."

"Well, they're interested in you, Marilyn, it's only natural." Nora Johnson was gone, having said she wanted to know every little detail about Marilyn Vine and having asked or discovered absolutely nothing at all.

After Ria's mother left, Marilyn took out again the wallet of photo-graphs that she had been given. She had to know who these people were when they all turned up as they would, so when Gertie arrived, slightly hesitantly, Marilyn recognized her at once.

"Let's not be awkward about this," Gertie began. "I know Ria told you I need a few extra pounds a week, but it seems unfair on you to have to dig into your holiday money . . ."

"No, that's perfectly fine and I'd love to know that this beautiful house is being kept the way it always is."

Gertie looked around her. "But you've got it looking great, there's not a thing out of place. It's just putting out my hand and asking for charity."

"No, that's not the way I see it."

"I'm not sure if Ria explained. . . ." Gertie began.

"Oh, totally. You are kind enough to come and help to keep her house in its fine condition twice a week."

"Yes, but if that's all right with you?" Gertie had big black circles under her eyes. There was some background of dependency here. Marilyn knew Gertie was both friend and employee, still, it was none of her business. "And would you like me to make you a cup of coffee?" Gertie began.

"No, thank you."

"Well, shall I start doing the cleaning then?"

"I'm sure you know this house very well, whatever you think . . ."

"Well, she always liked the front room polished."

"Sure, that would be fine."

"And would you like me to do anything for you, like ironing maybe?"

"That's very kind. I hate ironing. I'm going out now, so shall I see you next time?"

"That's fine, and you're very welcome here, Marilyn."

"Thank you," Marilyn said. She took her keys and walked up Tara Road. Lord but this house was going to be full of people. Not exactly the rest she had been looking for.

Gertie thought that for a woman who absolutely hated ironing, all Marilyn's clothes were very crisp and well pressed, and that she had already found time to take out Ria's iron since her arrival. But she decided not to argue it any further. There was something appealing about Marilyn. She didn't seem to want to know why Gertie, who already ran a laundromat, needed extra money in cash, nor did she seem eager to talk about her own situation. In a life where too many people wanted to move in and alter the situation, Gertie found this lack of involvement very pleasing indeed.

"What does it say?" Brian asked.

"It's an American woman's voice saying she's not there and to leave a message for the people who are there," Annie replied.

"There aren't any people . . . there's only Mam."

"Shut up, Brian. Hallo, Mam, it's Annie and Brian, and everything's fine and it's just that we'll be going out to a big dinner with Dad and . . . well, what I mean is that we'll be going out to dinner in Colm's restaurant on Saturday so we won't be back until maybe eleven o'clock our time. We didn't want you to ring and find nobody at home. That's it, Mam. Brian's okay too."

"Let me say I'm okay," Brian cried.

"You're not to waste the call, Mam *knows* you're okay."

Brian snatched the phone. "I'm okay, Mam, and getting on at the swimming. Finola says the coach told her that I'm making fine progress. Oh, Finola's Bernadette's mother by the way. She's coming to the dinner too."

Annie snatched the phone back and hung up. "Aren't you the greatest eejit in the whole wide world to mention Finola? Aren't you a fool of the first order?" she said to him, her eyes blazing.

"I'm sorry." Brian was crestfallen. "I'm so sorry, I just didn't think. I was excited leaving the message for Mam."

He looked so upset even Annie Lynch's hard heart relented. "It's not the end of the world, I suppose," she said gruffly. "Mam won't mind."

Ria came in from the pool wearing one of Marilyn's terry cloth robes. For the first few times she had just flopped around luxuriating in the cold water and the beautiful flowers and the lovingly kept garden all around her. But she had taken to reading Dale's sports books all laid so neatly in his room. There had been a section of swimming and how many lengths he and his friends had done on different days. One entry said, *Mom has decided to stop behaving like a dolphin and be a proper swimmer. So she's doing four laps each time, it's nothing but she's going to build it up.*

By the time Dale stopped writing his records, Marilyn Vine was doing thirty laps. Ria felt there was a message for her here. By the time her children came out she wouldn't be like a dolphin anymore, she would be purposeful, competitive even. She had done six lengths today and was utterly exhausted. What she needed was a cup of tea and a rest.

She saw the little red light flickering on the phone and rushed to play back the message. She sat at the breakfast bar listening to her children speaking to her from thousands of miles away. The tears poured down her face. What was she *doing* out in this place, wearing herself out playing silly games in a swimming pool? Why was she not at home with them instead of leaving them to become bosom pals with Bernadette's bloody mother? And why was Danny being so cruel and insensitive as to go back to the very restaurant where they had such a scene on the night she first learned of Bernadette? And would Colm make a fuss over them and offer them a complimentary drink as he always did?

The Lynch family on an outing, the same as usual, only a few small things changed. The wives, for example. The one put out to grass and a newer model installed. The mothers-in-law. Nora Johnson wouldn't be there, but Mrs. Dunne with her shiny copper shoes and her smart suit would. Like probing a sore tooth, she insisted on playing the message over and over. She couldn't even smile at the argument between the children. She knew that once they had hung up Annie had laid into Brian for his tactlessness. At this very minute some huge argument was taking place. How would Bernadette react? Would she stop their fighting or would she pretend not to notice?

Ria didn't care which she did. It would be the wrong thing to do anyway. And maybe this woman who was somehow Finola to Ria's children and yet was Mummy to Bernadette was now a huge influence in their lives. She was going out to dinner with them, for heaven's sake. That hurt more than anything.

It was too much to bear. Ria put her head down on the breakfast counter in the sunny kitchen and cried and cried. She didn't see a man come to the glass doors and pause before knocking. He, however, saw a woman doubled over in grief. He couldn't hear her sobs or the choked words. He picked up his canvas bag and moved silently away. This was not the time to call and say that he was Greg Vine's brother passing through and that he had come to see Marilyn. He walked down to his rented car and drove to a motel.

It had been such a house of tragedy since the accident he had hardly been able to bear visiting it. And now he had come across a strange woman in a terry cloth robe, crying with a kind of intensity he had never known. Still, he had promised his brother that if work took him east he would look up Marilyn. He had thought wrongly that it would be better to come without warning, otherwise she would have certainly found some excuse not to meet him.

He had a shower, a cool beer at the motel, and then he telephoned his brother's house. The words said Marilyn and Greg were both away but to leave a message for the people staying in the house. On a whim he spoke.

"My name is Andy Vine. I'm Greg's brother, passing through Stoneyfield staying at the . . . sorry . . ." he hunted for the name and number of the motel. "I know Greg's in Hawaii obviously, but perhaps you might call me and tell me where Marilyn is? I would much appreciate this. Many thanks in advance."

Ria sat listening to the message. She did not pick up the receiver. Marilyn had mentioned no brother-in-law. Perhaps there was a coldness. If he was a brother of Greg Vine's then surely he'd know that Greg's wife was in Dublin. If he was a brother-in-law of Marilyn and had thought she was at home, why had he not called around? But then was she being ridiculously suspicious over nothing? And would it be childish and nitpicky to call Marilyn in Ireland and check? It would also be somehow involving herself in Marilyn's doings, which she realized now was the last thing Marilyn seemed to want. She couldn't ask Carlotta and Heidi since they seemed to know nothing whatsoever about their friend Marilyn's lifestyle. She decided she would call Greg Vine in Hawaii.

She was put through to him with great ease. He sounded younger and more relaxed than his photograph had suggested.

"Yes, of course," he said when she gave her name.

"First, I must assure you that there's no problem here. Everything in your beautiful house is in fine shape," she said.

"That's a relief, I thought you were going to tell me the plumbing wasn't working."

"No, nothing like that, and I suppose in a way because I'm living in your home . . . I wanted to introduce myself to you . . . but not at length on your phone bill."

"That's most courteous of you. I hope you have everything you need." His voice was polite but cold.

Ria told him about the call from the motel. Greg assured her that he did have a highly respectable brother named Andy who worked in Los Angeles but came to Boston and New York City on business from time to time.

"That's fine then, I'll call him. I thought it wiser to check it out because he didn't seem to know anything about Marilyn's movements."

"I appreciate your caution very much. But Marilyn was, let us say, a trifle reserved in telling people anything about her movements." His voice was bitter and cold.

Ria decided to ignore the tone. "Well, you'll be glad to know she's arrived there safely and is as well installed as I am in Tudor Drive. It would be good if you had the chance to go over there yourself."

"Oh, I don't think that's in the Master Plan." Again his voice sounded cold.

"I asked would you be going, she said she didn't know."

"Really? And will your husband be joining you in Stoneyfield?" he asked.

Ria took a deep breath. Marilyn had certainly been fairly short on her explanations of anything to anyone. "No, Danny is now my ex-husband. He is living with a much younger woman called Bernadette. It's the reason why I am actually here in your house. My son and daughter will, however, be joining me here next month. Did Marilyn not even tell you that much?"

There was a pause then he spoke. "Yes, she did, and I apologize for my manner. It was uncalled for. I was confused by Marilyn's not wanting to come here. I still am."

"That's perfectly all right. I think it was a search for somewhere completely different."

"Obviously."

There was a little pause.

"And your son?"

"Yes?"

"He likes Hawaii?"

"I beg your pardon?"

"I suppose it's a place that all young people would like." Ria felt flustered, although she did not know why.

"Oh, yes. Certainly."

"I expect he's missing his mother."

"I'm sorry?"

"They never pretend, but they do in a way that they can't even define." She knew she was gushing. "Boys . . ." said Ria nervously.

"Well, yes." He seemed anxious to end the conversation.

"I won't keep you any longer," she said. "I'm not clear about what's going on in anyone's lives these days, but just be sure that your house is in fine shape. I had hoped to reassure you of that anyway."

"Of course, of course. And is it working for you being over here?"

"It was," Ria said truthfully. "It was working quite well but I just got a message from my children on your answering machine."

"Are they missing you? Is that the problem?"

"No, Greg. They're not missing me, *that's* the problem."

"Marilyn? This is Rosemary Ryan."

"Oh yes, thank you for your note."

Rosemary was to the point. "I wondered can I take you and Gertie to Colm's restaurant on Saturday for dinner? He has a special seafood evening, and you might enjoy it."

"I don't want to intrude."

"This would be a casual easy girls' night out. Gertie doesn't go out socially. Do say yes."

"Thank you so much, Rosemary, I'd love to join you," said Marilyn Vine.

Ria called Andy Vine at the motel, told him who she was and where Marilyn had gone.

"We both needed a little space in our lives and thought it would be a good idea," she said.

He seemed happy enough with the explanation.

"And in the normal turn of events would you be staying here on Tudor Drive, I mean if Marilyn had been at home and everything?"

"Well, I might," he said.

"So you shouldn't be paying for a motel really, should you? If you expected to stay here in your brother's house?" She was eager to do the right thing.

"No, please, Maria. Please don't think like that. It's your house now just as the house in Ireland belongs to Marilyn."

"I feel bad about it. How long are you going to be in Stoneyfield anyway?"

"I had thought that maybe I'd spend tonight and Saturday night here, you know, if Marilyn were around . . . then drive up to Boston on Sunday. The conference starts on Monday morning."

"I'm sorry she didn't think of telling you. It was all arranged in a bit of a hurry," Ria apologized.

This couldn't be the woman he had seen crying like no one had ever cried before. "I had been going to ask Marilyn out to dinner at a new Thai restaurant."

"Maybe next time," she said.

"Would *you* like a Thai dinner, Maria?" he asked.

She paused. It was the last thing on earth she thought would happen to her in America, a man who hadn't even seen her inviting her out to dinner within a week of her arrival. But it was a Saturday night. Back in Ireland tomorrow night her children were being taken to Colm's restaurant with a lot of strangers. "Thank you so much, Andy, I'd be delighted to accept," Ria Lynch said.

"Monto wants to bring in a crowd tonight," Colm said.

"What did you tell him?" Caroline was immediately anxious.

"I told him we were full."

"Oh."

"He said I was to have a word with Caroline and that he'd call back later and see if we had an unexpected cancellation for six people."

"Give it to him, Colm."

"Why? It upsets you when they're here. We don't need the business those guys bring in, six overdone steaks and round after round of double gins."

"Please, Colm . . . ?"

"It's utterly terrifying for me to see you so afraid of him." He looked at her big, sad eyes with such compassion that he could see the tears form in the corners. "Still, I'll do what you say. Which table will they be least noticeable at, do you think?"

She gave him a watery smile. "Look, do you think I'd be like this about him if there was any other solution?"

"There *is* a solution."

"We've had this conversation a thousand times."

"I'm so sorry, Caroline." He put his arms around his sister and she laid her head on his shoulder.

"What have you to be sorry for? You've done everything for me, you've saved my life."

He patted her on the back as he held her and behind him he heard the cheery voice of Orla King.

"Well, hello everybody. I thought I'd be on time to show you my sheet music but, boy, did I come a little early."

Bernadette's mother had decided to teach Brian Lynch to play chess.

"Isn't it hard?" Brian asked suspiciously.

"No, it's not hard at all to learn to play, it's hard to be good at it. You'd pick it up in half an hour then you'd know it for life."

"Right then," said Brian agreeably.

"Would you like to learn too, Annie?"

"No thanks, Finola, if you don't mind."

"Not at all." She had known Annie would refuse to do anything in tandem with her younger brother, and also she might have felt it somehow disloyal to her mother. Bernadette was right. Annie was a complicated child, and of course fourteen and a half was the very worst age in the whole world.

Danny and Bernadette were out with Barney McCarthy meeting some possible investors in a new development. It had not gone well, they had asked rather too searching questions about previous financial returns and too many details about building specifications. Bernadette had been quiet and respectful, looking from one to another with interest but no understanding. Ria would have had some kind of sparky input into the conversation which might have taken the dead edge of an unsuccessful pitch for unlikely business off the whole thing.

Danny was tired when they got up to leave. "Will we go to Quentin's tonight?" Barney suggested.

"No. A family dinner. Long arranged."

"Never mind, I just thought it would be relaxing to drop by Tara Road, have a drink, a shower, and then just the two of us head off and sort out the financial problems of the world."

"It would have been," Danny said.

Then they both looked at each other in alarm. They had both actually forgotten that Danny didn't live on Tara Road anymore.

Possibly that was what made Danny drive home that way. It was only slightly out of his way to cut through that neighborhood. As he looked out at the house that had been his home, Danny Lynch saw a tall slim woman in dark jeans and a white shirt, quite striking in a sporty kind of way, digging urgently at the undergrowth in his front garden. On the tarmacadam drive was a huge sheet of plastic that held what she had already hacked out.

"What the hell does she think she's doing?" he said, slowing down immediately.

"Drive on, Danny." Bernadette's voice was calm but insistent.

"No, I won't. She's tearing my garden to bits."

"Drive on a little bit farther anyway so that she won't see you."

"She'll see me, by God she'll see me. I'm not letting her get away with that."

But he did go on farther, and parked near Rosemary's house.

"Don't go in, you're upset."

"But she'll have the whole place cut down," he protested.

"Don't upset her. She might storm back to America."

"Good."

"Then there'd be nowhere for the children to go on holiday," said Bernadette.

"They're having a bloody holiday with us next week on the Shannon, isn't that enough for them?" But he took her advice and drove home.

"I brought you martinis in honor of the visiting American," Colm said. It proved to be a great success.

Marilyn told them about her happy day in the garden, she was never happier than when up to her elbows in earth. If the other two thought that she might have checked with Ria before embarking on it they said nothing. And of course it was quite possible that she had. Gertie told them about a man in the launderette who came there every Saturday and washed an entire bag of women's black lacy underwear. Quite unconcerned as people saw him taking them out and folding them neatly into a big carrier bag. Gertie said that she'd love to be able to tell these little things to Jack but that sadly you never knew how he would take them, he might come rushing in and calling the man a pervert. And if the other two thought it was a poor life if you couldn't even tell your husband a pleasant story about work they gave no hint of it.

And when a good-looking blonde began to sing "Someone to Watch Over Me," they told Marilyn that this was about the most troublesome woman in Dublin who had been known to cause spectacular scenes in her time.

"She's a good singer, though," Marilyn said, struggling to be fair and looking at the woman who played and sang as if every word had a huge meaning for her.

"But a high risk factor. I always tell Colm, but when does anyone listen to me?" Rosemary said in a tone that suggested almost everyone else listened to her and was wise to do so.

"Maybe he just likes giving her a chance. Colm's great at helping the underdog," Gertie said.

"She doesn't look like much of an underdog to me," Marilyn volunteered. At that moment Danny Lynch and his party came into the restaurant and they were settled at a table across the room. Marilyn recognized them immediately from the photographs on the walls. "Is that Ria's husband?" she asked very directly. And the other two nodded glumly.

Until then, nobody had spoken of Ria. Now her whole personal story was here in the restaurant and they couldn't skirt around it anymore. A glamorous, well-made-up woman in a black sequinned jacket was being very much the center of things, pointing at where people were to sit.

"She doesn't look like a twenty-two-year-old to me, she's my age if she's a day," Marilyn whispered.

"You're not going to believe this, Marilyn, but that's the twenty-two-year-old's mother," whispered Rosemary.

"Mother!" said Marilyn in disbelief.

Then she saw, beside the two animated children familiar from their pictures, the waif in the shapeless blue jumper and skirt. A pale child with long straight hair who could definitely be taken for Annie's not-very-much-older sister. Marilyn felt a pain that was almost physical to think that Ria Lynch had to endure this. Danny Lynch was still the excitable boy that he had been all those years ago. And Ria loved him deeply still. How could anyone bear the pain of losing a man to this, this strange, unformed young girl? No wonder poor Ria had run three thousand miles away to get over the grief of it all.

Orla began to sing "The Man I Love." Colm frowned. He frowned even more deeply when she went straight into "But Not for Me."

"Cool it, Orla," he said as he passed with the steaks for Monto's table.

"Pure Gershwin, boss, as you suggested. Coming up with 'Nice Work If You Can Get It.' That should set a few hearts fluttering, don't you think?"

"You have a reasonably nice voice but you don't have all that much of a career. And while you're at it, if you go on like you're going on tonight, forget the Horse Show next month."

"Be fair, Colm. You said Cole Porter and Gershwin. George I've done. They liked it. I'm coming up to Cole now. 'I Get a Kick Out of You' and 'I've Got You Under My Skin.' Can I help it, boss, if the titles have a bit of innuendo? I don't write them, I'm only singing them at your request."

"Don't be a fool, Orla, please."

"Hey, who are you to ask me not to be a fool? A man who's in love with his sister. Great bloody role model, Colm Barry."

"I warn you, you'll be so very, very sorry tomorrow. I'll still have a restaurant, you won't have a job or a chance of ever getting one in Dublin."

"Do you remember something we used to hear every week called 'One Day at a Time'? Okay, this is my day, this is my time." Her eyes were too bright.

"Don't do it, Orla."

"He left me, he could have had me and he went for an old trout in a sequinned jacket."

"That's not who's with Danny."

"He's holding her bloody arm, who else is he with? The others are children."

"The one in the blue sweater; the black sequins is his mother-in-law." She looked over again astounded. "You're making it up."

"I'm not, but you're not going to have a chance to check it."

"She's under the age of consent, it's not legal. Any more than you and Caroline are." She was standing up now, prepared to go over to Danny Lynch's table.

"Orla, sit down, this minute. Play. Don't sing. Play 'Smoke Gets In Your Eyes.' "

"It's the kind of shitty philosophy you believe in."

"Play it, Orla, or leave. Now."

"You and whose army will make me?"

"Monto's army." He looked over at their table. Six rough, vulgar men whom he disliked intensely.

"They like me, why would they throw me out?"

"I'd ask them nicely."

"And I'd tell Monto that you're screwing his wife."

"And who would believe you, Orla? Out of control weakling that you are."

"Hey, where's the solidarity tonight?"

"Where did you put it? The drink? I was on to you the moment you came in, I checked your grapefruit juice."

She threw her head back at him and laughed. "It's in the flower vase, you fool."

First line of defense. Half-bottle of vodka in with the carnations.

He picked up the vase, emptied the contents into an empty wine bucket, and indicated to a waiter to take it away.

"What will I do with it, Mr. Barry?"

"Down the drain outside. Save the flowers, wipe the stems."

"You believed me." She looked both anxious and triumphant at the very same time.

"Not until I saw your eyes when I threw it out. Then I knew it was there, all right."

"Self-righteous prick," she said.

"Hey, Colm, are you going to stand there looking down the singer's tits all night, or serve us our steaks?" Monto called from his table.

A few people laughed nervously. Others looked away.

Orla got up, and taking her microphone with her began to wander around the room. "I'd like to do requests for people," she said. "I think this is what makes a night out special. But so often people don't always quite know exactly what they want to hear. So I thought that possibly tonight I could *choose* songs for people, something that could be appropriate. And sing a few bars at each table."

People were laughing and encouraging her. To the customers who didn't know her, Orla King was an attractive, professional singer. Now she was doing something a little more personal, that was all that there was to it. But many people in the room froze and they watched her edgily.

First she came to Rosemary's table. "We have three lovely ladies here," she said. "Feminists, oh, definitely. Lesbians? Very possibly. Anyway, no men. My grandmother used to sing a song called 'There Were Three Lovely Lassies from Bannion.' But it's a little too old even for this group. Suppose I were to sing 'Sisters' for them . . . ?"

"Did I do anything except help you all your life?" Rosemary asked with the mask of a frozen smile on her face.

"You had your reasons," Orla said. She judged that a few bars were enough and moved to Monto's table. "Six men, powerful men, rich men. Nothing pouffy about these men, believe me, I know." She smiled radiantly around the room. "Now what song should we choose for them? Oh, I know, there was one they all sang at this stag night, they asked me to perform and they loved it. No it was not 'Eskimo Nell,' everyone knows that. No, it was 'The Ball of Kirrimuir.' 'Four and twenty virgins came down from Inverness and when the ball was over there were four and twenty less.' " She smiled and moved to the Lynches' table.

At the same time Colm Barry was at Monto's table whispering feverishly. "Well, well, what a wonderful family group. Let me see." She smiled at them all, playing them like little fishes on a line. "What would you like?"

Only Brian thought it was a real question. He chose a Spice Girls song. "Do you know 'Wannabe'?" he asked eagerly.

His innocent face halted her in her tracks. Just for one moment, but for long enough to throw her. "What about 'Love and Marriage'? No, that's not permanent enough. What about that nice song 'Only Sixteen.' No, she must be older than that. This *is* your new wife, isn't it, Danny?" She was just turning to point to Finola, but as she turned Monto and one of his henchmen had lifted her bodily and were carrying her to the door. "Don't think people don't know, Danny. They know what you and I had, just as they know what Monto's wife had . . . and still has . . ."

Her voice was no longer heard. She was outside the restaurant. If Colm had hoped that he could get by with the help of some of his friends he was disappointed. The embarrassed silence that fell on the restaurant seemed to last forever. Rosemary, usually so quick to know what to do in a crisis, sat white-faced and furious at her table, with the new American woman from Ria's house confused and bewildered beside her. And with them was Gertie, terrified to see yet again firsthand the damage drink could do.

Monto's party was more triumphant and hilarious than could be imagined, imitating some of Orla's more drunken lurches.

Jimmy and Frances Sullivan, entertaining some guests up from Cork, embarrassed at the turn the evening had taken. Two fellow restaurateurs that he knew who had come in specially to see how his business was getting on. A party of two families getting to know each other before a wedding at the weekend. His sister, Caroline, standing stricken by the accusations that had been made. And Danny Lynch's party, he didn't even dare to look at. All of them upset by that destructive little Orla King. *Why* had she done it? Because she was unhappy.

But we're all unhappy, he told himself. Why should she have the luxury of throwing a scene and upsetting everyone else? He saw his waiters looking at him as if waiting for a lead. It could only have been seconds, he realized, since Orla's struggling body had been carried out of his restaurant. It felt like a lifetime but it was probably three or four seconds. Colm straightened his shoulders, indicated by a gesture that one table should be cleared, by another that the wine bucket should be placed nearer to another. He touched Caroline's shoulder and looked at the kitchen, and zombielike she walked that way.

Then he approached Rosemary Ryan's table. "Well, well," he said looking directly at Marilyn Vine. "You can't say we don't show you life in the fast lane in Dublin."

"No, indeed." Her face was impassive. He wished she didn't have to be so uptight. She was the guest, she should have said something warmhearted and funny to show that she was a good sport, to show that it didn't matter. But she didn't.

"I'm embarrassed that this should have happened the first time you come to my place," he said. Marilyn nodded her head as if accepting his apology. He felt a dark flush of annoyance at being dismissed so regally.

"She'll never work again, Colm," Rosemary said, but not with the solidarity he might have liked. There was a hint that he might have known this would happen, that the fault was partially his.

"It was all a bit like a cabaret really," said poor Gertie, trying to put some favorable gloss on it.

At the Lynch table they hadn't quite recovered either. "Sorry about the cabaret." Colm had decided to play it low-key, he wasn't going to crawl to these people.

"Was it something she ate, do you think?" Brian Lynch asked with interest.

"I very much hope not, speaking as a restaurant owner." Colm forced a smile.

"More like something you gave her to drink." Danny Lynch's voice was cold.

"No, Danny, you know I wouldn't do that. Like myself, Orla can't drink like all you people can, but she was upset by something and she had hidden vodka in the flower vase."

Bernadette clapped her hand over her mouth to stop the giggle. "The flower vase? It must have tasted *awful,*" she said.

"I hope it did." Colm smiled at the strange girl that he thought he would never speak to. She really *was* only a child, more a friend for Annie than for Annie's father. What a nightmare for Ria to take onboard. "Anyway, you'll have to rely on conversation rather than music," he said.

"That's better in a way," Annie said. "You can hear music anywhere, we'd rather chat as it happens."

"Yes, we were asking Bernadette whether the baby inside her had webs or legs," Brian said. "And we were wondering was that the American? You know Mam's friend Mrs. Vine, over there with Rosemary and Gertie?"

"Yes, that's Marilyn Vine," Colm said.

"Some welcome to Tara Road for her," Danny said.

"That's what I told her; she thought it was very funny," Colm lied, and moved on to placate the next table.

Somehow the night ended for everyone. Monto and his friend came back.

"Where exactly?" Colm hated having to talk to this man.

"We thought of a lot of places, but settled on an emergency room in a hospital eventually," Monto said with a smirk.

"She'll leave, she'll come back. Close the door of the restaurant."

"No, we gave a folding note or two to someone there who will make sure she doesn't."

"Thank you, Monto, I owe you for tonight."

"You owe me a lot more than just tonight and you know that. So you'll never tell me again that your restaurant is full."

"No, of course not, a mistake."

"Exactly."

At Danny's table they had paid the bill and were leaving. "I took the price of the wine off to compensate for the unpleasantness involved," Colm said.

"Thank you." Danny was cold.

"It wasn't Colm's fault," Annie said.

"Of course not." Danny was still chilly.

"Nor was it your father's fault that Orla picked on him specifically," Colm said in an even icier voice.

"No indeed, and thank you very much for your generous gesture of the wine," said Danny Lynch, changing his tack so swiftly it knocked them all off course.

"Was it a great dinner?" Ria asked her daughter.

"It was extraordinary, Mam. This singer got pissed or stoned or something and started going around with her bosom falling out upsetting everyone. Then she was sort of carried out. Mrs. Vine was there and the drunk singer headed straight for her table and said they were all lesbians! Honestly, Mrs. Vine, Gertie, and Rosemary."

Ria held her head in her hand. "Come again, Annie? Gertie, Rosemary . . . I don't believe any of this, Annie."

"Well, Mam, the only one who's going to confirm it to you is that brilliant observer Brian Lynch, who was there for it all and who's waiting to get on the phone."

"I'm sorry, Annie, of course I believe you, love. It just seems so unlikely. And did Bernadette and . . . um . . . Finola enjoy it all too?"

"Well, I think they were a bit stunned."

"I love you, Annie," said Ria.

"Oh, Mam, for heaven's sake. I'll put Brian on now."

"Mam?"

"Brian, was it a great night?"

"It was mad, Mam. You just wouldn't believe it. Mam, what's a lesbian? Nobody will tell me."

"A lesbian, is it?"

"Yes, whatever."

"It's a lady who likes other ladies more than she likes men."

"So, is that a big deal?"

"Not a bit, tell me about the night in the restaurant."

"Do you know any lesbians?"

"Yes, I know a few, sure."

"Are they awful?"

"No, of course not."

"So why do people whisper about them?"

"They don't, believe me."

"They did, Mam, tonight. Believe me."

"I'm sure you misunderstood."

"I don't think so. Do you want to say good night to Finola? She's just off." Ria could hear Annie scream.

"Brian, you are so stupid," she could hear Annie crying.

"Yes, sure, I'd love to say good night to Finola," Ria heard herself say.

There was a fluster and then a woman came on the line. "Well, I just want to say that your children are great company," she said desperately.

"Thank you for saying that. They seem to have taken to you greatly also," Ria gulped. "And I gather there was some kind of night to remember?"

Finola considered. "Unless there had been someone there with a video camera you would never believe it."

Neither used the other's name. Perhaps it was always going to be like that between them. "Good luck to you," Ria said.

"And great good luck to you too," said Bernadette's mother.

Ria hung up the telephone. She had two hours to get ready for her date with a man who was in technical publishing in Los Angeles and was en route to a conference in Boston. She had just finished a pleasant conversation with the mother of her husband's mistress. The apparently manic-depressive woman with whom she had exchanged homes had been out partying in Colm's restaurant. The world had tilted.

He didn't look at all like his brother when he came in and had a lemon drink by the pool, so she was glad she had telephoned Hawaii about him. About her own age or younger, slight and red-haired. Somewhat academic and assuming that she knew much more about university life than she did. "Forgive me, I keep making the wrong assumptions," he said when she knew nothing of any faculty or alumni association in either Ireland or the states. "I thought that's how you and Marilyn met."

"No, not at all. Other people thought we met over an obsession about gardens, in which I have no interest at all." She was all smiles and wearing her best summer outfit, a blue and white dress that she had gotten for a wedding last summer and had never worn since. It had looked great with a hat from Polly Callaghan, but there was never anywhere smart enough to wear it since. She should have dressed better. Would everything have been all right had she been an elegant wife?

"Do you know Thai food at all?" he was asking.

"Well, there *are* Thai restaurants in Ireland now, we are very international. But I've only been twice so I don't remember it all and I'd love you to choose for me when we get there."

This seemed to go down well. Maybe it was easier making fellows interested in you when you were old and way past it and it didn't matter anymore.

They talked easily in the Thai restaurant. He told her about the kind of publishing his company was involved in. Books that you would never hear of unless you happened to be in that field, and then you not only heard about them, you bought them because you had to. He explained how it all changed so radically because of technology and CD-ROMs. His grandfather had been a door-to-door salesman for encyclopedias. The man would spin in his grave if he saw the size of an encyclopedia now and knew how they were sold. Andy lived in Los Angeles in an apartment. He had been married, and was now divorced. There were no children.

"Did you leave her or did she leave you?" Ria asked.

"It's never as simple as that," he smiled.

"Oh, it is," she insisted.

"Okay, I had an affair, she found out, and she threw me out."

Ria nodded. "So you left really, by ending the marriage."

"So you say, so she said. I didn't want it to end but who listened to me?"

"Would you have forgiven her, if she were the one who'd had the affair?"

"Sure I would."

"You'd have gone on as if nothing had happened?"

"Look, Maria, people let each other down all the time, don't they? It's not a perfect life with everyone delivering on every promise. Marriages survive affairs if there's something there in the marriage itself that's bigger than the affair. I thought there was in our case. I was wrong."

"If you had your time all over again . . . ?" She was keen to know.

"You can't rewrite history. I have no idea what I'd do.

"Tell me, are you divorced also?"

"I think so," Ria said. He looked at her, startled. "That's not as mad as it sounds. You see divorce was only recently introduced in Ireland. We're still not entirely used to it. But the answer is yes, I am about to be."

"Did you leave him or . . . ?"

"Oh, he left me."

"And you won't forgive him?"

"I'm not being given the chance." There was a pause. "Andy, can I ask you about Dale?"

"What do you want to know exactly?"

"It's just that when I talked to Greg, well, I think I may have somehow said the wrong thing. He seemed a bit startled, upset almost."

"What on earth did you say?"

"I don't know, ordinary things, you know, good wishes, and so on."

Andy shook his head. "Well, of course people are not all the same the way they respond. Everyone takes things differently. Marilyn's never really accepted it, that's the way she copes."

"Can't she and Greg talk about it?"

"Greg wants to but she won't, apparently."

Ria felt stung by the way men shrugged about things. Dale was in Hawaii, his mother clearly missed him, and yet things were stuck in this impasse. She and Danny hadn't made a brilliant job of sorting the children out, but they had tried. Both of them, she gave Danny that much. This matter of Dale was very baffling. "Surely all Greg has to do is to work it out with her, dates and times and visits."

"He was trying to and then she disappeared to Ireland."

"But when does she think he will come back?"

"In the fall."

"That's a long time and she still leaves that room like that?" Ria was puzzled.

"What did she tell you about it all?" Andy asked.

"Nothing at all. She never mentioned she had a son at all."

Andy looked upset and a little silence fell between them. And then they didn't speak about the matter again. There were plenty of other things to talk about. He told her about his childhood in Pennsylvania, she told him about her mother's obsession with the movies, he explained the passion for baseball and she told him about hurling and the big final every year in Croke Park. He told her how to make a great Caesar salad and she explained about potato cakes. She enjoyed the evening and knew he had too.

He drove her back to Tudor Drive and they sat awkwardly for a few moments in the car. She did not want to invite him in in case it would be misunderstood. Then they both spoke at once.

"If ever business takes you to Ireland . . ." Ria began.

"The conference ends on Wednesday at lunchtime. . . ." Andy said.

"Please go on," she said.

So he finished what he was going to say. "And I was wondering if I drove back this way and made you a Caesar salad would you cook those potato cakes?"

"It's a deal," Ria said with a big smile and got out of the car.

Years ago when they went out with fellows, the big question always asked was "Are you seeing him again?" And now she was back in that situation again, a fellow had asked to see her again. With all that implied.

Ria stood in her bedroom and looked out on the beautiful garden that this strange woman had created. From what she had heard, Marilyn Vine spent every waking moment with her hands in the earth pulling and changing and turning the soil and coaxing the flowers and climbers to come up out of the ground.

She felt very out of place here. The friendship that she thought she might have with Carlotta and Heidi had not bloomed. Both women seemed embarrassed at the effusion of the first night, and had made no attempt to arrange another jolly threesome. Despite the admiration in Andy Vine's eyes she felt no real sense of being pleased and flattered. He was just a strange man from a different world than hers. True, Stoneyfield was peaceful and beautiful, a place of trees and a river and a gracious, easygoing lifestyle with superficial courtesy and warmth everywhere. But it wasn't home. And at home her children had gone out to Colm's restaurant for a hilarious evening with their new family. And Marilyn Vine had been across the room at a table with Rosemary. And I was here alone. Tears came down her face. She must have been mad to think this was a good idea. Totally mad.

It was dawn at Tara Road. Marilyn had not slept well. What an ugly scene that had been at the restaurant. Everything had suddenly slipped out of control. All these people were like characters playing their parts in a drama. And not a very pleasant drama. Rosemary and Gertie had filled her in on some of the background. Stories of Ria's broken marriage, the new relationship, the puzzlement of the children, the known unreliability of that offensive drunken singer, the possible criminal connection of the heavy men who had eventually taken her away. These people knew everything about everyone and were not slow in discussing it. There was no dignity, reserve, self-preservation.

Rosemary had talked about it being natural that people might assume she was gay, since she was single and had a sister who was already out with a partner who was a lawyer. Gertie had told her about her husband's problems coping with drink and violence. She spoke as if Jack had been prone to getting chest colds in the winter. Colm had approached their table with a casual apology over the incident as if it had not been the most excruciatingly embarrassing moment of her life. The two women had told her how they had initially thought Ria was mad to go to America and leave her children but they hoped it would all work out for the best.

Marilyn could not take in the degree of involvement and indeed interference that these people felt confident to have in everyone else's life. They thought nothing of discussing the motives and private sorrows of their friend to Marilyn, who was after all a complete stranger, here purely because of an accidental home exchange. While she felt sympathy for Ria and all that happened to her, she also felt a sense of annoyance.

Why had she not kept her dignity, and refused to allow all these people into her life? The only way to cope with tragedy and grief was to refuse to permit it to be articulated and acknowledged. Deny its existence and you had some hope of survival. Marilyn got out of bed and looked down on the messy garden and the other large redbrick houses in the neighborhood. She felt very lost and alone in this place where garrulous people wanted to know everything about you and expected you to need the details of their lives too.

She ached for the cool house and beautiful garden in Stoneyfield. If she were there now she could go and swim laps in her pool, safe in the knowledge that no one would call and burden her with postmortems about last night. Clement the cat who slept on her bed every night woke up and stretched and came over to her hopefully. He was purring loudly. The day was about to begin, he was expecting a game and a bowl of something.

Marilyn looked at him sadly. "I don't usually talk to animals, Clement, but I'm making an exception in your case. I made the wrong decision coming here. It was the worst decision I ever made in my life."

"Do you think when we're talking to Grannie we should call her Nora?" Brian asked.

"What?" Annie looked up from her book.

"You know . . . if we call Bernadette's mother by her first name maybe we should do the same with Grannie." Brian wanted to be fair.

"No, Brian, and shut up," said Annie.

"You always say shut up, you never say anything nice, not ever at all."

"Who could say anything nice to you, Brian, honestly?"

"Well some people do."

"Who apart from Mam and Dad? And they *have* to because you're what they got."

"Finola often says nice things."

"Tell me one nice thing she said to you today, go on tell me."

"She said it was good that I had remembered to let my knights command the center of the board."

"And had you?" Annie still refused chess lessons but she couldn't accept that Brian had mastered it.

"Well, only by accident in a way. I just sort of put them out there and they were commanding and she was very pleased with me." Brian smiled at the triumph of it all.

Sometimes he was more pathetic than awful, Annie thought. You could feel sorry for him. And he didn't really understand that their lives were going to change. He thought that after the summer everyone would go back to their own homes. He had even asked Bernadette's mother if they could go on playing chess in the autumn when they came back from America. Their games wouldn't have to end then, would they? Finola had said that they could surely continue to play whenever he came to visit his dad and she happened to be around. Stupid Brian had just looked bewildered. In his heart he thought that Dad might be coming home. He hadn't taken onboard that this was the way things were always going to be.

Kitty had said that Bernadette must be very, very clever to have gotten her claws into Annie's father. Despite the ban, Annie still managed to see Kitty by visiting the library. Since Annie read a lot now, from sheer lack of anything else to do as she kept telling them, it was considered legitimate that she visit the library. Kitty would come along too and report on the real world of motorbike rallies, of discos, and of great crowds who hung out in bars. Annie listened wistfully to the freedom of it all.

But Kitty was more interested in the sexual side of it, and was fascinated by Bernadette. "She looks so dumb and half-asleep you'd never have thought it. She must be like one of these sirens, one of these famous courtesans who had captured people by wiles. There *were* women who could make men their sexual slaves. It would be interesting to know exactly how."

"She's hardly likely to tell me," Annie said dryly.

"But you all get on so well," Kitty said, amazed. "I thought you'd hate her taking your mother's place and everything."

"No, she hasn't taken Mam's place, she's just made a new place. It's hard to explain."

"And she lets you do what you want, that's good anyway."

"No, I said she doesn't bother us, that's a different thing. She doesn't make any rules except about you. She's obviously got a heavy message from Dad that you're a no-go area." Annie grinned.

Kitty was puzzled. "I always thought he liked me. I even thought he fancied me a bit, that I was in there with a chance. Your mother was on to me—that's why *she* didn't want me round the place."

Annie was shocked. "Kitty, you wouldn't have."

"I wouldn't have wanted to be your stepmother. I thought a bit of clubbing, going to fancy places . . ." Kitty wiggled her hips. "A bit of you know . . . he's a good-looking man, your dad."

Annie looked at her with a sick feeling. Kitty had had sex with fellows, and she said it was usually great. Sometimes it was boring but mainly it was great. Annie shouldn't knock it until she'd tried it. But Annie knew she was never going to try it, it was frightening and urgent and out of control and horrible. Like what she had seen in the lane that day. And like Orla King, the woman who sang and made all the trouble in Colm's; she had been singing and talking about sex. It was a horrible, upsetting, confusing business. She remembered her mother explaining it all to her years back and saying that it was very good because it made you feel specially close and warm when you loved someone.

Some good it had done poor Mam, feeling close and warm. And it wasn't as if at her age she was ever going to feel close and warm to anyone again, like Dad had done. So easily.

Ria decided to have her hair done for her date with Andy on Wednesday night. But she would not go to Carlotta's. She would not let these women think that she was clingy and dependent, even if it were true.

There were other beauty salons in Stoneyfield or nearby. In fact she remembered seeing one in a shopping mall she had driven to not long ago. She would go and investigate. Expertly she backed Marilyn Vine's car out of the carport and by chance met Carlotta, who was collecting her mail.

The greeting was warm. "Hi! Now isn't this lucky, I was hoping to see you."

"Here I am," Ria said with a smile fixed to her face.

What did the woman *mean,* she was hoping to see her? She lived next door, for heaven's sake. "Yes, well, I didn't want to keep bursting in on you. I know Marilyn values her privacy . . ."

"Marilyn is Marilyn," Ria said tartly. "I'm Ria." She felt it was a childish, petulant outburst, something Brian would have said a few years ago. She must be getting unhinged.

If Carlotta was startled she managed to hide it. "Sure, well, what I was going to say was that Tuesday evening we have a hair product company coming to the salon, you know? They want us to buy their line, so as an encouragement they offer four or five of our regular customers a special, shampoo, treatment, conditioner, the works . . . then if we all like what we see we buy their line. It happens with various companies a couple of times a year. I wondered, would you like to take part? It's not being a guinea pig or anything, they won't turn your hair purple!"

Ria was astounded. "But you must have more regular clients."

"Do come," Carlotta pleaded.

"Well, of course, what time?" It was all arranged. Ria wished she could feel more pleased.

Carlotta was obviously not being cold and distant as she had thought, and it would be good to meet some neighbors. But her heart wasn't in it. Her feelings from Saturday night were still with her. This was a strange place, not her home. It was foolish to build up hopes that she would fit in and get to know everyone.

She had been meaning to ring Marilyn in Ireland but couldn't think of anything to say. Still, she shrugged to herself, it was something. And as Hilary would say, it was a free hairdo.

Marilyn braced herself for endless discussions about the scenes in the restaurant when Gertie next arrived. But the woman looked frail and anxious, and wasn't at all eager to speak. Possibly Jack had not appreciated the girls' night out and had showed it in the way he knew best. Gertie for once seemed relieved to be left alone to iron and kneel down and polish the legs of the beautiful table in the front room.

Marilyn worked in the front garden. She always left Gertie's money in an envelope on the hall table with a card saying thank you. Colm worked in the back garden; there was no communication there either. Rosemary had driven by but hadn't felt it necessary to call. Ria's mother and the insane dog hadn't been by in two days.

Marilyn felt her shoulders getting tense. Perhaps she had managed to persuade them that she didn't want to be part of some big vacation camp with them all.

As Gertie was leaving, she paused and congratulated Marilyn on the work she had done. "You have a fierce amount of energy, Marilyn," she said.

"Thank you."

"I hope it gets better for you, whatever it is that's wrong," Gertie said, and then she was gone.

Marilyn flushed a dark red. How *dare* these people assume there was something wrong? She had confided nothing to them, answered their very intrusive questions vaguely and distantly. They had no right to presume that there was anything wrong. She had been tempted to tell Ria during that very first conversation the extent of her grief, but now she was very glad she hadn't. If she had told Ria Lynch, nerve center of all the information and concern of the city it appeared, then it would probably have been published in the newspapers by now.

Marilyn had intended to call Ria today but held off. There was nothing to say.

The phone rang in the sunny kitchen where Ria was busy making her scrapbook of Things to Do for when the children arrived.

"Hi, Ria? It's Heidi! I've found a course for beginners on the Internet. Shall we sign on?"

"I'm sorry to be such a wet blanket, Heidi. I don't know if I'd understand it, I might be left behind."

"But it's *for* people like us who aren't computer literate. It's not for bright kids. All we need is basic keyboard skills, you've got those."

"If I can remember them."

"Of course you can, and it's only five lessons."

"Is it very expensive, Heidi? I hate sounding like my clinically mean sister and brother-in-law but I do have to hold on to my dollars for when the kids come out."

"No, it's not expensive at all, but anyway it's my treat. We get a discount through the faculty office and anyway I want someone to go with."

"I can't."

"Wednesday and Friday this week and then three days the following week, and hey, we're on the World Wide Web."

"Oh, I'm not sure about this Wednesday," Ria began.

"Come on, Ria, you're not doing anything else, are you?"

"No, no, it's not that . . . it's just . . ."

"I'd love you to come, it's only for an hour—they think rightly that we can't concentrate any longer . . . it's twelve to one."

"Oh it's in the *day*time," Ria said with relief. "Then of course I'll come, Heidi. You tell me where to go."

Greg telephoned Marilyn from Hawaii.

"Thank you for your letter," he said.

"It was still very stilted, I tried to say more," she said.

"Still, we're talking, writing. That's good. Better anyway."

She didn't want him to begin defining things too much. "And are *you* all right, Greg?"

"I'm okay . . . summer courses, kids who know nothing, then graduate. Then there are graduate students, far too many bright kids who'll never get appointments. What else is new in the world of academics?" He sounded relaxed. This was as near as they had been to a real conversation for a long time.

"I wish they had E-mail here," Marilyn said.

"You could have taken your laptop, I suppose?" he said.

"I know. I didn't think of it at the time."

"I spoke to Ria Lynch by the way. She called me here. She sounded very pleasant."

"Nothing wrong?"

"No, just to check if Andy was who he said he was. He was passing through Stoneyfield and wanted to contact you."

"That was good of Andy. And did Ria meet him?"

"No, no she just called him at the motel."

"I hope she's getting along okay. I don't want to call her there too often; it sounds as if I'm checking up on her," Marilyn said.

"I know what you mean," Greg said. "And what sort of feeling do you get about her, from being in her home?"

"What do you mean, feeling?"

"Does she sound odd or anything?"

"Why do you ask that?" Marilyn's voice was cold now. "I thought you said you had a conversation with her yourself?"

"Sure. I just got the impression that she might be very religious, spiritual or something."

"I never got that," Marilyn said, puzzled. "In Ireland, of course, the place is coming down with churches and bells ringing and statues, but I didn't think she was into all that."

"No, maybe I got it wrong. It was just something she said."

"What exactly?"

"Well, no, nothing important I guess. As I said, I got it wrong. What's the place you're staying in like?"

"It's a beautiful house, everything's so old here. People are different, they keep dropping by but they don't stay long. Oh, and there's a cat, Clement, an enormous orange cat."

"That sounds good, and you have things to do?"

"Yes, I garden a lot, and I walk and . . . it's all okay, Greg."

"I'm glad you're happy," he said.

"Yes. Well."

"But you're all right anyway?" He sounded anxious.

"Sure, Greg, I'm all right," she said.

Marilyn went back into the garden and dug with renewed vigor. She would not ask Greg why Ria had sounded odd. It didn't matter. Nothing mattered except that she put in her time here and got on to whatever happened next.

A shadow fell over her and there was Colm standing beside her. She put up a hand to keep the sun out of her eyes.

"Hallo," he said.

"Hi," Marilyn said.

"I'm not a great believer in words as apologies, so I brought you some flowers instead."

"It wasn't your fault."

"It was my place where it all happened. Anyway, it's over. Please Almighty God may it be over! In all my anxiety dreams about running a restaurant, and they were pretty vivid let me tell you, I never thought up that particular scenario."

In spite of herself Marilyn found that she was smiling. "As you say, it's over. Thanks for the flowers. I also need your advice about where to get soil and fertilizer when I've cleared that undergrowth."

"I'll take you." Colm looked amazed at her achievement. She had done the work of three men uprooting and cutting back. Soon the earth would be ready to function.

"Danny Lynch must be very grateful to you."

"What on earth for?" She was genuinely surprised.

"For improving the value of his property, that sort of thing is a big priority in his life."

"You don't like him very much."

"I don't like what he did to Ria and how he did it, that's true. But I don't know now whether I liked him before or not. I think I probably did." Colm tried to remember.

"I'm not doing it for him, I'm doing it for Ria and the house," Marilyn said.

"Well, same thing. They'll have to sell it eventually."

"Never!" Marilyn was shocked.

"Well, how can he keep two families *and* keep this place going? But enough about Danny Lynch and all the trouble he causes everywhere he goes."

"Was he the problem with the little blond chantoosie, as my dad used to call them?"

"Chantoosie! That's a marvelous word. Yes, he was one of her problems, another was a carnation vase filled with vodka." She looked at him, openmouthed. "Come to Ireland, Marilyn, and see it all, nature red in tooth and claw. Will you come out to dinner tonight? I want to check out some of the opposition. I'd love your company."

"Thank you so much," said Marilyn Vine.

She would not mention it, however, when Gertie next came in to clean the house and iron her clothes. Nor did she refer to it in the thank you note she wrote and left at Rosemary's elegant house. No need to overburden people with information.

"I was wondering, would you like me to call you Nora, Grannie?"

"Have you gone off your head, Brian?" his grandmother answered.

"Told you but you wouldn't listen," Annie said triumphantly.

"What's all this about?" Nora Johnson looked from one to the other suspiciously.

"It's one more sign that he should be in a straitjacket," said Annie.

"Well I know you're pretty old, Grannie, but you're not *that* old, are you? And I thought it would be more friendly, make us all the same somehow."

Annie raised her eyes to heaven. "And will you call Dad 'Danny' when we go down to the boat tonight? And will you have a few more upsetting things to say to your friend 'Ria' when she rings up from America next?"

Nora Johnson looked at her grandson. His face was troubled. "You know what, Brian? I'd actually like to be called Nora, on reflection I would. That's what they call me in St. Rita's."

"But they're a hundred and ten in St. Rita's," cried Annie in rage. "Of course they call you Nora."

"And of course Pliers calls me Nora," said her grandmother. Annie looked at her in horror. "The *dog* calls you Nora, Grannie?"

"In his heart he does, he doesn't think of me as a Mrs. Johnson figure. Yes, Brian, I'm Nora to you from now on."

"Thanks, Grannie, I knew it was for the best," said Brian happily.

Annie raised her eyes to heaven. The entire family was going mad. And now they had to go to Tara Road and say hallo to Mrs. Vine before they left for the boat on the Shannon. Mam wanted it. It would be friendly she said, and courteous. Mam lived in a different world when all was said and done.

Mrs. Vine had a plate of horrible gingersnap biscuits that would break your teeth and she had made some ham sandwiches.

"Nothing, thank you," Annie said firmly.

"But please do, I got them ready for you."

"I'm very sorry, Mrs. Vine, I don't eat dead animals, and I find the biscuits a bit hard, so is it all right if I just drink the tea?"

"Of course, let me see . . . I have some frozen cheesecake, I could defrost that for you, it won't take long."

"I eat ham sandwiches," Brian said. "I'll eat them all so that they won't go to waste. I mean apart from the ones you'll be eating yourself." He reached out for the plate. "We could divide them up."

Annie didn't have to say "Brian," her face said it fairly loudly.

"Or indeed, leave them where they are and eat them as the urge comes on us," he said apologetically.

Marilyn felt that she couldn't have made a worse start. "I hope you'll both have a good time in Stoneyfield," she began.

"Do they have proper biscuits there?" Brian wondered.

"Yes, quite a range," Marilyn assured him.

He nodded, pleased.

"I'm sure it will be great, Mam says she loves it. We were talking to her on Saturday night." Annie was trying hard to be polite and to make up for rejecting both kinds of hospitality. "I think she's getting to know the place, she was going out to dinner in a Thai restaurant."

This was puzzling. Who could have invited Ria to that new place that had opened a couple of months back? Or would she have gone on her own? "Does your mother like different foods?"

"She's always cooking, certainly."

Brian looked around the kitchen on Tara Road, empty of its normal wire trays filled with scones, breads, and cakes. "You don't do much cooking yourself, Mrs. Vine?" he said slightly censoriously. "Daddy's friend Bernadette doesn't either. Her mother, Finola, does but only when she's in her own place. Though I think she's going to cook on the boat . . . do you think she is, Annie?"

"I hadn't given it much thought," Annie said through gritted teeth. "And I'm not sure Mrs. Vine wants to hear all about it either."

"I wonder if I could ask you both to call me Marilyn?" she asked them suddenly. The much-repeated address of Mrs. Vine was beginning to grate on her nerves. The girl resented her somehow for being in their mother's house. Or maybe she resented her mother for having gone away.

Brian accepted that eagerly. "Yes, I think it's much better if you ask me," he said.

"Is that you digging up the garden or is it Colm? We saw an awful lot of stuff out there."

"Well, it's mainly me, I just love it. But Colm *is* going to help me get new soil and plant things where they can reach the light. Maybe you'd like to choose some plants?" she asked without much hope.

The telephone rang just then. They heard the sound of their mother's voice on the machine. "Hi, Marilyn it's Ria. I was just calling to say—"

"It's Mam," cried Brian, running for the phone.

"Brian, wait," Annie called.

"No, please," Marilyn insisted.

"Mam, Mam, it's Brian, we're here, how did you know?"

Marilyn and Annie's eyes met. Somehow in that moment Marilyn felt the hostility beginning to depart. It was if they were both adults looking at the baby Brian who thought his mother had tracked him down.

"Yeah, she's fine, she's chopped down most of the front garden."

Annie sighed. "You get to expect a lot of that sort of thing with

Brian," she explained to Marilyn. "He always manages to say the one thing you don't want him to say. I'll sort it out."

And to give her great credit she did sort it out.

"Hi, Mam. It's Annie. Yes we're here having tea. Yes, very nice indeed. I read a lot . . . it's all so boring in Dad's place I've had to become a compulsive reader. *Catch Twenty-two* and *The Thorn Birds*. Yes, she did ask us to call her Marilyn. No, that is just Brian being mad this time, but don't mind him about the garden, it's only a few weeds, and Colm's helping her so stop panicking. And we're off tonight, but we'll ring you on Saturday."

When Marilyn finally did get on the telephone Ria was very apologetic.

"I'm so sorry, I didn't mean to make it a family conference."

"It was just good timing. It's all going well?"

"Oh, yes, brilliantly, and with you?"

"Couldn't be better."

"You were at Colm's restaurant, I hear?"

"Yes, the resident pianist drank a vase of vodka. And they tell me *you* went to the new Thai restaurant. You liked it?"

"Yes, terrific, lovely green shrimp curry." Ria didn't say that she had been there with Marilyn's brother-in-law. "Look, it's silly us talking now, why don't you call me back later tonight using my phone?"

"I'm going out tonight."

"Oh, good, where are you off to?"

"I arranged to go out to the movies, there's one I really want to see," lied Marilyn, who did not want to say she was going to dinner with Colm Barry.

They agreed to talk later in the week.

"Is Bernadette up to high don packing and everything for the holiday?" Barney asked.

"No, not at all." Danny was constantly surprised at how gently she moved through life. There would be no lists, no plans, no checking through things, emptying fridges, canceling people, phone calls. Twenty minutes before they left she would put a few items in a bag. He would pack his own case. The children had lists of what they should take taped to their own cases by Ria. "No, she's amazing, Barney. I don't know where she gets her serenity. It's infectious too, seriously, it's catching. Sometimes when I get fussed, I only have to be with her for ten minutes and it's all all right again."

"What do you get fussed about, Danny?"

"Lots of things. Money, work, a madwoman living in my house cutting down my front garden, Ria being so unaccepting of everything that's happened."

"Hey, is it that bad?" Barney asked.

"I don't usually give a long list of moans, but you did ask and today's not a good day. There's a long drive ahead, then a cramped cruiser for seven days that I can ill afford to be out of the office, Bernadette's mother thinking I'm made of money, and the kids seem to be on top of us all the time."

"And there was a bit of trouble with Orla King on Saturday night?"

"God, you know everything, Barney! How did you hear that?"

"A friend of Polly's was with Monto's party. He said the owner came over to them with barked instructions that Orla be gotten out before she went to your table. It wasn't quite in time."

"No, but nearly."

"You'd want to watch it, Danny."

"Tell me about it. I'm watching it so feverishly I'd need a dozen eyes."

The river was full of families getting on to their Shannon cruisers.

Bernadette's mother had arranged a box of groceries from a local store. "I telephoned ahead to order them," she explained to Danny.

"Great, Finola." He seemed relieved.

It had been a long car journey. In the beginning, as they left in the Dublin late afternoon traffic, he was tense. His shoulders were cramped, he had a dozen worries, and his conversation with Barney had not helped. Twice he had made foolish mistakes, pulling out of the traffic without checking. Tactfully Finola had offered to drive and eventually he accepted.

Bernadette sat in the front and played them tapes that she had assembled specially for the holiday. It was a restful choice, gentle Irish music, harpists or uileann pipes, nonstrident Greek bouzouki, nocturnes by Chopin, deep soulful French songs that none of them understood, pan pipes, violin music that none of them recognized. Danny sat in the back of his own car between his daughter and son and slept fitfully as Finola Dunne drove them to the Midlands.

He dreamed that Ria was waiting for them on the boat. "Aren't you going to go home?" she asked Bernadette in the dream. And Bernadette had just shrugged and said, "If you like." Danny had wanted to run after her but his feet were rooted to the ground. The dream was still very real to him as they got out of the car and began to settle into their boat.

"So will you then?" Finola said to him.

"Will I what?" Danny was genuinely puzzled.

"Will you pay this man for the groceries?"

"What? Yes, of course." He took out his credit card; the man shook his head, so he took out a checkbook. He saw the last check stub. It was a payment for their mortgage to the Building Society. The grocery bill was enormous. The cost of the cruiser was on his credit card. He didn't even want to think about it.

But he knew he would *have* to think about it one day soon.

Colm took Marilyn to Quentin's. He said he wanted to show off Dublin's finest. Also he knew the Brennans, who ran the place.

"Very full for a Monday, that's the booming economy for you," he said approvingly, looking around the many tables that were occupied.

"Nonsense, Colm. You should explain to Mrs. Vine that they come because the food is so brilliant," said Brenda Brennan.

"This I can believe," Marilyn murmured politely.

"I see you've got Barney McCarthy in with a crowd," Colm observed.

A shadow crossed Brenda's face. "Yes, indeed we have," she said. Colm raised his eyebrows as if to ask what the problem was. "I'll let you study the menu," Brenda Brennan said, and moved away.

"Does she not like those people?" Marilyn had picked up a vibe.

"No, it's not that. I think she may have had the same problem as I've had."

"Which is?"

"A very big check returned from the bank."

"Really!" Marilyn put on her glasses and studied the party by the window. "They look like very substantial people, not the kind who would bounce a check."

"No, they never did before. And the problem is they're important.

They know everyone; you wouldn't want to insult them, *and* also to be fair they have brought in big business in the past. So it's all a bit tricky." He looked over at the large man who was being expansive as a host to nine other people. A smart, much younger woman was laughing.

"Is that his wife?"

"No that's Polly. His wife's at home in a mansion."

"Will you sue him?"

"No. I'll be full next time he books, I'll just kiss one big bill good-bye. No point in going to court over one dinner."

Marilyn looked at him admiringly. "You're so right. In the States we are much too litigation-conscious. You're sensible to think of it as one big dinner and not to worry too much about it."

"But I do worry about it. Barney McCarthy more or less owns Danny Lynch. If he goes down, so will Danny, and what will happen to Ria then?"

Rosemary was legendary for the speed of her weekly business meetings. They were held early in the morning, with a large dish of fresh fruit, a lot of strong coffee, and a rapid agenda. Accountant, office manager, marketing manager, and her own personal assistant, all trained to present speedily their reports and follow-ups. They went rapidly through Accounts, New Business, Overtime, and What the Rivals Are Up To. Then it came to Problems.

"A really big check returned from the bank, I'm afraid," the accountant said.

"How much? Who?"

"Eleven thousand, Barney McCarthy."

"That's an error, that's a bank oversight," Rosemary said, about to go on to the next.

"I see Polly's Dress Hire is for sale in this morning's paper." The accountant was laconic.

"Thanks. Then it's not an oversight. I'll call the bank."

"They won't tell you anything."

"They'll tell *me*," said Rosemary.

When the meeting was over she dialed Danny Lynch's mobile phone. It was not picking up. "You're not doing this to me, Danny, you little bastard. You've done enough to everyone, and I can tell you straight out you're not doing this to me, not after all we've been through." But she was speaking to herself not to Danny, since he was on the Shannon without a care in the world.

Hilary said that she was going to invite Marilyn to come for a swim out in the Forty Foot bathing area. They could go out on the DART.

"That's an unusual idea," her mother said.

"Martin suggested it. He said it would save the cost of buying her a meal."

"True," said Nora Johnson.

"And still be entertaining her."

"It would."

Nora Johnson sighed a deep sigh. How had she raised a daughter who thought only in terms of saving money? Hilary hadn't been like that as a child, surely she hadn't. They never had much when she worked in the dry cleaners and the mother and two daughters were all wistful and slightly envious about what they would buy had they the money, but it had not been obsessive. Martin had changed her, dragged her down. Still, at least he hadn't abandoned her for a teenage waif. Nora sighed again. Sometimes she felt it was all very hard.

Hilary looked at her in concern. She didn't like all this sighing. "Mam, don't you think it's about time you moved into Ria's house?"

"What?"

"Well, not when Marilyn's there of course, but as soon as she goes."

"What would I do that for?"

"To have company for you and to pay Ria some rent."

"I don't need company."

"Of course you do, Mam. But whether you do or not Ria will definitely need someone to pay her something when Danny's grand plans are all sorted out."

"You can't be serious."

"I am. Get in there, Mam, before she asks someone else."

"Hilary, have you a brain in your head? Poor Ria will be out of that house by Christmas."

"What!"

"Barney McCarthy's on his uppers. I saw in today's paper that Polly

Callaghan's business is for sale. If he's selling the floozy's dress hire outfit he must be down to looking in kiddies' money boxes. And when he goes for the high jump then so will Danny Boy. Your brother-in-law will have one of his boards up outside that house before Ria gets back."

They all took turns at steering the boat. It was simple while you were still on the river, but when it broadened into a lake there were real rules. You had to keep the black buoys on one side and the red on the other. They waved to Germans and Dutch people they had met already, more expert at mooring and casting off than they were. They bought ice creams when they drew in and tied up at the small villages, or went to pubs where they played darts.

"Wouldn't Mam love this!" Brian said once as a flight of birds came out of the reeds and soared above them. The silence was worse than any number of people telling him to shut up.

"Sorry," he said.

Bernadette spoke dreamily. "Brian, of course you must mention your mother, she's not dead or anything. And maybe one day you'll take her on a trip like this."

Annie and Brian saw Danny reach out and stroke Bernadette's face in gratitude. He sort of traced it with his fingers and pushed her hair back. There was such love and tenderness in the gesture it was almost embarrassing to watch.

The boy Hubie who taught the course "Don't Fear the Internet" looked about sixteen. In fact he was not much older. This was his first venture into business, he said, and he wanted to make sure all the customers were satisfied so if there were any areas they didn't understand then he wasn't doing his job right.

Ria felt to her surprise that she seemed to understand it. It wasn't a world that only people like Rosemary understood, it was quite ordinary. A way of getting in touch. She saw how easy it would be to get sucked in and to spend all day browsing, looking up amazing facts, and talking to strangers on the screen.

She had lunch with Heidi afterward and they went over what they had learned and what they should practice before meeting with Hubie again on Friday. He had asked them to send him messages, which he would answer. It was easy for Heidi, she had all the computers and word processors in the alumni office. But where would Ria go?

"Marilyn has a laptop that she didn't take away with her. You could use that."

"Oh, I'd be afraid I might break it."

"No, of course not. Tell her on the phone you want to use it and I'll set it up for you."

"Do you think it would be intrusive?"

"No, it's only machinery. But Ria . . . I don't think you should mention that Hubie is our teacher."

"Why ever not?"

"Well, he was a friend of Dale's, you see."

"Well, what's so bad about that?"

"You know . . ."

"I don't know. All I know is that Dale's in Hawaii. . . ."

"What?"

"Well, with his father. Isn't he?"

Heidi was silent.

"Heidi, where else is he? He's not here, he's not in Ireland. His room is there waiting for him."

"Dale's dead," Heidi said.

"No, he can't be dead. You should see his room, that's not the room of someone dead."

"Dale's dead, that's what it's all about. Marilyn won't accept it."

Ria was more shocked than she had been for a very long time. "Why didn't she tell me?"

"She won't speak about it. Not to anyone. Not even to Greg. That's why he's in Hawaii."

"He left her?"

"No, he thought she'd come with him but apparently not, they had been there once with Dale."

"How old was Dale?"

"Not quite sixteen."

Oh God, thought Ria, Annie's age. "How did he die?"

"A motorcycle accident."

"But surely he was too young to ride a . . . ?"

"Exactly."

"Why on earth didn't she tell me?" Ria shook her head. "I was coming to live in her home after all. She'd know I'd see his room. I even dust it, for heaven's sake."

Heidi was gentle. "She doesn't have the words to tell people."

"When did it happen?"

"March of last year. They turned off the machine in August."

"The machine?"

"Life support machine."

"Poor Marilyn. What a decision to have to make."

"She thinks they made the wrong one, that's why she has no peace."

"Well, if she has no peace, I sure as hell wonder whether she'll find it on Tara Road," said Ria.

Marilyn lay in her bath and Clement sat on the bathroom chair as if he were somehow guarding her. Gertie had told her that Clement didn't normally go upstairs.

"Well, he does now," Marilyn had said.

"It's just that when Ria comes back, he might, you know, being only a cat, still think he's welcome up here." Gertie had tried to be tactful, but wasn't doing a good job of it.

"I'm sure Ria's doing things in my house that I don't approve of either but we agreed that we would put up with that for the summer." Marilyn sounded brisk and firm.

"But are there any living things in your house?" Gertie wanted to know.

"No living things," Marilyn had said.

As Marilyn added more hot water to her bath Clement yawned a great yawn.

"I fought for you, Clement. Don't yawn at me like that," she said.

Clement closed his mouth and went to sleep. Marilyn wondered at all the living things that Ria had left behind her.

Andy arrived with a cold bag full of food. He had also brought a bottle of wine. "You look very nice," he said appreciatively. "Very nice indeed."

"Thank you." It had been so long since anyone paid her a compliment. *You look fine, sweetheart* was the most Danny had said to her for ages. And in the last years Annie had said little except *you look absolutely terrible in that color.* Rosemary had said she looked well when she dressed up but the implication was that it was not often enough. Hilary had remarked that fine feathers make fine birds. Her mother had said there was nothing to beat a good navy costume and a white blouse and that it was a pity when people with as much class and opportunity as Ria wore dowdy clothes that you wouldn't even see on a halting site. True, Colm sometimes said she looked well. But it was more a compliment to the house or the garden, or Ria as part of the scene rather than in herself.

So it was unusual to be admired openly by a man.

Then the cooking began by rubbing the garlic around the bowl for the Caesar salad. There was a lot of gesture, flourish, and fuss but it tasted very good. And then they began on the potato cakes.

"Oh, they're latkes," Andy said, a little disappointed. He had thought it was something totally unknown.

"Are they?" Ria was disappointed too.

"But I actually like them a lot. And these are Irish latkes so that makes them special," he said.

So they laughed over that and over a lot of things. He told her about the conference and the crazy woman organizing it who was at such a level of stress she was almost ready to ignite. Arranging the seating plan for the conference dinner, a matter of no importance whatsoever, had her on heavy sedation.

"How did it go, the dinner, in the end?" Ria asked.

"No idea, it's tonight."

"And you didn't wait for it?"

"I thought this would be more fun, and I was right," he said.

Ria had made a strawberry shortcake, which they had with coffee.

"You mean you didn't buy this at a gourmet shop?"

"No, it's made by my own two hands," she laughed, and stretched out her newly manicured hands.

"But you bought the pastry, surely?"

"No way. I make pastry quick as looking at you." Andy was very impressed. She was enjoying this in a childish way. She told him about the Internet lessons and asked did he think Marilyn would mind her using the laptop.

"Not a bit, I'll set it up for you."

"I should ask first."

"Look, it's like using someone's telephone, or the vacuum . . . it's not like a finely tuned piano or anything."

"But suppose . . . ?"

"Come on, where does she keep it?"

"It's in the study."

They went into the pleasant book-lined room and Andy opened the machine. "I'll show you how to boot it up then you'll be able to do it for yourself." As he spoke the telephone rang and because they were not in the room with the answering machine Ria answered it automatically.

"Hallo?" she said as if she were back in Dublin and this was her phone.

"Ria? It's Greg Vine."

"Oh, Greg. How are you?" Her eyes met Andy's across the desk. The natural thing, the normal thing would have been to say "You won't believe it but your brother is here." That's what people would say if it were an ordinary situation, surely. But then it might need a lot more explanation than was necessary. And might imply things that didn't need to be implied. So she said nothing about Andy Vine being four feet away from her with a half smile on his face as he watched her.

Ria listened to Greg's apologetic request that she find a file for him. It was in the study. "I'm in the study as we speak," Ria said.

"Oh, good." He sounded pleased. "Very technical books I'm afraid, and lots of student papers. That's what I want you to get for me, can I direct you?"

"Sure."

From Hawaii, Greg Vine directed her to the wall with student notes on it and gave her a year, then a name, then a subject. Each time she repeated them Andy moved and found the document.

"It's just the first page and title of the publication this kid has done, and we need it today."

"Today?"

"I was going to ask Heidi and Henry as a huge favor to call around and pick it up and E-mail it to me."

"Heidi and Henry to come around here to pick it up and E-mail it to you tonight?" She repeated every word as if she were a half-wit but she wanted Andy to get the other end of the conversation. He understood immediately. He pointed to the piece of paper, to the laptop, and to his own chest. "I could send it to you by E-mail myself if you let me use Marilyn's laptop."

"You know how to E-mail?" Greg was surprised and pleased.

"Well, yes, by chance I do, I went to a lesson this morning with Heidi."

"Well, well, what amazing luck. I don't need to get Heidi and Henry out at all." He was overjoyed at the good timing.

Andy had written down *get the password and his E-mail address.* And in moments the information was put in, and the message sent.

"It's on my screen now, I can't thank you enough. Who is giving this course anyway? You learned pretty quick."

Ria remembered that Hubie had been a friend of the dead Dale. "Oh some man . . . I didn't get his name."

"Never mind. He saved us all tonight, whoever he was."

When she hung up they looked at each other. One bridge had been crossed almost accidentally.

"Well now, since they think in Hawaii that you're an expert at this, let's make you one," he said.

Was he sitting a little too close to her, she wondered. "Let me get my notes." She jumped up and went for the sheet of paper that Hubie had given them all at the class.

Andy looked at them. "My God, Hubie Green, he was one of the kids with Dale on the night of the accident."

Ria looked at him levelly. "Why didn't you tell me Dale was dead?"

He was shocked. "But you knew, surely?"

"No, I didn't. I had to wait until Heidi told me."

"But you mentioned his room, the way it was all laid out."

"I thought he was in Hawaii. I asked you when was he coming back, you said in the fall."

"Oh, my God, I thought you meant Greg."

There was a silence while they each realized how the misunderstanding had happened.

"You see, they're so very cut up they can't even bring themselves to talk about it. To mention that you knew Hubie Green would bring it all back."

"I know," said Ria. "That's why I pretended I didn't know his name."

"You did it very well." Andy was admiring.

"You know a funny thing? At home I am always so honest and undevious, and since I came out here I haven't stopped pretending and covering up things for no reason at all."

"Oh, there's always a reason," he smiled.

"Pure misguided niceness, I think," she said ruefully.

"Okay, so we have to pretend one more thing, which is that you understood this whole getting on the Net thing by yourself and then we can stop pretending, okay?"

"Okay," she said a little anxiously.

He was definitely sitting too close for friendship. "Who do we know with E-mail?" he asked.

"Hubie! He said we could send messages any time."

"Hubie. Yeah."

"What's wrong? He's a nice kid."

"Sure."

"Tell me. I know nothing about what happened, nothing at all. Well, I get the feeling that Marilyn's so private. I felt she wouldn't want me to go round asking questions, that she'd tell me what she wanted me to know, and it's not very much."

"Do you resent that?"

"I think she should have told me her son was dead. I don't want half of Dublin telling her about poor Ria, poor old Ria whose husband took off with a teenager. So since I get the feeling she's not going to be demanding information from my friends, I shouldn't from hers . . . it's just . . . it's just . . ."

"It's just what, Maria?" He had never got the shortened version of her name and somehow she quite liked him calling her something different. It made whatever there was or might be between them something that was out of time.

"It's just that there's a mystery here. There's no mystery in my case, it's as old as time. Man marries wife, man sees newer younger fresher model, man says good-bye to wife. The only mystery is that there's not more of it."

"Maria, please, you sound so bitter."

"What, should I be overjoyed about it? At least it's plain to see what happened. Here it's different, quite different. There's like a conspiracy of silence about it all. That room is like a shrine to him. The fact that nobody mentions the accident."

"But you see—" Andy began.

"No, to be honest I don't see. Do you know what I said to your brother, Greg, when I was talking to him in Hawaii? I'll tell you what I said, I asked him how Dale was enjoying it out there. My flesh is creeping when I wonder why he thinks I said what I did."

"He'll know." Andy soothed her. "He'll realize that Marilyn couldn't have told you."

"Look, I'm as sorry as hell that it all happened. I went into that room again and I cried over the child that I thought was out surfing in Honolulu. I cried to think he's dead and buried, but still we should be able to talk about it. Not all the time, as people say we do in Ireland, but just acknowledge it. She left his room like that and didn't tell me. That's not natural, Andy. Even you freeze up at the mention of that kid Hubie's name. Maybe if nobody else tells me what happened I'll talk to Hubie about it."

"Don't do that."

"No, of course I wouldn't but I am pointing out that it's odd."

"Don't you think we all know that?"

"What do you mean?"

"Listen, in this world there was only one marriage that any of us could think was truly happy, and that was Greg and Marilyn's. And yet from the night of the accident they were never able to relate to each other as human beings again."

"Did they blame each other or something?"

"Well, there's no way they could have. Hubie and two other kids and Dale were all crazy about motorbikes, but they were too young and they all had parents who would have as soon let heroin into the house as let a motorbike into their backyards. So on Hubie's birthday the kids went out somewhere. It was meant to be a picnic, I know because I was here at the time." He got up and started to walk around the study. "And they drank some beer and they found two bikes and they decided that this was a gift from the gods."

"They *found* them?"

"Yes, found as in stole them outside a restaurant. Hubie and the other kid who died, Johnny, were a little bit on the wild side. Not hugely wild but the signs were there. Older too, but not much. But at that age a few months counts."

"I know." Ria thought suddenly of Kitty, a year older than Annie but several years ahead of her always.

"And they went for what was described at the inquest as a kind of test drive and they went around a corner and one of the bikes was hit by a truck. Which wasn't surprising, really, because the bike where Dale was hanging on to Johnny was on the wrong side of the road. Johnny was killed instantly. Dale was on a life support machine for six months and then they agreed to let him go."

They sat in silence at the tragedy that had come to this house.

"And Marilyn said that she would never forgive any of them as long as she lived, and Greg said that they would have no peace until they learned to forgive."

Ria had tears in her eyes. "And is that what drove them apart?"

"I imagine so. Greg doesn't say much about it. You know how hopeless we men are at talking about feelings."

"You're not too bad; you've told me that story very sympathetically and it wasn't just idle curiosity on my part, you know."

"I know," he said.

"Do you understand how I felt sort of protective about her, how I didn't want to ask Carlotta and Heidi and anyone else?"

"Sure I do, and you understand also why it wouldn't be good to ask Hubie. That kid has had a lot to live with: his birthday, he got them drunk, his friend Johnny driving a stolen bike, and he and another kid walk away alive. I'm kind of impressed with him that he's setting up something like this class to pay for his college tuition."

"I know, and of course you feel bitter about him," Ria said.

"It wasn't his fault; he didn't set out to kill Dale or anything," Andy soothed her.

"But it's awkward, isn't it? I'm sorry to have become involved."

"Look, it's got nothing to do with you. Come on, Maria, homework time; let's get our assignments done."

They sent Hubie a message and he sent back CONGRATULATIONS MRS. LYNCH, YOU'RE A NATURAL. Then they sent one to Heidi.

"She's going to die when they tell her in the alumni office tomorrow that there's a message for her from me!" Ria pealed with laughter.

"I wish we knew someone else with E-mail," she said.

"Well, we could send one to my laptop back in the motel," he said.

"And you could ring me tonight to say that it had arrived," she said.

"Or tomorrow?" he suggested gently. It took a moment for it to dawn on her what he was saying. "It's so nice here, so good to hear laughter in this house again," Andy said. "And you and I have no ties, nobody who will be betrayed or hurt. Wouldn't it be nice if we spent the rest of the evening together?" He had a hand under her chin, lifting her face up toward his.

She swallowed and tried to speak. He took the opportunity of her not speaking to kiss her. Gently but firmly. And he put his arm around her shoulder.

She pulled away, startled. Ria Lynch would be thirty-eight this year. In November, on the anniversary of Clark Gable's death. Nobody had kissed her since she was twenty-two except the man who had tired of her and told her that there was nothing left in what she thought was a fine happy marriage.

"I must explain," she began.

"Must you?"

"Yes, I've had a lovely, lovely evening, but you see I don't . . ."

"I know, I know." He was kissing her ear now, gently nuzzling in fact, and it was rather nice.

"Andy, you have to forgive me if I have been giving the wrong signals. I couldn't have had a happier evening. I mean that truly, truly I do, but I don't want it to go any further. I'm not playing games, I never did, not ever, even when I was a kid going out with fellows. But I was often misunderstood and the fault is all mine if you thought things were different. I'm a bit inexperienced, you see."

"I had hopes when you didn't tell my brother that I was here," he explained.

"I know, I know." She knew that was a fair perception.

"But I agree it was a delightful evening. It doesn't *have* to end in bed, it would be much much nicer if it did, but if it's not going to let's remember the good parts."

"They were all good parts." She smiled at him, grateful that he hadn't turned on her, outraged that he had been misled.

"Those Irish latkes. Eat your heart out, Jewish cooking," he said.

"That Caesar salad, emperor of Caesar salads," she said.

"And that strawberry shortcake. Home baked pastry, yet."

"And the stylish wine in its coolbag."

"Hey, there's lots of good parts," he said.

"Look on your machine tonight, there may well be a message pending," he said and left.

She cleared up everything and went into the study to see if there were any messages for her. There were two. One from Hubie. JUST A TEST MRS. LYNCH TO SEE IF YOU CAN RETRIEVE AS WELL AS SEND! HUBIE GREEN. And then there was one from Andy. THANK YOU SO MUCH FOR THE MOST ENJOYABLE DINNER I HAVE HAD IN YEARS. I WILL DEFINITELY BE BACK FOR ALUMNI WEEKEND AS WILL GREG BUT IF THERE'S A CHANCE WE COULD MEET AGAIN BEFORE THAT I WOULD SO MUCH ENJOY IT. YOUR NEW FRIEND, ANDY VINE.

Imagine! Boring old Ria Lynch, poor deserted Ria, dreary mumsy tiresome Ria had a new friend called Andy Vine. And had she not said a persuasive no, then she could have had a lover of the same name as well. She looked at herself in the hall mirror and wondered what it would have been like. She had never made love with any man except Danny. Danny, who knew her body so well and brought her such pleasure.

It would have been awkward getting undressed in front of this man. How did people do it? Be so instantly intimate with people they hardly knew? People like Rosemary. But then Rosemary looked like Rosemary. As near perfect as possible. Ria was afraid that her own bottom might be a bit saggy, that she would look floppy when naked. In a way it was a relief not to have to go through the motions of getting to know another body and fear the possible criticism of her own. Yet it would have been nice to have had arms around her and someone wanting her again.

She sighed and went into Dale's room. She turned over the pages of Dale Vine's scrapbook, the pictures of motorcycles, the advertisements, the cuttings about various motorcycle heroes. Marilyn had been strong enough to leave these here, reminders of the machines that had killed her only boy, and yet she had not been able to tell the woman who was going to live in her house that her son was dead. This was a very complicated person indeed.

———

Marilyn had refused so many invitations that she feared that she might now be causing offense. She had better go out with Hilary, Ria's discontented and unprepossessing sister. The woman had been very insistent, she had called several times to mention a picnic on the coast. It would be good to swim again, and Marilyn told herself she was a match for any of these inquisitive Irish, just answer vaguely and ask them about themselves. Then they were off, all you had to do was sit back and listen.

Hilary arrived bristling with energy and fuss. "We'll miss the rush hour on the train, which will be good," she said.

"Good. I'm ready whenever you are."

"Merciful God, Ria'll go mad when she sees all that work in the garden. Are they digging for treasure or what?"

"Just some clearing out the undergrowth, it will be perfect when she comes back. Your sister has a very beautiful house, doesn't she?" Marilyn said.

"I'll tell you straight out what I think, I think that Ria and Danny got their money too easy and these things have a habit of coming home to roost."

"What do you mean exactly? Should we have a cup of coffee or would you like to get on the road, the train?"

"We could have a cup of coffee, I suppose. Were you not cooking, baking, like?" Hilary seemed to look around the kitchen with the same disapproval as Brian had, looking for something that was not there.

"Well, no. We're going out, aren't we?" Marilyn was startled.

"I thought we might have a picnic out there."

"Yes, yes what a good idea, will we pass a delicacies shop on the way?"

"A what?"

"You know, somewhere we could buy things for the picnic."

"But it would cost as much to buy a picnic in one of those places as to have a meal out. I really meant sandwiches."

Marilyn was beginning to regret this bitterly, but it was too late to turn back. "We could hard-boil two of those eggs, and take a couple of tomatoes and two slices of ham, bread, and butter. Wouldn't that be just fine?"

Hilary seemed to be restored to good humor. The two of them prepared the very basic picnic and caught a bus to the station and then took the little electric train out to Dun Laoghaire. It traveled south along the coast and Marilyn commented with pleasure on all that she saw.

"Martin and I knew you'd enjoy this." Hilary was pleased.

"Tell me how you met Martin," Marilyn asked. She listened to the strange, downbeat story told with great pride of a house saved for and bought, investments made, savings tucked away, economies arranged. They got out of the train and walked along the coast to the place they were going to swim. And as they walked by the shining but very cold-looking sea, Hilary talked about property prices, about Martin's brothers getting the small farm in the west, about children of fourteen getting pregnant in the school where Martin taught and where she worked in the office.

When they got to the swimming place Marilyn cried out in delight. "Look at the Martello Tower, and the Joyce Museum! I know where we are. This is where *Ulysses* opened. It's the very spot."

"Yeah, that's right." Hilary was not very interested in James Joyce.

She pointed out the much-photographed sign that said "Forty Foot Gentlemen Only," and said she remembered her mother telling her about the feminists first swimming in there to claim it back for everyone.

"But that can't have been in your mother's time, surely?"

"It was probably in *my* time! I'll be forty this year," Hilary said gloomily.

"So will I," Marilyn said.

A first mark of solidarity between two totally different women. They had a swim, which froze Marilyn's blood to the marrow, and then ate their makeshift picnic. Hilary did most of the talking.

"Tell me about Ria's marriage," Marilyn asked.

They talked about Ria. Hilary told the whole story as she knew it. The sudden announcement and he was gone overnight. The utter folly of it all, the comeuppance that was near at hand. Barney McCarthy wasn't a golden boy anymore, and his political pals were not in power. It was curtains for Mr. Danny Lynch.

"Did you ever like him?"

"I was nervous about him, he was too smart for Ria, too good-looking. I always said it and it turned out I was right in the end. It gave me no pleasure being right. I'm happily married myself, I'd prefer her to have been.

"Are you happily married?" Hilary asked suddenly.

"I don't know," Marilyn said.

"You *must* know."

"No, I don't."

"And what does your husband think?"

"He thinks we're happily married. We have nothing to say to each other. But he wants to go on as normal."

"Sex, do you mean?" Hilary asked.

"Yes. It was good once. But now, it would be empty. I had a hysterectomy two years ago, so even if a forty-year-old woman could conceive, which they can, there's no chance for me."

"I think you're lucky that he still wants to be with you in that way. I can't have children and so Martin thinks we shouldn't have sex. And so we don't."

"I don't believe you," Marilyn said.

"It's true."

"But since when?"

"We're married sixteen years . . . about eight years I'd say, since he knew we couldn't have children."

"And did you know before?"

"I always knew. I went to a fortune-teller, you see. She told me."

"Did you believe her?"

"Totally. She's been right about everybody." Hilary tidied up the remains of their food, and put it into a paper bag.

She was so sure and confident in everything, including the fact this psychic had told her she wasn't fertile. This was a very strange country. "Is she a psychic?"

"I don't know, she just knows what's going to happen."

"Is she a medium? Does she get in touch with the dead?"

"I don't think so," Hilary said. "I didn't want to anyway, I only wanted to know about the living."

"And what else did she tell you?"

"She said I'd be happily married, which is true, and that I'd live in a place with trees but that hasn't happened yet."

Marilyn paused for a moment to think about a woman who considered herself happily married to a man who thought about nothing except interest rates and didn't believe in sex without the possibility of procreation.

"Is she still around, this woman?" Marilyn asked.

They were getting the best weather ever known for a week in July. Everyone said it. The children were suntanned and loving it all.

"Can we take the dinghy out, Dad?" Annie asked.

"No, Annie, it's too dangerous."

"Why did they give it to us then?"

"They gave it to *us,* Princess, not to you, not to children."

"Let them, Danny," Bernadette said.

"No, sweetheart, they don't know about boats."

"Well, how will they ever learn?" Bernadette asked. "Suppose they go where we can see them, would that do?" It was a compromise that did fine. Danny looked on proudly as his son and daughter rowed the little boat along the shore.

"You're so good with them, but you're fearless. Ria would have wanted to swim along beside them like a mother duck."

"You have to let children go free," she said. "They hate you otherwise."

"I know, but when we have our baby will you feel the same?" He laid his hand on her stomach and thought about the son or daughter who would be in their home, a real person by Christmas.

"Of course!" She looked at him in surprise. "You don't want children, free spirits, all herded into some kind of corral do you?"

Danny realized that this was exactly what he and Ria had built and why he so badly needed to escape. He lay with his head in her lap and closed his eyes. "Sleep on, I'll look out at the dinghy," she said.

"Isn't that amazing?" Finola Dunne was reading them extracts from the newspaper.

"What's amazing?" Danny asked. He was still lying in the grass and Bernadette was making a series of daisy chains that she was spreading over him like threads tying him to the earth.

"Polly's is for sale! That's been the main dress hire place in Dublin for years."

"It's never for sale." Danny sat up suddenly.

"Well, so it says here."

He took the paper and read the paragraph. "I have to make a phone call," he said. "Where are those goddamn children on their bloody boat, and what the hell did you let them go off for?"

"Danny, they've tied up the dinghy. You were asleep. They've gone to get ice creams. Please, please be calm. You have no idea what's going on."

"I have a fair idea."

"Well, what do you think it is? Do you think that if Polly's is being sold Barney's running out of money?" Bernadette asked.

"And you can sit there making daisy chains if you think that?"

"I'd prefer to make daisy chains than to have a heart attack," Bernadette said.

"Darling, darling Bernadette, the world might be about to end for us. You don't understand, you're just a child."

"I wish you wouldn't say that, you've always known what age I am," she said.

"I have to talk to Barney, find out what's happening." Danny's face was white.

"You should wait until you are calmer. You won't understand anything the way you are now."

"I won't *be* any calmer, not until I know. And maybe not even then. I can't believe he wouldn't tell me, we're friends. I'm like a son to him, he's said so often."

"Then if he *is* in trouble maybe it was harder to tell you than anyone else." She saw it quite simply.

"And aren't you worried, frightened?"

"Of what?"

"Of what might be ahead?"

"You mean being poor? Of course not. You've been poor before, Danny. You'll live, you did before."

"That was then, this is now."

"You've a lot more to live for now."

He held both her hands in his. "I want to give you everything. I want the sun the moon and the stars for you and our baby."

She smiled at him, that slow smile that always made him feel weak. She said nothing more. This was what made him feel ten feet tall.

Bernadette didn't busy herself wondering was this strategy better than that. Having urged him to be calm she was now staying out of it. She was leaving it all to him.

"Where's Dad, we got him a choc-ice?" Annie asked.

"He went to make a phone call," Bernadette said.

"Will he be long, do you think, or should we eat it?" Brian wanted a ruling.

"I think we should eat it," said Bernadette.

"It's Danny."

"Didn't *you* get the weather! I bet it's beautiful down there." Barney sounded pleased for him.

"Barney, what's happening?"

"You're worse than I am about not being able to cut off and take holiday."

"Were you looking for me? My mobile's not charged up, I'm ringing from a bar."

"No, I wasn't looking for you, I was letting you have your holiday in peace." He sounded very unruffled.

"I saw the paper," Danny said

"The paper?"

"I saw Polly's is on the market."

"That's right. Yes."

"What does it mean, Barney?"

"It means that Polly wants a break from it, she got a good offer and we're just testing the market in case there's an even better one out there."

"That's bullshit. Polly doesn't want a break, she's hardly ever in there anyway."

"Well, that's what she says. You know women . . . unpredictable."

Danny had heard Barney so often talking to clients like this. Or when speaking to accountants, lawyers, politicians, bank managers. Anyone who had to be kept at bay. Simple, homespun, cheerful, even a little bewildered. It had always worked in the past. But then he had never talked like that to Danny before. Suddenly he thought of something. "Is there anyone with you as we speak?"

"No no one at all, why?"

"Are we okay, Barney? Tell me straight out."

"How do you mean?"

"You know what I mean. Have we our heads above water? Are we in the black?"

Barney laughed. "Come *on*, Danny, has the sun softened your head? When were we ever in the black? The red is where we live."

"I mean will we be able to climb out this time?"

"We always did before."

"You've never had to sell Polly's before."

"I don't *have* to sell it now." There was a slightly steely sound to Barney's voice. Danny said nothing. "So if that's all, will you get on with having a holiday, and be in good shape when you're back here on Monday."

"I could come back now if you needed me. I'd just drive straight up, leave the others here."

"See you Monday," said Barney McCarthy, and hung up.

Danny bought himself a small brandy to stop the slight tremor in his hand. The barman looked at him sympathetically. "Family life all cooped up in a small boat can get a bit ropey," he said.

"Yes." Danny spoke absently. His mind was far away in Barney McCarthy's office. He had been dismissed on the phone, that was not an exaggeration. He had seen Barney do it so often to other people. Now he was at the receiving end.

"How many kids?" the barman asked.

"Two, and one on the way."

"God, it must be pure hell for you," said the man, who had seen a lot of human nature in running a lakeside pub, but had never seen a face as white and strained as this fellow's.

"I'm going to go to a psychic with your sister," Marilyn said to Ria on the phone. "May I use your car?"

"I'm going to lessons on the Internet with your friend Heidi. Can I use your laptop to practice on?"

Sheila Maine was delighted to hear from Ria. Gertie hadn't told her that she was coming, what a marvelous surprise.

"Does Gertie write a lot then?"

"Usually an air letter every week. She fills me in on all that's going on."

Ria's heart lurched to think of the fantasy life poor Gertie needed that she had to write a catalog of imaginary goings-on. "Gertie's great, I see her a lot," Ria said.

"I know, she tells me. She's in and out of your house all the time, she tells me."

"That's right," Ria said. Gertie didn't write and say *why* she was in and out of the house on Tara Road, that she was usually down on her hands and knees scrubbing floors in it to make Jack's drinking money. Still, people had to have some area of dignity. This was Gertie's.

"Will you come and visit me in Stoneyfield? I've a lovely house for the summer. The children will be coming out too in a couple of weeks' time."

Sheila said she'd love to visit and that she'd drive over on Saturday with her children. Max was working shifts so he wouldn't be able to come. It was only an hour away. "And you tell that handsome husband of yours that I'm really looking forward to seeing him again. He was so welcoming to us when we were at Tara Road that time."

With a shock Ria realized that Gertie's letters about the never-never land that was Dublin must have failed to include mention of *any* kind of marital disharmony. Not only her own. She decided to wait until Sheila Maine arrived before telling her the story. It was too long and wearying for the telephone. It was a story told too often and becoming more incomprehensible with each telling. People thought she was over it all by now, they didn't realize that Ria still felt the phone would ring and it would be Danny. "Sweetheart, forgive me" is what he would say, or "Can we start again?"

Ria had answers for both questions. She would say yes and mean it. He was the man she loved and this had all been a terrible mistake. A series of incidents that had escalated and gotten out of control. Ria told herself that if she didn't think about, pray for it, and hope for it too much, it would happen.

Rosemary said that Mrs. Connor was amazing, Marilyn would be astounded by her. Rosemary looked particularly good today, Marilyn thought, in a very dressy rose silk dress. It was the kind of thing you might wear to a wedding rather than to entertain a neighbor. She poured tea in the beautiful roof garden where they had been admiring the planting that had been done by a nursery. Rosemary said that Mrs. Connor should be investigated by the fraud squad. She saw nothing, revealed nothing about the future, charged a fortune, and looked more and more poverty-stricken and tubercular.

"You've been to her?" Marilyn was surprised.

"Yes, a couple of times when we were kids. I went with Ria and Gertie."

"And what did she tell you?"

"Nothing at all, but she told it with great pain and anguish in her face. She puts on a good show, I give her that." Rosemary was being fair.

"But she must have told you something specific?"

"Interestingly, she told me that I was a bad friend." Rosemary laughed.

"And were you?" Marilyn had a lightly disconcerting way of asking questions directly.

"No, I don't think so particularly. Look, I'm in business, you have to be a bad friend to someone every hour doing deals."

"I guess."

"But I was a very good friend to Polly Callaghan last week. She came in and wanted a brochure printed. You know, full color, big pictures and everything. And I knew somehow that the bill might *just* not be paid. Now I like Polly. I didn't want to lose her friendship over this so I said let's do a straight swap. I take something from your stock and you have the printing free. And I got this dress. How about that for enterprise and the barter system?"

"And did she know why you did it?"

"She may have." Rosemary was thoughtful. "Barney McCarthy would know, certainly, when she tells him. Anyway, enough about all that. Why are *you* going to Mrs. Connor anyway?" she asked Marilyn.

"To talk to the dead," Marilyn said.

And for once in her life the cool, confident Rosemary Ryan was at a loss for anything to say.

Marilyn realized that if she were to drive Hilary to this remote place where cars parked in a field she had better put in a little driving practice.

Even though she drove an automatic car at home she had been used to driving a stick shift too, so the gears were not beyond her. She had been warned by everyone about Dublin traffic, the way people fought for parking places and were leisurely about indicating when they moved from one lane to another. Nothing prepared her for the number of near accidents she encountered in her first outing. Shaking, she came back to No. 16 Tara Road. Colm saw her getting rather unsteadily out of the car and asked was she all right.

"I swear they pull out right in front of you," she said. "I nearly wasted a dozen pedestrians. They just roll across the road no matter what color the lights are."

He laughed easily. "The first day is always the worst, anyway you're home now and are going to have visitors by the look of things." He nodded toward the gate where Nora Johnson and Pliers were making their entrance.

"Yoo-hoo, Marilyn," called Nora.

"Oh, hell," Marilyn said.

"Tut-tut, Marilyn," said Colm in mock disapproval, but he slipped away out to the back garden and let her cope with the visit on her own.

"Hilary and I were going to have lunch together, we wondered would you like to join us?"

"Thanks, Mrs. Johnson, but I don't really feel like going out just now. . . ," Marilyn began.

"Well, never mind, we can eat here."

"Here?" Marilyn looked wildly around the garden.

Nora Johnson was almost inside the house already. "Wouldn't it be much nicer, easier for us all?" she said. She was not a person who would sense when she might not be welcome. Not anyone to be rebuffed by a little coldness. There was no hint heavy enough to move her.

What the hell, Marilyn said to herself. I coped with Dublin traffic, I can make a lunch, can't I? Forcing a smile on her face she beckoned Ria's mother to come in.

Hilary came in not long after. "Mam said we'd meet here, where are we going?"

"Marilyn's going to cook for us," Nora said, pleased.

"It'll be like old times in this kitchen then," said Hilary, settling down happily. "What are we going to eat?" There were chicken pieces in Ria's fridge and some potatoes from the garden in a wire basket. "I'll peel those," Hilary offered.

"Thank you," Marilyn said, struggling to take in a recipe pinned to the inside of a cupboard. It didn't look too daunting, it involved honey, soy sauce, and ginger, all of which seemed to be on hand.

Pliers had settled down in his own corner, Clement on his own chair. It was, as Hilary said, like old times in this kitchen, only with a different woman standing at the stove.

Annie and Brian had remembered something very important. If they were to enter Clement for the cat show the form had to be handed in today.

"You'll be back in Dublin in two days," Finola protested.

"But that's too late," Annie wailed. "We thought Clement could get a Highly Commended. The form's probably on the hall table with all the mail at Tara Road."

Bernadette shrugged. It was one of the many things in life, good or bad, that just happened. She was sympathetic but offered no solution. Danny was out phoning, he wasn't there to help.

Finola Dunne recognized a crisis when she saw one. "Go and ring Mrs. Vine," she suggested.

Gertie rang on the door of No. 16 Tara Road. "This has to be the most embarrassing moment of my life, Marilyn."

"Yes?" Marilyn was flushed and anxious. The mixture of honey, soy sauce and ginger looked very glutinous and was sticking to the bottom of the saucepan while the chicken still seemed raw.

"But you know the way I come tomorrow . . . could I come today instead?"

"It's not really suitable, Gertie, I'm cooking a lunch."

"It's just, it's just it would help matters greatly at home if I were to—"

"I'm so sorry. But if you want to be away from home would you care to join Ria's mother and sister for lunch?" Marilyn felt her head buzzing. She was dizzy from her first attempt to cope with Dublin traffic. She was cooking a complicated dish for people she had not wanted to entertain, under the eyes of a menagerie of watchful animals. Now she was asking a third and very stressed woman to join them.

"Ah, no thank you, Marilyn, that's not what it was at all." Gertie was fidgeting with her hands, her eyes looked frightened.

"Then what is it, Gertie? I'm sorry, I'm not sure—"

"Marilyn, could you give me the money for tomorrow and I'll do the work, of course, later . . . ?" It was so hard for her to ask.

So hard to hear. Marilyn flushed. "Yes, yes, of course," she muttered, embarrassed, and went to find her wallet. "Do you have any change?" she asked without thinking.

"Marilyn, if I had any change would I be here like this asking you for tomorrow's money?"

"No, how stupid of me. Please take this."

"This will cover tomorrow and all of next week," Gertie said.

"Sure, fine, whatever you say."

"You could ring Ria in America and she'll tell you I always honor it."

"I know you will, and well . . . good-bye now."

Marilyn came downstairs flustered and unsettled by the conversation. "That was Gertie," she said brightly. "She couldn't stay."

"No, she had to get Jack's drinking money to him," said Nora Johnson succinctly.

At that moment they all realized that one of the saucepans seemed to be on fire with what looked like a toffee coating on the bottom.

"That will never come off," said Hilary. "And those are very expensive saucepans."

They left the saucepan to soak and Marilyn began again. As Hilary had said, it was a mercy she hadn't wasted the chicken fillet, the other bit was only old sauces.

The telephone rang. It was Annie and Brian from the River Shannon. Could Marilyn please find this form? She went upstairs again to the front room where she kept all the mail neatly on the sideboard. She found the form and called them back at the pub where they were waiting for news.

"Great," Brian said. "All you have to do now is drive it around to the address with a one-pound entrance fee."

"Yes, well . . ."

"Thanks very much, we'd hate for him not to enter." Annie had taken the phone by now.

"I don't have to take Clement to the show myself?" Marilyn asked anxiously. "Walk him around a ring or anything?"

"No, they sit in cages actually, and to be honest I'd quite like to do that myself, but if you'd like to come along or anything . . . ?"

"Yes well, we'll see." Marilyn ended the conversation.

"Are they having a good holiday?" Nora sniffed at the unlikely prospect of this.

"I didn't ask them." Marilyn cried with a great wail because she saw the second saucepan was burning and neither of these two women who were used to Ria Lynch being in total charge had lifted a finger to rescue it.

Was this what she had come all the way to Ireland for? This ludicrous, exhausting kind of day? Getting more and more enmeshed and involved in the lives of total strangers?

There was a letter from Mam in the mailbox on Tudor Drive.

> *Dear Ria,*
>
> *I should have been better about writing letters but somehow God does not put enough hours in the day. And talking of God as we were, I hope you've found a Catholic church out in that place for my grandchildren to go to on Sundays. Marilyn said that she gave you all the details, phone numbers and mass times and everything, but you don't have to pretend to me that you are a regular mass-goer, I know better. Marilyn doesn't go to the Protestant church here, and of course she might be of the Jewish faith, but I didn't like to suggest the synagogue to her. She's a grown woman and can make her own choices. I'd be the last one to interfere in anyone else's life.*
>
> *She was a bit stiff in the beginning but I think she's getting used to our ways all right. A mother should not criticize her daughter's friends, and I don't intend to but you know I don't like Lady Ryan and never will, and I regard Gertie as a weak slob who deserves what she gets by putting up with it. Marilyn is different, she's very interesting to talk to about everything, and very knowledgeable about the cinema. She drives your car like a maniac and has burned two saucepans, which she has replaced. She's going to be forty on August first. I'm twenty-seven years older than her but I get on with her just fine. I think she's sleeping with Colm Barry but I'm not certain.*

*The Adulterer is still prancing around the place. The children get
back from the ludicrous boat holiday tomorrow. I'm going to
take Annie out for a pizza and hear all the gory details. Annie's
anxious to bring her friend Kitty as well, so we may include her
in the party and then let them go home together.*

Lots of love from your Mam.

Ria looked at the postmark wildly. Five days since her mother had
written all this. Five whole days. And she hadn't known anything that
had been going on. What kind of friends or support system was there
that nobody had told her all of this vital information? It was eight o'clock
in the morning. She reached for the phone and realized that since it was
lunchtime in Ireland her mother would be out on one of her insane
perambulations. Why did people write letters like this that took five days
and five nights to get there instead of using E-mail? She realized that it
was a little unfair of her to blame her mother for not being on the Net
since she herself had hardly heard of it a couple of weeks ago. But
honestly.

She rang Marilyn. The answering machine was on but she had
changed the message. "This is Ria Lynch's house but she is not here at
present. Messages will be taken and relayed to her. Marilyn Vine
speaking. I will return your call." How *dare* she do that? Ria felt a huge
surge of rage. She could hardly contain her hatred of Marilyn.

This woman had gone into her house, driven her car into the ground,
chopped down the garden, gone to fortune-tellers, burned Ria's
saucepans, slept with Colm Barry. What else was there to discover about
her?

Ria rang Rosemary. She was at a meeting, her secretary said. She rang
Gertie in the launderette. "You're so good to entertain Sheila and the
children, she loved her visit to you. She phoned and told me all about it.
Loved it she did." Gertie's voice was happy. What she was really
thanking Ria for was keeping up the fiction that Gertie and Jack lived a
normal life.

More lies, fantasy, pretense. Ria was so impatient she could hardly
keep it out of her tone. "What's Marilyn up to, Gertie?"

"She's great, isn't she?"

"I don't know, I never met her."

"Is she sleeping with Colm?"

"Is she *what*?" Gertie's laugh from the busy lunchtime launderette was like an explosion.

"My mother says she is."

"Ria, your mother! You never listened to a word your mother said before."

"I know, did she burn my saucepans?"

"Yes, and replaced them with much better ones. You'd be delighted. She got herself a couple of cheap ones in case she burned them again."

"What is she . . . accident-prone?"

"No, just not any good as a cook. But you should see what she's done with the garden!"

"Is there any of it left?"

"Ria, it's fantastic."

"Like are there any trees or bushes? Anything I'd recognize? Brian told me she'd cut it all down."

"You listened to Brian?" Gertie asked.

"She's not working in my thrift shop with Frances Sullivan as well, is she? I mean, in between doing tunnel excavations in my garden."

"What *is* all this, Ria? She's a lovely person, she's *your* friend."

"No, she's not. I never laid eyes on her."

"Are you upset about something?"

"She's taken over my house."

"Ria, you gave her your house, you took hers."

"She changed the message on the phone."

"You told her to when she was ready."

"She's ready all right."

"Annie helped her decide what to say."

"Annie?"

"Yes, she comes round to the house a lot."

"To Tara Road?" Ria asked through gritted teeth.

"Well I think she misses you, Ria, that's why she comes round." Gertie sounded desperate to reassure her.

"Yeah, I'm sure she does," Ria said.

"She does, Ria, she said that the holiday on the Shannon was bizarre, that was the word she used. She said that Brian said every day 'Mam would like this' and she agreed."

"Did she?" Ria brightened a little.

"Honestly she did. I was talking to her this morning when I went up to the house. She's actually gone out with Marilyn today. The two of them have gone shopping."

"What?"

"Yes. Apparently Annie has some voucher or something for clothes, which your mother gave her. She wanted to use it so they went off to Grafton Street."

"I suppose she's there now, plowing up and down the pedestrian precinct in my car."

"No, she went on the bus. I honestly don't know why you've turned against her, Ria, I really don't."

"Neither do I," said Ria.

And she hung up and burst into tears.

There had been three false attempts to meet Mrs. Connor. Each time the line of cars had been too long. The anxious-looking boys who protected the vehicles said that it wouldn't be worth their while to wait. Fourth time lucky.

Marilyn looked into the haunted face of the thin woman.

"You're welcome to our country," she said.

"Thank you."

"You came to find something here."

"Yes, I suppose we all do."

"It's not here, it's where you came from."

"Can you talk to my son for me?"

"Is he dead?"

"Yes."

"It wasn't your fault, madam."

"It *was* my fault, I should never have let him go."

"I can't talk to the dead, madam." The woman's eyes were very bright in her thin face. "They're at peace. They are sleeping and that's how we must leave them."

"I want to tell him I'm sorry."

"No, madam, it's not possible. And it's not what the people who are sleeping would want."

"It *is* possible."

"Not for me. Would you like me to look at your hand?"

"Why can't you talk to my son, tell him I'm so very sorry? That I let him go that day, that I agreed they should pull out the plug? I took him off the life support machine. After only six months. They might have found a way to get him back. I sat there and watched him take his last breath." Mrs. Connor looked at her with great sympathy. "I held his hand in mine at the end and in case he could hear. I said, 'Dale, your father and I are turning this off to release your spirit. That's what it will do.' But it *didn't* release his spirit, I know that. It's trapped somewhere and I'll have no peace unless I can talk to him just once to tell him. Can't you find him for me?"

"No."

"I beg you."

"You have to find your own peace."

"Well, why am I here?"

"Like everyone else who comes in here. People come because they are unhappy."

"And they're hoping for a little magic, I suppose?"

"I suppose so, madam."

"Well thank you for your time and your honesty, Mrs. Connor." Marilyn stood up to go.

"Take your money, madam, I gave you nothing."

"No, I insist."

"No, madam, I insist too. One day you will find your peace. That day go out and give this money to someone who needs it."

In the car going home, Hilary asked almost nervously, "Was she any help to you, Marilyn?"

"She's very wise."

"But she didn't get to talk to the dead for you?"

"No, she said he was asleep."

"And couldn't she wake him for you?"

Marilyn felt a rush of affection for Ria's lonely, ungracious sister. "Well, we agreed why wake him if he's peacefully asleep."

"And was that worth it? I mean you didn't think you paid her too much?"

"No, not at all, it was good to know he was asleep."

"And do you feel better about him now?" Hilary was hopeful.

"Much better," lied Marilyn Vine. "And now tell me, what did she tell you?"

"She told me that it was up to me to find the trees, that we had enough put by to choose where we lived."

"And would you *like* to live somewhere with trees?" Marilyn asked.

"Not particularly. I've nothing against them, mind, but I never yearned for them either. Still if it's what's meant to be out there for me I think I should look for them."

The line of cars waiting for Mrs. Connor had still been long as they left. People all looking for a little magic to help them through. That woman had said that everyone who came to her caravan was unhappy. What a sad procession. But somehow there was a curious strength about it. Everyone sitting in those cars had a sorrow. Marilyn Vine wasn't the only woman in the world racked with guilt and loss. Others had survived it too. Like people needing medicine, they had to go to a caravan or something similar occasionally just in case there was any magic floating by that would help.

She smiled to herself. Hilary saw the smile and was pleased.

Ria changed the message. "This is the home of Greg Vine, who is in Hawaii, and Marilyn Vine, who is in Ireland. Ria Lynch is living here at the moment and will be happy to forward your messages to the Vines or return your calls."

She played it back several times and nodded. Two could play at that game. That would sort Ms. Marilyn out.

She called Heidi. "I'm having a little supper party here, won't you and Henry come? Carlotta's coming and that nice couple we met at the Internet class, and those two men who run the gourmet shop you told me about. I've gotten friendly with them but I have to show off to them seriously with my home-cooked food. I'm hoping they may give me a job."

"Mam?"

"Hi, Annie."

"Mam, aren't you funny, you say hi instead of hallo."

"I know, I'm a scream."

"You didn't call us so we called you."

"I did call you. And I also left a message for your father. To which he hasn't replied yet, you might tell him."

"He's out, Mam, he's out all the time."

"Well, when next he comes in tell him that I'm waiting."

"But it's only a message about business, Mam."

"I know, but I'd still like to hear his answer."

"Will it be a fight?"

"Not if he returns my call, no."

"And how are you, Mam?"

"I'm fine. How was your outing to the pizza place with Grannie?" Ria had a bit of steel in her voice that Annie recognized.

"It was fine. Gran gave me a marvelous waistcoat. You'll see it, I'll take it over with me."

"And did Kitty join you there?"

"No, she didn't as it happens."

"How did that happen?"

"Because Bernadette rang Grannie and said Dad had a Rooted Objection to Kitty."

"How disappointing."

"Well, I was disappointed, Mam, but there you go. You and Dad don't like Kitty, so what can I do?"

"I'm glad your father's looking after that side of things anyway."

"He didn't do it, he wouldn't know what day it was these times. I tell you, it was Bernadette."

"And tell me about your shopping expedition with Marilyn."

"Have you a fleet of detectives on me or something, Mam?"

"No, just friends and family who tell me about things I'm interested in, that's all."

"You're not interested in clothes, Mam, you hate clothes."

"What did you buy?" Ria hissed at her daughter.

"Pink jeans and a navy and pink shirt."

"Sounds great," Ria said.

"Mam, are you in a bad mood at me over something?"

"Should I be?"

"I don't think so, I'm having a shitty summer to be honest, everyone's upset the whole time. I'm not allowed to see my friend Kitty. Grannie's going to live in an old people's home. Mr. McCarthy's gone off somewhere without letting Dad know where. Rosemary Ryan is like something wired to the moon, looking for Dad to give him urgent messages. Brian has Dekko and Myles back in tow again roaring and bawling and driving everyone mad. Dad had some kind of row with Finola and she's not around anymore. Bernadette's asleep most of the time. Aunt Hilary's lost her marbles and keeps looking up into trees. Clement was coughing up fur balls and he had to go to the vet. Colm took him. It's not serious . . . but it was very frightening at the time. And then I ring you and you're in a snot with me about something that I don't know about. And honestly, if it weren't for Marilyn I'd go mad."

"She's helpful, is she?"

"Well at least she's normal. And she recommends me books to read. She gave me *To Kill a Mockingbird*. Did you ever read it, Mam?"

"I love you, Annie."

"Are you drunk, Mam?"

"Of course I'm not drunk. Why do you ask?"

"I asked you did you read a book and you said you loved me. That's not a conversation."

"No, but it's a fact."

"Well, I suppose. Thank you, Mam. Thanks anyway."

"And you? Do you perhaps love me?"

"You've been too long in America, Mam," said Annie.

Danny Lynch was standing on the steps ringing the doorbell of what used to be his own house.

Marilyn, kneeling under the huge tree inside the gate, was invisible to him as he stood fidgeting and looking at his watch. He *was* a handsome man with all that nervous, eager energy that she remembered from years back but now there was something else, something she had seen in the restaurant that night. Something anxious, almost haunted. Then he took out some door keys and let himself in. Marilyn had been about to get up and approach him but now she moved very sharply from her planting and ran lightly up to the house and let herself in.

He was standing in the front room looking around. He called out: "It's only me, Danny Lynch."

"You startled me," she said with her hand on the chest, pretending a great sense of alarm and shock. After all, if she *had* come in without knowing he was inside she would have been very shocked.

"I'm sorry, I did ring the bell but there was no answer. And you're Marilyn. You're very welcome to Ireland." Despite his restlessness he had a practiced charm. He looked at her as he welcomed her. He was a man who would look at every woman he talked to and make them feel special. That's why she had remembered him, after all, when she had forgotten so many other people.

"Thank you," she said.

"And you're happy here?" He looked around the room taking it all in as if he were going to do an examination on its contents.

"Very. Who wouldn't be?" She wished she hadn't said that. Danny Lynch had obviously not been happy enough to stay here. Why out of courtesy had she made that stupid remark?

He didn't seem to have noticed it. "My daughter says you've been very kind to her."

"She's a delightful girl. I hope she and Brian will enjoy visiting my home as much as I like being in theirs."

"It's a great opportunity for them. When I was Brian's age I had only been ten miles down the road." He was very engaging.

And yet she didn't like the fact that he had let himself in. "I didn't actually know that there was another key to the house out. I thought Gertie and I had the only two."

"Well, it's not exactly having a key *out*," he said. "Not *my* having one surely?"

"No it's just I misunderstood, that's all. I didn't realize that you come and go here, Danny. There were very precise notes about Colm having a key to the back gate and everything. I'll tell Ria that she forgot to tell me about you and how I thought you were an intruder." She laughed at the silly mistake but she watched him carefully at the same time.

He understood what she was saying. Carefully he took the key to Tara Road off his key ring and laid it on the table beside the bowl of roses. "I don't come and go, actually. It was just today I needed something and since you weren't in I thought . . . well, you know, old habits die hard. It was my front door for a long time." His smile and apology were practiced but nonetheless genuine.

"Of course." She was gracious, she could afford to be. She had won this little battle, she had got Ria's door key back too. "And what was it you wanted?"

"The car keys actually. Mine has packed up so I need to take the second car."

"Ria's car?"

"The second car, yes."

"For how long? I'd need it back in an hour."

"No, I mean take it, for the duration."

"Oh, that's impossible," she said pleasantly.

"What do you mean?"

"I mean I paid the insurance company an extra premium to cover my driving that car for eight weeks. Ria will be driving your children around in my car. My husband can't suddenly appear and claim the car from *her* . . ." She paused. The rest of the sentence hung there unspoken.

"I'm sorry, Marilyn, very sorry if you'll be inconvenienced but I have to have it. You don't need it, you're here all day digging in the garden. I have to go out and make calls on people, earn a living."

"I'm sure your company will provide you with another car."

"It suits me to have this one, and since you don't need—"

"Excuse me, you don't know what I need a car for. Today as it happens I'm meeting Colm to arrange for some organic fertilizer for the garden to be delivered, and the nursery where we are meeting is not on a bus route. I am driving your *first* mother-in-law and three old ladies from St. Rita's to a bridge tournament in Dalkey. Then I'm picking up your daughter and son and driving them to meet your *second* mother-in-law, with whom you have apparently had some quarrel, for swimming lessons. Then I meet Rosemary Ryan, who has been trying to get in touch with you urgently by the way, and she and I are going to a charity fashion show. I agreed to drive." He looked at her, openmouthed. "So can we *now* agree that regretfully there isn't a question of my giving you Ria's car?" Marilyn asked.

"Danny?"

"Jesus, Barney, where are you?"

Barney laughed. "I told you, a business trip."

"No, that's what we tell the bank, the suppliers, other people, it's not what you tell me."

"That's exactly what I'm doing, on the business of raising money."

"And tell me you've managed to raise some, Barney, because otherwise we're going to lose two contracts this afternoon."

"Easy, easy. It's raised."

"Where are you?"

"It doesn't matter, ring Larry in the bank and check. The money's there."

"It wasn't there an hour ago."

"It's there now."

"Where are you, Barney?"

"I'm in Málaga," Barney McCarthy said, and hung up.

Danny was shaking. He hadn't the courage to ring the bank. Suppose Larry said he knew nothing of any money. Suppose Barney was in the south of Spain with Polly and wasn't coming back. It was preposterous, of course, but then people did that sort of thing. They left their wives and children without a backward glance. Hadn't he done it himself?

"Mrs. Ryan on the line for you, *again*," the secretary said to him, rolling her eyes to heaven, pleading with him to take the call this time.

"Put her through. Sweetheart, how are you?" he said.

"Five calls, Danny, what's this?" Her voice was clipped.

"It's been hell in here."

"So I read in the papers and hear everywhere," she said.

"It's okay now, we're out of the fire."

"Says who?"

"Says Barney. He's saying it from Spain, rather alarmingly."

Rosemary laughed and Danny relaxed.

"We have to meet. There are a few things we must talk about."

"Very difficult, sweetheart."

"Tonight I'm going to one of Mona's dreary charity things with the woman who's living in your house."

"Marilyn?"

"Yes. Have you met her?"

"I don't like her, she's a real ball breaker."

"Come round after ten," Rosemary said, and hung up.

Somewhere Danny found the courage to ring the bank. He must sound cheerful and confident.

"Hi, Larry, Danny Lynch here. Is the red alert over? Can we come out of the bunkers?"

"Yes, some last-ditch Mafia money turned up."

Danny went weak with relief but he pretended to be shocked. "Larry, is that any way to talk to respectable property people?"

"There are some respectable property people; you and Barney aren't among them."

"Why are you being so heavy?" Danny was startled.

"He left a lot of small people who could ill afford it without their cash, and then when it started to get ropey he went down to the Costa del Crime and got some laundered drug money from his pals."

"We don't know that, Larry."

"We do."

Danny remembered hearing that Larry's son was in a detox center. He would have very strong feelings about money that might have been made through the sale of heroin.

Greg called Marilyn. "No reason. Just to chat. I miss the E-mails."

"So do I, but I gather Ria's making great progress on my little laptop. She sent an E-mail to Rosemary Ryan, a woman here—I'm going out to a fashion show with her shortly—and one to her ex-husband's office. They nearly collapsed."

"Oh, I know, she sends them to me too."

"She does? What about?"

"Oh, this and that . . . arrangements for the alumni weekend . . . Andy will be coming up too, and her children will be there, so it will be a full house."

"Yes." Marilyn couldn't quite explain why this slightly irritated her, but it did.

"Anyway, she seems to be getting along very well, she's cooking for John & Gerry's a couple of hours a day."

"She's *not*!"

"Yes. Isn't she amazing? And Henry told me that he and Heidi were at a dinner party there. . . ."

"Where?"

"In the house. On Tudor Drive. There were eight of them apparently and—"

"In our house? She had eight people in our house? To dinner?"

"Well, she knows them all pretty well now. Carlotta comes in for a swim every morning, Heidi's around there for coffee after work. It didn't take her long. . . ."

"It did *not*," said Marilyn grimly.

Mona McCarthy was on the committee. She sat smiling at the desk and had their tickets ready for them when they went in. People often wondered how much she knew about her husband's activities, both in business and private life. But they would never learn from Mona's large face. There were no hints there. A big, serene woman, constantly raising money for good causes. It might have been trying to put something back in order to compensate for the many sharp deals where Barney might have taken too much out.

"And a glass of champagne?" she offered.

"I'd love one," Rosemary said. "*And* I have a chauffeur." She introduced Marilyn.

Marilyn was being unusually silent tonight, as if she were thinking about something miles away.

Mona's face lit up. "And little Ria's out in your house at the moment, isn't she?"

Marilyn nodded with a bright smile. She was wondering what percentage of the population of Stoneyfield was now installed in Tudor Drive tonight. Oh, no, it was just after lunch back home, maybe a buffet party for thirty at the swimming pool. But she had to say something pleasant. "Yes, I gather she's having a good time, settling in well."

Mona was pleased. "She really needs that, how wonderful you were able to provide it for her."

"She's even got a job I hear, in our local gourmet shop." Marilyn wondered whether there was a tinny note in her voice, and she wondered further why there should be.

"Ria should have got a job years ago," Rosemary said. "That's why she lost everything she had."

"She didn't lose everything," Mona said quietly. "She still has the children."

Rosemary realized it had not been the right remark to make in front of the stay-at-home wife of Barney McCarthy, who was in the south of

Spain with his mistress. "Yes, of course. That's right, she has the children, and of course the house."

"Do you think that Danny Lynch's liaison, for want of a better word, is . . . permanent?" Marilyn wondered.

"No way," Rosemary said.

"Not at all," Mona said at the same time.

"And would Ria take him back when it does end, do you think?" Marilyn couldn't believe that she was asking these personal questions. Marilyn who was legendary about her reserve had changed entirely in this country, she had become a blabbermouth and busybody in a matter of weeks.

"Oh, I think so," Mona said.

"No question of it," said Rosemary.

If everyone seemed so sure . . . if it were all going to end with everyone back in their own homes as they had been . . . then what a terrible amount of pain and hurt for the whole summer! And what would happen to the baby who was waiting to be born?

As they drove back through the warm Dublin night, Marilyn talked easily to Rosemary. She spoke about Greg out in Hawaii. At no stage did she give any explanation for why he was on one side of the earth and she was on the other.

When Marilyn parked the car outside No. 32, Rosemary thanked her for the lift. "It was wonderful, it meant I could have four glasses of champagne. And I loved them. I would ask you in for coffee but I have such an early start . . . I thought I'd give the plants in the garden a drink of water and then go to bed."

"Heavens, no. I want to get an early night too."

Marilyn drove in and parked the car in the garage.

Just then she remembered that she had left the signed program she had gotten for Annie in Rosemary's purse. Annie and her friend Kitty were mad about two of the models. Marilyn had gone to the trouble to get the right ones, now she had stupidly left them in Rosemary's elegant black leather bag. She looked at her watch. Rosemary wouldn't be in bed yet. She had only left her two minutes ago, she would be watering the garden. Marilyn would just run up the lane, it would be quicker. They didn't lock their back gate in No. 32.

It was such a pleasant neighborhood in so many ways; she had been very lucky to find it. She looked up at the sky, slightly rosy from the lights of the city, a big moon hidden from time to time by racing black clouds that looked like chariots hastening across.

She wished that she didn't feel so mean-spirited about Ria's antics in Stoneyfield, but it was really most unfair of her. She was setting up precedents, establishing patterns, which could now not be broken. Marilyn didn't *want* Carlotta's voluptuous figure diving into her swimming pool, she didn't *need* Heidi coming for coffee every day. And she felt absurdly jealous of what Ria would do for everyone at the alumni picnic.

She was at the back gate of No. 32 now and she pushed it open. She expected to see Rosemary in her bare feet, having taken off her expensive shoes, directing the hose toward the beautifully planted herbaceous border.

But there was nobody there. She walked quietly across the grass and then she heard two people talking in the summer house. Not so much talking, she realized as she got nearer, more kissing. Rosemary had indeed taken off her expensive shoes and her expensive rose silk dress, the one she had got from Polly Callaghan in exchange for a printing job. She lay in a coffee-colored silk slip across Danny Lynch and she had his face in her hands.

She was speaking to him urgently. "Never, never again as long as you live, leave me with five phone calls unreturned."

"Sweetheart, I told you . . ." He was stroking her thigh and raising the lacy edge of the slip.

Marilyn stood there frozen. This was the second time she had watched Danny Lynch without his seeing her. She seemed to be condemned to spy on this man. She was utterly unsure of which way to move.

Rosemary was angry. "Don't, Danny. Don't play with me. There's too much history here. I've put up with too much, saved you, warned you too often."

"You and I are special, we've always agreed that, what we have is something that's outside everything else."

"Yes, I put up with your housey-housey marriage, with your affairs, I even put up with you getting that child pregnant and moving away from this road. God knows why."

"You know why, Rosemary," Danny said.

And Marilyn fled. Back to the safety of her garden where she watered Colm's vegetables and everything else in sight with a ferocity that they had never known and might not indeed have needed.

Clement came and watched her gravely, sitting at a safe distance. She was using that hose like a weapon. She was astounded at how shocked and revolted she felt. This was the falsest friend she had ever known. Poor, poor Ria, so unlucky in her man, which could happen to anyone. But so doubly unlucky to be advised and betrayed by her best friend as well. It was beyond understanding.

In a fit of generosity, Marilyn decided she didn't care if Ria was entertaining whole truckloads of people in 1024 Tudor Drive, serving them platefuls of homemade delicacies. She deserved it. She deserved whatever bit of pleasure she could get.

Ria was in fact on her own on Tudor Drive, bent over Marilyn's laptop.

Hubie Green had given her a computer game. She was going to master it and be able to show it to them when they got here. Sheila Maine's children had lots of these and both Annie and Brian did of course work on computers at school, but Ria had known nothing about them and had never been interested. Still, this game was defeating her.

She sent Hubie an E-mail. *Hubie, it would only take you thirty minutes to explain this game to me. It's worth ten dollars of my time to learn it. Do you think you could come by at some stage? A seriously confused Ria Lynch.*

The kid must live beside his screen: he answered immediately. *It's a done deal. Can you call me on the telephone at this number and tell me where you live?*

She called him and gave the address.

There was a silence. "But that's Dale's house. Dale Vine."

"That's right." She was solemn now. She had somehow thought he would have known. But then why should he know?

"Oh, I couldn't go there, Mrs. Lynch."

"But why not?"

"Mr. and Mrs. Vine wouldn't like it."

"They're not here, Hubie, I'm living in the house. Marilyn's in my house in Ireland, Greg's in Hawaii."

"Did they split up?" He sounded concerned.

"I don't know," she said truthfully.

"You must know."

"I don't, as it happens, they didn't tell me. I think after Dale's death they needed to get away."

"Yeah, sure."

"But of course I understand, Hubie, if you don't want to come round here, if it has bad memories for you. I'm sorry, I should really have thought."

She heard him take a breath. "Hey, it's only a house, they're not there to get upset. Your kids have to play this game and ten dollars is ten dollars. Sure I'll come, Mrs. Lynch."

It was so simple once he explained it, and also quite exciting. They played on and on.

"That was much more than half an hour, I'd better give you twenty."

"No we agreed ten. I stayed because I enjoyed it."

"Would you like some supper?" She brought him into the kitchen and opened the fridge.

"Hey, you've got one of those great Irish flag quiches they sell at John & Gerry's!"

"I make them," she said, pleased.

"You make them? Wow," he said. "My mother bought two of them for a party."

"Good, well, I'll give you some Irish soda bread with currants in it to take home to her when you leave, then I don't feel too bad keeping you out for so long."

He walked around the kitchen, restless, maybe uneasy to be in this home again. Ria said nothing about the past. Instead she busied herself talking about the visit of Annie and Brian. Hubie picked up a picture of the children. Ria kept it out where she could see it.

"Is this her? Your daughter? She's real cute," he said.

"Yes, she's lovely, but then I would think so, and that's Brian." She looked proudly at the son who would be here soon. Hubie showed no interest at all. They sat and talked companionably over the meal. Hubie used to come here a lot, he said. Great swimming pool and always a welcome. Not food like this, mind you, but cookies from the store. This was the house where the kids came. In fact his parents were quite friendly with Mr. and Mrs. Vine before everything.

"And now?" Ria was gentle.

"Well, you see how she is, Mrs. Lynch. You know what she's like now."

"No, the funny thing is I don't know what she's like, I've never met her and I've only seen one photograph of her."

"You don't know her? You're not a friend?"

"No, it was a home exchange, that's all. She's in my house, you see, digging up my garden, buying my daughter pink jeans."

"You don't want her to do that? Why don't you tell her?" To Hubie it was simple.

"Because we're old and complicated, that's why. Anyway, to be fair I'm doing something now that she mightn't like, having you to supper."

"She wouldn't like this, believe me, Mrs. Lynch."

"It wasn't your fault."

"Not the way she sees it."

"I really don't know all about it, people don't talk and I don't like to ask. I just heard it was on your birthday."

"Yeah, it was."

"But why is she upset with you?"

"You really don't know her?" He wanted to be reassured. "You're not a friend of theirs?"

"No, I promise you, we just got in touch by accident. I had problems of my own, you see."

"Did someone die?"

"No, but my husband left me and I felt bad and upset over there."

"Oh."

"And Dale's mother obviously couldn't come to terms with what had happened around here so . . ."

"Yes, that's true. She went insane, I think."

"People do for a while, but a lot of them get better." Ria tried to be encouraging.

"She hates me."

"Why should she hate you?"

"Because I'm alive, I guess." He looked very young and sad as he sat there trying to make sense of what had happened. And the lights went on in the garden as the darkness came down, as it did so quickly here in America, unlike at home where everything seemed to move much more slowly.

"But surely if she were to hate anyone it would be the other boy, the one who died?"

"Johnny?"

"Yes, Johnny. I mean he was the one driving. *He* was the one who killed her son."

He said nothing, just looked out at the garden lights and the sprinklers beginning to play on the lawn.

"She can't hate Johnny. Johnny is dead, there's no point in hating him. We're alive, David and I. She can hate us, it gives her life some purpose."

"You sound very, very bitter about her."

"I do, yes."

"But it must have been so terrible for her, Hubie. So hard to forgive. If Johnny hadn't been drunk . . ."

"Johnny wasn't driving. Dale was driving." She looked at him in horror. "Dale stole the bikes, Dale set it up. It was Dale who killed Johnny."

Ria felt her heart turn over. "That can't be true."

He nodded sadly. "It's true."

"But why? Why did nobody . . . how did they not know?"

"You don't want to think what that wreck looked like, you don't want to think about it. I saw it and David saw it so we have to think about it for the rest of our lives."

"But why didn't you . . . ?"

"Everyone assumed it was Johnny driving and at that time we thought Dale was going to get better. They said he might survive; they had him on this machine. I went in once to see him, before she had orders issued that I wasn't to be let near him. I told him in case he could hear me that we'd let people go on thinking it was Johnny. He was underage you see, and also he had these parents who worshipped him. Johnny had nobody."

"Oh, God," said Ria.

"Yes, I know, and now I don't think what we did was right but we did it for the best. We did it to help goddamn Mrs. Vine and then she wouldn't even let me come to Dale's funeral."

"Oh, God Almighty," Ria said.

"You won't tell her, will you?" he asked.

Ria thought of the room along the corridor, the shrine to the dead son. "No, Hubie, whatever else I may do in my life I won't tell her," Ria said.

CHAPTER

SEVEN

"MARILYN, THIS IS RIA. Sorry to miss you. Nothing really. Just to say that the Dublin Horse Show will be on next month, you might enjoy it. And Rosemary can get you tickets for the show jumping which is very spectacular. She's terrific about things like that, she'd do anything to help. She sent me an E-mail to your laptop and she's dead impressed that I know how to do it. Then maybe you might hate the horse show. I don't know why I'm burbling on, I think it's just I want to make sure you're having a good time. I hear from Gertie that you've done wonders in the garden, thank you so much. Okay. Bye now."

Marilyn listened to the message. She felt such a surge of rage against Rosemary Ryan that she was glad she wasn't holding her coffee mug in her hand. She would surely have crushed it into her palm. She would not return the call yet because she didn't trust herself to speak about Ria's friend who was so terrific about things that she would do anything to help.

"Ria, this is Marilyn, sorry I missed you. Our machines are playing tag as they say. No, I won't ask Rosemary for any tickets to the show jumping but I may well go to the Horse Show when it's on. I see a lot of advertisements for it already. You must tell me more about your Internet lessons. They seem to have worked very well for you, it took me ages to get familiar with it all. Glad to hear that you are getting to know everyone. Annie and Brian are coming to dinner here tomorrow. I was terrified of cooking for them but Colm said he'd leave something suitable. The children are really looking forward to seeing you again. Bye for now."

Ria listened to the message. For the first time she didn't feel excluded and annoyed that the children were going to supper with Marilyn. That woman needed any bit of consolation she could get. And she couldn't return the call because she had to work out with Heidi what they would say about Hubie Green.

"What did you and Dad fall out about, Finola?" Brian asked.

"Brian!"

"No, Annie, it's a reasonable question. And the answer is money."

"Oh," said Brian.

"People often do fall out about that." Finola was brisk and matter-of-fact. "I asked your father to tell me how his company was doing, I wanted to know whether he had enough funds to look after you both, your mother, and Bernadette as well."

"And has he?" Brain asked fearfully.

"I don't know, he asked me to mind my own business, which was fair enough in a way. It's actually *not* my business, but that's why we fell out."

"Will you ever make it up?" Annie asked.

"Oh yes, I'm sure we will." Finola was bright. "And anyway I want to thank you both very much indeed for coming to say good-bye, I really appreciate that."

"You were very good to us, with the swimming lessons and everything," Annie said.

"And with talking to us when Dad and Bernadette were being all sentimental and soppy on the boat." Brian remembered it all with some distaste.

"I was going to give you a little present for the trip but I thought I'd give you twenty dollars each instead," Finola Dunne said.

Their faces lit up. "We shouldn't really take it." Annie sounded doubtful.

"Why not, we're friends, aren't we?"

"Yes but if you and Dad . . ."

"That will be blown over by the time you come back, believe me." They believed her at once and pocketed the money with big smiles. "And . . . I do hope it's all nice for you out there, the holiday with your mother." Finola meant it.

"It will be," Brian said. "I mean she's quite old, Finola, like you are, there won't be any soppiness going on out there."

"Brian!" Annie said.

"I'll see you both in September." Finola had never thought she would like Danny Lynch's children and be sorry to see them leave Ireland for a whole month.

Greg Vine telephoned to say that he would like to stay at Tudor Drive for the alumni weekend in August. "Normally I would leave you the house to yourself and stay in a motel, but there won't be a bed for miles around. Even Heidi and Henry won't have any room."

"Heavens, no, you must stay here. And Andy too."

"We can't all descend on you, surely?"

"Why not? Annie and I can sleep in one room. You have two guest rooms, you and Andy have one each. Brian would sleep standing up, he doesn't have to be taken into consideration. And anyway there's a canvas bed that we can put anywhere for him."

"That's very good of you, it will only be for two nights."

"No, please it's your house, stay as long as you like."

"And when do your children arrive?"

"Tomorrow, I can hardly wait."

When he had replaced the receiver, Greg realized that she hadn't suggested that Brian sleep in Dale's room. It would have been perfectly acceptable. To him anyway. But not to Marilyn. Ria Lynch must have worked that out. She had been so odd the first time, talking about Dale's spirit being in Hawaii and the dead boy missing his mother. But maybe he had misunderstood her. This time she seemed highly practical and down-to-earth.

Marilyn went to Colm's to get the food.

"I'd have brought it down to you," he said.

"Nonsense, I'm grateful enough to you already. What have I got here?"

"A light vegetable korma for Annie, with some brown rice. Just sausage, peas, and chips for Brian, I'm afraid. I did nothing special for you, I presumed you'd eat from both not to show favoritism."

Marilyn said that seemed like an excellent plan. "I'll get my wallet."

"Please, Marilyn."

There was something in his face that stopped her. "Well, thank you so much, Colm, truly."

"Let me get you a basket to carry them." He called out to Caroline, and his pale dark sister, whom Marilyn had only seen in the distance before, came in carrying the ideal container, with a couple of checked dinner napkins. "You have met Caroline, haven't you?"

"I don't think so, not properly anyway. How do you do, I'm Marilyn Vine."

Caroline put out her hand hesitantly. Marilyn glanced at her face and realized that she was looking straight into the eyes of someone with a problem. She didn't consider herself an expert but as a young graduate she had worked for three years on a rehab project. She had not a shadow of doubt that she was being introduced to a heroin addict.

"Do you think Dad has lost all his money?" Brian asked on the bus from Finola's house.

"No, don't be an eejit," Annie said.

"But why does Finola think he has?"

"She doesn't know. Anyway, all old people like Finola and Gran ever think about is money."

"We could ask Rosemary, she'd know," Brian suggested. "We'll be passing her house anyway."

"If you so much as open your mouth to Rosemary about it I'll take your tonsils out with an ice cream scoop, and no anesthetic," Annie said.

"All right, all right." Brian wasn't going to risk it.

"But if we *are* going to Tara Road we might as well call in on Gertie," Annie suggested.

"Would she know about Dad's money?"

"Not about Dad's money, you moron, to say good-bye, like we did to Finola."

"Oh, do you think she'd give us anything too?" Brian was interested.

"Of course she wouldn't, Brian, you *are* a clown. You get worse all the time." Annie was exasperated with him.

"No, well, I don't suppose she'd be cleaning the house for Mam if she had any money herself." Brian had worked it out.

"I think Mam would like it if we called on her," Annie said.

Gertie was very pleased to see them. "You tell your mam that the house is fine, won't you?" Gertie said.

"I think she's forgotten all about the house," Brian said philosophically.

"She remembered that you told her the whole garden was cut down," Gertie said.

Brian felt there was some criticism implied here but was not sure why. "I was going to tell her that Dekko got into an over-eighteen film because they said they were dwarves, but I thought she might prefer to hear about the garden," he said by way of explanation.

"We're going to be meeting your relations out there, Gertie, Mam told us." Annie was hoping to steer the conversation into safer channels.

But Gertie didn't seem all that pleased. "Won't there be plenty of young American boys and girls for you in your own place without going all the way to Sheila's place or dragging them over to you?"

Annie shrugged. It was impossible to please people sometimes. "Sure," she said.

"And will you be sure to tell your mother that everything's fine with me too, just fine, for weeks on end. She'll know what I mean."

Annie agreed that she'd tell that to her mother. She knew what Gertie meant: Jack hadn't lifted a fist to her recently. Gertie was right, Mam would be pleased. Annie felt her eyes fill with tears. Mam was so kind in many ways, it was just that she didn't understand anything at all that was going on in the world. She knew nothing about clothes, and people's friendships, and how to keep Dad or get him back once he had gone away. And Mam didn't understand why she should put Brian down more and how awful Rosemary was. And she'd probably be terrific for the first ten minutes and then go back to being hopeless and understanding nothing. Annie sighed a deep sigh.

"Won't you have a great trip, the pair of you?" Gertie said.

"We will. Finola gave us twenty dollars each to spend on the way," Brian said cheerfully. Annie tried to stand on his foot but he was too far away.

"That was grand. Tell me, who is Finola?" Gertie asked.

"You know, Bernadette's mother," Brian said. Annie raised her eyes to heaven.

"That was kind of her, she must have plenty of money to give you all that."

"No, she's broke, that's why she fought with Dad."

"I don't think Brian quite understands the whole scene," Annie began.

"But she told us, Annie, she *told* us, you're always saying *I'm* a moron and I'm brain-dead, but you must be deaf. She said she fought with Dad over money."

"Brian, we'd better go now. Marilyn's expecting us, and we have to call in on Grannie as well," Annie pleaded.

"Well, I hope she'll have more than those gingersnaps," he grumbled, red-faced and annoyed.

"No, don't worry, Colm's making your dinner," Gertie said.

"Oh, good." Brian brightened up. Maybe he could talk to Colm about football and videos and not have to listen to Marilyn Vine and Annie talking about clothes.

"Listen, maybe I shouldn't have said that. If she doesn't tell you that he made it don't say anything, please. She might be passing it off as her own." Gertie was contrite now.

"Oh, I'm sure Brian Lynch would be able to cope with that, Gertie— tactful, diplomatic, he'll handle it beautifully."

"She's always picking on me, even before I do anything," Brian said. "Don't worry, Gertie, I'll say, 'It's terrific, Marilyn, haven't you become a good cook!' that's what I'll say."

Gertie put her hand into the pocket of the pink overall she wore in the launderette. "Here's a pound each, I'd love to be able to give you more, but it'll get you an ice cream at the airport."

"Thanks Gertie, that's terrific," said Brian. "Hey, I wonder if Marilyn will give us anything."

"Why don't we just stand at the gate of our house at Tara Road and shout out how much we want? Wouldn't that be a good idea?" Annie said with her face set in a fury as she marched her brother out of the launderette.

"Sheila, won't you come up this weekend?" Ria asked Gertie's sister on the phone.

"But you'll want to be alone with the children."

"Don't believe it, they'll be bored with me in twenty minutes. I'd love you to bring your two over again."

"They won't wait to be asked twice, they've never stopped talking about the pool," Sheila said. "So if you're sure?"

"I'm sure. Imagine in only a few hours they'll be getting on the plane. I can't believe it."

"You know, I've been going over and over the conversation we had when you first came. I'm so sorry about thinking Danny was with you and asking about him. You must have thought I was so crass."

"No, no." Ria remembered her own conversation with Greg Vine. "How could you expect to be inspired? If people aren't told things, how would they know?"

"Gertie certainly keeps things very secretly to herself," Sheila Maine said.

It was all quite clear now to Marilyn why Colm was so protective of his sister. The woman was hooked on drugs. Her husband, a coarse and flashily dressed man who had been present on the night of the restaurant debacle, did not look as if he would be any great help in such a situation. In fact he might well be part of it. Marilyn wished now that she had listened when Rosemary and Gertie had gone nattering on about Monto or whatever the man's name was. She couldn't remember what he had done for a living or if it had been at all clear. Perhaps he might even have been involved in what his wife was addicted to.

What a truly extraordinary cast of people she had met since she had come to Ireland. Not for the first time she wished she were talking to Greg properly and she could tell him. But at the moment she couldn't tell him anything.

———

"There's going to be a party at my house next weekend, Mrs. Lynch, if your daughter would like to come along."

Ria bit her lip. Hubie had been so helpful and straight with her. Yet she didn't want to let Annie go to a party with a whole lot of young people she didn't know. All she *did* know was that some of them had been involved in drinking and stealing motorbikes.

Hubie saw her reluctance. "Hey, it's not going to be anything wild," he said.

"No, of course not." Suppose Annie got to know that her mother had refused a party for her before she even arrived, the summer would be off to a very poor start. And that appalling Kitty wouldn't be here to lead her astray. Ria forced a cheerful smile to her face. "Hubie, that would be great, but we will have friends staying here that weekend and the boy, Sean, is about Annie's age . . . can he be included too?"

"Why not?" Hubie was easy.

Annie's social life was hotting up already. At least she would enjoy it more than the boat trip, Ria thought with some satisfaction.

"When we go in to Grannie, if you ask for money I'll kill you there and then and let Pliers drag your body up and down the street before he devours it," Annie said.

"I never ask anyone for money, they keep giving it to me," Brian said. "Howarya, Nora," he said cheerfully as his grandmother opened the door. Annie still insisted on addressing her grandmother in a more traditional way.

"I'm fine," Nora Johnson said. "You don't have Kitty hidden in the hedge or anything?"

"No," Annie sighed. "I suppose Bernadette was on red alert about that. God, she missed her vocation, she shouldn't be teaching music, she should be running a prison."

Nora Johnson smothered a laugh. She had been amused by the phone calls from that strange, waiflike girl Danny Lynch was shacked up with. Bernadette Dunne was no better herself than Kitty. What was she but a fast little piece making off with someone else's husband, proud as punch to be an unmarried mother?

Still, to give her her due, she did follow Ria's instructions, which was more than Danny did. Danny seemed to be on another planet, and everywhere Nora Johnson went heads were wagging over his future. She had even broken the habit of a lifetime and asked Lady Ryan if there was any truth in the rumors. Rosemary Ryan had bitten the head off her. "There's nothing wrong with Danny and Barney's business except gossiping old biddies trying to spread scandal about him because he left Ria." Nora hoped that she was right.

"Imagine, this time tomorrow night you'll be in America."

"I wish Marilyn had children," Brian grumbled.

"If she had she'd have brought them with her, you wouldn't have them to play with out there," Nora said.

"Mam didn't take us with *her,*" Brian said unanswerably.

"She does have a child but he's with his father in Hawaii, Mam told us ages ago, you just didn't listen."

"Well, he's no use to us in Hawaii," Brian said. "Were you about to make tea, Nora?"

"I thought the pair of you were going down home for your supper."

"Yes, well . . ."

Nora got out orange squash and biscuits.

"Why did you never go to America, Grannie?" Annie asked.

"In my day working-class people only went to America to emigrate, they didn't go on holidays."

"Are we working class?" Brian asked with interest. "I thought we were higher than that."

"You are now," Nora Johnson said. She looked at her two confident, bright grandchildren and wondered what class they might consider themselves at the end of the summer, when according to informed opinion their beautiful home would be sold. But she said nothing of that.

"You're to have a great holiday and you're to send me four postcards, one a week, do you hear?"

"I think postcards are dear out there," Brian said.

"You're as bad as your auntie Hilary . . . I was going to give you a fiver anyway for spending money."

At that time by chance Pliers gave a great wail.

"I didn't ask for the money," Brian cried out, remembering that Annie had threatened to feed his body to the dog.

"No, Brian, of course you didn't," Annie said menacingly.

It was very odd to go into their own home as guests. And even more odd to find the place so quiet. When they had been here with Mam only a month ago there were always people coming in and out. It wasn't like that now.

"Where's Clement?" Annie asked. "He's not in his chair."

"He may be upstairs. I'm sure he'll come down when he smells the food."

"Clement doesn't go upstairs," Brian began, then catching Annie's eye he changed hastily. "What I mean is . . . he used not to be much interested in going upstairs. But maybe he's changed now."

Marilyn hid a smile. "I've got a wonderful supper for us from Colm," she said. "I checked what you'd both like."

They helped her set the table as the food was warming in the oven. It was so different from the time when they had first come and she had found them difficult.

"Have you packed everything?"

"I think so," Annie said. "Mam E-mailed a list of what we should take to Dad's office. Imagine her being able to use machines."

"She uses all these machines here." Marilyn waved around at the food processors and high-tech kitchen equipment. Recently she had felt a very strong, protective sense about Ria. She wouldn't have anyone criticize her, enough bad luck had come into her life already.

"Oh, that's just kitchen stuff," Annie said loftily. "Mam would learn anything if it had to do with the house."

"Maybe she's broadening out."

"Are you broadening out here?" Brian was interested.

"In a way yes, I'm doing things that I wouldn't normally do at home. It's probably the same for your mother."

"What do you do that's so different?" Annie was interested. "I mean, you liked gardening and walking and reading at home you said, and you're doing all that here."

"That's true," Marilyn said thoughtfully. "But I feel different inside somehow. Maybe it's the same with your mother."

"I hope she feels more cheerful about Dad and everything," Brian said.

"Well, being away from the problem is certainly a help."

"Did it help you feel better about your husband?" Brian wanted to know. He looked nervously at Annie, waiting for her to tell him to shut up and call him a thicko but she obviously wanted to know too, so for once she said nothing.

Marilyn shifted a little uncomfortably at the direct question. "It's a little complicated. You see, I'm not separated from my husband. Well, I am of course, since he's in Hawaii and I'm here, but we didn't have an argument, a fight or anything."

"Did you just go off him?" Brian was trying to be helpful.

"No, it wasn't that, and before you ask I don't think he went off me. It's just we needed some time to be alone and then perhaps it will be all right, maybe at the end of the summer."

"Do you think Mam and Dad might be all right after the summer too?" Poor Brian's face was so eager that Marilyn felt a lump in her throat. She couldn't think of anything helpful to say.

"There's the little matter of Bernadette and the baby," Annie said, but she spoke more gently than usual.

"And did your husband not have anyone young who was going to have a baby?" Brian was clutching at straws.

"No, that wasn't it at all."

"Well, then there's not much hope," Brian said. He looked as if he were about to cry.

"Brian, can you do me a favor? I have a horrible feeling that Clement may have gone to sleep on my bed, on your mother's bed, and we don't want him to get into bad habits. Do you think you could go up and rescue him?"

"He's really Annie's cat." Brian's lip was trembling but he knew too well Annie's territorial attitude toward Clement and didn't want to risk being bawled out over it.

"It's okay, get him down," Annie agreed. When he had gone upstairs Annie apologized for him. "He's very dumb," she said.

"And young," Marilyn added.

"He still thinks it will end all right," Annie sighed.

"And you, Annie, what do you think?"

"I think as long as Mam is able to keep this house, she'll survive somehow."

———

Danny came home late. Bernadette sat curled in her armchair, the table was set for two. "Where are the children?" he asked.

Bernadette raised her eyes slowly to him. "I beg your pardon?" she said.

"Where are Annie and Brian?"

"Oh. *I* see. Not . . . hallo, Bernadette, or I love you, sweetheart, or it's good to be home. Well, since you ask where the children are, try to remember back as far as breakfast when they said they were going to make a series of visits saying good-bye to people like your mother-in-law, my mother, Marilyn, whoever, and you said they were to be home by ten at the latest."

He was instantly contrite. "Jesus, Bernadette, I'm so sorry, I'm so sorry and crass and stupid and selfish. I had a day—boy, did I have a day, but that's not your fault. Forgive me."

"Nothing to forgive," she shrugged.

"But there is," he cried. "You've given up everything for me and I come in and behave like a boor."

"I gave up nothing for you, it was you who gave up a lot for me." Her voice was calm and matter-of-fact as if she were explaining something to a child. "Let me get you a drink, Danny."

"It might make me worse."

"Not a long, cool, very weak whiskey sour, it's mainly lemonade."

"I'm no company for you, a grumpy old man harassed by work."

"Shush." She handed him the drink and raised the level on the stereo a little. "Brahms, he works magic all the time."

Danny was restless, he wanted to talk. But Brahms and the whiskey sour did their work. He felt his shoulders relaxing, the frown lines going from between his eyes. In many ways there was nothing to talk about. What was the point of giving Bernadette a blow-by-blow account of the unpleasantness in the office today? How Larry their bank manager had been downright discourteous on the telephone. How a big businessman had pulled out of a consortium that was going to do a major development in Wicklow because he said Barney and Danny were unreliable, possibly tainted partners. How Polly had called to warn them that the word was out they were on the skids. How Barney had proved elusive and distant over all these matters as if it didn't really concern him.

And worst of all, Danny's niggling fear that the personal guarantee he had given to Barney on No. 16 Tara Road would be called in and that he would lose the house. And not only would there be no home for Ria and the children but there would be nothing to sell. Some things were too huge to talk about, Bernadette was quite right not even to attempt it.

Clement sat in his chair but glanced wistfully at the door that would take him back to the big, comfortable bed with its white spread where he had been sleeping happily for so long.

As she served Colm's food, Marilyn told them more about Stoneyfield. She explained the alumni weekend and how everyone would come back and tell each other how young they looked. "My husband will be coming back from Hawaii so you'll meet him then."

"Will he be staying in the house, your house?" Annie asked.

"Yes, apparently your mother very kindly said he could."

"Will your son be coming back too?"

"I beg your pardon?"

"Your son? Isn't he in Hawaii with Mr. Vine?"

"My son?"

Annie didn't like the look on Marilyn's face. "Um, yes."

"Who told you that?"

"Mam did."

"Your mother said that Dale was in Hawaii?"

"She didn't say his name but she said his room was all there ready for him to come back."

Marilyn had gone very white.

Brian didn't notice. "Will he be there when we're there? Maybe we could have competitions with the basketball?"

"Did your mother say anything more?" Marilyn's voice was scarcely above a whisper now.

Annie was very alarmed. "I think she said she'd asked Mr. Vine about him but she didn't get any details so she doesn't know if he's going to be coming back or not."

"Oh, my God," Marilyn said.

"I'm very sorry . . . should I not have asked? Is anything . . . wrong?" Annie began.

"What is it?" Brian asked. "Is he not in Hawaii? Did he run away?"

"I see *now* what he meant," Marilyn said.

"What?"

"Greg said that your mother sounded very religious. . . ."

"She's not a bit religious," Brian said disapprovingly. "Nora always says she's heading for the hob of hell."

"Shut up, Brian," Annie said automatically.

"What a stupid thing to do. I never stopped to think that of course that's what she would imagine." Marilyn looked utterly anguished.

"So he's *not* in Hawaii?" Annie asked.

"No."

"Where is he then?" Brian was getting tired of this.

"He's dead," Marilyn Vine said. "My son, Dale, is dead."

Danny felt a lot calmer after an hour. Perhaps he was just exaggerating the situation. Bernadette drifted into the kitchen to prepare the smoked chicken salad. There was never any hiss of pots boiling, soufflés rising, pastry-making covering the whole place with flour. He had never known how gentle and undemanding life could be, how free from frenzied activity. And there was more than enough of that in the office.

"Have I three minutes to make a call?" he asked.

"Of course."

He dialed Finola. "This is Danny Lynch. I wanted to apologize very sincerely for my bad temper with you."

"I expect the children asked you to do this."

"No, not at all, they're not here."

"Or Bernadette?"

"You know your daughter better than that, she has never mentioned it. Not once. No, this is from me. I was out of order."

"Well, Danny, what can I say?" She sounded totally nonplussed.

"The answer to your question is that our company *is* in financial trouble, but I am utterly certain we will get out of it. We have plenty of assets. Bernadette will not be left destitute, believe me."

"I believe you, Danny, and thank you. Perhaps I should not have asked. It's just that you have so many other responsibilities as well as Bernadette."

"They'll be looked after, Finola. Are we friends now?"

"We always were," she said.

He hung up and saw Bernadette watching him from the doorway. "You are a hero," she said. "It's just as simple as that."

In the kitchen of No. 16 Tara Road a silence had fallen.

Eventually it was broken by Brian. "Did he have an awful disease or something?" he asked.

"No, he was killed. A motorcycle wreck."

"What did he look like? Did he have red hair like you?" Annie asked.

"Yes. Even though we have no Irish blood at all, both Greg and I have reddish hair, so for poor Dale there was no escape. We're both tall, so he was tall too. And lean. And sporty. He had braces on his teeth, you know lots of the kids in the States do."

"It's coming in here a bit too," Brian said, not wanting Ireland to be left behind.

"Sure it is. He was one great kid. Every mother thinks her son is the best in the world, I was no different."

"Have you a picture of him, a photograph?" Annie asked.

"No, none at all."

"Why not?"

"I don't know. It would make me too sad I suppose."

"But you have pictures of him at home; Mam said he was very good-looking and he had a lovely smile. That's why I was sort of hoping he'd be there," Annie said.

"Yes."

"I'm sorry."

"No, it's all right, he was good-looking."

"Did he have any girlfriends?"

"No, Annie, I don't think so, but then what does a mother know?"

"Bet he did, you can see it in all the movies. They start very young over in America," Brian said wisely.

And they sat and talked on about the dead Dale until Annie realized that Commanding Officer Bernadette would be on the warpath and they'd better go.

"I'll drive you," Marilyn offered.

They saw Rosemary on the street. Marilyn looked at Annie as if asking whether she wanted to stop and say good-bye to her mother's friend. Imperceptibly Annie shook her head. Marilyn accelerated so they wouldn't be noticed. She was very relieved. She found it increasingly hard to give the barely civil greetings that were required between neighbors. Interesting that Annie seemed to feel the same way.

Marilyn left the children at the end of their road. She had no wish to engage in any kind of conversation with Danny Lynch or his new love. She drove back to Tara Road, her mind churning.

When she parked at No. 16 she realized with a sense of shock that she didn't really remember the journey. Yet she must have taken the correct turns and given the appropriate signals. Marilyn felt very ashamed. This was how accidents were caused, just as much as by speeding, people driving with their minds somewhere else. She was shaking as she parked Ria's car and let herself into the house. She went and sat down at the table. Ria had left three cut-crystal decanters on the sideboard. In her note she had said that they were mainly for show, since she and Danny had always drunk bottles of inexpensive wine. She hoped that the contents were still drinkable and if so Marilyn was to help herself. There was a little brandy in one, something that looked like port in another, and sherry in the third. With shaking hand Marilyn poured herself a brandy.

What had happened today? What had changed so that she could talk about Dale, tell strangers that he had freckles on his nose and braces on his teeth? Admit that she couldn't carry a picture of him in case she would convulse with grief just by looking at it? Why had the direct questions of two children whom she hardly knew released these responses that her husband, friends, colleagues could not make her give?

It was almost dark now and but the reds and gold of the sunset had not disappeared totally from the sky. She was living in a house and a city that Dale had never seen. Nobody here had known her when she was a mother, a loving, fulfilled mother with a future ahead of her. They only knew her as frosty, buttoned-up Marilyn Vine, and yet some of them still liked her. She had met people who had problems as bad as hers. For the very first time since the tragedy she now knew this was true.

People had told her to count her blessings but had not been able to think of one blessing that was worth mentioning in the context of her own great loss. And nothing Greg or anyone had said had helped at all.

It was stupid to think that she had turned a corner in one night.

Marilyn was not a person who believed in miracle cures. It was an emotional occasion, that was all. These two living children were going to go to 1024 Tudor Drive where Dale Vine had played and slept and studied in his short life. They would make friends as he had done, and swim in the swimming pool where he had dived. They might even find the stopwatch and time each other and their mother as he had timed her when he was alive. "Come on, Mom, you can do better than that," he would shout. And she had done better.

She sipped her brandy and noticed that there were tears on her hand. She hadn't even realized she was crying. She had never let herself cry before and had dismissed as pop psychologists those who told her she must let go and give in to sorrow. Now she sat in this darkening room with the sounds of a foreign city around her, the different traffic noises, the cries of children with Irish accents, and the birds with unfamiliar calls.

A great orange cat sat looking at her on another chair. She was drinking brandy and crying. She had said Dale's name aloud, and the world had not ended. Annie and Brian had asked questions about him. What would he have done as a career? Did he eat meat, who were his favorite film stars, what books did he read? They had even asked what kind of a motorbike he was riding when he was killed. She had answered all these questions and volunteered more information, told them stories about funny things that had happened at Thanksgiving, or Dale's school play, or the time of the great snowstorms.

Dale. She tried again, fearfully, but no, it hadn't disappeared. She could say his name now. It was extraordinary. It must have been there the whole time and she hadn't known. And now that she knew there was nobody she could tell. It would be cruel and unfair to telephone her husband, poor baffled hurt Greg, wondering what he had done wrong and how he had failed her. It would be so wrong to call him in Hawaii, and say that something had happened to unlock her prison. It might just be because she was here in a place he had never known. But Marilyn believed that it was more than that. She wouldn't fear going to a place he had been, somewhere where she had seen him smile and rush up with yet another new enthusiasm.

She always knew that Dale had loved her own spirit of adventure, her willingness to learn. She had followed his lead in everything, to be a stronger swimmer, a demon at computer games, a sumo wrestling fan, and a gin rummy player. Only at motorbikes had she turned away from him. For month after weary month she had agonized in case it had all been her fault. Suppose she had promised him a bike when he was the age to drive one, then he might not have gone along with those wild boys and their dangerous drunken plans. But tonight somehow she felt a little differently.

Annie had said in a matter-of-fact way that of course you couldn't let him mess around with motorbikes, it would have been like letting him play with a gun. And Brian had said, "I expect up in heaven he's very sorry he caused you all this trouble."

And nothing anyone had said before, since the moment she had been told the news about the accident, had made any sense at all until this. She put her head down on the table and cried all the tears that she knew she should have cried in the past year and a half. But they weren't ready then, they were now.

Ria drove to the next town and caught the Stoneyfield Airport Limo. A month ago Marilyn had made this journey, a whole month. And in another thirty days Ria would be going home. She closed her eyes and wished hard that this would be a wonderful, unforgettable month for the children. It was no longer a matter of trying to outdo what Danny and Bernadette had given them. That seemed unimportant just now. They deserved a holiday, a good time, the feeling of hope, the prospect that the future might not be grim.

She would *not* lose her patience with Annie and boss her and tell her what to do. Annie was a young woman, she would let her find her own level in this quiet, sheltered place. Much, much safer in many ways than a capital city like Dublin. And mercifully three thousand miles away from Kitty. She would *not* let Brian's gaffes irritate her. There was no way you could impress anyone with Brian, she must learn to stop trying. He would say the most insensitive things to everyone. He would ask John and Gerry why they weren't married, Heidi why she didn't have children, Carlotta why she spoke funny English. There were acres of minefields for Brian to plow through. At no stage would she be ashamed of him or urge him to be more thoughtful.

She ached to put her arms around him and for him not to pull away in embarrassment. She yearned for Annie to say, "Mam, you look terrific, you've got a suntan, I really missed you." All the way to Kennedy Ria forced herself not to live in a world of dreams. It wasn't going to be perfect just because they hadn't seen her for thirty days.

Remember that, Ria, remember it. Grow up, grow up and live in the real world.

Danny rang the bell of Rosemary's flat. It was ten o'clock at night. Rosemary was working at her desk; she put away her papers. She looked at herself in the mirror, fluffed up her hair, sprayed on some expensive perfume, and pressed the buzzer to let him come up.

"Why won't you take a key, Danny? I've asked you often enough."

"You know why, it would be too much temptation, I'd be here all the time." He gave her the lopsided smile that always turned her heart over.

"I wish." Rosemary smiled at him.

"No, I suppose the truth is I'd be afraid I'd come in and find you *in flagrante* with someone else."

"Unlikely." She was crisp.

"Well, you have been known to indulge," he accused.

"Unlike yourself," Rosemary said. "Drink?"

"Yes, and you'll need one too."

Rosemary stood calm and elegant in her navy dress by the drinks trolley. She poured them two large Irish whiskeys, then sat down on her white sofa, her back straight and ankles crossed like a model.

"You were born graceful," he said.

"You should have married me," she said.

"Our timing was wrong. You're a businesswoman—you know that the secret of the universe is timing."

"All this philosophy didn't stop you from leaving Ria for someone else, not me, but we've been through all that. What are we drinking to? A success or a disaster?"

"You never lose control, do you?" He seemed both admiring and annoyed at the same time.

"You know I do, Danny."

"I'm finished. . . ."

"You can't be. You've a lot of fire insurance."

"We've called it all in."

"What about the Lara development?" This was their flagship, the forty-unit apartment block with the leisure club. The publicity had been enormous, every unit had been sold and resold long before completion. It was what was going to make them turn the corner.

"We lost it today."

"What in God's name is Barney at? He's meant to have these hotshot advisers."

"Yes, but apparently they need collateral . . . that we're not so strong on." He looked tired and a little rueful.

Rosemary could not accept the seriousness of what he was saying. Anyone else whose business had been wiped out would be hysterical, fuming with rage, or frightened. Danny looked like a small boy who had been caught in somebody's orchard. Regretful, that was how he appeared.

"What are you going to do?" she asked.

"What *can* I do, Rosemary?"

"Well, you can stop being so bloody defeatist, you can go out there and ask. Ask somebody for the support. Stop being so goddamn noble about it, it's only money when all's said and done."

"Do you think so?" He looked unsure now, not the cocky Danny who could conquer the world.

"I *know* so. And you know it too. We are two of a kind, we didn't get where we are by bleating. We've all had to humble ourselves from time to time. By God I know I have, and you've had to too."

"All right, I will," he said suddenly. His voice was stronger than before.

"That's better," she said.

"Lend me the money, Rosemary, lend it to me now. I'll double it as I did with everything." She looked at him openmouthed in shock. He went on. "I won't let Barney near it, he's past it and I owe him nothing. This will be my investment, our investment. I'll tell you what we'll do. I have a complete business plan. . . ." He took out two sheets of paper with columns of figures written on them.

She looked at him aghast. "You're serious?" Rosemary said. "You really are."

He appeared not to notice her shock. "Nothing's typed up, I didn't want to use the machines in the office but it's all here." He moved to sit beside her on the sofa to show her what he had written.

Rosemary leaped to her feet. "Don't be ridiculous, Danny, you're embarrassing us both."

"I don't understand. . . ." He was bewildered.

"You're demeaning us, what we have, what we were to each other. I beg you don't ask again."

"But you have money, Rosemary, property, a business . . ."

"Yes." Her voice was cold.

"You have all that, I have nothing. You have no dependents, I have people hanging out of me at every turn."

"That's your choice to have people hanging out of you."

"If you were in trouble, Rosemary, I'd be in there helping you."

"No, you wouldn't. Don't give me that line, it's sentimental and it's not worthy of you."

"But I would, you know I would," he cried. "You're my great friend, we all help friends."

"Neither of us helped Colm Barry. He asked us both to invest and we wouldn't. You wouldn't even bring clients there until it was successful."

"That's different."

"It's not. It's exactly the same."

"Colm was a loser, I'm not a loser."

"He's not a loser now but by God you will be, Danny, if you go round asking your lovers for support to help you keep your wife and your pregnant mistress."

"I don't *have* any lovers except you, I never did."

"Of course. Perhaps Orla King has hit the big time now as an international singer and *she* might bankroll you. Grow up, Danny."

"I love you, Rosemary. I always have loved you. Don't throw everything back in my face. I just made a mistake, that's all. Surely you've done that occasionally?"

"You made two mistakes, one called Ria and one called Bernadette."

He smiled slowly. "Yet you didn't leave me over either of them, now did you?"

"If that's your trump card, Danny, it's a poor one. I stayed with you for sex, from desire, not love. We both know that."

"Well, even then, can't you see that this would work . . . ?" He indicated the papers again, thinking even at this late stage that she might read them and reconsider. She put her glass down firmly, showing that it was time to go.

"Rosemary, don't be like this. Listen, we're friends as well as . . . as well as the passion and desire bit. Won't that make you think that you might be able . . . ?" His voice trailed away as he looked at her cold face. He made one last try. "If I had my own business, sweetheart, and you were involved in it, we'd be able to see each other much more often."

"I've never had to pay for sex in my life and I don't intend to start now." She opened the door of the apartment that they had so long planned for. They had spent hours on their own, planning what they jokily called a love nest, while in front of Barney they had called it a stylish investment property, and for Ria they had called it an elegant new home for Ria's friend.

"You're throwing me out," he said, looking at her, head to one side.

"I think it's time you left, Danny."

"You know how to kick someone so that it hurts."

"You did that twice to me. You didn't know you were doing it when you married Ria, but you sure as hell knew it when you couldn't even tell me about Bernadette and I had to hear it from your wife."

"I'm sorry," he said. "There are some things which are so difficult . . ."

"I know." Her voice was momentarily softer. "I do know. It's not that easy for me to let you go to the wall. But Danny, I will not even contemplate financing two different homes for you, while I sit here alone. If you can't understand that then you understand nothing and you deserve to go under."

When he was gone she went out on her roof garden terrace. She needed the air to clear her head. There was almost too much to take in. The only man she had ever fancied in her whole life had groveled to her. He had not been his old slick, confident self. He had really begged her to help him. It gave her no pleasure to remember how she had refused him. There was no sense of power in withholding money from him. But there would have been huge weakness in giving it to him, in paying him for his mistakes.

It gave her no satisfaction to let him go under. What she wanted was for things to be different. For Danny to desire her so strongly and permanently that he would give up everything else for that alone. This, she realized, is what she must have wanted him to do all the time. Rosemary had always thought that she was so strong, she was a woman like Polly who could live her life and keep love in its place.

In so many ways Barney and Danny were alike, urgent and ambitious, men for whom one woman would never be enough. What they needed were tough, strong partners, women who could provide them with passion without irritating demands. Danny and Barney were so alike in the belief that they could conquer the world.

And suddenly she realized that they were alike in other ways too. They loved two kinds of women, the ones they married and those they kept on the side. They married madonnas—the quiet, worthy Mona and the earnest, optimistic Ria. But to her great annoyance, Rosemary realized that Bernadette had been cast in the madonna role too. She hadn't realized how angry that made her feel. How had Bernadette sneaked in there somehow?

Was it possible that after all Rosemary did love Danny Lynch? She had told herself a million times that the words she would use were *desire*, *appreciate*, and *fancy*. Love was never meant to be any part of it. Surely it couldn't be developing at this entirely inappropriate stage?

At times like these Ria wished she were taller. It was infuriating to have to jump up and down but unless she did she couldn't see the passengers coming through. And then she saw them. They wheeled a luggage trolley with their two suitcases on it, their eyes raking the crowds. They each had a small carry-on bag. Those were new. Ria wondered with a pang who had bought those particular gifts. It was a good idea to have something that would hold sweaters, books, comics, games. Why had *she* not thought of that?

She forced herself not to shout out their names, neither of them would want the attention called to them. Instead she ran to a corner where she could reach out when they passed by. Don't hold them too long or too tight, she told herself. She waved with all the Irish Americans who waved for their families and friends. And they saw her. With a lump in her throat Ria saw their faces light up and they both broke into a run.

"Mam!" Brian cried, and ran toward her. It was he who hugged longer.

Ria had to release him to reach for Annie. She seemed taller, slimmer, but this couldn't be. Not in four weeks. "You're beautiful, Annie," Ria said.

"We missed you, Mam," Annie said into her mother's hair.

It was as good a reunion as Ria could have wished for as she had sat in the airport limo, impatient for their arrival. Ria had thought she would take them into Manhattan, show them the big sights, take them on the Circle Line tour, and behave like a native New Yorker, pointing out everything from the Hudson to the East River. She had already done this tour herself, she knew what it could offer. But then she thought, they'll be tired, and everything in America will be new for children anyway. Take them to Tudor Drive, let them swim, let them see their new home.

Back on Tara Road, Ria would have had many people to discuss this with over the past few days. There would have been phone calls and cups of coffee and the whole thing would have been argued to the bone. Here there was nobody. It would seem feeble somehow to lay such issues in front of Carlotta, and Heidi, young Hubie Green, and John and Gerry. Nowadays Ria Lynch made up her own mind about things, matters were no longer arranged by long committee discussions with coffee and shortbread.

"We're going straight back to Stoneyfield," she said, an arm lightly round each of their shoulders. "I want to show you your summer home."

They seemed pleased, and with her heart light and happy Ria marched her little family to the airport limo.

Heidi was looking at her E-mail with amazement. There was a message from Marilyn in Dublin.

Heidi, I found a cyber cafe and decided to seize the opportunity. Thank you so much for your letters, you are good to keep in touch. I miss you and Henry. There are lots of things I imagine myself telling you about Dublin and the way people live. I've been through Trinity College, which is quite beautiful, and absolutely in the center of the city, it's as if Dublin were built all around it. I'm glad to hear that you have been socializing with Ria, she sounds like a great cook and a wonderful homemaker. Her children are going over to Tudor Drive today, a very bright girl named Annie, just a year younger than Dale, and Brian, who should be the hero of some cartoon series and one day will be. I'll miss them. I wonder if you could possibly arrange some kind of treat for them? If there's anything like a circus or a pop star or Wild West show coming to the area. It's just that I'm afraid they'll find Tudor Drive dull after Dublin and I really do want them to have a good time. I'd so much appreciate it, Heidi. You can't E-mail me back here sadly but I'll be in touch again. Love, Marilyn.

Heidi read the screen three times, then she printed it out to take home and show to her husband. Marilyn Vine wanted people to get involved in her life. She thought Tudor Drive might be dull for two strange children. But most startling of all she had mentioned Dale. She had actually used his name.

Polly Callaghan heard Barney's key in the lock. He looked a little tired but not as tired as he deserved to look with all that was happening to him.

"Come in you poor devil," she said with a big warm smile.

"It's not good news, Poll."

"I know it's not," she said. "Look, I've got the evening paper, I've been looking through Accommodations to Let for places to stay."

He put his hand on hers. "I'm so ashamed. First your business, now your apartment."

"They were never mine, Barney, they were yours."

"They were ours," he said.

"So what's the bottom line? What date do I leave?"

"September first."

"And your own house?"

"Is in Mona's name."

"As this flat is in mine."

"I know." He looked wretched.

"And is she being as good a sport as I am? Giving it up without a murmur?"

"I don't know, she's not in possession of all the facts, if you understand."

"Well, she will be this week, you'll be declared bankrupt."

"Yes. Yes. We'll get back, Poll, we always did before."

"I think this may be a bit heavy," she said.

"They tell us to take risks, they advise us to be adventurous, entrepreneurs even, and then when we do they bloody leave us in the gutter." He sounded very bitter.

"Who do? Banks?"

"Yes, banks, big business consortiums, civil servants, architects, politicians . . ."

"Will you go to jail?"

"No, not a possibility."

"And you do have some money outside the country?"

"No, Poll, hardly anything. I was vain, you know, I believed my own publicity. I brought it all back for plans like No. 32 Tara Road, like the Lara development. And look where it got me."

"Talking about Tara Road . . . ," Polly Callaghan began.

"Don't remind me, Poll, telling them is as bad as telling Mona."

They chattered all the time on the trip to Stoneyfield.

There had been a well-known singer on the plane, up in the front in first class, but Brian and Annie had seen him as they went to view the flight deck. They asked him to sign his menu. Annie had seen him first but he could see Brian's disappointment so he had signed another for him. The pilots did nothing on the plane at all except sit there apparently. The whole thing was done by radar and computers on the ground. You didn't have to pay for Coke or Pepsi or orange on the plane, it was free.

Grannie was fine, they hadn't seen Hilary, but apparently she and Martin were looking for a new house. Gertie had sent a message. What was it? Brian couldn't remember.

"She said to tell you Jack wasn't belting her," Annie said. Ria was startled.

Brian looked up with interest. "She didn't say that, I'd have remembered," he said.

Ria intervened. "That was just a joke," she said.

Annie caught the tone. "Of course it was a joke, Brian you've no sense of humor," she said. "What Gertie said was to tell you that everything was going fine in the launderette and everywhere, and that you'd be glad to know that."

Ria smiled at her daughter. Annie was growing up. "And how's your dad?" She kept the question light.

"Fussed," Annie said.

"Broke," Brian said.

"I'm sorry to hear both of those things." Ria knew this was a slippery slope and she must leave it as soon as possible. "Look, I brought a map to show you where we're going." She pointed out the route and told them about thruways and highways and turnpikes, but all the time her mind kept going back to these two words. Fussed and broke. Danny had been neither of those things when he lived with her. What a fool he was! What a stupid fool to leave her and his children, and to end up not blissfully happy as he had thought but broke and fussed.

They couldn't believe that Mam could drive on the wrong side of the road. "It's sort of automatic unless you're coming out of a gas station, then it's dangerously easy to set off on the left instead of the right."

"Coming out of a what?" Annie asked.

"Petrol station. Sorry, I'm picking up the language," Ria said, laughing.

They loved the house. "My God, that's like a film star's swimming pool," Annie said.

"Will we have a swim now?" Brian wanted to know.

"Why not? I'll show you your rooms and we'll all change."

"You're going to swim too?" Annie was surprised.

"Oh, I swim twice a day," Ria said. With her first earnings from work, she had bought a smart new swimsuit. She was anxious to show it off to the children. "Annie, this is your room, I put flowers in it, there's lots of closet space. And Brian, you're over here."

They flung their suitcases on their beds and began to throw the clothes out. Ria was touched to see the E-mail that she had sent to Danny's office telling them what to pack taped to the inside lid of Annie's suitcase. "Did Dad do that for you, help you pack?" she asked.

"No, Bernadette did. Mam, you wouldn't believe Dad these days . . . he honestly hardly noticed we were leaving."

"And *is* he broke, do you think?"

"I don't know, Mam, there's a lot of chat about it certainly but if he were he'd tell you, wouldn't he?" Ria was silent. "He'd have to, Mam."

"Yes, of course he would. Let's all get changed and go swim."

Brian, already in his bathing trunks, was investigating the house. He opened the door to Dale's room that Ria had meant to lock until she could explain. "Hey, look at all this!" he said in amazement, looking at the posters on the wall, the books, the music center, the clothes and the brightly colored cushions and rug on the bed. *"This* is a room."

"Well, I must explain . . ." Ria began.

Annie was in there too, she was running her hand across the photographs framed on the wall. "He *is* good-looking, isn't he?"

"Look at all the pictures of wrestlers! Aren't they enormous!" Brian was examining pictures of giant sumos.

"And this must have been his school play," Annie said. "Let me see, oh, *there* he is."

"I must tell you about this room," Ria began.

"I know, it's Dale's room." Annie was lofty, she knew everything.

"But what you don't understand is that he won't be coming back."

"No, he's dead, he was killed on a motorbike," Brian said.

"How do you know?"

"Marilyn told us all about it. Let's see, can you see the braces on his teeth? Look, they're only like little dots." Annie was examining a close-up picture of Dale shoveling snow. "That must have been when they had the snowstorm and Dale dug out a path for them in the middle of the night as a surprise."

"She told you all this?" Ria was astounded.

"Yes, why did *you* tell us he was in Hawaii?" Annie wanted to know.

"Not to upset us maybe?" Brian suggested.

"I got it wrong," Ria said humbly.

"Typical Mam," said Annie as if this was no surprise to her but no big deal either. "Come on, Mam, let's swim. Hey, that's a nice swimsuit. And you're much browner than we are, but we'll catch up, won't we, Brian?"

"Sure we will."

Gertie was walking past No. 32 Tara Road when Rosemary came out. "You're the very person I wanted to meet," Rosemary called.

Gertie was surprised. Rosemary rarely wanted to meet her and when she did she seemed very scornful of Gertie's lifestyle. Also, there was a telephone in the launderette if she needed her. But life was good these days. She had asked those children to tell Ria, it wasn't a thing you'd put in writing but Jack hadn't touched a drop for a week and he had even given the launderette a coat of paint. The children were at home again, watchful and wary but at least they were home. "So now you found me," Gertie said brightly.

"Yes, I was wondering when Ria's children are off to the States. You see Ria sent me an E-mail no less, and she was talking about a big faculty picnic or some smart thing in the college town she's living in. Anyway I thought I'd send her over a couple of dresses, you know, things I don't need anymore. She might find them useful for socializing. She doesn't have anything particularly stylish herself."

Rosemary's eye always seemed to go up and down you as she talked. It began at your feet and went as far as the crown of your head, as if she were a teacher inspecting pupils to see if they were suitable for a public parade. Gertie had known it for many years, and the eye always seemed to linger on the stained part of the pink nylon overall or the hair when it was uncombed and greasy. "But they've gone already," Gertie said. "They went the day before yesterday, they'll be settled in now."

Rosemary was irritated. "I didn't know that."

"It was always August first that they were going out there, remember?"

"No, I don't. How can I hold everything in my head? They never called to say good-bye."

"They came to say good-bye to me," Gertie said. She had very few satisfactions, she would savor this one.

"Maybe I was out," Rosemary said.

"Could be." Gertie put a lot of doubt in her voice.

"And where are you off to?" Rosemary wanted to change the subject.

"I have a busy morning." Gertie sounded on top of the world. "I've hired a girl to do ironing and I want to ask Colm if he'd give me a trial to do his tablecloths and napkins. We do his towels already."

"Oh, I think for a restaurant like that he'd need a proper laundry, and particularly for Horse Show Week." Rosemary poured cold water on the scheme.

"Colm will know, and then I go in to Marilyn, do her floors and ironing. And she's going to drive me to this place where they do cheap electrical signs, and we're going to have one put up over the launderette."

Gertie looked so pleased with the modest plans for the day that

Rosemary was touched. Gertie, who used to be so handsome when she worked in Polly's all those years ago with Ria, Gertie who had lost everything for loving that madman. "And Jack. How is he these days?"

"He's fine, Rosemary, thank you. He gave up drink entirely and it suits him," said Gertie with a big, broad smile.

Hubie telephoned to know if he could call by the house and welcome Annie to Stoneyfield. Brian too, of course, he added as an afterthought.

"Please do, Hubie. They both love it here and they've been playing that game you set up every evening."

"Great."

The admiration in his eyes for shapely blond Annie was obvious. "You're even cuter than your picture," he said.

"Thank you," Annie said. "That's very nice of you."

Where had Annie, who was not quite fifteen, learned such composure? Ria wondered over and over. Certainly not from her mother, who was still unable to accept a compliment. Possibly from Danny who had managed to appear calm no matter what was happening.

As Hubie, Brian, and Annie went up to the pool she decided she would call Rosemary to find out about Danny. It would be nine o'clock at night at home. Rosemary would be in the cool, elegant penthouse. At her desk maybe, with papers. Watering the plants in her roof garden. Entertaining three people to one of her brilliant and apparently effortless meals? In bed with a lover?

Ria realized this summer for the first time how lonely parts of Rosemary's seemingly perfect lifestyle must be. When you live by yourself your life is not dictated by others, you have to choose. And if you don't plan something you sit staring at the walls. No wonder Rosemary spent so much time with them in No. 16.

There was nobody at home. Rosemary might be out at Quentin's, or in Colm's? Possibly she was with Marilyn, they had become friendly and gone to a fashion show organized by Mona.

"Rosemary, it's Ria. Nothing really. Only a chat. The children have arrived and everything's just wonderful. I wanted to talk to you about whether Danny and Barney's business is in any trouble. I can't call Danny obviously, and I thought you might know. Don't call me back about it because the kids will be here and if there is anything to tell I don't want them to hear. But you can see how I'm a bit out on a limb here and you're the only one I can ask."

Barney had asked Danny to meet him in Quentin's.

"We can't go there, Barney, we owe them, remember?"

"I remember. That's been settled, and I told Brenda it would be cash tonight."

"With Bernadette or without?"

"Without. Nine o'clock okay?" He was gone.

Perhaps at the very last moment he had pulled something out of the fire. Barney was an old-time wheeler and dealer. He had come from making tea on building sites in England to being the most talked-of builder and property developer in Ireland. It was inconceivable that he would declare himself and the company bankrupt next week, which was what was now on the cards.

Danny wore his best jacket and his brightest tie. Whomever he was being brought to meet would need to see a buoyant Danny Lynch, nothing hangdog. He had been putting on an act for years, that's how you bought and sold houses for heaven's sake. Tonight would be the biggest act because so much depended on it.

"I might be late, sweetheart," he said to Bernadette. "Big Chiefs meeting called by Barney, sounds like light at the end of the tunnel."

"I knew there would be," she said.

Brenda Brennan directed him toward the booth. Danny knew that this was where they would be since the person Barney was bringing might not want to be seen supping publicly with McCarthy and Lynch. Their names were not so good at the moment. He was surprised to see only Barney there. He was even more surprised to see the table was only set for two.

"Sit down, Danny," Barney said to him. "This is the day we hoped never to have to see."

"Everything?" Danny said.

"Everything, including No. 16 Tara Road," said Barney McCarthy.

Rosemary was also having dinner in Quentin's. With her accountant, her manager, and two men from a multinational printing company who wanted to buy her out. They had approached her, she had not gone to them. They were suggesting very attractive terms but were finding it difficult to persuade her how lucky she was to be approached in this way.

One man was American, one was English, but they knew that their nationality had nothing to do with their incomprehension about this beautiful blond Irishwoman with her flawless makeup, shining hair, and designer outfit.

"I don't think you'll ever be able to realize capital in this way again," the Englishman said.

"No, that's true, nobody wants to take me over as much as you do," she smiled.

"And there's nobody apart from us with the money to do so, as well as the will, so it's not as if you can play us off against anyone else," said the American.

"Quite true," she agreed.

Rosemary had seen Danny go into the booth with Barney McCarthy. Nobody had joined them. That was a bad sign. She knew that if she agreed to this deal, if she sold her business, she could save them. It was almost dizzying to think that she had that much power. She lost track of what the two men were saying.

"I beg your pardon?" She went back to the conversation.

"We were just saying that time is moving on and as you approach forty you may want to get a life for yourself, rest after all this hard work. Put your feet up, take cruise, live a little."

It had been the wrong thing to suggest to Rosemary Ryan. She didn't see herself as a person putting her feet up. She didn't like strangers telling her that she was approaching forty. She looked pleasantly from one to the other. "Come back to me in about six years. You will of course have worked out that by then I'll be half of ninety. Ask me again then, won't you? Because it really has been such a pleasure talking to you."

Her mind wasn't fully on what she was saying, she had just seen Barney McCarthy, white-faced, storming out of the restaurant. Danny was not with him. He must be still sitting in that booth where people went when they wanted really private conversations. Rosemary Ryan would not rescue him from bankruptcy but neither would she leave him on his own after a body blow.

"Gentlemen, I'll let you finish your coffees and brandies on your own. I'm so grateful for your interest and enthusiasm, but as you said for me time is moving on and I can't afford to waste any of it. So I'll say good night."

The men were only struggling to get to their feet when she was gone.

"Rosemary?"

"Brandy?"

"Why are you here?"

"Have you eaten?"

"No, no, there wasn't time to eat." She ordered a large brandy for him and a bowl of soup and some olive bread. A mineral water for herself. "Stop playing nursemaid, I don't want to eat, I asked you what are you doing here?"

"You need to eat. You're in shock. I was at another table, I saw Barney leaving . . . that's why I'm here."

"My house is gone."

"I'm so sorry."

"You're not sorry, Rosemary, you're glad."

"Shut the hell up . . . pitying yourself and attacking me. What did I ever do bad to you except betray your wife, my friend, by sleeping with you?"

"It's a bit late to be getting all remorseful about that, you knew what you were doing at the time."

"Yes, I did, and you knew what you were doing playing with Barney McCarthy."

"Why are you here?"

"To get you home."

"To your home or my home?"

"To your home. My car is outside, I'll drive you."

"I don't want your pity or this soup," he shouted as the waiter laid down a bowl of parsnip-and-apple soup.

"Eat it, Danny. You're not functioning properly."

"What do you care?"

"I care because you are a friend, more than a friend."

"I told Barney McCarthy I never wanted to lay eyes on him again. You're right, that wasn't functioning properly."

"That's business talk, panicky business talk, that's all. It will sort itself out."

"No, some things can never be forgotten."

"Come on, you and I were bawling out each other the other night and here we are sitting talking as friends. It will happen with Barney too."

"No, it won't, he's very shabby, he told me he'd settled up the bill here and it turns out he hasn't."

"Why did he want to tell you here?"

"He said he needed neutral ground. All he was doing was humiliating me here in front of the Brennans, people I know and like."

"How much is the bill?"

"Over six hundred."

"I'll pay that now on my card."

"I don't want your charity. What I want is your investment, I told you."

"I can't do it, Danny, it's not there. Everything's tied up." Out of the corner of her eye she saw the group of four leaving, her own office manager, her accountant, and two bewildered people who had come to offer her a huge sum of money, more than enough to bail Danny Lynch out and leave her plenty to live on. She caught Brenda Brennan's eye. They had known each other a long time. "Brenda, there was a misunderstanding. An old bill. It was never settled. Here, can we do it now on my card? No receipt to be sent to Barney McCarthy, this is Danny paying if you get my drift."

Brenda got Rosemary's drift. "The table was booked in your name, Mr. Lynch, otherwise Mr. McCarthy would not have been able to get a reservation," she said crisply. "He said that he was your guest when he arrived."

"Which, as it turned out, he was," said Rosemary.

"Drive along Tara Road," Danny asked her.

"Stop punishing yourself."

"No please, it's not taking us out of the way."

They came at Tara Road from the top end, the corner near Gertie's launderette.

"Look, she's got a new sign up: GERTIE'S. What a stupid name," Rosemary said.

"Well, it's better than calling it Gertie and Jack's, I suppose." He managed a weak smile.

They passed No. 68, the old people's home. "They're all asleep in St. Rita's, and it's not even ten o'clock," Rosemary said.

"They're all asleep there at seven. Imagine, I won't even be able to afford to go there when I'm old and mad." They passed Nora Johnson's little house at No. 48. "It must be about time for Pliers to go out and foul the footpath," Danny said. "Pliers always likes to go where it will cause maximum discomfort to everyone."

The little laugh they managed over that got them past No. 32, the elegant renovation with its beautiful penthouse where Danny and Rosemary had spent so many hours together. Frances and Jimmy Sullivan were putting out their trashcans at No. 26. "Kitty is pregnant, did you know that?" Rosemary asked.

"No! She's only a kid, Annie's age." He was shocked.

"There you go," Rosemary said.

They were at No. 16. "It was a beautiful house," Danny said. "It always will be. But I won't be living there anymore."

"You'd moved out already," Rosemary reminded him.

"I don't like that woman Marilyn at all. I can't bear to think she's living there in the last few weeks that I own it," he said.

"She's gone off me," Rosemary said. "I don't know why, she used to be perfectly pleasant, but she's curt to the point of rudeness now."

"Madwoman," Danny said. They were passing Colm's restaurant. "Plenty of cars," Danny said. "We were mad to not give him a start. Look where I'd be tonight if I had a piece of that restaurant."

"We weren't mad, we were careful."

"You may have been. I was never careful, I was just wrong, that's all," Danny Lynch said.

"I know, how did I fancy you so much?" Rosemary said wonderingly.

"Can you turn the car?"

"Why? This is the way."

"I want to come home with you. Please."

"No, Danny, it would be pointless."

"Nothing between us was ever pointless. Please, Rosemary, I need you tonight. Don't make me beg."

She looked at him. It had always been impossible to resist him. Rosemary had already been congratulating herself that her infatuation had not let her sell her company for this man. And he wanted her. As he had always wanted her more than his prattling little wife and the strange, wan girl he lived with. She turned her car in the entrance of Colm's restaurant and drove back to No. 32.

Nora Johnson, taking Pliers for his nightly walk, saw Lady Ryan driving up the road with a man in the passenger seat. Nora squinted but couldn't see who it was. For a moment she thought it was Danny Lynch. Lots of people looked like that. She had liked Danny and loved him calling her Holly. And she had thought he was handsome when she met him first. But when all was said and done what Danny had was cheap good looks.

Danny started to caress Rosemary before she had even put the key into the front door of No. 32.

"Don't be idiotic," she hissed. "We've been so careful for so long, don't blow it now."

"You understand me, Rosemary, you're the only one who does."

They went upstairs in the lift and as soon as they were in the door he reached for her.

"Danny, stop."

"You don't usually say that." He was kissing her throat.

"I don't usually refuse to save your business either."

"But you told me you couldn't, that your funds were all tied up." He was trying to hold her and stop her slipping away.

"No, Danny, we have to talk."

"We never had to talk before."

She saw her message light winking on the answering machine but she would not press the button. It might be one of the men she had dinner with increasing the offer, raising the stakes. Danny must never know what had been turned down only feet away from him in the restaurant.

"What about Bernadette?"

"It's early, she won't expect me for a long time."

"It's foolish."

"It was always foolish," he said. "Foolish, dangerous, *and* wonderful."

Afterwards they had a shower together.

"Won't Bernadette think it odd that you smell of sandalwood?" Rosemary asked.

"Whatever soap you get I get the same for our bathroom." He wasn't being smug or proud of his cunning, just practical.

"I remember Ria always had the same soap as I did," she said. "I used to think that she was copying me but it was you all the time. My, my."

Rosemary wore a white bathrobe. She glanced at herself in the bathroom mirror. She did *not* look like someone for whom time was marching on, nor a woman approaching forty. Those men would never get their hands on her company.

"I'll call you a taxi," she said.

"I needed you tonight," he said.

"I suppose I need you too in ways, otherwise you wouldn't have stayed. I don't do anything out of kindness."

"So I notice," he said dryly.

She called a cab company, giving her own account number. "Remember to get out at the end of your road, not your house, the less these drivers know the better."

"Yes, boss."

"You'll survive, Danny."

"I wish I could see how."

"Talk to Barney tomorrow. You're both up the same creek, there's nothing to be gained by fighting each other in it."

"You're right as usual. I'll go down and wait for the cab." He held her very close to him. Over her shoulder he saw the light on her machine. "You have a message," he said.

"I'll listen to it later, probably my mother demanding that I find a suitable man and get married."

He grinned at her, head to one side. "I know I should hope you will, but I really hope you don't."

"Don't worry, even if I did I expect we'd cheat on him as we have on everyone else."

The honeymoon period was still on at Tudor Drive. Ria could hardly believe it though; she walked on eggshells. Sean and Kelly Maine proved to be perfectly satisfactory friends for Annie and Brian.

"I wish Sean was younger," Brian complained. "It's the wrong way round. Kelly's okay but she *is* a girl."

"I'm glad Sean's not your age. I think he's fine the age he is," Annie said with a little laugh.

Ria opened her mouth to say that Annie wouldn't want to do anything silly with both Hubie and Sean fighting for her attention but she closed it again. These weeks of having to think before she spoke were paying dividends. It had been no harm learning to live in entirely new and different surroundings where people might judge you by what you actually did and said here and now and not in the context of years of friendship. Ria felt she had grown up a lot in a way she never had to at home. After all she had never lived alone, she had gone straight from her mother's house to Danny's. No years in between like girls who lived in flats might have known. Girls like Rosemary.

She had gotten an E-mail from Rosemary saying that Dublin was Rumor City and that it was impossible to separate the truth from the fiction but it had always been that way. Still if there was anything to tell, she *would* tell it, and of course Danny wouldn't keep her in the dark if there was anything serious. Rosemary wrote that the children had disappeared without saying good-bye, which was a pity because she had intended to send out a couple of dresses for Ria to wear at the picnic.

"You didn't say good-bye to Rosemary?" Ria asked them before she headed out to the gourmet shop.

Annie shrugged.

Brian said, "We forgot her, we called on everyone else." He seemed to think that it was a source of income they had overlooked.

"Brian, she wouldn't have given you a penny," Annie said.

"You don't like Rosemary, Annie, do you?" Ria was surprised.

"You don't like Kitty," Annie countered.

"Ah, but that's different. Kitty's a bad influence."

"So is Lady Ryan on you, Mam, giving you things, patting you on the head. You can earn money to buy your own dresses, not wear her castoffs."

"Thanks, Annie, that's true. Now, will you two be all right? I'll only be gone three hours."

"It's so funny to see you going out to work, Mam, you're like a normal person," said Brian.

Ria drove Marilyn's car to John & Gerry's, her knuckles white with rage. This was the thanks she got for staying on Tara Road to make the place into a home for them all. Danny leaves her saying she was as dull as ditch water and they had nothing to talk about. Annie thought she was pathetic and Brian thought she was abnormal. Well by God she was going to make success of business anyway.

She parked with a screech of brakes and marched into the kitchen.

"What thought have we given to making special alumni cakes?" she barked. The two men looked up, startled. "None I see," she said. "Well, I suggest we have two kinds, one with a mortarboard and scroll of parchment, and one with hands of friendship entwined."

"Special cakes for the weekend?" Gerry said slowly.

"Everyone will be entertaining, won't they need something festive? Something with a theme?"

"Yes, but . . . ?"

"So we'd better get started on them at once, hadn't we? Then I can get the graphics up and running and get young people at home to do work on the advertisements, posters for the window and leaflets." They looked at her, openmouthed.

"Don't you think?" Ria said, wondering had she gone too far.

"We think," said John and Gerry.

"I'm finding it very hard to see you alone," Hubie said to Annie. "Last weekend there was the party with all the other guys around, and then Sean Maine was everywhere like a shadow, next weekend is the alumni weekend and then you're going off to stay with the Maines."

"There's plenty of time left." They were lying by the pool sailing a paper boat from one side to the other by flapping the water with their hands.

Brian was practicing his basketball at the net.

"Maybe I could take you to New York City?" Hubie asked.

"I'd better not. Mam wants to show it to us herself, it's a big deal for her."

"Do you ever say no to her, Annie, and do what you want to do?" Hubie wanted to know.

"Yes I do, quite a lot. But not at the moment. Things are hard for her. My dad went off, you see, with someone not much older than me, it must make her feel a hundred."

"Sure, I know. But somewhere else then?" He was very eager that they should have a date.

"Look, Hubie, I'd love to but not the moment, we've just got here, okay?"

"Okay."

"And another thing, I was writing to Marilyn and Mam said I wasn't to say you come here."

"Marilyn?"

"Mrs. Vine. This is her house, you *know* that."

"You call her Marilyn?"

"That's what she wanted."

"You like her?"

"Yes, she's terrific."

"You're so wrong. You have no idea how wrong you are, she's horrible and she's crazy." Hubie got up and gathered his things. "I have to go now," he said.

"I'm sorry you're going. I like you being here but I have no idea what all this is about."

"Think of yourself as lucky."

"I know you were with Dale when the accident happened, my mother told me, but that's all. And I'm not going to say that Marilyn is horrible and crazy just to please you, that would be weak and stupid." Annie had stood up too, eyes flashing.

Hubie looked at her in admiration. "You're really something," he said. "Do you know what I'd really like?"

Annie never discovered what Hubie would really have liked just then because at that moment Brian arrived on the scene. "You were very quiet up here, I came to see if you were necking," he said.

"What?" Hubie looked at him, startled.

"Necking, snogging, you know, soul-kissing. What do you call it here in America exactly?" He stood there, his shoulders and face red, his spiky hair sticking up and his round face as always interested in something entirely inappropriate.

"Hubie," said Annie in a dangerously level voice, "is just leaving and the way things are he may never come back."

"Oh, I most definitely will be back," said Hubie Green. "And as a matter of fact I would like you to know that the way things are is just fine with me."

"Hubie fancies Annie," Brian said at lunch.

"Of course he does. He fancied her before he met her, he was always looking at that photograph."

"That's nonsense, Mam. Stop encouraging Brian." Annie was pink with pleasure from it all.

"Well, we need Hubie here tonight, so you'll have to use all your powers of persuasion to get him to come over."

"Sorry, Mam, impossible."

"I need him, Annie. I want him to design a poster for my cakes on the computer."

"No way, Mam, he'll think I put you up to it."

"No, he won't. It will be a professional job, I'll pay him."

"*Mam,* he'll think you're paying him to come and visit me. It would be terrible. It's not going to happen."

"But it's my job, Annie, I need him here." She stopped suddenly. "I'll tell you . . . suppose you go out somewhere, then he can't think that you're after him, can he?"

Annie thought about it. "No, that's true."

"In fact it might be playing hard to get, he'd wonder where you might be?"

"And where *would* I be, Mam?"

Ria paused to think up a solution to this problem and then suddenly it came to her. "You could go to work in Carlotta's salon for two or three hours, you know folding towels, sterilizing hairbrushes, sweeping up, making coffee . . . you know the kind of thing?"

"Would she let me?"

"She might if I asked her nicely, as a favor for tonight, since I know you want to be out of the house."

"Please, Mam, would you? Please?"

Ria went to the telephone. Carlotta had already suggested it days back, but Ria knew better nowadays than to suggest it to her daughter straight out. She came back from the phone. "Carlotta says yes."

"Mam, I *love* you," Annie cried.

Barney McCarthy said he would meet Danny any place and any time. How could there be hard feelings about what was said last night? By either of them. They had both been in shock, they knew each other far too well for mere words to create a barrier. They met in Stephen's Green and walked around the park where children were playing and lovers were dawdling. Two men walking, hands clasped behind their backs, talking about their futures and their past.

On the surface they were friends. Danny said that he would never have had the start in business without Barney McCarthy. Barney said *he* owed Danny a great deal for his insights and hard work, not to mention his quick thinking the night of the heart attack in Polly's flat.

"How's Polly taking it?" Danny asked.

"On the chin, you know Poll." They both thought for a few moments about the elegant dark-haired woman who had let any chance of marriage pass her by just waiting in the background for Barney. "Of course she's still young, Poll," Barney said.

"And with no dependents," Danny agreed. There was another silence. "Have you told Mona?" Danny asked.

Barney shook his head. "Not yet."

He looked at Danny. "And Ria?"

"Not yet."

And then they walked in silence because there was nothing left to say.

"I think Sean is greatly taken with your Annie," Sheila said on the telephone.

"I know, isn't it amazing?" Ria said. "It only seems such a short time since they were both in prams, now they're talking romance."

"I guess we'll have to keep an eye on them."

"Much good it did anyone keeping an eye on us," Ria laughed.

"But we weren't as young as they are," Sheila said. "I don't expect Annie's on the Pill?"

Ria was shocked. "Lord no, Sheila. For heaven's sake she's not fifteen yet. I was only talking about kissing at the cinema and all that."

"Let's hope that's all they're talking about too. Anyway you're coming to stay with us the weekend after next."

"Indeed we are."

Ria was troubled by this conversation, but she hadn't much time to think too deeply about it. The orders for her alumni cakes were unprecedented, they had to take on extra help at the shop, *and* she had to organize the house for her guests *and* prepare a huge lunch buffet for the friends of Greg and Andy Vine while trying to keep a low profile so that Marilyn's nose would not be put out of joint by it all. Apparently Marilyn had served olives and pretzels anytime people came at alumni weekend.

And she had to make sure that the children had activities. Oddly, Annie and Brian were the least of her worries. Brian had found a new friend called Zach four houses away, and had taken to wearing a baseball cap backward and using phrases he didn't understand at all. Hubie was always calling for Annie and taking her out to see cultural things, and since it was always in broad daylight Ria could not object. Every afternoon at four o'clock Annie went to Carlotta's salon, and came home with amazing stories about the clientele. Ria had rented a chest freezer for a week and she cooked, labeled, and stored way into the night.

As she was going to bed at two a.m. on the Thursday before the big weekend she remembered suddenly that she hadn't thought about Danny all day. She wondered, could it be that she was getting over him, but then when his face did come back to her, the whole bitter loss was as hurtful, lonely, and sad as ever. She missed him as much as she always had, it was just that she had been too busy to think about it until now. Maybe this was as good as it was ever going to get.

Marilyn brought a cup of coffee out to Colm in the garden. "What are you on today?" she asked.

"Sweet fennel," he said. "It's only to please myself, prove I can grow it. Nobody asks for it much in the restaurant." He grinned ruefully.

Marilyn thought again what an attractive man he was and wondered why he hadn't married. She knew about his love affair with alcohol, but that never stopped people from marrying. "How long does it take?"

"About four months, or thereabouts. The books say fifteen weeks from sowing."

"The books? You learned your gardening from books?"

"Where else?"

"I thought you came from a long line of addictive gardeners, that you grew up with your hands in the soil."

"Nothing as nice and normal as that, I'm afraid."

Marilyn sighed. "Well, which of us ever had the childhood we deserved?"

"It's true, sorry for the self-pity."

"Hey, you don't have any of that."

"Have you heard how they're all getting on, Annie and Brian?"

"Well, just great, they seem to know half the neighborhood, dozens of kids in our pool."

"That doesn't bother you?"

"Why should it? It's their house for the summer."

"But you're a very private person."

"I have been since my son died last year."

"That's a terrible tragedy for you. I'm very sorry. You didn't speak of it before, I didn't know."

"No, I didn't speak of it at all."

"Some things can be almost too hard to talk about; let's leave the subject if you prefer." He was very easygoing. Marilyn knew that he would have left it.

"No, strangely, I find recently when I *do* talk about it now it becomes a little easier to bear."

"Some people say that, they say let some light in on it, like plants your problems need light and air."

"But you don't agree?"

"I'm not sure."

"Which is why you don't talk about Caroline?"

"Caroline?"

"This country has unhinged me, Colm. In a million years I would never have interfered or intruded in anyone's life like this. But I'll be away from here in less than three weeks; I'll never see you again. I think you should let a little light and air into what you're doing for your sister."

"What am I doing for her?" His face was hard and cold.

"You're running a restaurant to feed her habit."

There was a silence. "No, Marilyn you've got it wrong, she works in my restaurant so that I can keep an eye on her. Her habit is paid for by somebody else entirely." Marilyn stared at him. "She is very well supplied by her husband, Monto, a businessman—one of whose most thriving businesses is heroin."

"Ria?"

"Hallo, Andy?"

"Just a quick question. When I come to stay next week are we meant to have met?"

"Oh, I think so, don't you?"

"Certainly I do, but I was letting you call the shots."

"It will be good to see you again, and have you meet my children."

"Sure. Will we have any time alone together do you think?"

"I feel that's going to be very unlikely, simply because I have so much to do."

"I'll keep hoping. See you Friday."

"Zach says they're going to be very old and very boring," Brian pronounced.

"Isn't it amazing the way Brian crosses the Atlantic Ocean and in minutes he finds a friend like Myles and Dekko!" Annie sighed.

Brian saw no insult in this, in fact he saw huge possibilities for the future. "Can Zach come to stay at Tara Road?" he asked.

"Certainly, we'll discuss it next year," Ria said.

"Do you think we'll still be at Tara Road next year, Mam?" Annie was thoughtful.

"Why ever not? Did you have plans for moving anywhere?" Ria laughed.

"No, it's just . . . it's quite dear and everything . . . I was wondering would we all, Dad and everyone, be able to afford it?"

"Oh, that will be fine, I'm going to work when we get back to Dublin," Ria said airily.

"*Work*, Mam . . . ? What on earth would you do?" Annie looked at her mother surrounded by food.

"Something a bit like this probably," Ria said.

Greg Vine was tall, slightly stooped, and gentle. He was courteous and formal to the children. He seemed overcome at the hospitality that Ria was providing for his friends. "You must have been slaving for weeks," he said as she took him on a tour of the freezers, and the rented trestle tables and linen.

"I didn't want to use Marilyn's cloths in case something happened to them."

"I don't think she'd mind," he said, unsure, uncertain.

"She has been meticulous about my home, they all tell me, I don't want to be any less with hers." She showed him all the replies to the guest list he had sent out. "I'll leave you to settle in your own house," she said. "I didn't put anyone to sleep in Dale's room . . . and on that subject I must apologize."

He interrupted her. "No, it is we who must apologize, it was unpardonable for you to come here without being told the whole story. I'm very, very sorry. All I can say in explanation is that she doesn't talk about it to anyone, anyone at all." His face was full of grief as he spoke. "I think she genuinely believes that if you don't talk about a thing it hasn't happened . . . if you don't mention Dale at all then his horrific death didn't occur."

"Everyone's different," Ria said.

"But this has gone beyond reason, to let you into this house, to see that room without knowing what happened. It probably doesn't matter now what she and I have left to say to each other, but for Marilyn's own health she will *have* to acknowledge what has happened and talk about it. To someone."

"She's talking about it now," Ria said. "She told my children all about him, everything. From when he got braces on his teeth to the time you all went to the Grand Canyon and he cried at the sunset."

Greg's voice was a whisper. "She said all this?"

"Yes."

His eyes were full of tears. "Maybe, maybe I should go to Ireland."

Ria felt a pang of jealousy like she had never known before. Marilyn was going to be all right. Her husband still loved her and he was going to go over to Tara Road. Lucky, lucky Marilyn Vine.

"I can't ask anything at all about his business," Finola Dunne said to her daughter.

"No, that's true."

"I accepted his apology for sharp words and he gave it generously so now you see my hands are tied. But you can, and you *must,* ask him, Ber. It's only fair, on you and the baby. You have to know is he bankrupt."

"He'll tell me, Mum, when he thinks I need to know."

The alumni picnic party on Tudor Drive was long talked of as one of the events of Stoneyfield. Ria had asked Greg if Hubie Green could come to the house as a waiter, and young Zach as an assistant.

"Hubie?"

"Yes, he taught us the Internet, and has been most helpful."

"He's a wild and irresponsible young man," Greg said.

"I know that he was with Dale that day. He says it was the worst day of his life."

"I have no objection to his being here, I never had. Those were all Marilyn's . . . I suppose in a way I'm advising you to keep him away from your daughter." Ria felt a shiver of anxiety but she couldn't allow it to develop, there was too much to do.

When Hubie arrived he went straight for Greg. "Mr. Vine, if my presence here is unwelcome I understand."

"No, son, I'm glad to see you in our home again," said Greg.

Ria let out a slow sigh of relief. That was one hurdle safely crossed. And then surrounded by friendly faces and food Ria felt very much at home. She made sure that Marilyn's name was constantly mentioned. She said that she had been speaking to her the previous evening and she had sent her love to everyone.

"I think Greg's brother sort of fancies you, Mam," Annie said after the party.

Annie and Hubie had been a delightful double act filling the wineglasses and serving huge slices of the mouthwatering cake that had been such a success.

"Nonsense, we're geriatric people. There's no fancying at our age." Ria laughed, admiring the sharp young eyes of her daughter.

"Dad was able to find someone else, why wouldn't you?"

"What a matchmaker you are. Now don't go encouraging me or I might stay over here cooking and fancying old men. What would you do then?"

"I suppose I could stay here studying and fancying young men," Annie said.

There was no time for Andy to meet Ria properly on her own. "I could come back another weekend," he said.

"It wouldn't be fair to ask you, Andy. I'll be up to my elbows in cooking and children and I couldn't concentrate on you."

"You didn't, even when you could." He was reproachful.

"I was very flattered to be invited to concentrate."

"I'm not giving up, I'll think of something."

"Thank you, Andy." She looked around to make sure there was nobody in sight and kissed him playfully on the nose.

"I wish you weren't going off to that hicksville town to see the Maines," Hubie said to Annie.

"No, it will be fun, they're nice people."

"And Sean's a good-looking guy," Hubie said gloomily.

"Is he?" Annie pretended to be surprised.

"Remember . . . I'm in Stoneyfield, he's in the boondocks," Hubie said.

"I'll remember," Annie promised. Kitty wouldn't believe all this. Two men fighting over her. But then Kitty would ask, "Which of them did you sleep with?" And Annie wasn't going to sleep with either of them.

"What did Mona say?" Danny asked.

"Nothing at all."

"Nothing?"

"Total silence," Barney said. "It was much worse than any words. And Ria?"

"I haven't told her yet."

"But Danny, you'll have to tell her. She'll hear."

"I must tell her face-to-face, I owe her that much."

"You're going to get her home?"

"No, *I'm* going out there."

"On whose money, might I ask?"

"On your money, Barney. You've got my house, for Christ's sake. You can give me a lousy air ticket."

They were sitting by the pool planning what to pack to go to the Maines.

"Are you still into lists, Mam?"

"I think so," Ria said. "It makes life easier." The telephone rang, Ria went to get it.

"Sweetheart, it's Danny."

"I did ask you not to call me that."

"Sorry. Force of habit."

"I'll get the children."

"No, it's you I want to talk to. I'm coming out there tomorrow."

"You're what?"

"I'm coming out to see you all for the weekend."

"Why?"

"Why not?"

"And is Bernadette coming too?"

"Of course not." He sounded irritated.

"Forgive me, Danny, but you do live with each other . . ."

"No, I mean, I'm coming to talk to you and Annie and Brian. Is that all right or has America been put off-limits?"

He sounded very edgy. Something in her throat began to constrict. Was it over with Bernadette? Was he coming to ask her forgiveness? A new start. "When do you arrive? Do you know how to get here?"

"I have all the details you gave the children about the airport limo and everything. I'll call from Kennedy."

"Yes, but Danny, we were going away for the weekend . . . up to Gertie's sister."

"Gertie's sister! That can be changed, surely." He was very impatient.

"Yes," she said.

"See you tomorrow," he said.

Ria went slowly back to the pool. This was too big to blurt out. The new Ria nowadays thought before she spoke. She wouldn't tell them yet until she thought about it. She wouldn't cancel Sheila Maine either. Perhaps the children could go for one night. And leave her alone with Danny.

He was coming to see her, after all. That's what he had said on the phone. "It's you I want to talk to." He was coming back to her.

CHAPTER

EIGHT

THE DOORBELL RANG at No. 16 Tara Road. It was Danny Lynch. The smile was very warm. "I hope I'm not disturbing you, Marilyn?"

"Not at all, won't you come in?"

"Thank you."

They went into the front room where Marilyn had been sitting reading. Her book and glasses were on the table.

"You like this room," he said.

"Very much, it's so peaceful."

"I liked it too. We didn't live here enough, it was always down in the kitchen. I'd like to have sat here of an evening reading too."

"Yes, well of course it's easy for me, I'm on my own. When there's a family it's different."

"True." She looked at him inquiringly. "I'm flying to New York tomorrow, I'll be staying on Tudor Drive. I thought I'd pay you the courtesy of telling you."

"That's very kind of you, but not at all necessary. Ria's free to have whomever she likes, but thank you anyway."

"And I need some documents to take with me."

"Documents?"

"Yes, they're upstairs. I wonder if I can go and collect them?"

"Ria didn't say anything about—"

"Look, I appreciate your caution, but pick up the phone now and call her. This is kosher, Marilyn, she knows I'm coming."

"I don't doubt it for a moment."

"You do. Call her."

"Please, Danny, please don't speak like that. Why shouldn't I believe you? You've given me no reason to think you might be deceiving Ria in any way." Her voice was cold and her eyes were hard.

He seemed to flinch a little. "You can come with me, I know where they are."

"Thank you."

They walked up the stairs in silence to the bedroom. Clement lay asleep on the bed. "Hey, how did you get up here, fellow?" Danny said, tickling the cat under the chin. Then he went to the chest of drawers, and opened the bottom one. There was a plastic envelope called "House Documents." He picked out four sheets of paper and returned the rest.

Marilyn watched him wordlessly. "And if I'm talking to Ria tonight what shall I say you took?"

"Some correspondence about the ownership of this house . . . she and I need to discuss it."

"She'll be home in under three weeks."

"We need to discuss it now," he said. He looked around the big, airy bedroom with its high ceiling and long window. Marilyn wondered what he was thinking about. Did he remember fifteen years spent here with Ria or was he in fact working out what price the house would go for?

Marilyn hoped that in this complicated network of friends Ria had a good lawyer. She was going to need one. It was only too clear why Danny was going out to Stoneyfield, to ruin the rest of Ria's visit. He was going to tell her that they had to sell Tara Road.

Ria was singing as she made breakfast.

"You never sing, Mam," Brian said.

"She is now." Annie defended her mother's right to croon tunelessly.

"Bernadette sings a lot," Brian said.

"That's so interesting, Brian, thank you for sharing that with us," Annie said.

"What kind of things does she sing?"

"I don't know. Foreign things." Brian was vague.

"She only hums, Mam," Annie said. "Not real singing."

Ria poured another cup of coffee and sat down with them.

"You'll be late for work," Brian said disapprovingly.

"Well at least Mam and I *do* go out to work," Annie said. "Unlike some people who throw a ball with Zach all day."

"I'd go out to work if there was a job," Brian said earnestly. "Honest I would."

"I think you're safe enough for the next twenty years, Brian, I mean who'd want to close down their business by employing you?" Annie consoled him.

"I have something marvelous to tell you," Ria said. "Something you'll be very pleased to hear."

"What is it?" Brian asked.

"You have a boyfriend?" Annie suggested.

Brian looked appalled. "Don't be disgusting," he said to Annie. "Mam wouldn't do anything like that." He felt that somehow he had said the wrong thing as he looked at their faces. Slowly to his mind came the notion that his father after all had a new girlfriend and everyone was going along with that. Perhaps he shouldn't have said it was disgusting. "Without telling us, I mean," he said lamely.

"Your dad is coming to stay for the weekend," she said.

Their mouths were open with shock.

"*Here,* here in Stoneyfield?" Annie said.

"But he said good-bye to us and he didn't say," Brian said. "Isn't that fantastic? When does he get here? Where will they sleep?"

"They?" Annie said.

"Well, isn't Bernadette coming too?"

"No, of course she's not, eejit," Annie said.

"Does that mean he's left her and he's coming back to us?" Brian wanted to be clear about what was happening.

"Oh, Brian, we've been through this a thousand times. Your dad didn't leave *you,* he went to live in another place, he'll always be your dad."

"But has he given her up?" Brian insisted on knowing.

"No, of course not. He wanted to come out and see you both and he got a chance . . . through work."

"So they can't be broke after all," Annie said with relief.

"He'll be here about five o'clock. He's coming on the airport limo."

"But we're going to the Maines this weekend," Annie remembered in horror.

"I've spoken to Sheila. You're going up on the bus tomorrow just for one night then come back on Sunday and we'll all have a big good-bye dinner for your dad."

"I can't believe it. Dad coming here. He'll even meet Zach."

"Well worth flying thousands of miles for," Annie said.

"Dad could well put a stop to you and Hubie and your goings-on when he comes," cried Brian, stung by the attack on his friend.

"Mam, there *are* no goings-on," Annie appealed.

But Ria didn't seem interested in whether there were or there weren't. "Let's think what we'll do tonight when your dad comes. Will we drive him around and show him the sights? Would he like a barbecue here by the pool? What do you think?"

"Dad's gotten much quieter, you know," Annie said thoughtfully. "He sits and does nothing a lot nowadays."

For some reason that made Ria feel uneasy. The picture of Danny sitting still wasn't an easy one to create. Danny, who never sat down, who was always on the go. What was making him quiet these days? Annie was observant, she wouldn't have imagined that. And from what Ria had heard, Bernadette was no ball of fun at keeping the conversation going. It seemed to be a silent house as it had been an eventless holiday on the boat. So different from what the energetic, quick-moving Danny Lynch had wanted all his life.

But she gave no hint of her anxiety. "Well, if your dad would like to be quiet . . . then hasn't he picked a great place for it? Now, I'm out of here, as they say, to work, while I still have a job to go to. See you lunchtime."

When she had gone the children looked at each other across the table.

"You're a little thug, a combination of a rat and a thug and that's saying something," Annie said.

Brian looked at her mutinously. "And you do nothing but jeer, horrible, scornful jeers. What has Zach done to annoy you? Nothing at all, and you're always making fun of him." His face was red and upset.

"Okay, peace?"

"No, not peace. It's only peace until you see Zach again and start groaning."

"Okay, not peace, but it's going to be great to have us fighting when Dad arrives."

"Why do you think he's coming?" Brian asked.

"I have no idea. But I don't think it could be anything bad," Annie said reflectively.

"No, like he's given all the bad news already. It might be something good though, mightn't it?"

"Like what?" Annie wondered.

"Like he's leaving Bernadette?" Brian sounded hopeful.

"Didn't look much like it, did it though?" Annie said. "They're very lovey-dovey."

"Do you think Dad will sleep with Mam when he's here?" Brian asked suddenly.

"I don't know, Brian, but can I beg you on bended knees not to ask them if they're going to? Either of them."

"What do you think I am?" Brian asked indignantly.

Ria came home from the shop with two big brown paper bags. "Now we've lots of work to do, will I make a list?" she asked them.

They exchanged glances. "What needs to be done?" Annie asked.

"We want to clean the place up and show Dad what a great house this is, scoop the leaves off the pool, make a super meal, and make up the bed . . ."

"Will he not be sleeping with you, Mam, in the same bed?" Brian asked. There was a pause. "Sorry," he said. "I didn't mean to say that."

Danny was packing his things in the office when the phone rang. "Rosemary Ryan?" The girl raised her eyebrows questioningly.

"Put her through," Danny said.

"I hear that you're going out to America," she said.

"You could hear the grass grow, sweetheart."

"I didn't hear it from you," she said crisply. "When we were last talking. In bed."

"I gather you're not in the office," he said.

"You gather right, I'm on my mobile in my car very near your office. I'll drive you to the airport."

"There's no need, honestly."

"Every need," she said. "Ten minutes' time I'll be parked outside."

He came out of the building where he would probably never work again. The offices would be repossessed on Monday. Danny had the carry-on he was taking to Stoneyfield, and two large canvas bags, the contents of his desk. "Do you know what would be wonderful? If you could keep these for me until I came back, save me going out to Bernadette and dropping them at home. And I can't leave them at Tara Road; that Kamp Kommandant will hardly let me pass the door."

"It was actually she who told me you were going to America," Rosemary said as she negotiated the traffic along the canal.

"Did she now?" He wasn't pleased.

"Yes, I met her this morning on Tara Road and she asked me whether I had heard anything of your plans. I told her she could call Ria to check. She said she didn't want to make waves. That was her expression."

"Was it?" he grunted.

"You don't think she could *know* about us, do you, Danny?"

"I certainly didn't tell her."

"No, it's just that she looks at me coldly and says things like 'your good friend Ria' . . . with what sounded like heavy sarcasm. Did she say anything to you?"

"She said something about . . . 'You've never done anything that would make you think you weren't trustworthy, have you'? It seemed a bit odd at the time, I'm trying to remember the words. But . . . no, I think we're only imagining things."

"Why are you going, Danny?"

"You know why I'm going. I have to tell Ria face-to-face."

"It won't make it any better for either of you, it's a wasted journey."

"Why do you say that?"

"Even if you do tell her she still won't believe that it's going to happen. Ria doesn't believe unpleasant things. She's going to say 'Never mind it will all turn out fine.' " Rosemary put on a childish voice to imitate the way Ria might speak.

Danny looked at her. "What did Ria ever do to you to make you despise her so much? She never says anything except good things about you."

"I suppose she let me walk off with her husband under her nose and didn't notice. That's not a clever way to be."

"Most people don't have to be so watchful of people that they think are their friends." Rosemary said nothing. "I'm sorry, that was smug and hypocritical."

"I never loved you for your fine spirit, Danny."

"It's not easy, what I'm going to do, but fine spirit or no fine spirit, I think she deserves to hear it from me straight out."

"Did you tell her what you were coming out for?"

"No."

"She probably thinks you're going back to her," Rosemary said.

"Why on earth would she think that? She knows it's over."

"Ria doesn't know it's over. In twenty years she still won't believe it's over," said Rosemary.

At the airport Danny met Polly Callaghan.

"Fleeing the country?" she asked him.

"No, going out to discuss the whole sad tale to Ria. And you? Deserting the sinking ship?"

"No, Danny." Her eyes were cold. "You know better than that. I'm giving Barney a little space with Mona for the weekend, he needs it. You're not the only one with a long, sad tale to discuss."

"Polly, I have spent the morning apologizing to people for things. I'm upset, I lash out. Forgive me."

"People will always forgive you, Danny. You're young and charming and you have a whole life still ahead of you. You'll be forgiven and you'll start again. Barney may not be so lucky."

And she was gone before he could say any more.

The van drew up outside the carport. Danny stared up at the house where his family was spending the summer. It was much more splendid than he had imagined. He wondered would he have liked Marilyn Vine under more normal circumstances. Possibly. After all, she had remembered him from a chance meeting half a lifetime ago. They might well have been friends, business associates. And now he was walking into her home.

He could hear Brian shouting: "He's here!" and his son hurtled down the slope to meet him and hug him.

A boy with a ball and a baseball cap on backward stood watching closely. Brian's new friend no doubt. Annie, slim and tanned in her pink jeans, was right behind him. The hug was as warm as when she was four years of age. At least he hadn't lost them.

Danny had tears in his eyes as he saw Ria. She too had come out to meet him but she didn't run to him as she would have done in times gone by. She stood there serene, pleased to see him, big smile all over her face. This was the Ria who hadn't realized that the marriage was over, the Ria who had lost all dignity and control the very night before she left for America and who had begged him to leave Bernadette. But she was a different woman now, surely. Confident and aware of the real world for the first time.

"Ria," he said, and stretched out his arms to her. He knew the children were watching.

She hugged him as she would have hugged a woman friend, and her cheek was against his. "Welcome to Stoneyfield," she said.

Danny let his breath out slowly. Thank God Rosemary had been wrong. All during the flight he had been wondering had he given the wrong message to Ria on the phone. But no, he knew that she saw him coming just as a friend. What a tragedy that he would have to change this mood entirely when he told her about Tara Road.

There was no opportunity to tell her the first night. Too much, far too much happening. There was a swim in the pool, a couple of neighbors or friends dropping in. Trust Ria to have gotten to know everyone. Admittedly these people didn't stay long; they were introduced, Heidi, Carlotta, two cultured gay men who ran a business in the town, a student who obviously had great designs on Annie. They had all dropped by, they said, to say hi to Annie and Brian's father. He wasn't being presented in some cozy way as a current husband, Danny noted with relief. A glass of wine and club sodas in the garden and a platter of smoked salmon, then they were gone and there was a family barbecue beside the pool.

Danny learned that the children were going to stay with the Maines the following night. Ria must have realized that they needed to talk alone and she was packing them off there on a bus. He looked at her with admiration. She was handling it all so much better than he could ever have hoped. All he had to do now was to give her some realistic options about the very bleak financial future that lay ahead of them, something that wouldn't make her believe that her whole world was ending.

"It's eleven o'clock for us but four a.m. for your dad, I think we should let him go to bed," Ria said, and they all carried the dishes back down to the house.

"Thank you for making it so easy, Ria," he said as she showed him into the guest room.

"It *is* easy," she smiled. "I've always been delighted to see you, so why not now and in this lovely place?"

"It's worked well for you then?"

"Oh, very much so." She kissed his cheek. "See you in the morning," she said and left. He was asleep in under a minute.

Ria spent much of the night in her chair staring out into the garden. She saw a little chipmunk run across the grass. Amazing that she had never seen an animal like this before she came to America. There were squirrels in the trees, and Carlotta had a raccoon, which she was trying not to feed because you shouldn't encourage them, yet he had a lovely face. Weren't they funny little things!

Brian was going to smuggle one home, he said, and start a chipmunk shop in Dublin.

"You'd need two if you were going to breed them," Annie had said. "Even you should know that."

"I'm going to bring a pregnant one," Brian said.

Ria forced herself to think about things like this rather than about the man who was sleeping in the room next door. Several times during the evening she had to shake herself to remember the events of the past few months. They seemed such a normal, happy family, the four of them. It was almost impossible to believe that he had left them.

Surely he realized that it had all been a terrible mistake. That was the only reason he could be here. Ria wondered why he hadn't said it straight out. Asked her to forgive him and take him home. He had already thanked her for making things easy for him. She must continue in the same manner, rather than throw herself into his arms and tell him that nothing mattered anymore. It was like some kind of game, you had to play it by the rules. Danny was coming back to her and this time she was going to keep him.

Mona McCarthy listened to the story without interrupting. Her face was impassive as she heard the events unfolding.

"Say something, Mona," he said eventually.

She shrugged her shoulders slightly. "What is there to say, Barney? I'm sorry, that's all. You put so much into it, I'm sorry that in the end you won't be able to sit back and enjoy it."

"I was never one for sitting back," he said. "You haven't asked how bad it is."

"You'll tell me."

"This house is in your name, that's one thing anyway."

"But we can't keep it, surely?"

"It's all we have, Mona."

"You're going to let all those people lose their jobs, all those suppliers go without payment, and Ria Lynch lose her home and expect me to live in this mansion?"

"That's not the way it is."

"What way is it then?" she asked.

He couldn't answer. "I'm sorry, Mona," he said.

"I don't mind being poor, we've been poor before, but I won't be dishonest."

"It's business. You don't understand, you're not a businesswoman."

"You'd be surprised," said Mona. "Very surprised."

There was an E-mail from Rosemary on the laptop.

Ria, Danny, you should access the Irish Times *this morning. There's an item about Barney that would interest you. All may not be lost after all. Enjoy the visit.*

Ria read it several times. What did she mean? She would bring the *Irish Times* up on the screen later but not just this minute. She brought Danny a cup of coffee to his room.

"We usually have a swim before breakfast, will you join us?"

"I didn't bring any swimming trunks."

"Now that was bad, if you'd only made one of my lists . . ." she mocked herself. "I'll get you something from Dale's room."

"Dale?"

"Their son."

"Will he mind?"

"No, he's dead." Ria went off and found him a pair of swimming shorts.

"Dead?" Danny said.

"Killed. That's why Marilyn wanted to get away from here."

"I thought her marriage broke up," Danny said.

"No, I think her marriage is fine actually."

"But isn't he in Hawaii? That doesn't look very fine to me."

"I think he's on the way to Ireland this weekend," Ria said.

"Can't you stay longer, Dad?" Brian asked.

"No, I have to go on Monday night, but I have three full days here," Danny said as they came down from the pool to the omelettes that Ria had made for breakfast.

"What did you come for, really?" Brian asked.

"To see you all. I told you that."

"It's a long way," Brian said thoughtfully.

"True. But you're worth it."

"Mam said your visit had to do with your work."

"In a way, yes."

"So when will you do it? The work part?"

"Oh, it will get done, don't worry." Danny ruffled his son's hair affectionately.

"Dad, what would you like me to be when I grow up?"

"I don't mind. What would *you* like?"

"I don't really know. Mam says I might be a journalist or a lawyer because I have an inquiring mind. Annie says I should be bouncer in a casino. Would you like me to be a real estate agent and work in your office with you?"

"Not really, Brian. I think people should choose their own line of work, follow their own star."

"What did your parents want *you* to do?"

"I think they hoped I'd marry a rich farmer's daughter and get my hands on some land."

"I'm glad you didn't. But suppose I did want to be an agent. I could, couldn't I? Then I could see you every day in the office, even if you didn't come home to live again."

"Sure, Brian, I'd love to see you every day, we'll work something out."

"And even when Bernadette's baby comes, you'll still have time for us?" Brian's face was anxious.

Danny couldn't find the words to speak. He gripped Brian's shoulder very hard. When he did speak his voice was choked. "I'll always have time for you and Annie, Brian, believe me. Always."

"I knew you would, I was just checking," said Brian.

They took Danny on a tour, pointing out all the sights of Stoneyfield and ending up at the burger place beside the bus station where Annie and Brian were catching the bus to the Maines'.

Zach and Hubie turned up to say good-bye. "It's going to be real dull with you gone," Zach said.

"It's going to be fairly dull with Kelly, she's a girl, you know," Brian said. Zach nodded sympathetically.

"If that guy Sean Maine puts a hand on you, I'll know and I'll be up there so quick . . ." Hubie said.

"Will you stop talking about people putting hands on me? My parents are listening to you," hissed Annie.

Danny and Ria got into the car and drove back to Tudor Drive.

"You were right to bring them out here, it's a great holiday for them."

"Well, you paid their fares." She was giving credit where it was due. In her list she had written down: *Make it easy for him. Be cool and calm rather than eager. Don't let him think he is a villain. Don't gush. Don't say that you knew he'd come back. Make no plans for Bernadette's future, that's up to him.* Ria smiled to herself. They might laugh at her lists, but they had their uses.

"You're happy here?" Danny said.

"I'm fine," she agreed.

"What's that place over there?" He pointed to a cluster of trees in the distance.

"That's Memorial Park, they keep it beautifully."

"Could we go and walk there, sit there for a bit?"

"Sure, but would you not prefer to go home? The garden on Tudor Drive is as good as it gets."

"I'd prefer somewhere . . . I don't know . . . somewhere a bit separate from things."

"Right, Memorial Park it is. The parking lot is around this way."

They walked together and looked at the names of the men from Stoneyfield who had died in the world wars, in Korea and Vietnam.

"What a waste war is. Look, that boy was only four years older than Annie," Ria said.

"I know, he could have been one of those old men playing chess there instead of a name on a piece of stone," Danny said.

She longed to touch him but she remembered her advice to herself. They sat down on a wooden seat and he reached out to hold her hand in his.

"You probably know what I have to say," he said.

She worried slightly, just a little. Surely he should say what he *wanted* to say not what he *had* to say. Still it was only words. "Say it, Danny."

"I admire you so much, I really do . . . and I hate to have to tell you bad news. I can't tell you how much I hate it. The only one thing you'll have to give me some little credit for is that I came out to tell you myself."

She felt a big, heavy stone suddenly develop below her throat, under the jaunty scarf that she had tied so cheerfully that morning.

"So?" she said, not trusting herself to say anything more.

"It's very bad, Ria."

"No, it can't be all that bad." Ria realized that he was not coming back to her. This is not what this was all about. Her list hadn't been necessary at all. It didn't matter now whether she was calm or cool or gushy, he wasn't coming back.

She heard herself speaking. "Danny, I've already *had* the worst news, nothing will ever be as bad as that. There can't be anything else you have to tell me."

"There is," he said.

And on a bench in Memorial Park, Stoneyfield, he told Ria that her home was gone. Part of the assets in the estate of Barney McCarthy, which would be out into the hands of the receiver very shortly.

"There's a party tonight, we can go to it," Sean Maine said the moment Annie arrived.

"Do we have to take Brian and Kelly?"

"No way. My mom got them a video to watch."

"I don't have any party clothes," Annie said sadly.

"You look just great." The admiration in Sean's eyes was plain.

Kitty wouldn't believe it. What a pity she wasn't here to watch this triumph! But of course Kitty would have the jeans off him by this stage, Annie thought disapprovingly. There would be none of that sort of thing as far as Annie was concerned; she must make that very clear from the start. Hubie had said it was totally unfair to look as good as she did and then not play. It was like putting delicious food on the table and then taking it away before people could eat it, he said. Really, it was all very complicated.

"All right, Hilary, what is it? What are you trying to tell me?"

"And how did you know that I wanted to tell you anything, Mam?" Hilary asked.

"You're like Pliers. He goes round in a circle when he's trying to let you know he wants to go for a walk, you're doing the same."

"Nothing's written in stone, Mam."

"Tell me."

"I mean if Ria were only here I'd sound her out before telling you anything at all . . ."

"Do I have to beat it out of you, Hilary?"

"Martin and I were wondering would you mind if we went to live in the country?"

"The *country*?"

"I knew you'd mind. Martin said you wouldn't."

"Whereabouts in the country?" Nora Johnson was astounded.

"Well, Martin's old home. You know none of his brothers want to live there and the house is falling down and there's a teacher's job in the local school, and I'd be able to get a job there as well."

"You'd live in the West?" Nora Johnson as a Dubliner regarded the country as a place you went for holidays.

"If you wouldn't be upset by it, Mam, yes, we would."

"I wouldn't be upset by anything. But Hilary, child, in the name of God, what would possess you to go over there?" She should have known.

"It's going to be much cheaper, Mam. We've done our sums, the cost of living is much lower there, less petrol on commuting, and of course we'll get a little nest egg from selling our own house."

"And what will you do with the little nest egg?"

"We'll just hold on to it, Mam, it would be great comfort to us as we grow older."

Nora nodded her head. For Martin and Hilary it might be the only comfort. "And what made you make up your mind?"

"When we were there last I looked up and wasn't the place all surrounded by trees," Hilary said. "I knew then it was right for us."

"I suppose you have sex with the customers?" Jack roared at Gertie.

"Ah, Jack, will you give over." Gertie struggled to get herself free of his grip. "What are you talking about?"

"You're my woman and you're not going out like any old cheap tart just to have a tenner in your handbag."

"Let me go. You're hurting me, Jack, I beg you."

"Where do you do it? Up against the wall, is it?"

"You know this is only madness." She was terrified now; she hadn't seen him like this for a long time. She knew that Ria and the children were up visiting the Maines this weekend. What a different story Ria would tell. Suppose Sheila could see her now.

"You knew I'd discover, didn't you?"

"Jack, there's nothing to discover."

"Why did you send the kids to your mother's last night then? Answer me that."

"Because I could see you are a bit . . . under the weather. I didn't want anyone getting upset."

"You didn't want them hearing that their mother did it for a tenner with anyone who came in." He hit her.

"Jack."

"I'm a normal man, this is what a normal man would feel about a wife who couldn't explain ten pound notes in her handbag."

"I scrub floors for them, Jack."

"Where? Where do you do that?"

"In Marilyn Vine's house where Ria lives, for Polly Callaghan sometimes, for Frances Sullivan . . ."

He laughed. "You don't expect me to believe that."

Gertie wept with her head in her arms. "Well, if you don't believe me, Jack, then kill me now, because there's not much point in going on," she said through her tears.

"I've never had a real girlfriend before," said Sean Maine to Annie. They sat on a window seat at the party. There was dancing in the room and they were building the barbecue in the garden. Sean had his arm around her shoulder proudly, protectively almost. Annie smiled at him, remembering she must not encourage him to think she was going to go any great distance. "It's just my luck that the girl I like is going back to Ireland in a short time."

"We can write to each other," she said.

"Or maybe I could come over to Ireland, stay with Aunt Gertie and Uncle Jack, go to school and be near you."

"Yes, I suppose." Annie sounded doubtful.

"Wouldn't you like that?"

"Oh, I would it's just . . . it's just . . ." She wasn't sure how to finish. Mam had told her not to go into details about Gertie's life, it wasn't necessarily known over here. She knew that somehow it was important. "It's just that I think Gertie's pretty busy," she said lamely.

"She'd find room for family." He was confident.

"Sure."

"It was a big surprise, your dad coming back?" Sean knew the story.

"I'm not sure he is actually back."

"But Brian said . . ."

"Oh, Sean, what does Brian know? It's just that Dad looked a bit sad. And he *was* very taken with Bernadette. I can't see he's given her up already, with the baby and everything."

"Still, he's at home there in Stoneyfield with your mom, that can't be bad."

"No," Annie agreed. "That can't be bad at all."

The shadows of the trees in Memorial Park grew longer as Danny and Ria sat on the wooden bench. They held hands, not like they used to do when they were young. Not even like friends, but like people in a shipwreck, holding on for fear of letting go and being totally alone. Sometimes they sat and said nothing at all. Other times Ria asked questions in a flat voice and Danny answered. At no stage did he call her sweetheart, and he offered no false hopes and glib reassurances that they would be all right.

"Why did you come over to America to tell us?" she asked. "Couldn't it have waited until we came home?"

"I didn't want you to hear from anyone else."

They were still holding hands, and she squeezed his as thanks. There were no recriminations. They had both known that the personal guarantee was there. It was just something that neither of them ever thought would be called in.

"Was he very sorry about us and Tara Road?" Ria asked.

Danny struggled to be truthful. "He's so shell-shocked about himself, to be honest, that it's only one part of it."

"Still, he sent you out here to tell me, he must care a bit?"

"No, I insisted on coming out."

"And Mona?"

"Barney said Mona said nothing. Nothing at all."

"She must have said *something*."

"If she did, he didn't tell me." This was a very different Danny. No longer certain of anyone, anything. Even the great Barney McCarthy was no longer a fixed point in his life.

They spoke idly of what Danny would do now. There were other real estate agencies where he might get a job. But he would go in on a very low rung of the ladder.

"What about Polly?"

"She's giving up her flat, getting a job. Barney says she's a brick or a sport, I can't remember which."

Ria nodded. "Yes, it would be one or the other."

"And the staff, that's another very hard bit," he said.

"Who told them?"

"*I* did as it happens."

"You've had a lot of the telling to do."

"Yes, well, I rode high and had a lot of the good times when they were there too."

"I know you did, we both did."

The silences that fell were not anxious or uneasy. It was as if they were both trying to take it all in.

"And what does Bernadette say about it all?"

"She doesn't know."

"Danny?"

"No, she doesn't, truly, I'll tell her when I get back. She'll be calm. Her mother won't, but she will."

A wind blew lifting some of the leaves and blossoms up from their feet.

"Let's go back to the house, Danny."

"Thank you so much."

"For what?"

"For not screaming at me. I've had to give you the worst news anyone could ever give anyone."

"Oh, no," she said.

"What do you mean?"

"You gave me much worse news than that before."

He said nothing. They walked together across the Memorial Park back to Marilyn Vine's car.

Colm Barry called to No. 16 Tara Road.

"You really did work on a rehab program?"

"Oh yes, certainly."

"So can you help?"

"You know I can't. Caroline will have to want to do it herself, *then* I can help."

"But we can't drag her there?" He sounded very lost.

"There is a place, a center?"

Colm nodded. "Yes, a fine place. But what use is it?"

"You could go there, check out the program, meet some of the people. Tell her about it."

"She'd only close her ears."

"She doesn't love that guy Monto?"

"No, but she loves what he provides for her, and now he's doing deals in my restaurant."

"You're not serious."

"Last night, I know that's what they were doing, I know it."

"You can't have this, Colm. He'll get the place closed down. What would you or Caroline do then?"

"What can I do? I can inform on him, but that would be to destroy her."

"You and Caroline have shared enough and have had enough history for you to be able to talk to her. Tell her that you may lose your restaurant, beg her to give this center a try. Tell her I'll go with her and sit through the assessment with her if she likes."

When he left, Marilyn looked at herself in the mirror. She still had the same auburn hair, slightly longer now than when she arrived. Her eyes were still watchful, her jaw firm. Yet she was totally different inside. How could she possibly have changed so much in these few short weeks? Getting involved with strangers and trying to alter the course of their lives. Greg wouldn't believe it was possible.

Greg. She decided to telephone him, but to her surprise they told her that he was taking some reading days. That wasn't like Greg, but she called him at home. His machine said that he would be away for a week. For the first time in their married lives he had not told her where he was going or what he was doing.

Suddenly she felt very lonely indeed.

When they got back to Tudor Drive, Ria suggested they have tea.

"No, Ria sit down, talk to me . . . try to talk, don't bustle about doing things like you used to do at home."

"Is that what I did at home?" She felt very hurt, annoyed.

"Well, you know, whenever I came in and wanted to talk there was this in the oven and that on the burner and something else coming out of the deep freeze and people coming and going."

"Only the family, our children if I remember."

"And half the neighborhood. You were never there to talk to me."

"Is that what a lot of this was about?"

"I suppose it was to cover what wasn't there," he said sadly.

"Do you really believe that?"

"Yes, I do."

"Well, of course, I won't get tea, I'll sit down and talk to you now."

That didn't please him either. "Now I do feel a shit," he said. "Come on, let's have tea."

"You make it," she said. "I'll sit here."

He put on the kettle and took out the tea bags. Maybe she should have let him do this kind of thing more.

"You have a message on the machine," he said.

"Take it for us, Danny, will you?" The old Ria would have leaped up with a pencil and paper.

"It's Hubie Green, Mrs. Lynch. I didn't catch Annie's telephone number and I thought it would be good to give her a call during her weekend away. I did leave you an E-mail about it but I guess you don't have time to look to your messages now with all the action going on. Say hi to Mr. Lynch for me."

"Do you want to call him with her number?" Danny asked.

"No. If Annie had wanted him to have it then she'd have given it to him," Ria said.

Danny looked at her admiringly. "You're right. Shall we check your E-mail in case there are any more messages?"

"I thought you wanted to talk, now who is putting it off?"

"We have the evening, the night to ourselves."

The old Ria would have started to fuss about what they would eat for supper and whether it should be earlier or later. But now she just shrugged. "Right, come into Greg's study and see how good I am at it."

Expertly she went for her mailbox and saw three messages. One from Hubie, one from Danny's office, and the one from Rosemary Ryan.

"Do you want the office?" she asked.

"No, who needs any more grief?"

"Well, will I see what Rosemary says?"

"More bad news, surely," he said.

"She knows? Rosemary knows?" Ria was startled.

"She had heard already from her own sources, then I met her yesterday just as I was leaving. She drove me to the airport."

Ria had brought her message up on the screen. "She says we should look up the *Irish Times,* the business gossip column."

"Can you do that?" he asked, impressed.

"Yes, hold on a minute."

Very shortly they had the Website and got the item. The paragraph said that rumors around the city seemed to suggest that Barney McCarthy's financial death might be like that of Mark Twain, somewhat premature. The word was that there had been a rescue package from sources outside his company. Things didn't look as dire as had been thought. Ria read it aloud, her voice getting lighter all the time.

"Danny, isn't that magic?"

"Yes."

"Why aren't you more pleased?"

"If there *was* anything, Barney would have phoned me here; he has the number. This is just him doing the PR job."

"Well, let's see what your office says on this. He might have sent you an E-mail."

"I doubt it, but let's call it up anyway."

"Message for Danny Lynch could he please phone Mrs. Finola Dunne at her home number urgently."

"I *told* you it would be grief," Danny said.

"Do you want to call her?"

"No, I can get the earful about how irresponsible I am when I get back," he said.

"You'll probably get a similar earful from *my* mother too," Ria said ruefully.

"No, to give poor old Holly her due, she'd put it all down to That Adulterer, as she calls him. Though these days it's hard to know who she'd describe as that."

They had gone back into the kitchen and picked up their mugs of tea. The garden lights went on automatically, lighting up the place. Ria sat down and waited. She ached to speak, to reassure him about that paragraph in the newspaper, to encourage him to ring Barney and Mona at home. But she would do none of these things, she would wait. As apparently she should have waited in the past.

Eventually he spoke. "What are you saddest about?" he asked.

She would *not* say that she was most sad because she thought he had been coming back to her. That would be the end of any meaningful conversation between them again. She tried to think what was the next most awful thing on the list.

"I suppose I'm sad that your dreams and hopes are ended. You wanted so much for the children and indeed for us all. It will be different now."

"Will we tell them together tomorrow, do you think?" he asked.

"Yes, I suppose so. I was wondering if we should let them have their holiday in peace but that would be lying to them."

"And I don't want you to have to do it on your own, make excuses for me as I know you would," he said.

"There are no excuses to make. Everything you did, you did for us all," she said. Danny looked quite wretched. She determined to cheer him up. "Right, they'll be home tomorrow, let's try to guess what horrific thing Brian will say." He forced a smile and Ria went on determinedly. "Whatever we guess it won't be *quite* as bad as what he'll come up with."

"Poor Brian, he's such an innocent," Danny said.

Ria looked at him, calmer than she had been for a long time. He really did love his family, and this was Danny without any disguises. Why did she not know what to do to help him or make things better? She just knew what *not* to do. Almost everything that her instinct told her would be right would only annoy him.

Tears fell down her face and splashed off the table. She didn't lift her hand to wipe them away, half hoping that in the fading light he would not see. But he came up to her and gently took her tea mug out of her hand and placed it on the table, then he pulled her up from the chair and held close to him and stroked her hair.

"Poor Ria, dear, dear Ria," he said. She could feel his heart beating as she lay against him. "Ria, don't cry." He kissed the tears from her cheeks. But more came in their place.

"I'm sorry," she said into his chest. "I don't mean to."

"I know, I know. The shock, the terrible awful shock." He still stroked her and held her away from him, smiling at her to cheer her up.

"I think I *am* a bit shocked, Danny, maybe I should lie down for a bit."

They went to the bedroom where she had been hoping he might join her tonight. He sat down and gently he took off her lilac and cream-colored blouse, which he hung carefully on the back of the chair. Then she stepped out of her silk skirt and he folded that too. She stood in a white slip like a child being put to bed with a fever, and he turned back the sheet and bedcover for her.

"I don't want to miss your visit. I want to get value out of your being here," she said.

"Shush, shush, I'll stay here beside you until you get a little sleep," he said.

He brought a face cloth from the bathroom wrung out with water and wiped her face. Then he stroked her hand as he sat beside her in the chair. "Try to sleep, dear Ria, and to know how fond of you I am, how very fond of you."

"I know that, Danny."

"That never changed, you do know that?"

"Yes, I do." Her eyelids were heavy. He looked so tired as he sat there minding her, his face half in the light that came in from the garden. She sat up on her elbow and said, "It will be sort of all right, won't it?"

He put his arms around her and held her again. "Yes, Ria, it will be sort of all right." His voice was weary.

"Danny, lie down on the bed and sleep too, just close your eyes. It's been worse for you." She didn't mean any more than that, lie down in his clothes on top of the bedspread and sleep beside her for a couple of hours.

But he clung to her and she realized that he wasn't going to let her go. Ria didn't allow herself to think about what might be happening. She lay back in Marilyn Vine's bed and closed her eyes while the only man she had ever loved gently removed the rest of her clothes and made love to her again.

Greg decided to tell Ria that he was going to Ireland but the answering machine was on. He debated whether to leave a message and decided against it. He stood in the phone booth at Kennedy and debated calling Marilyn. But suppose she told him not to come? Then they would be worse than they had ever been. His only hope was to call her and say he was in Dublin. Which he would be very soon.

He heard his flight being called. It was now too late to call his wife, even if it was a good idea.

There had been no reply from Danny. Rosemary was very annoyed. She had driven him to the airport, he was in a house with an E-mail facility, a telephone. He would have known what to make of that cryptic piece in the paper. He would be tired of playing Happy Family and trying to bolster up Ria. Why didn't he call her? Rosemary told herself, as she had told herself many times before, this was not going to continue.

What she felt for Danny Lynch was neither sensible nor in any game plan. It was in fact the most basic urge imaginable. No other man would do. She had put up sharing him with Ria for years, and with others like that disgusting Orla King. She had even put up with the infatuation for the wraithlike Bernadette. But he had always been civil and courteous before. He wasn't even that these days.

She was glad that she had not rescued him; she was just quivering with curiosity to know who had. The woman who wrote this column in the *Irish Times* was very informed. It would not be a flier, something deliberately planted. Rosemary believed that Danny Lynch and Barney McCarthy were genuinely going to be pulled out of the fire. All she needed to know was by whom.

"Frances, you know the way I told you never to tell Jack I did a bit of cleaning for you?" Gertie said.

"And I never have," Frances Sullivan said.

"No, but things have changed now. Now I do need him to know I come here, you see he thinks I get the money somewhere else."

"Yes, but surely he won't come and ask me?" Frances looked fearful.

"No, but suppose he does, it's all right now, I'd prefer him to think that this is where I get the money."

"Yes, Gertie." Like a lot of people Frances was becoming increasingly wearied by the menacing presence of Gertie's Jack Brennan in her life.

"Thanks, Frances, I'll just go and tell Marilyn and then Polly and it will all be out of the way."

Marilyn was in the front garden in jeans and a T-shirt. She looked very young and fit for her years, Gertie thought.

"I hate having to burden you with my problems."

"Sure, what is it, Gertie?" Marilyn listened and with great difficulty controlled her impatience. In her newly directive mood, she could easily have urged Gertie not to be so foolish, such a hapless victim encouraging more senseless violence and even neglecting her own children in the process. But one look at that haunted face made Marilyn retreat from any such action. "Sure," she sighed. "It's okay this week to tell him, let me know if it changes next week."

"You're lucky and strong, Marilyn, I'm neither, but thank you." She left to go to the bus stop across the road. Polly Callaghan was the third person she must warn.

Rosemary drew up her car. "Can I drive you anywhere, Gertie?"

"I was going over to Polly, I wanted to give her a message."

"She's in London, back Tuesday."

"Well, I am glad I met you. Thanks, Rosemary, you saved me a trip, I'll just walk up home then."

"They did invent a telephone system, you know, you could have called her," Rosemary said. It sounded somehow very dismissive and cruel.

"Are you cross with me about something, Rosemary?"

"No, I'm in a bad mood. Sorry, I didn't mean to bark."

"That's all right." Gertie never held a grudge for long. "Man trouble, is it?"

"What kind of man trouble do you think I might have?" Rosemary asked with some interest.

"I don't know, choosing between them I imagine," Gertie shrugged.

"No, it's not that. I'm sort of restless, I don't know why, and people are being difficult. Your woman in there hasn't spoken to me for ages. What did I do to get up her nose?"

"I don't know. I thought you were great friends, going to fashion shows and all together."

"Yes, we were, that was the last night she spoke to me," Rosemary said in wonder.

"So was there any coldness?"

"None at all. She drove me home . . . I didn't ask her in."

"Well, she'd not be sulking about that."

Rosemary remembered back to that night, and Danny coming to the summerhouse. But there was no way, no possible way that Marilyn could have . . . She pulled herself together. "You're absolutely right, Gertie, I'm imagining it. All well at home?"

"Oh fine, thank you, just fine," said Gertie, who was relieved that Rosemary wasn't really interested anyway.

They slept wrapped up together as they had done for years at Tara Road. When Ria woke she knew she must not stir. So she lay there going back over all the events of the day and evening. She could see the time; it was eleven o'clock at night. She would like to get up, have a shower, and make them both an omelette. Together they would sit and talk about what was to be done. They would make their plans as they had long ago. And it was all going to be all right. Money wasn't important. Even the house they had built up together could be replaced. They could get another one, a smaller one. But she would take no initiative, she would lie there until he moved.

She pretended to be asleep when he got out of bed, picked up his clothes, and went to the bathroom. When she heard the shower being turned on she joined him there with a towel wrapped around her. She sat down on one of Marilyn's cork and wrought iron bathroom chairs. She would let him speak first.

"You're very quiet, Ria," he said.

"How are *you*?" she said. There would be no more taking the initiative. The wrong initiative.

"Where do we go now?" he asked.

"A shower, a little supper?"

He seemed relieved. "Sandalwood?" he said about the soap.

"You like it, don't you?"

"Yes, I do." He seemed sad about something, she didn't know what. He went to his own room to get clothes. She followed him into the shower, then put on yellow trousers and a black sweater.

"Very smart," he said as they met in the kitchen.

"Annie says I look like a wasp in this outfit."

"Annie! What does she know?"

They were walking on eggshells. No mention of what had happened. Or of what might happen next. Nor did they talk of Barney McCarthy or Bernadette, or the future or the past. But somehow they filled the time quite easily. Together they made an herb omelette and a salad; they each drank a glass of wine from the fridge. They ignored the message lights winking on the answering machine. Whoever it was could be dealt with tomorrow.

And when it was half past midnight, they went back to bed. In the big double bed that belonged to Greg and Marilyn Vine.

The phone kept ringing, as if someone was refusing to accept that there was nobody to take the call.

"Technology," yawned Danny.

"Hubie Green, desperate for our daughter's telephone number," giggled Ria.

"I'll get coffee for us. Will I put whoever it is out of their misery?" Danny suggested.

"Do, of course." Ria was chirpy and cheerful as she heard the message tape winding backward. Anything at all he did was all right with her today. She was just pulling on her swimsuit, ready to go to the pool when she heard the fevered voice on the answering machine. "Danny, I don't care what time it is, or Ria or whoever is there, you've got to pick up, you have to. This is an emergency. Please pick up, Danny. It's Finola here. Bernadette's been taken to the hospital, Danny, she's had a hemorrhage. She's calling out for you. You've got to talk to me, you've got to come home."

Ria put a dress on over her swimsuit and went quietly out to the kitchen. She filled the percolator and switched it on. Then she took out a directory with the numbers of airlines in it and passed it to Danny without comment. He would go home today, and she must do absolutely nothing to stop him.

She caught sight of her reflection in the mirror. She had a half smile on her face. She must lose this immediately. She must not let a hint of what she was feeling escape. If Bernadette was losing the baby then their problems might be over.

Danny looked at her with anguished eyes.

"Get dressed," she said. "We'll get you on a plane."

He came over to her and held her very tight. "There never was and never will be anyone like you, Ria," he said in a broken voice.

"I'll always be here for you, you know that," she said into his hair.

Marilyn had seen Rosemary stop and talk to Gertie at the bus stop. She was relieved that she hadn't used the opportunity to come and call. It was getting harder to disguise her resentment of such a betrayal. She dug on furiously, wondering whether in this Catholic country they would think she was breaking the Sabbath by working in the garden. But Colm Barry had reassured her, it would be regarded as purely recreational, and weren't all the shops open on Sundays now, football games played.

She heard another car draw up outside. Surely not a visitor, she didn't want to talk to anyone now. She wanted to lose herself in this work. There were so many things she did not want to think about. Strange. Once there had only been one topic that had to be forced away. But today, as well as banishing Dale from her mind, she did not want to think about Gertie's violent husband, Colm's addicted sister, or Rosemary the faithless friend.

She heard voices outside the gate of No. 16. And as she knelt, trowel in hand, Marilyn Vine saw the slightly stooped figure of her husband come into the drive and look up at the house. She dropped the trowel and ran to him crying out. "Greg . . . Greg!"

He pulled back from her first. Months of rejection had taken their toll. "I hope it's all right . . ." he began apologetically.

"Greg?"

"I did plan to call you from the airport. I sat there until it was a civilized time," he explained.

"It's all right."

"I didn't want to disturb you, or invade your time, your space. It's just . . . it's just . . . well it's only for two or three days."

She looked at him, openmouthed. He was apologizing for being there? How terrible must have been the coldness she had shown to him. "Greg, I'm delighted you're here," she said.

"You are?"

"Of course I am. I don't suppose you'd think of giving me a hug?"

Hardly able to believe it Greg Vine embraced his wife.

There were bus timetables there too, so Ria looked up an earlier bus back for the children, then she called Sheila. "Could you be very tactful and get them on it for me? I'll explain everything tomorrow."

Sheila knew an emergency when she heard one. "No bad news?" she asked.

"Not really, very complicated. But Danny has to leave tonight and I want him to be able to say good-bye to the children himself."

"How much will I tell them?"

"Just that plans have changed."

"I'll do it of course, but I want you to know the courage it will take to tell that to Sean Maine and Annie Lynch."

"Dad, it's Annie. I can't believe what Mrs. Maine has told me, she says you're going back tonight."

"That's right, Princess, I'd love if you could get back."

"But why Dad, *why*?"

"I'll explain everything when I see you, Princess."

"We were going to go to a picnic and then come back this evening *and* we were all going to go to Manhattan tomorrow for the day. Now it's all changed."

"I'm afraid so, my love."

"Did you have some awful row with Mam? Did *she* send you home, is that it?"

"Absolutely not, Annie. Your mother and I have had a wonderful time here together and we both want to talk to the two of you this evening, that's all."

"Okay then."

"Sorry to upset all the romance," he said.

"What romance, Dad? Don't be old-fashioned."

"Sorry," he said, and hung up.

On the bus Annie and Brian tried to work it out.

"He's coming back to live at home?" Brian was hopeful.

"They wouldn't bring us back to tell us that," Annie grumbled. She had missed a marvelous picnic by a lake. Sean had been very sulky about her departure. Even suggested she wanted to go back to Stoneyfield to meet Hubie Green.

"Well, what then?" Brian asked.

"He's broke, I think that's it."

"I always said that." Brian was triumphant.

"No, you didn't, you kept bleating that Finola was saying it."

"We'll know soon." Brian was philosophical. "We're almost there."

When they got off the bus Hubie Green was waiting. "Your mom asked me to pick you up and drive you back to Tudor Drive," he said.

"Are you sure, you're not just kidnapping us?" Annie asked.

"No. I *was* glad for the chance to see you again, but she really did ask me." They climbed into Hubie's car. "Did you have a good time?"

"It was all right . . . ." Annie began with a careless shrug.

Brian decided that more information should be given. "She and Sean Maine were disgusting, almost as bad as the two of you. I can't understand it myself, I think it would choke you and I honestly don't know how you'd breathe while you're doing it."

Bernadette's face was very white. "Tell me again, Mum, what did he say?"

"He said I was to listen carefully and repeat these words: 'He was flying home tonight, he'd be here tomorrow, and nothing had changed.' "

"Did he say he loved me?" Her voice was very weak.

"He said, 'Nothing has changed.' He said it three times."

"Why do you think he said that instead of that he loved me?"

"Because his ex-wife may have been there, and because he wanted to tell you that if you *did* lose the baby, which you won't, Ber, it would still be the same."

"Do you believe that, Mum?"

"Yes. I listened to him say it three times and I believe him," said Finola Dunne.

"Sit down, Barney, we have to talk," Mona McCarthy said.

"But you wouldn't talk at all when I was trying to," he complained.

"I didn't want to then, but we have to talk now. A lot of things have changed."

"Like what?"

"Like that paragraph in the newspaper."

"Well, you *said* that you had something put by over the years and you were prepared to rescue things."

"We haven't yet discussed in what way. And I certainly didn't expect you to start telling the newspapers." She was calm and confident as always, but this time with a steely hint that he didn't like.

"Mona, you know just as well as I do the need to build up confidence at a time like this," he began.

"You'd be most unwise to build up anyone's confidence until we have discussed the terms."

"Look, love, stop talking in mysteries. What do you mean, *terms*? You told me you'd put something away, something that would rescue us."

"No, that's not what I said." She was placid. She could have been talking about a knitting pattern or a charity fashion show.

"What *did* you say then, Mona?"

"I said I had something, a way which *could* rescue you, that's a very different thing."

"Don't play word games, this isn't the time." There was a tic in his forehead. She couldn't have been fooling him, leading him along. It wasn't her style.

"No games, I assure you." She was very cold.

"I'm listening, Mona."

"I hope you are," she said. Then in very level tones she told him that she had enough money saved over the years in reputable pension funds and insurance policies that, when cashed in, would bail him out. But they were all in her name and they would only be cashed in if Barney agreed to pay his debtors. *And* to sell this mansion they lived in and buy a much smaller and less pretentious house. *And* to return the personal guarantee on No. 16 Tara Road to the Lynches. *And* that Miss Callaghan be assured that any relationship with him, financial, sexual, or social, was at an end.

Barney listened, openmouthed. "You can't make these demands," he said eventually.

"You don't *have* to accept them," she said.

He looked at her for a long time. "You hold all the cards," he said.

"People can always get up and leave the card table, they don't have to play."

"Why are you doing this? You don't need me, Mona. You don't have to have me hanging around the place as some kind of an accessory."

"You have no idea what I need and what I don't need, Barney."

"Have some dignity, woman, for God's sake. At this stage everyone knows about me and Polly, we're not hushing anything up that isn't widely known already."

"And they'll know when it's over too," she said.

"This will give you pleasure?"

"These are my terms."

"Do we have lawyers to fix it up?" He was scathing.

"No, but we do have the newspapers. You've used them already, I can do the same."

If anyone had ever suggested to Barney McCarthy that his quiet, compliant wife would have spoken like this to him Barney would have laughed aloud.

"What's brought this on, the thought of being poor?" His lip was twisted as he spoke.

"I pity you if you really think that. I never wanted to be rich. Never. It always sat uneasily on me. But anyway, as it happens I *am* rich, and I'll be richer if I don't help you out of the hole that you are in."

"So why then?"

"Partly from a sense of fairness. You did work hard for what you got, very hard, and I enjoyed a comfortable life as a result. But mainly because Helen is pregnant, she's going to have a baby, and we will be grandparents. I would like us to move with some grace into that period of our lives."

He looked at her with tears in his eyes. "It will be done," he said.

"As you choose, Barney."

Hubie left them at the carport.

"Nothing is ever the way Brian says it is," Annie said to him sadly.

"I know."

"So will I see you again?"

"Of course. Anyway, neither Sean Maine nor I will ever see you again after this summer, so what the hell?"

"I'd hate to think that," she said.

"About which of us?"

"About both of you," she said.

And they ran inside. They saw Danny's packed bag.

"You really are going then?" Annie said.

"Did you think I was making it up?"

"I thought you might want to get us back from Maines," Annie said.

"You'd want to have seen Annie and Sean Maine. . . ." Brian began.

"No, we wouldn't," Ria said. "We wouldn't have wanted to at all, even more than we'd want to have seen the way you left your bedroom here, Brian. But let's not waste time, we only have an hour before the airport limo comes. There are a lot of things to be said so we must all talk now."

"Zach might have seen me coming home, he could call in," Brian began.

"Well, he'll just be asked to call out again," Annie said.

Danny took control. "I came over here to tell you that there are going to be a lot of changes, not all for the better."

"Are any of them for the better?" Brian asked.

"No, as a matter of fact," his father said. "They're not."

They sat silent, waiting. Danny's voice seemed to have failed him. They looked at their mother, but Ria said nothing, she just smiled encouragingly at Danny. At least she wasn't fighting with him, and it reassured them. A little.

He cleared his throat and found the words. He told them the story. The debts, the gambles that hadn't worked, the lack of confidence, the end result. No. 16 Tara Road would have to be sold.

"Will you and Bernadette sell the new house too?" Brian asked.

"Yes, yes of course."

"But Barney doesn't own that one?" Annie asked.

"No."

"Well maybe we could *all* live there, couldn't we?" Brian enclosed the whole room in his expansive gesture. "Or maybe not," he said, remembering.

"And I would have told you all this tonight, with more time for us to discuss what was best and to tell you how sorry I am, but I have to go home."

"Is Mr. McCarthy in jail?" Brian asked.

"No, no, it's not that at all, it's something else." There was a silence. They looked at Ria again; again she offered nothing but a look of encouragement for Danny to speak. "Bernadette isn't well. We've had a message from Finola. She's had a lot of bleeding and she may be losing the baby, she's in the hospital. So that's why I'm going home early."

"Like it's not going to be born after all, is that it?" Brian wanted to make sure he had it straight.

"It's not totally formed yet so it would be very weak and might not live if it were born now," Danny explained.

Annie looked at her mother as she listened to this explanation, and bit her lip. Never had things been so raw and honest before. And Dad had been telling the truth on the phone, they were not rowing and fighting.

Brian let out a great sigh. "Well, wouldn't that solve everything if Bernadette's baby wasn't born at all?" he said. "Then we could all go back to being like we were."

Danny gave the taxi driver the address of the maternity hospital. "As quick as you can, and I have to pay you in U.S. dollars, I don't have any real money."

"Dollars are real enough for me," said the taxi driver, pulling out in the early morning sunshine and putting his foot down on the empty road.

"Is this the first baby?" the driver asked.

"No." Danny was curt.

"Still, it's always the same excitement, isn't it? And every one of them different. We have five ourselves, but that's it. Tie a knot in it, they told me." He laughed happily at the pleasantry and caught Danny's eye in the mirror. "Maybe you're a bit tired and want to have a bit of a rest after the flight."

"Something like that," Danny said with relief, and closed his eyes.

"Well, make the most of it, you'll have plenty of broken sleep for the next bit, there's a promise," said the driver, a man of experience.

Orla King was having a routine checkup at the hospital. Something had shown up on a smear test but it had proved to be benign. Her blood tests had also showed much improved liver function. Apart from the catastrophic lapse at Colm's restaurant, she was keeping off alcohol.

"Good girl," said the kindly woman specialist. "It's not easy but you're in there winning."

"It's a funny old world. I stay off the booze and God says: Okay, Orla, you don't have cancer this time." Orla was cynical.

"Some people find that kind of attitude helps." The doctor had seen it all and heard it all.

"Fantasists." Orla dismissed them.

"What would help you?"

"I don't know. A singing career, the one fellow I fancied to fancy me . . ."

"There are other fellows."

"So they say." Orla went out into the corridor and walked straight into Danny Lynch. "We do meet in the strangest places," she said.

"Not now, Orla." His voice was hard.

"It can't be baby time *yet*, surely?"

"Please, excuse me." He was trying to step past her.

"Come and have a coffee in the canteen and tell me all about it," she pleaded.

"No. I'm meeting someone, I'm waiting."

"Go on, Danny. I'm sober, that's one bit of good news, and a better one, I don't have cancer."

"I'm very pleased for you," he said, still trying to escape.

"Look, I behaved badly some time back. I didn't ring or write or anything, but you know I didn't mean it, it's not the real me when the drink takes over."

Across the corridor was a men's toilet. "I'm sorry, Orla," he said and went in the door. When he was inside he just leaned over the hand basin and looked at his haggard face, sunken eyes from a sleepless night on the plane, a crumpled shirt.

He had been told she was still in intensive care, and he could see her in an hour or two. Her mother would be back shortly, she had been there most of the night. Oh yes, she had lost the baby; there had been no possibility of anything else. Bernadette would tell him everything herself; it wasn't hospital policy to tell him whether it had been a boy or a girl, the woman would do all that. In time. Go and have a coffee, they had urged him, and then he had met Orla King of all people in the universe.

His shoulders began to heave and the tears wouldn't stop. Another man, a big burly young fellow, came in and saw him.

"Were you there for it?" he asked. Danny couldn't speak and the proud young father thought he had nodded agreement. "I was too. Jesus, it blew my mind. I couldn't believe it. I had to come in here to get over it. My son, and I saw him coming into the world." He put an awkward arm around Danny's shoulder and gave him a squeeze of solidarity. "And they say it's the women who go through it all," he said.

Polly Callaghan came back from London early on Monday morning. Barney was waiting outside her flat.

Polly was thrilled to see him. "I didn't call you or anything, I wanted to leave you a bit of space. Aren't you good to come and meet me?"

"No, no not at all." He seemed very down.

Polly wasn't going to allow that. "Hey, I bought the *Irish Times* at Victoria Station in London and I saw that piece about you, it's wonderful."

"Yes," he said.

"Well, isn't it?"

"In a way."

"Well, get out of that car, come in and I'll make us coffee."

"No, Poll, we must talk here."

"In your car, don't be ridiculous."

"Please. Humor me this once."

"Haven't I spent a lifetime humoring you? Tell me before I burst. Is it true, are you being rescued?"

"Yes, Poll, I am."

"So why haven't we the champagne out?"

"But at a price. A terrible price."

"Polly, it's Gertie here. Is this a good time to talk? I have a bit of a favor to ask you."

"No, Gertie it's not a good time to talk."

"Sorry. Is Barney there?"

"No, and he's never going to be here again."

"I don't believe it! I knew he was in a bit of trouble but . . ."

"He's in no trouble now it's all been smoothed out for him, but he's not ever going to be here again, that's part of the deal. Actually *I'm* not going to be here much longer, that's part of the deal too."

"But how?"

"His wife. Wives always win in the end."

"No, they don't. Ria didn't win, did she?"

"Ah shit, Gertie. Who cares?"

"I do, I'm very sorry. Maybe he doesn't mean it."

"He means it. It was either or. What was your problem by the way?"

"Just . . . it doesn't matter, it's not big compared to yours."

"What was it, Gertie?"

"It's just that Jack got some silly notion in his head that I was earning the extra money, well, you won't believe how he thought I was earning it, so I had to tell him I was working for you. He might come round to check, so can you say yes?"

"Is that all? Is that the big problem?"

"It was quite big at the time, and might be again if he's still brooding about it."

"Were there any stitches this time?"

"No, no."

"Gertie you're *such* a fool, such a mad fool. I'd love to come over and shake every remaining tooth out of your head."

"That wouldn't help me. Not a bit."

"No, I know that."

"It's only because he loves me you see, he gets notions."

"I see."

"And you know that Barney loves you, Polly, he'll be back."

"Of course he will," said Polly Callaghan and hung up.

Marilyn Vine said to Greg that they were going to drive out to Wicklow for the day on Monday. It was less than an hour's drive, and very beautiful. She was going to make what would pass for a picnic.

"Here, I'll show you a map, you love maps," she said as she got out Ria's picnic basket. "Now, you can see where we're going and navigate if I take the wrong turn."

He looked at her in amazement. The transformation was extraordinary. The old enthusiasms were back. "We can go to the country in one hour?" he said surprised.

"This is an extraordinary city, it's got sea and mountains right on the doorstep," she said. "And I want to take you to this place I found. You can park the car and walk over the hills for miles and meet no one, see no one. You can't even see any dwelling places. It's like Arizona without the desert."

"Why are we going there?" he asked gently.

"So that nobody can interrupt us. If we stay here at Number 16 Tara Road we might as well be in Grand Central Station," said Marilyn, with the easy laugh that Greg Vine had thought he would never hear again.

Bernadette looked very white. His stomach nearly turned over when he saw her. "Go on, talk to her. She's been counting the moments till you got here," the nurse said.

"She's asleep," he said, almost afraid to approach the bed.

"Is that you, Danny?"

"I'm here beside you, darling, don't speak. You're tired and weak. You've lost a lot of blood, but you're going to be fine."

"Kiss me," she said. He kissed her thin white face. "Properly." He kissed her on the lips. "Do you still love me, Danny?"

"Darling Bernadette, of course I do."

"You know about the baby?"

"I'm sad we've lost our baby, very sad," he said eyes full of tears. "And, God, I'm sad I wasn't here to be with you when it happened. But *you* are all right and *I'm* here for you and that's what's going to make us strong forever and ever."

"You're not glad or anything, you don't think it sort of solves things just now?"

"Jesus, Bernadette how could you even *think* that?" His face was anguished.

"Well . . . you know . . ."

"No, I don't know. Our baby is dead, the baby we were building a home for, and you're so weak and hurt. How could I be glad about anything like that?"

"It's just that I was afraid, you being out in America . . ." Her voice trailed away.

"You know I had to go out to America to tell them face-to-face about the business. And that's done and I'm home now, home with you."

"And did it go all right?" Bernadette asked.

"Yes, it went all right," said Danny Lynch.

Ria rang Rosemary. "You haven't set out for work yet?"

"No. Hey, what time *is* it out there? It must be the middle of the night."

"It is. I couldn't sleep." Ria sounded flat.

"Is anything wrong?"

"Well, yes and no."

And Ria confided to her good friend Rosemary that Danny had gone home early because of Bernadette's miscarriage. She had nobody in Dublin to keep her informed of what was going on, could Rosemary keep an ear to the ground? Nobody else would tell her what was happening, but Rosemary saw Danny from time to time and she would be in a position to know.

Ria also told how she hoped to get into some kind of catering work when she got home. Everyone here had been startled and pleased with her work, she would try to get commissions from Colm for desserts and from the big delicacies shop to do specialist work. She said she thought that everything was going to be all right again.

"And how was Danny when he was out there?"

"He was fine, it was a bit like the old days," Ria said. She didn't go into details but Rosemary got the distinct feeling that more had happened than was being said. But even Danny Lynch wouldn't be so foolish as to sleep with his ex-wife under such circumstances. Surely?

When Rosemary went out to get into her car, still concerned about it, she met Jack Brennan. He did not smell of drink—but he wasn't sober. "Just a quick question, Rosemary. Do you pay my wife to clean your house?"

"Certainly not, Jack. Gertie is my friend, not my cleaner. I have cleaners who come from an agency twice a week."

"And do other people pay her? Ria and that one staying in Ria's house, Polly, Frances?"

"Don't be ridiculous, Jack, of course they don't," said Rosemary as she slammed her car door and drove to work.

Finola Dunne drove Danny to his office.

"I have to talk to Barney about what this rescue business is all about.

It may be nothing, only puff, but it just might be something we can cling on to. I'll be back to Bernadette before lunch."

"You'll need some sleep, you look terrible," Finola said.

"I can't sleep, not at a time like this."

"Ber losing the baby . . . at this time . . . ?" Finola was tentative.

"Makes me love her still more and want to look after her even more desperately than I did before." Danny finished the sentence for her.

"But there must be ways . . . ?"

"Surely you know, Finola, that I adore her, that I wouldn't have left my wife and children for her if I didn't love her more than anything else in the whole world. You *must* know that."

In the office, a full-scale meeting was taking place. The receptionist was surprised to see him. "They didn't think you were coming back until tomorrow," she said, startled at his disheveled appearance.

"Yes, well, I'm here now, who's in there?"

"The accountant, the lawyers, the bank manager, and Mrs. McCarthy."

"Mona?"

"Yes."

"And was anyone going to tell me about this summit or was I to hear about it when it was all over?"

"Don't ask me, Mr. Lynch. I'm on notice like everyone else here, I don't get told what's happening either."

"Right, I'm going in there."

"Mr. Lynch?"

"Yes?"

"If I could suggest you sort of . . . well . . . cleaned yourself up a bit."

"Thank you, sweetheart," he said. The girl was right. Five minutes in the men's room would take the worst edges off.

The sun shone through the trees as Greg and Marilyn sat at a wooden table and unpacked their picnic. They had walked and talked easily in the hills, looking at the sheep that barely gave them a second glance.

"Why did you come here?" Marilyn asked.

"Because Ria said you had talked to her children about Dale. I thought you might be able to talk to me about him too."

"Yes, of course I can. I'm sorry it took so long."

"It takes what time it takes," Greg said. He laid his hand on hers. Last night he had slept in the big white bed beside Marilyn. They really hadn't touched each other, not reached out toward the other but they had held hands for a little while. He knew he must be very gentle in asking questions. He wouldn't ask what had changed her. She would tell him.

And then she did. "There's always some stupid, unimportant thing, isn't there?" Marilyn said with the tears that he had never seen her shed in her eyes.

"I mean it's so idiotic that I can hardly bear to tell you. But it all had to do with those children. Annie said that of course we couldn't have let him play with motorbikes any more than you'd let someone play with guns. And Brian said that he imagined Dale was up in heaven looking down, sorry for all the trouble he had caused." The tears fell down onto their joined hands. "Then it all made sense somehow, Greg," she said through her sobs. "I mean, I don't think there's a real heaven or anything, but his spirit is somewhere, sorry for all the trouble. And I must listen to him and tell him it's all right."

"The wanderer returns," Danny said, coming in with a false smile and confident stance to the boardroom where the meeting was going on. The stolid figure of Mona McCarthy sat beside Larry from the bank and the two lawyers.

"I'm sorry, we didn't know you were going to be in the country, Danny, there was no attempt to exclude you," Mona said. Mona was speaking at a meeting like this?

"Well, tell the prodigal if the story in the *Irish Times* about a fatted calf was true." Barney seemed curiously mute, so Danny was playing to the gallery now, trying to take control, or raise it a little anyway.

"Less of the jokes, Danny." Larry from the bank had never liked him, but today he was speaking as if Danny were a schoolboy.

Danny was silent. And in the space of fifteen minutes learned that Mrs. McCarthy had, entirely without any legal or moral need to do so, decided to rescue the firm from bankruptcy. Everything would be wound up, the assets sold, the debtors paid. There would be no more work for Danny Lynch since the company no longer existed. The bank manager also let Danny know that it might be extremely difficult for him to find a position in any reputable agency. The word about the financial mishandling was well known.

The good news was that the personal guarantee on No. 16 Tara Road was now rescinded. The house would not be sold to pay Barney McCarthy's debts. Danny could feel his breath slowly beginning to return to normal. But Larry added that on the Tara Road front there was also, on a practical level, bad news. Danny had no assets, no job, and a considerable personal overdraft. The house would have to be sold anyway.

Fergal, a man that Colm knew slightly from AA, called to see him. He was a detective as far as Colm could remember. "You know the way we're all meant to be like the Masons or the Knights, looking out for each other?" Fergal said, slightly awkwardly.

"I know. And are you telling me something or asking?" Colm made it easy.

"Telling. The word is that your brother-in-law is dealing here in this restaurant. There could be a raid."

"Thank you."

"You knew?"

"I suspected."

"Will you warn him, move him on somewhere else, or what?"

"I'd like to see him moved on to jail but I have to do something else first."

"Will it take long, what you have to do? You haven't got long," Fergal said.

"Then it will have to be done quickly," said Colm and prepared for the worst conversation in his life. He had promised his sister that he would look after her. Looking after her had long involved turning a blind eye to her addiction. Colm hoped that Marilyn Vine would deliver on her promise to help.

Mona was still talking in the boardroom. Barney and Danny walked out together. They weren't necessary anymore.

Danny was determined to be bright. "In better times we'd have said this was the day to ring Polly and book Quentin's for lunch," he said.

"There won't be any more days like that." Barney was subdued.

"Part of the deal?"

"Absolutely. And how did it go with you out there?"

Danny shrugged. "You know . . ."

"Well, at least Ria will get something now this way."

"Yes."

"So what brought you back early, anyway?"

"Bernadette lost the baby."

"Oh dear, oh dear. Still there are ways that it might all be for the best."

"There are no ways that it's in any way for the best," said Danny coldly, and went out to get a taxi back to the hospital.

Greg had gone back to America. Marilyn longed to get on the plane with him. "I can't leave her house, I can't abandon ship now, leave a house she's going to lose anyway, it would be too cruel."

"Of course not," he had said.

"I'll be back on September first, back on Tudor Drive," she promised.

"So will I, in that week anyway," he said.

"Hawaii?"

"They'll understand." Greg was confident. "It was a compassionate posting anyway. They'll be glad we got better."

"It's just a pity that Ria didn't get better," Marilyn said.

"We don't know, maybe she did." Greg was hopeful.

"No, she wants that guy back and she's not getting him. I hear from the network here that he's back and glued to the girlfriend again."

"She'll survive," said Greg.

"What's she like?" Marilyn asked suddenly. "As a person?"

"I forgot you don't know her. She's very warm, innocent in ways. She isn't short of a word. There was a time I didn't think you'd like her but now I think you would. I think my brother, Andy, did too."

"There!" Marilyn cried. "We might end up being sisters-in-law."

"Don't hold your breath," said Greg.

After he had gone, she sat at the table talking to Clement. "You know we're going to get a cat just like you, you foolish animal."

Colm came in from the garden. His face was pale. "Glad to see you talking to the cat," he said. Marilyn was startled. Normally he never came in unannounced. He didn't wait for her to speak. "I've got to do it, I'm telling her today. Will you help?"

"You've been to the center?"

"Yes."

"And they'll take her if she's willing."

"Yes."

"Then of course I will," said Marilyn Vine.

"Ria, it's Danny."

"Oh, thank God, I was hoping to hear from you."

"Well, it was a bit fraught."

"How are you . . . ?"

"Well, we lost the baby but that was to be expected."

"I am sorry."

"Yes, I know you are, Ria."

"But in a way—"

"I know you're not going to be like these people who wrongly say it's all for the best," he interrupted her.

"No, of course I wasn't going to say that," Ria lied.

"I know you weren't, but people do and it's very upsetting for us both."

"I'm sure." She was confused but she must never show it. "Anyway, the children are fine, they're winding down to go home now, and then we'll all meet and make plans about the future."

"Yes, it's not quite as bleak as it looked on that scene," he said.

"What do you mean?"

"Mona had some savings, Barney doesn't get our house after all."

"*Danny!*" She was overjoyed.

"We'll still have to sell it, but at least this way you and I get the money, we'll find somewhere for you to live."

"Sure."

"So that's what I rang to tell you."

"Yes . . ."

"Are you okay?" He sounded concerned.

"Fine, why?"

"I thought you'd be so pleased. Out of all this misery something good has emerged in the form of Mona McCarthy."

"Yes, of course I'm pleased," she said. "Sorry, Danny, I have to go, someone's ringing at the door." She hung up. There was nobody at the door but she needed to go without him hearing the tears in her voice. And the total wretched realization that it had all meant nothing to him and that there were no plans for them for the future.

"Monto will have a table for six tonight and he'd like the one near the door," said one of the nameless friends who accompanied Colm's brother-in-law.

"We have no reservations," Colm said carefully.

"I think you have."

"Ask Monto to talk to me himself if he's in any doubt," Colm said. He had asked his friend Fergal to tell the Drugs Squad that Caroline was safely installed on a rehabilitation program. She could not be reached by Monto offering her more supplies.

"Monto doesn't like people playing games."

"Of course he doesn't." Colm was pleasant.

"He'll be round."

"I'm sure he'll believe *you* that there's no room for him here tonight. Why shouldn't he take your word?"

"You'll be hearing from him."

Colm knew he would. Fergal said he'd make sure there were a couple of guys in the vicinity, in an unmarked car. "Very good of you, Fergal, there'll always be a dinner for you and whoever here."

"Ah, my whoever didn't hang around after the drinking days," Fergal said sadly.

"And I never found a whoever at all. Right pair of eejits we were. Still, this should be the year." Colm pretended a much greater sense of ease than he felt.

Marilyn called to the restaurant. "I thought I'd invite Gertie here for dinner tonight."

"On the house and with pleasure," he said.

"I wouldn't hear of it."

"Look what you did for Caroline."

"She *was* ready, truly she was, she thought you'd feel let down if she went in, that's all."

"Aren't we all mad in our ways?" he said.

"Sure," she agreed with a laugh. "Still, Gertie and I will have a nice quiet time here compared to the first visit. Remember the singer who drank the carnations?"

"I'm not likely to forget her, but I wouldn't put money on it being quiet tonight."

"Can we have the Maines to stay? Our visit *was* cut a bit short when we were there."

"I know, Annie, but there was a reason."

"Still. Please?"

"I don't know. . . ."

"But Mam, this is the last good holiday we might ever have, you know, if we're going to be broke, and Dad gone and everything. It would be nice to have something to remember."

"It would," Ria said.

"Are you all right, Mam?"

"Yes. I don't want you getting too fond of a boy that you're going to have to say good-bye to in ten days' time."

"No, Mam, you'd much prefer that than one I might see every day and night for the rest of my life," Annie said, her eyes dancing.

"Ask them," Ria said. It didn't really matter now. Nothing did.

Rosemary called at No. 16. "Just passing by. I heard from Gertie that your husband came over."

"That's right."

"Good visit?"

"Very nice, thank you."

"And is there any news of Ria?" If Rosemary thought it odd that she was being left on the doorstep to ask these questions she showed nothing of it.

Suddenly Marilyn opened the door wider. "Yes, there is as it happens. Come in and I'll tell you about her news."

———

Bernadette was home from the hospital. She lay on a sofa and Danny brought her a bowl of soup.

"That's nice," she said. "What is it?"

"It's just a tin of consommé and a little brandy in it. To make you strong." He stroked her face.

"You're the kindest man on earth," she said.

"I'm useless. I have to sell our new home before we've even begun to pay for it."

"I don't care. You know that."

"Yes, I do."

"And what about Ria?" It was the first time she asked. "Is she all right about selling Tara Road?"

"I think she is," Danny said. "She seemed all right about it when I was out there but she sounded different on the phone, I don't know why."

"Phones are bad," Bernadette reassured him. "Did she say anything about the baby?"

"She said she was very sorry."

"I'm sure she is too," Bernadette said. "And the children too. Remember when Brian asked did he have webbed feet?" She smiled at the memory and cried at the thought of the little boy they had lost.

Marilyn sat opposite Rosemary in the beautiful room. "Would you care for a glass of sherry?" she asked in a very formal and courteous tone. She picked up a decanter and filled two of the small, cut-crystal glasses that stood on a tray. "Ria is thinking of going into business when she comes back."

"Ria going into business?" Rosemary tried to keep the amazement out of her voice.

"Yes. She won't need a premises or kitchens or anything but she's a very talented cook as I suppose you know."

"She's good, yes."

"And Colm's pastry cook has left so she can do that. I gather she'll have an introduction to Quentin's too to do something different that won't compete." Marilyn looked quite fierce and determined. Rosemary wondered where all this was leading. "She'll also approach that big gourmet shop, you know the one I mean, at the junction of three roads?"

Rosemary found its name. "Exactly . . . and do cakes for St. Rita's. Her mother and I have been there already discussing it."

"You *have* been busy." Rosemary was impressed.

"But what she really needs, Rosemary, is someone to help her professionally, someone like you."

"I can't cook. Heavens, I can barely open a tin," Rosemary said.

"To write and print a brochure for her, business cards, menu suggestions."

"Well, of course . . . if there's anything I can do to help . . ."

"And to give her a series of introductions, small receptions in your office, in places you visit."

"Come on, Marilyn, you're making it sound like a full-time job."

"I think you should invest a fair amount of time in it, yes, certainly." Marilyn's voice was steely now. "And even some money, Rosemary."

"I'm sorry but I don't really know what business—"

Marilyn cut her off. "I'll be talking to Ria again tomorrow on the phone. I'd like her to know how much is being set up in advance for her. She needs all the practical help she can get just now. She has loads of goodwill already, that's falling off the trees for her, what she needs is the hard, practical help that you can give her."

"I don't invest in friends' schemes, Marilyn," Rosemary said. "I never have. It's just been a policy I've always had. I worked hard enough for my money and I want to keep my friends. If you don't lose money in their businesses then you've a better chance of keeping them *as* friends, if you see what I mean."

There was a silence.

"Of course I'll be happy to mention her name," Rosemary said. Still silence. "And if ever I hear of anything . . ."

"I think we should get a list ready now of exactly what you'll do. We could write down what a good, kind friend like you has done for Ria while she was away." It sounded like a threat. Rosemary looked at her wildly. It couldn't be a threat, could it? "Because she needs to know that friends can do things as well as say them. What good would a friend be who betrayed her?"

"I beg your pardon?"

"Well, it would be a betrayal, wouldn't it, if a friend took the things she most wanted in the world, while still pretending to be a friend?"

Rosemary's voice was almost a whisper now. "What do you mean?"

"What do *you* think she wants most in the world, Rosemary?"

"I don't know. This house? Her children? Danny?"

"Yes. And of course you can't restore the house to her, her children she has already. So?" Marilyn paused.

"So?" Rosemary said shakily. The woman knew, she bloody knew.

"So, what you can help with is her dignity and self-respect," Marilyn said brightly.

Danny's name had been left out of the list.

They began to write down what Rosemary would do to help Ria's career.

Gertie had been ironing a dress for Marilyn. "That's a beautiful shade. Fuchsia, is it?"

"I think so. It doesn't fit me properly, I rarely wear it."

"That's a shame, it's a gorgeous color. Years ago when I worked in Polly's dress hire place we had an outfit that color; people were always renting it for weddings."

"Would you like it?" Marilyn asked suddenly. "Seriously, I don't wear it, I'd love you to have it."

"Well, if you're sure."

"Wear it tonight to Colm's, the color would suit you." Gertie's face seemed to have a shadow. "It's still on tonight, isn't it?" Marilyn thought she would kill Gertie if she chickened out now.

"But of course it's on, Jack's pleased for me. I don't think he'd like to see me wearing such a classy dress though. One he didn't buy for me himself."

"Change here on our way to the restaurant then."

"Why not? Won't it do me good to dress up?" said Gertie with that heartbreaking smile that made Marilyn glad she hadn't said anything terrible about Jack.

At seven o'clock Monto and two friends arrived at the restaurant. And headed for the table that they thought they had booked. The restaurant was still empty. No one would arrive for at least thirty minutes. This was better than Colm had believed possible.

"Sorry, Colm, there was some mistake. You didn't get the message that we are meeting some friends here. Two are coming over from England and one down from the North. We have an important meeting and this is where we are having it."

"Not tonight, Monto."

"Tell me a little more." Monto smiled a slow smile. He had very short hair and a fat neck. His expensive suit did nothing to hide his shape, and the regular manicures little to help his pudgy hands and square nails. Colm looked at him levelly.

"You have a short memory, not long ago you told me you owed me."

"And I paid you. You've done enough deals in this place."

"Deals?" Monto looked at the other two associates and laughed. "Isn't the word *meals*, Colm? That's what you run, it's a restaurant, isn't it. They serve meals, not deals."

"Good-bye, Monto."

"Don't think you can talk to me like that."

"I just have and if you know what's good and wise you'll go."

"Give me a reason or two."

"The number of the car from northern Ireland has already been taken down. Your guests from the UK will be interviewed. Everything you have will be searched."

"Big talk, Colm . . . and who'll look after your sister? She hasn't enough to get her to the weekend."

"She's being looked after, thank you."

"Nobody in this city will supply your sister, they know she's my wife. They know she's with me."

"Well, they know more than you do. She hasn't been with you for three days." Colm sounded very calm.

"You'd start a drug war in your own place just because you got her a new source?"

"No, I'm starting nothing, I'm asking you to leave."

"And what makes you think I will."

"The police in the car just outside."

"You set me up."

"No, I didn't as it happens. I told them that there would be no meeting, no deal here tonight or ever again."

"And they believed you?"

"They felt pretty sure that I meant it all right. Good night, Monto."

When Marilyn and Gertie arrived, Colm was calm again.

"Gertie, don't you look lovely! That's a color you should always wear."

"I will, Colm, thank you," she said, delighted with the compliment.

"And are we going to have fireworks tonight?" Marilyn asked.

"It's over, amazingly. All wilted at the first of a little winter frost," he said.

"You two have lots of secrets," Gertie giggled.

"Only the secrets of those who share a garden," Colm said.

Across the restaurant they saw Polly Callaghan. She was with a very distinguished-looking man.

"Isn't Barney very understanding that he lets her go out to dinner with other men." Gertie was full of admiration.

"I don't think Barney is in the picture these days," Colm said.

"You may be right, and come to think of it she's leaving her flat tomorrow, I hear," Gertie chipped in.

"Now how on *earth* do you know all these things, Colm?" asked Marilyn Vine, who would not have been remotely interested a few weeks ago.

"In a restaurant you see and hear everything and say nothing," he said, and left them the menus and moved on.

Rosemary Ryan waved at them from another table.

"Who is she with?" Marilyn asked.

"Her sister, Eileen, and her sister's girlfriend, Stephanie. And now they really *are* lesbians," Gertie giggled.

"Let's hope the lady who drank the carnations doesn't come back and out them all," Marilyn said.

"They're so out you wouldn't believe it. Rosemary hates it."

"Does she now?" Marilyn smiled.

Jack was sitting up waiting when Gertie came home. "Nice evening, was it?"

"Yes, Jack, it was a nice girls' night out."

"And who gave you the whore's purple dress?"

"Marilyn did, it doesn't suit her."

"It wouldn't suit anyone except a whore," he said.

"Ah, Jack, don't say that."

"All my life I loved you and all you did was betray me and let me down." He had never spoken like this before.

"That's not so, Jack. I never looked at another man, never."

"Prove that to me."

"Well, would I have stayed with you all these times you've been under the weather?" she asked.

"No, that's true," he said. "That's very true."

They went to bed. She lay there hardly daring to move in case she might feel his fist. Out of the corner of her eye she saw him. Jack Brennan was awake and looking at the ceiling. He was dangerously calm.

"Hallo, Marilyn, it's only Ria, don't bother to ring back, I'll be here and there and everywhere. I've no news. Sorry I sound a bit down. It's stupid to ring up and then sound like something from a depressive's ward. It's just . . . it's just. Anyway, the real reason I rang was to thank you *so* much for the E-mail you sent from the cyber café. Isn't Rosemary wonderful to do all that? Wouldn't we all be lost without our friends? I'll say good-bye now, I've got to drive the Maine children back home, and Annie's heartbroken, she seems to be crazy over Gertie's nephew. Everyone just laughs at first love, but then Danny was my first love and look how long it lasted. For me anyway. All the best, Ria."

The next morning Jack Brennan got very drunk very early. He went first to Nora Johnson's house at No. 48. "Does my wife clear up after your daughter and all her friends?" he shouted.

"I have nothing to say to you drunk or sober," Ria's mother said with some spirit. "I have never met your wife without telling her that she should leave you. I'll bid you good day."

He moved on to Rosemary's house. "Swear to me on a stack of bibles that Gertie never cleaned for you or anyone."

"Oh, get the hell out of here before I call the police," Rosemary said, and pushed past him.

Next he stopped at the dentist's house. Jimmy Sullivan saw him from the window and answered the door himself.

"Tell me."

"I'll tell you nothing, Jack Brennan, except that I fix your wife's teeth every time you hit her and I'm not in a mood to do so again."

Then he went and knocked loudly on Marilyn's door. "Did you give Gertie a whore's dress?"

"Did she say I did?"

"Stop being Mrs. Clever with me."

"I think you should go, Jack." She slammed the door and looked out the window to see where he went. She saw him run across the road to the bus stop.

Polly Callaghan had everything ready. Today she was moving to a rented accommodation. An unfurnished flat so she could take her own things with her. Those, at least, had not been seized by that woman, Barney's mouselike wife, who had been stacking away thousands upon thousands.

Last night Polly had gone to dinner with a pleasant man who had long been pestering her for a date. It had been a deadly dull evening. She dreaded to think of a lifetime without Barney. She wished she could hate him but she couldn't. She just hated herself for having made the wrong decision so long ago.

The moving vans had arrived. Polly sighed and began to give the directions that would dismantle a large part of her life. The phone was disconnected but her mobile was still in operation. It rang just at that moment.

"Poll, I love you."

"No, you don't, Barney, but it doesn't matter."

"What do you mean it doesn't matter?"

"It doesn't," she said, and clicked off.

She was going to drive ahead of the van to direct them to the new address. One final look and she was ready to close the door. Polly sighed. It was hard to say to Barney that it didn't matter, but she must be practical. She had always known Barney for what he was. He was like Danny Lynch, although as far as she knew Danny never had any strong partner figure like herself. Barney would always remain married to a safe-haven person like Mona. Danny moved from his safe haven, the faithful, loving Ria, to safe, compliant Bernadette. There had been some little dramas in between like that wild Orla King and one or two others. But that's the way things were. Polly did not think she had been fooled or betrayed. She had always known the score. And there was plenty of life ahead.

She gave one last glance out the window at the moving van. Everything was packed now, she only had her hand luggage to take. There were sounds of shouting, some drunk was yelling abusively. Polly couldn't quite see what was happening. Then there was a thump, an impact followed by a screech of brakes. There were screams from everywhere. The boy who was driving was being helped from his seat.

"I couldn't help it, he threw himself, I swear," he was stammering.

It was Jack Brennan. And he was dead.

CHAPTER

NINE

THE LAUNDERETTE WAS BUSY when they arrived. The shirt-ironing service had been a big success, and Gertie had gotten orders from several business concerns as well. Colm had been high in his praise of her and the personal recommendation was always very important. She looked up when she saw Polly Callaghan coming in and her hand flew to her throat when she saw that Polly was followed by two police officers.

"Jack?" she cried in a strangled voice. "Has Jack done something? He was grand last night, very quiet, not a word out of him. What did he do?"

"Sit down, Gertie," Polly said. One of the officers had organized a glass of water from among the inquisitive staff and clientele. "There's been an accident. It was very quick, he didn't feel a thing," Polly said. "The ambulance men said it would have been over in a second."

"What are you saying?" Gertie was white-faced.

"We would all be lucky to go so quickly and painlessly, Gertie, honestly, when you think of the length it takes some people to die."

The young policewoman handed her the glass of water. She had only been in uniform for a week. This was the first occasion when she had been sent to break bad news to someone about an accident. She was very glad that this Miss Callaghan had come with them. The poor woman who ran the launderette looked as if she were going to keel over and die herself.

"But Jack can't be dead," Gertie kept saying. "Jack's not even forty, he has years of good living ahead of him, ahead of both of us."

"Mrs. Vine, Marilyn, we met briefly. I'm Polly Callaghan. I'm with Gertie Brennan now."

"Yes?"

"There's been a most awful accident. Gertie's husband, Jack, was killed and of course she's devastated. I'm here with her now, and they're getting her mother and everything . . . but I do have to go to let people into a new apartment and I was wondering . . ."

"Would you like me to come to the launderette?" Marilyn asked.

"If you can, please."

Marilyn heard the urgency, almost desperation, in the voice. "I'll come right away." She called out to Colm in the garden. "I'm going out to Gertie, Jack had an accident."

"Nothing trivial I hope?" Colm said.

"Fatal, I believe," Marilyn said tersely.

To her surprise, Colm threw down his fork and ran with her. "Jesus, what a stupid remark to make, I'll come with you," he said. "But I'll run on ahead and tell Nora Johnson, she'd want to come too."

Marilyn thought to herself, not for the first time, that these really were extraordinary people. The very time when you wanted to be left alone with your grief they started assembling half the country around you. She tried to take it in. Jack Brennan, who had knocked on this door under two hours ago, was *dead*? Her last words to him had been, "I think you should go." Suppose she had asked him in for coffee, suppose she had tried to reassure him, would he be alive now? But Marilyn had been down that road before; she wasn't going to travel it again. What had happened to Gertie's husband was not her fault. She would no longer take on the guilt and responsibility of the universe. She would go and see what could be done for the living.

Ria's mother was exactly the right person to have alerted. She knew precisely what to do. She encouraged the staff to continue working. It's what Gertie would want if she were able to speak, Nora Johnson said.

No, it wasn't at all heartless to keep the business going, in fact it was only fair to customers. But if the staff would all like to give her fifty pence each she would go out now and buy a big bunch of flowers and a card so that they could be seen to be the very first to sympathize. They rooted in their apron pockets and Nora came back with a bouquet, which had cost three times what she had collected.

"What exactly would you write in a case like this?" one of the girls asked.

"Suppose you say: 'For Gertie, with love and sympathy,' would that cover it?" Nora Johnson knew that none of them any more than herself could bear to mention the name Jack on a card. Only a couple of hours ago she had shouted at him herself and said that she had always urged Gertie to leave him. Nora didn't regret it at all, it was what she had always felt. Not of course that there would be any need to say anything like that now to Gertie.

Marilyn watched in amazement as the little flat above the launderette filled with people. A buffet table was set up with cold ham and pâté, which came from Colm's restaurant. Jimmy and Frances Sullivan had sent a crate of wine and bottles of soda. Hilary had sent a message saying she'd come over after work and bring a bag of black clothes, which Gertie could borrow. The children, John and Katy, had arrived, stunned, confused, and taken from the summer course where their grandmother had paid for them to have some kind of normal holiday. Gertie's mother was there, her mouth a thin hard line, but her words kind as she went along with the general fiction that Gertie had tragically lost a great man, a loving husband, and devoted father.

It was entirely surreal, but Marilyn told herself over and over that this is what Gertie ached to hear and it was being delivered to her.

Ria was having coffee with Sheila Maine when the call came from Sheila and Gertie's mother with the news of Jack's death. She said it was hard to speak because there were so many people there. Ria realized that it was also hard to speak since she too had been sworn to support the story of the fairy-tale marriage.

Sheila was appalled. "What on earth will she do without him? She'll be devastated," she cried. "I mean, other people *think* they have happy marriages but this is one we all dreamed about and never knew."

Polly left a message at Rosemary Ryan's office. They told her that Rosemary was on another line and couldn't be interrupted.

"Just tell her that Gertie Brennan's husband is dead."

"Any more details, Ms. Callaghan?" Rosemary Ryan's assistant was as cool as she was herself.

"No, she'll know what to do," said Polly.

"Danny, I have to talk to you." Rosemary had phoned Danny Lynch's mobile.

"It's not appropriate now, Rosemary." He was sitting holding Bernadette's hand, as she drifted off to sleep.

"Go on, Danny, take the call if it's business," Bernadette said.

He took his phone into the next room.

"What is it, Rosemary?"

"You haven't got in touch since you got back."

"Well, quite a lot has been happening," he said.

"I know, and didn't I alert you out there?"

"Not about work. We lost the baby."

"Oh."

"Is that all you can say?"

"I'm sorry."

"Thank you."

"But life goes on, Danny, and you and I have a lot of worries which you should know about. Can you meet me?"

"Absolutely not."

"We have to talk."

"No, we don't."

"Is your business safe, your house?"

"The business has closed, the house will have to be sold, but at least not as part of Barney's estate. Now I have to go back to—"

"But you, Danny, what will you do? You must tell me. I have a right to know."

"You have no right to know. You couldn't help me when I was in trouble. You made that clear, and I accepted it."

"But there's more . . . wait . . . Marilyn knows."

"Knows what?"

"She knows about us."

"Really?"

"Don't go all distant on me, Danny Lynch."

"Please, Rosemary, leave me alone, I have too much to worry about."

"I don't believe this," she said.

"Rosemary, stop the drama. It's over."

She hung up, shaking.

Her assistant came in. "Ms. Ryan, I have a message here. Some bad news. It's to tell you that Gertie Brennan's husband is dead."

"Good," said Rosemary.

"We're going home two days early," Ria said. "I was able to get cancellations."

"Oh *no*, Mam, no. Not for awful Jack Brennan's funeral. You never liked him, it's so hypocritical."

"Gertie's my friend though, I like her," Ria said.

"You *promised* we could stay here until September first."

"Well, I'd have thought you would like to be going on the same plane as Sean Maine, but what do I know?" Ria said.

"What?"

"Sheila's taking the two children over to the funeral, we'll all travel together . . . but of course if you're violently opposed to that then I suppose . . ."

"Oh Mam, come on, you'd never win a prize for acting," Annie said, overjoyed.

Andy had a business meeting nearby. Or so he said. "Can I take your mother out to the Thai restaurant on her own?" he asked Annie and Brian when he came to the house.

"On a date, like?" Brian asked.

"No, just for boring grown-up conversation."

"Oh, sure, I'll go to Zach's house. Will it be overnight?" Brian asked.

"No, Brian, it will *not* be overnight," Ria said.

"I can go to the movies with Hubie," Annie said. "And before you ask, Brian, that's not a date and neither is it overnight."

———

"You have a delightful family," he said.

Ria sighed. "I must remind myself not to cling to them too much, not to be the mother from hell."

"You couldn't be that," he laughed.

"Oh, easily. I don't know what we're going back to; it's real uncharted territory. I must not use them as my pair of crutches through it."

"You don't need any crutches, Maria," he said. "Will you keep in touch with me, do you think?"

"I'd love to."

"But just as a friend . . . that's all, isn't it?" He was disappointed but realistic.

"I need friends, Andy, I'd love to think you were one."

"That's what it will be then. *And* I'll send you recipes, I'll actively seek them out for you to make you a legend in Irish cuisine."

"You know, I really do think it might get off the ground. My friend Rosemary is putting herself right behind it and she's a real dynamo."

"I don't doubt it for one minute," said Andy Vine.

"I didn't have sex with Sean Maine and I'm not going to have sex with you either, Hubie. Are we clear on both these matters?" Annie said.

"You're making the point very forcibly, yes," he said. "But the thing that really bugs me is that one day soon you *are* going to have sex with somebody and it won't be me because you're going to be miles away."

"I might *not*, you know." Annie spoke very seriously. "I don't mean become a nun or anything but I might just not do it, ever."

"Unlikely." Hubie dismissed the notion.

"I once saw two people doing it . . . years and years ago. I don't know how to describe it . . . it wasn't nice. It wasn't the way I thought it would be."

"But you were very young then," he said. She nodded. "And you probably didn't understand it."

"Do *you* understand it?" she asked him.

"A little, I guess, well, better than when I was a kid. Then it seemed full of mystery and excitement and you had to have it and yet you were afraid of it." He smiled at the recollection of how silly he had been when he was young.

"And now?"

"Well now it seems more natural, you know? Like the thing to do with someone you like."

"Oh?" She wasn't convinced.

"I haven't done it all that often, Annie, believe me. I'm not bullshitting you."

"But it was nice?"

"It was, and that's the truth," said Hubie Green who knew they were having a conversation about abstracts and not about how the evening was going to end.

"Will you be living in a trailer park when you get back?" Zach asked.

"No, I don't think so, why?" Brian was interested.

"Well, if your house is gone?"

"I don't know where we'll live, maybe with Dad, but I think *his* house is gone too."

"It's a real adventure, isn't it?" Zach said. "Will there be somewhere to stay for me when I come over there next year?"

"Oh, there'll have to be," Brian said airily.

"And will I meet Myles and Dekko?"

"Certainly."

"That's great," Zach said. "I never thought I'd be a person who would travel."

"That's funny," Brian said. "I always knew I'd travel, I'll probably go to planets and all. I was going to be a real estate agent like my dad and work with him but now that he's lost his business I think I'll be an astronaut instead."

"I'll miss you," Carlotta said. "I wish I'd gotten to know you better. Earlier on I suppose I felt inhibited. Marilyn has kept us all at such arm's length, we thought that as her friend . . ."

"I think you'll find that she has changed a lot in a couple of months. She talks about Dale now, and Greg's coming back here to live. Things will be much more open now."

"Does she know Hubie visits here?"

"Yes, I told her. She has no objection, though I don't think he'll be around so much when my Annie leaves!"

"And did you find what you came here for, Ria?" Carlotta asked.

"No, but I was looking for the moon," she said.

"I kinda thought you had found the moon that weekend when your husband was here," Carlotta said.

"Yes, so did I for a little while, but it wasn't the moon after all," Ria said.

"Greg has told us how wonderful your home in Ireland was, I'm so sorry you won't be able to go on living there," Heidi said.

"It's only a house, Heidi, only bricks and mortar," Ria said.

"That's such a very wise thing to be able to say." Heidi was admiring.

"I'm just practicing, rehearsing my lines," Ria admitted. "I think that if I say it often enough then I might believe it when I walk around it and have to say good-bye to it."

"And do you know where you'll go?"

"House property is very expensive in Dublin at the moment, so we'll get a good price for it but then we won't be able to buy anything in the area. I imagine that we'll have to move out a long way."

"It does seem such a waste. He and you got along so well when he was here . . . but then I'm only saying things you must have thought a thousand times in your head."

"A million times, Heidi."

John and Gerry said they really would miss her. Ria was to go home, set up a food export business, get written up in *Bon Appetit,* and they would be among her first clients.

"That's what I love about America. You really do believe dreams come true here," Ria said to them.

She telephoned Gertie just before they left.

"I can't believe you're coming home early for Jack's funeral, you changed your tickets and all to be here."

"Well, of course I would, Gertie. You'd do it for me if things were different."

"Thank you, Ria, and you do know that Jack was always very admiring of you. Remember the party in your house that he came to where he drank lemonade and helped serve the food?"

"I do indeed, Gertie." Ria bit her lip.

"They're taking him to the church tonight," Gertie said. "You wouldn't believe all the lovely flowers. Jack was very popular and well-liked in his own way."

"Of course he was, and we'll see you tomorrow morning," said Ria, who would be hard put to it to find one person who could say one good word about the late Jack Brennan.

Sheila Maine slept on the plane, Kelly and Brian played cards and watched the movie. Annie and Sean whispered plans for the future to each other.

Ria could not sleep. Her mind was full of pictures. The funeral, and the sustained pretense that Jack Brennan had been very different. The meeting with Danny to discuss their future. Arranging to sell No. 16 Tara Road. Finding a new place to live. The whole business of starting to cook for a living. Meeting Marilyn face-to-face after all this time.

Ria hoped she would like her. She knew so much about her now, more than Marilyn even dreamed she knew. There was a time when Ria had thought she would hate her, when she heard of Marilyn taking over her garden, her house, her friends, and her daughter. That was when she had thought Marilyn cold and unfeeling, wearing a prickly armor about her son's death and shutting out so much goodwill everywhere.

But the summer had changed that. Now she was touched by little secrets she knew about this woman. How she had a bottle of hair color labeled in her own writing "Special Shampoo." How she had inexpensive, discount toilet tissues in her storeroom, and instant cake mixes in her larder. Ria knew that Marilyn's friends had been hurt and distanced by her, and that her love of the garden was not considered admirable but far more obsessive.

But Ria also knew a far bigger secret. Something that would never be told. She knew what had happened on the day of Dale Vine's death. To know that would never make Marilyn stronger, it would ruin everything. She had reassured Hubie that it would never be mentioned and he believed her.

Ria hadn't told everyone else that she was coming home. She would meet them all at the funeral anyway.

Marilyn had promised to have breakfast ready for them when they arrived at Tara Road. They would have time for that, to get changed, and then they would all go to the church together. Ria smiled as she remembered their conversation. "The one good thing about this dreadful accident is that you and I get a chance to meet. Otherwise we would have passed in midair again," she had said to Marilyn.

"I think there's a lot more than one good thing about this dreadful accident," Marilyn had said. "Not, of course, that any of us will ever admit it." Marilyn had been in Ireland for two months. She was learning.

Just then the captain announced that due to weather conditions they were being diverted to Shannon Airport. He apologized for the delay, which would not be more than a couple of hours. They would certainly be in Dublin by eleven a.m.

"My God," said Ria. "We'll miss the funeral."

"I'm going to that eejit Jack Brennan's funeral," Danny Lynch said. Bernadette looked up. "Who was he?"

"A drunken bully. His wife, Gertie, was always in and out of Tara Road. If Ria and the children were here they'd have gone. I suppose in a way I'm going to represent them."

"That's very good of you," said Bernadette. "You're always thinking of other people."

"I met Lady Ryan on the road," Nora Johnson told Hilary. "She said she was going to Jack's funeral."

"Well, I suppose like the rest of us she's only going as a bit of solidarity for poor Gertie."

"She never had the civility to throw the time of day to poor Gertie," Nora sniffed.

"Ah, be fair, Mam, didn't we all say that Gertie should have thrown him out years ago?"

"We did and we were right, but we didn't say it with the scorn that Lady Ryan did. She treated Gertie like dirt, like something she found stuck to her shoe."

"You never liked her, Mam."

"Did you?"

"She's all right, she's funny I suppose, and she jazzes us all up," Hilary admitted grudgingly.

"No, she doesn't, she pats you all on the head, and you're all worth ten of her." Some of Nora's opinions would never change.

The delay at Shannon Airport seemed interminable. Sheila Maine telephoned her sister. "If we're not in time for the church, we'll go straight to the graveyard," she said.

Gertie wept her gratitude on the phone. "Oh, Sheila, if you knew how kind everyone's being. And if only poor Jack knew how much it turned out that people loved him."

"Well, of course he did. Didn't everyone know you had a great marriage?" Sheila said.

Ria rang Marilyn. "It seems we won't have that breakfast after all," she said.

"Then you'll never know what a bad cook I am," Marilyn said.

"I wish you didn't have to leave tomorrow, that you could spend a couple more days."

"I might easily do that. We'll talk later. . . . Oh, and another thing . . . Welcome home!"

"Jimmy, would you sing 'Panis Angelicus' at the funeral?" Gertie had asked on the phone.

"Now, you wouldn't want me croaking away. . . ." he began.

"Oh, Jimmy, please. Jack just loved that hymn, he really did. It would make it lovely for me if you sang it."

"I think it's more a wedding hymn really, Gertie, rather than a funeral one."

"No, it's about Holy Communion so it would be equally suitable at both."

"Well, if you'd like me to then certainly I will," said Jimmy Sullivan. He put down the phone and raised his eyes to heaven. "If there *is* a God, which I gravely doubt, then he should smite us all to the pit of hell for our hypocrisy."

"What else can we do?" Frances shrugged.

"We could have the balls to say that Jack was a mad bollocks and that the world is better off without him," Jimmy suggested.

"That would be *great* consolation to the widow and children," Frances said.

There was a black-edged notice on the door of the launderette saying that Jack Brennan, proprietor, had died, and giving the time of the funeral mass, so quite a few of the customers came out of respect to Gertie.

The church was crowded when Gertie, her mother, and her children arrived. Some of Jack's family, long-estranged, had turned up, with dark suits and white shirts and awkward handshakes. Gertie, pale and wearing the black dress she had borrowed from Hilary, walked up the aisle looking proudly from side to side at all the people who had come to say good-bye to Jack. At least now he might know that he had worth in people's eyes. Surely he was somewhere where he could see all this.

The mass had only just begun when Sheila Maine and her two children came up and joined the family. A little ripple of approval went through the church. The relatives had flown in from America, a further sign that Gertie was being honored and made much of.

Ria, Annie, and Brian slipped into a bench a little farther back. "My God," Nora Johnson said to Hilary. "Ria came back. Isn't she a great girl." Danny Lynch saw his wife and children. He bit his lip. It must have been hard to organize, Ria was certainly a loyal friend. Colm Barry saw them too. Ria looked magnificent, he thought, tanned, slimmer, holding herself taller somehow. He had known she would try to be here even though she wasn't meant to be back today. She and Gertie went back a long way.

Polly Callaghan sat by herself. She averted her eyes from the pew where Barney McCarthy sat with his wife. If Mona saw Polly in the church she gave no sign or acknowledgment any more than she ever had.

Rosemary had dressed carefully for the occasion as always. A gray silk dress and jacket, very high heels, and dark stockings. She was most surprised to see Ria and the children, nobody had told her they were coming back. But then she realized with a start there were few people to tell her anything. Apart from Ria herself, she didn't seem to have any friends anymore.

Frances Sullivan stared ahead of her as her husband's deep rich voice sang "Panis Angelicus." She knew how much it cost him to do this. He had despised Jack Brennan and felt that singing this hymn was in some way letting him win.

Ria looked around the church to see if she could identify Marilyn. She wasn't beside Rosemary, or Colm, or near Ria's mother. But surely one of them would have taken her under a wing. She couldn't concentrate on the prayers, she looked at the bouquets and wreaths all sent by people who had nothing but scorn for the deceased.

Where was Marilyn Vine?

It was when the congregation was singing "The Lord's My Shepherd" that Ria saw her. Taller than she would have thought, auburn-haired from the special shampoo bottle, and wearing a simple navy dress. She was holding up the hymn sheet and singing along with the rest. Just at that moment she looked up and saw Ria looking at her. They gave each other a great smile across the crowded church. Two old friends meeting each other at last.

The sun was shining, the unexpected gales and rainstorms of the night before had blown away. The people stood and talked outside the church, a Dublin funeral where there weren't enough minutes in the hour for people to say what they wanted to say.

Ria was being embraced and welcomed home by everyone. She broke free to hug Gertie.

"You're such a true friend to come back early," Gertie said.

"We traveled with Sheila and the children, we didn't notice the journey. And they'll be staying with you?"

"Yes, yes, we have the rooms ready. It's such a pity that they had to come for this reason, isn't it? I mean Jack would love to have welcomed them here again."

Ria looked at Gertie with shock. She realized that history was being rewritten here. There was no longer any need to pretend to Sheila that everything had been wonderful with Jack. Gertie had bought the story herself, she really thought it had been a great marriage.

Danny looked curiously like someone on the outside. Not the man who used to dart from group to group, shaking this hand, slapping that shoulder. Ria told herself that she must not think about him and care what became of him. He was not part of her life, the notion that they could go back to the old life was only in her head. She stood looking at him across the crowd. Soon the children would spot him and run over. But she would make no move. This is the way it was always going to be.

Annie had gone to talk to Marilyn, to introduce her new friend Sean Maine, to talk about Stoneyfield. Brian had gone to his grandmother to tell her about Zach's visit next summer. Ria could hear him. "We might be living on a halting site then but he's coming anyway," Brian's clear, carrying tones were explaining.

Hilary was trying to tell Ria all about the move. They would leave in the autumn and settle in. Martin's post would begin in January. Ria couldn't quite understand where they were going.

"You'll come and stay Ria . . . lots . . . won't you? It's full of trees. Like the fortune-teller said."

"Yes, yes of course." She was bewildered. There were too many people around, too much was going on.

"I'll give you twenty-four hours to get over your jet lag and then you start working for me," Colm said. "You look absolutely beautiful by the way."

"Thank you, Colm." She thought she saw something of the admiring look that had been in Andy Vine's eye, but she shook off the notion. She must not lose her marbles now and think everyone was fancying her.

Rosemary didn't come over, which was odd. She stood, a little like Danny stood, on the outside of a crowd where she knew many people. Ria went up to her, arms open wide. She saw Rosemary looking a little uneasily over her shoulder. Ria turned to follow her glance. Marilyn Vine had paused in her conversation with Annie and was watching them. Very carefully.

"Are you going to the graveyard?" Ria asked Rosemary.

"God no, here's bad enough."

"Gertie's so pleased to see everyone," Ria said.

"I know, and she's been on the phone to the Vatican to organize his canonization too. Believe me, Ria, that is not beyond the bounds of possibility."

Ria laughed. "God, it's good to be back." she said putting her arm into Rosemary's. "Tell me, was it a good summer?"

"No, it was a bloody awful summer one way and another."

"You're so good to put so much effort into getting *me* started up," Ria said. "I really do appreciate it."

"Least I could do," Rosemary said gruffly, looking over at Marilyn Vine again.

"It's a really beautiful house, Marilyn," Annie said. "You never told us how great it was."

"I'm so pleased you had a good time."

"You have no idea, it was like a house in the movies, honestly. And we swam before breakfast and even at night."

"Great."

"And we went on Rollerblades in Memorial Park and we ate huge pizzas, and we went to New York City twice and up to Sean's house on the bus all on our own. There was never a holiday like it."

"I'm so very happy it went well," Marilyn said.

She knew that she and Ria were almost putting off the moment they would speak to each other. And yet every time they took a step in each other's direction someone came to claim one of them.

This time it was Colm. "I didn't know Ria was coming back today. I'll leave you something over in the house, something from the restaurant. To save you cooking," he said.

"To save them being poisoned, you mean." Marilyn laughed at herself.

"You said it, not I."

Barney McCarthy had sympathized briefly with the widow.

"You're very good to come, Mr. McCarthy, Jack would have been very impressed at the quality of all the people who are here," Gertie said.

"Yes, well. Very sad," Barney mumbled.

"Polly Callaghan is devastated that it happened on her premises," Mona McCarthy said unexpectedly.

Gertie nearly fell down on the ground. Mona didn't talk about Polly, she pretended that she didn't exist.

Barney looked startled too. "Well, it wasn't exactly her premises. . . ." he began.

"No, that's right, she was moving house and poor Jack, poor, poor

Jack had called to her. . . . He wanted reassurance about something, you see." Gertie's lower lip began to tremble.

Mona rescued her. "I know, I heard the story. He wanted to be sure that you loved him. Aren't men like children in so many ways? They always like everything to be there in black and white." Gertie looked from Barney to Mona, bewildered. But Mona sailed on. "And Polly told him that of course you loved him, those were the last words he heard."

"Polly told me, but I wasn't sure if she was just being kind you know, telling me what I wanted to hear."

"No, no, whatever else you could call Polly, she isn't kind," Mona said. And moved away.

"That wasn't necessary, Mona," Barney hissed at her.

"Yes, it was. Poor Gertie had no life while that savage was alive, she's going to have one after he's dead, believe me."

"But how did you hear what Polly said or didn't say . . . ?"

"I heard," Mona said. "And don't think I have anything against Polly, I think she did this city a huge service by allowing her furniture van to kill Jack Brennan. She should be decorated by the Lord Mayor."

Then they finally met. They put their arms around each other. And said each other's names.

"I'll drive us to the graveyard," Marilyn said.

"No, no."

"I have your car, all shiny and clean from a car wash. I want to show it off to you."

"We cleaned your car too, Marilyn," Brian said. "And we got all the pizza off the seat at the back."

There was a pause and then Annie, Ria, and Marilyn broke into near hysterical laughter.

Brian was very startled. "What on earth did I say now?" he asked, looking from one to the other and getting no answer.

When they did get back to Tara Road there wasn't nearly enough time for all they had to say to each other. The children eventually went to bed. Marilyn and Ria sat at the table. It was unexpectedly easy to talk. They apologized for nothing. Not for encouraging Clement to sleep upstairs or for cutting back the garden, nor for inviting neighbors to become part of

Tudor Drive and taking up again with Hubie Green. They asked each other about the visits of their husbands. And each spoke thoughtfully and honestly.

"I thought Greg looked tired and old, and that I had taken away a year of his life because I couldn't help him over the bits that were just as bad for him as for me."

"And will it be all right from now on?" Ria asked.

"I guess he'll be cautious, even a little mistrustful of me from time to time. If I closed myself off so terribly before, I could do it again. It will all take time to get back to where we were."

"But at least you will." Ria sounded wistful.

"And nothing happened when Danny was over there to make you think that *you* might get back together again?" Marilyn asked.

"Something happened that made me certain that we *were* back together already. But I wasn't right. He told me all about the financial disaster, and losing the house and everything, in Memorial Park under big tree. Then we went back to Tudor Drive and . . . I suppose if I were being realistic I would say he consoled me in the way he knows best. But I took more from it than there was."

"That's only reasonable, and he probably meant it all at the time," Marilyn said.

"Timing is everything, isn't it?" Ria was rueful. "Just after that came the news that Bernadette was losing the baby and he was off like a flash. Even if we had had another twenty-four hours . . ."

"Do you think that would have made a difference?"

"No, to be honest," Ria admitted. "It might only have made me feel worse. Maybe it was for the best. The stupid bit was I kept thinking that it was all tied up with the baby. Once that no longer existed, perhaps the whole infatuation would go. But again I was wrong."

"Did you talk to him today at the funeral?" Marilyn asked.

"No. He looked as if he were going to speak but I didn't trust myself so I turned away. I couldn't think what he was doing there anyway, but he told Annie that he was there representing the family."

"That was a good gesture anyway." Marilyn's voice was soft and conciliatory.

"Danny's full of good gestures," Ria said with a smile.

Marilyn had been able to change her ticket. Now she was going to stay for an extra three days. This way she could arrive back at Tudor Drive at the same time as Greg. It was to be symbolic of their starting a new life together. And Marilyn said that by staying on a few days she could help Ria settle in and start to face the whole business of selling the house.

They talked about Hilary's plans to move to the country, the pregnancy of young Kitty Sullivan. They spoke of Carlotta wanting a fourth husband and how John & Gerry's had really taken off this summer. They didn't shy away from personal questions. When they spoke of Colm Barry, Ria asked whether Marilyn had been having a thing with him. "That was what I heard from a probably ill-informed source," Ria apologized.

"Totally wrong. I think he was much more interested in waiting until *you* came home," Marilyn said. "And on the subject, can I ask whether you had anything going with my brother-in-law?"

"No, your husband is quite wrong about that too," Ria giggled.

"But he might have liked to, we think?" Marilyn wondered.

"We don't know at all because we didn't allow such a situation to develop," Ria said.

And into the night they spoke of Gertie and how she was going to build a legend based on the dead Jack. They were both much more tolerant than they would have been a few weeks back. It wasn't just because Jack was dead. They sat in the beautiful front room of No. 16 Tara Road as the moonlight came in the window, and they each thought about the need to have some kind of legend in your life. Ria knew that for good or evil Marilyn must go on forever without knowing it was her drunken son who had killed Johnny and himself that day. And Marilyn thought that for better or worse Ria should not learn how the husband she still loved and the friend she still trusted had conspired to betray her for so long.

"Aunt Gertie's not as well off as I thought she was," Sean Maine said to Annie.

"Does it matter?" Annie shrugged.

"No, of course it doesn't, except I was just thinking it might work to our advantage."

"How's that?"

"Well . . . suppose I were to stay with her . . . you know, pay room and board and go to school here?"

"It won't work, Sean." Annie was practical.

"Not next week when school starts, okay I know it won't, but after Christmas I can find out what courses I'd get credits for . . . organize a transfer . . ."

Annie looked troubled. "Yes, well . . ."

"What is it? Wouldn't you want me here? I thought you liked me."

"I do like you, Sean, I like you a lot. It's just . . . it's just I don't want to sort of lure you on with promises of things we might do, I might do, once you got here. It wouldn't be fair to let you think that. . . ."

He patted her hand. "In time," he said.

"But probably not in short enough time for you," she said.

"I've never done it either," Sean said. "I'm just as confused."

"Really."

"It might not be as good as they say. But we could see what we thought," he said, and then looking at her face, "not now of course but when the time seems right."

"I bet Gertie'd just love having you stay," Annie said.

"I'm taking on more private pupils this year, Mum, can I do it in your house?" Bernadette asked.

"Of course, Ber. If you're well enough."

"I'm fine. It's just that I don't want to start them off in one place and then have to transfer them when we move from here."

"Does he know when he's going to sell?"

"No, Mum, and I don't ask him, he has enough pressures."

"Does he have great pressures about Tara Road? Is she on at him all the time?" Finola Dunne was always protective of her daughter against the ex-wife.

Bernadette thought about it. "I don't think so, I don't think she's even been in touch since she came back."

"I wouldn't mind seeing those children again," Finola said.

"Yes, I'd like to see them too, but Danny says they're all tied up with this Marilyn until she leaves. They're mad about her apparently," Bernadette reported gloomily.

"It's just because they stayed in her house, which had a swimming pool, that's the only reason." Finola tried to reassure her daughter.

"I know, Mum."

"Do you mind if we have Gertie and Sheila around for lunch?" Ria asked Marilyn. "Sheila's not staying long in Dublin and it would be nice for her to meet you . . . she's been in your house, remember?"

"Of course," Marilyn said. She would have preferred to talk to Ria on her own. There were still so many things to discuss, about Stoneyfield and about Tara Road. About the future and the past. But this was Ria's life, and lunch with these ladies came first. Marilyn had learned this. And she noticed that Ria had learned something too.

"I'm not going to spend the whole morning getting something ready. They want to talk, not do a gourmet tasting, let's you and I walk down to the shop and get something simple."

They walked up the road past No. 26 and waved at the swinging seat where Kitty Sullivan sat in the garden with her mother. Sixteen, anxious, and pregnant, she had suddenly found a way of communicating with Frances, which they never had before.

"Let's hope Annie doesn't find a similar one," Ria said wryly.

"Do you think she might be sexually active, as they say at home?"

"And as they increasingly say here," Ria confirmed. "No, I don't, but mothers know nothing, you'd know more about Annie than I would."

"I know a bit about her hopes and dreams, but I truly don't know anything like that side of things," Marilyn hastened to say.

"And if you did it would be sacred, you wouldn't have to tell me," Ria said, anxious not to appear curious and trying to beat down the slight jealousy that was always there. Why could Annie Lynch tell Marilyn her hopes and dreams? It was beyond understanding.

They looked into the grounds of No. 32.

"Does Barney still own any of that?"

"No, they sold it all at huge prices, it was the talk of the place at the time. Rosemary really knew what she was doing going in there." Ria was pleased for her friend.

Then they were at No. 48. No sign of Nora Johnson and Pliers; they must have gone on one of their many adventures. "Your mother will miss you if you move from here. Hilary going to the West, now you going too."

"It's not *if* we move away from here, it's *when*. This is Millionaires Row nowadays. Weren't we so clever to move in here when we did?"

"You weren't being clever, you went after a dream, didn't you?"

"I suppose Danny did. He wanted a grand house with high ceilings and deep colors. Often nowadays when I think about it, I don't quite know why, but that's what he seemed to want when he was young."

They walked on, an easy companionable silence between them. They passed the gates of St. Rita's.

"Future home of nice, soft cakes," Ria said, laughing.

"Nothing too difficult to chew," Marilyn giggled. "Not like those gingersnaps I bought Brian and Annie the first time, they were horrific."

They turned the corner and saw that Gertie's launderette was busy.

"I dare not mention the deceased, but would he have left any insurance?" Marilyn asked.

"Gertie's mother paid some kind of a policy," Ria said. "I think it was just a burial one."

"And will she be all right?"

"She'll be fine. She has the little flat upstairs there and of course she can have her children at home now that they won't be assaulted or have their poor nerves shot to pieces by that lunatic."

Gertie was so used to cleaning in No. 16 Tara Road that it was hard to get her to sit down.

"Will I do a bit of ironing for you to have your clothes nice for packing, Marilyn?" she said.

"Lord, Sheila, don't you have the kindest sister. I simply hate ironing and Gertie often helped me out."

"Yes . . . she was born caring about clothes, I never was," said Sheila, and the moment passed. Once or twice Gertie rose as if to clear the table but Ria's hand gently pressed her back. "Sean is so anxious to come back and study in Ireland after Christmas and find his roots," Sheila said. The other three women hid their smiles. "He has been around to all the various schools and colleges and of course I'd just *love* him to come back here," Sheila said.

"And Max?" Ria wondered.

"There's not much looking for roots in the Ukraine, they all came to the States from that village. Max will be okay about it."

Gertie was excited about the proposition. "There will be a small room in our flat, it's not very elegant but it's convenient for schools and libraries and everything."

"Stop saying it's not elegant," Sheila cried. "Your property is in such a good area. It's a wonderful place for him to stay, it's a happy home. I'm only sorry his uncle Jack won't be there to see him grow up."

"Jack would have made him very welcome, that's one sure thing," Gertie said, without any tinge of irony. "But we'll paint up his room for him to have it ready when he comes back. He can tell us what color he'd like. And maybe he'd get a bicycle. You know," Gertie confided, "a lot of people have asked me would I be financially able to manage without Jack?"

Ria wondered who had asked that and why. Surely they must have known that poor Gertie's finances would take an upturn now that she didn't have to find him an extra thirty or forty pounds drinking money a week by cleaning houses. And now that she could concentrate on her business. But then perhaps other people didn't know the circumstances.

"And of course I am fine," Gertie continued. "My mother's looked through all the papers and there was a grand insurance policy there, and the business is going from strength to strength. There will be fine times ahead, that's what I have to think."

Suddenly Ria remembered something. "Talking of what lies ahead, I wonder what happened to Mrs. Connor!"

"She told me she couldn't talk to the dead when I wanted to, and that one day I wouldn't want to anymore," Marilyn said. "I'd like to tell her that day has come."

"She told me I'd have a big business, I'd like to know how big," Ria said.

Sheila said that Mrs. Connor had said the future was in her own hands, and look at the way it all worked out. With her boy wanting to come back to Ireland to his own people! Gertie tried to remember what Mrs. Connor had told her. She told her that there would be some sorrow but a happy life, she thought. "Well, that was true enough," Sheila said, patting her sister on the hand.

"Should I make myself scarce while you meet Danny?" Marilyn asked as they cleared the dishes after lunch.

"No need, there'll be plenty of time after you've gone home. Let's not waste what we have."

"You should talk to him as soon as possible, listen to what he has to say, and add what *you* have to say. The more you put it off the harder it is to do."

"You're right," sighed Ria. "Yes, but it's a question of don't do as I *do,* just do as I *say!*"

"I'm only telling you what I didn't do myself."

"I suppose I should ask him to come over."

"I have to go and buy some gifts for people back home. I'll go down to that place I saw in Wicklow and leave you free for the morning."

"That's an idea."

"And you know what we'll do as a treat tomorrow afternoon?"

"I can't guess."

"We'll go see Mrs. Connor," said Marilyn Vine, who wanted to pay her debt to the woman who had told her the truth. That the dead like to be left asleep. They want to be left in peace.

"I have to meet Ria this morning," Danny said.

"Well it's better that you get it over with," Bernadette said. "Are you very sad?"

"Not so much sad as anxious. I used to laugh at middle-aged men who had ulcers and said their stomachs were in a knot. I don't know why I laughed, that's the way I am all the time now."

She was full of concern. "But you *can't* be, Danny. None of this is *your* fault, and you are going to be able to give her half the proceeds of that house, which is very big nowadays."

"Yes, true."

"And she knows all this; she doesn't have any expectations of anything else."

"No," said Danny Lynch. "No, I don't suppose that she can have any expectations of anything else."

———

"Brian, will you go and play with Dekko and Myles? Your dad is coming here and we need to talk on our own."

"Is it just *me* that you don't want to be here?" Brian wanted it clarified.

"No, Brian, it's not just you. Marilyn's going down to that craft shop, Annie's showing Sean the rest of Dublin. It's everyone."

"You won't fight, will you?"

"We *don't* now, remember? So will you go to Dekko and Myles for a bit?"

"Would you think it was okay if I went to see Finola Dunne? I bought her a present when I was in America."

"Yes, of course, that's a great idea." She laughed at his anxiety.

"That's not just me being awful and doing the wrong thing, is it?"

"You're wonderful, Brian," his mother said.

"But a bit different?" This was too much praise, he wanted it tempered.

"Very different, that's for sure," said Ria.

He came at ten o'clock, and rang at the front door.

"Haven't you got your keys?" she asked.

"I turned them in to Mrs. Jackboot," he said.

"Don't call her that, Danny. What would she have done with them, do you think?"

"Search me, Ria. Cemented them to a stone, maybe?"

"No, here they are, on the key holder at the back of the hall. Shall I give them back to you?"

"What for?"

"For you to show people around, Danny. Please let's not make it more difficult than it is."

He saw the sense in that. "Sure," he said and held his hands up as a sign of peace.

"Right, I have some coffee in a percolator up here in the front room, will we sit in there, and if you'll forgive the expression . . . make a list?"

She had two lined pads ready on the round table, and two pens. She brought the coffee over to them and waited expectantly.

"Look, I don't think that this is going to work," he began.

"But it *has* to work. I mean, you said we'd have to be well out of here by Christmas, I made sure that the children and Marilyn were out so that we could get started."

"She hasn't gone home yet?"

"Tomorrow."

"Oh."

"So who will we sell it through?"

"What?"

"The house, Danny? We can't use McCarthy and Lynch because they don't exist anymore. Which agency will we ask?"

"There will be a line of them waiting to dance on my grave," Danny said glumly.

"No, that's not the situation. Stop being so dramatic, there will be a line of people waiting to sell it so that they can get two percent of the price. That's all. Which one will we choose?"

"You've been out of the business for a long time. It's not two percent anymore, it's cutthroat nowadays, all of them trying to shave off a bit here and there."

"How do you mean?"

"It will be what they call the Beauty Parade, they all come in one by one, each one hoping to be chosen. This one says he'll take one point seven percent, this one will do it for one point two five. Then there's going to be some so desperate for the commission they'll say a flat fee."

"That's the way it is?"

"That's the way it is. Believe me, I've been in it, may even be in it again one day, who knows?"

"So who, then?"

"Ria, I'm going to suggest something to you. These guys hate me, a lot of them. I've cut right across their deals, stolen their clients. You must sell it on your own, and give me half."

"I can't do that."

"I've thought about it, it's the only way, and we must pretend to be fighting as if I'm giving you nothing, and your only hope is to screw as much out of this as possible."

"No, Danny."

"It's for us, for the children. Do it, Ria."

"I can't possibly hold a Beauty Parade as you call it, here on my own."

"Get someone to help you."

"Well, I suppose Rosemary could come in and sit with me, she's a businesswoman." Ria thought about it.

"Not Rosemary." He was firm.

"Why not, Danny? You like her, she really does have a head for figures; look at her own company."

"No, they'd walk over two women."

"Come on. What do you think it is? People don't walk over women in business anymore."

"Get a man to help you, Ria, it's good advice."

"Who, what man? I don't know any man."

"You've got friends."

"Colm?" she suggested.

He thought about it. "Yes, why not? He's got valuable property himself, more or less by accident but he's sitting on it. They'd respect him."

"All right."

"So when should I start?"

"I suppose as soon as possible. And tell these guys that you'll be in the market to *buy* a house too. They'll be even more helpful if they think there are going to be two bites of the cherry."

"The furniture and everything?" He shrugged. "Well, what will we do with it?"

"If you buy somewhere that suits it then of course you must take it," he said.

"But suppose *you* find somewhere that suits it?" she asked.

"I don't think we will, it will be small, and anyway . . . you know?"

"I know," Ria said. "Bernadette would prefer to start life with you having her own furniture."

"I don't think she'd even notice what furniture was in the room," he said. He sounded very sad.

She touched one of the balloon-backed chairs that they had found in the old presbytery, covered then with a rough and torn horsehair. Everything here had been searched for and found with such love. And now, less than two decades later, two people were shrugging about what would happen to it.

She didn't really trust herself to speak.

"So, it's not easy but we'll do it."

"I'll do it, apparently." She hoped it didn't sound too bitter.

"You understand why?"

"Yes, I do. And will you say I could have gotten more, or I shouldn't have chosen this or that one?"

"No, believe me I won't say anything like that."

She believed him. "Well, I'll ask Colm today. I'm eager to get it done and start trying to work for a living."

"You always worked hard," he said appreciatively and annoyingly.

Ria found that this made her eyes water a little. "And will you be able to get work?" she asked.

"Not as easily as I thought. In fact I was sort of advised to look into some other sector. Not too many agencies opening their doors, arms, or books to me, I'm afraid. Still, there's always something."

"Like what?"

"Like PR for the building industry or property companies. Like buying furniture from dealers. There are still houses throwing out beautiful stuff and filling themselves up with pine and chrome."

He was talking more cheerfully than he felt. Only someone who knew Danny Lunch would realize that. Ria gave no sign that she saw anything at all.

It was late in the afternoon when they went out to the halting site. Horses were tethered to fences, children played on the steps of caravans. Young boys hung around hopefully as cars drew up.

"Mrs. Connor?" Ria asked.

"She went away," said a red-haired boy with paper-white skin.

"Do you know where she went?" Marilyn asked.

"No, she just went overnight."

"But you might have some idea where she went." Ria made a move as if to open her handbag and look for a wallet.

"No, really, missus, if we knew we'd tell you. There's people coming here all the time looking for her, but we can't say what we don't know."

"And does she have any relations here?" Ria looked around the caravans that housed this particular traveling community.

"No, not to speak of."

"But surely a lot of you are family cousins, we really do want to find her."

"To thank her too," Marilyn said.

"I know you do, aren't there droves of them coming at night. And even now there's two cars coming in asking after her, my brother's telling them we haven't a God clue where she is."

"Was she sick do you think?" Ria asked.

"She never said a word, missus."

"And no one else took over her . . . um . . . work or anything?" Marilyn wondered.

"No. Wouldn't they have had to have the gift?" said the boy with the nearly transparent face.

They went to a last dinner in Colm's. Sean and Annie held hands and ate an eggplant-and-red-bean casserole. "Sean doesn't eat dead animals now," Annie said proudly.

"Sound man, Sean," Colm said admiringly.

"Finola Dunne said she saw your sister in a hospital. Her friend is there," Brian said.

Ria closed her eyes. Marilyn had told her the story. Brian was the last person in Ireland who should have learned it.

"Yes, that's right, she's been quite sick but getting a lot better now. Is Mrs. Dunne's friend getting better too?" Colm was ice calm.

Ria flashed him a glance of huge gratitude.

"I think her friend's a drug addict to be absolutely honest. But I *suppose* she could get better. They do, don't they?"

"Oh they do, Brian," Colm said. "They do all the time."

Barney and Mona McCarthy came up to the table. "I just wanted to welcome you home, Ria, and to wish you bon voyage, Marilyn." Mona spoke with confidence these days.

"Mam's going to be cooking things for money now if you still know any rich people who'd buy them?" Brian said helpfully.

"We know a few," Mona said. "And we'll certainly be able to put the word around."

Barney McCarthy was anxious to end the conversation. Colm ushered them to their table. You would never think from his manner that Barney had ever been at this restaurant with another woman. Or that his bills had remained unpaid until a solicitor had asked for any outstanding invoices to be presented.

The solicitor had been engaged by Mrs. and not Mr. McCarthy.

"Do you want us to call so that you can say good-bye to Rosemary tonight?" Ria asked Marilyn.

Annie looked up.

"I think I'll just leave her a note," Marilyn said.

"Sure, why not?" Ria was easy.

At that moment Colm asked Ria would she come into the kitchen. He wanted her to see the desserts that he had prepared for tonight so that they could discuss what she might dream up.

"Can I come into the kitchen?" Brian's eyes were excited.

"Only if you don't talk, Brian," his mother said.

"Sean, would you ever go with them and clap your hand over his mouth if he says anything at all?" Annie begged.

Sean Maine was pleased to be seen as a hero and went willingly.

Annie and Marilyn looked at each other across the table. "You don't like Rosemary," Annie said.

"No, I don't."

"Why don't you like her?" Annie asked.

"I'm not sure. But it's not something I need to say to your mother, they're friends over many years. And you, Annie? Obviously you don't like her either. Why is that?"

"I couldn't explain."

"I know. These things happen."

The taxi was coming at ten-thirty but Ria said Marilyn would not think she was getting away with leaving quietly. Colm was there with a gardening book for her, a very old one they had talked about, he tracked it down in an antiquarian bookseller's. Nora had come to say good-bye too. Hilary came to show a photograph of Martin's old homestead. A bleak-looking place with great tall trees. "There's a lovely sound in the evening when the rooks all come home," Hilary said.

"We went to see Mrs. Connor, I was going to tell her about you and the trees but it turns out that she's gone away," Ria told her sister.

"Well, her work is done," said Hilary, as if it was obvious.

Gertie came to say good-bye. "You were a great pal while you were here, and honestly, Marilyn, I wouldn't expect you to understand our ways, being a foreigner and everything, but you understood as well as anyone that Jack loved me and did the best for me. His problem was that he thought nobody really appreciated him."

"But they did," Marilyn said. "You only had to look at the crowds at his funeral to know that." Then it was time to go. "I could get a taxi, Ria," she began to protest.

"I'm driving you to the airport. Don't argue." The telephone rang. "Who now?" Ria groaned.

But it wasn't for her. It was Greg Vine from California. He was changing planes and about to check in for New York. He would wait for Marilyn at Kennedy. They would go back to Tudor Drive together.

"Yes, you too." Marilyn ended the conversation.

"Did he say I love you?" Ria asked.

"Yes, as it happens," Marilyn said.

"Lucky Marilyn."

"You have the children," Marilyn said.

And they held each other tight in a way they wouldn't be able to do at the airport.

Annie was coming to say good-bye, accompanied by Sean Maine and Brian. As they got into the car, Clement came out to say good-bye. It took the form of a huge yawn and stretch but they all knew what it was.

"I'm sorry about letting him into your bedroom," Marilyn said.

"No, you're not, but it doesn't matter, we'll be somewhere new soon and he'll have to relearn all his good habits."

Colm was in the back garden, he came out to wave them off.

"You are still working in that garden even though other people will get the benefit?"

"No, they won't get the benefit. I'm moving it all up to Jimmy and Frances Sullivan's garden, that's what I'm at."

"Why don't you do something with that awful concrete behind your restaurant? You could plant there."

"I'm hoping to build there," he said.

"Build?"

"Yes, proper accommodation at last, not just a bachelor flat."

"Great idea."

"Well, you never know."

"I hate to go," Marilyn said.

"When you come back we'll welcome you somewhere new."

"I don't suppose you could take anything *live* on the plane, could you, Marilyn?" Brian asked.

"Not really, except myself," she said.

"Then it's no use giving you a guinea pig for Zach, is it?"

"We can't go beyond here," Ria said at the passenger check-in.

"Aren't we magnificent?" Marilyn said.

"Yes, we really took a chance, didn't we?" Ria said.

"And how very well it worked out," said Marilyn.

They were still unable to say the good-bye.

Annie flung herself into Marilyn's arms. "I hate you going, I just hate it, you're quite different from anyone else, you *know* that. Will you come back so that I'll have someone to talk to?"

"You live in a place where there are plenty of people to talk to."

Ria Lynch wondered were people speaking about her over her head, but she must be imagining it.

"And you'll keep an eye on things from over there," Annie said.

"Yes, and you from here?" Marilyn begged.

"Sure."

Sean Maine shook her hand gravely and Brian gave her an embarrassed hug. Marilyn Vine looked at Annie Lynch. The blond, beautiful, nearly fifteen-year-old Annie walked up to her mother and put an arm around Ria's waist. "We'll keep the world ticking over until you get back," she said. "Won't we, Mam?"

"Of course we will," said Ria, realizing that it might be possible after all.